RAPTORS: THE COMPLETE SERIES

Aethon Books
www.aethonbooks.com

Print and eBook formatting, and cover design by Steve Beaulieu. Artwork provided by Luciano Fleitas

Published by Aethon Books LLC.

To both my little Sidekicks:
Oliver and Juneau
—J.C.

To my dad, who always believed in me.
—CJV

SIDEKICK

RAPTORS BOOK 1

CHAPTER **ONE**

Superhero.

It actually sounds pretty stupid when you say it out loud. Is it one word or two? Hyphenated maybe? Not sure. Most of us masked crime fighters don't use the term.

It also suggests someone has superpowers. Me, not so much. I have a really useful ability, but I wouldn't call it a superpower. It's kind of like an eidetic memory, only better. Most people would say it's a photographic memory, but that's wrong. I not only remember things, I can copy them. Perfectly.

Because of this, I can learn things really fast. Like martial arts skills.

Don't get me wrong; I've trained hard. Really, really hard. Enough to be a black belt in a bunch of different disciplines. But I basically just have to watch a Jackie Chan or Bruce Lee movie—or, better yet, an MMA or UFC match—and I can mimic every move perfectly.

Right now, I'm out on my nightly patrol after having spent the afternoon watching my favorite parkour channel on YouTube. I swear, every week these guys come up with something I've never even thought of.

From up here, the city looks beautiful. Before you judge me, New York is way different from above than it is at street level. From the rooftops, leaping from building to building, it's like the Fourth of July with all the lights. Call me weird, but I love the place. It's my city.

Bleep.

Groan…

"Go ahead," I say as I plant my hands on a low wall and dash vault to the building ten feet below.

"Sawyer, I'm receiving reports of some dirty boys three blocks north of your position."

That's Amber. She's an artificial intelligence built into my helmet. And yes, she always talks like that. It's really sort of off-putting if I'm honest. You see, my partner Frank—better known to the world as the Black Harrier—has a bit of a...

vice? I guess that's what you'd call it. My mom would call it womanizing—and she wouldn't be wrong.

This might be a good time to mention that my mom doesn't know I work with Frank. Actually, she doesn't even know him—no more than anyone else who watches TMZ or reads the viral gossip blogs everyone posts to social media.

Amber used to belong to him. He's since upgraded to Tiffany. I guess he likes the idea of a sexy woman in his ear all the time, and for some reason, he thought it was appropriate to hand this one down to a fifteen-year-old boy.

"Thanks, Amber," I say before taking a sharp turn and hopping to the next rooftop.

I'm about four stories up on an apartment building's fire escape. Down below, I can see at least a dozen gangbangers and one scared-looking thirty-something-year-old woman.

Silent as a jungle cat, a series of rail flows over and under the emergency ladder housings has my feet on asphalt. Three or four of the thugs notice me immediately.

"What, you've never seen a kid in a costume in October?" I ask.

Harrier hates the word costume—like it's a curse word. He calls it a uniform. Some of us would rather be honest about it. Sure, it's got technology built-in that most of the world can't even imagine, but it's still just a costume.

Now all twelve—make that thirteen, I just noticed the one sneaking up behind me—of them are staring at me. The good news is, their victim has recovered her purse and is now running away, leaving behind her high heels. They're expensive-looking. Like, what-is-she-doing-on-the-lower-east-side expensive-looking. I don't know, maybe I just still haven't gotten used to the new nightlife around this part of town.

"You screwed up, kid."

"Oh, without a doubt. For one, I forgot to turn off my old Xbox, and you know how hot those things get."

The jerks don't even give me a chance to finish my quip before they're attacking me. At least the real villains in the Big Apple like some good banter, but these guys? Ridiculous.

The first thug attacks me. I think I'll call him Bowl Cut.

Remember how I said I can replicate an MMA fight after watching it once? As I sidestep, I put that into practice, grabbing Bowl Cut's wrist with my right hand and then jabbing the heel of my left palm into his shoulder. I feel a satisfying *pop*, and I'm positive he won't be a problem anymore.

They're all a little scared now, I can tell. Though to their credit, the fight's on in full force. However, they're making the usual mistake of trying to take me on one or two at a time.

As usual, I'm kicking all their butts.

"*Behind you*," Amber says.

She can see things I can't, with cameras built into the helmet. That's why I'm able to elbow the guy sneaking up on me in the eye without even looking. You think eyes are off-limits? Did you miss the part where I said I was fighting thirteen guys?

And reminder… I'm only fifteen. For six and a half more minutes, anyway. At 10:34 p.m., I'll officially hit the big one-six. Yay. *Happy birthday to me.*

You'd think these losers would get the hint after I defeat five or six of them, no problem. I mean, the girl they were trying to assault is long gone now. But no, they keep coming at me, one after another. And even when they do land a punch, the armored parts of my costume—including the helmet housing Amber—make it so they hurt their hands more than they do me.

I can never understand what these guys are thinking. *I know he just took out five of my buddies without breaking a sweat, but I'm the one who's gonna beat him down.*

I have to admit that one of my favorite things to do is really petty. I find way too much joy in dodging and letting my attackers assault their buddies. Which is exactly what I just did.

Pock Mark—that's as good a name as any, I guess—is hunched over, trying to keep the blood in his nose with two cupped hands after… I don't know… Knock-Off Nikes walloped him in the face with said bo-bo brand shoe.

As I take these guys on, I do start to wonder why this seems to be happening so much more lately. Of course, there's always crime in the city—it's freaking New York—but the past couple of weeks, it's starting to get out of control. And not just a little bit. It didn't even build up over time. Just all of a sudden, my job was ten times harder than usual.

Well, not really that hard. It just takes me ten times as long to take care of it.

Punch to the solar plexus. Kick to the jaw. Knock-Off Nikes and another one goes down, but they keep on coming. Then the part that always seems to happen in these situations: the biggest, toughest guy they have steps up and the rest back away. I'm not sure why he's been hanging back, but I have a feeling he wanted the rest to wear me down so he can take me out easier and boost his reputation as a badass.

I'm gonna show him just how wrong he is.

Big Guns runs at me with a roar, and his fist pulled back above his head like he's about to bring down a sledgehammer he isn't holding. This guy obviously never had to learn to fight because he's so big and strong. I barely have to move to step out of his way and watch him plow into the wall behind me.

"That was hot," Amber says.

"Not now," I growl, sounding a bit too much like Black Harrier for my own tastes.

Big Guns says some words reserved for shows with M ratings on Netflix and spins toward me. He's really pissed off. And pretty dazed. After shaking his head like a dog just out of the water, he tries to grab me.

"Watch out for the ground and pound," Amber says.

I ignore her, but she's right. He probably wants to take me down to the pavement so I can't dodge him. I give him a knee to the junk—nope, that's not off-limits either. In fact, there's only one rule: *No killing.*

Every guy has felt that, but not many have experienced graphene armor to the groin. He slumps to his knees, holding his crotch, then falls over on his puckered face like a tree being cut down.

"Timber!" I shout, then step over his body.

The three baddies who are still conscious look at each other and try to escape.

"Nope!" I say while grabbing the two closest to me and slamming their heads together. Both fall unceremoniously to the ground. It's a little *Three Stooges*, but it works.

The third tries to limp away, and even though I'm barely breathing hard, I don't feel like chasing him. I toss my boomerang and tag him at the base of his skull, which may not have knocked him out. But when his face hits the corner of a dumpster on his way down, I'm pretty sure he's done with.

That's when I hear *him*.

"Not bad." That was a legit voice changer. In the middle of an empty alley at, like, 10 p.m. I hate it. So much. He does it when he's in costume. I've told him how lame it sounds, but he still insists on it, even when nobody's around to hear it except me.

"Not bad? I thought it was pretty damn good."

"*Mmmm, me too,*" Amber purrs in my ear.

You might have noticed the little *bleep* earlier before she started talking. It's a feature I added. Truth? She used to scare the hell out of me. I'd be leaping around the city, and suddenly some sultry voice starts whispering in my ear? God… she nearly got me killed more than once.

Now, that little *bleep* lets me know she has something to tell me. I call it an Amber Alert, and yes, I know how insensitive that probably sounds. It's set up kind of like my phone's screensaver. After three minutes of silence between us, she needs to alert me that she'd like to speak. Don't look at me like that. She's a machine. She's not real—no matter how insanely hot she might sound.

"Enough, Amber," I say.

She'll know that's an order for her to go back in her box. If she wants to talk again, she'll need to alert me.

The Black Harrier steps out of the shadows, where he's apparently been standing, watching me. With the almost all-black costume, it really isn't that hard for him to do. Unlike me, with my bright red *uniform* and blond hair.

"Language."

So ridiculous. He has no problem taking me into situations where I'm more likely than not to get killed or maimed, but I'm not supposed to swear around him.

"Yeah, sorry," I say. "How long were you standing there?"

"Long enough."

I'm serious, he sounds like Darth Vader or something. I almost wanna laugh sometimes.

"And you didn't think it might be a good idea to, I don't know, give me a hand?"

"You didn't need any help."

Wow. From the Black Harrier, that's pretty much the highest compliment you can get. Then, in typical fashion, he has to knock me down a peg.

"But there are still some things we need to work on to increase your efficiency."

I nod and decide not to ask him where he was all night, even though it's the fifth time in a couple of weeks I've had to patrol alone.

"Is tomorrow okay?" I always have to confirm things with him. Never assume.

"Tomorrow."

"Okay, then." I stand there awkwardly a bit longer, waiting for him to say something else. After a more-than-uncomfortable amount of time staring at one another, I say, "Well, I think I'm pretty much done here. Sounds like the cops are on the way. I need to get home to finish my homework and check on my mom."

He grunts. He always gets extra-broody when I bring up my mom. I swear, sometimes he's such a tool that I almost don't wanna be his partner anymore. I shoot my grappling hook at the top of the building next to me and prepare to go up.

"Kite."

I hate the way he says my code name. In fact, I hate that code name.

"It's 'Raptor' now," I remind him. "'Red Raptor.'"

"Right. I keep forgetting."

Yeah, sure you do. More like you're so mad I changed it without your permission that you refuse to accept it.

"But until it gets approved by—"

"...by the Guild, it's not 'official.' Yeah, so you keep reminding me."

The Guild... *guuuh.*

Basically, a hundred years ago or something, all the world's best supes decided it would be smart to inflict everyone with a bunch of laws and rules. Now, anyone who wants to fight crime has to go through them. It's like the worst kind of union imaginable, but Harrier is one of the guys in charge, so he's a real hardass about it.

He tosses me a package wrapped in newspaper. The guy's a billionaire, and he can't splurge on some gift wrap?

"Happy birthday," he says.

Dude, something strange is going on for sure. And who gets the newspaper anymore?

"Uh, thanks." This is so weird, I'm not even sure how to respond. I just stare again, waiting for something else. As usual, he just stands there, being all tough and silent.

I thumb my grappler button and rise up toward the rooftops. I cat vault upward and land on the retainer wall. I can't process the fact that I'm holding a birthday present from Harrier. I know you don't know him, but one time, a villain named Doctor Evo manipulated the genes of a Sea World–sized aquarium filled with bull sharks, and they grew legs, then proceeded to terrorize the city, somehow being able to breathe on land. This... this is way weirder than that.

As I turn around, I see Harrier pull something from his utility belt and examine it in the moonlight...

"Amber, zoom in?"

"*Anything you want, honey,*" she says.

Huh. It's some kind of business card and something scrawled on it in red ink. Even with Amber's magnification on my face mask, Harrier's moving it too much for me to read anything. I pause and watch while something changes in his demeanor. Yeah, he's wearing a mask, but I know him, and I can just tell. Whatever is written on there, it's for sure bothering Harrier.

Between his unusual absences, which have forced me to patrol alone, and giving me a birthday present—not to even mention this, something is wrong. And I can't shake the feeling in my gut that whatever has him acting so weird has gotta be really, really bad.

CHAPTER **TWO**

C*onfession.*

I didn't go home.

I needed some more time to process everything, so I decided to stay out a bit. Besides, with the growing crime throughout the city, I figure her streets need me more than usual—especially since Harrier wasn't doing much lately.

"Amber," I say, knowing I'm giving her the opportunity to gab my ear off.

"Yes, Master Vincent?"

That's my last name. Sawyer William Vincent. Lots of first names, really. She never calls me that, but she loves being sarcastic too.

I ignore the comment and ask, "What do you think that was? The card, I mean."

Amber hesitates, as if thinking. I know that's stupid, since she's just a machine, but Frank really gave her a personality and sometimes it's hard to differentiate between fact and fiction, you know?

"I don't know. Maybe an escort service?" she asks.

I roll my eyes and slide to a stop on a Chattahoochee stone rooftop.

"What in the world would he do that for?"

"Oh, sweet innocent Sawyer—"

"Okay, shut up. I know what an escort service is for. I just mean... he's freaking rich. And famous. He can get any woman in the city without even trying."

"Sometimes, it's nice to not have any… emotional attachments."

"What would you know about emotions?" I say as I start off again and clear a sizable gap.

"That's hurtful," Amber says.

"I just get the feeling it was important. That look on his face…"

I let the thought hang in the ether for a bit, and my mind is so distracted, I almost don't notice a figure standing on the rooftop as I sprint by.

Actually, I don't notice at all until Amber says, *"Proximity alert."*

It's another one of her features. She doesn't tell me when someone is nearby on street level because, well, she'd never shut up. But up here, high above the city, there are very few reasons for me to run into anyone, especially this late at night.

I stop and duck behind an HVAC system. Peering around the corner, I catch a glint of light coming off what looks to be white armor. There's definitely a figure standing in the shadows, obviously female, hard to tell her age. I see a blonde ponytail coming from under the back of her helmet, and I get a strange tingle in my stomach. What's that all about? I can barely even see the bottom of her face.

"Amber," I whisper, "see if you can tell me who that is…"

"Analyzing."

I swear, as soon as I'm in charge, I'm changing the voice to some kind of butler with a British accent. It's *way* too distracting, even when she's saying words like "analyzing."

When I was reprogramming her for various new tasks, I tried to change the voice, but of course, Harrier has it locked with some encryption not even I could break through. What a hill to die on, Frank.

My helmet's heads-up-display bursts to life with overlying green text. Some info about a new heroine known as "Osprey," but there's almost zero about her. It's really nothing more than some tweets from a guy called @byrdwotcher—and yes, based on the stuff he's saying, it's definitely a guy.

I decide that there's enough to prove she's on the good team. I have the sense enough to leave Harrier's present to me tucked between two of the dark green AC units. My hands are already up palms out, slightly raised, to show I'm not a threat as I step out from my hiding place. I don't even make it one step, saying, "Hello —" before she's jumping toward me with a flying kick that I'm barely able to block with my bracer.

"Whoa!" I gasp. I don't even know how she got to me so quickly.

The next thing I know, she's leaping off the roof and onto the one across the alley. It was super graceful, like a dancer or something. I don't know why she'd run away like that unless she has something to hide, so I take off after her.

"Wait!" I realize I probably won't be able to catch her because she's at least as fast as I am, so I pause long enough to devise a plan. It'll be hard for her to lose me with her white armor at night unless she has some tricks up her sleeve.

As if on cue, trick number one comes my way.

She turns and tosses a throwing star at me. There really isn't any danger of it hurting me through my graphene plate armor, but on pure reflex, I jump to the side. I successfully avoid it, but that gives her an even bigger lead.

I've got tricks too, you know, I think as I toss a bola at her to slow her down. I aim for her torso. I don't want her to trip and fall off the edge of the building. As if she knows it's coming, she goes into a slide and almost succeeds, but it still catches the top of her helmet and wraps around it in a weird, tangled way. Frustrated, she yanks her helmet off and tosses it at my head, forcing me to duck.

"Wow, she's hot," Amber says.

"Not now!" I shout, sending her into quiet mode.

While I'm distracted, both by the flying helmet and my sexy ear-partner, my quarry-turned-assailant dives off the other side of the building toward the street, which freaks me out. Can she fly?

I don't know the answer to that, but I know for sure that I can't.

Without a choice, I leap off after her and immediately shoot my grappler toward the building across the street. That's when I realize she's right in front of me, her strange, wing-like cape acting almost like a parachute. I catch a quick glimpse of her face, but she wears a white domino mask just like Harrier and me, only ours are black. Her fist is cocked back and—

POW! She punches me as my momentum takes me forward, and I start to fall until my grappler connects and starts to pull me toward the building across the street.

When I reprogrammed Amber, I included an emergency bypass in the programming. Still, the hardest part was figuring out how a machine could decipher a situation well enough to know when something really was an emergency.

Luckily, this time she's right.

"Alert. Colliding with pavement at this velocity will most likely lead to—"

"Yeah! I get it! I'd be dead."

The side of the building comes at me like a subway train. I barely have time to brace myself before slamming into it a lot harder than I want to. Despite my armor, the jarring motion alone has me feeling like I'm gonna pass out. Then I feel the line pulling me up. I get the sensation in my shoulder like a tiger just wrapped its jaws around my arm and wanted it for a toy.

Using as much effort as I have left, I throw myself over the lip of the rooftop. Hey, at least I'm not a puddle on the sidewalk below. When I turn around, I can barely see my opponent sprinting back on the other roof and grabbing her helmet.

I'm not positive, but I'm pretty sure she gives me a little wave before taking off in the other direction.

I change on the roof of my crappy apartment building as usual and take the stairs down to our little cracker box on the top floor. Looks like they painted the walls again in a sorry attempt to cover the graffiti. Never works. You can still see everything through the coat of cheap paint. And they don't even try to patch up the holes anymore.

The fight with Osprey bothers me, but I can worry about that later. That feeling I had earlier about Harrier is still nagging me a lot more. What was it about Frank that was so off tonight? That he was so nice to me, for once? And that business card. Maybe I'm paranoid. Everyone hands out business cards in New York. It was probably some shady electronics dealer who gets his merchandise when it "falls off a truck."

I haven't been home all day. I have an excuse ready to go, but then I realize it won't be necessary as soon as I walk in the door. Mom's asleep on the couch, red hair a tangled mess over her face. No big deal at eleven at night, right? Maybe she was waiting up for me.

Yeah, right.

The only reason the bottle of vodka she has nestled against her chest hasn't spilled is that it's just about empty. And the only reason the cigarette in her other hand didn't burn our building down is that the ashes fell onto a plate sitting on the floor.

I start to think she's forgotten my birthday again until I notice what's on the plate: a cupcake covered in wax from the melted candle planted in the center of it. Guess I should've stopped by after school before going out on patrol.

I grab the cigarette and the vodka and toss them, then take a frayed blanket off the back of our ratty couch and cover Mom up. I haven't eaten since lunch in the cafeteria, so I decide to try a taste of the cupcake. The paper comes off stiff, the burned portions sticking to it. Peeling off a chunk of the bottom, I take a bite that isn't covered in wax.

Then I gag. Maybe the wax would be an improvement. Well, at least she tried this year. I'll give her that.

As usual, it's up to me to clean up the mess in the kitchen even though I didn't cause any of it. The dirty dishes have been sitting here so long that they've become science experiments, and I just can't take the smell anymore. Maybe I'll discover the next wonder drug if I test some of this stuff on the rats that live in our walls.

I grab her coffee mug that's, no doubt, been there since this morning and the cupcake plate. Lifting it reveals a homemade birthday card with a balloon drawn on a regular piece of paper folded in half. "To Sawyer, Love, Mom." Hmm. It's not much. Just four words, but it's more than I usually get from her. That's almost as strange as Harrier giving me a present.

I swear loudly. I forgot about Harrier's gift after everything that happened with Osprey.

"Sawyer?" Mom says.

My chin falls to my chest, and I let out a heavy sigh.

"Oh, hey, Mom."

I assume she's gonna berate me for being late and missing her "special" birthday celebration, but she just smiles sleepily and says, "Happy Birthday, honey."

She sits up and reaches for the TV remote.

"Thanks," I say. "Why don't you, uh—you should go to bed."

What I really need is for her to go to bed so I can go get Harrier's present, and there's no way I'm gonna be able to sneak out now that she knows I'm here.

"What? No. It's early."

"You were asleep, though," I say, desperate.

"I was just resting my eyes. But you… you have school tomorrow." I start to turn when she says, "And Sawyer. Tomorrow we'll talk about you not coming home."

I don't respond, but I'm not really too worried. Her words are slurred enough that I know she won't even remember this in the morning.

Seven steps take me to my sanctuary: a ten-by-ten bedroom with a twin bed mattress on the floor and a desk made from cinderblocks and plywood. I flip open my laptop—the one I told Mom everyone at school got thanks to a new government program—and type in my password: redR@ptor15. That's a name I can live with. Being called "The Red Kite" made me feel like I'd never be taken seriously. I mean, nobody even knows it's a bird. I do need to change the number to sixteen before I forget, though.

I'll give Mom twenty minutes before she's out cold on the couch again, and I'll be able to go retrieve the gift, but until then, I'll check for anything I can find on Osprey. It's clear that, like me, she's patterned herself after the Black Harrier in her look and style. Unlike me, however, she isn't directly connected to Harrier. If I know him, which I do, he'll freak out when he finds out some girl is out there copying him without his permission.

No major articles or blog posts, just a poorly-made 1.0 style website called The Unofficial Osprey Fan Club.

I scroll through a bunch of nonsense and speculation until I find something that causes me to stop. Somebody managed to get a shot of her with his phone. It's not all that clear, but I can still make out the bottom half of her face under that white mask of hers. Man, she looks good in that costume. I'm pretty glad I don't have my helmet on. There's no chance I wouldn't be enduring ridicule by Amber right now.

I leave a couple of comments on the message boards, fishing for some info on where I can find her. It probably won't work, but you never know when something might be helpful.

Yeah, I know it all sounds kind of stalkerish, but what am I supposed to do? It's not like there's some clubhouse where teenage costumed heroes hang out. One way or another, I need to find her and figure out why she reacted like a crazy person upon seeing me. Absentmindedly, I rub my shoulder, which still hurts.

Careful to exit out of all open browser tabs and clear my history, I slap the laptop shut. Then, I sneak out to the short hallway that connects my room and bathroom to the living room where I hope to find my mom asleep again.

Bingo. Out like a light.

CHAPTER **THREE**

Relieved.

It's a little after midnight, and I'm back on the rooftop where I'd first met Osprey. Luckily, she hadn't found my newspaper-wrapped birthday gift.

I feel embarrassingly excited about what might be inside, so I waste no time tearing off the paper. I can see right away that it's a new cape.

Black. What a surprise.

But as I unravel it, I realize something is different. The edges turn rigid when they're snapped out. A glance into the box, and to my further surprise, there's something else. A new utility belt? Equipped with… jets?

Okay, I totally have to check this out. Now.

It takes a little while to figure out how to attach the cape. I was thinking too hard. The cape grabbed hold of the armor like a magnet, only that definitely wasn't what it was. Graphene isn't magnetic—which is good when you consider one of Harrier's enemies controls metal through magnetism.

Frank's company—oh, right... the Black Harrier, or Franklin Douglas III, is the CEO of Douglas Industries. Honestly, I don't even know half of what they do. They're one of those companies who has their hand in every pot but makes an insane amount of money.

So, they have a crazy-awesome R&D team led by a dude named Mr. Chen. He's always coming up with crazy stuff that Harrier and I get to use on the field. Being a bit of a tech-head myself, I can't wait to probe him over what the material is.

It looks like the cape extends into a sort of glider and attaches to my gloves just like the neck does. And the jet canisters are pretty small, so I don't think they're intended for long flight, just enough for short bursts to keep me high up while gliding.

Let's give it a shot.

I start out slow and jump off the AC unit. As the edges go rigid, I'm able to float down. After a couple more tries, I start to get the hang of it. Harrier and I have used gliders before, but those were big, bulky rigs. It's a lot different when it's my actual cape. More like those wing-suit things that lets you skydive without a parachute.

Standing on the edge of the roof, I look out over New York. Nine million people going about their lives, most of them never giving a thought to people like Black Harrier and me, out there protecting them every night. I find myself scouring for Osprey, like somehow I'm gonna see her again. Like she hung around, waiting for me.

Bleep.

"Yeah?" I say, opening up the channel for Amber.

"Is everything okay? Your heart rate has increased exponentially."

"You try jumping off a building," I say, totally lying. "Switch to silent."

I've jumped from rooftops more times than I can remember. My heart's going nuts because I'm thinking about Osprey. Damn teenage hormones. I physically shake my head in an attempt to clear my thoughts and look down at the street below.

Most people would probably hesitate at this point, but I didn't become a masked crime fighter because I was afraid of trying things. So I drop my helmet visor and leap. For a moment, I feel weightless. Then, as I start my descent, I extend the cape.

I'm able to stay in flight long enough to reach the building across the street, then I press the palm control for the jets to push me higher.

Nice. I could get used to this. Let's see how high I can go.

Getting a running start this time, I jump, straighten like an arrow, spin, and then *poof*, I let my cape snap out into rigid wings.

"Wooo!" I scream, and it gets buried in the sound of wind whipping past my head.

I cut a hard turn toward the nearest skyscraper and circle up to the top. It's an older building, probably built in the 1930s, and has those convenient ledges that Harrier likes to perch on like he's a stone gargoyle. Fits his personality.

I stop on one to take a short break, then take a dive off the edge, a good fifty stories above the street. I blast the jets again and straighten out. At this height, I could probably glide across half the city.

A red kite, believe it or not, is a bird in the Accipitridae family, which also includes other raptors like eagles, hawks, buzzards, and, of course, harriers. If people knew that, I wouldn't need to change my name. But right now, soaring like this? I feel more like my bird of prey namesake than I ever have before.

Bleep.

Guuuh. Not now.

I close my eyes and feel the air blowing against my face, and I realize I've never felt more free in my life. No mom, no school, no Black Harrier, no worries. Just flying through the night sky above the city lights. If I start getting around this way, I might miss the fun of leaping across the city parkour-style, but I think it'd be worth it.

I stay at a decent height to practice some more, figuring I'll circle down to my apartment building when I get close.

Bleep.

Another Amber Alert comes in as I'm coming up on another skyscraper closer to my neighborhood.

"What is it?!" I say at the exact moment I realize I'm not gonna clear the huge building, so I tap the palm control again.

"*You're out of fuel,*" she says. "*Bone dry.*"

She's absolutely right, but it's too late.

I try a sharp turn to get past the building, and it looks like I just might make it, but a gust of wind pushes me back at the last second, and I smack hard into the corner.

Ow! That effing hurt. Knocked the wind out of me, too.

"*Sawyer, you're heading—*"

"I know!"

Now I'm in free-fall. And it feels like I'm about to pass—

Wham! Something collides with me, and for a split second, I think I'm hitting the ground sooner than I expected. Or maybe the side of the building again. But instead of being, like, *dead*, I'm heading back up somehow.

Realization hits me about as hard as the pavement would have. Harrier was spying on me. Watching. He probably gave me this birthday gift as some kind of sick test to see how I'd behave in such a dire situation. That jerk. I can't believe it. I mean, yeah, he probably saved my life, but—

"Hold on. We're almost on the roof."

Wait. No robotic voice-changer. That wasn't Harrier. That wasn't even close to Harrier. It's a woman for sure, but not Amber.

As soon I feel myself lying on a rooftop, I retract my visor and do what anyone would after an experience like that. I throw up.

A lot.

At the absolute worst time possible, too. Because when I look up at my savior, I immediately realize that I'm finally face to face with the woman I love.

Well, technically, we just barely met. But still, I think I love her. Especially now.

"What happened?" I ask Osprey as she stands above me, closed fist on one cocked hip. So. Freaking. Beautiful. "How did you..." My voice is hoarse and sore from puking. I sound almost as ridiculous as Harrier.

"I thought I made it clear for you to stay out of my business," she says.

Whoa, whoa…

I think for a second she's gonna kick me or something. I toss up two placating hands and say, "I wasn't—I didn't—"

Real smooth, Sawyer.

"*Look at those curves,*" Amber says.

"Shut up!" I shout, slapping my helmet.

"*Excuse* me?" Osprey says.

My face goes as red as my costume, and I try to stand. It's not graceful, but I make it to my feet.

"Not you…" I say.

"There someone else up here?"

"I—uh…"

"It doesn't matter. I'm only going to tell you this one time. Whatever this is… it stops now."

What the actual eff is going on here? This is the second time tonight that she happens to be where I am, and she's acting like I was what—spying on her? Stalking her? I think about saying something, but she turns to walk away. Her costume is so much like Harrier's and mine, only… tighter.

"Hey!"

She stops but doesn't turn to face me.

"I... Thanks. Thanks a lot."

Then, she does something that makes my stomach flop around like a fish. She smiles at me. I can't believe she looks so good when she's not beating me up.

"Yeah," she says. "Just be more careful with your new toys next time."

"How did you know—"

My next words bounce around in my mouth, my tongue battling with my teeth like I'd never talked before. She's walking back toward me.

"Mind if I...?" She gestures at the new gear.

"Uh… yeah… for sure! Go ahead."

Osprey looks at the edges of my new cape, then checks out the small jets on the belt. She leans in close, and all I can think about is my breath.

Is my breath okay?

I just freaking threw up. Of course my breath isn't okay.

Omigod, I had that chili dog for dinner tonight. Better hold my breath. I need a mint. Why don't I have any mints? I need to add a mint compartment to my utility belt.

"Pretty sweet, but not much capacity for fuel. Which I'm sure you realized a few minutes ago as you were plummeting toward the asphalt." She laughs, and it's literally the most beautiful sound I've ever heard.

"Uh, yeah. Makes sense, really. It would be way too heavy otherwise."

As she stands, done examining my belt, she tucks a lock of blonde hair behind her ear. "Harrier's a smart guy. He's got it all figured out."

Why do I feel so jealous? Of course she worships him. Judging by her costume, she's practically *his* stalker.

But obviously, she's been keeping an eye on me also. I smile, just thinking about it. Then I hope she didn't notice me smiling as I return my face to normal. Crap. What's my normal face look like? I purse my lips a few times, trying to act natural.

"You okay?" she says.

"Yeah. Fine." My throat's still hoarse. Probably will be until I drink some water. I decide to take advantage of her sudden shift in demeanor. "So. You, uh, patrol around here much?"

"Just recently. I've been going around to different areas. Getting to know the city better."

"Oh. That's cool."

That's cool?

I'm a badass freaking crime-fighter, why do I sound like such a dork? Get it together, Sawyer. You're gonna blow this. "So, earlier…"

She looks down and seems a little embarrassed. "Yeah. I know. I'm sorry."

Sorry? I don't expect that at all.

She continues. "I was sort of following you, and when you caught me, I didn't know what to do. I… guess I got a little carried away."

"You were following me?" I say, hoping it doesn't sound too much like an accusation because I'm more than a little flattered.

I shrug. "Oh, yeah, I get it. Well, I guess you more than made up for it. By saving my life, I mean."

When she doesn't respond, I try to think of what to say next. And nothing comes to mind. Absolutely *nada*. The awkward silence feels like it lasts for days. I realize I'm staring at her like an idiot, and I probably still have vomity drool all over my chin.

Finally, she breaks the silence.

"Well, you take care of yourself. Next time, I might not be around when you get into trouble." She grins at me and shoots her grappler across the street. It looks like the same design Harrier and I use, attached to the bracers on our forearm.

"Wait!" Geez, could I sound any more desperate? "Do you think sometime we could... I don't know... patrol together or something? Maybe tomorrow night?" Smooth, d-bag. Real smooth.

She thinks for a couple of seconds. Then, to my utter amazement, says, "Sure, why not? But what would the Black Harrier have to say about it?"

I make a way-too-exaggerated wave of dismissal, along with a lame sound like air leaking out of a tire. Apparently, I'm just so bad at this. "It's not like he's my dad or anything."

"I wondered about that," she says. Before I can respond, she says, "Okay, it's a date. I'll meet you here at eight." She thumbs the button on her grappler and disappears into the night.

I almost can't move, stunned at hearing the word "date." Then I remember I have vomit all over my costume.

And my breath.

CHAPTER
FOUR

S*chool.*

Much worse than fighting crazy villains.

People assume the really evil guys like Doctor Delay or the Magnetist come from insane asylums or high-security prisons. I think they come from my high school.

Like my mom, the teachers have no idea who I am. No one does. They also don't know my special talent. Because of that, I purposely play dumb with them, so they don't expect too much out of me. I can live with Bs. And I don't need my guidance counselor trying to stick me in some AP class because she found out how smart I really am.

That's not me being arrogant. Things like complex math problems and spelling come as easy to me as fighting or parkour. If I see the solution once, I'll know it forever. Same with athletics. Nobody knows how good I am at sports, especially gymnastics and wrestling. Otherwise, I'd be spending all my free time after school practicing with a team.

There is one thing I'm not afraid to excel at in school, and that's technology. Between my computer class and robotics club, I get to use school hours to play around with things I'm working on without drawing any attention to myself. I've been able to make some pretty cool modifications to my costume and old utility belt. I even came up with the prototype for the retractable grapplers we use to get around the city, although Harrier was able to create much cooler ones based on my original idea.

Money makes everything easier, in case you didn't know.

Even there, though, I don't really fit in, because the tech geeks see me as just some skater dude who listens to loud music. But the skaters think I'm a poser. And the popular kids… don't get me started. They don't even notice me.

I'm pretty much invisible to just about everyone here. And that's just the way I like it. Who needs a bunch of friends always calling up, seeing if I wanna go hang out at… I don't know, like, the mall or whatever? Not me.

And, it's not like I'd have the time or the money to take any girls out on dates. That's why I don't bother asking anyone out.

Yeah, *that's* the reason.

For example, here comes the hottest girl in school—the captain of the cheerleading squad, Fabiola. All the girls trailing behind her in her entourage are nearly as hot as she is, too. They're walking by me when my skateboard falls out of my locker and rolls right in front of them. They step right over it and keep going without even looking in my direction.

See? That's me. I just show up in my plain T-shirt and jeans, no popular bands or brand names plastered all over my clothes, nothing to draw attention to myself. I keep a low profile and blend in with the crowd. It almost always works.

Almost.

Unfortunately, there's always some Neanderthal whose hobby is to spot invisible people like me and make us his next victim. My personal caveman's name is Logan, and I'm pretty sure his parents actually named him after the guy with the claws from the comics and movies. Except this guy only has the bad attitude without the Bushido code and dry wit to go with it.

He's also a lot taller than the Logan in the comic books. In fact, he's the tallest kid in school. He plays center on the basketball team and fullback on the football team. Not to mention a bunch of other stuff. But I'm not here to read his triumphal entry. He's pretty much everything that school-version of Sawyer William Vincent is not.

With all those things, he doesn't have a lot of time for stuff like homework, but it doesn't seem to bother anyone else or hurt his grades. Not even the teachers or administrators.

As long as he can manage to juggle his various sports schedules, what difference does it make if he actually learns anything?

I think I showed up on his radar a few weeks ago when he was picking on a kid smaller than me, and I decided to get in the way. He was tormenting this poor guy, and everyone was either too indifferent or too scared to do anything about it. Even though I made it look like an accident, my interference still drew Logan's attention enough that he abandoned the other kid and made me his new "buddy." Obviously, I could pretty much destroy him in two seconds, but like I said, I try to stay incognito.

So, I let him think he's pushing me around, and just make sure he never really connects with a punch or shoves me too hard into a locker. I've watched enough stuntmen in action films to know how to make it look real to everyone else, including Logan.

Meanwhile, the smaller kid I saved, Javier, has attached himself to me in kind of an annoying way. We definitely don't hang out after school or anything, but he tries to sit with me at lunch and stuff. And he isn't much of a conversationalist. I try not to be mean, but a lot of times, I find myself trying to lose him or make an excuse to get away.

Today, he sneaks up on me in the hall like a little ninja as I'm putting my skateboard back in my locker.

"Hey!" His voice is high-pitched, like it's perpetually in the process of changing but never quite gets there.

"Hey, Javi." I hope I don't sound as annoyed as I feel when I greet him.

His unibrow creases as he searches for something to say. I can tell he wants to talk to me really badly but has no idea what topic to bring up.

"Um… did you… do your math homework?"

I toss the books I'll need for my next couple of classes into my backpack and pull out the ones I'm done with. "Yeah."

"Me too! How about history?"

"Yeah," I say again as I slam my locker and double-check the lock.

"Cool. I did it, too. What about—"

"I did all my homework. No need to go down the checklist." I try walking away without being too obvious that I'm trying to ditch him.

He follows behind me. *Come, little doggie.*

"Yeah, I finally finished it all, too. I was up until almost nine-thirty working on it. I thought my mom was gonna kill me for being up so late."

"Well, I'm glad to see you survived." Ugh. Why did I do that? I'm just encouraging him.

"I was wondering if you wanted to hang out after school sometime. Are you into collectible card games?"

"Uh… not really. I can't afford them." I try speeding up. Nearly to class, then I'm home free.

"Yeah, I have to save my allowance for weeks to get a single pack. Um… I don't have a skateboard, but I could watch you do your tricks. I don't mind."

"I don't know if that would be very fun for you. I'm sure we can figure something out one day. When I'm not too busy." I'm *always* busy. That's my secret loophole without lying to him.

He starts to sound desperate. He must be able to tell he's losing me. "Maybe we could—"

Suddenly, Javier freezes like a rabbit who just spotted a wolf. His eyes widen as he stares past me and starts to get this weird twitch. He makes a strange, high-pitched squeaking sound.

I turn around and spot Logan coming toward us, and mentally prepare myself for the idiocy. Javier scurries off in the opposite direction like the rodent he resembles. One of Logan's minions tries to trip him, but he manages to hop over the guy's leg and get away. Wow, that kid can really hop, too.

The bell rings, and I use the excuse to follow after Javi. I try to play it cool since I'm not actually afraid of the muscle-for-brains bully, but I also don't want him to know I'm not afraid.

It's really a delicate game I play, and it sometimes gets tiring. There've been more than a few times I almost clocked the dude.

I'm not gonna get far, anyway, since Logan and Javi are both in my history class, and so is…

Fabiola.

I take my seat one row behind and a seat diagonal to her. Logan plops down directly behind me and shoves his desk into my shoulder blades.

A few giggles issue from his equally brainless cronies, but Mr. Peel appears in the doorway just in time to shut everyone up.

"Mr. Andrews," he says to Logan. "Why don't you come sit in the 'special' seat?"

He motions to a spot at the front where no one likes to sit because the ceiling tends to leak on rainy days. I snicker a little. It's raining. In the olden days, he'd probably be wearing a "dunce" cap.

"I'll get you later, loser," he grunts in my ear as he shoves by. Then to Mr. Peel, he says, "Thank you, sir. I love sitting this close to your desk."

"Mmm-hmm. Turn to page three hundred and ninety-four."

I absentmindedly turn to a page bearing a picture of Ulysses S. Grant, while watching Fabiola flip her long, straight, black hair over her shoulder. The smell of fresh lilacs wafts toward me.

Then, I can't breathe when she turns and stares at me. Her eyes are so green, especially when contrasted with her chestnut skin tone. I smile awkwardly, but she definitely doesn't smile back. She, instead, makes a little face like I'm a clump of dog poo on the bottom of her sandal.

It's about that time that I realize *everyone* is staring at me. Then I hear my name.

"Mr. Vincent… Sawyer… are you listening?"

I snap out of it and realize Mr. Peel is talking to me. I look at him.

"If you're done gawking," he says.

The whole class starts laughing, as if that's what I need.

"I was… I..." I've got nothing, so I shut up.

"Right," he says. "So, can you tell me anything about Ulysses S. Grant?"

What I didn't say is: *Actually, I can tell you everything about Ulysses S. Grant. I know way more than you do about our eighteenth president who was supposed to be with Lincoln the night Abe was assassinated, who won the first battle for the Union in the Civil War, hated wearing uniforms, and whose real name is Hiram, by the way.*

Instead, I say, "Looks like he was in some kind of war."

The class laughs again, only at me this time.

Mr. Peel turns around to write on the whiteboard, and I feel something wet hit the back of my neck. I reach up and pull down a spit-soaked ball of paper. I turn to see one of Logan's lackeys laughing and prodding his friends.

Two seconds. It's all I need, and they'd never walk again.

The rest of class goes pretty much as usual, and I try to keep my head down and get to lunch.

When the bell finally dismisses us, Mr. Peel yells something about homework, but I don't hear him as I shove past Logan's goons and rush back to my locker. I was hoping to make it to the cafeteria before Logan can catch up, but a voice behind me says I had my hopes too high.

"Guess what day it is today, loser?" Logan invades my personal space as he towers over me. I act as casual as possible under the circumstances. He makes absolutely sure he's loud enough for everyone in the hallway to hear. They do, and now, they're all staring in our direction. Everyone.

I should just stay quiet and play dumb. But I don't. I recently read that some expert somewhere says we have like eighty emotions in addition to the ones we already recognize. Right now, I'm feeling all of them coursing through me. Probably more than I can even identify. From worry over Harrier and what might have been on that business card to concern that my mother might actually remember how late I was out last night and try to ground me when I get home. Then, there's anger toward Logan, and excitement over meeting Osprey tonight to patrol together.

So, no. I should stay quiet, but I don't.

"I'm pretty sure your mom said it was her birthday when I was with her last night."

Logan is slightly infuriated at this. No, that's not true. He's pissed. Especially when everyone else, including his friends, laugh so hard at my answer. They start egging him on, asking if he's gonna take this crap from some "little pleb" like me. He responds in the only way someone as dumb as he knows how. He grabs the front of my shirt in his huge hand and tries to be more clever. He fails for sure, but hey, it's the effort that matters, right?

"Wrong. It's the day you finally get your ass beat." His face is red. Like, redder-than-my-costume red. He shoves me into my locker.

Don't say it, don't say it, don't say it… I'm gonna say it. "What's the matter? Did I wake you up when I was sneaking out of her bedroom?"

He swings. I move. He ends up punching a fist-sized impression into the locker.

Enraged and in pain, Logan screams. The string of obscenities would be seriously impressive if it wasn't aimed at me. Harrier would have a stroke if he heard me talk that way.

The crowd scatters as campus security rushes over. My first instinct is to disappear into the crowd, but that's the crimefighter me, not the high school student me. Sure, I might be able to get away, but there are too many witnesses around, so I'm gonna get busted anyway.

So much for my "powers of invisibility."

A few minutes later, Logan and I are sitting across from Principal Blanchard. If I'd ever felt okay with using the term jarhead, it would be about Mr. Blanchard. He used to be in the Marines before he became a P.E. teacher and, eventually, a principal. He still acts like he's in the military—and looks like it, too. I wouldn't be surprised if he really did eat crayons.

I have a lot of respect for veterans. Harrier saw combat in Afghanistan himself. But this guy? He's a real putz.

I look around his office at all the sports memorabilia, trophies, pennants, and I can't help but wonder, does this guy actually give a damn about education?

"Logan, your parents are on their way to pick you up and take you to the emergency room. The school nurse thinks your hand may be broken."

My eyes can't physically roll back any farther, and I think Mr. Blanchard notices because he gives me a little look like he thinks I should be doing pushups or something.

On the other hand, he looks very sympathetic toward Logan even though he knows he regularly bullies kids smaller than him. I know he knows, and he knows that I know he knows. But he still doesn't do crap about it.

Logan just nods. I think he's trying really hard not to cry from the pain, and he's afraid his voice might crack. *Aww, poor widdle bully.*

"Sawyer, we can't seem to be able to get a hold of your mom." He pauses for me to respond. I don't. "We just have the one home phone. Is there another number where we may be able to contact her, such as a cell phone?"

Did you try Reilly's Pub?

"No, sir. I'm not sure where she is."

I try not to look at Logan, who's holding his bandaged hand and staring me down like a pit bull on a leash. Whenever the principal isn't looking at him, it's like he's ready to rip my throat out with his teeth.

"A work number, perhaps?"

If she had a work number, it would be on the freaking student information card that took me an hour to fill out at the beginning of the year.

"No, sir. She, uh… she's between jobs right now."

I see the side of Logan's mouth go up in that combination sneer-grin he does so well. A short fantasy of me taking Blanchard's giant football-shaped trophy and bashing Logan repeatedly in his stupid skull plays through my mind. I try not to smile at the thought.

"I see. Then we'll just have to hold you in the office until after school. We can't have either of you walking around campus after such a display, since it would give the appearance that you did nothing wrong and that there were no repercussions for actions like this."

"Like what?" I say before I can stop myself. "What *did* I do wrong?" Then I add, "If you don't mind me asking."

Mr. Blanchard looks confused as to how I could ask such a question. "Mr. Vincent, Logan's injury could cause him to miss a significant part of the season. Surely, even you could understand how serious that is."

Even me? Wow.

"Yeah, he punched a locker because I ducked. How exactly is that my fault?"

Mr. Blanchard stands and rounds the desk. He looks down at me, hands behind his back, drill sergeant style.

"Several witnesses—trustworthy students, I might add—"

In other words, Logan's popular friends...

"—heard you making inappropriate comments to purposely anger Logan. Obviously, and understandably, he was unable to control his emotions."

"So you're saying that my witty retorts to his threats were somehow just as serious as him trying to take my head off with that meat hook of his?" I'm sure my incredulous expression is just getting me into even more trouble.

Mr. Blanchard draws a straight line with his lips but is saved from whatever nonsense justification he was about to spew by a knock at the door.

"Logan's parents are here to pick him up," his secretary says. She shakes her head and looks sympathetically at Logan's hand, then shoots me the stink eye.

"Tell them to come right in."

When I see the worried look on Logan's mom's face, I almost feel bad. Then I remember the sociopath she raised, and any remorseful feelings vanish. She immediately starts to dote on him, helping him out of his chair, and hugging him. He's gonna milk this thing as long as he possibly can. He starts now by playing it up for his mom. He's all hunched over, holding his hand, and she totally buys into it.

His dad seems to kind of know better. Surprisingly, he looks pretty angry at Logan. Then I realize he's as big a douche as his son is when he says, "I hope this doesn't affect your scholarship chances, son."

Logan's mom gives his dad the *shut up, or you're cut off for a long time* look.

Mr. Andrews turns to the principal. "Thank you. We'll be back tomorrow for the meeting."

"I'll see you folks then." Mr. Blanchard looks worried, too.

Again, I know I should keep my mouth shut. And again, I can't help myself. "It was nice seeing you again, Mrs. Andrews."

Logan's mom gives me a confused look, which totally makes sense since we've never seen one another before in our lives.

Logan turns back, and his look tells me I'm a dead man once his hand is better.

But it was worth it. Totally worth it.

CHAPTER
FIVE

Exhausted.

That's what I am by the time the third death bot comes at me. It's not the most original name, I know, but it's really, really accurate.

Humanoid—that is, it has two arms, two legs, and a head—it lunges at me. Its movements are slow but superfluid, almost exactly like a man its size would move. And the only man I know of its size is that old basketball player, Shaquille O'Neal.

That can't be his real name, right?

I dodge left, barely avoiding a circular saw blade attached to its right arm. It had come down vertically. Anyone knows that's the most ineffective way to attack. It covers the least amount of ground. Now, if I'd have programmed this thing...

I swear as it does exactly what I was gonna say. Its second blade spins toward me in a horizontal swipe, while the first comes back three feet below that one in the exact opposite direction.

There's a taxi directly behind me, so I'm forced to crouch and jump. While tucked into a little ball, I spread out flat, still in the air, then push off the taxi with my feet, kind of like an Olympic swimmer, and spear the robot where the solar plexus of a human would have been. Had this been a human, the sheer force of it would've driven the wind from his lungs, and I'd have been able to finish him with a kick to the side of the head.

But this isn't human. Not one bit. My shoulder feels like it cracked in half, the same one I hurt when fighting Osprey in midair above 9th Street.

Even so, I manage to roll clear of its reach and wall run to safer ground.

Its head spins to follow me. The movement is hella creepy since it's now walking in reverse with just one single eye fixated on me. Legs and arms technically still backward, it raises an arm, and I immediately know what it's planning.

On cue, one of those spinning blades soars through the air, intent upon taking off my head. I dive and slide over the hood of a '73 El Camino. Cool car. I land in a crouch just behind the vehicle and scan my surroundings, looking for anything that might save my hide.

It's dark... really dark. The streetlights are all dead. That was my fault. I thought maybe I could shut down the robots with an EMP grenade. Apparently not. Whatever was powering the bots was completely impervious.

It's not like we've never seen stuff like that. Before I was his partner, Harrier and the first Red Kite—I'm actually the third—had to deal with a literal alien invasion. It all got covered up, but Frank's still got CCTV footage from several places, as well as satellite imagery his company was able to procure.

For whatever reason, the creatures—the Tuldarians—haven't returned. Or maybe they have, and I'm part of the masses not privy to it.

I mentally shrug away the thought since I currently have far more pressing matters to deal with.

At the end of the street, another death bot ambles toward me. I have one advantage: they're as slow and lumbering as hundred-year-old tractors.

I check my utility belt but find nothing of real use. Boomerangs and bolas aren't gonna do much against these metal monstrosities. But I have to come up with something because they are now closing in on me from both sides. I'm just lucky the new one wasn't desperate enough yet to expend one of its blades by shooting it my way.

I stand and break into a run toward the newcomer, and just as I'm about to strike, Harrier appears in front of me.

"Kite," he says, voice muffled and airy through his device.

I skid to a stop.

When I say he appears in front of me, I mean precisely that. He walks right through the death bot like it doesn't even exist, which, since this is a simulation, I guess it doesn't.

Out of breath, I say, "What is it?"

He stands there looking at me, while everything else on the fake New York City street stands still as a frozen lake.

"Hello?"

"I know about her."

An eighty-pound sledgehammer to my chest couldn't have been more jarring.

"You… what?" I ask. But I know exactly what he's gonna say…

"The girl. I know about her. You're done seeing her."

I often wonder if he's capable of forming sentences with more than five syllables until I remember that he's also the incredibly articulate CEO, philanthropist, billionaire playboy Franklin Douglas III.

I take one more look around at the simulation I've been working my ass off to complete for well over an hour now. "Isn't there a better time for this?"

"No."

With that, he turns and walks away, and within seconds, the sim ramps back up again, and the death bot's sawblade slices into my chest.

Everything goes red, and the illusion disappears.

It didn't hurt. I didn't even feel it, but that wasn't the point. I take my training seriously, especially when I was so damn close that time.

Stepping out of the practice room, my teeth are grinding, and my heart is pounding. Who the hell does he think he is, anyway? He can't just tell me what to do.

But he can. He absolutely can. He may not be my father or anything like that, but everything I currently know is because of him. I would just be some lame kid living with his mom in the slums. Sure, I'd still have my awesome ability to maintain and recall anything I ever see, but I wouldn't have the training to control it. That was Frank. He taught me to own it, so it didn't own me. You wouldn't believe how overwhelming it is to remember everything.

At that thought, my ire wanes… sort of. I'm still shaken over what he said about Osprey.

Things with Harrier weren't always like this. When I first became his partner, I was in awe of him. Before the Black Harrier existed, this city was like a war zone with all the criminals and gangs terrorizing everyone. He brought order and justice and did it almost single-handedly.

Problem is, Harrier put down all the mob bosses and crime lords, but then the "supervillains" started rising up.

During the day, he went around town like a carefree celebrity, but that was—and still is—a load of crap. He's hiding the fact that he's never gotten over his dad's death. His mom had died giving birth to him, and his dad raised him alone until he was killed by a gang of criminals when Frank was a teenager. Frank was reckless when he was younger, out of control, even after his dad died. But something made him turn his life around and dedicate himself to fighting crime.

I still don't know what that was.

I met him by accident. It was just after my thirteenth birthday, and I was skateboarding home from school. Some bangers in my neighborhood whose crew I'd refused to join jumped me and pulled me into an alley. They were gonna give me a serious beating. Maybe even kill me.

I was surrounded. They'd smashed my board in half. Then, like hyenas, laughing and everything, their circle started moving in, and they were shoving me between them. No matter how much danger I've been in since then, it's never approached the fear I'd felt at that moment. I was sure I was dead.

Suddenly, Harrier appeared out of nowhere, which was strange because he's very rarely out in the daylight. He told me to run, and I almost did. But then something happened. As I watched him fight, I suddenly felt like I could do the same thing. After half a minute, I'd seen enough of his moves that I decided to try some.

The next thing I knew, I was bending a guy's leg backward with a kick to the knee, then breaking the jaw of another guy with a palm to the face. There I was, fighting back-to-back with my hero. It was amazing. Exhilarating. I'd never felt anything quite like it.

I'd always found it really easy to learn tricks on my board if I saw someone else do it or watched a video. But it still felt like I was learning it on my own. But there, in that alley, watching Harrier, it was like something on the inside of me unlocked. Okay, that's cheesy, but there's no other way to explain it.

Maybe it was the surge of adrenaline or the feeling that I'd become powerful enough to take on those guys, but this was something on a whole different level.

Harrier noticed, and I thought for sure he was gonna yell at me to run again. Instead, he stood there and watched me take out the last two guys by myself.

Even with his visor retracted into his helmet, I couldn't see his eyes behind those tinted lenses on his mask. However, it was obvious that he was doing some serious thinking. He walked over and stared at me for a long time. But it wasn't like he does now. Now, he just broods. Then? It was like he was assessing my worthiness or something. For the next five minutes, he questioned me about everything: me, my mom, school—just… life. I had no idea what was going on, but I wasn't about to lie to him or keep quiet. He'd just saved me.

Finally, he asked me if I'd like him to train me to defend myself. It didn't even take a second for me to respond. Was he kidding? Of course I wanted the best fighter in the world to train me.

The rest is history.

The memory helps wash away the rest of my anger just in time. A large metal door swishes open like we're on the bridge of the Starship *Enterprise*.

The Aerie.

That's literally what Harrier calls it. As if the whole bird of prey theme isn't stupid enough already, he uses a name for a place that practically nobody else knows about except for me. And he couldn't keep it simple and call it "The Nest" either. It had to be a fancy name for it. I've never had the heart—or the guts—to tell him that actual black harriers have their nests on the ground.

Not that I normally mind being here. Harrier's penthouse is nice enough, sitting on top of one of the tallest buildings in the city. Douglas Tower has the best restaurant in town on the ground floor, along with a few high-end shops. The next several levels are offices, including Douglas Industries. And then the upper section is reserved for the most expensive condos in the city, with the top few floors belonging to Harrier himself.

But the secret level above the penthouse, that's a whole different thing. The fastest computers I've ever seen, a helipad that lifts when the ceiling opens, and more high-tech gadgets than an E3 convention. The entrance from the outside allows me to come and go without people wondering what a teenager is doing here all the time and Harrier to enter and exit while in costume.

There are also several training facilities, including the simulation room I was just so rudely interrupted in, and the one where Harrier trained me three years ago. I almost hate to admit it, but everything he shows me does make me better. It's been that way all along. No matter how good I feel like I am, he's always able to help me improve.

In my opinion, though, the coolest things here are the various Black Harrier costumes lined up in their plexiglass lockers. One for every occasion; fighting, detective work, base jumping, scuba diving, even skulking around in the sewers. Some are lightweight for stealth, others are heavily armored, but they're all mostly black with some gray or silver thrown in. And they all have the white on the underside of the cape, like an actual black harrier, only to be seen when he's swooping down from above.

The only thing I don't like about the Aerie—other than the name—is the shrine to the two previous Red Kites. I'm not even sure how he gets those costumes to stand up like that… almost like they're on invisible mannequins, or even freakier, like someone is still inside of them. They simultaneously make me feel like a poser and make me worry about what's in store for me.

"I hope I was clear about how I felt regarding that girl." Harrier doesn't even bother to look up from his super-computer when we have these talks, as if I'm simply a distraction he's trying not to pay too much attention to. I mean, okay, so he's probably doing something super important. Still, he could at least act like we're having a conversation. And—so annoying—he's *clacking* away at a keyboard from, like, the '90s or something. He can *so* afford the latest in touch screen and even holographic technology, too. But, of course, he prefers the "old-fashioned" way.

"I wouldn't exactly call her a girl."

He actually stops typing for a second.

"What would you call her then?"

Him and me. All alone. Voice-changer still on.

Even so, he's got me there.

Woman? Chick? Smokin' hot superheroine?

"Why can't you give her a chance?"

He's back to typing again. "She's unsanctioned."

"By who?"

Uh oh, here it comes.

"*Whom*. By me. By the law. And, most importantly, by the Guild."

"Yeah, yeah. Definitely don't want to be stopping crime and saving people without your union membership card, right?"

Clack, clack, clackity, clack, clack.

"Stay away from her."

And we're back to five syllables.

"Okay! I got it." I turn and hit a practice dummy extra hard since I can't take it out on Harrier. I'm sure he notices.

Another pause in the *clacking*. "I need your help tonight."

Another hit to the dummy. "I'm busy. I have a project due at school tomorrow."

"The project can wait. This can't."

"It's gonna have to," I say. "I'm already missing some assignments in science class, and if I don't turn this in, I'm gonna be failing."

"And?"

"*And* I don't want to fail science."

"Fine. I'll handle it by myself."

Sometimes I'd prefer it if he'd just yell at me. These stone-cold statements followed by icy silence are almost unbearable.

It's nearly eight, and I'm meeting Osprey whether he likes it or not, but I can't help feeling like a total jerk. Especially after he'd just given me a birthday present. Barely ten seconds go by before I feel too guilty to stay quiet.

"Look, maybe I can help out for a couple of hours, then—"

"I'll be fine."

Geez, I thought only women pulled this passive-aggressive crap. My mom's an expert at it.

I start walking toward him, but I don't really know why. It's not like I'm gonna reassuringly place my hand upon his shoulder or anything.

When I'm a few feet away, I say, "Are you sure? I—"

In a swift movement, Harrier swipes something off the desk and shoves it into his lap without moving any other part of his body, then goes right back to typing. I'm pretty sure it was the same business card from last night.

I curse internally.

Why didn't I notice that before? I could've put this whole mystery to rest if I'd just seen it. However, just because I didn't get to see what it says, doesn't mean I don't now know without a doubt that it's something he doesn't want me to know about.

"In fact," he says, "maybe you should go now. Get a head start on finishing your… *science project*."

Now's my chance. *Take it. Take it. Take it.*

"If you say so." I turn to leave the Aerie.

Just as I'm about to reach for the exit hatch, he says, "Say hello to Osprey for me."

I freeze in my tracks and swallow hard. He knows. *Of course* he knows. And he knows her name? Who is this guy? Sometimes, it's easy to forget he's the greatest hero alive.

I'm too ashamed to even apologize. I spin toward him and for the first time, notice what he's working on. Up on the screen is a photo and intel on his former arch-enemy, Chef Maléfique. Stupid name for a supervillain, I know. Apparently, it's French for "Evil Chef." And, no, I have no idea why he called himself that. Any time I bring him up, I get shut down.

But why would he be looking him up? Chef Maléfique blew himself up before I even started working with Harrier, so I can't think of any reason he'd be working on this.

I almost say something, but I swallow the words as it hits me again—the nagging feeling that something is wrong, and this time it comes on like a panic attack. I clench my teeth and try to insist I'll go with him, but the words just won't come out. I stand there for about thirty seconds, trying to do the right thing.

Instead, I open the hatch and glide out into the evening sky without even looking back.

CHAPTER SIX

Weird.

Not sure what it is lately, but I'm used to my mom being gone or passed out, and again, there she is, wide awake and watching some stupid reality show. Instead of putting on my costume and sneaking through my window, I have to change on the roof and stash my clothes somewhere.

I sling my backpack over my shoulder and try to cross the room as quickly and quietly as possible.

Mom turns down the volume on the whiny voice of some so-called reality star. "Where are you off to?"

"Library. Science project."

"I need to talk to you about—"

"Sorry. Gotta go." I close the door before she can get out another syllable and rush up the stairs before she can follow me. I'm pretty confident she's heard all about my little scuffle with Logan by now, and the meeting she's supposed to have with Principal Blanchard tomorrow.

Before I don my costume, I sniff it to make sure it doesn't still smell like puke. The bleachy smell from the cleaner I used last night isn't much better, but it'll have to do.

I always wonder, when I'm changing like this, if someone in one of the nearby buildings ever spots me and is curious about what I'm doing. Not that New Yorkers care much about what other people do—especially this close to Halloween—but it would definitely be weird if they did.

As I'm putting on my new cape, my mind wanders to Harrier. What's he doing tonight that he would need my help? He's never asked me like that before. Does it have something to do with why I've been patrolling on my own so often lately? I'm sure he'll be okay.

After making sure my costume's in order, I glide to the building where Osprey and I met. The butterflies in my stomach and weakness in my limbs make me second-guess the idea of patrolling with her. What if I'm not focused enough? I could actually get killed out there.

But as soon as I see her waiting for me—and she sees me—I know there's no way I could ditch her. I don't want to either. The way she looks, the way she stands, the way her costume…

Bleep.

"Heart rate?" I ask.

"Not even a hello? I've missed you," Amber says.

"Yeah, it's just the new cape. Still getting used to it."

"Mmmm-hmmm."

"Silent mode," I say, then retract my face shield. My domino mask still covers my eyes and the top half of my face, but I figure it's a bit weird to show up to a "date" with my face covered.

Osprey doesn't seem upset that I'm a little late thanks to Mom, so that's good.

"Kite," she says as I touch down on the rooftop. When she says my old codename, I don't mind it as much.

"Hey, Osprey." Did my voice just crack? Dammit. Stay cool. Stay. *Cool.* "I actually go by Raptor now. Red Raptor."

"What was wrong with Red Kite? I kind of liked it."

And I kind of like you.

"Nothing, as long as someone knows it's a pretty awesome hawk. But most people think of a toy that flies in the air."

Osprey laughs. "I have to admit, I did think that when I was a kid. But I guess that must've been a different Kite back then."

"Yeah."

As expected, she knows her Black Harrier lore.

"When did you take over?"

"I'm actually the third. I've only been his si—partner for a few years."

I almost said sidekick. I *never* say sidekick. This girl has me off my game like no one ever does.

"I never realized that," she says.

I can't blame her. Most people don't know there were three of us. Harrier and Frank, since sometimes they seem like totally different people, rarely talk about the previous Kite. Not even I know what happened, just that one day he was gone and I was him.

"What happened to the other two?"

I knew that question was coming.

"I wish I knew. He won't talk about it." And I've asked. I've asked a *lot.*

"That doesn't sound good."

She pushes a strand of hair behind her ear, and just like it had the first time, the action makes me weak. What the hell is wrong with me? I'm the freaking Black Harrier's partner!

"Yeah. Tell me about it. That's the other reason I wanted to change my name. I don't like having to live up to what those other guys did." It feels good to tell somebody this. I certainly can't tell Harrier.

A bit of his paranoia washes over me, and I can hear his voice in the back of my head. *The girl. I know about her. You're done seeing her.*

Maybe he's right? Maybe he knows something I don't. Why am I trusting her so much? I really have no idea who she is or what her real agenda might be.

"How'd you come up with the new name?" she asks before I have the chance to worry any more.

"I don't know. It just kind of came to me."

Liar.

I spent hours trying to find something that wasn't either already taken by a real crimefighter or trademarked by some comic book company or movie studio. But it makes the most sense. Harriers and Kites are raptors. And fun fact: so are Ospreys. Though she probably knows that.

"Red Raptor. I like that too. But now you have a similar problem to the one you had with Kite."

"What's that?"

"Everyone might think you were named after a dinosaur instead of a bird of prey."

"Yeah, I guess. But it's a lot better than a diamond-shaped toy on a string."

"I suppose I can't argue there," she says. Then, "So... where should we start?"

Every time she smiles at me like that, my chest constricts. What is up with that? I clear my throat to make sure it doesn't crack again.

"Ummm…"

Grab some dinner? See a movie? Followed by some serious making out?

I continue to try to appear as nonchalant as possible. "Whatever, I guess. Where do you usually go?"

"Well, I have my earpiece tuned in to the police scanner. When I hear something's going on, I try to beat the cops there."

Wow. That's smart. I mean, I have Amber to tell me of anything strange happening in the city, but I can't expect someone without Harrier's resources to be able to afford a super-smart A.I.

"Yeah. That sounds pretty good." I do my best shrug. I wish I could see her eyes, but she has those same reflective lenses in her mask that Harrier uses. I bet they're blue. Or green. Or brown… like caramel. Hazel maybe?

"Until then, we can just... patrol."

"Right. Cool."

I need to get a book with things to say to girls that won't make me sound like a total dork.

Patrolling with Osprey for the first time takes me back to when I first started with Harrier. I had no idea what I was doing, and he had me stay off to the side and observe for a long time before he allowed me to get in on the action. I was still in my regular clothes then, so nobody suspected I was with him.

Meanwhile, he was training me at the Aerie and showing me all the moves he knew. Since I picked up everything so quickly, it was just a matter of going through all the different styles of fighting and then practicing them for a week or so. His style is a combination of a bunch of various martial arts and fighting techniques, but he wanted me to learn everything from the easy beginner moves up to the most complex combinations for each discipline.

Within a few months, I had so many choices every time I made a move that it was kind of overwhelming. But soon, I narrowed down the hundreds of options to certain ones that I liked and were the most effective for me. My style isn't even the same as Harrier's. I use a lot of kicks while he prefers punching most of the time. I think it's part of his anger management program.

He drilled it into me to "Never fight angry." He was preaching to himself, so to speak. We always most easily see our own sin in others.

It wasn't all just training me to fight, though. Harrier also became my mentor. I didn't have a dad around growing up, and even though he isn't much of a father figure, he's still a strong role model for me. He's helped me to learn a ton of things about life that I just haven't gotten growing up with a single mom.

Plus, he bought me practically anything I wanted or needed. The only problem was that most of the time I couldn't bring it home.

Eventually, he gave me my Red Kite costume and made it official. It was pretty close to the others' costumes, but there were some mods and improvements. I've made some changes of my own over the past three years, too—even changing the symbol. Which, like the name change, Harrier didn't embrace easily.

But across all three Kites, one thing that's always consistent is the red, black, and white coloring.

There's a popular joke among crimefighters that the heroes like to dress their sidekicks in bright colors, so they make better targets and keep the heat off of them. But I don't think that's true, at least in Harrier's case. I think the red is so I always stand out no matter how many people are around, so he can keep an eye on me and make sure I'm safe.

Plus, I'm not his sidekick. I'm his partner.

At least, that's what I always tell myself.

"You see that?" Osprey says, pulling me back into the present.

In New York, you never have to patrol long before spotting a crime of some sort. Most times, it's a mugging or a robbery. It almost always involves some loser with a fake gun.

This time, it's a little different—but I can still see the old "there's a gun in my pocket" thing going on.

Below, a dude is arguing with an old man to get out of his car. From the roof, we can't hear the words, but I've heard it all before. The old man has his hands up in surrender, and he's moving slow to get out of the car while the young guy motions frantically with his pocket-gun hand.

"You go behind him," I tell Osprey. "I'll take the front. If he runs, take him down?"

She nods.

Using our capes, we glide down. I snap mine shut just above the car hood and land with a loud metal *thud*.

"Nice night for a carjack!" I say.

The guy with the fake gun turns on me, a wild look in his eye. This guy is whacked out on something strong for sure.

Crouched, I spin and sweep the man's hidden weapon aside, then lash out with my other boot to his face. He staggers backward and into Osprey, who finishes him off with a gut punch.

When the criminal is moaning on the ground, I zip tie his wrists together.

"Call it in, Amber," I say.

"*Your desire is my duty,*" Amber says.

"Yeah. Silence mode, please."

The last thing I need is Amber's sexual innuendos while I'm patrolling with Osprey.

I stand and clap my hands together, turning to face the victim. I have a huge smile on my face, and I expect him to as well. Instead, his scowl almost says as much as his words.

"You motherbucker!" The guy says, except that isn't what he says.

"Whoa, whoa!" I say, backing away.

"Look at my car!" He stabs a finger at the hood where there's a distinct impression of my booted footprints.

Behind him, Osprey is giggling at me.

"I'm sorry," I say. "I was just trying to help."

"Help do what, you idiot? That guy had no weapon, and I got insurance. Now... now, what do I do? Tell them it was foot-sized hail?"

"I'm... I'm sorry?" I say. It comes out as a question. I've literally never experienced anything like this with Harrier. People are usually thrilled to be saved and even more thrilled to meet Harrier.

"Buck you!" he doesn't say. "Get the hell out of here."

I cross the pavement to where Osprey stands, hand to her mouth, covering a smile, and leave the guy to his bucking.

"Wow," I say once we are back on the rooftops. "Can you believe that?"

"It's New York. Of course I can believe that."

I shake my head as we start to parkour across the city once again. For the most part, Osprey keeps up, which is impressive. Granted, I'm going pretty easy on the moves. Doing my best to show her some cool stuff, but not look like I'm showing off. I think it works.

Bleep.

At the same time I receive my Amber Alert, Osprey says, "Hold on a sec." She puts a finger to her ear and listens for a moment.

"Yeah?" I whisper to Amber, not sure I'm ready for Osprey to know I have a sex demon talking in my ear.

"Okay, got something," Osprey says.

Then together, she and Amber both say, "Corner of First and Houston."

Before I can respond, she leaps off the roof. Sure enough, she's already copied the design of my new cape, and she's gliding toward First Street faster than I can keep up. I don't see any jets, though. If she figured out the cape in one day, that'll probably only take, like, another week or so for her to tackle.

I leap off the rooftop after her and realize I still need to practice this some more. I'm used to jumping around on rooftops and swinging from my grappler line. Gliding through the air is totally new to me, and since I haven't seen someone else really do it, I have nothing to imitate. It's definitely fun, though.

"What's going on, Amber?"

"A group of naughty robbers at J. Jewelers."

"How many?"

I'm moving too fast to see the looks on the faces of the people below, but I can see them looking up and pointing at us. Some of them are recording us on their phones. I bet we make the papers tomorrow.

Too bad nobody reads the papers anymore. Maybe we'll be all over social media. Not that I have time for that sort of thing. I'm a little busy with the whole crimefighting and, you know, generally saving the world thing.

"Her butt looks amazing in those tights," Amber says, her voice slathered with sex.

"Amber, please, focus." What I really mean is that I can't lose *my* focus. "How many robbers?"

I swear whenever I speak to the AI that way, there's a slight pause like she's mad. That's gotta be in my head, right?

"Only nine."

Only.

"Thanks, Amber. Silent mode, please."

As I follow Osprey, I start to fantasize about her being my partner instead of Harrier. We could be together all day and hang out, then patrol at night. Then we could go home and—*whoa*! I need to pay attention. I almost hit that power line and fried myself. Definitely need to focus.

But what would happen to Harrier? Would he just go on alone? Find a fourth Red Kite? Why do I really care? Most of the time, he just acts like I'm a pain in the ass anyway. Except today… when I abandoned him for Osprey.

The guilt runs deep, but I'm gonna have to deal with it at another time.

Osprey swoops down, and I follow. We arrive on the scene, but I have no idea what to expect. Amber was right—it's J. Jewelers, a chain of high-end diamond dealers here in the city. All I see is a building with its alarm going off and broken glass everywhere. When Harrier and I work together, we always have a plan. Osprey apparently just jumps in and improvises.

As we close in, I can see that it looks like a typical jewelry store robbery. Bust through the window, get in, grab what they can, get out fast.

Unless Harrier and I happen to get lucky, we don't usually come across this kind of action. So why did Amber pick it up this time?

I start to ask her, but Osprey lands outside the store's entrance just as the first masked robber exits with his bag full of goodies. She smashes him in the face with a roundhouse kick before he even notices she's there.

Okay, I guess we really are just going in with no plan at all. No time to worry about it now.

Another advantage of the new glider cape is that I'm moving pretty fast when I slam feet first into the next guy out the door. He flies backward into another, and they are both out cold with no more fuss. Osprey gives me a big smile, which unfortunately means I'm not paying attention when a fourth guy starts taking potshots at me with his pistol.

Bleep.

Yeah, that doesn't do me a lot of good after the bullet leaves the gun. I'm really gonna have to tinker with her emergency programming.

Luckily, the thug's aim sucks, and the bullet whizzes by without touching me. It seems whatever the cape is made of is at least as strong as my graphene armor. The bullet stops dead and falls harmlessly to the sidewalk.

The guy looks at me, stunned. I toss one of the throwing stars from my belt at his gun, and it lodges in the end of the barrel, just like it's supposed to. As I leap forward and knock him down with a foot to the face, I recognize the mask he and his buddies are wearing. From afar, it looked like a typical bank robber type setup, but up close, I see the multi-colored, spandex-looking things…

No. This is *not* good. They're the henchmen of—

"La Cucaracha!" Osprey calls him out like we're in a cartoon or something. It's the first thing she's ever done that I didn't totally love. Taunting one of New York's most dangerous?

Now I know why Amber picked up on this.

Why the hell didn't you tell me? I think, but I don't dare say to her. The last thing I need is her voice in my ear, further distracting me.

Right now, my instinct is to run. To call Harrier for help. But I don't want to look weak in front of Osprey.

"I don't believe we've had the pleasure, *Mija*."

Like any good boss, La Cucaracha stands inside the jewelry store, watching his men get pummeled.

I'm not sure the guy is even Latino, but he always throws in some Spanish words to keep up his shtick. Why someone so huge would name himself after an insect never made any sense to me. And for anyone to adopt the moniker The Cockroach? Blech.

But I'm pretty sure super-intelligence isn't one of his powers. I mean, Spanish isn't my best subject, but shouldn't it be 'El Cucaracho' or something? He's all strength and looks like one of those Photoshopped bodybuilder guys who are too huge to be real.

From what I've heard, he's actually sort of an outlaw hero back in Mexico, like some kind of Robin Hood or something. I guess he robs wealthy Americans and sends it all back there. I'd almost applaud him… but the problem is, he isn't just stealing, he's also hurting a lot of people along the way.

"It's Osprey," she says, flicking her wrist and producing a stick that extends on both ends into a five-foot staff. "And trust me, jerkwad, we've met."

He tilts his head like a dog.

"Oh, well, I'm sure it was a pleasure," he says. "Now if you'll *perdóneme*. We have work to do."

"I promise this is going to be one of the *least* pleasurable experiences you've ever had."

Witty banter. I like that. Usually, Harrier just grunts and barks orders. But it's also kind of stupid. Like I already said, La Cucaracha is huge, and she darts into the store and leaps straight at him. I can't see his face because of that half-green-half-yellow *luchador* mask he wears. But I can imagine he's smiling. He's also stronger than any bodybuilder out there with his exoskeleton that gives him super-strength —and, hey, it does make him look sort of like a cockroach now that I think about it.

She doesn't stand much of a chance against him on her own. She's fighting out of what seems like anger, and like I said... Black Harrier has always taught me, that's the worst place you can be. That's when you make mistakes.

It's a good thing I'm here with her.

She swings her collapsible staff at him, and he grabs it away from her with no effort whatsoever. Then, he bites down on the middle of it, pulls down on the ends, and snaps it into three pieces with his mouth. The guy's a brute even when the exoskeleton isn't enhancing his strength.

As La Cucaracha swats Osprey away, she crashes through the storefront glass and slides to a stop by my boots. Luckily, her armor seems as sturdy as mine, so she wouldn't have been hurt too badly.

"What are you doing?" I ask.

"I hate bugs," she says.

Oh, okay, the banter continues even when the villain can't hear. Wonderful.

"Well, he's gonna kill you," I say as I throw one of my smoke bombs at him.

While he stomps around in confusion, I help Osprey up. She starts rushing toward him again, and I yank her back. She practically snarls at me and holds her arm like it's injured. I don't think she has any experience fighting actual supervillains, and she's probably embarrassed by how easily he took her down. I get the impression that, up until now, this has been some kind of game to her.

"Come out, *parajito*, and face me." He flexes, and his muscles bulge so much that I think I can hear them.

"We need a plan," I say, keeping my voice low even though he probably wouldn't hear me over his own bellowing. "Get ready to slam into him from the back. I'm gonna come in low and sweep his legs."

Osprey nods, if a bit reluctantly, and I watch as she uses the cover of smoke to duck behind the U-shaped cases filled with priceless gems and metals. She disappears into the smoke and moves around behind La Cucaracha. I give her a few more seconds to get into place, then I run straight at him. As the smoke starts to clear, he sees me and reaches forward like he's gonna grab me. This also forces his momentum to follow. At the last second, I turn sideways and roll the last few feet into his shins. Osprey hits him in the back just at the right time, and he falls forward like a bowling pin. The exoskeleton may make him stronger, but it also impedes his movement.

His face slams into one of the display cases, and it smashes to pieces under his weight. We jump out of the way as glass shatters all over the place.

Any average person would be lucky to be alive after that. I'm pretty sure we just pissed him off. He struggles to get up and screams with rage, blood covering his now-shredded mask.

"He's too strong. We need to disconnect his power source. I'm gonna distract him. You try to grab onto those cables and yank them out." I make sure Osprey nods her understanding, and then rush the big bug again.

I try to land a kick to his chest, but he grabs my leg while I'm in the air. I know people talk about someone's grip being like a vice all the time, but his really is. There's no way I can break it. He swings me around in a move like we're fighting a Hell in the Cell match or something and tosses me through the *other* front window of the store. Despite my disorientation, I manage to wrap myself in my cape before I skid across the sidewalk and back onto the street.

One of the first things Harrier taught me was how to land without getting hurt, so I'm in pretty good shape as I try to figure out my next move. I just hope Osprey—

No. He must have caught her as she tried to pull out the cables that deliver power from the large battery in the middle of his back. La Cucaracha holds her up with one hand around her neck, The Undertaker style. But I get the distinct impression he's not about to smash her down with a chokeslam. With that grip, she doesn't have long.

Since his back is to me, I should have one chance to do this.

One deep breath. It's all I have time for. Then I run and flip through the gap in the storefront window, landing just behind him. I pull a cyclone blade from my belt and slice the cables.

He immediately screams and drops Osprey. Smoke rises from his back as his technology seizes up on him, and sparks fly from the cables. He falls headlong to the ground, and broken glass falls free from half a dozen display cases and both windows.

I hear the sirens, and the street is filled with blue and red flashes as the cops finally show up. I'm really not in the mood to give a report right now, and some police officers really don't appreciate us doing their jobs for them. I quickly help Osprey to her feet, then we take off out the back door.

CHAPTER **SEVEN**

"What the hell was that?" I ask, and I can barely believe I'm talking to Osprey like this. The girl I've been pining over. Who'd consumed most of my thoughts for the last twenty-four hours. And I'm yelling at her. But she deserves it, right? I mean who does that? That was freaking La Cucaracha.

We are now safely above the city again, watching from a distance as the police do their job and toss the robbers into their squad cars. It would have been pretty romantic if I wasn't so pissed. As they drive away, I'm surprised and a little frightened by the absence of La Cucaracha in the walk of shame. Has he gotten away?

"What was what?" she has the audacity to ask.

Bleep.

"Not now!" I scream.

"What?" Osprey says.

"Nothing."

"What is your problem?" Osprey asks.

Me? What's *my* problem. Are you kidding me? That was amateur hour back there, and we both almost died.

To her, I simplify it. "That was stupid."

"You're stupid," she says in what could be the most immature response I've ever heard.

"Wow," I say. It's all I can even come up with.

I bailed on Harrier for this. To gallivant around the city with someone I, apparently, barely know, diving headfirst into supervillain battles.

He was right. He's always right. I should have stayed far away.

I shake my head. "You know what? I gotta get home. I'll see you later, maybe."

"You're acting like I did something wrong," she says to my back. I turn to her, and she's standing with her arms crossed in a totally defensive posture.

"You *did* do something wrong!" I want to leave, but for some reason, I can't let this go. "You don't just leap into a situation with one of the world's most dangerous criminals without even discussing a plan. You could have—*we* could have been killed."

"Don't you do this, like, for a living, or whatever?" she argues.

"Yeah, and I'm approved by the Guild to do so." And there it is. I am actually Harrier now. All I need is the stupid voice-changer.

She looks to the side like she's disgusted. "Whatever. If you're afraid of a little bug, maybe you shouldn't be doing this."

"Enough with the 'little bug' stuff. That guy is massive, and he could have been the one squashing us like bugs. What were you thinking?"

That question seems to give her pause. She turns her back to me and takes a few steps. I consider following, but I give her space and wait.

Maybe she's right. Who am I to question her? I agreed to go along with her, didn't I?

That's when it hits me. Like a two-by-four to the face.

"You knew about the robbery, didn't you? You were using me."

I don't even need a response. I know it's true. Good thing too, because she's silent as a ghost.

"You went from attacking me and almost killing me, to what—us out on a 'patrol date?'"

How stupid am I? I can't believe I fell for this. What an idiot. *Hi, I'm Sawyer and I become a complete doofus the moment a pretty girl smiles at me.* Well, not anymore. I'm nobody's fool.

"Unless you've got an answer for me, I'm out of here."

It looks like she's about to say something when I hear the sound of stone cracking and little rocks bouncing like a tiny, little avalanche. Her eyes go wide, fixated behind me, and I spin to see a green and yellow head appear just above the low wall of the rooftop. True to his name, the freaking cockroach is using his exo-suit to crawl up the side of the building.

"That was *no muy bueno,*" he says.

"Look, I'm sorry," Osprey says to me. "Just please don't leave me here alone with him?"

I worry that I'm falling for it again. She's using me again, like twenty minutes later. But there's more than just desperation in her voice. It's like she's begging. What am I, heartless? Harrier wouldn't leave her. If I did, I'd be breaking the only rule, killing her by not helping.

I take a deep breath and turn to face La Cucaracha. "How did you get out of there?" I ask. I'm sure he'll answer. Let's have a seat, maybe a spot of tea, Mr. Skuzzy Bug.

To my surprise, he does just that.

"Do you think I'm *estúpido*?" The Spanish thing is becoming incredibly annoying and more than a little bit racist. "Backup battery."

By now, he's standing fully on the roof, towering over us and looking even more imposing, silhouetted in the light of a giant full moon. With Halloween coming up, why not bring out all the crazies?

I look to Osprey, who doesn't even have her staff now, and she looks scared. I don't blame her. I'm terrified. The only thing going for us is that there aren't eight more of his men waiting to take our heads off. Problem is, he's probably enough all by himself.

I nod, and we both rush in.

Unlike ignorant back alley thugs, we don't attack one at a time. She and I engage him with a flurry of blows, and all of them connect. He, however, doesn't even flinch. It's like we're hitting steel with Q-tips.

He grunts and says, "My turn." Then, with a roar that barely sounds human, he punches forward with both closed fists. They connect and send us both soaring across the roof. I hit my head hard on something, but I'm too woozy to care what it is. Even with my helmet on, it rattles me.

I look to the side and see Osprey stand and disappear out of sight before my world goes black.

I come to confused. Really, really confused.

I'm still on the rooftop, staring up through my visor at a starless sky. Harrier says that the movies and TV shows are all wrong, that if you're knocked out for more than a minute, you risk brain damage. Since my brain feels fine, I'm guessing I wasn't out very long.

Then I remember La Cucaracha and Osprey. I bolt upward, and my head becomes a swivel.

Nothing.

No one.

"Amber," I say.

"It's about time," she says. *"I was getting lonely."*

"Yeah, yeah. Where's Osprey?"

A slight pause?

"Always a bridesmaid, never a bride."

You know, it's one thing for my artificial intelligence to have a voice like a high-end stripper, but add a measure of snark to it, and it's difficult to get anything done.

"Amber, where is she? This is important." I can't believe I'm doing my best to keep the frustration out of my voice, so I don't upset the computer voice in my helmet.

"How do you expect me to know the answer to that, Sawyer?"

I have been dreading this moment and hoping it wouldn't come. I rub the back of my neck. "I… uh… sort of slapped a tracker on her."

Amber is silent and judgmental. Not really, she's just a computer. Maybe it's my own embarrassment.

Shameful, perhaps, but now I'm glad I did it. When I helped her up during the first fight with La Cucaracha, I'd grabbed her hand with my right hand, and when bracing her back, I tagged her.

She'll be mad at me for all of two seconds once she realizes that's the only way I can help her if La Cucaracha has her.

"I see a restraining order in your future," Amber says.

"It's not like that, and you know it. I didn't know if I could trust her. I needed to be able to find her, no matter what."

Wait a second. Why in the name of everything holy am I explaining myself to Amber?

"You know what? Just find her, would you?"

"Triangulating."

Damn right, she is. I'm the boss.

Just then, I hear a scream, and I know it's Osprey. I speed for the ledge, and without even looking first, I push off, and I'm Eaglestar, flying through the air. Snapping my cape, it becomes rigid, and I glide swiftly toward the sound.

"Osprey is one block east," Amber says.

"Thanks. Keep me posted on her movements."

"Oh, you'd like that, wouldn't you?" Amber says.

Then I see her, ground level. She's giving La Cucaracha hell, but I think he's toying with her. I break into a dive, gaining crazy speed. Just as I'm about to hit him face-first, I flip around and nail him with two stiff legs right in the back of his head. If he saw me coming, he sure didn't do anything about it.

Using his head like a springboard, I shove off toward Osprey. Without even thinking, I wrap an arm around her, extend my other one with my grappling hook tight in hand, and fire toward the nearest building. Together, we rise above the city streets.

"What are you doing!" she shouts. "I had him!"

"You absolutely didn't have him," I say. "He was playing with you."

We land on a nearby rooftop.

She looks at me like I've stolen her milk money.

"You could say thank you," I say, really tired of the games.

The expression on her face is not what I expected. She looks... impressed.

"We can talk about this later. For now, are you okay? Can you run?"

"Yeah. I think so."

"Good, follow me."

She does her best to keep up as I parkour from roof to roof until we are a respectable distance from La Cucaracha, and I'm satisfied that he won't be sneaking up on us again.

"I'm not helpless, you know," she says, seeming pretty sore as we cross another rooftop.

I stretch a hand out for us to stop. "Look, I know you're mad about what I said, but La Cucaracha isn't someone to take lightly."

"You think I don't know that?" she says. She spins away and kicks at the rooftop stones. They clatter in silence.

Unchartered territory here, Sawyer, I tell myself.

I, of course, was right. I don't know what to say, so I just shut up.

A few minutes later, I'm rewarded for my patience.

"You were right," she says.

I was?

"I'm sorry."

You are?

"That's why I had to draw him away from you. I couldn't live with myself if I got you hurt, or worse."

Is this another manipulation tactic? Is she just trying to cover up for her dumb mistakes? I don't know, but I have to give her the benefit of the doubt.

Now my own bout of silence lingers on.

"Can you say something?" she asks, her voice meek.

I clear my throat a couple of times. "I... I've fought the guy so many times with Harrier. He's dangerous. Really dangerous. A lot of villains want to play games and pull elaborate stunts. Not him. La Cucaracha will tear your limbs off for the fun of it."

"I know. Really. I'm sorry."

"It's okay," I tell her. "From now on, you stick with me, no matter what. Okay?"

"From now on? So you forgive me?" She almost sounds like Amber. Definitely at least some minor manipulation there.

"Yeah," I say. "I guess."

"*Awwwww*," Amber says. "*Not tell her about the tra—*"

"Silent mode," I say, unable to believe everything we'd done had happened within the three-minute period I allot Amber before an alert is required.

"What does that mean?" Osprey asks.

I explain to her about Amber, and she says, "Whoa!" I left the part out about her sounding like a super horny streetwalker.

"It sounds cooler than it is," I tell her.

"I doubt that. I didn't even know tech like that existed. Can I talk to her?"

The thought of Amber talking to the girl I like is even more horrifying than introducing Osprey to my mom.

"I'd rather you not," I say. "Not yet, at least."

She looks a bit dejected but seems to accept my response.

"What's it like?" she says. "Being his—"

"Sidekick?" If I haven't mentioned it, I *hate* that word.

"I was going to say 'partner.'"

"Oh. Sorry. Little sensitive about that, I guess."

"Why?"

Do you have a few days to talk about it?

"It isn't easy living in the shadow of someone like the Black Harrier."

"I'd give *anything* to be his partner."

Not sure what to say to that. But I remember feeling the same way once.

"Yeah. It's kind of one of those, 'Be careful what you wish for' type of things, you know? When I first started working with him, I was in awe. But just like everything else, it wears off."

"I guess I really don't know what it's like for you, but I can't imagine ever getting sick of it. He must teach you so much."

Now I'm feeling guilty. What *is* my real problem with Harrier? Is he really that bad, or is it me? Am I being an ungrateful little brat? A typical rebellious teenager? Or maybe just a grade-A jerk?

"Um, yeah. I guess he does. Now it's my turn."

"For?" she says, skepticism oozing off her.

"What happened between you and La Cucaracha?"

The look on her face makes me wonder if I'd accidentally killed her puppy.

She takes a deep, shuddering breath.

"About a year ago, I fought him."

"A year? You've been doing this for a year?"

"No, I was out of it for a while after that fight. He... he put me in the hospital. Almost killed me."

I can't even form words. I think I say, "Wow," or something similarly inappropriate.

"I told my parents I got hit by a speeding taxi while I was walking down the street. Luckily, I didn't have a costume back then, so when I showed up to the hospital, bloody and broken, they didn't suspect anything—or at least if they did, they never said anything.

"Even after I recovered, I didn't really recover, if you know what I mean."

I do. I guess that's the reason Harrier is so adamant about heroes being licensed.

"So why go after him again?" I ask.

"What would you do?" Her tone is slightly accusatory, but I guess the question makes sense.

She isn't wrong, either. If I were her, I'd have an archnemesis for life. Actually, it's kind of cool that she has one, even if he had no clue what he'd done. Oh. Ouch.

As if she read my thoughts, she says, "Crapface didn't even remember me."

"I'm sorry," I say, and I know it's not enough.

"Yeah, thanks."

Heh. Superhero problems.

We arrive back at our meeting place, too battered to do any more patrolling. Osprey walks up close to me and reaches out, then wipes some blood off of my face.

"Thanks for showing me a good time, hero."

Omigod omigod omigod, is this really gonna happen? Is it? She leans in close, and I close my eyes. Then she kisses me.

On the cheek.

I open my eyes, and she's already backed away. Osprey holds out her hand.

"Hey, before you go, I have something for you."

That smile. God, I love that smile.

"Really?"

She tosses me a small tin box. I look at the front. Not just mints—the really strong mints. I'm not sure whether to be insulted or hopeful.

"You might want to keep them in your utility belt." She shoots her grappler at a nearby rooftop and zips away into the night.

CHAPTER **EIGHT**

I'm so up from my night with Osprey, I don't even notice the light beneath my bedroom door.

But when I open it, and Mom's there, sitting on my bed, arms crossed, cigarette in hand, blowing smoke out of her nose like a dragon? I know there's gonna be a long discussion. At least there's no bottle this time.

She doesn't even wait before she starts laying into me, fiery hot as her hair.

"Where the hell have you been?"

She lowers her voice on the word "hell" like God was gonna hear her and smite her. For Mom, that was a curse word as bad as any.

"I was out," I say, nonchalantly entering and lowering my stuff to the floor.

"Out where?" She stabs the cigarette into a paper plate, which I can't imagine is a smart idea, and drops the butt into an empty diet soda can.

"Just out. With a girl."

Since when do you care?

She rolls her eyes. "I hope you used protection. The last thing you need is to be paying child support for the next eighteen years."

"Mom, it's not like that."

But I sure wish it was.

She stands and gets in my face. "You think I'm stupid?"

"Well, you did manage to get knocked up when you weren't much older than me, didn't you?"

Oh, man, that was dumb.

She slaps me across the face. Not in a child abuse sort of way. More like an old-timey, black-and-white movie sort of way.

I just fought Arnold Schwarzenegger on crack, and it still hurts, though.

"I shouldn't have said—"

"And where'd you get this?" she asks, pulling out my older, spare costume. She shoves it at me, and I couldn't be more shocked. I'm sure it shows on my face.

My heart pounds like it's holding a sledgehammer, and it's trying to break out of my chest cavity with it.

"That… that…" I can't get any words out because I can't breathe.

"Must have cost a fortune. Just for some stupid costume party, or... or comic book convention?"

The relief is so overwhelming that I almost collapse into a puddle of goo. I'm such an idiot. Why would someone assume I'm some kind of crimefighter just because I look like a cosplayer?

"But—"

She strikes up another cigarette and waves the smoke away with her hand like my whole room doesn't already smell like an ashtray.

"I called the school today to check the time of our meeting tomorrow about you beating up that kid."

"Oh my God, Mom, I didn't beat anyone up."

"That's not the story they tell. You are out of control, young man."

Young man. Is there any more derogatory term to be called by your parents? I don't think I've ever seen her this angry.

"While I was on the phone, I had a little hunch, and I asked about your computer. You know what they told me? They said there's no government program, and they don't know where you got it from. And this..." She tosses something at me, and I almost don't catch it in time. "This... i-thing—"

"Tablet."

Damn, I thought I'd hidden that pretty well.

"Whatever it is, it's even more expensive than the laptop. I think it's pretty obvious what's going on here."

"It is?" *Wait.* So did she figure it out or not?

"You're selling drugs."

I can't help it. I bust out laughing. It's like one part humor and a hundred parts relief. I really need to learn some self-control.

"What's so funny?"

"You think I'm… I'm…" I laugh some more. It's just so stupid. A drug dealer? I literally took down a drug dealer two nights ago. Oh, man. I sigh. That's rich.

What I don't think about is how disrespectful this must sound to her.

"You stay out until all hours. You come home with bruises and cuts that you can't explain. Like this one. And this… What the heck happened to you tonight? Jesus. And you buy all these expensive things when we don't have any money. What else can it be?"

Hmmm. Good question. What else could it be?

She blows out a puff of smoke, filling my room like a nasty biker bar. "Things are going to change. I'm getting my act together, and so are you." This causes her to think twice about her cigarette. She looks at it, then smashes it out.

"What?" That took a turn. I don't think I could have expected that in a million years. No, a billion. I can't believe where this is going. How did things turn so crappy so fast?

"Yes, you heard me. Things are going to change."

"I can't wait," I say, and plop down on my bed with my head in my hands.

Life just keeps getting better and better.

"I like to think of my students as delicate flowers," Mr. Blanchard says from the other side of his desk.

Ho-lee sh—

"And, Ms. Vincent, I'm afraid your son is wilting."

"Wilting?" my mom says. Her hand reaches for her mouth, her words almost a whisper like she's in shock.

"Mmm-hmm. And I fear it's partially my fault." He shakes his head dramatically.

I can't believe the level of garbage going on here.

"Oh, gosh, no. Mr. Blanchard. Don't even think that."

I'm sitting here in a metal folding chair that Hector the custodian brought in for my mom and me, stunned that this conversation is even being conducted, while Logan and his mom sit in the plush chairs.

Apparently, Logan's dad was too busy at work, selling used cars, to be bothered to show up.

"I should've seen the signs," Blanchard says. "Mr. Treasure, the overseer of our Robotics Club says your son has been working on 'questionable projects.'"

My mom looks at me, and I just continue sitting there in shock.

"Mr. Peel, our esteemed history teacher, says that Sawyer here is a constant distraction and never pays attention."

Logan smiles, then quickly wipes it off his face when Mr. Blanchard looks to him. With those acting skills, he should be auditioning for the school play.

"And poor Logan here. Even worse, his mother. The things Sawyer said can't even be repeated in the presence of you two lovely ladies."

"Well, I think I've heard enough," Mom says. "Mrs. Andrews, I am so sorry for my son's behavior."

"Mom!" I protest.

She turns and shoots daggers at me with her eyes.

"Mom," I say softer. "You're not really buying all this crap, are you?"

"Sawyer, have some respect," she says. Then she does that silent "I'm sorry" thing that adults do to Mr. Blanchard. You know, the one where you mouth the word and gesticulate with your hands?

"Mom, he hit *me*."

"Then why is he the only one injured?" she asks.

"Because I ducked, and he hit my locker! The dent is still there. Geez. I'll show it to you."

"That won't be necessary," Mom says.

"Or possible," Blanchard adds. "Mr. Hector takes good care of our school, and he didn't notice any dents, new or old."

"Unreal," I say, shaking my head.

"You've got to understand, Mrs. Vincent, Logan is our star athlete. He's going to be on the bench, nursing that broken hand for quite some time. This could affect his entire future. We have to make an example of your son. Otherwise, we're going to have a school full of students who think they can just pick fights whenever it strikes their fancy."

"This is bullshit," I say under my breath.

"Sawyer!" Mom says.

"Mr. Vincent!" Mr. Blanchard says at the same time.

"My word," Mrs. Andrews whispers.

After everyone has recovered from what they act like was the first time any of them had heard a swear word, my mom says, "I understand, Principal Blanchard."

Aaaand, why wouldn't she? After all, she was head cheerleader in high school before she got pregnant at only eighteen during her senior year.

"Again, Mrs. Andrews, I'm so sorry," she says to Logan's mom.

"At least it's good to know he comes from good stock," Mrs. Andrews says.

Good stock? What is this, the medieval times? God, kill me. Just end it now.

After Logan and his mom leave, the meeting changes focus to my "Underachievement." Apparently, my aptitude scores were off the charts, so the only way I could be doing this badly in school is laziness.

Me. Lazy. Right.

When the new semester starts next week, I'm gonna be placed in honors and AP classes, and I'll be expected to work extra hard to catch up. I'll also be placed in a special program for "at-risk" kids, where I get free tutoring after school and for a few hours every Saturday. And, to top it off, my mom is gonna start dragging me to church on Sundays, followed by Bible study.

I'm totally screwed.

P.E. class.

Hate it. I ditch it, figuring I can't get into any more trouble than I'm already in. Not only is Coach Carmichael my least favorite teacher, but it's right before lunch. This is the only chance I'll have to tell Harrier I won't be around for a while, since my mom found my phone and took it away, assuming it was part of my dark, shadowy secret life slinging drugs.

Can't help but snigger at the thought.

Calling Harrier from a landline won't be possible because I have no idea what his number is. It was pre-programmed into the cell phone he gave me, and there was some kind of app on there that masked the number. Besides, who has a landline anymore?

So, I head to the Aerie as quickly as I can. Without my costume, new cape, especially, the trek is a bit longer than it could've been. But in New York, no one even looks twice at a kid my age leaping and vaulting up and down walls. Hopefully, I can be back before lunch ends after P.E., so I don't have to miss history class also since I now know that Mr. Peel thinks I'm some kind of a trouble-student.

But when I get to the Aerie, Harrier isn't around. I check everywhere and even go down to the penthouse in case he's still asleep after a long night. It would've had to have been a night of debauchery since I know for sure he wasn't patrolling. No luck. And his bed doesn't look like it's been slept in—or *not* slept in, for that matter.

I guess he could be at some kind of board meeting or something downstairs at Douglas Industries, but he rarely shows up for those kinds of things. He always lets Mr. Chen—the one other person he trusts besides me—take care of all the business stuff.

Then again, maybe he just got lucky and stayed in a hotel or… *gasp*… at her house. I did see him on TV a couple of days ago, out on a date with that one actress. I can't think of her name, but you'd know her if you saw her. She's been in a bunch of stuff.

He pretends the billionaire player thing is just an act, but I know him well enough to see that it's the one thing he legitimately enjoys about being a handsome, rich guy. Franklin Douglas III usually crests any "most eligible bachelor" list, leaving even the most popular movie stars and athletes in the dust. As a matter of fact, he even beats out Black Harrier, since nobody knows they're the same person.

I teased him about it once, but after the harsh overreaction I got, I never brought it up again. The way he acted, you would've thought I'd made a joke about his dad being murdered or something.

Back in the Aerie, I look around the place, and I consider Osprey's words. How she'd give anything to be Black Harrier's partner. Now that I'm grounded for the next millennium, I feel like I should've enjoyed the place more when I'd had the chance. It has everything, and I've just taken it for granted. Why do people always do that?

It's seriously weird, him not being here. He's always here, and if he's not, Frank Douglas is on the news. I haven't really thought about that business card, I've been so preoccupied with Osprey, but I look around for it with no luck.

I promise myself that if this blows over and things go back to "normal"—I can't help but smile at that word—then I'm gonna appreciate being here a lot more. And I'll appreciate him a lot more, too.

I leave Harrier a message on the desktop of his giant computer screen to make sure he doesn't miss it. The heavy clack of the keyboard under my fingers feels surprisingly satisfying, and I might actually understand why he likes it so much. I tell him I'm not sure when I'll be able to go back to crime-fighting, or when I'll even be able to contact him.

I leave out the fact that I'm starting to feel like I may never see him again.

CHAPTER
NINE

Groan.

The next couple of weeks are the worst ever. It's all about going to school, improving my grades, and being punished for stuff I never even did. Plus, Logan's always mad-dogging me and making sure I know he's my stalker now, even though he's waiting to get his revenge. Oh, and to round out the pile of dung? His hand wasn't even broken, and it's getting better fast. Now he just has to wait for the right time.

And it turns out I did get into even more trouble for ditching P.E. Now I'm the towel boy for the wrestling team on top of everything else. And three guesses who the star of the wrestling team is.

Actually, I bet you can get it in one.

Meanwhile, I don't see Harrier, I don't see Osprey, and I don't get to do any crimefighting. In fact, without my tablet, my phone, and my laptop, I feel like I'm living in the Stone Age. I even had to hide my costume really well on the roof of our building, since my mom regularly ransacks my room now.

One day after wrestling practice is over, I'm getting ready to put away the mats when I hear someone approach me from behind. From the heaviness of the footsteps, I correctly assume it's Logan.

Everyone else has already hit the locker room, and Coach Carmichael is in his office. Logan's had the bandage off for a couple of days now, so I know what's coming. The difference is, this time, he can't have any witnesses because of what happened last time.

"Hey, loser." I can hear the sneer in his voice.

I try to ignore him, knowing that it isn't gonna work.

"Hey, I'm freakin talking to you, butt nugget."

Oh, butt nugget. That's a good one. Bullies, dumb as dirt, every time.

"Turn around," he commands me.

Figuring I have to play the part of helpless nerd, I turn around slowly and face him. As much as you can face someone who's more than a foot taller than you, anyway. He looks down at me, his lip curled into a snarl. He even looks like he's shaking like a crazy person. If he only knew I've squared off with La Cucaracha.

"My hand is better."

"Bet you missed it at night."

"Yeah, funny. Won't be laughing long, though." He makes a fist and punches his own palm to illustrate his point.

"You don't want to do this, Logan."

"What the eff are you talking about?" He looks at me suspiciously.

"I don't want to hurt you again."

He laughs. "You didn't hurt me, loser. I hurt myself. But this time, there's no locker, and I'm not gonna miss."

He swings, and I easily step out of the way. But as he loses his balance, he decides to barrel into me with his shoulder, a move so stupid that I wasn't prepared for it at all.

We both fall to the mat, and he tries to get on top of me. He's actually a really good wrestler, but I'm... well, you know. I turn him around and grab his arm, twisting it behind his back. With my other hand, I tap a pressure point—the brachial plexus—that paralyzes him.

"Had enough?"

I guess he hasn't. "You better freakin kill me, 'cause I *will* get you for this."

How do you even deal with a psycho like this? Obviously, I can't kill him. What am I supposed to do?

"Gentlemen!" Coach Carmichael really knows how to yell. "What's going on here?"

I look up, and he's standing in front of the entire wrestling team, most of which have looks of utter disbelief etched on their faces.

"Did you see that?" one says.

"What a freak," whispers another.

"Daaaayum, Logan got owned."

I let go of his arm and jump up. Logan collapses onto the mat, and I hear a quiet groan leak out of him.

"Uh... Logan was just teaching me some wrestling moves, Coach."

"Well, he must be quite a teacher. I've never seen anyone pin someone who outweighed them by so much like that." The shock is as apparent in his voice as it is visible on his face.

Dammit, Sawyer. This is not how you stay invisible.

"I, uh... I'll just finish with the mats and the towels, sir."

"Forget the towels! You're an official member of the team now."

The other wrestlers look at one another in shock, and I look down at Logan, who's struggling to get up.

When is this hell gonna end?

At home, Mom has been staying sober and going to AA meetings. I never thought I'd be mad that she got her act together—okay, reality? I never thought she'd get her act together at all—but it's the worst time ever for me. Suddenly, she thinks she's super-mom just because she makes me some toast in the morning before school and isn't passed out drunk when I get home.

She also doesn't currently have any boyfriends, something which has definitely been an underrated joy in my life. Don't misunderstand. Most of the guys she's dated were complete losers who made her look like a great catch, and the ones that weren't were obviously only after one thing—and that thing isn't something a kid wants to think about when it comes to his mom. But at least they kept her attention off of me.

I'm not sure where she got her inferiority complex because it's painfully obvious that most men like her—a lot. And yet she always ends up with the worst guys possible.

More than half the time they're married or have serious girlfriends, which has led to endless fights between my mom and other women. Some of them have even shown up to our apartment at all hours, demanding to know where their men are.

To make matters worse, we live in a one-bedroom, so when she does have a guy over, they're either in the middle of the living room or—grossest of all—in my bed.

A few of them have even tried to hit me, but once I learned to fight, that came to an abrupt and bloody end. They never tried it in front of my mom, so that left me free to break some wrists, noses, and ribs before these ass-hats knew what hit them.

To top it all off, she's making a little extra money now by watching the neighbors' little kid while they're at work, which is a lot. In fact, I think they pretend they're at work quite a bit more than they actually are to get a longer break from him. So, in addition to not having any privacy, I have the little monster running around the house when I get home. And the shows he watches… with those songs that get stuck in your head… I literally feel like I'm going insane.

Between my mom's reality shows, trailer-trash talk shows, and the little asswipe's cartoons and annoying sing-song crap, I can't even watch the news.

I'm totally out of touch.

I walk in our front door, and Mom is making dinner. It appears to be an attempt at spaghetti, only the sauce looks like ketchup, and there are cut up hot dogs in it instead of meatballs. I know I shouldn't be so picky, but Harrier usually gets us takeout from the best restaurants in town, many of which he owns, which are not only healthy but delicious. I'm gonna have a hard time keeping this stuff down.

The brat she babysits, Aiden—even his name bothers me—doesn't seem to have a problem with it, though. He's scarfing it down like he hasn't eaten in days, and it's all over his face. When he opens his mouth to show me what's in there, I gag.

"Have a seat. I'll get you some." Mom's proud of this crap?

I sit on one of our rickety, mismatched wooden chairs, and the rug rat stares at me from across the tiny table, still chewing with his mouth open. All of a sudden, he stops eating and closes his eyes. The next thing I know, he sneezes right at me, spraying me with greenish snot and red and white bits of food.

Totally disgusting.

"Gross!" I shout, and Aiden laughs like the little imp he is.

My mom, of course, doesn't even notice it's all over me.

"Bless you!" she says, tussling Aiden's black mop. "Sawyer, you might not want to get too close, he's pretty sick."

I do my best to wipe everything off me. "Yeah. Thanks for the warning."

Mom dumps some of her pasta-ish stuff into a plastic bowl and sets it down in front of me. For the first time in my life, I wish we had a dog just so I could feed it under the table.

Except that might be cruelty to animals.

"Sawyer, there's something I've been meaning to talk to you about."

Uh-oh. I don't respond. I just look up from my food.

"I know I haven't set the best example for you. When I said things are going to change, I meant it. We're going to make something of ourselves."

Mom is full of staggering sentiments lately, this one ranking high on the list.

"I—uh, okay?"

She smiles and says, "How was school today?" She looks at her watch. "You're home late. You're still grounded. You know that, right?"

"Yeah. I…"

I decide to tell her since she's gonna find out soon enough anyway. "Coach, um, made me part of the team."

"What?" She really could've turned down the shock a little bit to spare my feelings.

"The wrestling team. I'm on it now." As much as I hate the situation, I have to admit I enjoy telling her now that I see how low her expectations are for me.

"That's... amazing. How did it happen?"

Okay, Mom, you can pick your jaw up off the floor already.

"I just tried a couple of holds with some of the guys after practice, and the coach said I was pretty good."

Can't tell her the truth, that's for sure.

"Huh. Well, I certainly wasn't expecting that to happen. But good for you. I'm glad you finally found something you're good at."

Ouch. Not that I'd know from personal experience, but moms aren't supposed to talk to their kids this way, are they?

I take a drink of the watered-down grape Kool-Aid she gave me to wash down the bad taste in my mouth. From the food *and* her comments. It doesn't help.

"That's not true. I'm good at... at..." *What?* Go ahead and tell her: Krav Maga, Kung fu, Karate, Tae Kwon Do, Judo, Jiu-Jitsu, Muay Thai, kickboxing, nunchakus, acrobatics, computers, detective work, parkour, swinging from rooftops, *freaking flying…*

She raises her eyebrows, waiting for an answer. The kid is staring at me, too, snot running down over his lip, dangerously close to his mouth.

"I don't know. *Stuff.*" I stand up and set my bowl in the sink, then stomp off to my room like a three-year-old.

Busy feeding Aiden, who now has spaghetti on the top of his head, Mom doesn't even look at me.

Why am I so upset? I've spent years covering up the fact that I'm so good at everything. Apparently, I'm really good at making believe I'm not good at *anything.* Is it really unreasonable that people believe it?

As I'm passing the TV, which mom must've left on, I spot Harrier in the little box above the news anchor's right shoulder. I stop and turn up the volume since the brat is singing some song from one of his shows at the top of his lungs back in the kitchen.

"Where is the Black Harrier?" The anchor is a pretty woman with blonde hair. Kinda reminds me of Osprey. "With our favorite night-time avenger absent, the city is experiencing a noticeable uptick in crime. From robberies, carjackings, and muggings to rapes and murders. Has New York stepped into a new era overnight?"

That's not good. If other people are noticing Harrier being gone, that means I'm not being paranoid. Of course, Harrier has done this before when he's had missions in other countries or went deep undercover, but I decide I should probably look into it anyway.

"Notorious supervillains have been spotted all over the city. Sources tell us, La Cucaracha's gang has hit more than twelve jewelry stores in just the past week. So, I ask again, where is Black Harrier?"

If anyone knows where he is, I'm guessing it'd be Mr. Chen. I guess a trip to Douglas Industries is in order. Good thing tomorrow's Saturday.

Since my mom doesn't have a regular job, she sleeps a lot during the day and stays up most of the night to make sure I'm in bed. She probably won't even notice I'm gone.

CHAPTER
TEN

Snacks.

Everyone needs them. While skating on the way to meet with Chen, I stop at the Mini-Mart on the corner for some junk food. Luckily, Mom still hasn't found the debit card Harrier gave me for things like this. I grab a bag of my favorite spicy chips and an energy drink and head for the checkout, but I notice something's wrong.

The guy behind the counter has his hands in the air, and there are five guys a little older than me grabbing the money out of the register and anything else they can carry. I look up at the security mirror and see that three of them have guns pointed at the guy. Unlike that carjacker from the other night, these guns look real. Two Sigs and a Glock. Not exactly cheap either.

I swear under my breath and duck behind a rack of gummy snacks. They haven't noticed me yet, so I decide to take them out as quickly and quietly as possible. I crouch and silently approach them from behind. But the clerk blows it by looking directly at me as I'm about to attack, and the bad guys immediately turn and point their weapons at me.

Now it'll probably get messy.

I jump on my board and throw my energy drink at the one farthest one from me. It explodes all over his face as it cracks him in the nose. I hear a gun fire, but I don't feel anything. Scared shooters rarely hit their targets. The problem is, that means someone else might have been hit, included anyone who happened to be walking by. I take solace in the fact that I heard no glass shatter, and in a split second, I'm right on top of them.

Now that I'm closer, I grab the gun arm of the guy closest to me and spin him around so that he's in front of me. Luckily, I'm right in thinking that his friend isn't gonna shoot him to get to me. But he does try to shoot over his friend's shoulder and hit me in the face with the bullet—except he fires wide and it smashes the glass on the refrigerated display nearby, busting a forty-ouncer, which sprays all over the place.

The destroyed fridge upsets the clerk so much that he starts yelling at the shooter, which is about as stupid as stupid gets. The only good thing about it is that the guy turns to point his gun at him instead of me, which will give me a chance to make a move.

I karate chop a pressure point on the neck of the guy I'm holding, and he drops. Then with a swoop of my legs, I have Trigger Happy down on the ground. A quick blow to the face, and he's out cold, leaving only two more to handle.

Leftover Punk Number One goes to shoot me, so I kick my skateboard up into my hands and swing it at him. It knocks the gun free, which allows me to take him down with a combo move that ends with my knee against his temple. Four down, one to go.

Number Five is too scared to shoot. He drops his weapon and just looks at me, which is a reaction I get a lot from someone who's seen me take down several of his friends. I start to smile, but then I realize I don't have my mask on.

And then, I recognize this kid from my history class. I think his name is Benji… yeah, dumb name. We stare each other down for a few seconds. Then, as if an unspoken agreement has taken place, he nods at me and runs out of the store. That's when I notice there's someone else in the store with us.

I turn and look down one of the aisles, and Javier is standing there so still, with his mouth so wide, he could catch flies. Bowling balls pop out of his eye sockets, and he drops the chocolate milk and mini-donuts he's holding.

Crap.

He looks like he's afraid of me, and he takes off running out of the store. Before I can go after him, the clerk starts berating me in a language I don't understand, as if stopping a robbery and possibly saving his life isn't enough.

He's mad that I messed up his store and let one get away.

So now, not only am I stuck on the wrestling team, but some kids from my school know I'm not what I appear to be. I wonder if any of them have the brains to put together that one of their classmates can take down criminals the same way as the famous teenage sidekick who operates in the same neighborhood. I doubt those goons are very bright, but Javier could be a problem.

So what happens to me if everyone finds out I'm Red Ki—er, Raptor, anyway? Do they lock me up for assaulting so many people, even though they all deserved it? Do they give me a medal for helping to put so many criminals behind bars? Do the police throw me into an interrogation room and question me until I give up the identity of the Black Harrier?

I have no idea.

While other kids my age are worried about having a sweet pair of kicks or getting rid of that zit on the end of their nose before their date Saturday night, these are the things I have to think about. Hiding my secret identity. Pretending to be a loser who sucks at everything in life. Oh yeah, and trying not to get murdered by one of a dozen supervillains.

It's strange rolling up to Douglas Industries on the ground floor. I can probably count on one hand the number I've times I've entered the building this way, and have fingers left over. All of those times, it's been to eat at the restaurant. I stop and check myself in the blue-tinted reflection.

Am I a mess after kicking those dudes' asses? I've canvased my body ten times in case of blood or anything else that would get security suspicious, but I guess it was a pretty clean fight, all in all.

I kick my board up into my hands and sling it to my backpack. I look up at the impossibly tall building in the middle of Manhattan and stride toward the doors.

The doorman looks down his nose at me as I approach the lobby entry.

"Can I help you with something?" His voice is dripping with condescension.

Dude, if you only knew who I was and how many times I've hung out in the penthouse. You open a freaking door for a living. "Oh, sure, you can leave that package with me… Ma'am, I believe you just dragged poop in on your shoe… Let me get that for you."

"Nah, I'm okay," I say as I reach for the door handle myself, not expecting him to do it for me.

He puts his foot in front of it, and the door shudders, making our reflections ripple. "I'm sorry, do you have business here in the building?"

I hate to say this, but I may have to get this guy fired. Assuming I ever talk to Frank again, that is. Does he even know how his employee treats people down here? Probably not. I mean, it's not like he's gonna act this way in front of the owner of the building.

"Yeah, as a matter of fact, I do. I'm meeting with Mr. Chen." That's a lie. He has no idea I'm coming.

The doorman gives me a disbelieving look. "At Douglas Industries?"

"Bingo, that's the Mr. Chen I'm talking about. Now, can I…?" I try pulling on the door handle again. His foot remains planted.

"Look, kid. I can't let in every teenager with a story. You got some sort of… proof?"

Okay, he's got a point. Maybe I won't get him fired. In fact, he should probably get a raise. I didn't even think I'd need proof. I don't even know what proof would look like.

Damn him for actually making some sense. Now how am I supposed to hate his guts?

"Is it common practice to not let people into a public building?"

The guy pretends to pick some lint off his sleeve. "As a matter of fact, this building is private. Do you have any proof of your meeting with Mr. Chen?"

I shake my head. "No, I don't have a note from him saying I'm allowed to enter the building if that's what you're implying. I don't get it, is there a problem here? Why are you giving me such a hard time?"

Just then, a couple of guys in two-thousand-dollar suits walk up to the door, and the doorman puts his hand on my chest to hold me back as he opens the door, smiles, and nods at them. He closes the door immediately.

Yeah… okay… back to firing.

I really wish I could break his wrist as he removes his hand from my chest. Remember, Sawyer, you're one of the good guys.

"How come you didn't ask those guys if they have any business here?"

Frustrated, he suddenly drops what he probably thought was a super-professional demeanor. "Because they *look* like they belong here, and because I see them every day. You think you're the first kid trying to get in who doesn't work or live here and isn't visiting someone who does?"

"I just told you, I *am* visiting someone who works here. Mr. Chen?"

"Luis Chen is a very public personality. Everyone knows he works here. Anyone could say they are visiting him. My job is to obtain proof before letting in riffraff."

"Oh, I'm riffraff, now?" I say.

He looks me up and down, then shrugs.

"What if I just wanted to go to *Le Meilleur Plat*?"

Best French food in the whole city. Super expensive. Super delish. My mouth starts salivating at the thought.

"Dressed like that?"

Riiiight.

"Come on, kid. You're wasting my time. Unless you can show me that you really have a meeting with Mr. Chen, then I can't let you in. My job's at stake."

I go to pull out my phone to try to dial up to Mr. Chen to let me in, then realize I don't have it. It's only about the zillionth time I've done that since Mom took it away. I'm such an idiot. I should've figured out a way to make an appointment to see him. I mean, it's Saturday. He might not even be here.

"I don't know what to tell you. I'm supposed to meet with him about doing some community service for the Douglas Foundation, but he didn't give me anything to get me in the door."

He looks me up and down again, but this time it seems like he's softening a little. "Charity, huh?"

I try to do my best puppy dog eyes. I have no idea if it's decent or totally ridiculous. "He visited my school last week. Found out I was a... a trouble-student. 'At-risk,' they said." A good lie has a bit of the truth, right? "But then my robotics teacher showed him some of my gadgets, and he offered to show me around his lab. He offered to take me under his wing."

He still doesn't appear convinced, but I'm wearing him down.

"Please, Mister. This is my last shot before I end up in juvie. Or, at least, that's what my mom said. If I go home without paperwork from Mr. Chen saying I can start this internship, I'm screwed."

The doorman looks up to the sky for a second and lets out a breath. I think he's about to give in, but instead, he goes into a long story about this being his first break. He shows me gang ink on his wrist and tells me how Mr. Douglas gave him this opportunity. He tries to give me his phone number in case I need some accountability or something. I think he actually cries.

"If it wasn't for this place," he says, lovingly tapping the door, "I'd be doing hard time. I know it."

"Uh. Yeah." I rub my neck. "So, can I go in?"

"Okay. Fine. I'm a sucker for a redemption story."

"Really?"

"Yeah. You go get 'em, kid. Just don't get me into any trouble for this."

"Thanks! I really appreciate it." I rush through the door before he changes his mind.

From behind me, he makes that sound you do to a dog when you want it to stop whatever it's doing, and I turn.

"Board stays here," he says.

"Yeah. Okay. Sure," I say.

"You know what? Just leave the bag, too. Can't be too careful."

I groan as I remove the backpack, skateboard still attached, and place it behind a podium by the door.

"Nothing better be missing when I get back," I say.

The doorman juts his chin out and lets the doors slam shut.

"A-hole," I say under my breath.

Douglas Tower is easily one of the most lavish places in the city. The lobby looks like something straight out of a science fiction film starring Tom Cruise. Glass and metal everywhere. No crystal chandeliers like the other snobby places. Instead, these huge LED discs hover about twenty feet above me, varying in sizes, but many of them are up to a couple dozen feet in diameter. It's all unbelievably impressive and lights the room in a soft, white glow.

Four glass elevators rise up from the center of the lobby and break through a ceiling—also made of glass—about four floors up. They'll continue out in the openness of the outside air another, like, fifty stories.

Currently, one set of elevator doors is about to close, so I sprint over and jam my foot in just in time to stop them. They open up to an already-crowded elevator full of business executives and wealthy residents. Every one of them looks pissed at me as I squeeze in amongst them and reach over to press the button for the main office of Douglas Industries.

The doorman wasn't wrong. I feel really out of place in my T-shirt, jeans, and hoodie with them all dressed in expensive suits and dresses. At first, the only sound in the elevator is the muzak they play over the speakers—really horrible stuff. Then, two of the business bros start a conversation about TPS reports that makes me wish for the muzak by comparison.

The elevator is so crowded that when it stops at a floor, half of us have to step off momentarily to allow others to exit.

Then, it starts up again, and we "burst" through the glass above us—I mean, not really, it doesn't break, but it looks like you're heading right for a ceiling, and then you're looking at the city. Best view there is other than Frank's penthouse.

After what feels like an eternity, we finally get to my floor, and I feel the exhilaration of a prisoner being set free from years in the slammer.

There are no fake greens, no magazines in waiting rooms, no TVs playing silly advertisements for products. Just like Black Harrier—all work. Really, it's Mr. Chen's influence, though. He runs the place.

I approach the reception desk as Douglas employees rush around in all directions, in and out of the many glass doors leading to various offices and conference rooms. The giant DI logo looms above the head receptionist, who sits in the middle of a long, round desk surrounded by four other people answering the phone lines.

A gorgeous redhead with lips the color of ripe plums stares and is genuinely surprised to see someone like me walking in. Makes me wonder if hiring receptionists is one job Frank does himself around here. "Can I help you?"

For a second, I'm speechless. Now, *she* is what I would expect from Frank Douglas.

"I'm, uh, here to see Mr. Chen."

She's taken aback by the statement. I'm sure the only thing that would have shocked her more would be if I'd asked to see Frank. "Do you have an appointment?"

"No, I didn't really think about it. I guess I really should've called ahead."

Somehow, she gives the impression of rolling her eyes even though those beautiful green lovelies never move a millimeter.

"I'm afraid there's nothing I can do for you." She slides a business card across the desk at the same time as she lowers her gaze back to her work. "Give us a call and make an appointment."

"Can't I make one now? It's kind of important."

She looks up, probably annoyed. Sighing, she says, "I'm sorry, it doesn't work that way. You have to call our appointment department. It's the 800 number on the card I just handed you."

The white linen card has a small DI logo and the word "Appointments," along with a phone number, just as she'd said. No names. No other information. There's an entire department just for making appointments?

"Please," I say, drawing her attention again. "There's no way you can just call him and ask if he'll see me?"

"Mr. Chen is a very important person. And he's in a meeting right now with other very important people."

Got it. I'm not important.

"And he gave explicit instructions not to be disturbed. The only person he would take a call from right now is Mr. Douglas."

Oh, the irony. The whole reason I'm here is that "Mr. Douglas" seems to have disappeared.

"I guess I'll give this number a call, then."

"You do that. Have a pleasant day." She immediately goes back to whatever she was doing before I'd walked in, and it's like I never existed.

I start the trek back to the elevators, feeling totally defeated, and press the 'down' button. Just as the doors open, I hear a voice from behind me. "Sawyer?"

I turn and see Mr. Chen exiting one of the conference rooms. In one hand—oh right... he has a bionic hand—he holds a tablet similar to the one my Mom ganked from me. I never asked what happened, but I'm pretty sure Frank met him in the service, so it might be an old war wound. And with all the crazy technology DI develops, I can guarantee that hand is state-of-the-art.

He passes the tablet to someone else and tells the rest of his people to go on without him.

Relief hits me like a wave, and I smile broadly while walking toward him. He does the same, then shakes my hand with his human one, a big smile on his face. "What brings you to our offices?"

"I was actually hoping to talk to you for a minute? Guess I should've called first." I look over at the receptionist, who now wears a shocked expression. I won't lie, it feels good.

"Nonsense. I always have time for you." Mr. Chen looks over at her as well, and her face turns redder than her hair. "Let's head back to my office."

He guides me down a long corridor, glass cubicles on both sides, little worker ants doing little worker ant things in each one. We go all the way down to the end, where a set of double doors have a brass plate saying, "Franklin Douglas III, President and Chief Executive Officer."

Instead of entering Frank's office, we turn to the one next to it, which indicates that Mr. Chen is the "Senior Vice President and Chief Operating Officer." Like I said, he's the one who really runs things around here.

It's funny, I've been working with Frank for almost three years, and I've never been here. Never seen anything beyond the receptionists' desk, and even then, it was only from the elevator doors.

Mr. Chen's office is gigantic, so I can't even imagine how big Frank's must be. Shelves full of boring-looking books and binders line two of the walls. Three TV sets with giant screens are mounted on the same wall as the office door, each showing a different news or financial channel. He has a fireplace on one of the walls with books, which seems like a fire hazard to me, but whatever. Above the mantle, a painting of Frank hangs, as if he's looking down upon everything that happens around here.

Mr. Chen sees me eyeing the painting and smiles. "That's sort of an inside joke. Frank and I know how ridiculous it is, but everyone who comes in here wonders about it. You know, did Frank make me put it up—or did I put it up to kiss up to him? That sort of thing. Keeps people distracted and off-balance when I'm making business deals."

"Uh, yeah. That's… pretty hilarious." The painting is so realistic, and the eyes look like they're staring into my soul. I see what he's talking about. I wish I was kidding when I say there are probably little cameras behind the eyes, so Frank really can watch what goes on from the Aerie.

Chen motions to a black leather chair in front of his desk, and I've never seen anything more comfortable-looking. He lowers himself into a plush captain's chair situated behind his giant mahogany desk and lets out a sigh. "Please, have a seat. You look parched. Let me get you something to drink."

"No, I'm actually—"

He holds up a finger to stop me while he presses a buzzer on his desk. "Pam, please have a beverage cart brought in."

"Right away, sir."

"And please continue to hold all my calls."

"Yes, sir."

So, while the rest of Douglas Tower looks crazy-modern and sleek, Mr. Chen's office is all dark wood and amber light. Behind his desk, on a credenza, is a picture of him with his wife and daughter, whom I've never met. There's also what looks like a graduation picture of his daughter, who's… wow… really cute.

I think he notices me staring, cos a second later he says, "That's Amy. She's starting college this year."

I just nod. What am I supposed to say, *Oh, she's really hot, sir?*

A young woman—another redhead… *Geez, Frank*—enters the office with a cart full of drinks and wheels it right over to me. There's everything: water, coffee, hot tea, iced tea, lemonade, soda… I don't know where to even begin. I grab an ice-cold water bottle and crack open the cap. The woman hands me a glass full of sphere-shaped ice, and I thank her.

"Thank you. That will be all, MJ." She nods in response to Mr. Chen's dismissal and quickly leaves the room. "So, to what do I owe the pleasure of your company today?"

"It's about Frank." His face betrays absolutely no emotion as he leans back and adjusts something on his bionic hand before flexing it once. When he says nothing, I continue. "I haven't seen him in a couple of weeks, and I was wondering if you could tell me where he is or what's going on."

"I'm afraid I can't do that, Sawyer."

"Because he told you not to tell me?" I think the question comes off sounding way more accusatory than I'd intended.

"No," he says, drawing the word out cautiously. "Because I don't know where he is."

Something I'm sure resembles panic comes bubbling from my lips. "What? Crap. Really? I don't know… Seriously? Then what—"

"Calm down, son. Frank has disappeared before. He always comes back. You know that."

"But for this long? And what about the company? And what about…" I lean forward even though nobody else is around and practically whisper, "…*you know what*?"

Mr. Chen drums his metal fingers on the desk, looks at me with a small smile, then stands, and heads to the drink cart. I'm pretty sure he's just trying to hide his face from me. It's a practiced action, for sure. I haven't spent so much time detecting with Frank to be so easily deceived.

"He doesn't really have much to do with the day-to-day operations of Douglas Industries," he says over the distinct sound of carbonation and crackling ice. "That's why he has me. As for his… *nocturnal extracurricular activities*, I believe there are others who can pick up the slack. Including yourself."

Yeah, if I wasn't grounded. I make a little noncommittal sound.

"How do you like the new cape?" he asks, almost as if trying to change the subject.

"It's amazing. Like flying."

"Good, good." He finishes pouring and leans against his desk, looking down at me. "I see you've recently made some modifications to Amber."

Shoot. I didn't know Mr. Chen would be able to see those adjustments.

He must notice the emotion wracking my features because he lets out a laugh and says, "Don't worry. I'm not upset."

"No?"

"Quite the opposite. I'm really damn impressed, Sawyer. As a matter of fact, if you ever decide you want a day job *in addition* to your nightly duties with the boss…" he nods his head to the big painting of Frank, "… I think we could use someone like you in R&D."

I won't make believe I'm not flattered and more than a little tempted. A job at DI could get Mom and me out of that crap-hole of an apartment and into a decent neighborhood. I hadn't even really thought about it. Now that I'm sixteen, there'll be a lot of new job opportunities open.

"Wow. Thanks, Mr. Chen. I… well… I don't—"

"You don't need to answer now. Just think about it, okay?"

I nod, then say, "You don't think we should be worried?"

He chuckles. "About Frank? Son, Frank Douglas is the last person I would ever worry about. If ever there was someone who could take care of himself, it's that man right there." Again he points to the painting.

I'm not convinced, but I still say, "I guess you're right."

"Is there anything else?" he asks.

"No, that's pretty much it. Thanks for seeing me."

"Thank you for coming to me with your concerns. But I'm sure everything will be just fine."

I shake his hand. But just as I'm turning away, I detect a flash of worry in his eyes. He's not as confident about Frank as he's letting on.

As I open the door to leave, I hear him behind me.

"And Sawyer..."

I turn back.

"Think about the job. It could be good for you and your family."

Back at home, Mom is making lunch for Aiden, who's running around in circles until he gets so dizzy that he falls on his face. Looks like he's feeling better. As soon as I walk in the door, she's on me.

"Where've you been? I don't think you're taking your grounding seriously enough."

"Relax. I went to talk to someone about doing the community service that I'm supposed to start." The "supposed to start" part is true, anyway. Another one of Mr. Blanchard's gifts to me for effectively dodging Logan's fist.

"Where did you go?" She looks at the skateboard hanging from the backpack slung over my shoulder. "How do I know you weren't just out with your friends?"

I thought about this on the way home. I knew she'd have to be up by now, so I had everything planned out. "I figured you wouldn't believe me, so I grabbed a business card. I'm hoping to do some work for a charitable foundation."

Wow. Mom looks ashamed. That's a new look.

Then, I hand her the card I got from the receptionist. When she sees it, her expression morphs to surprised and lands somewhere in the neighborhood of angry. I have no idea why. "Douglas Industries? Why? Why them?"

"I don't know. I heard something about all the charity work they do, so I thought I'd check it out."

"No. You don't need to have anything to do with some big corporation. After church tomorrow, we'll talk to Father Pulliam about doing community service there." She tears the business card into little pieces and sprinkles it in the trash.

Well, that escalated quickly. So much for that job offer.

CHAPTER **ELEVEN**

M*onday.*

I jolt awake with a start. It takes me a bit to figure out where I am, even though it's my own room. I wanted to try to catch the late-night news on my laptop before sneaking out to patrol, but I must've nodded off. And, right away, I figure out why. Headache, chills, clogged sinuses, sore throat. That little germ-incubator got me sick.

After sneaking out Saturday morning, I decided to chill out last night so Mom wouldn't have any more reason to be suspicious.

I look at my clock, which is blurry from the sleep in my eyes, and see that it's after three a.m. Mom was kind enough to drape a blanket over me before calling it a night, but I listen at the door to make sure she's really asleep out on the couch. She's snoring. Not loud, but she's definitely out.

Then, I dip into the bathroom.

Uh, yeah… heroes have to pee, too.

It takes a lot of effort not to sneeze or cough, but I can't wake up Mom.

Back in my room, I put on my costume, which I'd retrieved from the roof earlier, and sneak out the window. It's not something I like to do because if someone spots me, they'll know precisely where Red Raptor lives—at least if they see me changing on the roof, they only know which building it is—but I can't sneak out the front door.

I scale the fire escape and stand on the edge of the roof. The cold, early morning air is fresh. Between that and being back in costume, I feel so good that I don't even mind when Amber greets me.

Bleep.

I take a deep breath—which is more labored than I care to admit—before plunging off into the darkness. My cape snaps out, and I glide down the street at about fifty feet up.

"Hey, Amber."

"I love the way you say my name."

"What's the scoop? Any news on the net about Harrier?"

"Just rumors and gossip streams." As if she senses my unease, she adds, *"I'm sure he's okay, Sawyer."*

Her tone is uncharacteristically... normal. Not trying to seduce me or anything. Just like... Mom... or something. I clear my throat.

"Yeah, thanks," I say. "What are you picking up? Anything close?"

"Traffic cams are picking up a mugging in front of Gentleman's Clearance House. Half a block south."

I flip mid-flight and let the swoop and dip pull me in the opposite direction. Most times, I'd have Amber make a call to the police, especially with how bad I'm feeling. However, with Harrier gone, someone has to remind these scumbags that there's still someone watching over the city.

Amber is never wrong. She's got eyes like the government—probably better. That's why it scares me that she has no idea where Harrier is.

I whip around the corner and see some dude, clearly heading to work, having his wallet taken away by a couple of guys with shaved heads and more metal in their faces than a scrapyard. Not much of a challenge, but my being sick will give them a little more of a chance. Should be fun.

I dive down and stomp the guy who's thumbing through the wallet with both my feet, sending him into a twenty-foot slide ending in a subway stairwell. I think he keeps tumbling down the stairs. I feel a little bad because that's an ER visit at best. Hopefully, it doesn't ki—

My thought is interrupted by a punch to my lower back.

I swear because now I actually have to do some work.

I assumed that after what I'd just done to his friend, the other assailants would have been hightailing toward the docks and into hiding. I turn to see another fist coming at my helmet. I don't understand that move. Who punches armor?

I duck, for no other reason but so the guy doesn't break his hand.

"What are you hoping to accomplish with that?" I say, my nose all stuffed up.

I dodge about three more attacks, each one lazy and unfocused. Then, I slam him into the metal lamp post and lower his unconscious body to the sidewalk.

I take a few steps and pick up the dude's wallet.

"Give it over, hero," the third guy says. He didn't run either? Geez. What's wrong with these guys?

I look up to see that he has the victim in a headlock, holding a knife up to his face. Suddenly, this isn't so fun anymore.

I start to reach for one of the throwing stars in my belt, but he's watching me carefully. He touches the blade to the man's face. "Move and I cut him."

I lift up my hands. "Okay, man. Stay calm."

"Give me the wallet." His hand shakes, which makes me nervous that he's gonna cut him whether he means to or not. "Slide it over here. Now!"

I toss the wallet over to him, and it lands next to his feet, credit cards and stuff spilling out. I can tell he wants to pick it up, but he's afraid I'll attack the second he no longer has the knife up to his victim.

He's right, but I try not to let him know that. "Just pick it up and let him go."

This is the point at which all criminals internally weigh the odds of escape. They know they've been caught, and that makes them a bit unpredictable. If he's got priors, he won't wanna go back. If he's a newb, he might not realize the consequences of his actions and do something rash. If he's a pro…

"How do I know you won't follow me?"

Yeah, he's somewhere in between. At least he's asking the right questions.

This isn't the first time I've dealt with someone like this. "You have my word," I say. "Just don't hurt him, and you can leave."

"Your word don't mean crap to me." He thinks for a second. And it turns out this guy is smart. "Take off your mask."

"What?" It's so unexpected, it doesn't even register at first. There's a first time for everything. How did this go downhill so fast?

"Your mask. I wanna see your face."

"I can't really…"

"I've alerted the police," Amber says into my ear. I can't answer her, but that's exactly what I needed to hear.

If I can keep him talking…

"Now." He pushes the point of the knife against his victim's face, and it draws a little blood. The dude whimpers like a beaten dog. I mean, I'm sure it's scary for him. But the thug has such a light grip, and if this guy had bothered to take even an introductory self-defense class, he'd be free, and the would-be-stabber would be on the ground clutching his nuts.

Instead, I have no idea how to handle this. Heroes and villains have an unwritten code where we don't do this type of thing. If everyone finds out our identities, it's all over. But this is just some low-level street thug.

"Okay, okay. Just stay calm." I retract my visor, and he just looks at me. "Happy?"

"Take off the damn mask, too, stupid."

My heart is racing. I have no idea what Harrier would do in this situation. I don't think I have any choice but to show the guy my face.

"I'm nobody," I say.

"Yeah. No crap. But that ain't the point. Mask. Off. Or..." he digs the knife in a little deeper, and the guy literally starts whining like a hurt puppy.

I lift my hand to my mask. I guess there's no real harm in it. He probably won't even remember what I look—*oh, no.*

The mugger pulls a cellphone from his pocket with his free hand. Another easy opportunity for the guy to escape. Anyone living in New York should really sign up for anti-mugging classes. The thug holds his camera phone up, waiting for me to lower my domino mask.

"Say cheese."

THWACK!

A boomerang flies out of the alley and knocks the phone out of his hand, followed immediately by a bola that binds his ankles together. He falls flat on his face, and I see a tooth bounce out of his mouth as his jaw hits the sidewalk.

I take my hand away from my mask, thankful that I hadn't had to remove it and run over to the victim to see if he's okay. The guy starts thanking me profusely, but I don't hear a word he's saying as I watch Osprey walk out of the alley and step on the mugger's neck. In my mind, it's like she's moving in slow motion.

"I hope you have insurance because you're going to need it."

Witty quips, judges? Six out of ten? Not bad. Not really good either. But she just saved my butt, so I certainly won't say anything.

She kicks him in the face, and he's unconscious. After picking up some things that fell out of the wallet, she walks over to return them. I don't hear anything as the guy thanks Osprey either, and I realize I must look pretty ridiculous standing there with my mouth hanging open. I just hope I'm not drooling.

I shake my head out and turn to the guy.

"Hey, take a self-defense class at the Y or something? We might not always be around."

"Y-yeah. I—thank you. Thank you."

He stands there, stumbling over more words to Osprey while I jog over to grab the thug's phone off the ground. Looking at the screen, I can see he hadn't taken any pictures, but I'm taking no chances. I pull off the back and yank out the memory card. I put it between my teeth and crack it in half. I toss it and the battery into the sewer drain, and stomp the crap out of the rest of the phone until it's tiny jagged pieces of glass and plastic.

"You good to go?" I ask the victim.

The dude tells us he's fine and that his work is only about a block away, so we watch to make sure he makes it okay.

I turn to Osprey, and I'm so happy to see her, but at the same time embarrassed about everything.

"So... I guess you saved me again."

She smiles that mind-melting smile, and for a second, I see something familiar there that I can't place, and I hadn't noticed before. Before I can think too hard on it, she's talking. "That's right. So we're no longer even. I guess I'll have to think of a way for you to pay me back."

"I'm sure she'll think of something," Amber says.

I clear my throat. "I'm sure you'll think of something. How'd you find me? You stalking me again?"

"You wish. It came across on the police scanners."

Oh, right.

"Thanks, Amber," I whisper.

"You know… I've been coming by this neighborhood a couple of times a night for the past few weeks, hoping to see you."

"That's the definition of stalking," I say with a little smile.

She gives me a playful shove, but I'm still processing things.

She's been looking for *me*? Of course she was. Why wouldn't she? I'm good looking. I'm badass. I'm…

"Yeah. About that..." What am I supposed to say? *My mommy grounded me from crimefighting*? "I've been working on an important assignment, and it's been keeping me really busy."

"You sure? Because I was afraid that maybe you didn't like me or something."

You could not be more wrong about that.

"Oh, no, no, no. That's definitely not it. Not it at all."

"Is this special assignment the same reason Harrier's been missing?"

Well, I certainly can't tell her I have no idea where my partner's been all month. "Uh, yeah. Kind of. In fact, I'm on my way to see him now."

She perks up when I say this. "How about I come along? Then we can call it even again."

And there it is. Is she using me again? This time to get to Harrier?

Stop being paranoid, Sawyer. She likes you.

"I really wish I could, but not tonight. This whole thing is really sensitive."

She looks deflated.

"I'll talk to him, though, and see if he'd be okay with you meeting him some time."

Sure. Like when hell freezes over.

"Promise?"

"Of course. Thanks again for your help." I go in for a hug, then immediately feel weird about it, and we do the awkward dance. I decide to shake her hand instead, and she gives me a weird look. So, I shoot my grappler across the street and get out of there as fast as possible.

Ugh. I'm such a freaking loser.

CHAPTER
TWELVE

W*orried.*

I think about what I'm gonna do if I don't find Harrier. It's early morning; Mom will be awake soonish, and I don't exactly have a lot of time to go searching for him right now. Plus, I feel like absolute garbage. I wipe my nose with my cape, ignoring the fact that it immediately begins to drain again.

I could try to contact the Guild, but I'm not entirely sure how to do that. It's not like I have a number for them. Or an email address. Not even Amber is programmed to access the Guild Hall without Frank's passcode.

This kind of situation is precisely why the Guild was started, and I'm confused as to why no one seems to be more worried about Frank. Most of the time, they're just more adults making rules for no reason. But, I'll give them on thing... I used to think that if someone wants to fight crime, they should be able to fight crime without getting permission from anyone. However, Osprey's latest actions made me question that at least a little bit. Still…

I've met the Guild once. Well, most of the members anyway. It was when I first started working with Harrier, and he needed to introduce me to them. I'm sure it was just to get their approval, as if one of the head honchos needed their collective consent for his choice of partner.

He even put a blindfold on me so I wouldn't know where their headquarters was located—something about me not being able to reveal the location if I ever got captured and tortured or brainwashed. To be honest, the fact that they even consider that a possibility makes me kind of nervous. Anyway, I was excited about the opportunity to meet these people.

But like I said, some of the members weren't there. Cupid, the archer guy who flies, was pretty cool. His name would make you think he's a fat little baby, and you'd be right, minus the baby part… oh and he isn't little. And the super-speed guy, Fastlane—funniest guy I've ever met. Hands down. Bastet caught me looking through her boob window, and just smiled and winked at me. But most of them acted like they couldn't care less about meeting me. Firefly and Omar the Defenestrator were even hostile toward me. And Eaglestar, the guy I figure would have had the most say in it, didn't bother to show up.

In a way, it's like getting a bunch of movie stars together in a room. They act like they get along, but you can feel the tension because they all have such big egos, and they're trying to figure out who's more important. I guess it's hard for them when they're so used to being the most famous person anywhere. They all claim to be doing what they do because they want to help people, but I don't think anyone could do this without some level of self-importance and overconfidence.

Maybe even mental illness.

Some of them have their own partners, but most of them are labeled sidekicks, and I *know* Harrier doesn't care about *them*. So, I'm not sure how they'd react to me contacting them even if I could figure out how to do it.

Just another example of Harrier treating me like a kid. Because he doesn't give me access to information, I'm wandering around in the dark now that he's not around. How am I supposed to grow up if he never trusts me or gives me any responsibility?

Entering the Aerie, it feels cold and abandoned—lights are off, heat's off, totally silent. Scratch that… I do hear something coming from the control room.

Clackity, clack, clack, clack, clack…

My heart stutters a bit at the thought that Harrier's here and okay. I take a few quick steps, then think better of it. Although I assume it's Harrier, just to be on the safe side, I move in quietly. Good thing, too. There's someone standing at the main computer, but it's definitely not Harrier. With everything dark except for the computer screens, the figure is just a silhouette, and I can't tell much other than that it looks like a guy, and he seems to be in a costume. I can tell that he's smaller than Harrier but still bigger than me.

I silently climb onto the metal support beams above so I can literally get the drop on him. As I wait to make sure he hasn't noticed me, I can't see much more than I could before. Whoever it is had no problem getting into Harrier's system, so he must be really good at tech stuff. I go through a list of enemies who might have that capability, but none of them match the dark figure I see below. Either way, it's sort of a good sign, because most of the geeky villains who can handle that sort of thing aren't so good in the combat department.

I hop down, prepared to knock out the intruder, but I don't even come close. Before I can touch him—before I touch the ground, even—he casually grabs a staff that he has leaning against the terminal next to him and whacks me like Babe Ruth.

I barely feel it through my graphene armor, and I think he might've known that too.

Whoever this guy is, he's good.

I toss some throwing stars. It's more as a distraction than anything since I know he's gonna knock them down. I follow up with a flying kick at his head. He slaps me and the stars out of the air with almost no effort. Then, one of his heavy boots sends me sailing against the same terminal, stealing the wind from my lungs.

I can only hope he's not out to kill me because it looks like he'll be able to without breaking a sweat.

He approaches me, and now that my eyes have adjusted, I realize who he is. I've never met Redhawk—a name I really wanted, by the way. He lives in Boston —why would a hero from Boston break into Harrier's base?

"You ready to talk, or do you want to keep sparring?" It sounds like he finds the situation humorous.

"Redhawk?"

"And you're the new Kite, I presume?"

"It's Red Raptor now. And I'm not sure three years qualifies as 'new.'"

"Has it really been that long?" He smiles, and extends a hand to help me up, and I take it a little reluctantly. But like I said, if he wanted me dead, I'd probably already be.

Standing, I take a tentative step back, distancing myself from his staff.

"Red Raptor. Huh. Not bad. Aren't you worried people are gonna think you're supposed to be in Jurassic Park?"

"Maybe a little. But it's better than 'Kite.'"

"Tell me about it." He holds out his hand. "Name's Alex, the original Red Kite."

CHAPTER THIRTEEN

"Huh?" I say with all the intelligence of a baboon.

I've known about Redhawk for years. Sure, he lives and serves a few hundred miles away, but everyone knows Boston's guardian.

"You didn't know?" he says to me.

I feel like yelling at him. I feel like punching him. I feel like an idiot. Why hadn't Harrier told me? Was three years not long enough to earn his trust?

Instead, I just say, "No."

"Ah, well, you know Frank… you do know his name is Frank, right?" I open my mouth to respond, and he waves his hand. "Just kidding, man. Don't get your panties in a bunch."

"I'm not getting my panties in a bunch."

Bleep.

Amber can't let a comment like that go, and I know it. Too bad she won't get a chance to say anything.

"Well, I know all about you," he says and pulls a card from his pocket—his Guild I.D. He's listed as a hero, not a protégé, like me, so he'll have the advantage of having seen my files. Me? I'd be lucky to get invited to the Christmas party. Oh, and if there is one, I don't know about it.

"That's great," I say.

"Come on, kid. Don't be like that. I'll tell you anything you wanna know. Even playing field, so to speak."

I sit in one of Harrier's leather rollie-chairs. "Was he always a dick?"

I mean it as a joke, and I think it came across that way, since Alex laughs, but I immediately feel the guilt, knowing that Harrier is missing.

"You know, when I met him, he wasn't much older than I am now. But what's crazy is I thought he was an old man. It was early on in his crime-fighting career. I think he realized he needed some help, but really didn't have anyone to trust—except maybe Luis Chen."

He practically spits Mr. Chen's name. There's something there, and I'm not about to ask. It also doesn't surprise me that Mr. Chen has known about Harrier for so long.

"I think Chen even tried his luck at the whole thing too. Successfully put away more than one supervillain."

Okay, that surprised me.

"Luis Chen?" I said. "I thought he'd always been a pencil-pusher or something."

"Yeah, more the 'or something' part. Ever heard of Yahtzee?"

"The game with the cup and dice?"

Alex chuckled. "No, back when I was a kid, Yahtzee was one of the biggest supervillains in New York. Now, he's locked up in the Trench."

The Trench is an underwater, super-security prison where only the world's most vile villains get stored when no one knows what else to do with them. As far as I know, no one has ever escaped. They get penned in and forgotten.

"I'm surprised I haven't heard of him," I say.

Truth is, I'm in a sort of shocked state. I feel like there's an entire lifetime worth of information Harrier hasn't shared with me, and I won't make believe it doesn't hurt.

"I'm not. You were a kid… maybe not even born yet. I was barely a teenager, part of the police explorer's program. Wanted to be a cop. Part of me still does. I grew up around where you're from, actually. You know how rough that neighborhood can be. I learned everything I could—black belt in more than one martial art, as well as boxing and wrestling. I don't have your gift… took me years to learn to do what I do."

"Sorry," I say. I'm not sure why, it just feels wrong being able to pick up things so quickly while knowing the other Kites didn't.

"Not your fault. And I don't regret it either. I had more than enough reason."

I wait, hoping he'll continue without prodding, but he returns to the computer console and starts typing again. I'm patient. I don't know what he's doing, but as the first Kite, I think he's got more than enough right to do whatever it is. He punches the enter key, and a green progress bar starts inching across the screen.

He turns back to me, spinning in his chair. "So here it is. Even playing field. Just like I said." He leans forward. "One day, my whole family's out to dinner. You know that place in Bushwick—used to be a brewery, now it's some Italian joint? Pictures of tomatoes and vines all over the wall. A mural of a naked woman, leaves covering her good stuff. The servers all wearing bright white shirts, even though they're all shucking red sauce around. Classy joint. Mom even ordered wine.

"Anyway, we were just eating. I think I got veal parmesan because Dad just got a bonus check, and he said to get whatever we wanted. I didn't even know what veal was, just that it was expensive. I took my first bite when I heard it. Gunshots."

I lean forward, just like him. This guy can tell a story!

"Wasn't meant for us, but bullets don't care what names we put on them. Dead in an instant, both of them. I remember thinking how much their blood looked like the sauce. I was young… didn't get it, not really. My brother was even younger, though I almost think he knew more than me, cos he was crying in his highchair and wouldn't stop."

"That's awful," I say. I can't even imagine.

"There was a lot of screaming and people running. Someone took out a gun at the table next to us and started shooting back as they ran to the sidewalk. But it was too late for my parents."

"I never knew my dad." I have no idea why I said it. Seriously, like watching your parents get shot and growing up not knowing who your dad was are even remotely the same thing. It's just—what do you say to something like that?

"I know. And that's awful, too. Maybe a different kind of way, but still sucks."

"So, how'd you end up with Harrier?" I ask.

"After that, my brother and I ended up in the system. At Saint Barnabas Home for Boys. Not far from where you live. During a charity benefit for the orphanage, Frank, in his ten-thousand-dollar suit and shoes, sat down at the table with me and the other eight-year-olds. His knees practically touched his chest on that little chair, but he didn't seem to care. Even so many years ago, Frank always carried himself with an air of maturity. That was one of the most surreal moments of my young life."

I can't help but smile at the vision of that in my mind. Frank isn't a small guy, not by any definition.

"He just started talking to me, asking questions. Whatever. Then, it was my turn to perform. We all a special little thing we were supposed to do as a part of the evening's entertainment. I was supposed to perform some stunts as part of the benefit. I think he liked what I was able to do with my bo staff, but really, I don't know what it was. He never told me... Frank, right? Starting that night, Harrier began sponsoring me in competitions and training me in other forms that he knew."

"So, he adopted you? That's awesome."

Something like anger washes over Alex's features, but he hides it almost immediately. "I didn't say that," is all he says, and I let it stay that way.

I guess I hit a nerve because he doesn't really offer any more information, at least not freely. I ask a few more questions and find out that Harrier eventually let Alex in on his secret and allowed him to tag along on patrols.

"At first, I just wore a ski mask and body armor, but after a while, Harrier had the first Red Kite costume made for me."

"Why Kite?" I ask. It comes out as a groan.

"Why ask me? I hated it. Still do."

"What?" I've always assumed the first Kite had come up with the name himself.

"It was Harrier's idea. I wanted the name Red Hawk from the beginning, but Harrier thought it sounded too Native American or something."

"Wow," I say. Knowing Frank, he probably just didn't want the code name to sound as cool as his.

"Why are you back?" I ask. "I mean, why now? After so long, why now?"

I suspect I know the answer, but I want to hear him say it.

"Truth? I think something horrible might have happened to Frank."

Maybe I didn't want to hear him say it. My stomach does a flip and then crawls up into my throat. Between my own feelings and the news stations, I already felt like something was wrong, but I guess I'd let Mr. Chen's false confidence rub off on me a little. Now, every ounce of fear is back on me, and it's brought friends.

There's a ping on the computer behind Redhawk, and I see a familiar and horrifying face pop up.

"And this is gonna sound crazy," he says, spinning back toward the computer. "But I think Chef Maléfique is back."

"What? No way," I say. "He's dead."

"We don't know that. Not for sure. Chef Maléfique is nothing if not devious and resourceful. I have reason to believe he faked his death and has been biding his time."

"That's insane," I say.

"*He's* insane," Alex agrees. "And he's the only person I've ever seen Harrier come close to killing. And you know his one rule."

"No killing."

"Yeah, but you try being Frank and trying and failing to capture the same guy over and over again. It nearly drove him mad."

I may not know everything, but I know Chef Maléfique is the one villain Harrier could never ultimately defeat. Could never capture. It started to drive Harrier to the edge of what he would normally do as a hero. But I never thought he'd even come close to breaking his hard and fast "no killing" rule when it came to the "evil chef."

"They never discovered Chef Maléfique's true identity or his motivations," Alex continued. "He wasn't after money... in fact, most of his plans cost way more than he ever made from them. His purpose in life seemed to be to destroy Harrier—not kill him but destroy everything he stood for, and everything he did."

"Well, he didn't succeed back then, and if he is back, which I still don't buy, he won't succeed now."

"You know what happened to Toby?" Alex asks.

The second Red Kite, Toby, is an absolute enigma to me. I know less about him than I do about Alex. As a matter of fact, I didn't even realize they were separate people until I'd been with Harrier for almost a year—when I'd finally asked him about all the old Kite costumes.

"Hold on a sec…" Alex—Redhawk—click-clacks the controls of Harrier's supercomputer and works them like he's been using them for years… which he probably had.

"There's something I can show you if it's still here, but I have to warn you… it's pretty disturbing."

He taps a few more keys, and an image appears on the giant screen in front of us. A closeup of a terrifying face. Chef Maléfique. I can't see his body at this angle, but let's just say he's rotund. A sloppy, painted-on black domino mask and white makeup stain his face, and he has a thin handlebar moustache. Except for the actual chef hat he wears, he looks more like an old cartoon villain than anything else.

In the upper left corner of the video is a timer, and the demented villain appears to be filming himself while he talks directly into the camera.

I swallow hard. "Show it to me."

"Are you sure?"

I nod in silence, Alex hits the space bar, and the video begins to play…

CHAPTER FOURTEEN

MALÉFIQUEFOUNDFOOTAGE.MP4

0:00

I What I really like best is the popping.

You know when you get that bubble wrap and squeeze those little cushion things? How good that feels? It's like that.

No, I'm not talking about *eyeballs.* Why would you think that? Those are more like grapes. Olives, maybe.

I'm talking about windpipes.

I'm sorry, is that a little too much? Maybe you better get off this ride here, then. It's only going to get juicier.

Must be this tall to ride.

No participation trophies here, folks. You have to be in it to win it.

Where was I? Oh, yes, the windpipe thing. It's always a difficult decision for me. It's my favorite way to do it—because, y'know, the *tingles*—but it's a little too quick for my taste. There are so many other ways to snuff out a candle that'll really last.

So, I try to be a good boy and not always go for the speedy, intense burst of joy. Let it sort of marinate, as it were.

That's how it is with my "friend." See what I did there? I put "friend" in air quotes because, if I'm being *frank,* we aren't all that friendly. I mean, I *am* always trying to kill him, after all.

Of course, I've had my chances to do it quickly. But where's the fun in that?

Torture? Sure. That's a given. When the time comes. But that's going to be the… the… what do you call it? *Amuse-bouche.*

No, no, no. That's not it, dadburnit.

Pre-dessert. Ha. How could I forget something that simple? Yes, the torture, when the time comes, will be like a brown sugar panna cotta with grapefruit *espuma* and cranberry gel, topped off with some crunchy dark chocolate crumble.

Mmmmm. Yummy.

Then—and only then—will we move on to the best part. The actual dessert.

NO. Not some tiramisu, you hillbilly. I'm talking about roasted pears with espresso mascarpone cream. Or rhubarb and pistachio pavlova.

WAIT! Wait. Hold on. No, that's not it.

Strawberry, currant, and mint tart with mascarpone.

Yes, *that's the ticket.*

Remember that? I used to love that guy. Why doesn't he ever work anymore?

That's the ticket. Still makes me giggle.

7:57

But I'm getting way ahead of myself here. It'll be years before I'm ready for that. Right now, I'm somewhere in the middle, perhaps the removes or sorbet of my wicked menu. The kidnapping of a loved one. Yes, indeed.

One of the classics, to be sure. All the worry, the hand wringing, the popping of the acid-reducers that can be milked out of that one. It's just such a satisfying feeling to know the person you despise with every fiber of your being is going through the worst personal hell imaginable. It's even better when you're the one putting them through it.

The problem is, my friend has no loved ones. I'm not going to keep putting friend in air quotes, as I'm fully aware that will become tedious. You'll forgive. I'm sure of it.

Awww. No loved ones. Alone. All alone. Yes, it's all so very sad.

Mother died in childbirth. Father died—was *murdered*—sometime later by… oh no, I mustn't give that away. That would be so very spoilery of me.

No siblings. Nary an uncle, aunt, or cousin to his name. What to do, what to do?

Oh my, but the answer was quite simple, really. No, it couldn't be children, since he didn't have any—or *DID* he?—so it would have to be the next best thing.

A ward. Two words. Not like a trophy or plaque. A. Ward.

Ha! Now I have you thinking, "What the devil is he talking about? Does this story take place in the nineteen-aughts or some such? Chef Maléfique, that's so very Edwardian of you. Who has a ward nowadays?"

Don't worry, I'm going to answer that question, and you're bound to smack yourself silly when you realize it… A hero. A masked crimefighter. A person who runs around in a ridiculous costume.

Oh, giggle, giggle, tee-hee, but I'm one to talk, am I right?

But he gets his jollies by beating up people like… well, *moi.*

Yes, yes, now it's dawning on you, isn't it? They call them sidekicks. I'm not certain, but I believe the word comes from the ancient Greek word for "human meat shield."

What? You never realized it? They take some poor kid, dress him—or her, mustn't be a misogynist. Not in this sensitive political climate—up in spandex and bright, colorful tights, and train them to jump straight into the fray while spouting loud insults at the poor supervillain or bank robber. What's a criminal to do, just sit idly by and take it? Of course not.

So they send them into danger like a canary in a coal mine, scoping out what kinds of traps lie in wait, or how many henchmen may be hiding on the mezzanine above with machine guns, or what have you. Meanwhile, the "hero"… there I go using the air quotes again… skulks in the shadows in his—or her, yes, yes—dark-hued body armor, waiting for an opportune moment to strike.

No wonder they tend to go through them like a snack bar goes through fried butter sticks at a county fair.

Say what you will about those of us on the wrong side of the law. At least we hire minions of their own free will. And pay them, for Pete's sake. We don't bring in some poor orphan off the street and turn him into a little punchy-kicky machine.

They think they're the good guys, but I'm telling you, they're on the dark side of the game when it comes to that.

5:42

You were thinking that was a clock, weren't you? It's quite all right, no need to be embarrassed. But you're a smart one, and now you've figured it out. It's a timer. And it's counting down. And when it—Oh! There you go trying to get me to reveal spoilers again, you cad.

So, my friend's sidekick is a young man—let's call him Toby (because his name is Toby)—who dresses up in red, black, and white and uses the same code name as his predecessor, who left some time ago for personal reasons I don't have time to go into at the moment (you can see the time ticking away, after all). It is—get this—Red Kite. Kite. Isn't that a gas? And it had to be red. Because just plain Kite was taken, maybe? I don't know how these things work.

And you may wonder—because I sure as hell did—"Why would a hero name his human meat shield after a children's toy?" Or maybe it makes sense to you. I don't know, we've never met. I have no idea where your head is at.

See, the thing is, you're wrong whether you're asking the question, or whether you think you know the answer. Because a kite is not just a children's toy. It's also a fabulous bird. Go do a search on it, I'll wait.

Whoops. I just told you we didn't have time, and now I'm putting things on pause so you can type away on your typie-thingie and look at pictures. Shame on me.

But see? Fabulous, just as advertised. And, if you're really smart, you looked up "red kite," species name *Milvus milvus*, and were treated to something extra, extra fabulous after you sifted through all the nonsense about my boy, Toby. Because those little hawks are quite lovely indeed.

Sure, Toby is fabulous, too, I guess. By all accounts, the nicest young man you could ever meet. Of course, I've only met him when he was trying to shove his fist down my throat and his foot into my sensitive squishy parts. But even I am quite enamored of the boy.

I have, after all, been watching him for quite some time now. Not in a creepy way.

Well, okay, it's obviously creepy, but you know what I mean. It's not like I'm trying to do anything naughty to the tyke. Well, not like you might be thinking, anyway.

I've just been trying to figure out the best way and the best time to kidnap him so that I can tie him up and use him as bait.

. . .

3:31

Goodness, I just realized I'm nearly out of time, and I haven't even told you who my friend is. He didn't just randomly choose the name Red Kite for his meat shield. He appears to have some sort of fetish for birds of prey.

He goes by Black Harrier. Or *The* Black Harrier. It's not very consistent, to be honest, and that bothers me quite a bit.

I'm not going to tell you to do a search to look up what a Black Harrier looks like because, as I said, we're almost out of time, so you'll probably have to just wait until we're done here. But let me assure you, it's quite a beautiful and formidable creature.

I'm ignoring the fact that you may be, instead, thinking about a fighter plane, because the United States military decided to use that name for a jump jet. But I do want you to understand there's a reason they'd name a powerful fighter jet after such a bird. It really is magnificent.

(If instead, you're thinking about a yappy pup, then I can't *even* right now. Shame on you.)

Anyway, you may have already guessed that I have a somewhat complicated relationship with my friend. Perhaps even an unhealthy obsession with him. After all, the bird he's named after has the classification, *Circus maurus*. How funny is that? I love to put on makeup and put on a magnificent show, and… oh, you get it. Yes, I know circus has a different meaning here, but let's be honest: we both know I'm not all that concerned about that sort of thing.

To be fair, I feel like the preoccupation is mutual, but I suppose I've never really asked him. Maybe that's just wishful thinking on my part.

So we go round and round playing this game of hawk and mouse (because why would I say cat when this analogy makes so much more sense?) and having a great deal of fun. Okay, *I* have a great deal of fun, and he gets very angry and assaults me to within an inch of my life.

But my point is, we have this thing going on, and I'm trying to keep it interesting by upping the ante. Pushing the envelope.

2:20

Why use Toby as bait? Why, why, why, why, WHY!

Sigh… Because I know that it will drive my friend bonkers. He will be searching for him, and I will leave clues, and some of those clues will make no sense whatsoever. Why should I make it easy on the man? He's trying to put me away, after all.

Wait. Did I say will? I'm having trouble with my tenses here. Actually, I already did capture young Toby and tied him to a chair. I didn't just use rope, either. I've seen all those old films and television shows where the hero cuts through the rope, and so have you.

What do I look like, a silent movie villain, twirling my mustachios? Okay, so maybe my moustache threw you off a bit, I quite understand. No, I tied him up with rope, zip ties, titanium-alloy cable, and duct tape (you know, I used to think it was called "duck" tape, then only later realized you're not supposed to use it on waterfowl—but not until it was too late).

You may think this sounds like overkill, but believe me, this kid is resourceful, and if I didn't go to such great lengths, he'd find some way out. So, I made absolutely, positively, undoubtedly, unquestionably, undeniably... What was I saying? Nothing important, I guess.

So... I set the timer. Tick tock.

I know you want to ask me why I need a timer, but I'm sure you've already figured it out, and are just hoping that you're wrong about the answer. I assure you, you're not.

Most supervillains only have one reason for setting a timer, and it's not like I'm trying to be extra creative here. What's the best way to wound a superhero without physically harming him?

You already know.

1:06

At the risk of sounding foolish, I'm going to be candid with you and admit that I'm getting a bit worried here. You see, I didn't believe for a second that Harrier would be cutting it this close, and I did set quite the pile of explosives to detonate when the timer was done.

Perhaps I shouldn't have left such perplexing clues or so many red herrings. Now, it appears my entire plan, like chocolate, crumbles before my eyes. Dissolving. I may never get my dessert. Or my pre-dessert even.

I fortified this place so well to make it difficult for him to get in, and let my henchmen go home early so they wouldn't mess anything up, as they have a habit of doing.

I'm not sure this is going to work out at all.

Are you getting worried? You should be. There's a young boy here about to be turned into hamburger meat, and there's no way anyone is going to save him in time. Besides. That's not the main course I had in mind. Roast bird. Yum.

Me? Of course, I don't care if he goes splat. That was my plan. But Harrier was supposed to show up, and we were going to fight, and he'd realize it was too late to save Toby without everyone turning into bits and kabobs, and he'd have to say goodbye and be wracked by guilt forever.

Well, not *forever* forever. Just until I made him dessert. By which I mean, made him *into* dessert.

0:24

You see, unfortunately, he was supposed to find a way into this impenetrable room here, and then I would escape whilst he agonized over the fact that there was no way to get through the rope, the zip ties, the titanium-alloy cord, and the duct tape and then get out at the last second, as he is so famously wont to do.

Problem is, my henchmen aren't too bright, and they locked the door on the way out. But my copy of the key is out there. And, while I've been telling you this story, I've also been trying to open this—

The video glitches, and the screen goes black. It takes me a few moments to recover from seeing that.

Redhawk seems shell-shocked as well, even though it's obviously not his first time seeing the video. In fact, he appears to be pretty traumatized. When he finally speaks, he just keeps staring at the blank screen rather than look at me.

"Apparently, he was going to film it all and send it to the news. But he, ah, never got the chance. Harrier found it in a mini recorder buried in the wreckage before anyone else could get a hold of it. I'm pretty sure he showed it to me later to make me feel guilty for leaving. I don't know."

"Sounds like Frank."

I ask Redhawk what Chef Maléfique was like in person. He thinks for a second before answering. "You know the evil clown from *It*?"

"Yeah." I've seen him in the movie anyway. Never read the book.

"Imagine that clown, running away, screaming from something that terrifies him. That something would be Chef Maléfique."

I'm not sure I've ever shuddered before, but I do it now. "That bad, huh?"

"More evil than you can imagine. And the few pictures of him that were taken before he died don't do him justice. In those, he looks like a sad, fat cook, just like in that video. In-person, he was scary as hell to look at. Especially his eyes."

"What's with the whole chef thing?" I ask, now that I finally have the chance for answers.

Alex shakes his head. "Who the hell knows? I'm sure it has something to do with why he's a homicidal maniac, but your guess is as good as mine. There are rumors about him being some sort of… cannibal or something. But I've never seen any evidence to back them up."

Wow. That's a whole new level of scary.

"So, this is why you're here?" I ask.

"Frank couldn't stop Chef Maléfique from killing Toby, and I'm not going to let it happen again."

I swear. "You think it's that bad?"

Redhawk shrugs. "Can't be too cautious, I don't think. I'm going to hit the streets today and see if I can dig anything up. It's been a while since I did any patrolling around here, though. You think you might be able to go with me?"

Redhawk is known in Boston as a hero who is around when you need him. Night or day. Not like me and Harrier, who mainly patrol at night and let the police do their job during the day.

"I, uh, can go later on tonight," I answer. "But I kind of have school today, and I can't miss it."

"Then I'll do what I can on my own, and you can join me later on."

He turns, and so do I. Him for the gym and me for the window.

"Hey, Alex?"

He looks over his shoulder at me.

"If you're gonna train anyway, think you could show me a few moves on the staff?"

"It's not like one session—" He stops, and I think he realizes that it would only take one second with my particular talent. "Alright, yeah. Come on."

Once we're in the gym, he shows me some basic moves and, even with my cold slowing me down, I pick them up immediately. Impressed, he gets more complicated quickly, and I'm still able to keep up. Within an hour, he's shown me everything he knows, and I can duplicate it all perfectly.

I always wondered why Harrier never trained me with a staff, and I realize it's because it would remind him of Alex.

"That's it, man. That's all I got," he says.

"Awesome," I say, wiping my nose. "Thanks."

"Kinda makes me feel like I've just wasted my whole life learning stuff you picked up in one session." He laughs. "I'm kidding. Pretty cool gift you've got."

"Yeah," I say.

As we're about to leave, Alex suddenly has an idea, and we head back to the control center to try one more thing. He opens a compartment on the main computer panel that I've never noticed before and types in a code, then presses a red button.

"Ever met Eaglestar before?"

I'm puzzled by the question of whether I've ever met the most powerful being on Earth. It seems so random.

"No. He wasn't there the one time I was at a Guild meeting. Why?"

"Because you're about to." He looks at my slack-jawed expression and grins. "Don't get too excited, though."

"Why?"

"Cos he's kind of a douche-bag."

Just then, there's a sonic boom, and the Aerie rattles as if there's an earthquake. Redhawk opens the helipad doors, and I see the most amazing thing ever. Eaglestar, costume all red, white, and blue, floats down from the sky and hovers a couple of feet off the ground. His eyes glow, which creeps me out more than I would have thought.

Eaglestar was a World War II fighter pilot who shot down a lot of enemy planes and became a national treasure along with his squadron. They were sent on a secret mission to take down an airship the Nazis were using to transport some kind of artifacts—supposedly something of alien origin—and the rest of his squadron was killed during the fight. He managed to take down the other enemy planes escorting the airship singlehandedly but ran out of ammo in the process. So he did the only thing he could and rammed his plane into the ship, which erupted in a fiery explosion.

But instead of being killed in the crash, he was given extraordinary powers, including super-strength, invulnerability, flight, apparent immortality, and the ability to shoot some sort of energy out of his eyes. Yes. Laser-beam-eyeballs. Sometimes, the whole "I got powers from..." thing makes no sense at all, but it's happened enough that we all just have to accept it.

At first, the government used him as a secret weapon to help win the war—and hunt down the Nazis who also gained powers in that explosion—but it wasn't long before the word got out. Now, he's the world's greatest hero, and everyone loves him.

Then again, *everyone* hasn't met him in person.

"Where is he?" With his strange, hollow voice, it's hard to tell if he's angry or not, but it sure seems that way.

I look at Redhawk nervously, but he doesn't seem fazed by this. "He's not here. That's why I called you."

"*You* called me? That signal is for Harrier. And only Harrier." Redhawk was right. He does sound pretty douchey.

"Yeah, well, Harrier has been missing for a few weeks. I was hoping maybe you could—"

"Harrier goes missing frequently. Cases in other nations, undercover work, that monastery in Tibet... there are also missions with the Guild, even off-world on occasion." Eaglestar sounds more dismissive than anyone I've ever heard.

"Is there currently a Guild mission in progress?"

I can't believe Redhawk is talking to the guy this way. He scares the crap out of me.

"No."

"Then why bring it up?" Now he's even challenging him. Redhawk's got guts, I'll give him that.

"My point is that Harrier often disappears without warning, and he always returns. Why are you so concerned?" I wish he wouldn't keep floating that way. It's like he's too good to stand on the ground like the rest of us.

"Well, for one thing, his partner has no idea where he is."

Eaglestar turns his gaze on me as if he's noticing I'm there for the first time. I'm pretty sure I pee a little in my costume.

"Has he ever performed missions or left the country without informing you of his whereabouts?"

"Well—" I have to clear my throat because my voice is cracking from nervousness. "He's done it once or twice... for a few days. And there were a couple of times he took... um... women on trips. Like, vacation?"

"Is that a question or a statement?"

Confused and flustered, I look to Redhawk for some help. He speaks up. "We don't think any of those situations is currently the case. We're not even sure he's alive. As I was saying, I was hoping you—"

"Until you have some evidence of foul play, I suggest you stop worrying. Harrier can take care of himself." Eaglestar starts floating toward the helipad doors. "And don't use that signal again unless there's a major threat to this city or a planetary emergency. I'm not at your beck and call."

"Sorry to bother you then." Redhawk's tone is so sarcastic I feel like I could learn a thing or two.

Eaglestar stops his ascent for a moment and fixes his glowy, icy stare on Redhawk.

"In the time we've had this conversation, three-hundred seventy-two incidents occurred in which I could have prevented a crime or an accident. Nine lives have been lost. If you believe you were simply 'bothering me' then you are mistaken."

Eaglestar takes off so fast that he's nothing but a blur, and a sonic boom follows. Redhawk closes the helipad doors.

"Well, then. I guess we're on our own."

CHAPTER **FIFTEEN**

My head is pounding. It's like my sinuses are the Hoover Dam and the Snot-arado River is building up behind it.

I think about Eaglestar the entire way home. I never thought that meeting one of my heroes could freak me out so much. Meeting Harrier was definitely a rush the first time, and even though that feeling eventually faded, and he even started to annoy me sometimes, he's never treated me as badly as Eaglestar just had. I guess maybe I should give him more credit for the way he acts, considering who he is.

With Eaglestar, I felt like I didn't matter. Totally insignificant.

I like to think Harrier knew what a giant ass Eaglestar would be, and that's why he never introduced me to him.

I know they went on missions together and stuff, especially with the Guild. I kind of always assumed they were friends. But for him to not care at all that Harrier is missing and could even be dead… wow.

"Amber," I say, swooping down to my roof.

"*How can I please you tonight*?" she asks.

"Do you sit around thinking about the dirtiest way to say innocent things?"

"Was I being… dirty?"

I ignore her. "Still nothing on Harrier?"

"I'm sorry. Nothing."

"Thanks. We're done for the night. Silent mode."

I manage to sneak through my window, strip off the suit, and climb under the covers just in time for Mom to come in to wake me up for school. I try the old "too sick to go to school" routine, and even though it's for real, she won't have any part of it. It's a good thing I got several hours of sleep before I left because this flu or whatever is starting to knock me on my butt.

As I ride my skateboard to school, my head continues to throb, and my throat starts to feel like it's on fire. *Great*. So I'm supposed to go out searching for Harrier with my predecessor, and I'm gonna look like an amateur because I feel like I've been run over by a truck. Redhawk's gonna wonder why Harrier ever chose me as his new partner.

It definitely doesn't get any better once I get to school, either. All the loud noise in the halls makes my head hurt even worse, and it seems like everything is closing in on me.

After first period, Javier runs to catch up to me in the hall as I'm opening up my locker. I wonder if he's gonna bring up the incident in the convenience store yesterday.

"Hey, are you okay? You don't look so good." He's acting normal. Maybe he won't.

"I'm coming down with something. That kid my mom babysits sneezed and coughed all over me."

"Oh, that stinks," he says, taking a baby-step backward.

"Yep."

"So..." He seems kind of nervous now. "Yesterday at that store..."

Think fast. What's my cover story? Why didn't I come up with a cover story?

"Yeah, that was crazy, right? I'd just finished an energy drink, and I've been taking these karate classes, and it's like I just went nuts with adrenaline or something."

You sound like an idiot. Shut up.

"Yeah, it was pretty cool. Can you… uh… teach me?"

That's not at all where I thought this would go, but I need to do whatever it takes to keep him quiet and on my side.

"Well, I don't really know what I did, but sure, I mean, we could train together sometime."

He looks like a kid on Christmas, or more accurately, like a kid on Christmas who just got every single thing he'd wished for *and* found out he was going to Disney World.

As I feel my nose tingle, I do the Dracula thing and sneeze into my sleeve in the crook of my arm.

So, of course, I have snot on my sleeve when Fabiola—that really hot cheerleader—decides to talk to me for the first time ever. She flips her hair over her shoulder and giggles at the girls she's with.

"Hey. So I hear you're on the wrestling team now."

Even though the words she's saying are obviously about me, I still find myself looking around to make sure she isn't talking to someone else. "Um. Yeah. I guess I am."

"Great," she says. "Wow. I mean, that came out of, like, nowhere. Does that mean you're coming to my party?"

"Party?" Of course I've heard about The Party, but I have to play it cool. Everyone is gonna be there. Suddenly, my invisibility doesn't seem to matter much anymore.

"Halloween, silly." She playfully slaps my arm, and I'm pretty sure she hit the boogers. "It's a costume party, and I'm gonna wear the skimpiest costume I can find. Trust me, you don't want to miss it."

She ain't lyin'…

"I don't? I mean, yeah, I don't."

"Follow me online for directions. 'Kay? 'Kay."

"Okay. Yeah. Sounds good."

As she's walking away, Fabiola grabs my arm for a second and raises an eyebrow when she feels my bicep. Her mouth curves into a half-smile, and she doesn't break eye contact until she's around the corner. I keep watching the spot where she disappeared as if I can still see her through the wall.

Javi picks his jaw up off the floor as he stares after her also. "That-that-that was —" He ends with an odd squeaky sound.

"I know."

"And she, like, *talked* to you. And touched you. And invited you *to her house*."

"I know." I turn and close my locker, so I'm not late for class.

He finally looks at me instead of the empty space where Fabiola went around the corner. "Are you going?"

Let's see… Black Harrier is missing, Redhawk wants me to help search for him, and even if I don't end up dead, my mom has semi-permanently grounded me and won't let me out of her sight.

"Probably not." As I walk away, I can almost hear Javi's jaw hit the floor again.

Algebra 2 is a difficult enough class for me to stay awake in even under the best of circumstances. But when I'm sick, stayed up most of the night, and had the prettiest girl in school talk to me, my concentration is far from as good as it can get. My head feels like it's a blown-up balloon. Fire ants are crawling down my swollen throat, and I have chills.

Mr. Cross's voice sounds like it's coming from a TV in another room as he drones on about variables or whatever. I keep going back and forth in my head, thinking about Harrier and trying to figure out a way to go to Fabiola's party.

I start picturing Fabiola in Osprey's costume. Then I start to feel guilty. But why? It's not like we're dating or anything.

I have to stop letting my mind wander like this. I need to pay attention in class, or I'm gonna be in more trouble. Then I'll never be able to help figure out what happened to Harrier. That gets me thinking about Chef Maléfique. Even after having seen the video and pictures of him up close, I start imagining him like I used to, with glowing red eyes like Eaglestar's, and a tongue like a snake.

I go from feeling like I can't keep my eyes open any more to suddenly realizing I'm being woken up by the teacher, and the entire class is laughing at me. Worse, there's a puddle of mucus on my desk where I laid my head down, and a string of it stretching between the desktop and my face when I sit up.

When my teacher sees this, he quickly changes his attitude from annoyed to concerned. "Sawyer, maybe you should go see the school nurse."

"I think I'll be all right, sir." I sound like Rudolph when Santa made him wear the cap over his red nose.

"It's not a request. You look really sick, and I'm sure it's contagious. I don't want to spend my weekend in bed or worse, have my wife accuse me of getting my kids sick again. You need to go now."

"Yeah, okay."

I grab my backpack and head out the door, some of the other students still chuckling as I go. I'm so out of it I can hardly think straight, but I do start to worry about whether I'm gonna be able to help Redhawk out tonight at all. Then I hear a loud clanking sound coming from around the corner, like metal hitting on metal. I can't figure out what could possibly be making that noise.

Fear grips me when my imagination draws a picture of Chef Maléfique coming for me. It's a ridiculous thought, but I'm freaking delirious at this point.

As I turn toward the office, I see Logan out of class, running down the hall and slapping all the combination locks hanging from the lockers as he goes. I secretly smile, thinking Logan is finally gonna get busted for something, when I see Principal Blanchard come out of the teacher's lounge. But he completely ignores the racket Logan's making and makes a beeline to me.

He gets right up in my face like he's about to kick my butt or something. His breath smells like old coffee, and long hairs are coming out of his nostrils and eyebrows in all directions. "Mr. Vincent, do you have a pass to be out of class?"

You've gotta be kidding me. I point after Logan, and the loud clanking still coming from his direction. "Seriously? But—"

"Do you have a pass or not?"

I try to think through all the snot clogging my head as I feel around in my pockets. I come up empty and realize I left the classroom in kind of a hurry. "Uh… I guess Mr. Cross forgot to give me one."

"We'll see about that." He starts writing out a referral slip. "Where are you going?"

"To see the nurse." I start to feel the tingling again, as well as an overwhelming pressure building in my sinuses.

"Are you really? You seem fine to me. Are you sure you're not—"

That's when it happens. The biggest, grossest sneeze I've ever had, and I can't get my hands out of my pockets in time to cover anything.

It explodes from my nasal cavity, all over Mr. Blanchard. Green slime is everywhere.

I try to hold back a smile as I apologize. "I'm really sorry—"

He pulls out a handkerchief and starts wiping himself off, beginning with his face. "Just go! Get out of here. Now!"

I know it's mean, especially for a supposed hero like me, but I feel so much better after doing that. When I get to the nurse's office, it turns out she isn't even here today. Due to budget cuts, she's only at our school twice a week, and today isn't one of those days.

The secretary tells me I look horrible, and to go lie down on the cot in the back of the nurse's office until she can get call my mom to come pick me up. Knowing full well that she's never gonna get ahold of her, I drift off for a nice, well-deserved nap.

Of course, once I'm asleep again, the dreams start up thanks to the cold meds I took this morning. Only this time, it's a dream about the past.

In fact, it's so much like a "life flashing before my eyes" dream that I should probably be worried that I'm sicker than I thought, and I'm actually dying.

It's like watching an edited recording of my adventures with the Black Harrier, only instead of from my own point of view, I see everything from a distance. The early months of my training, going up against ordinary thugs on the street. Then my first encounters with costumed villains like Music Master and Creeping Death. Then the more dangerous bad guys such as Med-Evil show up, and things get really hairy.

As it goes on, I can remember how I felt all along the way. How the whole thing went from being a constant thrill to just hard work, and finally, a job that I dreaded showing up to every night. But it wasn't Harrier who changed. It was me.

He was the same hero, with his drive to clean up the city and bring justice to criminals. He treated me the same way from the beginning to now. But I somehow lost that feeling I had when we began, and now I'm acting… what? Ungrateful? Like I took it all for granted? Like my life would be better if I went back to being just some lonely skater dude who tuned out life listening to heavy metal with my earbuds in and spent all my time after school practicing tricks on my board?

The school secretary wakes me up to tell me school's over and it's time to go home. It takes me a minute to shake out the cobwebs and get over the disorientation of having slept in a place I'm not used to. The cold meds and the sickness don't help, and the dream felt like it lasted for years.

An overwhelming feeling of loss hits me when I think about Harrier being missing. Just when I realize I should be happier with my situation as his partner, he might be gone forever—and it could all be over with.

CHAPTER **SIXTEEN**

C*rap.*

That's the best way to describe what I feel like as I head for the Aerie. I had the unbelievable luck of Mom taking the brat to the theater to see some stupid 3-D kid movie, and because she could see how sick I really was, she left me in bed and trusted me to stay put.

Of course, when she gets home, she'll probably figure out right away that the lump under my covers is just a bunch of clothes and not really me, but I'll have to worry about that later. This is far too important.

As if being half-dead with the flu isn't enough, it starts pouring rain as I head out to meet Redhawk.

"Amber, anything new?" I ask as soon as my helmet's on.

"Your girlfriend isn't far away," she says. *"And she's so wet."*

"My… what? What is wrong with you?"

"It's raining, Sawyer. Golly, you have such a gutter-brain. She's eight blocks east of here and moving north."

"Oh, my tracker is still on her?"

"Mission: Stalk Osprey is a complete success."

"I'm not stalking her!" I scream. Regret becomes tangible when the feeling of icepicks drags along my throat.

"Silent mode," I say. As much as I want to see Osprey, I can't get distracted. Not now.

By the time I reach the Aerie, I'm thoroughly drenched and hacking up a lung.

I get there even earlier than Redhawk was expecting. I enter through the hatch, and he gawks at me and the puddle that's quickly forming around my feet. I let out a big sneeze.

"You're not looking so good." Redhawk isn't just making an observation like everybody else. He seems genuinely concerned.

"Yeah, so everyone keeps telling me."

"Maybe you shouldn't go with me then."

Bullcrap. I'm going.

"I'll be okay. I took a really long nap this afternoon."

He doesn't look too sure, but I have a feeling he really needs the help, so he doesn't want to push the issue too much.

Redhawk grabs his equipment and starts to put on his mask. I happen to look over at the glass case with his and the second Kite's costumes. Now I know what happened to the other one, but Alex still hasn't told me why he left.

I decide this could be the only chance I have to ask him, considering how dangerous our mission is. "Hey, Alex."

"Yeah?"

"You don't have to tell me if you don't want to, but… I've always wondered why you stopped being the Red Kite."

Redhawk sighs and looks over at his old costume himself. He considers for a long moment, then points to the same chairs where we sat when watching the Chef Maléfique video. I get some kind of PTSD flashback that sucks, and then I worry that he's gonna show me another one. However, I follow him anyway, and we each take a seat.

"I don't know what your situation is, but I get the impression you have a real life outside of… this. School, fun, friends. A girl… or boy?"

"Girl," I say quickly, then add, "Not that there's anything wrong with… you know, whatever. But girls, I like girls. Well, kind of one girl, but—"

Dude, shut up.

He laughs then gestures around the Aerie. "Yeah. Exactly. Well, that wasn't really the case with me."

"What do you mean?"

"Like I told you, I was an orphan when Frank met me, and all I wanted to do was to become a cop and bring criminals to justice. He took me under his wing and trained me until I was more effective than I'd ever be as a police officer."

So far, he hasn't told me anything I didn't already know.

"But what became even more important to me was for him to adopt me, since he was the closest thing I had to a parent in many years. He always made excuses about how a single guy couldn't adopt a teenage boy that way, but I know he just never really wanted the responsibility. Someone as rich as he is can hire lawyers to make pretty much anything happen, you know?"

I never really thought about any of this since I already had my mom. That must have been hard on him.

"So, even as Harrier trained me day in and day out, I lived at Saint Barnabas until I turned eighteen, unlike my brother, who'd been adopted as a baby. Then I had to find someplace else to go. I kind of assumed I'd be able to move in here once that happened, but when I brought it up… well, you know how he can be."

"Definitely. But what was his excuse for not letting you move in?"

"He was worried about 'the appearance of impropriety.' I'm not sure whether he was more afraid of it scaring off the ladies or the implication that would result from a young guy moving in with a rich bachelor like that."

It takes me a second to register what he means, just because it isn't something I would have ever considered. "Seriously? But it's not like you're—" I cut myself off when I realize I don't actually know if what I was about to say is true. But it's none of my business and shouldn't matter anyway. What Harrier did was messed up. "I mean, it's not like you would interfere with his dating life or anything, right?"

Alex just smiles. He knows I'm uncomfortable, and for some reason, he has no desire to alleviate it by telling me anything one way or the other. Which is fine. Because, you know—like I said—none of my business.

"Didn't help that his advisors were such hard-asses either."

Advisors? I don't know of any advisors other than…

"Mr. Chen?" I ask.

Alex's nonresponse said all I need to hear.

"So when I packed up my stuff and left the orphanage, I just kept on going and left town. Never even said goodbye to him."

Wow. So, that's nothing like I was expecting to hear. I don't know what I *was* expecting to hear, I just know it wasn't that.

"Alex," a voice sounds from the hallway leading to the simulation room. "Who are you talking to?"

Mr. Chen rounds the corner, dressed in a black turtleneck and black slacks. A far cry from his typical rich-man suits.

"Sawyer!" he says with enough excitement to share. Though upon second thought, it seems forced. Like he's caught off-guard by my presence.

What's he doing here in the Aerie? In all my years as Harrier's partner, I've never seen Luis Chen up here.

"Hi, Mr. Chen." I don't mean to, but I tag a little question mark on the end.

He gets closer, seems to compose himself, and gives me a once-over.

"You look like you got into a fight with death and barely won."

I laugh without much humor. "Yeah, well, at least I won, right?"

"What are you doing here?" we both say at the same time. Then, we both start to answer.

"You first," Mr. Chen says.

I don't think that's particularly fair, but I don't get the impression "age before beauty" is gonna work here.

"I'm here to help, uh, Redhawk with something."

"It's okay," Alex says. "Luis knows why I'm here."

"You do?" I ask. "I thought you weren't worried about Frank?"

"I wasn't… I'm not," he says. "But when a member of the Guild comes calling, I have an obligation to comply."

I snort mucous into the back of my throat. It's disgusting. "So, that's all this is? You *complying* with the Guild?"

"What's going on here?" Alex asks.

We both look at him, and I wait for Chen do answer, but he doesn't.

"I went to see Mr. Chen a couple days ago." Or was that yesterday? I'm so out of sorts I start to think maybe I should be at home sleeping. "And he told me there's nothing to worry about, and Frank can take care of himself."

Alex looks confused for a moment, but before he can speak, Mr. Chen chimes in.

"It doesn't matter anymore. We are all here now, and whether or not Frank needs saving, we've got the best there is working the case."

I almost roll my eyes at the attempt at flattery. Maybe it's the cold, but I'm pissed off. It's like every turn I take, someone isn't telling me something, or isn't being honest with me. I bet this is how Redhawk felt back in the day.

"Still sticking it to the Kites, are you, Chen?" Alex asks.

"That is unfair, Alexander."

"Is it? Things could have been completely different, had you not interfered." Resentment drips off his words.

"I was trying to protect you." Even though Chen's expression hasn't changed one bit, his tone has definitely softened.

"Right. And how did that work out?"

"You don't know Frank like I do," Mr. Chen says.

"I could have."

I realize I'm looking back and forth between them like I'm watching a tennis match.

"I don't know what you're complaining about," Mr. Chen says. "If I'd have advised him to let you stay, you wouldn't be your own hero. You'd still just be a Kite."

His words probably came out faster than he'd expected because his eyes went wide, and he looked at me.

"Yeah. Well. I guess that's that," Alex says. "Is that it?" He snatches something out of Chen's mechanical hand that I hadn't seen before.

"Sawyer, I'm sorry," Mr. Chen says.

I just stand there, swallowing against my scratchy, dry throat.

His eyes, pursed lips, tilted head—they all speak of some kind of sympathy or apology. To me, it doesn't matter. He said what he said. He'd meant it. It wasn't exactly untrue, either.

Redhawk hands me what he'd taken from Mr. Chen.

"Just push that button," he says.

I do, and what was a foot-long span of graphene extends into a full-length staff just like the one Osprey carries.

"Wow. Thanks."

"Anyway," Alex continues, "we have a lot to do, and that's all ancient history now. So, what do you say we go beat up some bad guys?"

I watch Mr. Chen, who just rubs his face.

"Yeah, sounds good," I say.

When I try to exit the Aerie in the usual way, Redhawk just crosses his arms and shakes his head. "I have a better idea."

"Be careful," I hear Mr. Chen yell at us, like he cares.

Redhawk takes me down a private elevator to a secret garage in a sub-basement under the building's regular parking levels. On top of everything else, I feel pretty angry and maybe a little jealous that Harrier's never shown me this area, but there's no reason to get into it now. For one thing, it's not Redhawk's fault Harrier never told me about it, plus Harrier's not around for me to discuss it with him.

"That guy's a prick," Alex says.

"Never thought so until now."

"But he sure knows his stuff." He points to my new staff.

"Oh, right. This was you?" I ask.

"Yeah, after seeing how awesome you did in training, I thought you should have one. I hope you like it."

He hopes I like it? It took Harrier three years to give me a gift. *Three years.* Here, I've known this guy for a day, and I've got a killer staff and entrance into a secret part of Douglas Tower I never knew about.

"I love it."

As the doors to the elevator open, the first thing I see is a giant black vehicle that looks like a cross between a Ferrari and a tank. How did I not know about this? Does Harrier not use it anymore, or does he just not use it when I'm around?

But what Redhawk really wants to show me is parked behind the big vehicle. A set of motorcycles, a big black one and a smaller red one.

I guess my expression at seeing these gives away the fact that I had no idea they existed.

"What's the matter?"

"I just… I never…"

I can tell from his expression that Redhawk didn't realize I had no idea about this stuff. "He was probably just waiting for you to get your license. But you're old enough now, right?"

"Yeah, probably," I say. Technically, maybe. I don't believe it, though.

He shows me how to start the bike, and then points out the other controls.

I turn the key, and the motor rumbles under me.

"Feels good, huh?" he asks.

"Hell, yeah," I say.

"Language."

I stutter over a response when he laughs. "I'm kidding. I used to hate him for that."

This guy… He's like the first person I feel like I can totally relate to. It's almost like he's been me.

He takes off, doing a little wheelie, and I follow, not doing a wheelie because at first, I have trouble just moving along on the thing. But then, like everything else, I get the hang of it from watching Redhawk. He's an expert rider, and it doesn't take long for me to replicate his ability.

Once I know what I'm doing, it's the most fantastic thing I've ever done. Even better than gliding around above the city. I thought skating on my board was cool, but this is about a billion times cooler.

Our helmets have mics and speakers in them, so we sync them up to communicate.

As we're riding, Redhawk tells me about the time after the second Red Kite was killed by Chef Maléfique. He and Harrier hadn't spoken much since their falling out, but he'd gone to visit Harrier after the funeral. Harrier had stopped putting on the suit and was spending all of his time sitting around his penthouse, drinking. That was when he showed Alex the video.

He wasn't sure what brought Harrier out of his depression a couple of months later, but he did see news stories about Harrier and me, the new Red Kite, together all of a sudden, so he always figured getting a new sidekick had something to do with it.

In other words, I somehow managed to drag Harrier out of his despair. Not something I would have ever considered.

Bleep.

"No way," Alex says.

"What?"

"He gave you Amber?"

"Oh, yeah. I guess she was his when you were with him?"

Redhawk switches lanes, and I follow.

"Dude, I used to fantasize about her growing up. In my mind, she looked like that chick from that one high school show in the 90s."

I have no idea what he's talking about.

"What are you waiting for?" he asks. "Answer her!"

I can't believe how excited he is about this, but I do what he says. "Hey, Amber."

"OMG," she says. A phrase I've literally never heard from her virtual lips. *"Is that little Alex? Hmmm. Not so little anymore, are you?"*

As always, her words are laced with innuendo, and I can almost hear Redhawk blushing if that's possible.

"What can I do for you, Amber?" I ask.

"Ask not what you can do for me, but what I can do for you..."

"Enough," I say.

"Hey, let the lady talk," Alex argues.

"There's a disturbance two blocks over to the east," she says.

"What kind of disturbance?"

"Oh, you'll see."

Just like it had with Osprey, being out on patrol with Redhawk, it reminds me of the early days with Harrier. The main difference is that Redhawk actually has a sense of humor.

We roll up on the disturbance, and I'm not sure either of us knows how to respond. That is until I watch Redhawk leap off his bike and charge toward several men—I think they're all men?—dressed in Black Harrier masks. Some even have the whole outfit on.

"Wait up," I say, dismounting and doing my best to keep up. The cold is in my chest now, and I'm trying my hardest to not cough.

"What is this?" Alex growls. At first, he sounds like he's using a voice manipulator like Harrier, but he's not. That's just his anger roiling.

He slams one of them against the wall, and it's immediately evident that none of these people are fighters. A couple run. Some try to stop Redhawk, but very timidly, like someone trying to keep a lion away from their friend. You don't want to do nothing, but you know you have no chance.

Alex repeats himself with another slam. "What is this?"

"Wh-wh-what's wr-wrong with you?" the guy mumbles.

"Why are you dressed like that?"

I step in and try to keep the others away from Redhawk. He hasn't seen how they're acting. They're all terrified.

"It's Halloween, man!"

"It's *not* Halloween for a few days," Redhawk reminds them.

"Tis the season, dude."

"And what—all of you decided to dress the same?"

The guy pinned against the wall is still stumbling over his words, and one of the others by me says, "Someone paid us to do it, man. Even gave us the costumes. Let him go, dude. C'mon, let him go."

Redhawk punches the wall right beside the guy's head before dropping him the six inches to his feet.

Breathing heavily, Redhawk turns toward me and then the guy who'd spoken up.

"Who?"

"What?" the guy answers.

"Who paid you?"

"I… I don't know… just some guy."

"You didn't think it was weird that 'some guy' paid you money to dress up like Black Harrier?"

"This is New York, man! People act crazy all the time. We ain't gonna say no to free money."

"What did he look like?" Redhawk asks.

"We didn't see him. He told us to meet at Holy Mother Catholic Church. We talked in the confessional, I swear. Then, he said to wait five minutes, and everything we'd need would be in the priest's booth."

"What was in there?"

"The costumes… and a stack of these. He said to give them to anyone who commented on our costumes. I promise, man. We aren't doing anything wrong."

He hands Redhawk something…

A business card. But it's blank. Redhawk turns it over and moves his thumb. It's not blank.

"A handlebar moustache?"

Redhawk says a word my mom would probably kill me if she heard me say it.

"Get lost," he tells the Black Harrier wannabes.

They all fan out and run in different directions without looking back.

"Chef Maléfique?" I ask.

"Or someone who wants us to think it's him."

I tell Redhawk about the business card Harrier had on my birthday.

"What was on it?"

"I don't know. It was too far away. I couldn't see it. But then Harrier had it again in the Aerie on the same night he was researching Chef Maléfique. Can't be a coincidence, right?"

He shakes his head. "Let's go."

We get back on our bikes and zip around town, rounding up thugs and questioning everyone we can find who might know something. That wasn't the only group of Harrier cosplayers, either. They all had the business cards. Thankfully, Redhawk didn't beat the mess out of the other groups, but he did have some choice words for most of them.

Word must get around fast, because soon whenever we catch sight of any criminal-types, they scurry away immediately like rats.

I'm a bit confused by Redhawk's behavior—like he's bipolar or something. He goes from pissed off and punching walls to cracking jokes and making quips. I tend to throw in some comments here and there, but he goes at it all the way. At first, I don't get why he would waste his time joking around so much with bad guys who obviously don't appreciate it. Then I realize it's a tactic. Not only do they not take him as seriously as they should, but I can tell they're really distracted and frustrated when he does it.

We hadn't been successful in capturing any of these lowlifes enough to question them, but one that we do is way too overconfident for his own good. As we approach and the rest of his gang runs away, he stands right in front of our bikes and flips us off with both hands and smiles. I toss him into an alley, my favorite place to take care of scum like him.

"I see you got a new boyfriend, Kite," he says. "Harrier getting too old for your taste?"

I hit him in the stomach. "What have you heard about Harrier?"

He has trouble talking with the wind knocked out of him. Guess I hit him a little too hard. "Nothing."

I bring my knee up and drive it into his face. Then I grab him by the shirt collar and yank him up. Blood drips from his probably-broken nose. He smiles, and I shove him hard against the dumpster. "I find it hard to believe someone in your line of work hasn't heard anything at all about this city's hero disappearing."

He wipes away the blood and sneers at me. "I don't care if you believe me or not."

"My new friend here is just as anxious to find out some information. I'm gonna let him ask a few questions now."

"Oh, I get it. The old 'good cop/bad cop' routine. It ain't gonna work, kid."

"I wouldn't be so sure about that. See, the thing is, *I'm* the 'good cop.'"

He looks nervous as Redhawk pops his knuckles and approaches him. Yeah, it's cheesy, but it's effective. I actually turn around because I'm feeling kind of nauseous, so I'm not really sure which bones Redhawk is breaking when I hear the screams and cracking sounds.

CHAPTER **SEVENTEEN**

N*othing.*

He didn't know anything.

How do I know?

There aren't many people outside of Black Ops who could have withstood Redhawk's interrogation. I kind of felt bad for the dude. Kind of.

Then we stumble across another gang who broke way easier. Finally, after hours of not being able to get any useful info, we have the name of a certain low-life snitch who supposedly knows something. Warren "Weasel" Wilson is never tough to find once you're looking for him. Every cop in town knows to go to Weasel if you can't get anything out of anyone else, and every criminal knows to stay away from him because he's under the cops' protection. And Harrier's as well.

He's not just called the Weasel… around the city, he's known as "the Net." Get it? His initials? W.W.W.?

We confront Weasel as he's pulling a con on some tourists downtown. A bunch of people who don't know how dangerous it is to be in this neighborhood at night—or even in the daytime for that matter—stand around while he plays the cup game with the rubber ball on top of a cardboard box. A couple of the guys watching, who I'm sure he planted, win a few dollars, and the rest get confident and start throwing down fives, tens, even twenties.

I have to admit, Weasel's good. And from past experience, I know he's even better at lying than he is at getting people to willingly hand over their money. But with the right, ummm... motivation, I guess? He's definitely a pretty reliable informant.

Before we can even get close, Weasel has taken a couple hundred bucks from them.

"Oh, hey Weasel," I say, pushing through the crowd.

"Kite," he says in his nasal tone. "Come on, I'm workin' here."

"Oh, right… just trying to make an honest living."

Since I'm familiar with the game, I pull the ball out from his sleeve, and the crowd starts to get angry.

He licks his lips and his eye twitches. Man, he really looks like a weasel. The teeth, the snout, the beady eyes…

"Give the money back," I say. "Now."

He has both hands up, palms out while the crowd starts to close in.

"What kinda hero are you?" he says. "Pickin' on the little guys."

We make him give back the money as best he can, and most of the suckers are happy. Some of them probably even got back more than they'd put down.

Once everyone's gone, he says, "That was pretty messed up, Kite."

"Cry about it," I tell him. "And it's Red Raptor. And this is Redhawk."

"Like the color red, huh?"

"Shut up," Redhawk says, literally slapping him in the face. I almost laugh when Weasel turns back, flabbergasted that someone had just slapped him.

"Who slaps?" he argues.

"Would you rather I punch?"

"What the hell is wro—"

We grab Weasel and follow procedure, taking him into a nearby alley. For some reason, he's much less talkative than usual, so we decide to take him to a nearby rooftop to loosen him up some.

"How is this necessary?" he squeals.

Harrier found out years ago that Weasel is afraid of heights, so usually, as soon as he's uncooperative, we grab him and pull him up top, and he starts to sing. But even after I take him on a little ride with my grappler and we're on the edge of a high building, he's still tight-lipped. That's when Redhawk decides to pull one of Harrier's favorite moves and hang him upside-down from the ledge.

Weasel screams, and his voice comes back half a dozen times.

"Shut up, or you'll wake up the whole neighborhood," Redhawk says.

"Listen, stop. Come on. Please. You don't need to do this."

"We could have avoided it," Redhawk says. "But you had to be all... difficult."

From the smell, I can tell immediately that he's crapped his pants, but he's still afraid to talk. Redhawk and I both lean over him as he hangs there, looking straight down at the pavement ten stories below. Redhawk tries to get him to open up a little more, this time playing the "good cop" part.

"What are you so afraid of? You know you're untouchable in this town. Harrier's always had your back."

"Harrier ain't been seen in weeks. Who's gonna help me when—when—when… *someone* comes after me? C'mon. You seen it. The cops are afraid to leave their patrol cars lately."

"Well, maybe if you help us out, we can find him, and he can protect you."

Redhawk gives him a little shake, and some loose coins fall out of his pockets, clattering on the pavement.

"I-I-I-I don't think that's gonna happen."

"Why?" Redhawk asks.

"I can't tell you, man. Please."

That was my cue to be "bad cop."

"Let's just drop him, Hawk. If he won't talk anymore and he isn't any help finding Harrier, then what good is he?"

Redhawk looks like he's having too much fun with this. "I don't know, Raptor. It's a long way down."

I eye the alley again. "I know. I want to see what happens. Besides, once everyone he's ever snitched on realizes nobody's protecting him anymore, he's gonna be dead anyway."

Even with our lousy acting, Weasel is terrified.

"Wait! Maybe you guys can ensure my safety, huh? Like, keep me somewhere safe until things blow over."

Redhawk grins at me. "That sounds fair. Now, tell us what you know about Harrier's disappearance."

Weasel starts shaking, and at first, I think it's just because he's so scared of us dropping him. Then I realize he's sobbing uncontrollably, and it's because of what he's about to tell us. "The chef has him."

"Maléfique?"

"Y-you know another chef?" Weasel asks, but there's no bravado in his tone.

Redhawk couldn't have looked more shocked if he found out Santa Claus was holding Harrier at the North Pole. Between the business card and everything else, I think we both know this was a possibility, but to hear it from this guy's lips… Instead of expressing shock, it comes out as pure anger. "Maléfique's dead."

"Yeah, well… I guess he got better."

My turn again. "You better not be lying to us, or next time we hang you from the top of Douglas Tower."

"I swear, man. I swear. I seen him myself."

My mouth is so dry, I have trouble getting my next question out. "Is Harrier alive?"

"Last I heard. But word is, he won't be for long."

"Where is he holding him?"

"I don't know. Somewhere nearby, I think. But you better bring backup."

"Why?" Redhawk says.

"'Cause Maléfique's gathered everyone… all the big-time crooks in town to work for him, and some from other places, too. In fact—"

BLAM!

Weasel's brain spatters all over the side of the building as a bullet plows through his forehead. I almost throw up right when it happens, but I don't need Redhawk and Osprey both thinking I can't stomach being a hero, so I manage to hold it down. I'm used to violence and a certain amount of blood. Bullets to the head, not so much.

Nearly too far away to see, I catch a glimpse of the assassin repelling down the side of a building, sniper gun still in hand. It's hard to tell at this distance, but I'm pretty sure it's Deadeye. If it is, I'm not sure why Redhawk and I are still alive. He's such as good shot, and so fast, he could have taken down at least one of us before we even knew what was happening.

I guess we really couldn't protect Weasel. *Whoops.*

We glide down to the street as fast as we can, since the next shot could still be for Redhawk or me. We jump on our bikes and speed off in the direction of the shooter. Deadeye is on a bike also, so we're pretty far behind him thanks to his big head start.

I try to remember everything I know about the sharpshooter. He's pretty unpopular, even with other criminals, because he uses guns. In many ways, the whole hero/villain thing is kind of a game, like with the mask thing. So using firearms is sort of cheating as far as most of us are concerned. It's fine for normal henchmen and minions, but it's definitely not cool when it comes to bosses. Either way, the truth is, if somebody wants someone else dead, he's the man to hire.

From what I know, he was special ops in the military, but I don't know what branch or anything more specific. The rumor is that he was part of some kind of experiment the government conducted on its own soldiers. It worked, but it also made him kind of crazy. On his first mission to clean out some village in the Middle East, he finished the job a little too well and then went after the guys on his own team.

With all the heroes and villains created by government experiments, you'd think it was all on purpose. Maybe they're all just trying to screw up in order to create the perfect super-soldier. Who knows? Either way, I think it's time to give it up. Even Eaglestar is a freaking psychopath.

I hear Deadeye's bike roar ahead. He's an expert at practically everything, and Redhawk's a good rider, but I'm sure Alex is holding back for my sake. So why is it that we're gaining on Deadeye?

As we start to catch up, I notice there seem to be a lot of cars around for this late at night. Then, all at once, twenty car engines turn over, and they start to move. Before we know it, vehicles of every kind pull up and surround us: cars, vans, trucks, more bikes. The hunters have become the prey.

Every side street we pass, more vehicles join the posse escorting us. It's no longer a chase. It's become a parade. All that's missing are the balloons.

Redhawk gives his bike more gas, and I follow close behind him, but our "escort" is quickly closing in. My rear tire gets a bump from what looks like a hearse, and the bike skids forward a bit.

At this point, I don't even see a way that we can get out of here, even if we wanted to. It's like we're at the center of a swarm of bees, and they're buzzing ever closer. So what's gonna happen?

"Amber."

"*Yes, Sawyer?*"

"You know, this is the kind of emergency you're supposed to warn me about."

"*I'm sorry. The shooter was fully incognito, even to me.*"

That's a scary thought. Amber was supposed to see everything. Douglas Industries has satellites dedicated solely to Harrier's A.I. systems.

"Can you see anything up ahead?"

"*Nothing. It's like a big black blotch over everything, including you.*"

"Well, that's fantastic," Redhawk says.

I can see a dozen ways this could go down, and none of them seem good. Are we gonna stop somewhere, or will they just try to shoot at us from all directions as we drive along? I assume not even these thugs are stupid enough to risk the crossfire, so I don't worry much about that option, yet.

Ahead, Deadeye's gunning for the big suspension bridge, and I notice there are no cars around other than the ones that are closing in on us. Something's happened to the typically heavy traffic crossing the river, and I'm guessing it isn't a welcome party for Harrier's favorite sidekicks—er, partners.

Not the good kind of welcome party, anyway.

After speeding up for most of our chase, Deadeye suddenly stops on the bridge and turns to face us on his bike. The dude is a serious badass. I mean, if I weren't worried he was gonna kill me right now, I'd probably be impressed. He's fully clad in leather. Not like a lame hair band from the 1980s, but awesome leather pants, a biker jacket with little silver spikes, and gloves to match. He climbs off and straightens his helmet, the full facemask painted like a skull, then slowly adjusts all of his weapons to make sure they're ready. I can clearly see a staff, a sword, and several sidearms. Plus lots and lots of ammunition. Like bandoliers across his chest, and magazines strung to his hips. I definitely can't see any way this is gonna end well.

We slow down as we approach him, and I notice there are now cars coming from behind Deadeye, driving the wrong way on this side of the bridge. On either side of us, the vehicles are pulled in close to each other, which fences us in. There must be somewhere between fifty and a hundred of them surrounding us now, each with at least a couple of guys getting out. It's hard to tell the precise number with so many stretching out into the dark in both directions.

We're good, but we're not that good.

As Redhawk slowly flips up the visor on his helmet, he doesn't seem too bothered by the whole situation. Which is in direct opposition to me, feeling like I'm about to pee my pants again. He climbs off his bike and starts walking toward Deadeye as the increasing number of criminals moves in on us.

Now that I have a chance to scope things out, I notice the variety of thugs in the group. Rival gang members who would usually kill each other on-sight are strolling side-by-side. Low-level costumed villains who I know were in prison very recently are scattered throughout the crowd as well. Right away, I spot Med-Evil in his doctor's getup and zombie makeup. At least I hope it's makeup. I wonder if the hearse is driven by Morty Mortician, but I don't dare turn to find out.

A lot of them are wearing costumes. Most of them aren't actual supervillains, but as we've been reminded time and time again, Halloween is coming up, so maybe they're just in the mood for dress-up.

I always hate this time of year. Not only is it hard to spot the actual costumed criminals among the partiers, but people seem to get crazier and braver. Just as some women feel like it's okay to dress up way more provocatively than they ever would any other time of year—as a "sexy schoolgirl" or whatever—so many jerks want to put on a mask and carry a weapon. Even guys who would generally cower in a situation where they'd have to fight, suddenly think they're invincible.

What I don't understand is why all these villains, who are normally willing to take on Harrier and me by themselves, are holding back when they have all this backup.

I follow Redhawk's lead and try not to look too scared. Redhawk keeps his collapsible staff in a sheath under his cape. He pulls it out and extends it, all in one smooth motion. It almost looks like it appears out of nowhere. I pull out the one he gave me, but it's not quite as smooth because I'm so nervous. I need to practice with this thing for sure. My brain may have learned how to do it immediately, but my muscles have some catching up to do.

Deadeye doesn't bother to unholster any of his many guns. Instead, he pulls out his own staff. His doesn't have the "push to extend" feature like ours, but something tells me that won't matter in a fight. Because his mask completely covers his face, I have no idea what expression he has. But I have a feeling it's a straight lip and furrowed brow.

He holds up his hand, and the mob of bad guys stops closing in on us, forming a circle that looks like a human arena.

Redhawk doesn't look at me, but he speaks just loud enough for me to hear him in our helmets. "I want you to hang back and let me take care of this. If you see a chance to escape, take it."

"But—"

"Just listen to me. Please. I don't need your death on my conscience." I step back as Redhawk lowers his visor and gets within striking range of Deadeye.

I said Deadeye is an expert... but really, he's the best assassin in the country. Maybe the world. He's a proficient marksman, and as dangerous as Harrier at hand-to-hand combat. Actually more, when you consider the weapons he uses and his lack of a "no killing" rule.

Redhawk is almost as good as Harrier. But somehow I don't think "almost" is gonna cut it. He shows off some of his fancy moves, spinning his staff around his body and over his head. Another one of his tactics to distract his enemies. Deadeye is a statue, watching like a cobra ready to strike.

In the middle of what looks like an ordinary spinning technique, Redhawk swings his staff directly at Deadeye with what should be a surprise move. Deadeye moves so fast to block it that it's too quick for me to follow. Then he strikes back immediately, hitting Redhawk's visor and cracking it.

Redhawk is obviously stunned, but he shakes it off right away, and ducks before Deadeye's next swing can catch him on the side of the helmet. Then he jumps up as Deadeye's next swipe tries to take out his legs.

Instead of coming straight down, Redhawk uses his staff almost like a pole vault and lands his first blow, a kick to Deadeye's chest. This is the assassin's turn to be surprised, and he stumbles back a couple of steps but manages to stay on his feet. As Redhawk descends, he uses his body's momentum to swing his staff over his head and come down hard on the top of Deadeye's skull. It seems to ring his helmet but doesn't do much in the way of damage.

Deadeye returns with a jab to Redhawk's chest using the end of his staff, but Redhawk's Kevlar body armor takes the brunt of it. It turns out to be just a diversion anyway, as Deadeye's foot shoots out and lands a smack across Redhawk's face that shatters the already-cracked visor on his mask and knocks him back to the ground. He follows up with another swing of his staff, and this one makes contact with Redhawk's knee.

Redhawk manages to flip backward and up onto his feet just before Deadeye can land another blow. He pulls off the remnants of his cracked visor so it won't interfere with his vision and tries to catch his breath for a moment.

I start to move forward, but Redhawk holds up his hand immediately and gives me a warning look. He gets his second wind and goes on the attack, getting in several hits that Deadeye barely has time to block. He swings down hard from above, and when Deadeye blocks, the assassin's staff shatters.

Deadeye isn't the type of person you want to make look bad in front of all these people. He unsheathes his sword and goes after Redhawk mercilessly. Even though Redhawk is able to avoid any serious wounds, Deadeye does cut him a few times by connecting in the spaces between his armor, and the blood is starting to flow pretty heavily.

I hear movement behind me and spin to see a few brave henchmen are sauntering toward me. What? That's the only word I can think of to describe it. It's like they are hesitant still, but gaining confidence as they watch their fearless leader taking on Redhawk. They probably don't even consider how much better Deadeye is than them.

"You sure you wanna do this, fellas?" I ask. I'm more than sure that even with this cold or whatever, these guys'll be a cakewalk. But then a few more close in.

Behind me, Redhawk and Deadeye continue to dance around one another, but Deadeye continues to cut Redhawk more and more, while Redhawk lands fewer and fewer hits in return. It's evident that he won't be able to keep up much longer at this rate.

One of the thugs, let's call him Scraggly Beard, lunges for me, and I sidestep, grabbing his scraggly beard and thrusting him into the pavement. I don't bother to make sure he's gonna be down for a while. Two more come at me at the same time for a change. I use a set of moves I learned from watching Joe Lewis videos, blocking, and slapping down their attacks. Then, I combine those with a few one-inch kung fu punches, and both of them are flat on their backs in a matter of seconds.

The remaining would-be attackers back off.

At first, I think it's because of my expert display of martial arts, but I turn to see something new transpiring behind me.

Redhawk knows he won't be able to beat Deadeye in this condition and uses his staff to vault up into the crowd of bad guys. Using their shoulders and heads, he jumps and flips parkour-style until he's on the railing at the edge of the bridge. He's holding his side, where there's a pretty deep gash in his costume between the armored pieces. That's the problem with Kevlar; if you want to be able to move, there's gotta be some unprotected areas.

Some thugs in the crowd start reaching for him, but he knows just what to say. "What's the matter, you don't think Deadeye can finish me off himself? He needs help from you losers?"

They respond immediately by stopping their advance, not wanting to incur Deadeye's wrath.

Redhawk turns and looks me in the eye, and I know precisely what his look is trying to tell me: *Don't let this be in vain.* I hear a shot ring out, and with a jerk, Redhawk goes over the edge of the bridge. I almost scream "No!" like they do in the movies, but then I realize how stupid that would be. I need to escape, and drawing any more attention to myself like that wouldn't make any sense.

I turn to see Deadeye holding his smoking pistol up, but he's shaking and breathing hard from his battle with Redhawk. He may not be severely wounded, but he's at least winded, which might give me just barely the edge I need.

The criminals are all either looking over the side to see Redhawk hit the water, or cheering and slapping each other on the back. Now's my chance.

I can't just get to the suspension part of the bridge up above—I'll still be surrounded, and Deadeye will have no trouble picking me off. I need to get as far away as possible, fast, while he's distracted. Unfortunately, we're almost to the middle of the bridge, so nothing else is close by.

I shoot my grappler away from the bridge, but I'm too far from any buildings, and it retracts without hitting anything. I run back toward the beginning of the bridge, but there are a bunch of guys in my way. I start fighting them one by one, thinking about how confident I just was. Now, with Redhawk gone, I feel like a lost little kid, separated from his mom at the store. How many could I take down if I had to? This time it's like an endless supply.

I determine the thinnest part of the blockade of minions in my way and start to plow through. Most of them go down with a punch or a kick, but with so many, some of them get in some good hits.

I need to try my grappler again because I won't be able to keep fighting like this, but I'm still not sure if I'm close enough. I try to calculate how many more steps I need to manage before I can successfully connect. Almost there…

I point my grappler and shoot. It extends as far as it can go, and I hear a satisfying *thunk* as the graphene hook buries itself into the brick, barely catching the closest building. I hit the button to be reeled in, and a bunch of thugs try to grab me as I soar over their heads.

Despite everything, I feel myself laugh a little as I zip up out of their reach and head away toward someplace safer. I must be more than a little feverish. I'm only about twenty feet off the ground, but that should be enough to get me to safety before—

CRACK!

I hear another shot ring out, and my line goes slack. I know immediately that Deadeye severed it with a bullet.

As I plummet toward the ground, everything feels like it's moving super slow. What a stupid way to die after everything I've been through.

The instant I feel my back hitting the ground, everything goes black.

CHAPTER EIGHTEEN

Bleep. Bleep. Bleep. Bleep.

"Amber?"

"And who might Amber be?" I hear the voice and am so confused. I'm in strange surroundings, including a bed that's way too comfortable to be my own.

My eyes open, and I see nothing but brilliant, blurry light. All I can hear is an annoying beeping sound and an even more annoying song being sung by the brat.

"Mom?"

And I have a stabbing pain in my... well, everything. But, hey, on the bright side, it looks like my cold is finally gone. Or everything else hurts too much for me to notice those symptoms. How long have I been out?

As my eyes focus, I see my mom staring at me with a worried look. She lets the whole Amber thing go, thankfully.

"Thank God you're awake. Father Pulliam was here praying with us just a bit ago. It's like a miracle! They were afraid that with such a serious head injury, you might be out for a long time."

"Head injury?" I look around at my hospital room. Yeah, about what I'd expect with the sorry government health insurance we have. At least nobody is in the other bed next to me.

"It's a good thing your friend was there to call the ambulance for you, or you might not have made it."

Did Alex survive?

"Friend? What frien—"

Mom moves aside, and I see an Asian girl standing behind her, giving me a small wave. She's cute, and sort of familiar-looking. With those glasses, she has kind of a sexy gamer vibe going on. The type of girl who can destroy you in *Call of Duty*, and you still want to make out with her later. She seems really shy, though.

Then something else hits me. Oh, hey. That's Mr. Chen's daughter, from the picture in his office. Does she know me? I don't know her. How did she find me? These questions and a million more cycle through my mind.

"Hey," she says, and I feel like Weasel, brains splattering on the wall behind me as my mind is blown.

Holy crap! That voice. I know it. Like, *know it* know it.

Osprey is Mr. Chen's daughter.

What was her name? Annie? Alli? Amy? Suddenly, a whole lot of things start to make sense.

"She's like your guardian angel." Mom smiles at her.

"Yep, that's me. I watch him like a *hawk*." That's definitely her voice. But it can't be. It is. Who else could it be?

"Thanks. I guess I owe you one." There's no way we can talk about stuff now, but there's gonna be a whole lot to discuss later.

"Yeah. *Another* one, actually." She is not what I expected Osprey to be like in her civilian identity. But, then again, most people would probably say the same thing about me. It helps that she wears a wig with her costume. No wonder the blonde ponytail is so prominent. It's like she's saying, "Hey, look at me, I'm blonde." And those shiny, reflective eye covers in her mask...

I feel bad that I led her on about visiting the Aerie. Or maybe the reason she was watching me in the first place was to try to follow me there. Even so, I can't stay mad at her now.

Mom's look and voice change now that she's not so worried about me. "Then there's the matter of why you were out when you're sick *and* grounded. The first time I trust you in weeks, and you blow it. And what the h-e-l-l were you doing skateboarding without a helmet?" She literally whisper-spells the word, but I'm too confused to even snicker.

"Skateboarding?"

Mom starts to look suspicious at me, not knowing what she's talking about.

From behind her, Osprey gives me a warning look. "Must have lost your memory," she says. "You know... because of the head injury. The doctor said that might happen with a concussion. It's a good thing you wiped out into that pile of garbage, or it could have been even worse."

"Uh... yeah, I must have. I actually don't remember anything from before my accident." I squint at her. "In fact, I don't remember *you* being there at all. I do remember another friend being with me. Do you know what happened to him?"

Osprey gets a sad look. "Haven't heard anything. Sorry."

I don't know how Redhawk could've possibly survived that fall, especially with his injuries. But I can't worry about that right now.

Mom is looking at us like we're crazy, and then she gets kind of bitchy with me. "Anyway, when you get out, we're going to have a long talk about why you didn't follow the rules. And what kind of additional punishments we're going to have to add."

Osprey looks uncomfortable about the way my mom is talking to me. I'm not sure if she doesn't like it, or if she just thinks it's weird that Mom's acting that way in front of her.

Osprey starts moving toward the door. "Well, now that I know you're going to be okay, I think I'll get going." She seems pretty nervous for some reason. Something more than just not liking the way my mom is talking to me.

My mom grabs her arm. "I was just about to get a diet soda. I'll walk you out." She turns to the brat. "Aiden, you stay here with Sawyer for a minute and make sure he doesn't try to leave. Can you do that?"

He slumps in the vinyl chair.

"If you're good, I'll bring you back a candy bar."

Now the kid nods excitedly. Just what he needs, more sugar. My mom and Osprey leave the room, and Aiden stares at the beeping machines. I try to tune him out as he starts singing his song again.

"Do do do-do do do."

Guuh, so annoying.

So, Osprey was watching me again. She not only saved me, but she showed up in her civilian identity to check on me. Despite my pain, I can't help a big smile. Maybe she isn't just using me to meet Harrier. Maybe she *is* a little bit interested in me for me.

And now, we know each others' names. Amy Chen.

The kid reaches up to one of my monitors like he's about to press a button or something. Leave it to that brat to ruin my moment.

"Don't touch that."

He gives me the side-eyed look he always wears when I reprimand him, then flops back down into his chair with his arms crossed. My mom pretty much gives him the run of the apartment, so I end up being the disciplinarian a lot of the time. Yet another reason why we don't like each other.

"Your mom was wheelly sad when you was sweepin'."

"Was she?"

"Yeah. She kept cwying and cwying and cwying."

"I didn't realize that."

For the first time, I wonder what she would do if I actually got killed, fighting criminals. It never seemed like I was important to her before, but things have changed a lot lately.

"It's a good fing the fat man was here with us to make her happy."

"Fat man?" I try to picture everyone my mom knows. Old boyfriends, neighbors… none of them were very fat. Even in my grogginess, I know something isn't right.

"You know. The chwef."

"Chwef? Who's a chwe—" I feel the blood rush out of my face. "There… there was a chef here?" I hear the beeping get faster on the machine.

Aiden nods emphatically. "He was super nice, too."

"What did he look like?"

"I don't know. A big, fat chwef wiv a curly moustache."

"Okay, okay. But—"

"He gave me this." The kid reaches under his chair and pulls out something that was apparently a gift from the fat "chwef" man.

A red kite.

I jolt upright in bed, and the vitals monitor starts going crazy. My heart rate speeds up so much it sets off the alarms. I pull the IVs out of my arms and try to stand up, knocking over the IV pole in the process.

My head is swimming, and I have tunnel vision as I hear doctors and nurses running down the hall outside. I slam against the doorjamb as I try to exit the room. Mom and Osprey turn around at the end of the hallway and are running back to me just as everything starts to spin.

Then I black out again.

CHAPTER **NINETEEN**

Uhhhh.

My eyes crack a hair, and I can see blurry shapes at the foot of my bed. One is clearly Mom. Even through the fog, her fiery-red hair is unmistakable. The other, I assume, is a doctor. I can hear them, but it's like they're talking into a can at the end of a string like they used to back in the day.

In a strong but gentle voice, the other woman says, "Ms. Vincent, these injuries are just not in line with what one would expect from someone who 'fell on their skateboard.'"

I can tell she's using air quotes on that last line.

"His friend said he landed in a pile of garbage. That would explain the various cuts and bruises, no?"

"This looks more like he got into a very intense fight. Or worse..."

"Are you implying that I beat my son?"

"Gosh, no," the doctor says. "But do you know anyone who might have it in for him? A school bully or something?"

I want to hold on. I want to listen more, but I can't any longer, and I fall back into a dreamless sleep.

The next time I wake up, I'm in less pain, but I'm more heavily medicated. It's the middle of the night, and my room is so dark, I can't see anything until my eyes start to adjust in the dim light from the machines. I try to lift my arms and discover I'm strapped down to the bed like a criminal. They must not want me trying to leave again.

I nearly have a heart attack when I suddenly hear a voice in the darkness at the end of my bed.

"Sawyer William Vincent." I can just barely make out the outline of a figure who appears to be looking at my chart. A very large, very round figure. "You know what that sounds like to me? It sounds like a backwards name."

"Who are you?" I ask, but I'm sure the words come out mashed together. "What do you want?"

"Oh, I'm a trained professional. Don't mind me. I'm merely checking up on you."

Everything is blurry… really blurry, and the figure before me swirls around, and there's three of them.

"Are you my doctor?" I ask, noticing what looks like a white coat.

"Oh, no. Nothing like that. But I do have to make sure the doctors do a good job of patching you up for the big finale."

"The what?" With my question comes a sort of clarity. Not just in what I'm saying, and what he's saying, but literal clarity. I can see the big fat chef in front of me. The same one I'd seen in the video at the Aerie. He was alive. Very much alive.

I struggle against the restraints, but there's no way I'm getting loose all drugged up this way.

"The climax of the story. The big confrontation. The *dessert.*" He lets that word linger on the air while he thumbs through my papers so quickly he couldn't possibly be reading anything. "It certainly won't be very enjoyable if you aren't in superb fighting condition."

"Maléfique."

"Oh, you *do* recognize me! And it's *Chef,* if you please. You see, it's more than just a name. It's a *title.*"

"Do it," I say. "Kill me now."

"That wouldn't do. That wouldn't do at all." He's shaking his head vigorously, which brings back a bit of my confusion. "You see, I'm going to kill you in front of Harrier like I did his last little boy toy. And then I'm going to finally put him out of his considerable misery."

"You son of a bitch."

"Wow. Do you kiss that smoking hot mother with those lips?"

"Don't you even think about my mother," I warn. "What have you done with Harrier?"

"You'll see, child. You'll see. Once you're up and about, come to this address." He pulls out a small business card. This one, I can see writing on it, just like Harrier's. Then, he lifts up the end of my blankets. He starts to place the card between my toes, then makes a harsh slicing motion, and gives me a giant paper cut. "Oopsie."

He lets the card dig in between my toes, pushing it into the paper cut. I grit my teeth but refuse to give him the satisfaction of anything else.

"Oh, and do make sure you're by yourself, little birdie. I'd hate for something horrible to happen to that pretty mommy of yours. She's aged well. Like a fine wine." He covers my feet back up and then pats them a couple of times.

Chef Maléfique walks to the door, and when he opens it, I can see his broad back in the light from the hall. Then he turns. He's wearing a white coat, but it's not like the ones the doctors wear. His pulls tight across him, buttoned over his right breast. There's blood spattered all over it, smeared in large swathes.

"Although… if you wanted to bring your little girlfriend, I suppose I would allow that. I would very much enjoy seeing her again."

He slowly closes the door behind him. I struggle against the restraints, knowing full well I'll never get out of them in my condition. I spend the next few hours wondering how I'm ever gonna get through this until I can't fight the drugs in my system and drift off into some of the worst nightmares I've ever had.

It's night. Full moon. Foggy.

I'm an actual bird—some kind of hawk, probably a kite, I guess—and I'm flying around looking for something. Through the darkness, I spot an injured black harrier attempting to take flight from its nest on the ground next to a river. The white undersides of its wings bob up and down, but it's unable to stay in the air.

I swoop into a steep dive to help, but then a white osprey catches my attention, and I fly off after her. Maybe it's mating season or something. I don't know, you know how dreams are.

When I remember the harrier, I turn and fly back toward it, but before I can get there, an alligator jumps out of the river and chomps it in half in its jaws. The alligator turns, and I see that it has a white face. It seems to grin at me, its teeth full of black feathers.

I wake up and try to figure out why I would have a dream that was so on-the-nose for my situation. It's like my brain is trying to tell me something, but all this medication is messing things up. Is Osprey a distraction, keeping me from finding Harrier? Or is she really someone who can help?

CHAPTER **TWENTY**

Excruciating.

That's how I would describe the next few days in the hospital. I'm either lying in bed by myself with my head spinning, trying to figure out my plan for saving Harrier and defeating Chef Maléfique, or I'm putting on a show for my mom, pretending everything is okay and I can't wait to go home. Even worse, the kid brings the red kite with him every time they visit, reminding me of my situation.

The upside is I can finally watch the news. The downside, I don't want to. The crime spree continues to worsen on the streets, and now that I know Chef Maléfique is behind it, the signs are everywhere. Gangs of criminals are now wandering the streets, dressed in Harrier costumes, doing whatever they want to, and ordinary people are hiding in their homes at night. The cops are either too overwhelmed or too scared to put a dent in the situation.

"The problem, hon," says a bald Englishman on the TV I recognize as an ex-Guild member named Baron Steele, "is that no one wanted to listen to me a decade ago. This goodie two-shoes superheroing just ain't the way to stop crime."

"So what do you propose?" asks the anchorwoman in the other box, doing a pretty solid job not reacting to being called "hon."

"Same thing I did back then, right?" Baron Steele says. "Look, you ever meet a kid whose parents clearly never put a belt to their arse? They act out. Think they rule the roost. That's what we've got going on here in our beautiful city—a bunch of spoiled brats who've never been beaten within an inch of their lives. They need a firm hand."

The anchorwoman begins a retort but I decide I can't take any more and lower the volume. I think I might fall asleep for a bit, but otherwise, things are brutally boring.

I do have one break in my misery when Fabiola shows up to visit me. Not something I was expecting at all, but I'm definitely not gonna complain. I don't even know how she heard about me being in the hospital.

Despite the nippy October air, she walks in wearing a pair of ripped jeans and a white cotton tank top that perfectly contrasts her silky dark skin. She's so gorgeous it hurts to look at her.

"O-M-God... I heard your accident was bad, but holy crap." She touches the bruises on my face lightly and parts of me tingle.

"It's not as bad as it looks." I try to act tough, but just what little pressure she's applying hurts like hell.

She runs her fingers along the straps holding me down. "What's this all about? Are they afraid you're going to fall out of bed?"

"I tried to walk out of here when I first woke up. You know, 'cause of all the drugs they have me on. So now they keep me strapped down to make sure I don't try it again."

For some reason, she really likes hearing this. "Oh, a bad boy, huh? That's intense."

I smile, which feels really stupid.

"So you… can't move at all?"

I make a demonstration of trying to pull on the restraints.

"Interesting," she says as she leans over me, and her hair brushes against me. She licks her lips. I swear. It's not the drugs. I'm pretty sober and become more sober by the second. She licks her lips again, and I'm fully aware that I'm naked under the thin dressing gown.

She speaks, and the scent of her strawberry lip gloss overwhelms me, makes me lightheaded. "I hope this doesn't mean you aren't coming to my Halloween party. Are you going to be out by then?"

"I..." My voice cracks, and I clear the frog out of my throat. "I'm not really sure when they're releasing me."

"Well, don't worry. I'm wearing a naughty nurse costume, so even if you're still hurt, I'll take care of you if you show up."

This is so bizarre that I start to think maybe I *am* just having another weird dream because of the medication. The thing is, I don't even like this girl. She's never even said 'hi' to me before I was on the wrestling team. I mean, yeah, she's really *really* hot, but her IQ is probably lower than her bra size. I fight the temptation to check to see if I can figure out what that might be.

"Well, I should let you get some rest. Get better quickly. I don't want you to miss out on the fun." I didn't think she could get closer, but then she leans in and kisses me on the lips. A real kiss.

My first real kiss. From the hottest girl in school.

Maybe things are gonna start getting better for me. Maybe.

Yeah, except for being in the hospital, having my mentor kidnapped by a homicidal maniac, and getting ready to confront that same maniac on what is probably the most dangerous mission of my life. Things are really looking up.

Fabiola turns to leave, and there's Osprey standing in the doorway. To say she looks surprised would be a major understatement. Fabiola looks at Osprey, then back at me. With a little wave in my direction, she opens the door and disappears around the corner.

Osprey finally shows up so we can talk, and it has to be right now. At the worst possible time.

"Who was that?" she asks coldly as she watches Fabiola leave the room.

That can't be jealousy, can it?

"No one." Real smooth, idiot.

"Sure, I always go around kissing no one."

"She kissed *me*," I say.

She looks me up and down. Her eyes linger on the "down" a bit longer than I would want. I quickly readjust myself as she smiles, and says, "Looks like you enjoyed it."

"What do you care, anyway?"

"I *don't* care," she says, shoving a lock of her black hair behind her ear.

As cute as she is, I still have a hard time imagining her as the same person I was fighting criminals with except for that little movement. I'd seen her do that enough as Osprey. She's a little bit skater-girl, maybe a little goth, but mostly kind of nerdy, and definitely not someone you'd think of as a costumed crimefighter.

Then I realize that must be how people see me. To most of the people at school who even notice me, I must seem like some quiet loser without any friends. Except maybe Javier.

As if I'd summoned the little pipsqueak with my thoughts, Javi leans in and knocks. Two short, succinct taps.

Does the whole world know I'm in here?

"H-hey, uh, Sawyer," he says.

"Javi, what are you doing here?" I'm afraid the question comes out like an accusation, but he smiles anyway and shuffles in. He's wearing a shirt with that dwarf from that one old fantasy movie. It says, "No one tosses a dwarf," in big gold letters. Poor kid is such a geek, but I can't help liking him.

"I heard you were here. Then I saw Fabiola..." He stops talking abruptly as if he saw Osprey... or Amy... or whatever, standing there for the first time. "Oh. Hey?"

Osprey smiles and introduces herself. "I'm Amy. Sawyer's told me all about you. Javi, right?"

That is a total lie. I've never mentioned him to her even once, but his face lights up like Times Square.

"Wow, really? Wow..."

He stares at his shoes for a moment.

"What's up, Javi?" I ask.

"Oh. Uh, yeah. My abuela is on the third floor. She's got something bad. I don't know. I can't pronounce it. But I'm pretty much here every day. Maybe... maybe when you're not so busy we could hang out? Maybe tomorrow?"

"I hopefully won't be here tomorrow," I say.

His face looks like a balloon that just got popped.

"But, I still owe you some karate lessons, remember?"

That perks him up, and he nods. "Right. Absolutely. Yeah. As soon as you're better?"

"You bet."

He starts backing away. "Cool. Well, I gotta go. Feel better."

"Thanks, Javi."

"Hope your grandma feels better too," Osprey says as Javi closes the door.

I should be nicer to him. He really is a good kid, and I can't blame him for wanting to be friends with the only person at school who's nice to him.

And if you add the fact that a lot of the other students blame me for sidelining the quarterback for a few weeks, they probably don't like me very much either.

But isn't that what I want? Isn't that exactly what someone like me or Osprey looks for in a secret identity? Then why do I feel so bummed about it right now?

Probably because, unlike with Fabiola, I can picture Osprey and me as normal teenagers who are boyfriend and girlfriend. Hanging out, playing video games, going out for burgers. Whatever "normal" teenagers do.

You know what? She doesn't even know that I know who she is, and she hasn't even offered to level the playing field.

"What was that all about?" I asked.

"What?"

"I told you all about him?"

"Look, believe it or not, when I was in high school, I was a total nerd."

I laugh. "Wasn't that like, last year?"

"So?"

"I just mean—"

She cuts me off. "You try being... like me... and being a Mathlete, concert violinist, and captain of the debate team."

"Whoa," I say.

"Yeah, pretty dorky, right?" she says.

"No... I mean, that's awesome. You play violin?"

She rolls her eyes, and I let it go.

"So, now that you know who I really am, are you gonna tell me your name?"

"No." She says it so matter-of-factly, as if she's answered the question a billion times.

"Why not?"

"You won't let me into your world. Why should I allow you into mine?"

Ouch. Good point. "Okay. I guess I deserve that."

"Let's be honest. The only reason you've been stringing me along is to get into my pants—tights, whatever. Until you're ready to introduce me to Harrier—or ask me to help you find him—it's going to be strictly professional."

I consider denying it all, but I'm afraid it will just make things worse. Because then I'd be lying to her, and she'd know it. For now, I'll have to pretend I don't know her true identity.

"I *would* like your help. Especially now that Redhawk is gone. He believed Harrier's disappearance was because he was investigating Maléfique, even though he's supposed to be dead."

"Chef Maléfique? Do you think someone is getting some sort of revenge for his death?"

I hesitate to tell her the truth. I still don't know her very well, and I really don't know how much I can trust her.

"We weren't able to find much out at all. From the computer or informants."

"You don't think Chef Maléfique could still be alive, do you?" she asks.

I calculate the risks of telling her versus the help she could provide and decide to let her know everything.

"From what I know about the explosion that he was supposedly killed in, I wouldn't have thought it was possible. But something really strange happened to me."

I told her about the night Chef Maléfique gave me the card. I also try to figure out when that was. Yesterday? Two days?

She then tells me about the day the chef showed up in my room when I was unconscious, and about the creepy way he kept staring at her.

"You didn't think it was weird that a chef came to visit me?" I asked.

"I don't know," she said. "People are chefs, right? Like... how would I know it was an evil supervillain and not just some guy who worked at the Olive Garden?"

"Yeah, that's fair. What day is it?"

"The thirtieth."

I show her the card he left. One side has the handlebar mustache logo. The other has an address scrawled on it, along with tomorrow's date and a time: Halloween, 9:00 p.m.

"I have to go there," I told her.

"Don't you think it's a trap?"

"Of course it's a trap. And Chef Maléfique knows I know it's a trap. But he also knows I'll go anyway."

"You can't." Wow. She genuinely looks worried about me.

"I have to. Harrier will die. If he isn't dead already."

"I'm going with you."

"No," I say, shaking my head. "No way. It's way too dangerous."

"So, it makes more sense for you to go alone?" I've never seen her this serious before. At least, not since she first beat me up.

"I can't put you in that kind of danger."

"Oh, the big strong man, huh? Gotta protect the little girls."

"You know that's not what I meant."

"You're not 'putting me' into anything. I'm making my own decision."

"But I can't—"

"Look, I don't want to embarrass you, but I'm actually older than you, and, unlike you, technically an adult. I'm going to go with you whether you like it or not, and I don't think there's a whole lot you can do about it."

I sigh. She's right. This is a woman who, without any assistance, became a crimefighter just by making her own costume and training herself to be a great martial artist and acrobat. Who am I to tell her what she can or can't do?

Besides, as I yank on the restraints, I don't think I can even get out of this bed without her help.

CHAPTER
TWENTY-ONE

Osprey does a bit of recon work, going to check the address on the business card Maléfique gave me. Turns out, it's an old warehouse down at the docks. We devise a plan for me to sneak out of the hospital just after the nurse comes by during her rounds tonight. Now, we just have to figure out a way to get me there in time for my little meeting with the evil chef.

First, Osprey loosens the restraints that have been holding me down. I expect bells and whistles to go off, but nothing happens. I consider myself lucky for once this month. Then, she has to go back to my place and basically break in to get my spare costume because she'd dumped the one I'd been wearing somewhere along the way on our way to the hospital. I'm not sure what I had on when I got here, but I don't ask because I don't really want to know the answer. Chances are she got the clothes off of a homeless guy or out of a dumpster, not to mention that she had to undress and redress me while I was unconscious.

When—*if*—I ever get back to the Aerie, I'll be able to track Amber from Frank's computer and at least find my helmet… hopefully, my whole costume. But until then, I'm living in backup city.

It's almost as uncomfortable to think about her going in through my bedroom window—which I have rigged to be able to get into from the outside with a special trick and a screwdriver—and rifling through my stuff. It's not like I was expecting to have her over and cleaned up my room beforehand or anything. I just hope she doesn't do any snooping other than just looking for the costume and getting out. That could end up being really awkward. I have to force myself to stop going through the list of things she might come across that would make me want to die.

Oh, man. If she sees my browser history, I'm screwed.

All I can think of is her finding out I'd been net-stalking her.

"Okay, just breathe," I tell myself.

At least Mom didn't throw out the spare costume or give it away, even though she thinks I paid for it with money from "selling drugs." But it's is the old version, without the attached grappler, glider cape, and jets.

And no mints in the utility belt. Maybe I can stop by the hospital gift shop on the way out. Man, my priorities are seriously out of whack.

Probably the worst part is the helmet won't have Amber installed. Even though she'd missed a couple of emergency warnings, I'd much rather have her with me than without.

Nerves are really getting to me now. It's that anxious feeling you get right before boarding a rollercoaster.

The nurse rolls her little cart in and does some checks on me and then moves on to the equipment. As she checks on everything, I watch the news on the TV in the corner of my room like I'd been doing for days. In addition to the usual Halloween stories, they show the continuing rise in the crime throughout the city. I turn up the volume.

"In an unprecedented event, more than three dozen prisoners have escaped from Dellgate Prison, including several of the city's more deranged 'supervillains.' As of yet, there's no news on how, and Commissioner Mahlberg has declined media comment. I—"

She stops and touches her ear like she's listening to a voice lodged in there.

"This just in... we have a camera crew live at Times Square..."

A new feed pops up, taking over the whole screen. In the middle of Times Square is a massive gathering of people in costumes, jumping up and down to music playing from gigantic speakers.

When they show who's playing the music up on stage, I recognize him immediately. You can't mistake Music Master with his stupid colorful costume, a patchwork of post-grunge meets old lady quilt shop and bright orange hair. He reminds me a bit of that one comedian I used to watch with Mom when I was younger. He's playing a keytar, and whatever song it is, really seems to be riling up the crowd. His music can't exactly control someone's mind, but I know that he's able to cause people to feel different and intense emotions, and he's definitely pushing a hostile vibe with his spooky Halloween tunes.

The police surround the crowd as the dancers start moshing into one another, and some of them even break into rioting. The feed becomes smaller and shrinks into the top right corner of the TV, once again showing the news anchors.

"An impromptu concert in Times Square has really stirred some buzz," the female news anchor says. "Officials say there were no plans for this event, but after seeing and hearing a sample of the band's demo, they simply couldn't resist."

"I think I've seen this guy before," says the co-anchor, a guy who looks like he's had more than a little work done on his face. "I can't place him, though."

"Yeah, Dale, he *does* look familiar."

The song ends, and Music Master starts to talk. The camera zooms in. Up close, I can see his makeup. It's like some kind of drugged-out drag queen.

"Looks like he's saying something. Let's have a listen."

The full screen returns to Music Master. The volume of the audience gets louder, and I hear that sickly sweet voice. Everyone quiets immediately.

"Kite, Kite, protector of night, what will you do on this evening of fright? Danger, danger, I know you're no stranger to the man who will die if you don't find a game-changer. Scarier and scarier, can you break the barrier? So many of us between you and Black Harrier."

"Oooo," Dale says, smiling. "Freaky. Perfect for this Hallow—"

The screen goes black, and then a shaky black-and-white feed appears. In the corner of the screen, I can just make out an eyeball that's way too close to be clear.

"SWV. SWV. SWV." Finally, as if the cameraman figures out how to zoom out, Chef Maléfique appears. "SWV. SWV."

He keeps saying my initials over and over. Behind him, I can see what is probably the same warehouse Osprey checked out, but there's no sign of Harrier.

"Time is… ticking." He does a little dance. "Tick. Tock. Tick. Tock." But since the guy doesn't laugh or smile, it's super strange and makes me even more uncomfortable. "Didn't you know its rude to miss your reservation?"

Then, I consider what he just said. Tick tock? Crap. Is there another bomb? Is this Toby all over again?

"I hope you deciphered our little rhyme. Who am I kidding? Any idiot could have figured that out. Are you smarter than an idiot?"

I sit up a little in bed despite the restraints, but when the nurse glances over at me, I try to act natural.

"Our little bird must leave the nest to save daddy bird," Chef Maléfique continues. "But you know, if someone doesn't stop Music Master, the whole city will be moving-and-a-grooving to his particular tunes. Better hurry, I'm preparing the chef's special!"

You've gotta be kidding me. Did he just call me out on live television?

"What is this scary movie you're watching?" the nurse says. "A young man like you shouldn't be watching such filth."

"You're right," I say. Hoping to get rid of her, I turn off the TV.

She grumbles about "kids these days" and pushes her cart out. After I know she's gone, I pull one hand loose from the restraints, then free myself completely.

I glance at the clock. Man, the nurse was late on her rounds. I've only got a few hours to stop Music Master from turning Manhattan into an angry murder zone, and get to the warehouse before Chef Maléfique does to Harrier whatever he's planning to do.

I make sure everything is unhooked from me. At least the IVs are out of my arms now. I hop out of bed and—whoa, that's not good. It's been too long since I've stood up, and I'm pretty shaky here. I'm sure the hospital food, with all that Jell-O and broth, isn't helping much either. I wonder if I have time to stop for a burger on my way to Times Square.

I have no idea what will happen if I don't make the meeting with Maléfique, but from what I've heard about him, I shouldn't take a chance on finding out.

My legs are so wobbly that I feel like I'm walking on noodles. How am I ever gonna do this?

Power through, Sawyer.

After the very short pep-talk, I crack open the door to my room and peek out to assess the situation. A couple of orderlies are talking down at one end of the hall, and a doctor is going through some paperwork at the other. When the doctor turns his back to me, I sneak out and head in that direction, then slip into the first non-patient room I come across. It's some kind of locker room. I thought it was empty at first, but then I notice a doctor asleep on a cot in the corner.

I'm gonna need to get out of this hospital gown if I plan to out of here without drawing attention to myself. I quietly check a couple of the lockers, but it looks like they're all locked. After searching for a minute, I find a couple of paper clips lying around and pick the lock on one of the lockers. There are scrubs inside, but they're pink. I need to try another one.

Damn, that doctor is waking up. No time to be picky about the color. I quickly pull on the pants and shirk the gown. Since Dr. Sleepyhead is sitting up now, I pull the scrub shirt over my head as I exit the room, hoping nobody is standing right outside to see me.

The pink scrubs are both too big and too short for me at the same time, and I look completely ridiculous. If anything, I'll probably draw more attention to myself than I would have by wearing the gown.

I manage to make it down to the end of the hallway, but just as I start to open the door to the stairwell, I see my nurse exit my room. Why was she back in there?

She peers down the hall in both directions and spots me just as I'm going through the door.

"Mr. Vincent! Wait there, young man!"

Great. Now security is gonna be after me. Why are they treating me like a criminal?

I head down the stairs as fast as my noodle-legs will carry me, which isn't very fast at all. Up above, I can hear handheld radios and a couple of security guys talking as they rush down the stairs, so I know I don't have a lot of time.

Just then, I see Osprey on her way up to meet me, still in her civilian clothes. She laughs. Which is fine. I look stupid. But before I can say anything, she rushes past me, dropping a duffel bag. A couple of flights up, the security guys shout in surprise, then make some unpleasant noises just before I hear what has to be their limp bodies hit the stairs and roll down.

Poor guys. They were just doing their jobs. But, better them injured than other people dead.

Osprey comes back down to join me and picks up the bag. I try to give her a stern look.

"I was hoping to avoid hurting anyone here at the hospital."

"Couldn't be helped," she says. "And you're welcome. What are you wearing?"

"It was this or my bare butt flapping in the wind."

She shrugs with a little smile as if to say, "That wouldn't be so bad." However, I'm sure that's just my hope speaking.

We exit the stairwell at the bottom near the lobby. A bunch of security guards have gathered there, knowing it's my only way out.

Osprey looks at the guards, then at me. "You ready for a fight?"

"No. And I said I don't want to hurt anyone."

She grabs me around the waist and pulls her grappling gun out of the bag. "Then I guess we'll have to improvise."

She shoots her grappler at the front doors of the hospital just as someone is walking in. The hook barely avoids taking the guy's head off and connects with a pole just outside the doors. When she hits the button to retract the line, we start to slide through the lobby fast. The guards try to grab us, but they end up running into each other like they're in an old-fashioned comedy film.

Just as we're about to go through the doorway, I notice a kid standing by the door holding a Happy Meal. I grab it out of his hand. "Sorry!"

I immediately feel guilty about taking the kid's food, but it had to be done. Sometimes stuff happens when you're working for the greater good.

As soon as we're through the door, Osprey disconnects the grappler again and shoots it up to a nearby rooftop. Before anyone can even follow us out, we're gone.

Once we're safely on a nearby rooftop, I open up the box. "Dammit!"

Osprey looks worried. "What is it? What's wrong?"

"Nuggets. I was so craving a burger. Even a crappy one. And look at this! Apple slices! I don't even get fries."

"You poor baby. Maybe we can stop—"

"No. There's no time. Did you see the news?"

"What? News? No, how the heck did you expect me to see the news while I was sneaking into your bedroom. Your mom was home, by the way. Almost caught me."

"None of that matters," I say, tossing a McNugget into my mouth. Chewing, I tell her about Music Master and Chef Maléfique.

"Holy crap. How are we supposed to get to Times Square and stop a mad man *and* get to Maléfique in time?"

"Dunno."

It's the most genuine answer I can come up with. I know what Harrier would want, even though it might not be my first instinct. If it comes down to him dying or dozens or even hundreds of citizens… he'd gladly sacrifice himself. That's what being a hero is all about.

"I'm not even sure we're going to get there in time as it is," she says.

I scarf down the food—even the apples—and get my costume on as quickly as I can. It fits kind of snug since it was made a couple of years ago, and the design is a little bit different from the newer one. It also doesn't offer as much protection because it's Kevlar instead of graphene. Plus, it doesn't have some of the newer pieces of armor attached to my new one. But there's an old grappler in the bag. One of Osprey's, I assume. As well as some other random equipment that might come in handy.

It's also missing the glider cape, which means traversing the city will be extra tricky.

I try not to gawk as Osprey changes into her own costume, but it's really difficult. I'm probably gonna be dead within the next couple of hours anyway, what do I have to lose? I sneak a peek, and she immediately busts me.

"Eyes forward, soldier."

"Sorry. It's... you know." My face must be redder than my costume right now.

She smiles. "It's okay. I know how irresistible I am." She finishes pulling on her costume and her wig and walks over to me. "Don't worry about it. I had to strip you down before I took you to the hospital, so now we're even."

She's standing so close to me that I can feel her breath. I should try to kiss her. What difference will it make? I'm going on a suicide mission. I start to lean forward.

But what if she doesn't want me to? Is she giving me a signal right now? How do I know? Why am I such a geek? I think she wants me to. I'm gonna go for it. But what if she doesn't?

She leans in and gives me a small kiss. On the lips. The *lips*! But then she pulls away. What does that mean? Was that a real kiss? Or a "hope you don't die" kiss? Or an "okay, I feel sorry for you" kiss? Maybe her seeing Fabiola kissing me wasn't so bad after all.

I don't have time for this!

"We better get going."

She isn't happy taking orders. "Yes, *sir*."

"I'm sorry. You didn't see that crowd at Times Square. And I've seen what that guy's music can do to people. I hope I'm wrong, but there's a good chance people are already dying. And, if Chef Maléfique is as insane as I've heard, I'm not interested in finding out what happens if I'm late."

"Alright, alright. I get it. Let's go."

She thinks I don't realize that she just turned the tables and gave the orders, but I do. And I don't care. We just need to go, and egos be damned.

We take off across the rooftops in the direction of Times Square, but Osprey still wants to talk. "You don't really think he'd kill him, would he? I mean, he's had him for weeks. Why would he all of a sudden kill him now?"

"Maybe you missed the part where I said he's insane." That came out harsher than it should have. I should be happy about the kiss. Why does it seem like I'm upset about it?

"Just seems like he went through a lot of trouble to capture Harrier and lure you there… even keeping you alive when he could have easily had you killed, or even killed you himself."

"I don't know about easily," I say under my breath. But again, this is no time for egos.

"Even for a crazy person, that doesn't make any sense."

"He's punishing Harrier, and I'm somehow part of that plan. I just don't know what part."

Actually, I do, assuming he was telling me the truth. He wants to kill me in front of Harrier to torture him. He knows Harrier will blame himself for getting another kid involved after what happened to the last one.

But I can't let Osprey know any of that.

As we run across the roof of one of the nicer buildings in the neighborhood, I hear loud music, and at first, I think it might be Music Master. Then, I look and see that a bunch of teenagers are out front and talking really loudly. It sounds like there's some kind of fight going on. If only that was it.

Even though I tell myself to stay out of it and focus, I still glance down to check out what's happening. In a coincidence I wouldn't believe if I saw it in a movie or TV show, it turns out to be Fabiola's party. The biggest event of the school year. And I'm missing it.

But the noise isn't because of a simple fight like I thought it was. Someone dressed in a Black Harrier costume is shoving someone dressed like… me? And the Red Raptor guy isn't fighting back. A group of teenagers in other costumes starts to surround the smaller kid.

I know I'm repeating myself when I say I don't have time for this. But something tells me I'd better *make* time.

My old helmet may not have Amber, but it still has the onboard microphone and amplifiers, as well as sound dampeners. I turn up the volume and listen in. I immediately recognize "Harrier's" voice. Of course, it's Logan. Who else? But what really surprises me is the voice of "Raptor."

It's Javier.

"I'm sorry. I'll leave," Javi says.

"Not until I'm done with you, loser. The only reason we invited you was to get your idiot friend to come."

It's not like I can see Javi's face under that mask, but there's no doubt in my mind he's terrified.

"He's in the hospital," he says.

"I know, you stupid moron. So why did you bother to show up?"

From my utility belt, I fish out a… well, fishing line. It's hyper-durable and strong, made for situations just like this. I attach it to a drainpipe and rappel down the side of the building just as Osprey notices I'm not keeping up with her. She glides down after me. "What are you doing?"

"I have to."

"There's no time!" Osprey shouts.

"I have no choice."

I get closer and see Fabiola come out with her naughty nurse outfit on. Even in the middle of all this. *Yowza.*

I shake the impure thoughts away and watch as she stomps toward the altercation. It's a major relief, her being there, since I'm sure she'll put a stop to it and I won't have to step in. I almost turn to head back to the rooftops when she grabs Logan's arm.

"Just hit him and get it over with. I can't believe he had the nerve to come to my house."

Wow, was I ever wrong.

Just as Logan cocks his fist back, I squeeze between them. He gives me a strange look. "Who the hell are you?"

"I'm the *real* Red Raptor."

"He's called 'Red Kite,' you freakin' 'tard."

I look at Osprey, and she smiles as she says, "You're right. We had no choice."

I haul off and pop Logan square in the face. Even in my weakened state, it's plenty hard enough to knock him unconscious. There are a hundred other ways I could have taken him down, some of them without hurting him. But that just wouldn't have felt right.

Fabiola rushes to his side and lifts up his head. "Logan! Logan?" She stands up and shoves me as hard as she can and then gets in my face.

"What did you do to him? How did you—?" She stops and tilts her head. She squints, and I can tell that a hint of recognition is starting to form.

POW! Osprey knocks her on her ass with one punch, then turns to me, wearing a crooked grin. "Well, I knew *you* weren't going to do it."

The rest of the crowd backs away, afraid to mess with us.

We turn to leave, and Javier calls after us. "Hey!" I turn around for a second to give him a chance to thank me.

"That's Kite's old costume, you know. You really should update it."

I can't even catch a break after saving someone.

But his comment does remind me that I'd transferred most of my tools and weapons to my new utility belt when I got it, which means I only have basic stuff with me on my most dangerous mission ever. I look down at my old, slightly faded backup threads, then turn to Osprey. "Are you sure you don't remember where you dumped my good costume?"

CHAPTER
TWENTY-TWO

C*raziness.*

As we head toward Times Square, I start to see that the news stations don't begin to do justice when explaining the situation on the streets. That's pretty odd since networks live to stir up fear and exaggerate everything. But there's more crime going on in the city than I've ever seen. I'm not talking about typical Halloween pranks. There's serious looting, brawling, and rioting all over. Osprey and I try to do what we can along the way, but it's a drop in the bucket. Scratch that—it's a bucket in the ocean. And as much as I want to stop every little thing from happening, say it with me… we don't have time.

Sadly, the police aren't even coming close to getting a handle on the situation, either. They're all pretty much wandering around trying not to get shot.

Harrier isn't the only hero in the city, but he's definitely the most famous. I start to wonder where everyone else is when I realize they must already be at Times Square. I don't think any of them will be a match for Music Master, though. Then the thought strikes me… *Will I*?

A short while later, we are standing on the precipice of the busiest tourist trap in America. Just close enough that we can hear the beginnings of Music Master's music. I've been debating when would be the right time to do this, and I admit, I'm still not sure. But there's a good chance we're gonna die, and I might as well just get it out of the way.

I inhale deeply. "Did your dad make that helmet?"

"Yeah, but I made some modi—" Osprey answers before she realizes the implications. Then, even through her lowered visor, I can see her mouth part, and words start to form.

I smile.

"You're joking. How long have you known?" she asks.

"Since the hospital."

"But how?"

"I visited your dad a few weeks ago. He has a picture of you on his desk."

"And what—you just remembered my face?" she asks, skeptical.

I probably blush a little, but my mask is down, too. "Kinda hard to forget."

For the first time since changing, I'm so glad Amber isn't installed on my old helmet.

I don't think she knows what to say either.

I decide to break that awkward tension. "Okay. So if your helmet is like mine, you have dampeners?"

"Yeah," she says. "I've never used them, though."

"We should be able to sync up our microphones." I reach for her visor, and we make eye contact. "I..." I clear my throat. "There we go."

I adjust mine and say, "Can you hear me?"

"Loud and clear."

"Can you hear anything else?"

"No. Creepy."

"Yeah, but you'll be happy when you're not being controlled by that loser's hippie music. Now or never, you ready?"

"Nope."

"Good. Let's go," I say.

This time, she doesn't argue, and we take off together.

The closer we get, the more we're slowed down by crowds, and the more I worry about not getting to my "reservation" before it's too late. This is all just part of Chef Maléfique's plan. Music Master is working for him, just like all of the other criminals in town seem to be now.

It continues to worsen until I feel like we're wading through a horde of zombies. Most of them are ordinary people, which makes it both easier and more difficult at the same time. It's easier to take down a normal person than an experienced criminal, but it's more difficult because we really don't want to hurt them.

"Make way!" I scream.

"Does that ever work?" Osprey asks.

I shove people aside as gently as I can, but they keep attacking me, full of rage. I can't hear Music Master's music, but these people are clearly being affected by it. How long does its effect last? I don't have any of the information I desperately need. That's always been Harrier's job.

"No."

I am not prepared for what I see when we arrive in Times Square. Yeah, there're the typical glowing signs and billboards, larger-than-life Victoria Secret models, and, of course, that seafood place from that one movie. But there's also absolute mayhem, and even the police are involved. Except, they aren't helping. They're just as crazed as everyone else, throwing stuff, screaming, punching, kicking. Then, as if that's not enough, my heart plummets into my nether regions.

In the middle of it all, Gargantuan Grey and Royal Rampage, both Guild-affiliated heroes, a bipedal werewolf and fully-sentient great ape who, for some reason, wears a giant gold crown, are tearing through the crowd with abandon.

"You seeing this?" Osprey asks through our linked-up helmets.

"Yeah, unfortunately."

A bright green blur appears out of thin air about a hundred yards in front of us, then disappears in a crackle of dark energy.

"Was that..."

"Stygian," I finish for her.

Stygian is a hero too. No one knows for sure since he doesn't speak any known language, but we all think he's from another dimension. He looks human enough, but he's green and covered in scales. Oh, and he can teleport.

"Are they all possessed or whatever?" Osprey asks.

"That's what it looks like. We've gotta do something."

"Riiiight... but what?"

Before I have a chance to answer, I'm grabbed from behind and pulled. I spin, ready to clobber whoever it is and stop, my fist an inch away from beating a woman. A pregnant one at that.

"Don't hurt anyone," I say to Osprey, my eyes fixated on the twenty-something-year-old who'd just attacked me.

I peel the woman's fingers off my arm and back up.

"You don't want to do this," I say.

She screams something, pointing at her bloated belly, but I can't hear it through my dampener. The look on her face is just pure rage.

Music Master is definitely drawing out their anger. I mean, we all have it, buried deep inside. Memories of our dads who beat us, or weren't there at all, teachers who told us we'd never amount to anything, bullies like Logan. Whatever it is that causes it, the anger is there. Now Music Master is taking advantage of it.

There are thousands of people, a lot of them tourists, clearly on family vacations and checking out the most famous spot in the city.

Imagine?

"Hey, honey, let's take the kids to New York to see Gulliver's Gate. Maybe we'll even get possessed by a supervillain and watch our children gut-punch homeless people."

"We have one advantage here," I tell Osprey while I continue to fend off Violent-Femme. "Music Master is expecting *me*. Not you."

"How is that an advantage? There are literally dozens of supers out there who could probably kill either of us just by stomping hard enough."

"I don't know. I'm still trying to figure that out."

How do we use that to our advantage? How... how? I've literally got nothing. I don't even think Harrier has seen anything of this magnitude.

"We've gotta get closer. We're running out of time."

"Not without a plan," I say.

"You and your plans."

With that, Osprey whips into action. She goes for the Canadian Shield, who is easily twice her size. But she has surprise and sanity on her side. Even so, he still bats her away with his massive shield. She uses the momentum and falls into a roll, coming up in a perfect Brazilian jujitsu stance. Who is this girl?

The Canadian Shield rushes her, and she snatches his wrist, then lets her body roll along his arm. Her other elbow connects with his jaw, and the big man goes down.

I'm sure he'll recover quickly enough, but I don't watch the rest of it. Instead, I parkour through and over people, using them as objects, I make it to the throng of the concert in a matter of minutes. I have to dodge punches, and I get caught in more than one mosh pit—why is anyone moshing to this crap? I'm just glad I can't hear it.

I feel my ribs crack, and I'm flying through the air. Cool. I'm out there for four seconds, and I'm dead. Awesome.

I land hard on my back and slide, slamming into several citizens along the way. Not being able to hear anything is disorienting at best. I stand and see my attacker, Royal Rampage, well, rampaging toward me. So, that crown... I'm guessing the film studio that owns the name *King Kong* wanted to charge too much for him to use it.

At one time, he was an ordinary gorilla being transferred from the Central Park Zoo when the driver of his truck collided with a GenLabs hauler. GenLabs is a shady tech company out of Jersey. Yeah, I know... anything from Jersey, right?

Turns out, their hauler, which was supposed to be carrying "harmless chemicals" across the harbor, was actually carrying some sludge. It killed the drivers of both vehicles on contact, but it left Barry the Gorilla with the intelligence of a ten-year-old and the strength of a god.

Oh, and they were transporting him because he broke the record for the largest gorilla ever. So I guess, not exactly ordinary. He's a thick mass of muscle and bone. Six feet two inches and over nine hundred pounds, and all of that is hurtling toward little hundred-and-thirty-pound me.

Both of his fists pound the pavement, cracking it and sending spiderwebs out. They're like freaking bowling balls. He roars when he nears me. I can't hear it because of the dampeners, but oh, my, God can I feel it. It literally shakes my chest, and I think I feel spittle. He lowers his head and goes for another spear.

I dive to the side, avoiding him but crashing into a group of pedestrians who turn on me. Now, I'm blocking punches and kicks from all sides while hoping Royal Rampage doesn't eat me. I could really use Amber's warning system about now.

One of the teenage girls—purple hair, *My Little Pony* shirt—starts swinging her metal-studded purse at me. It clearly doesn't hurt, but it's a perfect example of just how chaotic this place is. I'd have a better chance of catching every raindrop in a thunderstorm than quelling this crowd without first stopping Music Master.

I "feel" Rampage's roar again and turn to see him barreling toward me. His fist hits my chest with the force of a pickup truck on a straightaway. I fly back fifteen feet and smash into a stack of speakers. It topples, and out of the corner of my eye, I see Osprey swoop in to knock two men aside before the weight of it crushes them to death.

I stand and turn just in time to see Gargantuan Grey, long fangs, sharp talons, and yellow eyes coming at me.

Still recovering from that last hit, I have no choice but to brace myself and prepare for impact. That's what I do, but there is no amount of preparation I could have done. Every ounce of air evacuates my lungs, and I'm gasping even as I land.

Music Master's crappy song assaults my ears, and I feel a fire inside of me. My helmet must've come off. I start to look for it, but it's no use. Everything around me goes red. Logan's dumbass, pudgy face... I see it on everyone around me. I lash out, hitting things, people, anything within striking distance.

Then, Frank fills the forefront of my mind. Everything he ever did to piss me off—not trusting me enough to tell me what happened to my predecessors, not telling me about the garage below Douglas Industries, his stupid voice-changer. I hate him.

He didn't even trust me enough to tell me about the business card he clearly got from Chef Maléfique. Am I his partner or not?

Chef Maléfique. Frank. The warehouse.

I blink and focus, recalling every YouTube video I'd ever watched about centering my chi. I calm just long enough to see my helmet on the floor and make a leap for it.

When it's in my hands, I stare at it. I hate this helmet. I hate this costume. Red Kite. What a stupid name, and it was Frank's idea. I hate him.

A scream rings out, and I think it might be mine. Though, it sounds more like a howl. It *is* a howl.

I recognize the battle going on inside of me, but it's just so difficult to fight. I almost don't want to fight it. I like the anger. It's like an old friend.

I feel my helmet slip over my head, but it's not me doing it. When silence comes, I see Osprey standing in front of me, and Gargantuan Grey laid out on his face a few yards away.

"Are you okay?" she says.

"Did you do that?" I ask, pointing at the werewolf.

"Couldn't let him kill you now, could I?"

I can't see her eyes with those reflective covers, but I imagine she's winking at me.

"Look out!" I shout as I see Gargantuan Grey rise, head tilted to the sky and howling.

We leap out of the way as he lunges. He continues until he smashes into the iron fence surrounding the stage where Music Master continues to pound away on his stupid keytar. I glance up at him, but he's just as distracted as everyone else, lost in the music, like I'm not even there.

While Grey recovers, I turn to see Osprey is gone. I look out over the crowd, hoping to see her somewhere, but I have no luck. There's just too many people.

"Where are you?" I say into my microphone.

"A little busy," she says, sounding winded. "You'd better stop this guy, quick."

"Me?"

Her response is a series of shouts and moans as she fights whoever she's fighting.

I turn back and see Rampage and Grey beating on each other now. Better that than focusing their super-strength on helpless people.

I rush the stage and leap up there. No one even tries to stop me. Music Master stands several yards away, playing his instrument. His head snaps toward me, but again, barely even seems to care about me, just a few strides away. His music isn't the only thing loud about him. His stupid, colorful costume and bright orange hair hurt my eyes just looking at them.

Obviously, he's controlling the sound, so if I can take him out, it should stop. I look around the stage, expecting to find a full band, but it's empty except for the speakers. I try to walk, but a sudden, sharp pain in my side drives me to my knees. Had Rampage actually broken something? Jumping onto the stage must have aggravated it. I also feel nauseous. Great… puking is gonna end up becoming my signature move.

Through the pain, I can't concentrate enough to hit him or his keytar with my throwing stars. If only there was some way of reaching him from here. I can't even crawl over to him.

Then, remembering Osprey's solution to reaching the door at the hospital, I pull the old grappler off my belt. It's a piece of junk compared to my new one, but it'll do for what I have planned. Music Master's expression goes from passive to curious. Then it changes to realization a second too late as I shoot the hook at him, and it attaches to his keytar, which is strapped around him. His playing stops immediately.

I brace myself and retract the cable, and because he wasn't ready for it, he's pulled toward me extremely fast. Just as he's about to reach me, I muster all my strength and do a flying kick, allowing the grappler to launch me toward Music Master as he continues moving in my direction. I grit through the pain in my side, and my kick nearly takes his head off. He drops to the ground like a sack of potatoes. I check to make sure I didn't kill him, but he seems to just be unconscious.

I unhook the keytar from its strap and smash it against the stage as hard as I can, even though I know he has many of them, and this won't stop him the next time he gets out of jail. It takes everything I have not to bash him over the head.

Everyone is still going crazy in the crowd. Why? Why didn't it stop? I look at the soundboard, next to where Music Master had been standing. Lights are still moving up and down on the board's indicators. He was just playing along to some music he'd pre-recorded. I swear and start turning down all the knobs and flipping switches, but it doesn't seem to do anything. How can I stop this thing?

Then I remember another hero I'd caught a glimpse of in the crowd. Darkstryke...

He controls electricity. If I can spot him…

As I search the chaos, a couple of guys from the mob climb up onstage and attack me. I do my best to take them down as gently as possible, but I don't have time to be too careful. Then I spot what looks like a small lightning storm nearby.

I climb up on one of the giant speakers so I can see Darkstryke among the rest of the rioters. There he is, purple and silver leotard, V-shaped headband-thing, and long blond hair. He kind of looks like a wrestler from the 80s or something.

I try shouting to him, but he can't hear me over the music and the yelling. So I pull out my boomerang and toss it at him as gently as possible, just to get his attention without injuring him too badly. The last thing I need is to knock him unconscious and ruin my plan.

The boomerang hits him on his back, and he flinches in pain, but he doesn't go down or anything. Turning around, he spots me waving my arms at him. "Hey, Dorkstryke! I'm over here!" I taunt, grimacing as the movement makes my side burn.

He throws a ball of electricity at me, and I leap out of the way. It fries the one speaker and leaves scorch marks, but the rest of the speakers are still functioning.

I move directly in front of the soundboard and flip him off with both hands, which I can see enrages him even more. His eyes narrow, and he points both fists at me as they start to glow and crackle. I'm not that familiar with his powers… how long do I wait before I jump out of the way without him moving his aim? I guess if I wait too long, at least I'll have gone out saving thousands of people. I decide to just count down and hope for the best. "Three, two, one…"

I spring from the stage just as Darkstryke unloads with everything he's got. The lightning blast temporarily blinds me and, I assume, everyone else. The soundboard, the PA system, the speakers—they all blow, sending sparks and smoke all over the stage.

Aaaarrrrgh. I lie in agony, but everyone around me starts to settle down, looking around in confusion as their eyes recover from the brightness of the blast.

"Amy," I say. It's the first time I actually use her name. I like the way it feels, saying it.

"You okay?"

I groan. "I'm hurt. This… dumb… armor…"

I look down and see that there's a piece of the Kevlar cracked and sticking into my ribcage. I yank it off, and the pain immediately subsides.

"What happened?" Osprey asks.

"I think I stopped him… but it was too—"

I was gonna say "too easy" when Osprey swears and shouts, "Look at the screens!"

I do as she says, and I see the giant visage of Chef Maléfique, bigger than anyone would ever want to see him. I chance switching off my dampeners and hear him.

"Tick, tock, tick, tock, tick, tock. So much time you're wasting." He points to an imaginary watch on his arm. "Better hurry up. Don't be late."

The camera pans to a fuzzy figure in the background, but it's only up there for a blink before it's gone.

"Was that Harrier?" Osprey asks from wherever she is.

"I couldn't tell. I hope so. He was moving, at least."

We both meet up and take the least amount of time possible to make sure Music Master is tied up, and everyone else is okay. We leave things in the capable hands of the other supers—who, by the way, are very apologetic and thankful—and the NYPD before grappling up to the rooftops and starting toward what I hope isn't our final destination.

CHAPTER TWENTY-THREE

Isolated.

We finally arrive at the address. Talk about the shady part of town. I think I saw a dead body in the gutter a couple of blocks back. This is the kind of place the mafia owns to store their guns and lie low while the fuzz searches for them.

A bit of false hope comes. I start thinking I'm actually gonna be on time for my "reservation." But reality is a bitch, and it slaps me hard.

"There's no way this is opening," I say, tugging on the massive roll-up door. There doesn't appear to be any other way in, either.

"You didn't mention the place looks like something out of a Marilyn Manson music video."

"I'm sorry," Osprey says. "I didn't really think that was pertinent information."

The place is huge—like an airplane hangar. It's covered in graffiti. Giant spiderwebs, creepy dolls with red eyes and bloody noses, black and white skulls, amongst other stuff like gang tags and symbols indicative of this neighborhood. Right in the center are two giant butcher knives, crossed… and a handlebar moustache.

It's scary as hell on the outside. I figure most of it is Chef Maléfique's work, though, trying his best to elicit fear.

We circle the perimeter, pushing our way through waist-high weeds. It must have rained here recently because I'm ankle-deep in mud, and it's starting to get cold. I'd forgotten that this suit didn't have built-in heat.

Sure enough, aside from the massive garage door, there are no other entries, and all of the windows are covered with sheets of metal and welded shut.

"Well, now what?" I say.

"The roof?" Osprey suggests.

"It's either that or dig. The roof sounds like a better first option."

We grapple up to the roof and, honestly? I start to panic about what's gonna happen as Maléfique's deadline passes.

I remember my dream about the black harrier getting eaten by the alligator while I was distracted by the white osprey. I'm sure it was just a dream, but I can't help but worry that Frank is being devoured, even now.

Bye-bye, hope.

On the roof, there's nothing there. Same problem. No doors, no skylights, no way in at all. The entire area is covered in junk and stupid horror stuff, as if someone put up Halloween decorations years ago and never bothered to take them down.

Just as I'm about to give up, Osprey whisper-shouts, "Over here!"

I run to see that she's found a small hatch buried in the far corner, hidden in some debris. She also figures out how to open it, since it's not obvious just from looking at it.

As it cracks, smoke pours out. But… it's not smoke... it's a chemical smell… like a fog machine.

We start the climb down into who knows what. I go first, looking up at Osprey, wondering if I'd have made it here without her help. She's been anything but a distraction.

CHAPTER
TWENTY-FOUR

Explosions.

Really cool and fun in an action movie. Not so much up close in real life.

You know what you never consider when thinking about explosions? First of all, we all realize you can be blown to pieces, or struck with shrapnel. But the heat... The fire is so hot without my climate-controlled suit, I can feel sweat pouring down my spine. Explosions are just one of the traps Chef Maléfique has waiting for us when we get inside. If he wanted me dead, he could have killed me a bunch of times by now. He could have sliced my throat in the hospital. Deadeye could have shot me instead of killing Weasel. The entire mob of bad guys could have converged on me on the bridge and taken me down with the sheer force of numbers.

It's the same with all the explosions. None of them are big enough or close enough to kill me, but they do make me dizzy and knock out my hearing for a while. I consider switching the sound dampeners on again, but the last thing I need is to be caught unawares in this hell-house.

There's fog machine smoke everywhere, and every now and then, one of the things hisses and expels more. I'm a little embarrassed when one goes off to my left, and I jump. Truth is, I'm completely on edge. I know the explosions aren't deadly, though. Probably not even loud enough to bring the cops, if he has as much soundproofing as I imagine he does. So I go in knowing that he doesn't want me dead—yet—but I still have to worry about what kind of shape I'll be in by the time I reach him.

It feels like a thousand years ago when I saved that woman in the alley from that group of a dozen thugs. But somehow, this reminds me of that. Like when the biggest, toughest gang member hangs back while the others soften me up. All this nonsense is meant to just make me weak, break my will.

Unlike that night, now I have to worry about Osprey's safety. I'm sure Maléfique probably knows that Harrier doesn't give a damn about her, so the only reason for him to allow her to come with me would be to hurt or kill her in front of me. Demoralize me further. Just one on a long list of reasons why I should have figured out a way to prevent her from joining me.

Like a carnival funhouse, albeit one with deadly traps, Chef Maléfique has the entire warehouse set up in some sort of maze, with everything in it meant to disorient me. The "walls" are made of kitchen stoves, each one's timer going off, beeping incessantly. Hallways shrink and then widen, then turn back on themselves.

The hallway opens into a small room with walk-in freezers wide open, pouring out freezing-cold air. Thick cuts of meat hang... like animal legs or... human torsos. No, I'm gonna go with cow legs. In addition to the explosions, loud French-style music blares from hidden speakers like we're in some bistro in Paris. It's absurd. He isn't even French. Doesn't sound French. But there's this whole stupid schtick.

Every fifty yards or so, there's a big flatscreen TV with the sound blasting over the music. Right now, they're playing recorded news stories about how Harrier hasn't been seen in so long. Another tactic to throw me off, I guess.

I turn to Osprey. "Stay close. The last thing we need is to get separated in this madhouse."

She shakes her head. "Oh, you don't have to worry about that. I have to admit, I'm pretty much terrified."

"Right."

We continue forward through a wall of hanging streamers. When I shove them aside, a blast of liquid hits us. Immediately, I begin to worry that it's acid or some chemical, but I'm soon convinced it's... wine?

"This guy is insane," I say.

At one point, the hallway narrows until it's nothing more than a crawlspace. In fact, he probably just led us up into the actual crawlspace of the building now that I think about it. It's really dark except for the TV screen up ahead, suddenly filled with Chef Maléfique's face.

"Welcome to my kitchen, wee little birdies. Or is it dinosaur now? Raaahr. None of it makes *SENSE*."

He really emphasizes that last word, and I catalog it for later, in case it means something more than just the ramblings of a madman. However, he did say birdies, plural. That means he knows Osprey is with me.

He continues. "We're going to have *so*. Much. Fun. But first, I suppose you'll be wanting to see how Harrier's doing at some point. Well, no time like the present." Maléfique steps back from the camera, and now, that fuzzy figure is clear as a bell.

It's horrible.

Harrier and I have been in bad shape after some really intense fights, but nothing like this. His uniform, except for his mask, is almost completely gone, and what's left of it is hanging in tatters from his bruised, bloody body. He, himself, is suspended from chains that are cuffed around his wrists, and he's covered in cuts from head to toe. He's obviously been tortured.

I must have let out some kind of sound when I first saw him, but I can't tell you what it was. This time, I don't need Music Master's keytar tones to feel the anger well up inside of me after the shock wears off. I can't wait to get my hands on that evil bastard. He won't know what hit him.

"Oh, and by the way—this is for you being late." He reaches for something off-screen, and suddenly an electric jolt zaps Osprey and me. It starts at our feet and zips through us. Now I know what the wine was for. It wasn't too bad. I've been hit with a Taser before, and it was along those lines.

I whisper to Osprey. "Glad you came along?"

"I'll be fine," she says through gritted teeth. "We need to save him."

She looks back at the screen again. I'm gonna have to force myself not to think about the torture Harrier's been through while he's been here. I mean, Maléfique has a thing for butcher's knives. If I dwell on it too much, it's gonna throw me off my game and put all of us in even more danger.

While Osprey and I are focused on Harrier, a hidden trap door opens beneath her, and then immediately closes again, even as I dive after her. I'm met with nothing but steel. I hear her start to scream, but it cuts off as soon as it shuts. I have no idea how far she fell, or what she landed on at the bottom of the drop. It could be spikes for all I know. I may have just watched her die.

What if she *is* dead? What in the world would I tell Mr. Chen? How could I explain bringing his daughter on what I knew would be the most dangerous date of her life?

I try to pry open the trap door with my fingers, but I can't get a grip around the edges. I grab one of my throwing stars to see if I can force it open, but I don't have any luck with that either. In desperation, I start pounding on it, but I realize it's not gonna help anything.

"I'm gonna kill you!" I shout.

Snow fuzzes on the TV screen. "No killing," Chef Maléfique says in what I'm guessing to be his Black Harrier impression.

I whip my throwing star, and it smashes into the display, sending out shards of glass and puffs of smoke.

"Oh, so childish," he says, voice echoing over the speakers even without the TV. "That was expensive."

Once I calm down, I continue to crawl, determined to get through the maze as quickly as possible so I can save Harrier, and hopefully now Osprey also.

The crawlspace ends by opening up into a dark room that appears empty from what I can tell. I can't see the bottom, so I drop another star, waiting for it to ping. From what I can figure, the floor is only about a twelve-foot drop. I lower myself, then feel around with my foot, allowing my eyes to adjust to the darkness. Normally, I'd use my light, but I don't want to give away my position to anyone—or anything—that might be lurking in here.

Just as I start to be able to make out where I'm going, and I reach the center of the room, bright lights suddenly come on from all directions, blinding me now that my pupils have fully dilated.

I shut my eyes and fall to my knees. Why is Maléfique doing this? Why not either kill me now or let me get to where he's keeping Harrier so he can kill me then? Is he somehow making Harrier watch this, assuming it'll torture him? From what I saw on that video screen, it's hard to imagine Harrier being able to focus on anything right now.

This is apparently the stage portion of the "restaurant." Even with my eyes shut, the light is so bright that I can't think straight. They flash on and off, getting faster and faster until they produce a strobe effect.

"Hello, sweetie."

I turn around, and Sinsation is already behind me. There must be a hidden doorway somewhere in here.

No matter how many times I see her, I can never get over how hot she is. I've never been to a strip club, but I imagine this must be how the women look before they take their clothes off. Most heroes and villains don't actually have costumes like the ones in the comics. They wear some combination of lightweight body armor, Kevlar, and other microfibers. But Sinsation is a major exception, all in spandex and glitter, like she was drawn by a pinup artist.

So, idiot that I am around attractive women, I stand there with my mouth open instead of reacting immediately. That gives her plenty of time to roundhouse kick me in the helmet, knocking me to the floor, and again my helmet comes off and lands ten feet away. What a piece of—

She kicks me again while I'm down, and I flop over. Now my head's throbbing on top of everything else, and I think I strained my neck.

I'm not sure what kind of technology she uses, but she's able to do a lot of things with her light shows. Right now, I feel myself not being able to move very well or to track her with the strobe light flashing. I don't know whether it's a trick of the lights or if I somehow end up with gaps in my perception, but like the lights themselves, she appears to flash in and out of places. On top of that, she's an Olympic-level acrobat, cartwheeling and flipping all over the place.

The next thing I know, she's behind me again, this time using a flying kick to my back, which slams me into the wall, breaking the light fixture there. I can feel where the glass cuts into my face, and even through parts of my old costume that aren't armored.

I forgot what an excellent hand-to-hand fighter she is on top of the light show. Her stiletto boot slices across my face, and I feel the warmth as my blood trickles down. I can't see her. Then I realize what Chef Maléfique is doing.

Sense. That's what he'd said.

Music Master was the sound. Sinsation, the sight… he's toying with my senses.

Harrier taught me what I should do the next time we fought her. I close my eyes, listening for her footsteps. If I can't trust my sense of sight, I'd have to focus on the others. She's so quiet, I almost don't pick it up, but then I hear a nearly imperceptible crunch as she steps on a piece of shattered glass.

I hate hitting a woman—my mom would kill me if she ever found out—but I kind of think Sinsation deserves it. Oh, man, I hope that doesn't make me sound like some kind of a-hole who makes excuses for abusing his wife or something. I mean, she is helping a homicidal maniac who's trying to kill a teenager, isn't she?

And right now, she's doing a pretty good job of it.

I swing out my leg, and it connects with her stomach. From the sound she makes, I can tell I got her pretty good. I continue my momentum forward and punch for where her face should be, and I'm successful there as well. My next move is to sweep her legs out from under her, and I hear her fall to the ground.

I leap onto her chest and hold my forearm against her windpipe. "Turn it off."

She tries to wriggle out from under me, grunting with effort. Her voice sounds almost like a cartoon duck because of the pressure on her throat. "Get away from me, you little—"

"I said turn it off!"

Finally, she gives in and presses the buttons in her glove or whatever it is that controls her light shows. Now I have to figure out what to do with her. I can't have her showing up when I'm in the middle of my showdown with Maléfique. It's gonna be nearly impossible to defeat him as it is.

"Roll over," I say. Then I realize I'm subconsciously bracing for Amber to make a smartass comment before I remember she's not here and relax a little.

I pull a zip tie out of my utility belt. She does what I ask, but as I start to bind her hands behind her back, she flips over and gets me into a headlock with her legs.

I can't breathe at all, and I feel myself losing consciousness fast. Things start to go dark with little stars flying around as I feel for something to hit her with. My fingers close in on something... my helmet, lying on the floor just a foot away. I grab hold of it, and just as I feel like it's gonna be lights out, I get both hands around it and smash her in that smokin' hot face of hers as hard as I can.

Her leg-lock goes slack as she collapses to the ground. So much for going easy on her. I zip tie her legs together so she can't follow me even if she comes to. I wipe the blood off my face with her pink and grey half-cape, and it comes away really saturated. That boot was more than just a little scratch, I think, but it's too dark to make any real assessment.

All I can think about is resting right now, but I have to keep moving. Harrier may not have much time left, even if Chef Maléfique doesn't directly kill him, and I don't even want to think about what that wannabe-French-freak and his men could be doing to Osprey right now.

CHAPTER **TWENTY-FIVE**

My question is answered in the next room. It's set up like a sort of a makeshift bar. Dark wood countertop, a mirrored wall with bottles of various liquors. I'll give Maléfique one thing, when he picks a theme, he really leans into it hard. There's even a mannequin wearing a black shirt and jeans, frozen in the act of wiping down the bar. Above the bar, situated a few feet apart from each other, are another half-dozen flatscreens. Each one shows me the same room from different angles. Osprey, in a giant cage. It's hard to even worry about her; the relief that she's alive is so strong.

"Lookie, lookie, little birdie," Chef Maléfique says over the speaker system. "Have you ever seen an Osprey in a cage? It's like your own little private zoo. Maybe she'll perform for us? Oh, and who is this—is that the zookeeper?"

A chain-link door opens on the side of the cage opposite where Osprey is standing and in walks a dark figure. Despite being newer-looking televisions, the live feed is absolute crap. It isn't until he steps into the center of the cage that I can tell who it is.

Deadeye.

He wears his trademark skull helmet, which I figure he'd want to take off since he's not on his motorcycle, but I guess that's his way of shielding his identity. Now, there are no bandoliers full of ammo, and I can't see a single gun on him. For that matter, he doesn't even have a weapon. No blade. No staff. He cracks his gloved knuckles.

Osprey drops into a fighting stance. Thank God. She looks okay. My best guess is that the trap door led right into the room on these screens.

They circle each other for a second, and Deadeye looks like he's playing a game while Osprey seems prepared to fight for her life. She cartwheels in, and Deadeye is ready for it. He kicks straight out and catches her full-on. Still upside down, her body looks like a rag doll as it's launched across the cage.

Deadeye stalks toward her, no urgency to his movements at all. When he gets close, she does a whirlwind like she's breakdancing. Both feet catch him in rapid succession.

That's a badass move I'll have to remember. She winds up in a handstand that she uses to catapult herself to her feet. Two quick steps and she's on him, unwilling to give him the chance to recover. She gets a few really good hits in before he brings an elbow around, and she crumples.

The feed is cut the moment she hits the floor.

"No!" I shout.

"That's enough entertainment," Chef Maléfique says. "You may want a drink. I know, I know... underage, but I won't tell. We have so much more fun to be had firsthand!"

The mirrored wall shatters, and all the bottles of alcohol come toppling down toward me. I leap out of the way but still get hit by a few. They don't hurt, but it does distract me to the fact that more fog starts rolling in through the vents, but then I smell it, and it absolutely isn't fog.

This is typical of supervillains in this town. They come up with some hokey plan and think it's clever. First, they assault my hearing, then my sight. Now? Smell. Music Master, Sinsation, and… there's only one baddie who smells this bad. Creeping Death.

Who is Creeping Death? Imagine someone who smells like a fart and looks like a massive tarantula. It's just a ratty old costume, worse than one you'd pick up at a Halloween store, but that's part of what makes it so scary.

So who am I gonna face when I get to "touch," assuming I live that long?

I can't think about it right now. I just have to focus on the moment and worry about that if and when it comes up.

I follow the room toward a dark hallway I feel a... stickiness on the bottom of my boots. Soon, I notice webbing hanging down from the ceiling also. It doesn't get bad enough that I can't move, and I know from past experience with Creeping Death that it won't do any good to try to cut it. It'll just stick to the blade and keep pulling like the cheese on a good slice of pizza.

I can see up ahead that there's a dim light coming from an opening and more of his noxious gas. My helmet, even this old one, has an air filter built-in, but after having gone through so much with Gargantuan Grey, Royal Rampage, and Sinsation, the thing is cracked to hell and won't seal no matter what I do. I have to make a decision to either go through quietly and assess the situation, or rush in and try to take him by surprise. Again, these are the kinds of calls Harrier makes, and, again, I realize I'm not very good at it, having not had a lot of practice.

I decide to go in headfirst and fists blazing.

It's hard to get a running start with the stickiness, but I'm going at a pretty good speed when I burst through the opening and roll forward. I get up into a crouch and look around, but I don't see the Creepster anywhere. It does become immediately apparent that this is supposed to be the dumpster area behind a restaurant. Two large blue dumpsters take up half the room, adding to the stink. There's a thick, yellow haze, making it so I can't see more than a few feet in any direction. The smell is already beginning to burn my nostrils and my lungs.

I cough. A bunch. It almost makes me wish I still had a cold, maybe then I'd be too stuffed up to smell it.

I turn in circles as quickly as I can without making myself dizzy, hoping to catch him before he can get to me from any direction. Somehow, I didn't think about him coming from above like a spider, so when he lands on my shoulders, it's a complete surprise. He's bulbous with that stupid costume on, and I find myself off balance. Sharp fingernails dig into the sides of my head. He's surprisingly strong for a bony old man.

If you've ever seen Beetlejuice, turn him into a spider, and you can get a good visual for this guy. He's so disgusting.

Luckily, it doesn't take much for me to figure out how to get him off. I bend as if I'm gonna do a backflip, which ends up slamming his head into the floor. As soon as I hear the crack, I feel his hands loosen, and I jump away to get my bearings. But then he drops another one of his gas bombs, and it feels like napalm in my lungs. He uses the distraction to disappear again into the haze. These villains absolutely have the advantage on me. They've probably seen the hangar with the lights on. All part of screwing with my senses.

Okay, think, Sawyer. These crazies always do things according to their theme. What's he gonna do next?

Attack from below. I think of it a split second too late as I feel something clamp around both of my ankles. I can't move my feet. They're in some kind of cuffs that are attached to the floor.

I hear Creeping Death's cackling laugh. I don't know if this guys' been smoking two packs a day for fifty years, or if he's just breathed in too much of his own creations, but he sounds like he's gonna hack up a lung. Just like I can never tell whether his old, faded costume is part of his theme, or if he's just too cheap to get a new costume. It looks like it hasn't been washed in my lifetime.

Some kind of whip snaps at me from behind and wraps me, pinning my arms to my side so I can't move them. The old man dances around me in circles, wrapping his long whip, like a spiderweb, tighter around me. Between the dancing and the cackling, I'm almost sure he's completely lost it.

There's one idea I had a couple of years ago that Harrier gave me a lot of praise for. After continually being locked up by these costumed villains and not being able to get to our lock picks in our utility belts, I convinced him that we needed to come up with a way to hide them in our gauntlets. Because we wear bracers over our forearms, it wasn't too difficult to hide the tools up there. I squat down before he can get the whip around my legs, and my hands are able to reach the cuffs on my feet. In less than ten seconds, I'm able to unlock both cuffs without him noticing a thing.

I don't know what Creeping Death's plan is, or if he even has one, but it ends now. As soon as he gets to the point where he's directly in front of me, I launch myself forward, and the crown of my head smashes into his nose. He was not ready for that at all.

He drops his whip, and I roll in the opposite direction that it's wrapped around me. I'm free, but I still can't see him through the haze. Eyes shut, I hear him whimper from the ground where he's lying. I'm sure I broke his nose, but the old fart probably broke a hip or something, too, when he fell.

What? I'm supposed to feel sorry for this guy?

The whip starts to move, so he must be picking it back up. No way I'm letting him have another crack at me. I grab the end closest to me and yank on it as hard as I can. I think he's afraid to let go because he'll fall down again, so he's hanging on tight as I see his nasty old spider costume coming at me. I prepare to kick him hard, but at the last second, I sort of feel bad. I mean, he looks like someone's grandpa.

Instead, I step out of the way, and he runs into the nearest wall headfirst. He spins on me, hissing? What the crap?

He lurches forward and bites me on the neck. Actually bites me.

"You crazy old bastard!" I shout. All concern for his elderly ass flees me, and I punch him as hard as I can in the side of his wrinkled face. I stare down at his unconscious form. I reach up and touch my neck. It's hard to tell because there's still blood dripping from where Sinsation's stiletto got me, but it doesn't seem like he broke the skin.

Wrapping him up in his own whip to make sure he can't come after me, I decide I better check his pulse to make sure he didn't croak. It's weak, but still there. And, dude, his breath smells worse than his stink bombs.

I scour the room, and it turns out the only way out is an opening in the ceiling. I use the junky old grappler and shoot it up into the opening. It attaches to something solid. Rising up above the room, I notice tiny cameras in each corner of the ceiling. I didn't see any in the other spaces, but I didn't get up this high, so I'm sure they were there.

Apparently, all of this is part of a show for Chef Maléfique's entertainment.

I climb through the opening in the ceiling and crawl through what feels like a duct, thin metal bouncing under my movements. In the darkness, I start to notice a slight downward incline, and then it suddenly gets steeper. Too late, I realize it's actually moving, and the surface has gone from ordinary metal to something really slick. I start to move faster, and just when I'm about to put my hands out to the sides and stop myself, razor-sharp blades spring out.

Maléfique's voice booms from unseen speakers. "Anyone in the mood for Sawyer Allumette?"

I pull my limbs in as close to my body as I can so I don't get cut, but that makes me like a bobsledder hurtling down the slide.

As I spot a light up ahead, I prepare myself to be launched into whatever's at the end of this ride.

CHAPTER **TWENTY-SIX**

The slide dumps me out in a cavernous room filled with tables and chairs, all nicely decorated with white tablecloths and candles. I gotta hand it to him; it's really nice. Like someplace Frank would send me to get food to bring back to the Aerie. And I go crashing through all of it at very high speed.

My guess? It's time for the "taste" portion of the program. I have no time to even catch my breath before a giant hand grabs me by the cape and lifts me into the air like a doll. Perhaps we're skipping taste and going straight to touch.

La Cucaracha pulls me in close. I should have known.

"Hola, mi amigo."

Looks like he's back in fighting shape. And, with his body odor, he could have easily been the "smell" portion of their plan instead.

He doesn't realize it, but knowing what he did to Osprey gives me extra ammo to want to pound this oversized bug into the ground.

Who am I kidding? I'm exhausted, and I'm not sure how I'm even gonna make it through a fight with another boss, much less inflict any pain on them.

"Ay, Papi," he says, then chuckles as he flips me over, grabs one of my ankles, and lifts me completely above his head.

There's no way I'm defeating this monster in my condition. I might as well just give up now. He throws me at a thin metal sign that says, "Please seat yourself," but it might as well be a concrete wall. Groaning, I roll into another part of the gigantic room. When I come to a stop, I wanna lie there and just let him kill me. I'm ready for it to be over with.

But then I see them. Chef Maléfique. A couple regular Joe henchmen dressed like servers. Harrier. On the other side of the room. I'm so close to the end. I can't give up now.

La Cucaracha is gonna be on top of me any second now. I can hear him grunting as he walks toward me, his exo-suit making a whirring sound with each step. I feel around in my utility belt, trying to figure out what I might still have in there.

Most of the compartments are empty. Just a few throwing stars, but I know they're worthless against him.

My hand closes around a small metal tube. Pepper spray? I shrug internally. Why the hell not? Last-ditch effort. Go down fighting. He grabs me again. I spray it directly into his face, and he screams in rage. I'm not sure how much actually got into his eyes, though, because the eyeholes in his mask are pretty small. Either way, I can't believe that with all the high-tech weapons I usually have at my disposal, I took him down with something I can get at a convenience store for a couple of bucks.

I mean, I didn't actually take him down, but I slowed him long enough to gain a desperately needed advantage.

I pull out a throwing star and try cutting the cables again like last time, but it's useless. The new ones are made of some really strong material. I guess he—or, more likely, Chef Maléfique—wanted to make sure he couldn't be defeated as easily as he had been last time.

He starts spinning, metal appendages sticking out. He becomes a violent tornado, and I do my best to avoid him, but my luck has absolutely run out along with my energy. One hits me, and I'm sent staggering, and eventually, I'm on the floor again.

I lie there, trying not to just die, trying to will myself to move because if I don't, this guy is gonna recover and kill me. After a few failures where I topple into some of the dinner tables, I manage to stand weakly, and I grab something. I don't even know what it is. A chair leg? A signpost? It doesn't even matter what it is. Maybe I can use it to break the batteries in that power the suit. I know from past experience that when the suit's not working, La Cucaracha can barely move. Plus, he doesn't really know how to fight, so I'd be able to take him down quickly.

I swing directly at the batteries, but they're also made of something too strong to be affected by it. If I hadn't lost my new graphene staff on the bridge, I might have a shot, but now, I'm just desperately kicking and punching a couple of his more vulnerable areas. He barely notices as he spins and claws at his eyes.

Then, without warning, he stops and looks directly at me. His eyes bulge like an old cartoon, bright red, and full of hate. Two catcher's mitts grab me by my shoulders. His hands are absolutely massive. They lift me above his head again and tosses me across the room in Chef Maléfique's direction.

I allow myself to go limp, so I don't break anything as I hit the floor and roll once again to a stop. For a second, I feel like I can't move, and I'm worried I'm gonna be paralyzed. I wiggle my fingers and toes just to make sure I still can.

I look over at Harrier. He's seated—strapped to one of the chairs—at a table. The white tablecloth is stained red and pink from his blood. He tries to lift his head long enough to see if I'm okay and manages to get it up for a second, and in that second, I manage to squeak out an "I'm sorry."

La Cucaracha makes it over to me before I can even think about moving yet, and he's still in a rage. Looking at the bright side, if I live through this night, I don't think even Harrier could say he's gone head to head with this many rage-infected heroes and violent villains in one day.

La Cucaracha stands above me and, with a roar, lifts his foot for the killing blow. It's sort of funny in a morbid kind of way, him being a bug, doing what he's about to do. He's gonna literally stomp on my head, and I can just see every time I've ever killed a pest that way. Squish. Like a melon. There's no way I'm surviving this.

BLAM!

A shot rings out, and La Cucaracha slumps down, collapsing on top of me. He's so heavy, especially with the exo-suit, that it's only slightly better than having my head caved in under his boot. I keep thinking that the uber adrenaline people say moms get when their kids are in danger will kick in, but really, I might as well be trapped under a train or something.

Behind him stands Deadeye, once again holding an actual smoking gun in his hand. Chef Maléfique shoves him to the side as he throws a tantrum about La Cucaracha almost killing me.

"I warned him to stick to the plan. Why is it so difficult for everyone to stick to the plan?" He runs over and kicks La Cucaracha's lifeless body over and over, screaming like a little girl who had her ponytail pulled on the playground.

This is the first chance I have to get a good look at Chef Maléfique in person. So much different than in the pictures, video, and even while I was drugged up in the hospital. So much scarier. Who'd have thought a chef could be so terrifying? His face is painted like a mime... I guess more of the French influence. All black and white. His chef jacket is also stained with blood. And he's wearing one of those big floppy hats. He's way too overweight to be exerting himself this way, and he starts breathing heavily as the sweat smudges his makeup.

This is not what I was expecting at all. It's kind of... sad.

I try again to push La Cucaracha off of me, but he's far too heavy, or I'm way too weak. Probably both. Chef Maléfique finally stops and tries to calm himself, breathing heavily as if he'd just run a race.

"I never did like him anyway," Maléfique says. "Couldn't be even a bit original." He brushes his jacket off, smoothing out wrinkles. He snaps his fingers, and his two regular henchmen come over and—with a lot of effort—drag La Cucaracha off of me. Then they roughly help me get to my feet.

I thank them both by using my last bit of energy to knock them unconscious with roundhouse kicks to the head.

Chef Maléfique makes a tsk-ing sound. "Now, what did you go and do that for? Do you have any idea how hard it is to find good henchmen these days? And let me tell you, their union is a real problem. I can barely afford the overtime anymore."

I'm starting to see why criminals get so annoyed with the witty banter. It's no fun when you're on the other end of it.

Deadeye pulls his bo staff from its sheath on his back and faces me. I can barely stand, and my legs are shaking hard, but I try not to show it. He can probably kill me with one blow—what am I saying? He can *definitely kill me with one blow.* I've been going on fumes for too long now, and I don't think there's anything left in me. I've been ignoring my injuries because I'm afraid of what I'll find when I start to check them out. It's like I'm already defeated, and I haven't even gotten to my main enemy yet. I just have to go through the deadliest assassin on Earth to get to him.

"Where's Osprey?" I demand, but it comes out weak, just like me.

Deadeye shakes his skull-helmeted head.

No.

She's dead? She can't be dead. But if Deadeye is here, that means she lost.

"You bastard," I say. He pops me right in the mouth with the end of his staff and I taste blood. Really? After everything else, is that all there's going to be for the "taste" course of this meal?

I know if I let the emotion get to me, I'm a dead man walking.

So now, the only question left is whether Chef Maléfique had Deadeye shoot La Cucaracha to save me for himself, or if he wanted to give the assassin the honor of killing me. Thankfully, I get the answer right away.

"Mr. Deadeye," Maléfique says, huffing. "I believe I have this young man right where I need him at this point. Thank you for all your assistance with my grand plan—you were absolutely brilliant. Now go take the rest of the evening off."

Deadeye doesn't care about killing people. He's not one of those emotional thugs like Music Master or La Cucaracha. He's all about the money, and I'm guessing Maléfique paid him enough for his services already.

He just shrugs and puts his staff away. People always talk about letting out a breath they didn't know they were holding, and until now, I've always thought that was stupid. How could you not know you were holding your breath? But then, I notice I'm starting to breathe again. As Deadeye leaves the warehouse, I feel like I've been pardoned from a death sentence. Except the reality is that Chef Maléfique is far more dangerous than even Deadeye.

And now it's down to Chef Maléfique and me.

"Release Harrier. Now." With Deadeye gone, I get a little bit of confidence back, but I'm mostly faking it because I have nothing else to lose. I can't believe Osprey is dead.

"Oh… I see. You think you can just waltz into *my* restaurant and start barking orders. What in the world gave you that idea?"

I move toward him and make it clear with my body language that my intention is to beat him senseless.

"No. Nyet. Non. Nein. Don't step any closer, little bird. Or the girl gets it."

I look around. "What girl?"

Is she still alive?

Hope floods my chest as he walks over to a wine rack and swings one of the lower doors open. Osprey tumbles out to the floor, her hands bound with rope in front of her. She doesn't look too good.

Chef Maléfique holds Osprey by her hair—her real, black hair. Her costume is torn, and her cape is missing. She looks like she's nearly unconscious.

"I'm so glad you listened and brought your girlfriend, little birdie. She's oh-so-delicious. Once I'm done with you and Hack Derrière over there, I'm going to have *so* much fun with her." He sticks out his slimy tongue and licks her neck from her collarbone to her ear. She recoils enough to spit on his face, and he sticks out his tongue again to lick it off his own cheek.

I take a step toward him, but that causes him to yank her head back hard, so I stop. "Let her go. She isn't part of this."

"Isn't part of this? Of *course* she is. She was always part of the plan. You can't possibly think you met by accident, can you? Think about it. She was there when you needed her. To save you. To push you along. To make sure you got here. Did you think it was all a coincidence? Everyone works for the Chef."

What? *No.* He can't be telling the truth. What does he mean? That Osprey was working for him? For Harrier? What?

I go through everything in my mind. She showed up when I was falling, so she was watching me then. She was there when that punk tried to take my picture. And she somehow, she was there on the bridge, saved me from that criminal mob —Chef Maléfique's criminal mob—and took me to the hospital. Was she a spy for Chef Maléfique that whole time? Moving me toward coming here all along? Or is he just trying to get to me some more and make sure I don't trust anyone?

My features must give away what I'm thinking, because Osprey speaks even though it seems like it's a huge effort for her. "Not… true."

Chef Maléfique sneers. "Oh, don't be so modest, girl. You were wonderful. Don't denigrate your fantastic performance by pretending it was all real. I'm sure he knows deep down that someone like you would never want anything to do with someone like…" He turns and looks at me in disgust. "… *him*."

"You're lying."

"Oh, and her father…" Chef Maléfique says.

My heart drops further, if that's possible. He knows who she is? He knows Luis Chen is her father?

"Yes, yes. Luis Chen. I think he deserves the Academy Award for Longest Performance."

Chef Maléfique turns slightly toward Harrier.

"Played this sucker for the fool he is for… how many years?"

I just can't believe it could be true. The Chens working for Chef Maléfique? I've had my problems with Mr. Chen these past weeks, but he and Harrier go way back.

Osprey somehow gets up the strength to lift up her knee and then slam her foot back into his crotch. Maléfique snarls with rage and throws her down to the ground.

I run to her while the chef doubles over in pain, holding his junk. He makes a strange groaning noise that is gonna keep me awake at night if I ever get a chance to go to bed again after this.

Osprey looks up at me, her eyes pleading. She can barely get her words out through her sobbing. "Please. He's lying. Please don't..."

She passes out. She seems to be okay when I check her pulse and everything. I look back at Harrier to make sure he's still breathing. I'm done with this game. I have to get them both to a hospital right away.

At this point, I don't care who's telling the truth. Chef Maléfique's gonna pay for this. All of it.

I wipe blood from my face with my forearm—or it could be tears. Standing, I face Chef Maléfique, who is also trying to get up. The rage continues to build inside of me, and I can feel the adrenaline pumping again. I'm in bad shape myself. The injuries from my fight on the bridge hadn't healed yet, and now I have brand new ones that might even be worse, but I'm gonna finish this fight. And I'm gonna win.

Chef Maléfique holds up his hands. "Hold on. Before you get all punchie-hittie with me, there are some other things I think you're going to be very interested in hearing."

"This better be good."

Why am I even letting him talk? As long as he's talking, I can get some of my energy back.

"Oh, it's good. Very good. Much better than you can even imagine." He strolls over to Harrier and slaps him in the face. "You still awake, bird-brain? I'd hate for you to miss the most exciting part after three years of careful planning and moving everything into place."

Chef Maléfique grabs Harrier by the chin and lifts his head up. Harrier winces.

"Hands off him, or I kill you now," I say.

"You think he's trying to clean up the city because criminals killed his father? That *is* what he told you, yes?" He lets go of Harrier's chin, and Harrier grits his teeth as he tries to hold his head up. After a second, his neck gives out again. Silverware rattles as his head hits the table.

"Oh, no, no, no," Chef Maléfique continues. "You've got it all wrong, boy. The Black Harrier is just trying to clean up the mess his daddy left behind. As this city's top criminal. You see, his papa's death left quite a vacuum at the top of the underworld. And we've all been trying to fill it ever since."

I look at Harrier to see if there's any reaction to help me figure out if Maléfique is telling the truth, but he still can't lift his head.

I make a dismissive sound with my lips. "I don't care. Why should it matter to me *why* he does it? He's cleaning up the streets; getting rid of garbage like you."

"Why should it matter? Hmmm. Why *should* it matter?" He taps his index finger on his lip as if he's in deep thought, and turns back to Harrier. "What do you think, Frankie-boy? Should I tell him, or do you want to do the honors?"

With a considerable effort, Harrier raises his head and looks Chef Maléfique in the eye. His voice comes out as a rasp, but not like his voice-changer, not the kind I usually make fun of. It almost sounds like a death rattle. "… no…"

"Fine. Fine. Fine. I'll do it then." Maléfique waddles over to me and gets right up in my face, and I have to do everything in my power not to punch him as hard as I can.

"The first reason you should care, young man, is that your mentor here was the one who killed him."

No. It can't be. That's our number one rule. Our only rule. *No killing*. How could Harrier have started his career by killing his own father? I don't believe it. He's lying just like he's lying about the Chens.

"I know. Shocking, isn't it? But this squeaky-clean do-gooder just couldn't handle the idea that his father was such a notorious blaggard, and it simply drove him over the edge. But wait… there's more! It gets better."

It makes me sick to see Chef Maléfique relishing this so much. I'm not sure how much of my shaking is adrenaline, how much is due to my injuries and weakness, and how much is just from me wanting to thrash this evil bastard.

"The second reason—the most important reason—is that Franklin Douglas Jr., kingpin of crime for many years, and responsible for more death, destruction, and misery than anyone else in this city's long history... Oh… wait for it... This is so good. Is there someone to give me a drumroll?"

He looks around at the dead and unconscious men throughout the room. Then he does a little drumroll with his tongue.

"Was your granddaddy!"

As my head tries to wrap itself around what Chef Maléfique just said, I see a look of satisfaction stream across his face like I've never witnessed from another person. It takes a second for me to register exactly what he means, but when it hits me, it hits me hard—like getting the wind knocked out of me.

And then Maléfique literally knocks the wind out of me. I hadn't even noticed how close he'd gotten, and he punches me in the stomach, and I feel my diaphragm push all of the air out of my lungs. I lean forward and gasp for breath, and he hits me with an uppercut so hard that I feel myself standing up straight before falling back and hitting the ground.

Then he kicks me. First, in the ribcage, then again in the kidneys. That's when it becomes glaringly apparent that he's wearing steel-toed shoes. I cough, and blood comes up.

All fight is gone. I just wanna lay here. To let him finish me off. It can't be true. But what if it is?

Chef Maléfique looks down at me, and I imagine that he's gonna start laughing, but then I remember what Redhawk said about him being deadpan. In fact, I don't remember him laughing at all during the two times we've interacted or on video. He could kill me now, right in front of Harrier, but he's making sure what he revealed to me is sinking in.

My brain is trying to calculate how Harrier's dad could be my grandfather without it being the obvious answer. I met my mom's dad when I was little, before he died, so that can't be it. Could my dad have been Harrier's brother? No—he was definitely an only child.

That only leaves one other option. But it feels so wrong that my mind rebels against it. Pushes it out as if it's poison.

I force myself to my hands and knees, blood dripping from me like drool. I turn to Harrier. "Is it true?"

No response.

"He's just saying it to get to me, right? To mess with my head." Harrier continues to just sit there, his head pressed against the table, arms bound behind the chair. I crawl over to him and get up close. Close enough that he can see me without lifting his head. I can hear Chef Maléfique following slowly behind me. He wants this. He wants me to experience every second of it.

"Is. It. *True*?" I ask again.

His response is barely a whisper. If it wasn't so quiet in here, I wouldn't have been able to hear it. "Yes."

Flames well up inside of me. Ones that I have to release. But I can't take it out on Harrier. Not right now. I spring from my position on the floor like a wild animal and land on Maléfique's rotund chest, knocking him to the ground. He wasn't ready for it one bit, and his head smacks against the floor.

I start pounding on his face with my fists. One after another and then again. Even with all the violence I've witnessed and participated in, I've never seen anyone beaten as savagely as what I'm dishing out myself right now. It's like it's not even me—I feel like I'm watching everything happen on a TV show or in a video game. I don't even know how long it goes on for. My fists are stained with blood, and the makeup on Chef Maléfique's face is now just a black and white smear.

Through the rage and the hitting, I somehow hear it. I don't know how many times he said it before I noticed, but it barely registers in my ears. Harrier's raspy, almost inaudible voice.

"Stop."

I freeze, crouched on Chef Maléfique's chest, my right fist raised high, ready to piston down. I'm breathing heavily, and I can feel my heartbeat throbbing in my head. I look down at Maléfique's beaten, bloody face, barely clinging on to life. I watch as a drop of blood falls from my fist into the middle of his forehead and mixes with the swath of the stuff already there.

I look back at Harrier and see tears streaming down his face… the first time I've ever seen him cry.

Then Chef Maléfique spits out some teeth and talks to me, his speech distorted by his broken nose and busted lips. "Do it."

And he laughs. For the first time, I hear the bastard laugh, and it's more frightening than anything else he's done. Sick, twisted… evil.

And I suddenly realize why I'm really here. The truth about what's going on. Chef Maléfique didn't lure me down here to kill me in front of Harrier. He'd already done that before with another Red Kite, and Harrier came back stronger. than ever. He wanted me to kill *him* in front of Harrier. To break me. To get me to become the one thing Harrier and I could never live with: a murderer.

And it almost worked.

I roll off of him and look at his plump, broken face as he continues to laugh. At the very least, he has a concussion, a broken nose, and a dislocated jaw. Probably a detached retina. But he'll live if we get an ambulance here soon.

I manage to get myself up and stagger over to Harrier. Pulling my lock picks out again, I unlock the chains holding him and try to help him to prevent him from dropping to the ground and injuring himself even more. I lower him to the floor, and he lies there momentarily, near unconsciousness. I need to call for an ambulance now that the building is secured. There's no way I can handle this myself at the Aerie.

Somewhere in my periphery, I notice Osprey stirring.

Then, Black Harrier does something more superhuman than anything I've ever known even Eaglestar to pull off, and pushes himself up to his hands and knees.

"You should relax, Harrier, we'll have help on the way soon." But he ignores me completely. "Frank, it's over."

Harrier starts to crawl over to Maléfique, who continues his insane fit of laughter. He reaches his nemesis and leans over him, barely able to hold himself up. If anything, Chef Maléfique is laughing even harder now, gasping for breath. Maniacal.

Harrier grabs both sides of his mortal enemy's head. "Shut. Up." He twists Chef Maléfique's head quickly, and there's a sickening crunch.

And the laughter stops.

CHAPTER **TWENTY-SEVEN**

Dad.

Not a word I'm all too familiar with, especially when it comes to addressing someone. It's too weird for me to call Harrier that. At least for now. Plus, I don't think that's what he wants anyway.

Mr. Chen—who absolutely wasn't working for Chef Maléfique, by the way—helped create a story about how Franklin Douglas III had been kidnapped and held for ransom by some Middle Eastern regime that he'd fought against in the war. It explains his condition, as well as why Frank hasn't appeared in public for so long.

At first, I didn't wanna see him because I was so angry. I'd gone to the hospital, but only to visit Osprey—Amy Chen. She was in a wheelchair for a couple of weeks after the fight with Deadeye, but she was healing quickly and back on her feet in no time.

Turns out, her dad doesn't even know she's Osprey. She begged me not to tell him, and I agreed. How could I not? I keep it from my mom.

About a year ago, she was borrowing one of her dad's computers without him knowing and came across some information on Harrier and all the tech he uses. Because she's so good with all of that, she was able to not only access a lot more, but get a hold of some of the spare stuff at Douglas Industries. When I think about how much she did on her own, plus the fact that she's been able to hide it all from someone like Chen, I'm even more impressed with her than ever.

One day, I show up to see her, and she's gone. So, already there, I figure I'll swallow my pride, and wander down the hall to the private rooms where Frank is recovering.

I don't knock. He's just staring at the wall, sitting upright in a bed that is a million steps above the one I'd been given after my battle on the bridge.

"I guess I owe you an explanation," he says without looking at me.

"You think?"

I'd planned to go easy on him at first, with how bad off he is physically and after all the psychological torture he must have endured. But you know what? He's a big boy, and he's gotta own up to this. It's time for him to give me some answers.

I start with the most important part.

"Why the hell didn't you tell me I was your son? And what about Mom? Seriously? You live in a damn Manhattan penthouse while we eat crap in a dump of an apartment in Brooklyn? Please, try to spin it, but no matter how you slice it, Frank... it's bullshit."

I expect him to tell me to watch my language or my tone, but instead, he just says, "You're right."

I wait for him to say more, but he doesn't.

"Nope. Nu-uh. You don't get your five syllables or less answer. Not this time."

"All right." He takes a breath. "I didn't know you existed until just before I showed up in that alley. Your mom and I met when we were young. I had no idea she was still in high school. She got into a club I own with a fake I.D. I never saw her again after our one night together, and she never contacted me about being pregnant. I get the impression she wasn't sur—"

He cuts himself off, but I know what he's gonna say. She wasn't sure who the father was, because he wasn't the only guy she'd been with around that time. Knowing my mom, this isn't a surprise to me, and I'm long past it bothering me.

I'm still pissed at him for a lot, but I figure I'll let him continue. "So what changed?"

"A few years ago, I was contacted by a sleazy lawyer who claimed I had a child out there I wasn't aware of. Apparently, your mom had been dating him, and mentioned that she had, uh, been 'seeing' me shortly before you were born."

He pauses and takes a long drink from a hospital water bottle. Now that I think of it, I'm actually shocked they don't have him recuperating somewhere else. I mean, the private suite here is nice, but this is one of the richest men alive. And his next statement confirms that.

"A man of my considerable means and... reputation is always slapped with paternity suits, most of which turn out to be false. The few that aren't, I... well, I make sure they're taken care of."

I can only hope he means financially, but now isn't the time to ask him to be more specific about that.

"This guy was different. He was ready to go to the papers, the news channels, the entire internet. He didn't give a damn about me helping you or your mom; he was more interested in how much money he could squeeze out of me if he kept quiet about it. As you can imagine, I don't appreciate being blackmailed."

Derek—I vaguely remember my mom being with him for a month or so. He was a douche. Couldn't stand him. Frank hasn't even told me what happened next, and I already feel sorry for this guy. Not really...

"I'd been on a... break from crime-fighting, but it got me motivated again." I figure this must have been the time after the second Kite was killed. That would go along with what Redhawk told me.

"So, Harrier paid him a visit. It didn't take much for me to uncover several things that would not only get him disbarred but sent to prison, including jury tampering."

He smiles, and it kind of scares me because it isn't the fake Frank Douglas smile he uses in public. It's the smile Black Harrier gets on the rare occasion when he enjoys his job.

"I also maybe… roughed him up a bit. Just enough to make sure he left Frank Douglas alone, as well as anyone else he was thinking about extorting. I also found out that your mom had no idea what he was doing."

That's a relief. My mom isn't perfect, but I'd hate to think she's capable of such heinous things.

Derek… what was his last name?

I guess it doesn't matter, but I always wondered what happened to that guy. Not that my mom doesn't break up with guys often, but I do remember that relationship ending so abruptly that it puzzled her.

"Didn't it matter to you that you might actually have a kid out there?" I ask.

I notice the blip of his heart rate increasing a bit before he answers.

"Of course it did. Just because I wouldn't allow that ambulance-chaser to blackmail me doesn't mean I didn't want to make things right."

He's so vehement about this that I have no doubt he's being honest.

"I immediately started investigating the situation. You, your mom, everything I could find. My plan was to get ahold of some of your DNA and test it against my own. But I didn't need to."

"Why?"

"Because that day you were attacked while I was observing you… I saw you fight. You copied my moves exactly, and took out those thugs without much effort."

I think back to that first day we met. It's strange to hear about it from his point of view. This is also the most I've ever heard him talk at one time.

"Your ability is rare. Very few others have it, but I'm one of them. And I knew immediately you'd inherited it from me. That's why I took you on as a protégé and began training you. So you could use it properly and stay out of danger."

"But… how could you let me keep living in those crappy conditions when you knew I was your son?"

"Because I couldn't take you away from your mom, but I couldn't give her access to a lot of money either. I had Chen send a few checks from Douglas Industries at first—not much, but nothing to sneeze at, either—under the ruse that she was part of some class-action lawsuit against the company. I had to know how she would react." He takes another long drink.

"And...?"

"And she immediately blew it all on herself and her vices. From what I could tell, she didn't spend a red cent on you or make any attempt to make your life better."

The look on my face must be pretty bad, because he looks like he doesn't wanna go on.

"I'm sorry, I shouldn't—"

"No." I shake my head. "I wanna know the truth. All of it."

No matter how much it hurts.

"I was afraid that if she had even more money, she'd end up overdosing or drinking herself to death. So instead, I tried to help you out directly. Buying good food, electronic devices, letting you hang around the Aerie as often as possible."

So many things make more sense now, including why it seemed Alex got shafted out of things I didn't… like Amber. Shudder.

You know, I don't know what pisses me off more, the fact that he lied to me, or that I'm not even mad about it anymore.

"Well, I'm glad I know now. When will you be able to return to crimefighting?" I ask.

Just as he's about to respond, a doctor enters and starts talking about discharging Frank, finally.

"Look, Sawyer," Frank says. "I've got to handle this. Why don't you come by my place tomorrow night? We can talk more. I'll order in some *Le Meilleur Plat.*"

I cringe, and he adds, "Maybe something less... French."

We both laugh.

I wave and leave Frank alone with the doctor to discuss things.

The next morning, I'm up early, hoping to leave for school before Mom can stop me. I'd been more or less avoiding her since the whole "escaping the hospital" incident. Except she's already made me a Pop-Tart and is waiting with her purse by the front door.

"Oh, hey, Mom," I say, snatch the pastry from the counter. It's still hot, and I juggle it in my hand while doing my best to skirt by her.

"Not so fast, Mister," she says.

Groan.

I hate it when she calls me that.

"I'm taking you today."

"Wait… What? Why? You don't have to do that." I push by her again, and she grabs my arm, spinning me to face her.

"Actually, I do. You've been absent for so long that Mr. Blanchard called to say I needed to sign you back in. Besides, you haven't exactly been forthcoming with me lately, and I'm going to make sure you get to class. God, that still looks really bad." She pushes her thumb against my cheek, where Sinsation kicked me. Only moms do that. Touch the place where they know you're hurt, like somehow it's helping. I wince and pull away.

"So, what—you don't trust me now?" She'd be an idiot if she did. I don't let her answer. "You know how embarrassing it is for my mom to walk me to school?"

"Oh, you want to talk about embarrassing? How about having a son who *escapes* a hospital room in the middle of the night?"

She won't let it go… keeps harping on it day in and day out. Apparently, it's time for round thirty-two.

"I told you I was sorry. It was the drugs. I was freaked out and paranoid, and I just… I don't know? Snapped."

"So you've said."

She leaves it at that, then shoves me out the door. Not hard, but enough for me to know any argument will be moot.

We walk in silence all the way to my school. When we get there, I do my best to avert my gaze from everyone pointing and grinning at the loser walking through the front doors with his mommy.

First stop, the school office. Mr. Blanchard's secretary stares at me. It takes a moment for me to realize there's something like sympathy in her eyes.

"Mr. Blanchard should be expecting us," Mom says. "I'm Ms.—"

"Vincent," the secretary says. "Yes, yes. Sawyer, you look… Are you sure you're ready to come back to school?"

I turn to my mom whose face seems to say, "Yes, you are."

"Yeah. I… it looks worse than it is."

Mr. Blanchard comes out a few seconds later and gives my mom the same look his secretary gave me. Like he's apologizing to her for having to deal with me, or something.

"Mr. Vincent, why don't you go ahead and get to class? Your mother and I will get things squared away here."

Again, I eye my mom, and she nods me along.

"Yeah. Okay." I readjust my backpack, trying to keep my face straight as my textbooks poke into my bruised ribs.

I hear them talking in hushed voices as I leave, but I'm so beyond caring what they say or think. If they only knew I'd saved the Black Harrier and stopped the city from descending into absolute mayhem…

I round a corner toward my locker and see Javi standing there. He rushes to meet me midway.

"I heard you were coming back today. What happened? Are you okay? I—"

"I'm fine," I say. "Just a few bruises still healing."

"Looks worse than that," he says.

"Looks worse than it is," I say for the second time in as many minutes.

"That's good. I… so…" He starts a few sentences but I'm distracted.

Over his shoulder, I see Logan strutting toward us. His shiner from where I'd decked him at Fabiola's party is healed up, but I wouldn't mind giving him another one.

"You know what, Javi? I think it's time for your first karate lesson."

"What? Now? Here?"

"Sup, loser?" Logan says, literally shoving Javi aside. "The hell happened to you?"

I glance at Javi and smile.

"Oh, you didn't hear?" I reply.

Logan just stares at me like a gorilla in a cage. I wouldn't be surprised if he starts scratching his ass.

"I was down in Times Square when that concert was going on, and everyone went nuts."

"That right?"

"Yeah, I don't remember much of it. Police just said I cracked. Nearly killed a guy." I get a crazy look in my eye and step so close to him, I can smell his gross breath. "Now, I'm on all kinds of meds just to keep me from doing it again."

Logan backs away. Tries to make it look like he's just shuffling his feet, but I know when someone is scared. I follow him.

"They don't even know what caused it… neither do I. One minute I'm fine and then the next, WHAM!" I crack my hands together, and he stumbles back into the lockers behind him.

After a nervous titter, he steps aside. "Yeah, well... whatever. We didn't miss you, dork."

He doesn't stick around for me to respond and definitely walks away faster than normal.

I smile again, then turn back to Javi, who looks just as terrified as Logan.

"Whoa," he whispers. "That really happen?"

I shake my head. "Not a word..." That's not entirely true. I *was* in Times Square...

"So why—"

"Lesson number one: it's better to intimidate your foe into backing out of a fight than engaging in combat. Come on." I throw my arm around Javi's shoulder. "Let's get to class."

My mom thinks I'm going to Douglas Industries for my community service, so she doesn't give me crap when I don't come home after school.

I enter the Aerie through the hatch. It's dark and cold, but that's normal.

"Kite... Sawyer, right here," Frank says. No voice box, but still only five syllables.

I cross the room and find him standing by the display cases containing the Red Kite costumes. A new one is erected next to them, and in it, the black and gray "uniform" I've become so familiar with over the years.

"What are you doing?" I ask.

"I've been through too much," he says, adjusting the cape on the invisible mannequin. "I'm getting too old. And I broke the rule we're never allowed to break."

"What are you saying?"

He turns to face me. "I'm done."

"Don't be crazy." I laugh, but it's definitely just awkwardness. "This city needs you."

He grunts. "It's time for someone else to take over as the Black Harrier."

The shock is so much, I almost feel the blow physically.

"Me?"

He shakes his head and turns back to his uniform. "You're not ready yet."

As if on cue, the swishy door that leads to the training rooms opens, and someone comes through, dressed in a new Harrier costume. He's still pulling on the gloves as he approaches us. He's not wearing a mask yet, and I recognize him immediately.

"Alex!" I run over to him, full bore, without even thinking about it. "How did you—I thought you were—"

"Hey, kid. Yeah, so did I. Glad to see you're okay."

"What happened?" I ask.

"Don't know. Not really. I'm not sure how long I was in the river, but I woke up on a fishing boat after some guys pulled me out of the water. I wasn't in as bad of shape as I should've been, but it still took me a little while to recover. Not nearly as long as this guy though, right?"

He points to Frank.

I didn't see it before, but as Frank struggles, I notice the cane he uses to limp over to Alex. "How's it fit? Chen worked hard on it."

"Great."

"Wow," I say under my breath. His new suit is badass. So much cooler than Frank's ever was.

Alex—Harrier, I guess?—turns to me. "Well? Are you going to be my sidekick or what?"

"Whoa," I say. "We don't use the 's' word around here."

He laughs and stretches his hand out. Before I shake it, I turn to Frank. He nods, and I extend my hand, but this time, Alex pulls back and looks to Frank.

"You sure you're ready to do this? No turning back?"

"You're the Black Harrier now."

"Good. Because I've made my first big decision already. I figure I'm going to need some extra help out there until I get up to your level, so I invited someone else to come along."

Osprey steps through the entrance and takes in the posh surroundings of the penthouse lair. "Nice crib."

Frank gets his old look back. "I thought I said—"

"Ah-ah-ah. I'm the Black Harrier now, and I get to choose my own sidekicks."

Osprey and I both respond at the exact same time. "*Partners.*"

"Oh. Right. Sorry."

"My dad doesn't know. I'd appreciate it if everyone would just let me tell him my own way," she tells Frank.

"You're an adult. You make your own decisions," he responds. Then, he turns to Alex. "She gets approved by the Guild before she even talks about crime-fighting. That understood? I may not be the Black Harrier anymore…"

He lets his words linger on the air.

"Yes, sir," Alex says, saluting Frank. "I'll make sure of it."

Frank grunts again.

Alex shakes his head, laughing a little as Frank turns back to the display cases.

"Well, then," he says, heading toward the door. "Let's go, *partners*."

I follow him, and he stops.

"One more thing," he says, looking at me directly.

"Yeah?"

"I hope you don't mind… I took Amber." He smiles, and so do I, more than a little relieved if I'm being honest. "Let's go kick some ass?"

I'm definitely in the mood to beat up some bad guys.

EPILOGUE

BATTLEGEAR

Idiots.

That's what they are. Every last one of them. We had a whole team together, ready to finally take on the Guild. I had a perfect plan in place this time. It would have been big. The biggest. The greatest heist in the history of humankind.

We all could have been rich beyond our wildest dreams if they had just listened to me. But they have no self-control. The attention span of goldfish, the lot of them. That rotund chef threw a few silver coins in their direction, and they all abandoned our plan in an instant, said they'd get back to it.

"Just hold on, Battlegear, and when this is done we'll do your thing," they promised.

"Plus, we won't have Black Harrier in our way anymore. One less hero to worry about..." they surmised.

Yeah? How'd *that* work out for you, morons?

"Don't do it!" I said.

"The guy's insane. Literally!" I warned.

"There's no way this works out in our favor," I predicted.

Hey, but why listen to me? I only have one of the greatest intellects in the country. Plus a preternatural skill with technology. You think I became Eaglestar's archnemesis because I'm a pushover? Because I don't know what I'm doing?

What was it Maléfique had going for him again? Oh, yeah—he was batcrap crazy and liked to kill everything in sight, including his own henchmen and teammates. He liked to taunt heroes until they were so angry they went overboard and caused traumatic injuries to everyone they were fighting. That's beneficial! Oh, wait, I can see now why they went with him instead. It makes perfect sense, right?

They're all in prison now. Or worse. Look at the Cockroach. Bullet to the forehead—by his own employer, even! All except for Deadeye, anyway. But that guy was already a loose cannon. I think I'll pass.

You want to get rich living a life of crime? Don't work with the evil ones. Stay away from the crazy ones. Work with guys like me who are in it for the cash. Who can think straight. Who don't get off on blowing up sidekicks just because they want attention.

Oh well, back to square one. I was tired of working with those imbeciles all those years anyway. Time for some new blood. Some clay I can mold into what I need, rather than broken-down old has-beens like Creeping Death and Med-Evil.

I already have my new plan. I don't need people with powers. I'll provide the powers. I don't need pros with "experience" who are going to contradict me at every turn. All they need is a few practice heists, and we'll be ready for the big time.

And those feeble-minded fools—the ones who are still alive, anyway—can watch my new team execute our plan on the tiny television screens in their prison rec rooms and cry in their prison lunches and rock themselves to sleep in their prison bunks as they think about how it could have been them.

Now all I need is to find some young, naive people who are real lowlifes to set things in motion…

SUPERTEAM

RAPTORS BOOK 2

To my grandparents—Lou and Angela Puma*. Grandpa, I wish I could still hear you cheer me on, though I know you are…*

"Therefore, since we are surrounded by so great a cloud of witnesses, let us also lay aside every weight, and sin which clings so closely, and let us run with endurance the race that is set before us…"
Hebrews 12:1
—J.C.

To my family.
—CJV

PROLOGUE

ALEX

B*oston.*

A city I'd grown to love over the past several years. I moved here of my own choosing after leaving New York—leaving Franklin Douglas III, the Black Harrier—and I'm proud to say, I made it my own. One of the first decisions in my entire life I actually made for myself, despite being an adult at the time.

My parents were killed when I was young—really brutally in front of me and my brother. It was a mob hit gone bad and we were at the wrong restaurant in Brooklyn at the wrong time. After that, my guardians at Saint Barnabas Home for Boys made all my decisions for me. Haven't seen my brother in so long, I don't even know if I'd recognize him.

Then, Frank took over—but never as my legal guardian… never adopted. I became his sidekick, the first Red Kite.

It wasn't until he decided not to let me move in with him—a rejection I was not prepared for after everything I'd been through—that I left. I even got permission from the Guild, despite Frank's objections, something I now realize was a pretty amazing feat under the circumstances.

They were all too happy to have a new hero in Boston. About a year before I moved here, their resident masked crimefighter, the Fenway Flipster, died doing the thing he was best at. You guessed it. Flipping.

That guy was the best of the best when it comes to acrobatics. Trust me, I know a thing or two. I'm no spring chicken in that department. From the stories, he was chasing down a baddie and went to do his signature, a corkscrew 180 in which he would flip over the perp while spinning, land in front of them and take them out with any number of moves.

It was January. He slipped on some black ice when he landed, cracked his head open on the sidewalk. If I recall, the crime he was trying to stop was silly. A stolen watch or something. Definitely not worth the life of a stellar hero.

I've since made up with Frank, who—due to the physical and mental repercussions of his abduction by Chef Maléfique last year—is unable to continue as the Black Harrier. That mantle has been passed on to me. Sort of. I'm the Black Harrier now. Something I would have thought impossible for so many reasons, for so many years.

Basically the coolest, best thing that's happened to me in the jacked-up situation that I call a life. I couldn't be happier.

Or, should I say, if I was allowed to actually do it, I couldn't be happier?

Because the Guild giveth and the Guild taketh away.

We all assumed—me, Frank, Sawyer, and Amy—that there was no reason to think I wouldn't be able to immediately assume the position, and move back to New York, with Sawyer—the Red Raptor—and Amy—Osprey—as my partners. And for weeks, that's how we operated, just waiting for the Guild's official blessing. Its rubber stamp.

Oh, how wrong we were.

The Guild, primarily that egotistical blowhard Eaglestar, decided to force me to return and stay in Boston as Redhawk until they figure out what to do about replacing me there.

"We've already suffered this city for too long after the Flipster's death. To take you away now would cause pandemonium," he'd said.

And they can't just have Black Harrier suddenly showing up in Boston—that wouldn't make any sense, at least according to their logic. What, masked crimefighters aren't allowed to relocate? It's not like people don't understand that we're *actual* people. But you try arguing with the most powerful being in the world. Go ahead. I'll wait. No? Didn't think so.

So here I am, back in the red-and-silver, fighting on my own, two hundred miles away while my partners try to take up the slack in New York. I mean, sure, the city's secret crime lord, Chef Maléfique, was killed—by Frank b-t-dubs—and most of the other supervillains in the city—La Cucaracha, Deadeye, Music Master, Creeping Death, and Sinsation to name a few—were taken out or arrested in the process, so it's not like they have an impossible task. But the city's other heroes seem to have disappeared as well in the last year. And it's still New York, which means plenty of normal crime, so Sawyer and Amy are getting somewhat overwhelmed.

Being stuck in Boston sucks. And my resentment is causing me to hate this city more and more every day. I mean, why did I even choose Boston in the first place? Because my favorite show to watch in the boys' home as a kid was repeats of *Cheers*? I don't even remember.

Maybe I really didn't want to be all that far away from Frank, and was hoping he'd try to make amends and have me come back someday.

Anyway, I'm taking out my frustrations now on the local riff-raff. I almost feel sorry for them. But they're criminals, so I get over it really fast.

Currently, a group of very drunk guys come out of the most famous bar in Boston—yeah, that one—and starts following a couple of young women through the park across Beacon Street. They're dressed in very expensive suits and look like they're made of money. And they act like that entitles them to whatever they want. In this case, said women.

They catch up and start harassing the girls, even trying to grab them and get them to stop walking. To the ladies' credit, they calmly ask the guys to cut it out. But of course, they don't. It's, like, five on two.

No means no, boys.

Then they start to become more insistent. The guys, I mean. They circle around the women, easily preventing them from moving. That's my cue to swoop down and step in.

"All right fellas, better move along. Go home and sleep it off."

"Screw you, Redwing." The biggest guy says, slurring his words.

"It's Redhawk."

"Whatever. Screw you. We ain't ascared of you. Are we guys?"

His four buddies don't look so sure, but they're too drunk and too embarrassed to back down. They just shake their heads.

"See that, Tweety? Why should be we ascared of you? It ain't like you're the Black Harrier or something. Nobody even knows you."

That jab gets to me. I *am* Black Harrier. I notice my hands balling into fists.

"Tweety," I say with a little scoff. "I told you, it's Redhawk."

"See? That's my point. Nobody cares."

He's too drunk to realize I've been slowly inching toward him while he runs his stupid, rich mouth. He opens it again to say something snide and I punch him in the face. Way harder than I should. Blood flies from his nose as his eyes roll back in his head as he falls straight back, already unconscious before hitting the ground. It would be comical if I wasn't worried that I might have killed him.

"Amber, is he still breathing?" I ask under my breath.

Amber is the AI in my helmet that helps me out. It used to belong to Sawyer, and Frank before him, but one of the perks of becoming Black Harrier was taking her—*it*—back.

"Yes, Alex. His vital signs are stable. And wow, did you look good doing it. Perfect form."

"Cool. Thanks. Call an ambulance, please."

"Anything you say, sweetie. I'm on it."

The guy's friends decide to stick up for their ostensible leader and come at me together at the same time. Big mistake. Even if they weren't all fall-down drunk, I could take on all four of these schmucks with one hand tied behind my back. In my sleep. Too many idioms?

"Guys, that's not a good—"

They charge me and yell at the same time. I can smell the alcohol on their breath from a couple yards away, it's so strong.

As soon as they're close enough for me to reach them, I slip into a ducking roll and they slam together like some old-timey film. I'm in no mood to waste any more time on them.

They all stumble, and two fall limply to the ground like sacks of potatoes. This is the important work I'm doing for the fine people of Boston. Rounding up drunks.

I smile at the ladies, who are standing there watching, expecting a 'thank you' or something.

One of the remaining drunks, smartly, fumbles his way back toward the bar but the other comes at me and I sidestep, hook my boot around his feet and let him topple unceremoniously to the grass. He'll probably take a good nap there and wake up soaked from the sprinklers.

"Yaw wicked mean!" One of the girls says in a really strong accent.

"Yah. Ya didn't have ta knock em out that way. Ya could'a just told em to leave us alone Naw they're just lyin there in the middle ah the pahk."

They walk away shaking their heads. How does the saying go? *No good deed goes unpunished.*

Then I get a call on my helmet comm. I wander away from the scene so I can hear over the approaching sirens.

"Redhawk?" He asks in that booming baritone of his.

"Yeah?" I recognize the voice immediately, but it's such a shock to be getting a call from the big man himself, Eaglestar, that I still can't quite comprehend it. He continues before I can fully process who I'm talking to.

"Hello, Alexander. Is this a bad time?"

"Uh... no, I just finished knocking some heads together on the Common. Just outside the Bull and Finch, in fact."

There's a pause on the other end. He has no idea what I'm talking about. Why would he? The guy's a relic from World War II who doesn't age and just happens to shoot friggin laser beams out of his eyes. Among other things.

"Yes, well, I have something to speak with you about. Guild business."

My ears perk up at that. One of the many reasons I was so excited to become Black Harrier was that I assumed I would take over Frank's position in the core of the Guild instead of staying on as an ancillary member.

"Am I finally going to be Black Harrier?" I try not to sound overly excited, but it's hard not to.

"In a manner of speaking. You see, we still haven't found your replacement for Boston, and Osprey and the Red Kite seem to be staying on top of things in New York." He refuses to let Sawyer become Red Raptor. Still. After all this time...

"Okay...?" I have no idea what he's getting at.

"The thing is, people are starting to notice that Black Harrier hasn't been around for quite some time, especially when it comes to Guild missions."

What he means to say is *important* missions. Not meaningless, day-to-day crimefighting like slapping around some drunk hooligans in Beantown. He's talking about world-threatening events like alien invasions.

"Yeah, I kind of figured that." *No kidding, super-genius.*

"We were hoping you'd be of a mind to participate in a very special event next month as the Black Harrier in New York in addition to maintaining your position as Redhawk in Boston."

"You... want me to be *both*?"

"Yes. That would be ideal."

Ridiculous. I should reject this. It's asking way too much of me. Just like asking two teenagers to patrol all of New York is asking too much of them. *Of course* my answer is...

"Yes! I would love to! When do you need me there?"

ONE

SAWYER

Seventeen.

That's how old I'm supposed to turn tomorrow, but I'm pretty sure I'm not gonna live to see it.

No, it's nothing like that. No supervillain, hanging me upside down over a pit full of hungry cats—though that had happened once before, believe it or not.

And I don't mean tabbies. There was a lion, a tiger, a panther, and either a leopard or cheetah. I'm still not sure which since I was little too busy trying to escape to get a good look. All I remember was it had spots.

And big, sharp teeth.

It was when I'd first started working with Harrier. Back then, there was a new villain on the block. Guy named Dr. Delay. Now, he's kind of a joke among supervillains, but at the start, he'd actually come up with the occasional trap that worked. That was one of them. Big, hangry cats.

I was completely tied up and hanging upside-down, and the line was slowly lowering toward the pit. I'm sure, to them, I was just another slab of meat to fight over.

How did I get there? Let's just say I wasn't as good at my job back then and leave it at that. Thanks.

Fine. I guess I owe you something.

I'd just tracked Dr. Delay to some hideout in the Bronx when I felt a sharp pain in my neck. Reaching up, I pulled away a small dot of blood and a tranquilizer dart as I felt myself passing out and hitting the floor.

When I woke up, I was there, inside some kind of old warehouse. Isn't it always? At least Delay kept his place cleaner than most, I'll give him that. Though, it wasn't much of a consolation since my hands and feet were bound and I was hanging by a rope from a winch. And did I mention it was slowly lowering me? I think I did.

The guy is definitely beyond OCD. I remember everything being brand new and the cats even being well-groomed. Morbid a thought as it was, I also remember thinking there were worse places to die. I would hate for my final resting place to be some disgusting pit like the places where I used to end up fighting La Cucaracha before Deadeye killed him last year.

At the time, I had no idea where Harrier was. Before the whole tranq thing, he'd told me over comms to wait outside and he wasn't far away, but I wasn't given that luxury.

Now, I don't know if you've ever found yourself dangling just a few feet above a pit of deadly carnivores, but it's kind of nerve-wracking. They were jumping as high as they could and swinging katana-like claws at me like I was a superhero piñata. I figured I had less than thirty seconds until I was at the point where they could reach me, or at least give me a close buzzcut.

Then I'd have been lunch.

I'm not gonna insult you by not at least acknowledging that you *know* I didn't die. I mean, come on, I'm telling you the story. But still, it was really messed up. One of the craziest moments in my career. At the time, I really thought I was done for… then I heard it.

"Kite!" I'd never been so relieved to hear Harrier's stupid voice-changer. "Get some momentum and swing yourself back and forth."

I did as he said, but I wasn't sure how it was gonna help. I mean, there was no way I was gonna swing out past the edge of the opening to the pit. And there was no way he could've reached me in time.

Plus, by that point, I felt like the cats considered me a giant play toy, and were trying even harder to snatch me. You ever swung a ball of yarn or something in front of a cat? Turns out they like that, no matter how big they are. I bent my body as I swung past the middle, and it was just in time because the tiger only missed my head by a couple of inches.

I felt the line go slack and I started to fall.

I think I prayed. I don't know. I mean… you would've too.

SLAM! Someone plowed into me in midair, and we continued just past the edge of the pit and rolled away.

"How'd you do that?" I asked Harrier as he rushed over to help me out of the bindings.

He held up a version of his boomerang I hadn't seen before, with a sharp metal blade on the inside edge. Now, I carry one just like it everywhere I go.

"I'm still working on it," he said. "But it seemed like a good time to try it out."

"You think? I'm just glad it worked."

And that your aim is so good.

At that moment, I remember it like it was yesterday, Dr. Delay burst into the room with two of his minions. If I hadn't been so relieved, I probably would've burst out laughing. The dude's costume is pretty ridiculous—not the typical leather or armor-type getup that most crimefighters and villains wear at all. Still, to this day, he wears old-fashioned spandex tights, a pointless cape, and some fancy headgear that doesn't even match his theme. And don't even get me started with the symbol on his chest. I'm pretty sure it's supposed to be some variation of the "don't walk" sign when you cross the street. You know? Delay? So stupid.

"Get them!" he shouted.

I assume he was watching the whole thing unfold on a screen from some kind of evildoer control room. Henchmen shoved through the door behind him. More generic-type guys wearing brown leather and metal and stuff. They fired their weapons, but I'm think "never hit the hero" is in their contract.

Delay waved them back with a hooked hand that I think I'd heard was the result of a mishap with a shark tank trap he'd devised for another hero a while back.

"No! I was so close," he shouted like a shrieking old hag.

But he wasn't close. Not even a little bit. Even then, I realize that Harrier was using Delay's distraction to get the jump on him. Frank was absolutely unmatched in skill and professionalism. I also realized that I was bait. That night, when we got back to the Aerie, I had a bit of a yelling match with him about it. He assured me I was never in much danger, and I assured him that he hadn't felt the wind pass by his head from huge cat paws.

In the end, I know Frank had things under control. He always did.

It's something I wish I would have realized before I'd been such a brat and chose chasing Osprey over helping him last October. Maybe if I'd have paid more attention to my job, Harrier wouldn't have gotten kidnapped by Chef Maléfique, beaten to a point near death, and then left with a limp and a cane.

Maybe then, I wouldn't be in the situation I'm in now.

Okay. I know, I've built it up enough. It's third period and I'm in with Mrs. Darlings. Don't let the name fool you. She's awful. She reminds me of that old wrestler, Andre the Giant. You know, the guy from *The Princess Bride*? She's huge and her head is like an afro-poof.

I'd been so busy last night with my *nocturnal activities*—and no, unlike most high school students, that has nothing to do with a girl. Well, actually, Osprey was there. But not like that. I mean, I wouldn't have stopped it... but it was strictly professional. Unfortunately.

Aaanyway.

I'd totally forgotten that we had a huge trig test today. This year, I'm, like, borderline failing. It's not my fault. Frank quit crimefighting because of his injuries, both physical and mental, and the Guild still hasn't let Alex—Redhawk—leave Boston to come take over here since they forced him back there shortly after he'd become the Black Harrier.

Part of me is beginning to think they never will.

So, for now, it's just me and Osprey against a city full of lunatics.

The Guild also denied my billionth request to be called Red Raptor instead of Red Kite. You'd think no one would care about such a minor thing, but they are serious control freaks.

At home, my mom has been completely sober and well, really awesome. It's like she's a different person, especially lately. But that also means that she knows exactly what's going on at school and she's been trying to tutor me at home.

Mrs. Darlings places the test facedown on my desk. I run my thumb along the edge of the stapled pages. There are like eight of them. Front and back.

A whisper hisses my way. "What's the matter, loser? You look like you're gonna puke."

Betcha can't guess who that is?

As soon as Mrs. Darlings passes, I feel my chair being shaken from behind.

It's easy to ignore Logan Andrews when I know after this year, I'll be held back and he'll move on.

I'm so dead.

Turns out, I know trigonometry better than I'd thought. In case you forgot, I have this thing—I don't know, it's not really a super power—where, if I see something once, I can remember it forever. I guess after watching Mrs. Darlings scrawl stuff on the whiteboard for the last few months, I've retained more than I could've guessed. I don't know that I got an A or anything, but I definitely passed.

The rest of the day is pretty mundane at school. Javier and I have been hanging out a lot more. He's a good kid. Weird, sure, but he's got a heart of gold. Logan tries to act tough, but he hasn't messed with Javi once this school year. I count that as a win.

Later, after a quick work out at the Aerie, I head downstairs to our new place in Douglas Tower. Now that my mom has her act together, Frank has no problem funneling some cash her way and giving us the condo for free. Years ago, Mr. Chen, the guy who runs Douglas Industries—oh, yeah, and Osprey's dad—came up with an elaborate story about Mom being the beneficiary of some bogus class-action lawsuit against the company. When she'd proven untrustworthy, blowing the money on poor choices, he'd put an end to the payments. Now that she's straightened out her life, the checks not only started flowing again, but Douglas Industries is making up for missing a bunch of payments due to a "clerical error."

It's really just Frank's way of taking care of us because, wait for it… he's my father. The reveal came during Chef Maléfique's monologue in an old warehouse —always warehouses. It was kind of like a *Star Wars* moment, you know? I mean, not exactly "Sawyer, I am your father," or anything. But it was dramatic.

My mom doesn't think I know about it, but I've suspected for a while now that she *does* know the whole class-action lawsuit thing is bogus. But why ruin a good thing? We have a sweet apartment in the nicest building in the city, and enough money every month to eat well, and buy nice clothes and stuff.

And, best of all—for me at least—she no longer has to babysit the brat, Aiden. Can't stand that kid. But I also sort of miss him. Shhh. Don't tell anyone.

As I ride down the private elevator connecting the Aerie to my floor, my mind fixates on how exhausted I am from Osprey and my attempts to keep this city safe while the Guild twiddles their thumbs. And Eaglestar… That guy's such a… seriously… I have no word to describe how much I hate him now.

A few months ago, I was in Washington, D.C. I'd told my mom it was a summer wrestling trip. Luckily, she'd never asked Principal Blanchard or Coach Carmichael about it. It was the last time I was with Alex—Redhawk—in person, and Eaglestar used it as his opportunity to tell me and Alex both the bad news that I was stuck with the name Red Kite and Redhawk was stuck in Boston until the Guild could find a reasonable replacement. Frank hadn't argued either. I don't get it. It's like he's just checked out completely.

Ding!

I peek out and make sure nobody's around before exiting the elevator. It's at the end of a side corridor with no apartments, so there's really no reason for anyone to be there, but I always have to be sure. I don't need my neighbors wondering why some teenage kid is using the private elevator reserved for the penthouse. The coast is clear, as usual.

As I enter the apartment, I'm focused on my tablet, so it takes a second for me to register that someone is home. When I look up, I see Mom *kissing* some guy, but his back is turned to me.

Great. Another boyfriend.

It's been a long time, but I guess I knew it would happen eventually. I've even had a sneaking suspicion that something like this might be going on. Hopefully, this new guy is classier than the losers she usually ends up with. By the look of that suit he's wearing…

He turns around, and I can only imagine that the look on my face is as shocked as the one on his.

No no no no no no no no no. This is impossible.

"*Frank*?"

Now it's Mom's turn to look shocked. "You two know each other?"

We both freeze up. I have no idea what to say, and he obviously doesn't either.

Then, like complete doofuses, we both start talking at the same time. "Well, we met at—"

"I was taking care of Mr. Douglas'… fish, when—"

"—that thing, back when—"

"—out of town, and then… I fed his fish so good he asked me to walk his dog—"

My mom narrows her eyes at Frank. "I didn't know you had a dog."

Frank grimaces in my direction. "Well, I don't. Anymore. Sawyer here… *lost* him."

"Sawyer!" Mom yells.

I raise an eyebrow, not happy with the direction this improv routine is taking. "Well, to be fair, he *was* kind of a handful. Chewed through his leash and everything. At least your penthouse doesn't smell like pee anymore, right, Mr. Douglas? Or does it? That dog peed a whole lot."

Frank doesn't look happy with me either, but I know he's also uncomfortable with the whole situation. And honestly? I don't care. Of the three of us, he's the only one who really knows what was going on here. He's got some explaining to do.

Mom's stare jumps back and forth between us. She's legit confused.

Ditto, Mom. Ditto.

"It's fine," Frank said.

"Well," she says, "that's unfortunate. But I *am* glad to see you're being proactive about making some money. I know it's hard for teenagers to get jobs nowadays." Then, she gets that look, like a firework is going off in her head. "Frank, do you think maybe he could get a job with one of your businesses?"

She looks at me and says, "Frank owns a lot of business." Then back to Frank. "Just some part-time starting position?"

"Hmmm. I don't know," Frank says. He's not fooling me. He knows exactly what he's gonna say. Big smile. Snap of the fingers. "Wait a minute… I think I know just the place."

I've gotta put a stop to this immediately. "That's okay. I—I've got school and stuff, even when I'm ready for a real job, I'm sure I can find something on my own."

Mom looks hesitant now. "Sorry, Frank. I shouldn't have put you on the spot—"

"Oh, it's no trouble," he says. "In fact, come along with me, Sawyer, and I'll introduce you to someone right now."

With one hand, Frank grabs his cane, and the back of my arm with the other—a little rough, actually—and escorts me out the door.

We both turn back and smile at Mom as she closes the door behind us, and then, it's suddenly all business.

Frank whispers urgently, "Walked my *dog*? What were you thinking?"

"It's better than 'We met at that thing.' I'm not some business associate of yours. I'm a freaking teenager." I try not to yell. "And don't go trying to turn this around on me. What are you doing kissing my *mom*?" I inadvertently shudder at the thought.

Frank sighs and pushes me farther from the apartment door. "We ran into each other in the lobby a couple of weeks ago."

"Oh, so that's what this was really about? Put us in the building so you can 'randomly bump into her?'"

"Sawyer," Frank says, then lets out another exasperated breath. "She asked if I wanted to get a drink."

My eyes go so wide, I probably look like some kind of psycho. In fact, I hope I do.

Frank gets defensive and raises his hands, palms out. "Of *coffee*. She hasn't touched a drop of alcohol as far as I know."

"And you just started dating her without telling me?" My heart is *pounding*. Why is my heart beating so fast? It's not like I'm plummeting from a skyscraper or hanging over a tiger pit. It's a good thing Alex took Amber, my old helmet AI, or she'd be alerting me that I'm about to have a heart attack or something.

"It just sort of happened. I didn't plan it." Now he has to see the incredulity on my face. "I didn't plan it, Sawyer. Honestly. And I didn't intend to keep it a secret from you, but by the time I realized we were in a relationship, I couldn't figure out *how* to tell you."

Part of me actually believes him. Probably because he's using more than his standard five syllable sentences.

We start walking toward the elevator—the normal glass one that residents use. The lift doors slide open and we load in. It's empty, thank God.

"I'm gonna need some time to process this," I tell him.

"I understand. But whenever you're ready—"

"Don't. Please. I'll let you know when I wanna talk about it. Let's just put it on hold for now." Deep breath, Sawyer. Use those calming techniques you learned. "So where exactly—"

The elevator stops at the next floor down, and a couple gets on with us so we stop talking and ride the rest of the way down to the lobby in silence. As the awful Muzak plays overhead, they keep turning and looking at Frank like he's a celebrity—probably because he basically is—but they're afraid to talk to him. For the first time, I realize how old that must get. Well, after the novelty wears off, anyway.

As soon as we get to the lobby, we rush through as fast as Frank and his cane allow, and exit the building. It's not like he's an invalid or something. He's still more than capable, but I think there's something going on that's more mental than physical. It's hard not to feel bad for him.

To be expected, 5th Avenue is loud. Taxis whip past, some pulling over erratically, trying to be the first to pick up hailing pedestrians. The sidewalk is crowded as well. It's mostly businessmen and women here in this part of Manhattan, but there're a few pierced-up punks with those novelty things they called hoverboards which were really just a plank with two wheels. They pass by without causing too much trouble. I feel like I've been holding my breath for the past five minutes and I can finally breathe.

I inhale, ready to speak, but Frank gets his say in out of the corner of his mouth. "Before you say anything, I thought this through. I know you've been having trouble sneaking out for patrols, and it's the perfect cover for you to go out crimefighting at night. You work a couple of nights a week, and the rest of the time, you hit the streets. You can even go out after work."

I'm still not sure if I like the idea. Mr. Chen had mentioned something about working for him last year, but since we've now left the offices of Douglas Industries, I have to assume Frank has something else in mind. "Yeah, okay. So, where's the job?"

"Right in front of you." He points with his cane across the street.

"The bank?"

He shakes his head.

"That suit shop?"

"Try again," he says.

At first, those two places are all I see. Then I notice he's indicating the Big Frankie Junior's burger place between them. It's kind of old and rundown for this part of the city, but it has a fairly new sign with flashing lights and the whole thing.

"You can't be serious."

Frank just smiles.

"*You're* Big Frankie Junior?"

"No. I'm Franklin Douglas III, remember? Junior was my dad."

"Your dad made his money in fast food?" I asked before I remembered what Chef Maléfique had told me about my grandfather being some big-time crime lord.

"Not exactly. It was just one of many fronts for some of his less reputable activities. Of course, I didn't know that when I started working there as my first job. But now it's just a regular fast food chain."

"Wait, your dad made you flip burgers even though you guys were billionaires?"

"Well, at the time, we were only millionaires. But, yes. He wanted me to get my hands dirty. In more ways than one, as it turned out. That was when I started figuring out what was really going on with our family. Although it took me a lot longer to finally face up to it."

As we cross at the light, I stir up enough courage to ask him a question. "I know you probably don't want to talk about this, but ever since Maléfique told me about you… killing your dad… I was wondering how it happened."

"You're right, Sawyer."

"I am? About what?"

"I *don't* want to talk about it."

TWO

AMY

D*ivorce*

I know it happens to nearly half of all marriages nowadays—even more if it's a second or third marriage—but it still seems so traumatic when it's your own parents. Even when you're nineteen, like me. End-of-the-world type of thing.

You know what occupation has the highest divorce rate in the United States? Dancer. Guess what my mom is? Bingo. Or she used to be, before she went into modeling. I don't know what the rate is for models. But it's not as high as massage therapists (no big surprise there, is it?) or gaming cage workers.

Wait. *Gaming cage workers*? Massage therapists? Maybe they're talking about a different kind of dancer if those are the top categories. I don't know, whatever.

Okay, let me back up. My mom wasn't a stripper.

This is stupid. Point is, my parents are getting divorced.

It's been going on for over a year now. First, the separate bedrooms. Then, separate condos. Separate attorneys. Now that it's in the final stages, my mom wants to live in separate countries. And she wants me to go with her. Wants me to move back to the "old country" with her. Bulgaria. *Blech*.

Who wants to live in Bulgaria? Not even most Bulgarians, I bet. If my mom wasn't from there, I doubt I'd even know where it was on a map. She used to always talk about how much she'd hated it there. Why would she want to go back? That's a long trip just to get away from Dad. And he's not even a bad guy. As a matter of fact, he's one of the good guys. Luis Chen, Vice-President and Chief Operation Officer of Douglas Industries. Works directly for Mr. Douglas—the Black Harrier, though no one is really supposed to know that.

I do…

And, oh yeah, did I mention I'm a masked crimefighter? Can you imagine me jumping around on the rooftops of Sofia? You didn't know that was the capital of Bulgaria? Don't worry. *No one does!*

Some of those buildings are fifteen-hundred years old. One misstep and *crack-boom*. One dead birdie. At least there'd be plenty of organized crime there for me to fight. For a small country, they sure seem to have a lot of it.

I call myself Osprey. I've never tried to hide how much I look up to the Black Harrier. He's the best in the business. And here, with Sawyer, the Red Raptor, and all the others, I can get the job done and blend in. But if Osprey suddenly started fighting crime over there, right after Amy Chen moved there with her mom, that would be more than a little suspicious, right? Or would it? It would certainly show me how successful I've been at hiding who I really am.

Actually, the truth is, we'd probably live on the coast of the Black Sea in some mansion or something, with as much money as Mayka's going to have after the divorce. She was already independently wealthy from her own career before marrying my dad. He doesn't have Frank Douglas money, but he's definitely well into the top of the One Percent.

And I would do… what, exactly? Date a bunch of guys in the poorest country in the European Union? No thanks. Become a jet-setter like my mom, shopping in the ritziest, classiest shops in Europe, going on holiday to Monaco?

Yeah, I don't think so. Not my style. I'm a gamer, a geek, a loud-and-proud nerd through-and-through, no matter how much Mayka has tried to change me over the years. Oh, shoot. I'm sorry. Bad habit. "Mayka" is Bulgarian for "mom." Pretty ridiculous of me to expect anyone to know that, I guess. Sorry about the confusion.

How do I tell Mayka I don't want to go without destroying her? How do I tell my dad I want to stay here in New York with him even though he seems pretty indifferent about it? I need to go out and clear my head.

By knocking a few heads together.

I think about giving Sawyer a call to see if he can come out on patrol, but I feel like I need some alone time right now. Nothing against him. He's a sweet kid, but sometimes he's a little… *much*. I know he can't help being a teenage boy with raging hormones and everything, but sometimes, I feel like if I catch him staring at me like he does one more time, I'm going to have to knock him on his ass.

Okay, that's not fair. It was obvious from the moment we met that he had a crush on me. And I probably should've made sure to completely shut him down… immediately.

Hi, I'm Sawyer.

Oh, nice to meet you. Here's the friend zone. Don't move.

I guess I was a little flattered, since I don't get much attention in my civilian identity, and it's not like I'm meeting a lot of guys while crimefighting (unless I'm shoving my fist down their throats, of course). He's also kind of cute, and funny, and if he wasn't only sixteen maybe we could have dated or something. Not only would that be a bad idea, it's totally illegal and gross. By the time he's eighteen—

Oh, *crap*. That reminds me. Sawyer's turning seventeen tomorrow and I haven't even gotten him a present or anything. I'll have to think about it while I save the world or whatever far less interesting situation I happen to come across while patrolling.

This feels a little like one of those confessional videos on a reality show. You know, where the producer or whoever is just offscreen asking questions and the contestant is answering? I always figured they'd answer and then the bigwigs would say, "Yeah, I'd rather you say something else." It's all staged, right?

Well, I *do* have a confession to make. I dated one guy while crimefighting, but it didn't work out so well. Alexander Garner. Redhawk. Last winter, when he first became Black Harrier, we were working together, and things kind of just... happened? I guess? And we totally had to hide it from Sawyer because that would've been awkward on so many different levels. But then we broke up and the Guild made him go back to Boston, which makes zero sense. They have him being Redhawk up there most of the time, and then sometimes he has to go on a Guild mission where he's Black Harrier because Frank just straight up won't. If people found out Harrier was gone from New York and the Guild and everything, there'd be mayhem. But I don't see them working very hard to replace either hero. Whatever.

Some things don't last, right? And I don't want to talk about it. Now he wants to come back, and he's been texting me and...

No. I don't want to discuss it. I want to kick the crap out of someone who deserves it. It's so much more satisfying than Pilates. Or hitting a punching bag. They just don't have that same *give*. And no crunching. I like the crunching. And I'm so beyond what they're doing in my old martial arts classes that I started causing some major injuries to my classmates, so that's not an option either. I need someone I can hit and feel good about it, you know?

Speaking of which, look what we have here. Three idiots trying to steal an old lady's purse at knifepoint. Real tough guys. Seriously? She's like eighty years old and she's hitting one of them with her purse.

Badass bitch. I better be as tough as her when I'm that age. Give it to em, grandma!

Oh. Shoot. I've gotta get down there.

Sawyer told me how he gives these bad guys nicknames when he's fighting them to keep them straight and pass the time. It sounded like fun, so I started doing it myself. I'll dub these morons Moe, Larry, and Curly, since one of the few cherished memories of my dad when I was a kid was watching the Three Stooges with him. Sure, the Stooges didn't have tattoos and hipster beards, but let's roll with it anyway.

First, my signature move. After doing some calculations on my trajectory (star mathlete here), I jump from a nearby rooftop and glide down. Both feet connect with the biggest one—Curly—in the back of the head, causing him to face plant into the sidewalk. They usually lose a few teeth that way, which is far less than someone deserves for robbing and terrorizing a woman two decades shy of a century. I'm a little bit afraid that one of these days, taking the full brunt of my glide from a rooftop might cause more damage and paralyze or kill one of these trolls, but honestly? Serves them right.

No, I'm not evil. Just pragmatic. They could also get shot in the back running from the police, or try robbing a Second Amendment nut and take a bullet between the eyes. It's a chance they take anytime they decide stealing other people's money is easier than obtaining their own by legal means. If they're willing to risk that, I'm willing to risk hurting them more than I probably should. And I'd be lying if I told you I don't enjoy it.

Sawyer hates when I talk this way. He really takes the whole *no killing* rule seriously. Me? It's more like a guideline, or a suggestion. Before someone starts quoting me on the internet, let me make this perfectly clear: I'm not about to start shooting criminals or dropping them from ledges or anything, but I'm also not going to lose any sleep over some ogre who's in a wheelchair for the rest of his life because he was ready to gut a senior citizen for seventeen dollars and some change.

The one I call "Moe" points at me and sneers. "Cut that slut!"

Hey, what do you know? I picked the right one to call Moe, since he's apparently the leader. Oh, and you know how many times I've heard a criminal call Sawyer some male equivalent of "slut?" Zero. With me, it's a regular thing. Like I'm supposed to be equated to some kind of whore for daring to challenge these Cro-Magnons. Add sexism to their list of crimes.

Larry jabs at me, and I barely have to pull my belly in to avoid his blade. I retract my helmet's visor and blow him a little kiss, since my family drama has me in the mood to play with my prey before devouring them, bones and all. More cat than hawk, I know, but I'm not into the whole bird theme as much as Frank. I just thought ospreys were badass birds of prey. I still do. Have you seen one in action? Kind of like the animal kingdom version of what I'm doing to these losers. Especially dropping down on them unexpectedly. That's why they're called "ambush hunters."

"Come on, you can do better than that," I tell him. "Don't be such a—"

He takes a swipe at me and I block it with my bracer. The collision of metal-on-metal causes a spark and probably hurts his hand way more than it hurts me, which is not at all.

"Good boy! At least you connected that time."

He hops around like a snow monkey I saw at the Central Park zoo once. That monkey ended up throwing some poop at everyone and then eating some of it and I still think it was smarter than this idiot.

"I'll give you one more free shot." I stand perfectly still while he figures out his next move. Then, after a caveman-like grunt, he lunges for my face. My foot turns, springs out, and nails him in the gut. I can feel his fat ripple from the impact. Trash cans play like the Philharmonic and he lies unmoving in the midst of them.

Moe eyes him with disgust and yells at him even though he's obviously unconscious. "Geez, Larry, you're pathetic!"

Oh, my god! His name *is* Larry! That's too funny, and almost creepily coincidental. I love when stuff like that happens, but then it kind of freaks me out at the same time, you know? Maybe I'm psychic too?

"So, that makes you Moe, right?" I ask the leader.

"What?" His confused look proves that he has no idea what I'm talking about. People are so uncultured these days.

The old lady, who is no longer cowering against the wall, tilts her head and stares at him like he has a screw loose.

"Moe! From the Three Stooges, you moron," she says. Wow, she really does have spunk. No wonder she hasn't run away by now.

"Three Stooges? What the hell is that, you old bag?"

"I'll show you an old bag!" She shouts and swings her giant purse at his head again. It connects, and she must have something heavy in there because Moe seems like he really feels it. He becomes enraged and brandishes his knife above his head, ready to plunge it into her chest.

Are you kidding me?

"Playtime's over, Asshat," I say just before unleashing a high roundhouse kick which knocks the knife out of his hand. I follow it up with a leaping kick, which he takes under the chin, causing his neck to snap back. I hope he has whiplash on top of whatever other injuries I'm about to inflict on him. Unfortunately, Moe is tougher than I thought. He's still standing after taking a couple of hits that normally flatten guys like him.

"Oh, you did it now, bitch." Again, with the sexist nonsense. If only he realized it's only going to make me hit him even harder. He picks up his knife and licks his lips.

Ewwww.

He grins at me and says, "Just for that, I'm gonna do some *nasty* things to you once I have you down on the ground."

Here we go. Another thing I've never *ever* seen Sawyer have to deal with—threats of a sexual nature. Like he has a chance in blue hell. Even if, by some miracle, he knocks me down, let's see him deal with the razors that pop out when someone tries to take off my uniform leggings without triggering the failsafe first. I may be confident in my abilities, but I'm not a complete idiot. I had to warn Frank, Sawyer, and Alex about it early on to make sure they didn't lose a finger if I were ever unconscious and they needed to remove my costume in order to save me or something.

I'm almost tempted to let Moe try just to watch him bleed, but I can't stand the thought of him getting that close to me. In fact, it makes me throw up a little in my mouth. Instead, I taunt him.

"I'm *so* frightened of the big, scary man who makes his money robbing grandmothers with his big, scary knife. Oh, please, Moe… *please,* don't hurt me." I'm laying it on extra thick and even acting it out. I know how much it riles guys like this and causes them to make even more mistakes. It works every time. I'm telling you—*every* time.

"I'll kill you!" He runs at me at full speed, knife going straight for my stomach. I flip over his head and come around, grabbing his neck in a chokehold on the way down. I saw it on TV once and always wanted to try it, and now seemed like as good a time as any. Even though the move I watched was rehearsed a million times first and I'm doing it on the fly, it still succeeds.

He comes down hard with a loud "Oof!" and the knife flies from his hand. I hold him down, my forearm on his windpipe, and he struggles to breathe.

"You want to tell me again what you're going to do to me? Do you?" I hope I sound as angry as I am. I'm pretty sure I do.

His eyes start to bulge and he tries to say "no" as he shakes his head.

"That's what I thought. Now, listen to me carefully. I'm going to be watching you and your friends. If I ever see or hear about any of you stealing from senior citizens—or anyone—or, especially threatening to rape anyone like you did to me, I will find you. And next time I won't be so nice. If you're *lucky,* you may just end up in a wheelchair. If you're not, I may have to make sure you can never use your probably pathetic little package on anyone whether they're willing or not."

He's quaking now. Eyes tearing up. Though that might be because I still haven't let him breathe.

"One more thing. I'm sure you've heard that Black Harrier has a no killing rule. Well, let me tell you a little secret…" I lean in close and whisper the last part. *"I'm not Black Harrier."*

I stand up and kick him in the face, knocking him unconscious.

The little old lady actually starts clapping. Like she was watching a play or something.

"Bravo!" she says, a big, denturey smile on her face.

"Are you okay?" I ask.

"Oh, you were wonderful, dear," she said. But then she tilts her head at me the way grandma's do. "But you really should watch your language. It's unbecoming of a young lady."

I'm almost speechless until she says, "But he really was an asshat, wasn't he?"

We laugh together and I take her by the arm.

"Where's home?" I ask.

As we pass Curly, I notice he's coming to with a groan. I step on his back, hard, letting my toe dig in at the base of his neck.

Then I realize I haven't thought at all about what I'm going to get Sawyer for his birthday. Hmmm… what do you get the boy who's dad is one of the richest people in the world?

THREE
SAWYER

Ugh.

If Frank thinks this is some kind of punishment for how I'd behaved when I caught him kissing my mom… he's right. If I had to make a list of things worse than this, they'd all have something to do with the most painful kinds of genital diseases.

I'm in a tiny office in the back of the burger joint, being interviewed by the manager—who looks like he probably has one or two of those. I had no idea Frank owned this place until now. Well, the whole chain, believe it or not. Of which there are about a hundred in the tri-state area.

Big Frankie, Jr. isn't just the name of the restaurant, either. It's also the name of the stupid cow character on the signs and in the commercials. He wears a chef's hat and holds a spatula, which suggests that he's cooking burgers.

A cow. Cooking burgers. So, the fun-loving kids' character is, like, a bovine cannibal, right?

Now that I think about it, it reminds me a lot of Chef Maléfique. Whoa. The cow even has the handlebar mustache…

One thing you learn quickly in this business—crimefighting, not burger flipping—is that there's this weird sort of incestuous thing between the heroes and their archenemies. It can be disturbing at times and makes you wonder if that's why none of them end up dead or behind bars very long. I did, however, watch Frank snap Maléfique's neck. So, if he comes back, he'll look a lot more like Med-Evil than himself.

I wonder if the office I'm sitting in is a repurposed broom closet. It barely fits the small desk, an office chair, and the hard metal stool that he told me to sit on. A bulletin board hangs above the desk, full of thumbtacked paperwork, notices from corporate, and complaints from customers. On another wall, under an ancient-looking clock, is a one dollar bill, and below that, a girlie calendar that's totally inappropriate for any place of business except maybe an auto-repair shop.

The manager's creaky office chair groans as he slumps and stares at me. The guy, whose name tag says 'Mr. Kevin,' is in his late twenties, *maybe* thirty, but he's already a heart attack waiting to happen. I imagine he probably eats nearly every meal here. His skin is as greasy as the fryer pit, and I try not to focus on the giant zit on the end of his nose, but it's so… *there*.

I wonder if I should tell him about the smudge of ketchup on his cheek?

I think he's about to start talking, but instead, he goes into a coughing fit, not even bothering to cover his mouth. I would've been disgusted under any circumstances, but the fact that we're in the back room of a restaurant makes me extra sick to my stomach. On the other hand, it's almost exactly what I would have expected to happen.

He finally speaks. "Listen. Just cuz you got connections, don't think this is gonna be easy for you. You gotta work just as hard as everyone else here. Capiche?"

I nod politely. "Of course." Inside, however, I'm wondering if this guy is for real. Capiche? I know this is New York, but not everyone is a mobster. Especially not this overgrown toddler.

"Maybe even a little harder, to make sure it don't look like you're getting some kinda special treatment. That would be despotism, you know?"

"Okay. I guess. But I think you mean nepo—"

"You *guess*? Look, just cuz I gotta hire you as a favor to the owner don't mean I gotta like it." He takes a long sip of his 64-ounce soda until it hits bottom and makes that annoying sucking air sound as he rattles the ice around, making sure he inhales every precious drop of high fructose corn syrup before giving up because he runs out of breath.

I would love to tell him a few things. For starters, Frank isn't just "the owner." I mean, he is? But he's so much more than that. Secondly, the *owner* is my father.

Instead, I grit my teeth and keep my mouth clamped. It's obvious he considers this place his own little fiefdom, and I've just become one of his lowly subjects.

"I just hope this don't end up a disaster. I prefer to hire my own people." He tosses a folder full of paperwork on the desk. I eye it suspiciously, wondering if I should take it, and more than a little grossed out by the greasy fingerprints he left on it. "You gotta fill all this out, and then show up to Big Frankie University tomorrow for training so you can get yourself one of these bad boys."

He points with pride at a framed certificate on the wall with Big Frankie, Jr. printed on it in the company font. When I look back at him, he's nodding with an "*Oooohhh, yeeeaaah*" expression that's totally unjustified.

I try not to sound sarcastic, but I'm not very successful. "You mean that's real? It's really a thing?"

He squints at me. "Of course it's a thing. You think they give these out to just any jerk off the street?"

"Ummm..."

"*No*. The answer's no. You gotta go through *a whole day* of training. And take tests. It's not like you can just come in here and start frying up poppers and running the drive-thru without no education. I mean, I got seven years of college, and I couldn't have figured it out on my own."

"Seven years? What's that, like, a master's degree?"

He sits forward in his chair, bringing that zit just a little bit closer. "Actually,

I'm a few credits away from my associate's. You think it's easy running this place and taking classes at the same time?"

I'm careful to police the expression on my face and glare through the tiny office's open door. Bored employees stand around flipping burgers. They look like zombies as they dump frozen fries into vats of boiling oil and pull them up again when the timer tells them to.

"No. For sure. Definitely not," I agree.

"You got that right." He points to the calendar on the wall. "We run like a well oiled machine around here. So, being the new guy, you ain't gonna get the best schedule right away. Can you work days?"

"Um, no. I have school."

How can he not know this?

"I need someone for days. You can skip it sometimes, right?"

"Not if I don't want my mom to kill me?" I find myself saying things like questions and lilting my voice like I'm talking to a seven-year-old. Is this guy for real? "Oh, and I'd kind of like to graduate."

He lets out a long, exaggerated breath to make it clear that he's frustrated. With no shame at all, he picks his nose with his thumb, then flicks it nonchalantly toward the garbage can. I guess maybe it helps him think. Clears the airwaves to his brain.

I'm sure he'd love to screw me over, but he also has to keep in mind that the owner himself asked him to hire me. I can almost see those thoughts duking it out in his head.

"Geez, I knew this was gonna be a pain in my ass," he says, standing and squeezing his way past his desk toward the door. He opens in all the way, making it clear it's time for me to go. "I gotta figure out what I can do."

I try to sound thankful, but I really just want to get out of there. "I appreciate that."

"I'll see you in a couple of days—with your certificate—and we'll talk about your schedule then."

I know I should shake his hand, but there's no way I'm touching any part of this guy. I give him a small wave and get out of there as quickly as possible.

Back at Douglas Tower, I head straight for the Aerie. I'm not in the mood to deal with Mom right now, and she has no idea how long the job interview thing is supposed to last, so I have some oh-so-precious time. As I'm about to head into the training room, I notice a box about the size to hold a bowling ball sitting on Frank's computer console. It's wrapped in shiny black paper and has a silver ribbon with a bow on top. Is this a present? From Frank?

I look at the card attached to the bow. Sure enough, it says, "Happy Seventeenth. I know you've been needing some assistance out there, especially with Amber gone."

That's true. As much as I got annoyed at Amber sometimes, with her ridiculously inappropriate sexual innuendos and whatnot, having an AI in my helmet to help out and warn me about things was a huge help. But Alex, who had apparently always had some weird crush on her—it—has her—uh, it—now.

I can't believe how nicely this is wrapped. What a step up from last year when he wrapped my new cape in newspaper. Although I'm sure he didn't do this himself. Probably had Mr. Chen do it.

I pull on the bow and remove the lid. Inside, a shiny new helmet stares back at me. It's very similar to my old one, but upon closer inspection, it's closer to Frank's Harrier helmet, only painted with my color scheme, red, white, and silver. My helmet is already pretty amazing, so I'm not sure how this new one is gonna be an upgrade.

But hey, the guy hardly ever disappoints when it comes to tech. So, I slide it on over my head. Seems like the heads-up display is the same as my old one. Thin green lines create a small grid around me, showing distance and trajectory in semi-transparent numbers. I don't see what the big deal is so far. Then, suddenly —*BAM*. There's a gorgeous, scantily-clad woman standing right in front of me with—of course—bright red hair.

"Hey, there. I'm Tiffany," she says. *"You must be Sawyer."*

I pull the helmet off, but she's gone. If anyone else was in the room, I'd look like an idiot, searching under chairs and behind the computer console. She's totally gone. I slide it back on, and—

"Hey there!"

I've seen the women Frank goes to red carpet events with. Tiffany makes them look like homely housewives. She's wearing black leather. I would say head to toe, but her boots come up to her thighs and then there's a sizable gap of bare and creamy flesh before a pair of leather hot pants start. My face starts to flush as I look her up and down. My heart beats way too fast.

"Are you—?"

"All yours, honey. At your beck and call for… all *your needs."*

"I was gonna say, 'Are you a hologram?'"

"Well, that's not a very nice way to greet a girl you just met. But, yes, technically I'm a computer generated, artificial-intelligence-based, interference pattern which uses diffraction to reproduce a three-dimensional light field."

"That only I can see."

"That's exactly right. I appear right in front of your eyes inside your helmet, but using highly advanced artificial reality, it looks to you like I'm standing right in front of you."

"Can I touch you?"

"Wow, aren't you forward?"

"No, I mean… dammit. Are you real?"

"If you are asking if I'm tangible. No, but you can look all you want. Would you like to scroll through my different clothing options?"

"Uh, no, I'm good. No clothes right now."

"My, you jump straight to the point, don't you?" Suddenly, Tiffany's clothing disappears and she's completely nude.

I shut my eyes and throw my hands over my face.

"Whoa! That's… not what I meant. Just—just put back on what you had before you… you know."

"As you wish. You can also change the settings on my physical appearance any time you like. Would you like to fiddle with my measurements?"

"Absolutely not. There will be no… fiddling with anything right now. Please just go back in the bottle or whatever. I'll let you know if I need you."

"Yes, master. I will await your command."

"Sawyer?"

Osprey's voice startles me so much that I practically jump out of my skin. Geez, it was just an AI hologram. Why do I feel like I just got caught looking at porn?

"Oh! Hi! How's it going?" I yank the helmet off and try to shove it back into the box, only for some reason, it's at a weird angle or something so it doesn't want to go in. I start feeling like I'm doing a comedy sketch and finally give up, shove the box away, and hold the helmet under my arm.

"Are you okay? Who were you talking to?"

"Just—you know—Frank—"

"Frank is here?" she asks, looking around.

"No, no. You didn't let me finish. He, uh, gave me this new helmet with his old AI built in, and I was… trying her—trying *it*—out."

"Why are you acting so strange?" She's totally onto me. Panic hits me like Royal Rampage's big hairy fist when I consider… could she see Tiffany with her helmet, too?

"Strange? I'm not acting strange!"

Oh, my god, I'm acting totally strange.

"No, you're *definitely* acting strange."

She's got me. I've gotta know.

"Could you see the h-hologram?" I ask. "With your helmet?" I feel like I'm sweating buckets now. I swear my shoes are filling up.

"Hologram? No, not at all. Why?" She gives me a very confused look.

Relief. Sweet relief.

"Oh, I, yeah. Nothing. Never mind. So, what's up?"

"I wanted to be the first one to give you a birthday present, but I guess Frank beat me to it."

"He does have a way of ruining things, doesn't he?" I say, hoping to lighten the mood and act normal again.

"You remember when we first met and I couldn't wait to meet him?"

"Yeah, of course."

"Well, I got over it pretty fast once I actually did."

"Welcome to the club."

"Don't get me wrong," she says. "I have mad respect for him. None of this… *none* of it would have happened without him. And it's not like he had an easy time of it."

"That's very true. I need to remember that more often." Especially after finding out he's my dad.

"Not to mention what he went through last year. He still hasn't recovered physically."

"And he may never recover psychologically." Why do I feel like this has turned into small talk? And what about my present? Did she forget? "So, how's everything going with you?"

"It's… going," she says. Something's wrong. Why won't she talk to me? You'd think she'd feel comfortable talking to me by now. "How about you? School okay?"

"Meh. Same as usual. Y'know, pretty much hell." I notice for the first time that she has a large duffel bag with her. "What's in the bag?"

"What? Oh! It's your present. Duh. It's only the whole reason I came here." She unzips the bag and pulls out a fairly large box wrapped with really nice paper. What's funny, to me at least, is that where Frank used all black… his colors. She was thoughtful enough to use mine.

"Wow. Nice. You want me to… open it now?"

"Of course! Why wouldn't I?" She's super excited, which makes me even more excited.

I tear off the silver bow and rip into the red paper, revealing a plain, nondescript box. Glossy. Red. Long. But there's no indication of what's inside, and I still have no idea.

I peel open the top and what's there is absolutely the last thing I'd expected. But it's perfect. A brand new skateboard—the deck is my favorite brand, with the best trucks and wheels you can buy on it. And it even has a custom paint job with a really sweet looking…

"Remember when we first met and I told you people might think…"

"Whoa…"

It had a red dinosaur on it. Just like the ones in the movie, only… yeah, red. As far as inside jokes go…

"Yeah. This is amazing."

"Do you like it?" she asked. I could see anxiety in her features. "I was a little afraid you'd think I was being… I don't know."

"No way. This is so perfect. I love it. Thank you!"

"It's hard to shop for the son of a billionaire."

"Yeah, well, all he ever gets me is stuff for 'work.'" I indicate the new helmet.

"Well, I know it's not a helmet with holographic porn, but hopefully it's okay."

All the color drains out of my face and my mouth fills with cotton balls in less than a second.

"H-how did—?"

"Relax. I'm just kidding. What's wrong?"

"Nothing. Everything's great."

And it was. I returned my admiration to the skateboard. Maybe she *is* kind of into me?

FOUR
AMY

I *lied.*

I know I said I didn't want to talk about me and Alex, but ever since I mentioned it, it's been swirling around in my head, and now I'm not going to be able to sleep or do schoolwork or anything else until I work through things. That's the last place my mind can be. My parents pay really good money for me to go to Columbia University. And they didn't buy my way in or anything. Remember, it's a wig… not that all blondes are dumb. I didn't mean that… I just…

Moving on.

So, me and Alex. We've known each other since we were kids. Though, I didn't always know he was… you know, the Red Kite.

Right after he took over as Black Harrier for Frank, we started going out on patrol together a lot. Sawyer was with us sometimes, but since he's still in high school, there were times when it was just the two of us out there. Or in the Aerie. Or, eventually, at his apartment in Douglas Tower. Crimefighting can be sort of an aphrodisiac when it's two of you together and there's any kind of attraction—which is all the more reason I need to cut Sawyer some slack.

Things moved fast. Way too fast. Especially since I'd never been in a serious relationship before. Other than being a masked crimefighter, I'm still pretty sheltered. I grew up in Douglas Tower for God's sake. It doesn't get more sheltered than that.

I feel like he wasn't very experienced at relationships for someone his age, either. I guess running around most nights in a mask beating up on criminals doesn't leave a lot of time for a social life.

Unless you're Frank Douglas, apparently. I still don't know how he does it.

And even though I'm *technically* an adult, Alex is quite a bit older than me, and there was no way I was going to have my dad finding out we were dating… besides the fact that my dad knows that he's Redhawk—and is now Black Harrier, too—they don't seem to have a very good history together. I sort of had a huge crush on him growing up, and I think my dad knew. But then Alex disappeared for a long time. And I know why now, and I get it.

When he came back last year, and I found out who he was, and he asked me to be one of his partners, I kind of got swept up in the whole thing. That was just the first problem: things moving way too fast.

Then, right after we started patrolling together, he found out that I'm not licensed by the Guild. I'm pretty sure Frank brought it up, but I don't know for sure. He started making this *huge* deal, and wouldn't shut up about it. So I did all the paperwork, and Frank put in a good word, and that got straightened out pretty quickly. But, honestly, by then I was kind of getting sick of him and his harping about the rules and justice and all that. He fits the Black Harrier costume pretty well, if you ask me. While I just wanted to get out there and take down some bad guys, he was basically a cop in a mask.

Not that I don't like cops. Cops are great. They do their part and we do ours.

Okay, so at that point, things were already strained between us, and it had only been a few weeks, maybe a month. Then, out of the blue, the Guild tells him he needs to go back to Boston. I still don't understand it. Neither does Alex or Frank. We all just assumed that if he took over as Black Harrier, then he would just take Frank's place here in New York but they insist upon not losing "hero presence" in Boston. Oh, and he can't just be Black Harrier in Boston, because then people might suspect something, or criminals might just wait until they see Harrier on TV in Boston before pulling shenanigans here.

Last time he was in town, he and I hung out a little—I mean a very little—and he's been trying to talk to me ever since. He's convinced he'll be able to move back here permanently really soon, and it seems like he still considers us a couple. But I don't feel that way anymore. I don't know what to tell him.

Is it wrong that I feel relieved that the Guild sent him away? Even though it's making things difficult for Sawyer and me? No, I don't think so. We can handle things here, and maybe they *do* need him in Boston. I don't even know what kind of other masked crimefighters they have there. Maybe none. Well, probably some. But nobody big, that's for sure.

I need to get past this. I need to meet someone else. But how? Too bad there's no superhero dating app. Or at least just a way to meet other people like me, so I can be myself around them.

"Have you started packing, darling?" My mom asks over breakfast.

My mom is *gorgeous*. Not even just gorgeous. Like, there's no way to describe how pretty she is. When she moved here, it was for a thing with the New York City Ballet. I think that's when she met Dad and it wasn't long before they were married. Which is really sort of depressing now that they're getting divorced—such a romantic rom-com kind of setup, you know? Then, her production ended and my dad got her a job in the modeling industry. She has the look. Foreign. Tall. Thin, but not like, sickly thin like models had to look then.

She's sipping on an espresso, sunglasses on. I almost laugh at how diva she can be sometimes. But, she's Mayka, and I love her. I haven't had the heart to tell her I don't want to go with her to Bulgaria.

We're out on the balcony outside our condo in Douglas Tower, and right in front of us is a giant glowing billboard for "National Sidekick Day." It's got a really cool logo, and little generic superheroes jumping around and doing flips and kicks and stuff.

None of us has been told what it is yet, not even Sawyer. I think the Guild wants it to be a surprise, but the whole city—really, the whole world is invited to Times Square in just a few days for some kind of huge event. Our view overlooks 5th Avenue from the north side of the tower. I love coming out here and watching the city.

I used to sit out here with my dad all the time.

He didn't even take anything with him except for his clothes when he moved out. He just had a decorator come over and entirely furnish his new place, so ours looks just the same as it did when he'd lived here. And now we're—she's leaving, so I'm not really sure why *he* was the one who had to move out anyway. I guess Mom will keep this place, too, for whenever she's in the States. *If* she's ever in the States. I wonder if she'll decide to stay if I don't go? I don't want to live half a world away from her. Maybe she'll feel the same?

"No, Mayka, I've been busy." I absolutely have, but not doing the things she probably thinks I have.

"Doing what?" She has a really thick accent, but a really great vocabulary. She learned English as a second language growing up and you can tell. "You are out all the time, yet I have never met any of your friends, I don't see any posts on social media. I don't even hear anything about any boys."

Our maid, Julia, who we have had for like a thousand years offers to fill up my coffee again, and I politely wave her away and do it myself. Even growing up with it, I *hate* having servants. So awkward.

"I like to keep things private." And the award for Understatement of the Year goes to… Amy Chen of New York, New York! Come on up and give a speech, Amy…

"Do you not like boys? It's okay, you can tell me. I'm very open-minded. You know I am. If you want to bring a female lover home, I have no issues with—"

OMG, Mom.

"Mayka, I like boys, okay? It's not that. But I'm not bringing any 'lovers' home no matter what. That's gross." Not to mention very, very dangerous if it happens to be Alex. Wait, why am I thinking about Alex again? *Stop thinking about Alex!*

"We have such a big place, *dušička*." That means something like "sweetheart" in English. "You wouldn't bother me at all if you brought home a *gádže*,"—boyfriend—"I promise. You will have your privacy. When I was your age, I had many lovers."

"Mayka! I've told you a million times, I don't want to hear about it." She started trying to tell me this crap when I was little. Apparently, European countries are far more advanced when it comes to things of a sexual nature. Less prudish. I used to stick my fingers in my ears and make noise to drown her out. I'm perfectly fine not hearing about my mother's sexual escapades, thanks.

She holds both the cup of espresso and a cigarette in her right hand and she takes a slow sip. Everyone in Bulgaria smokes. It's like, smokers capital of the world now. I can't stand the smell so I've never bothered, but Mom has one lit all the time.

"Don't be such a prude. You are an adult now. We should be sharing these things. Just last night, I had the most wonderful—" *Lalalalalalalalala. I can't hear you.*

"There's nothing to share right now. I swear." And if the maid doesn't stop trying to fill up my coffee cup, I'm going to scream.

"When we get to Sofia, we'll start looking for you. The boys—and girls—there are so beautiful. There's no point in falling in love now, anyway, when we're leaving so soon."

Fall in love. Yeah, right.

"About that..." I start, but I can't finish it.

"Da?"

You need to tell her. Just tell her. You're an adult. You can make your own choices.

I chicken out. "Uh... how soon do I have to be finished packing?"

"You still have a couple of weeks, but with all of your things, you should not wait until the last minute."

"Yeah. I need to stop procrastinating," I say.

"I tell you what, my *dušička,* I will hire someone to pack your things for you. No need to worry."

"*No!* No, don't do that." That's all I need is a stranger coming across an old costume or stabbing themselves on a boomerang blade or something. I stand. "I'll get started right away."

"*Goosh*!" she says. It means she's asking for a hug.

I try not to look too put out as I oblige. She squeezes me tight, and I now I *really* realize how much I'm going to miss her.

"Ti znachish tolkova mnogo za men."

I don't know what I would do without you.

Great. One ticket to Guilt Trip City, no layovers or transfers.

"Me neither, Mayka. Me neither."

And there goes the maid, refilling my coffee while I'm occupied.

I had a few things to do before I left. One of them was to make sure if Mom did decide to have someone go through my stuff—you know how moms can be—they wouldn't find anything incriminating.

With a small duffel bagful of weapons and gadgets that I'll just leave at the Aerie for now, I head toward the apartment's front door. Julia, has the TV on while she cleans in the other room, and I've been listening and half-watching the news out of the corner of my eye.

"Reports say there's been some kind of an explosion in the financial district," says reporter Dale Edwards. "We haven't received information as to whether or not this was an accident or something more nefarious. However, the way things are these days, I wouldn't be—"

I don't hear the rest. With Alex in Boston, Frank doing... whatever Frank does... and Sawyer probably already at school, who else is going to take care of this?

"Mom!" I shout.

She slides the balcony's glass door open. "Da?"

"I gotta go!"

"Everything okay?"

"Just realized I'm gonna be late for class!" I grab my backpack—the one that's supposedly full of textbooks, but actually has my costume and helmet. So now I'm carrying a super heavy duffel bag filled with all the junk I hardly ever use that I don't want anyone finding and my—

"How many books do you need?" Mayka asks. Yeah, my backpack is sort of ridiculously big and bulging. The armor parts of my costume are lightweight, but it's still a lot.

"You know how it is. They overload you more and more every semester." I start toward the door.

"Goosh!" she shouts.

Internally, I groan. On the outside, I put on my best smile. She has no idea she's stopping me from anything more important than a boring lecture.

"Police confirm an attack—" comes Dale's voice from the other room.

I gently pull myself away from Mom's grasp, giving her a dozen kisses to ease the release.

"Love you, Mayka," I tell her, slinging my bag over my shoulder. Then, I head out the door, which closes softly behind me. Now, I break into a run. I can't waste any more time, especially if this is some kind of an attack. I grab the elevator for the highest floor it goes to, then take the stairs to the roof. You need a code to open the lock on the door to get out, but Sawyer and I know it. I've been using this as a shortcut to get around the city.

Just before I exit, I do a quick-change—which, I must say, I've gotten pretty good at—and stow my backpack and duffel. I take a moment to get my bearings. I can see practically anything from here, and it only takes a second for me to spot Wall Street, just beyond One World Trade Center. To see smoke rising in that location again…

I was really young during 9/11, but living in the city, you never stop seeing little reminders of what happened. I'd seen the video footage a million times.

I back up and get a few long strides before diving off Douglas Tower. The reason I call this a shortcut is that I can glide almost anywhere in Manhattan from so high up. I'm sure someone who's afraid of heights would be terrified doing this, but I've always been something of a daredevil, even as a little girl. My parents were always surprised that I wasn't a regular Mt Sinai Children's Hospital all the time because I was always climbing up some things and jumping off others.

I cut through the wind like a knife on my way south toward the disturbance.

People are always trying to commit crimes in the Financial District. I mean, put the word "financial" in the name, and everyone thinks they can make some quick cash. The 1st Precinct of the NYPD is great—they're the ones who patrol the area—but I know they're going to need some extra power.

My feet skid to a stop on a rooftop. I nearly facepalm when I see that the attack is on the Federal Reserve. Watch Diehard much? People, there's no way you're stealing gold bars from the Federal Reserve Bank. It won't work!

Police and fire crews are arriving at the same time, which just goes to show how fast I can get around when I use my shortcut. While the firefighters get their equipment ready, the cops stand in a state of confusion, most behind open car doors with guns drawn, waiting for whoever did this to come out.

I leap down behind the cops, hands positioned upward in a sign of goodwill. Now that I'm a registered member of the Guild, no one will give me much trouble, but the last thing you want to do is startle one of the good guys into opening fire on you.

"What's going on, officer?" I ask.

I have to admit, I put on a sort of a fake voice when I talk to the police or anyone else for that matter. I tell myself it's because I don't want to take any chances they might recognize Amy Chen, but I don't know. It's fun.

"We know what you know," the cop tells me, pointing toward the building where there's a huge hole with smoke still pouring from it.

"Any sign of the perps?"

"Nothing."

"Hostages?"

"None we can see," the cop answers. "Look, if you wanna know more, go talk to the captain. Yeah?"

Geez, fine. That's when I notice the guy is shaking. Like, really shaking.

I lean in and say, "It's gonna be okay, officer. Just rely on your training."

He looks over his shoulder at me and I think he's going to thank me or something, but then he wrinkles his face. "Get the hell out of here, will ya?"

Customers and employees of the bank are still streaming from the building and running in all directions. Some want to get out of there, while others are holding up their phones taking pictures and video. There's a reported two-hundred billion dollars worth of precious gold in that building, but it's five stories underground. I don't know what they were thinking! Then I hear another report on my police scanner that clues me in.

"Bank alarms going off on Fulton. Units respond."

Crap. It's a distraction. A really damn big one.

"Ah, not another one," the cop says. "Make yourself useful, will ya?"

"On it!" I shout.

I'm not high up on Douglas Tower this time, so it takes me a bit more effort to climb the few blocks to where the alarms are sounding. The scene here is totally different. No giant chasms in the brick, no flashing lights or pedestrians snapping photos.

I use some of the tricks I've learned from Sawyer to parkour on the rooftops, since my normal gliding technique won't cut it. I'm above the small alley between a Chase Bank and what looks like one of those co-working places that no one wants to use anymore. I can hear voices, people laughing. Below, there's a black van parked with two back doors wide open, and five guys in brightly colored armor, not too different from mine but with sort of a medieval flair, loading in bags full of what I assume to be cash. Each robber wears a different color, so neon it almost glows: red, green, blue, yellow, and orange. Honestly, it looks pretty ridiculous.

I hop down on top of their van, and it gives them quite a scare.

Then something happens that strikes me as being so funny that I can't help laughing despite whatever danger I might be in. When I was a kid, I didn't read many superhero comic books, but the ones I did usually had some villain or villains on the cover making a big announcement, proclaiming loudly about who they were or what kind of chaos they were causing while the hero or heroes stood nearby looking on. At least, that's how I remember it.

So these guys are marching in and out in their gaudy armor with giant bags stuffed with cash. One stops when he sees me there, the others follow suit. Behind me, I can finally hear the sirens and see the lights painting the walls.

The leader shouts, "Make way for the Neon Knights!"

That's the part where I start laughing.

Except it's not so funny when the one in orange lifts their hand and a glowing crossbow appears in it, aimed at me. A bolt of pure energy fires and I'm barely able to avoid before it explodes and shatters the brick wall behind me. In dodging it and the ensuing debris, I leap off the van and try to kick their apparent leader, Red, in the head. I'm sure he barely feels it through his heavy helmet, but it distracts him long enough for me to pull a roundhouse on Green who was just getting ready to bring a mace down on my back. I spin back to Red just as he draws a big sword with crackling energy coursing through it and swings it at me like a baseball bat. I'd hate to think what it might have done if he'd connected.

These guys are playing for keeps. Wow.

"Come on, little girl," Red says.

"Don't make this sexist," the yellow one says in what's clearly a feminine voice.

"Thank you!" I say to her just as she brings a glowing, spiked club across in a swipe at me.

I flip back, avoiding it, but just barely.

"This gives new meaning to going medieval on someone!" I say.

I get a good look at them and realize they are all pretty young. Younger than me, probably. It's like a teenage gang. Wow.

"That was stupid," Green says.

"I know," I admit.

He comes at me with his electricity mace or whatever it is, and I sort of don't know what to do. I can feel its heat.

Tires screech behind me. Police empty out of their cars. One of the cops, apparently whoever is the highest rank, shouts, "Drop your weapons!" But instead of dropping them, Orange shoots his crossbow and nearly kills the officer when the patrol car hood blows up.

The rest of the officers open fire, but their bullets just ricochet off the Knights' armor. In fact, a few of the bullets nearly hit me on the rebound. I probably look like a white version of these idiots. The cops either don't know I'm on their side or don't care. That becomes evident very quickly.

In my distraction, Green, Blue, and Yellow triple team me. So much for female solidarity! I'm just lucky none use their electricity weapons. I take a kick to the stomach, and even through my graphene armor, it hurts. One drives their boot into my helmet.

The thing about helmets is that, although I don't feel the actual kick against my skull, my head still rattles around a bit inside. I'm disoriented while they continue the attack but I do my best to fight back, rolling into a squat. I draw my extendable bow staff and raise it in time to block Green's mace. Sparks fly in all directions, blinding me. I do, however, manage to bring my staff around hard and crack Green across the neck where his helmet doesn't quite meet his armor. He staggers sideways and into the wall, where I jab him with the butt of the staff, then whip it back around on top of his helmet.

With him sort of disabled, I return my attention to Blue and Yellow, but they have already started charging at the cops. Were they that sure Green would take me out alone? They attack the police with their modern, energy-powered versions of medieval weapons. Yellow whips out her club with the spikes on the end—I think it's called a morning star. Blue flails his heavy axe. It literally slices through the door to the police cruiser. Thankfully, the police are smart enough to back off since their guns are basically useless.

I'm hurt, but not out. I stumble to the van and tear open the driver side door, stand on the edge and take a play out of their book.

"Hey, you psychotic highlighters!" I shout.

They all turn on me, leaving the police alone for a second.

Red points and shouts, "Get her!"

Slamming the door shut, the engine already running, I throw it in reverse and squeal out of the alley, watching in my side mirrors as bags cascade out and cash floats all over the street.

FIVE

SAWYER

"*Neon Knights?"*

"That's what he said," Osprey tells me over our communicators. They aren't phones. Phones are traceable. Then people might figure out who we are, and family members or friends will be in danger. Our communicators are private and run on Frank's satellite network with the best security money can buy. It's odd to think that giant hunks of metal are floating around space almost exclusively for my use—well, me and the rest of the Guild, but still.

"Are you okay?" I ask Osprey.

"I'm definitely shaken up," she says and I can hear it in her voice. "Those guys were tough and their weapons were legit."

"Where are you now?"

"Just dropped off the van at the police station. Gotta get to class, now."

"After that?" I ask. "You're going to class, just like that?"

"What else can I do? It's freaking Columbia University. It's like fifty grand a year. If I don't show up and Dad finds out, what do I tell him? Plus, I've got an exam in two weeks and I absolutely need to pass. You know how it is."

She's right about that. But wow. What a tough chick. I can't imagine a fight like that right before school.

"Another National Sidekick advert just went up," she says.

Guhhh.

"Where's this one?"

"Riverside."

You know how I hate being called a sidekick? Well, apparently, now there's gonna be a whole day dedicated to that insulting term. The Guild even calls us proteges, but not this time.

"Frank still hasn't told you anything more about it?" she asks.

"Not a word. I'm tired of asking. I'm surprised the Guild hasn't told you more."

"Apparently, they want it to be special for everyone. No spoilers. Hey, I gotta go. Good luck at *training*."

Guuuhhhh again. She's not talking about arms training, or martial arts or anything. Today starts job training.

"Thanks." I don't even try to hide the sarcasm.

Comms click off and I'm left with nothing to do but follow through with this ridiculous fast food thing. Thanks, Frank.

Training at a lot of jobs is OTJ… right? On the job training. But here, there's something called Big Frankie University. And, yes, it's just as ridiculous as you'd think. First of all, it's in a fancy office building that's *way* nicer than my school. Possibly even nicer than Osprey's. Brand new desks and white boards, textbooks with spines that still crack when you open them, vending machines in the hallways with good snacks and not that healthy crap they have in the ones at school.

Everything has the cartoon cannibal cow all over it—the textbook, the worksheets, the presentations, the videos—oh, man, the videos. You've never suffered like I have until you have to watch a preteen in a cow costume performing a dance, and excitedly dressing a burger while the narrator explains how to put lettuce on it. I get so tired of looking at him in the first few minutes but its like a trainwreck.

I even try bringing up to the instructor—we're supposed to call him "professor" if you can believe it, because he apparently has a PhD in fast food prep or something—about the fact that the cow is cooking beef. He's grilling his own kind. You would have thought I'd torn off my clothes and ran around on his desk naked, the way he looked at me. He told me that employees were never to speak of it, and that I'd better comply with that rule if I wanted to work for Big Frankie. As if the *cow* owns the restaurant chain.

Whatever.

There are lectures and tests and projects and everything. All on day one. I almost don't pass the first quiz. My special gift of memorizing and mimicking only works when I'm paying attention, and this crap is so boring that I'm not. This class is definitely pushing the bounds of my concentration, not to mention my preoccupation with the Neon Knights.

Who are these guys? Osprey said they had armor and power weapons, which hopefully means they don't have superpowers. The last thing we need is more superpowered villains running around while Frank is incapacitated and Alex is stuck in Boston.

Again, my mind is drifting and I catch the end of one of the *Professor's* last statement. How hot is the oil in the deep fryer? How often does it have to be changed? What type of vegetable oil is it?

Fun fact: I don't give a crap, and I don't understand why I have to know any of this. I'm gonna be going through the motions of either selling or cooking this stuff. That's it.

How many calories is in a chocolate shake? Vanilla? What if you mix the two? Do you just average them? And don't even get me started on strawberry shakes. Exactly four whole strawberries in each shake, and they have to fit in a one cup scoop. They are strawberries for God's sake. How does Frank own this place?

How can someone who has spent most of his life tossing bad guys in jail bother with this nonsense?

How many times do you have to shake the can of whipped cream before you spray? What should the exact height of the shake be with or without the whipped cream? And how long past the "best by" date can you still use the Maraschino cherries that we place on top of the whipped cream?

Anyone? Anyone?

I also have to create a presentation, and the subject he assigns me is a timeline of the history of the restaurant. But as stupid as the whole thing is, it's also very informative. Especially when it really hits me that the whole thing was started by my grandfather.

Grandfather.

So weird. My mom's dad died when I was little, so I never really knew him either. But at least I'd heard stories about him my whole life from Mom and her sister, Aunt Patricia—Patty. I didn't even know who my *dad* was until last year—and I'm still trying to wrap my head around it. Never mind my paternal grandfather. And it wasn't exactly great news.

I'm almost proud until I remember that he was the city's biggest crime lord. I guess I'd subconsciously been avoiding looking into Franklin Douglas, Jr. since I found out I was Frank's son. I'm not sure what I was afraid of… maybe that I'd see some of myself in him?

I study a picture that I pull up through a web search. It's from an old newspaper article about him opening the very restaurant I'm now gonna be working in. He's dressed in one of those big pinstripe suits you always see in the old movie. Doesn't look like a murdering psychopath or anything. He's wearing a big smile as he cuts the ribbon with the help of a little boy standing next to him.

Ho-Lee… Whoa! Hold on…

I go to the original article and read the caption. *"Business Leader Franklin Douglas, Jr., pictured here with his son Trey, age 8."*

Trey? What the—Ahhh… the *third.* Trey. Sure enough, it's Frank himself as a kid. No smile there, though. Frank was apparently always the serious person he is today, even as a kid. I guess maybe losing your mom at such a young age can do that to you.

I pull up everything I can find on Frank, Jr. being a criminal, but as you could expect there's very little, and what does come up seems to be based almost entirely on rumor and innuendo. I'll say one thing for granddad, he knew how to cover his tracks. From what I can gather, Frank—my dad—didn't even realize Junior was a criminal until just before he, well… killed him. And, now that I think about it, he must have covered everything up about his own father once he took over Douglas Industries. Maybe that's why there's almost nothing here. I can't even find mention of his death, anywhere.

Frank has probably spent many years and a whole lot of money making sure the family's dirty laundry stays buried. Is that a mixed metaphor? I'm not even sure. That's got to be wrong. Why would anyone bury dirty laundry?

Anyway, at first, it kind of bothers me that Frank kept it covered up, but then I think about what I would do—what I *will* do, when I'm the one carrying on the family legacy. Am I gonna admit that I'm the grandson of such a horrible human being, or just keep the skeletons in the closet where they've been for so long? That one's not mixed, I'm sure of it.

I guess it's hard to say what I'm gonna do decades from now, but for the moment, I'm content to let sleeping dogs lie.

Then, as I'm about to give up, I find some conspiracy site waaaay down the list of search results. And it's a veritable gold mine. There's a picture of a woman at the top. Shelly Charmane and next to it, a cracked open egg. The URL bar says shellycracks.com.

Oh, I get it. Shelly. Egg shells. Clever, I guess?

The headline: Shelly Cracks Biggest Cover-Up in New York History.

She gets very specific and sort of pieces everything together about how Frank, Jr. was such a respected business leader and philanthropist on the surface but underneath, was a kingpin. Here's an excerpt.

Franklin Douglas Jr.'s reach extended into every conceivable criminal enterprise in the city—in the tri-state area, really. From white collar crime to the mob, to biker gangs and street-level thugs, Frank, Jr. controlled everything from drug dealing to illegal weapons and ammo, to illegal gambling, prostitution and human trafficking.

Wow, you get the picture.

The craziest part is that even the supervillains seemed to bow to him. I can see why this isn't a popular or well-known website, because I even have trouble believing all of it, and I know that it's true. At least most of it, anyway. That makes me wonder how much of the other stuff I'd written off as conspiracy theories might actually be true. Yikes.

There are a lot of pictures here, most of them pretty bad quality. Some black and white, a lot of them grainy. But one really catches my attention. There's a young Asian man standing next to Frank, Jr. in a group picture, and I'm almost sure that it's Luis Chen. Mr. Chen is older than Frank, but he's not as old as Junior would have been if he was still alive. Great, now I'm gonna be wondering if Mr. Chen might be dirty? I don't really know anything about his history, and I've never had any reason to ask about it or look into it. I mean, he's always been really good to me.

He is quite a mystery, though. Now that I know he worked for Junior before Frank took over, it makes me wonder: Was Mr. Chen part of the whole organized crime part of the Douglas Industries, or was he strictly involved in the legit business aspects, like he is now?

At least, I assume he is now. Then again, he designs a bunch of our gear.

And what does Frank know about it? Would he have taken him on as his most trusted ally if he'd been a criminal before? Did Mr. Chen help Frank murder Junior? This has my head spinning.

Oh, yeah, and where did he get that bionic hand? It was from the war, right? Or was it?

My first instinct is to start saving all the pictures and screenshot the articles that I find on this website. But when it's all over, I just delete it all. Sure, I want to know my family history, but is it worth the cost if Frank ever finds out that I've been digging into it? Especially since he's worked so hard to keep it hidden?

But what if Mr. Chen is actually some kind of criminal mastermind and Frank doesn't realize it? I'm so confused. I don't know what to do. Frank isn't stupid. I know that. For now, I'll just worry about finishing up my presentation and concentrate on the fact that Junior started the company I'm now working for.

Okay, Sawyer, just focus.

So Frank, Jr. was a really bad person, but came across as a good guy who everyone loved. It was almost like he wore a mask to hide who he really—oh, crap. I guess in some ways I *am* like my grandfather. I hope that's all I inherited from him.

I add the picture of the two Franks together to the presentation and decide to leave all the rest out. I can't wait for Frank—er, *Trey*—to see this.

Before I quit my research for the night, I decide to check one more thing. I type "Neon Knights" into the search bar.

Mostly all that comes up is an old song from *Black Sabbath* but that was when Dio sang for them, so I've never really given it much credence. Always been an Ozzy guy, myself. What? I'm young... sure. But metal transcends age.

When I click the "News" tab, some stuff from today comes up. Reports on a gang of young kids robbing a bank, explosives. Yeah, this is what Osprey was talking about for sure.

Turns out, the one dressed in Green who went by Mace got arrested. Police say his real name is Martin Garza. The rest escaped.

I check out the "Videos" tab. Just a shaky cellphone video... Oh, nice! It's Osprey kicking the guy's ass. Damn, she's got some serious moves. Then they get the upper hand and she really starts taking a beating. The video ends with a police officer placing his and over the camera and telling the phone owner to get lost.

Poor Amy.

I consider the way this past year has gone and maybe I haven't made it clear, but the city is only getting worse. There's still no open mention of Black Harrier being gone, but I think maybe the bad guys know it.

I consider reaching out to the Guild, but I don't have that kind of access. Alex does, but he's got enough to worry about, I think. Frank... well, he's just not the same. But they all have time to throw a freaking festival or whatever for Sidekicks? Ridiculous.

We need help and if Frank and Alex aren't gonna do it, it's up to me.

SIX
SAWYER

I get home after dark and all the lights are off at the apartment. Good. That means Mom's probably out with Frank, so I can get some work done for school in peace. As I'm heading to my room, I hear some shuffling coming from the kitchen.

I almost crap myself when the lights come on and I hear, "Surprise!"

Mom, Frank, and a few others jump out at me, shouting and clapping. Mom carries a cake with a candle in the shape of a 17 on it, and they all start singing to me.

"Happy Birthday, sweetheart," Mom says when the song is through.

"Happy Birthday, kid," Frank agrees.

My heart is still racing from the shock as I blow out the candles. I had completely forgotten that it was my birthday.

"What did you wish for?" Frank asks.

Mom playfully slaps him and says, "You don't ask that. Then it won't come true."

"Oh, right," he says, smiling and rolling his eyes.

I don't know if I've ever, *ever* seen Frank roll his eyes. Or smile. No, that's not fair. But still, he's acting weird. Normal almost.

Other than Mr. Chen, the others are people I don't know very well—a couple of my mom's friends and a few neighbors. Nobody my own age. It makes me realize that I don't really have any friends. At school, I'm either alone or hanging out with Javier, but that's more because I can't get rid of him than because he's really my friend.

I have Alex, but he's quite a bit older and obviously, he's in Boston now. Then there's Osprey. It would be cool if she was here with her dad, but he has no idea we even know each other. It's not like we can really hang around in our civilian identities. It would make him way too suspicious.

We are all sitting around, engaging in conversations I highly doubt anyone really cares about. Mom gets up to do something in the kitchen and I decide to take advantage of it.

"So, Mr. Douglas," I say, "did you hear about those kids who tried to rob the Federal Reserve or whatever?"

Frank squints at me, then opens his mouth but my mom cuts him off.

"Oh, Sawyer," Mom says from the other side of the room, "let's not talk about such horrible things. This is a party!" I wouldn't be surprised to find out she has super hearing.

I keep trying to find a way to gauge Frank's thoughts on the subject but every time, my mom is there to thwart me.

Then, I try another tactic.

"How about this National Sidekick Day?"

Frank gives me a disapproving stare.

"Pretty stupid-sounding if you ask me," I say.

"No one did, dear," Mom says.

I throw my hands in the air internally. We end up sitting around eating cake, then I open some presents. By the time my party is over, I barely have enough time to finish my homework for school and the essay for my job training before going to bed.

Such is the life of a superhero, I guess.

School is, as always, a real joy the next day. I jump on my brand new board as soon as I'm out the door of Douglas Tower and the doorman gives me a "Good morning" and a wave. Hard to believe it's the same guy who wouldn't let me in last year when I needed to talk to Mr. Chen after Frank had gone missing. But he eventually gave in, so I forgave him, and now we get along really well. Actually, believe it or not, we hang out at the arcade next door every now and then. He likes to play this old game called *Time Crisis* and I like watching him lose. So, it's a win win.

I keep a lookout for anything weird or suspicious on my way, same as I always do. Only this time, my eyes are peeled for bright neon armor. The remaining four Neon Knights have, smartly, kept low since Mace got arrested. The news this morning had Osprey front and center, which is never really a good thing. Apparently, her quick response saved close to a hundred grand. But that means it *cost* the Knights that much too.

She's gonna be target *numero uno.*

I tense up every time I go past an alley or get to a corner. Not because I'm worried about the Knights, but because I'm afraid Javier is gonna suddenly appear. I'm beginning to think he waits for me and then makes it look like a happy accident. A conversation with him always ends up with me doing all the heavy lifting. Plus, it means walking instead of riding my skateboard. I mean, there's a reason I ride my board to school, and having Javier around sort of defeats the purpose.

Luckily, today I'm in the clear, so I make it to school with plenty of time to spare. Plenty of time to swing by my locker and grab some stuff before getting to class early and hopefully avoiding Logan too. But I don't make it inside.

Here's a lesson in life: If one thing goes your way—i.e. avoiding Javi—don't expect your next wish to come true also. Case in point? Logan's here early also and he's not alone. Benji Torres is with him. Remember that convenience store robbery I foiled last fall? The one where Javi saw that I had mad martial arts skills? This was the kid I recognized from school. He joined the wrestling team, and he and Logan have become really buddy-buddy ever since.

They approach me on the sidewalk outside, and it's obvious Logan has a bone to pick. We haven't had any major confrontations since last year, but it's not like we're friends now either. Or even get along. We barely tolerate one another. The word "hate" may have been tossed around.

"Hey, loser, why didn't you try out for wrestling last week?"

"Cuz I didn't want to?" I tell him.

"You're letting the team down!" He says it—yells it, actually—like it's some kind of life-or-death thing.

"If I'm such a loser, why would you *want* me on the team?"

"That's—it's—you know, cuz…" He gets that furrowed brow a lot. I know, I know, *thinking is hard,* right?

"Yeah, can we put a pin in this conversation for now? How about you get back to me when you recover your faculties."

"Recover? I'm not even injured. You don't know crap."

"Yeah, *I'm* the dumb one. I totally get it."

"You better shut it, bro, or I'm gonna meet you after school and shut it for you."

"That hasn't worked out well in the past," I say, trying to push by. He shoves me a bit and I have to bite my lip to keep from decking him.

"You got lucky. Plus, I've been training at that MMA place down the street."

"Me too," Benji says, finally speaking.

I've seen that place. It's mostly grandmas and kids working out in there.

"That's good," I say, even-toned.

"What's that supposed to mean?" Benji says, flexing on me.

It's really a stupid move considering he is one of the few who really knows what I'm capable of. Maybe he realizes I can't show it right here on the campus' front lawn.

"Nothing I just—"

Benji pushes me. I won't lie; I wasn't expecting it. I stumble backward and trip over a parking stop. There's no graceful way to do that, by the way. My board clatters away, and I scramble to my feet. I hear some girls laughing behind me, but I don't look.

"That wasn't smart, man," I tell him.

"You have no idea what I am capable of," Benji says. "No idea."

The threat is pretty well executed. If I were anyone else, I might have been scared.

It was my turn to ask, "What's that supposed to mean?"

"You'll see, twerp."

"Twerp?" Who still says "twerp?"

I decide to keep that to myself. It's not worth it. None of this is.

"All right, guys," I say, picking up my board. "I'm not looking for trouble. I just wanna get to class."

I push past them. Then I change my mind just as I'm rounding the corner and jump on my board.

"By the way, Logan, how's your mom? Tell her I miss her."

"Aaaaarrrrggh!" Logan tries running after me, but I'm long gone on my board. If this is any indication, I'm sure this is the start to another wonderful day. He's pretty fast on the football field, but he's definitely a fullback. He has to get his speed going, and then it's a short sprint and he's out of breath. Also like his mom. Just kidding. I don't know.

Fabiola and the rest of the cheerleaders are practicing their routines before school. There's some kind of pep rally today in the gym, so I'm sure they're gonna be doing their thing. They stop and watch, and I think that makes Logan quit, embarrassed that he looks like a gorilla chasing a gazelle.

I haven't spoken to Fabiola at all since the Halloween party last year. She kissed me in the hospital and I hate to admit how many times I've fantasied about that moment since. But afterward, she went right back to pretending I don't even exist, which is fine with me. I don't understand what I ever saw in her anyway other than oh, my God, she's hot.

But now that I know her and experienced one of her "mean girl" stunts personally, any desire I once had for her is long gone.

Pretty much. No, completely. Well, maybe a little is left. I mean, she's still hot. Who am I kidding?

The rest of school was boring as usual. I'd really only escaped Logan and Benji until third period, but they didn't try anything too stupid with Mr. Peel watching over us. Oh, yeah. I've got Peel for History class again. He still doesn't like me, but I get the impression he dislikes Logan even more. So every time Logan opened his mouth, Peel shut him up. It was nice for a change.

The pep rally was fine, I guess? It's not really my thing, people wearing uniforms and performing…

After school, I have to attend my graduation ceremony. No, not from high school. From Big Frankie University. I was gonna skip it until I found out that you can't get your certificate unless you attend the ceremony, and you can't work unless you have the certificate. So then I was gonna just show up and grab the stupid paper and leave, but I made the mistake of mentioning it to my mom. She got all excited and said she wanted to go.

Now it's a *thing*. She makes me dress up and even wear a tie. She puts on her nicest dress—one she wore for Easter church last year. And we ride down to the "university" together. Then things get crazy.

Mom invited Frank.

Can you imagine what happens when the owner of a fast food chain shows up to one of their stupid little training graduations? It's ridiculous.

Everyone is taking a picture either *of* him or *with* him. He's in full billionaire playboy mode, too, pretending to eat it up. What none of them realize is that it's all fake. Every bit of it. It was never Black Harrier that was the mask. It's always been Franklin Douglas III.

Oh, and my mom loves it, too. There's one thing a kid should never have to experience, and that's what Mom was like before you were born. Mom got pregnant with me *by Frank*—I'll never get used to that—when she was barely older than I am now. Wow. That's nuts. Frank is a good bit older than her. Don't worry, I did the math. It was legal. Sort of messed up, but legal.

Kevin, the manager, must have gotten word, because he shows up all covered in flop sweat and starts kissing Frank's butt. Then he starts cozying up to me in front of Frank. I feel his moist shirtsleeve against my neck, my face way too close to his stained armpit. He then informs Frank that he can already tell I'm gonna be one of his best workers. A bright mind. Quick on my feet. Superb communication skills. What a freaking suck-up. What happened to him being afraid of the appearance of "despotism?"

The whole affair is "catered" with burgers, nuggets, fries, and sodas. Fancy. They have a couple of cakes, which, having taken the extensive course to become an employee, I recognize as the ones they wheel out for children's birthday parties. Same with the decorations. But I guess it's nice that they did something for us.

Everything is fine until the "professor" starts bragging about how I gave the best presentation on the company's history that he'd ever seen and asks me to show it to everyone at the ceremony. Seriously? No warning? My mouth goes dry and my chest clenches up. Not just because I don't like going up in front of audiences—like any normal person—but also because I realize immediately that I hadn't shown it to Frank yet like I was planning.

Uh oh.

A projector and laptop are already on stage and everyone is already applauding for me to get up there, so there's no time to warn him. Mom is beaming with pride as I shuffle toward the front of the room. At least there's that. As far as she's concerned, I've never really given her much to be proud of.

If she only knew.

Remember the presentation is no problem due to my special gift, but that doesn't stop my voice from cracking as I talk through the introductory slides. I start with the construction of the first restaurant, the origins of the cannibal cow character, and how different the menu was back in the beginning—especially the prices. It started off as strictly a kids place. Parents wouldn't even eat when they went. Amazing how things change.

Then I get to the picture of Frank Junior and "Trey." I try keeping my voice neutral, but I'm actually really nervous about Frank's reaction, and it shows. My eyes sting with sweat. I've faced La Cucaracha head-to-head and I've never been this mortified. I try to read Frank's expression, but with the houselights off and the glare from the projector, everyone out there is just a silhouette. Then something even worse than I was expecting happens.

Frank stands and walks out.

SEVEN

AMY

N*ervous.*

I couldn't be any more nervous as I ride the elevator down from our condo to Douglas Industries headquarters. I rehearse over and over again what I'm going to say. The elevator *dings* and I'm met with the huge Douglas Industries logo backlit by a bright white light. Below that, the receptionist flashes teeth almost the same color.

"Hi, Pam! How are you?" I can't stand Pam. She's so fake, and I'm almost certain she's just waiting in the wings to be my new stepmom after my parents get divorced, even though she's barely a decade older than me. Plus, she's not my dad's type *at all.* Frank's the one who likes redheads.

"Amy! It's been so long." She trots around the desk on her high heels in one of those mini-step moves you see on TV but wouldn't think anyone would ever do in real life. Probably because her pencil skirt is so damn tight. Looks like she painted it on. She holds out her arms and gives me a big hug, followed by an air kiss on each cheek.

I repeat the gesture back to her. Yes, I know. I'm fully aware that it makes me just as fake. But I'm a superhero with a secret identity to maintain. I have an excuse.

"Is my father in? I need to talk to him." She runs back around to the other side of the desk and holds up her finger as she dials his office.

"Mr. Chen? Your beautiful daughter's here to see you. I hope I'm not interrupting your meeting." She pauses as she listens to his reply. "Okey-doke, I'll let her know." She never, ever spoke to him that way before my parents split up. It was all business before.

"He'll be right out. We haven't had a chance to catch up in *forever*. We really need to do lunch." We've never done lunch. We're never *going* to do lunch.

"Absolutely! Let's do that real soon." Luckily, I can now see my dad coming down the hall through the floor-to-ceiling glass, which saves me from having to actually set up a time.

"Oh, there he is," I say, practically sprinting away from her toward the doors.

"Hello, darling." We kiss each other on the cheek—a real one. "What a nice surprise. Come on back."

He rests his hand on my arm and escorts me down the hall. Pam gives me a fake smile and mouths "Call me" while doing that weird hand thing people do when they say that. I smile and nod before turning away. I don't have her number. She doesn't have mine. It's all a tiresome charade.

We get back to Dad's office and, as usual, the first thing I look at is that creepy-ass painting of Frank that hangs on his wall above the mantle. It used to scare the crap out of me, with its eyes that look like they follow you around. Oh, my God. When I was little and my dad left me in here alone while he went to do business or something? I would literally have nightmares about that painting. Now I just tend to think about how much Frank has gone downhill since his glory days when that was painted.

I sit in one of the plush chairs across from him at his desk. He used to have a picture of me at my high school graduation on the credenza behind his desk but now, there's a big empty place. I almost ask until I realize my mom was in that picture. All the pictures are gone. Wow.

"To what do I owe the pleasure of this rare visit to my sanctum sanctorum?" I don't know why he calls it that. I have no idea what it means.

Before I have time to think about it, I blurt out the words I'd been chewing on for the last hour. "I need to talk to you, and it seems like it's never a good time, so I decided to just do it now while I still have the courage."

"Oh, wow," he says, sitting forward a bit. "Can I get you something to drink?"

"What? No. I just need to tell you something."

He leans back into his chair and says, "Sure, honey. What is it that has you so worried?"

"I don't want to move. I want to stay here in New York with you."

The only visible reaction from him is a slightly raised eyebrow, but I know that he is definitely much more surprised than that. "I see. Well, that's certainly good news for me, since I would miss you tremendously. But… what about your mother?"

"That's what I need to talk to you about. I don't know how to tell her. And I'm running out of time."

"You're going to miss the chance to see the world."

"Dad, it's Bulgaria."

He laughs, which eases my tension just a bit.

"What do I do?" I ask.

He leans back in his chair and steeples his fingers in a gesture I can remember him doing my entire life. "That is quite a dilemma, isn't it?"

"Can you help me?" I ask, doing my best to give him a sad little girl face without it being too obvious about it.

"I can certainly try, but I'm concerned that any part I play in relaying your wishes will be interpreted by your mother as an attempt to manipulate you into staying." So calculating. Always so calculating. Which, if I'm honest, is exactly why I'm here.

"I know. But I just can't bring myself to tell her, Bàba. I don't expect you to do it, but I need your help figuring out how." I hope I'm not laying it on too thick. I know he can see right through me when I do.

"I'll certainly try to assist you in finding a way of letting her know without crushing her. But, I must ask first, what are your reasons? School? Friends? Have you thought about telling her the truth?"

I hadn't even thought about school. That's an easy one. What kind of universities do they have in Sofia?

"Um. Well, school, sure. But, it's a lot of things."

"Such as?"

He has me cornered. I may not share everything with him, but he knows I'm not that into college and that I don't have many friends. He's a lot harder to fool than my mom, that's for sure. I don't know what to say, and now I feel his eyes on me more than Frank's little beady painted ones. He's getting suspicious.

"Sweetheart? Is everything all right? Let me order us some drinks." Before I can deter him, he's buzzing Pam.

"Yes, Mr. Chen?"

"Can you have MJ bring in some beverages?"

"Mary-Jane's at lunch, but I'll gladly bring them in," she says.

Oh, I bet you would, you gold-digging hussy.

"That would be great," he says.

Then, he narrows his eyes at me. I hate when he does that. It's like he's some kind of robot analyzing me for data.

Since I don't know what to do, I just sit there for a moment.

"So, if it isn't just school, then what?" he says.

I didn't come in here to leave in the same position I started in. Desperate, I just blurt out—"I have a boyfriend!"

Crap! Why did I say that?

As soon as I do, the door opens and stupid Pam comes in with the cart.

"Oh, my God!" she says. "That's so wonderful, Sweetie!"

Sweetie? Are you kidding me?

Dad looks shocked. He clears his throat a few times and says, "Really? That's… uh… interesting news. I had no idea."

Pam oversteps every single boundary and pulls the other black leather chair close to me and sits with her hand on my knee. "You've got to tell us everything."

I turn back to my dad and I think I can feel my jaw dragging on the carpet.

"Well?" he says, as if his receptionist wasn't acting like she belonged in the Twilight Zone. "Is it anyone I've met?"

My mind is racing and coming up with nothing. Nada. Zilch. Blank.

"It's Alex." What. Are. You. *DOING*? I panicked. I said the first name that popped into my head. And I'm pissed at myself for that being the first name. Now I'm screwed.

"Alex… Garner? Frank's…" His eyes shift over to Pam and back to me. "Friend?"

Wow. He's more flustered than I am. And he's *never* flustered. I can't believe he almost let it spill to me that Alex was the Red Kite. I just bested dad. Score one for Amy. Except, it doesn't feel like a win because now I'm apparently dating Alex.

"He sounds *cute*," Pam says.

I'm pretty sure everyone's forgotten about drinks at this point.

"Yeah. Alex Garner." Okay, I've dug this ditch. Now I'm going to lie in it. And hope someone buries me.

"Didn't he move to Boston some time ago?" Dad asks as if he doesn't know.

I nod. "Yes. Yes, he did. But we sort of got together before that, and now we're having a… long distance relationship."

"I see. Very well, then." There goes that computer brain of his. I can see it going into overdrive.

"Do you have any pictures?" Pam asks.

I ignore her and address my dad. "Very well, then?"

"It's just. Darling, I'm not quite sure how you expected me to respond. He's quite a bit older than you, and I've known him for quite some time."

"Oh, an older man," Pam says. "I like older men."

Unreal.

Dad stands and circles the desk toward the drink cart. I guess he didn't forget. He pours something that fizzes. Pam is still brimming with unbridled elation. Doesn't she have phones to answer or something?

He hands me a drink, sits on the edge of his desk, and sighs. "But the reality is, you're an adult, and you can make your own decisions."

I can what? Wait. Yes. That's right.

"Yeah, well, I'm very mature for my age."

He raises an eyebrow at that also. It's his signature move, and the most anyone can usually get out of him. We both know that isn't true, at least as far as relationships go.

"Oh, very," Pam says, nodding with her head tilted a bit to the side.

"Perhaps you should just tell your mother the truth, then," Dad offers. "She certainly places a great deal of importance on… social relationships."

This isn't one bit how I expected or wanted this conversation to go. I almost swear but I restrain myself and take a sip of the ginger ale.

"That sounds like a plan," I say.

"Perfect," my dad says as he returns to his desk. "Glad we got that figured out, aren't you?"

"Sure."

"So glad," Pam says.

I stand to leave while dad sits and starts working on some papers.

"I'll walk you out, darling," Pam tells me, and I know she's purposely using the same name she heard my dad call me.

When we make it to his office door he says, "Oh, and the next time Alex is in town, perhaps the three of us can all go to dinner together."

"I'm sure he would love that." He would hate that. He would totally hate that.

Crap. Now I have to warn Alex before Dad says something to him. And I do *not* want to have that conversation.

NINE

SAWYER

F*alling apart.*

Yes, that's right. Things are falling apart in my life. Everything was going so well after the nightmare with Maléfique was over, with Alex being the new Black Harrier, Osprey being our new partner, and Mom finally turning her life around.

Then things started going sideways. Not just sideways… upside-freaking-down.

The Guild forcing Alex to move back to Boston. Mom dating Frank. Osprey and I were having enough trouble on our own without the Neon Knights showing up out of nowhere. And now Frank being all pissed off at me over my stupid idea of including that picture of him and his dad. How could I have been such an idiot? It's such an obviously colossal mistake now in hindsight.

I need to blow off some steam, and the neighborhood is in need of some clean up, so it's time to try out the new helmet and get out there. There's no way I'm gonna try this thing out with Osprey around. No way.

Standing on a rooftop, I switch on the AI. But nothing happens.

"Hello?"

In response, Tiffany appears in front of me, as if she's standing right there on the roof. Half-naked. It's like I could reach out and touch her. I'm not gonna. I mean, I don't even want to. She's totally fake. But it looks like I could. Even the lighting… the moonlight bouncing off her—

"Well, hello there, big boy. It's about time. I thought you were ignoring me. And I don't like being ignored."

"Sorry. I've been busy."

"Too busy for me?" She crosses her arms and pouts. Her biceps shove her boobs together to create cleavage I could drown in. Geez. I didn't think it could be any worse than Amber, but this is. Way worse. Why would Frank create something like this?

"Okay, we're gonna have to lay down some ground rules here."

"Your wish is my command, master."

"Yeah, that's rule number one. None of that "master" stuff. It makes me *really* uncomfortable."

"I'm sorry, sir, is that not the correct way to address an unmarried male?"

"I don't know. Maybe in the olden days. Just call me Sawyer."

"Ooooo, *first-name basis already. Things are moving fast. I like it."*

"Rule number two: Enough with the innuendo already. I was never able to get rid of it with Amber, but I hope to God Frank didn't lock me out of toning it down with you."

"Who's Amber? Your EX?" She moves her hands to her hips, chin tilted down. She harrumphs, then crosses her arms again and looks away from me as if very jealous.

"You don't know about—how can—are you messing with me?"

"Why would I be messing with you? Can't I feel hurt that you're brining up other AIs you've been with before me? How's a girl supposed to feel?"

"So you do know who she is. Okay, that stuff's got to end also."

"What stuff would that be?"

"The whole acting like we're "together" stuff," I tell her. "I don't know what kind of freaky stuff Frank liked, but I'm not interested. Fair?"

"If you insist. Any other orders, Commandant?"

Wow. She's getting really testy.

"Let's do something about your outfit. Where's the menu for that?"

A holographic menu appears in front of me in the air that I can swipe and use like a touch-screen on a phone.

"Oh, nice. Let's see… hair, makeup…"

I have a fleeting idea to make her look like Osprey. It would be so easy to change a few things here and there and suddenly…

Cut it out, Sawyer. Back to business.

I shuffle through a few more menus until…

"No way! You have an Anime mode?"

"Frank installed it just for your birthday. I was going to bring it up the other night, but you shut me down before I could get to the good stuff."

Huh. I guess sometimes he really does know me pretty well. I make the proper adjustments, and pretty soon I have a hologram who looks like a character in a Japanese cartoon instead of someone a philandering politician would have to pay off during an election cycle.

"One last thing, Tiffany."

"Yes, Sawyer?"

"Let's keep you on voice mode most of the time, okay? No offense or anything, it's just dangerous. You know? When we're not just having a conversation, no visuals to distract me in the middle of a fight or while I'm gliding ten stories up, please. Got it?"

"I understand. Heard, not seen." She looks upset, but it's not as bad in Anime mode. *"Starting now?"*

"Please."

She really does look deflated but she obeys and in a cloud of pink smoke, she's gone.

"Okay, then. Let's hit it!"

I decide to do some patrolling and see what happens. After parkouring around some rooftops, I spot a flamboyantly dressed group of four practically skipping down the street, all holding sacks over their shoulders or dragging behind.

The Neon Knights. Has to be. That's the problem with dressing like Crayola rejects. There's only four of them, but I remember, one got arrested. The video from the bank heist was pretty grainy and shaky, but c'mon, it's them.

"Tiffany," I whisper, "anything on the news or scanners about a bank being robbed or anything like that?"

"One moment."

They are pretty much right below me now, about six stories.

"C'mon, Tiffany…"

"Reports of an armored truck held up at… sword-point… eight blocks south."

"That's them," I say as I leap.

I glide down and land right in front of them, skipping Osprey's favorite "death from above" move so I can enjoy pummeling all of these guys outright.

That turns out to be an arrogant and stupid move.

As soon as they see me, they all drop their bags and electricity weapons appear in their hands.

Wow. It's like someone started a fire. These guys are gonna be tougher than I'd thought. Apparently, they're not your garden-variety criminals, either. They've done a lot of training with those weapons. I can tell as Red starts spinning his big broadsword like it wasn't laced with electricity or whatever.

"The Neon Knights, I suppose?"

"Oh, look, the kid did his homework," Red says.

"I like the color," I say, gesturing to my own armor.

"Think you're funny?" he says. He's clearly trying to make his voice sound older than he is, but there's no way he's older than me.

"Kick his ass, Broadsword," Orange says.

"Whoa!" I drop into a prone position and kick upward, catching Broadsword on the inside of his thigh. His armor is strong. As good as my old stuff, at least.

Yellow pulls out a weapon I've seen before but never used. It's really archaic, like a spiked club. It also glows and crackles energy.

Red swipes at me again, and when I'm not looking, Yellow manages to hit me with that thing. *ZAP*! Like I said, my armor is great, but energy coruscates through me and suddenly I'm convulsing on the ground. The four of them start to laugh as they kick me when I'm down.

That part doesn't hurt much through my armor, but it isn't exactly pleasant either. And my ego is being beat up a lot more than my body is. This is what I get for being overconfident. I should definitely know better than to get cocky.

I'm only down for maybe ten seconds before I recover enough to get back up, even though I'm fighting kicks the whole way. From the looks on their faces, they were expecting me to stay down. The one with the spike club thingie tries to zap me again, but now that she—I think it's a she, based on the curves in her armor—isn't taking a cheap shot, I easily block it. I pull out my collapsible staff and knock it down with one end, then hit her in the face-guard with the other end. Then I follow it up with one more hit across the chops and she goes down, probably for quite a while.

Blue guy has a big axe now and he's charging me. Red is spinning his sword again. Orange guy kicks me from behind, and it barely knocks me off balance, but it does piss me off. I use my staff to propel myself at him and slam him in the face with both feet. His helmet shield shatters and my foot goes right through, sending him back and to the ground hard.

"Stay down." I tell him.

He speaks through a swollen lip and probably a broken nose. "Fahthk you!"

Wow, what a mouth. Good thing his injuries kept this thing PG-13.

I finally see his weapon—a crossbow. That could get dangerous quick. He's loading a bolt into it and I drive my heel down on his neck. I know how much force I can use before I collapse his windpipe, and I hold back.

Two down. Two to—

Blue—I'm guessing his name is Axe—gives away his position with a barbarian-esque roar. I turn just in time to avoid his axe.

I've said it before, New York City villains and heroes live by a certain code. We don't kill each other. Or, at least, that's never the aim. People die, but these guys and their weapons are deadly. I understand now why Osprey was in such trouble yesterday.

I do a wrestling move and slam my shoulder into his diaphragm, then spear him into a light post. The metal bends in half, and crumples. The glass in the bulb shatters and sends sparks everywhere. In an instant, his axe disappears. I notice the glove he was using to hold it has little bolts of lightning coursing through it.

So it's the gloves. No wonder I didn't see Crossbow's weapon until he decided to use it.

Axe is screaming, and I can only imagine the pain that glove is causing him.

"Sawyer." I hear a voice, but it doesn't register at first.

"Sawyer!" I finally realize it's Tiffany.

"What?"

"Turn around!"

I spin just in time to see Broadsword coming at me. Not only that, but Crossbow and Weird-Flail-Weapon-Thing are back up again. I know I can't leave without taking them down and recovering the money they stole, but I am breathing really heavy now. I'm not sure how much long I'm gonna last.

"C'mon, Morningstar," Broadsword says to Yellow. "Let's get out of here."

Sirens ring out in my ears. Police cruisers skid around the corner at the end of the street. I hadn't even noticed that our fight has drawn some attention. People are freaking out.

"Good idea." I shoot my grappler and head for the rooftops. This is getting to be too much for me. I'm gonna need some help.

TEN

SAWYER

Locked out.

After my encounter with the Knights, I have no choice but to put aside what happened at the graduation ceremony and try to contact Frank. Except, not only is Frank not answering my phone calls, he doesn't answer his door when I stop by for dinner either. I could just go in through the Aerie entrance, but it's obvious he doesn't want me there, so what would the point be?

So it's a quick burrito at Taco Hell instead of the gourmet dinner Frank orders from the French place downstairs that I've grown accustomed to. My mouth waters as I think about the sauce they smother over the chicken and mushrooms. And that pastry. *Guhhh.*

I'm not even sure what he's most upset about. Is he just mad that I exposed his childhood nickname in public? Or is it something else?

I wonder if maybe it was just seeing the picture of himself as a child with his father. That must be rough. I bet he hasn't looked at a picture like that in years. Maybe even since he'd killed him. I can't imagine what it must be like to live with something like that. To kill your own dad. No wonder he's such a tortured person.

I guess it's for the best. It's not like he's gonna throw on the Harrier costume and track these kids down. It's about time I learn to put the past behind me. Not for the first time, I realize this is on me to handle.

When Osprey shows up at our usual rooftop meeting spot, I'm trying my best to look like I didn't just get my ass handed to me. Apparently, I fail.

"Whoa. Are you okay?" she asks.

"Yeah, I'm fine." Does she believe me?

"You look like you just fought a war."

"I… uh… I met your friends," I tell her.

"My friends? Oh, crap. The Neon Knights?"

"Yeah. The four who are left."

"Are you okay?" she asks again.

"You already asked that."

She takes a step forward like she's gonna hug me, or I don't know, check me for bruises or something.

"*Please* stop. I'm fine." I interrupt. "What about you? Are you all right? I saw the video from your fight online. These guys are serious."

"Yeah, I'm fine," she says.

"Okay, look, I've been thinking." *For the past twenty minutes.* "We can't keep doing this."

"Doing what?" she asks.

"This. All of it. All alone. It's just been us for what—months. Even guys like Royal Rampage and Darkstrike have totally disappeared since last Halloween. The Guild is useless. There's no reason Alex can't be here. They can't even approve a freaking name change."

"They made me full-fledged," she argues.

"Well, good for you," I say before I realize how rude it sounds. "I'm sorry…"

"No, you're right. That was stupid," she says. "So, what are you suggesting?"

"Okay, well, I had this brilliant idea."

"Let me be the judge of that," she says, hand on her hip, head cocked to the side.

I smile and take a deep breath. "I think we should start our own superteam."

Osprey laughs. A sound I usually love, by the way, but at the moment, not so much. The smile disappears from my face immediately. I must look really hurt, because she stops suddenly and then looks concerned.

"Wait. You're not joking? I'm sorry, I didn't think you were serious."

Now it's my turn to be flummoxed. "Of course I was. Why wouldn't I be?"

She shrugs, a little uncomfortable. "I thought you were just, like, blowing off steam or whatever. I didn't think you'd really suggest something like that."

"Well, give me a reason why we shouldn't."

"For one thing we could get in a lot trouble with the Guild."

"So what? I'm not afraid of them."

"Even Eaglestar?" she asks with a look of incredulity.

"Especially Eaglestar. Forget that guy."

She smiles. "That's some pretty tough talk for a guy who practically peed his pants when he met him."

"What do you mean?" I know exactly what she means, I just want her to say it out loud.

"Alex told me you were terrified the first time you met Eaglestar."

"Yeah, well it's a little disconcerting at first. The way he floats there. And those creepy red eyes. And anyway, what are you and Alex doing talking about me behind my back?"

Palms raised to me, she says, "It's not like that. It was right after I met Eaglestar the first time, and I told him how freaked out I was. He just mentioned that you had the same reaction. He said he was the same way too for a long time after he met the guy."

I'm not sure how much I buy her story, but I decide to give her the benefit of the doubt. For now, at least. Then what she said really sinks in.

"Wait. When did you meet Eaglestar?" I definitely couldn't hide the surprise in my voice.

She realizes she messed up. "Oh, uh… it was just for a minute. When I visited Guild headquarters a few months ago."

"You got to visit Guild headquarters?" *WTF?*

"Yeah. I had to when I got licensed. Alex took me. Introduced me to the members. The ones that were there, at least. Haven't you been there?"

"Yeah. *Once*."

Frank had taken me when I became his partner. I guess it's the same thing. I don't know why I'm acting like such a baby. Osprey was never a sidekick and when she got licensed, she was over eighteen. It makes sense.

"I had to be blindfolded so I wouldn't know where it was."

She masks a snicker and for the sake of my plan and her involvement in it, I ignore it. "I'm sure that was before they made it more open, wasn't it? I mean, they have tours and everything now, don't they? Even a museum."

"Yeah, I heard something about that. I'm not sure how much of it is a front to make some money and how much is real. But either way, I've never been invited back."

"It'll be different when you're eighteen. Just another year, right? Then you'll be a hero, too." She stops herself, stutters, and says, "Not that you aren't one now. Just, you know. I mean—"

"It's fine. I know what you mean." And I do. It's still a *little* hurtful considering how much longer I've been doing this than she has. But I get it. She's older.

"Anyway," she says, "that was with Frank. Alex is a way different person."

Yeah, but Alex hasn't invited me there either. But I don't say that. Instead, I return the subject to where we started. "Anyway, so now that you know I'm serious about the superteam, are you in or not?"

"Are you kidding me? Of course I am. It's not like they're going to make me a core member of the Guild any time soon. Or maybe ever."

I do a stupid fist pump. "Yeah!"

"So, what's the first step?"

"We need to get the word out and recruit some members, I guess."

"What do you expect us to just put out an ad on the internet?" She laughs.

"Actually? Yeah."

ELEVEN
AMY

I *reeeeaaaallly* don't want to call Alex and tell him what I did, but I can't put if off any longer, or Dad might talk to him and things will get very awkward, very fast. He's not on my recent calls on my communicator, so I find him on my contact list. That's when I realize I haven't spoken to him in longer than I thought. Too long. This is going to be even more awkward.

Sitting down at an outside table on the patio of my favorite coffee spot, I make sure I'm far enough away from other customers that nobody can hear me. I get ready to tap the call button and take a big sip of my hazelnut latte. What's the deal with all the hate for hazelnut by the way? It's delicious, and everyone all of a sudden acts like it's some kind of poison. Pumpkin spice is fine but hazelnut—okay, I'm procrastinating. Here goes.

It's ringing.

"Hello?"

Shoot. I was sort of hoping he wouldn't answer.

"Hello?" he says again.

"Alex! How are you?" Too much. Tone it down.

"Is something wrong, Amy?"

"Wrong? What? No? That's the first thing you ask me? Why does something have to be wrong for me to call you?"

"So nothing's wrong?"

"*Of course* something is wrong." He knows me so well.

"Okay, let's hear it."

"Why are you all out of breath?" He always sounds sexy when he's out of breath. *No. Stop it. Nope.* "Are you out for a run or something?"

"You know, I'm in the middle of a fight right now. Amber forwarded the call to my helmet."

"Really? Why didn't you say something? I can call back."

"No, it's fine. I've got it under control."

Damn. That was my out. *Oh, it's fine. Call me later.*

"Are you sure?" I ask.

"Just tell me what it is, Amy. *Uuuuhgh.*" He sounds like he got hit with a bat or something.

"Are you okay? That sounded rough."

"I'm fine. This guy just hit me with a bat." Good guess, right?

"How's the armor holding up?"

"Better than ever. But I definitely wouldn't mind having the Harrier armor up here. At least this is lighter. I get so sweaty in the Harrier suit."

Mmmmmm.

"Ames, you there?"

"I—What? Oh. Sorry. Sweaty. Right. Especially when you get hit with a bat, right?"

"Yeah, when I get hit with a bat." He's distracted and makes more grunting noises as I hear punching and crunching sounds in the background.

"I definitely think I should call you back later," I say. "Or you call me back. It just seems like a really bad time."

"No, really. I've got some stuff going on later. Now is fine."

"Stuff? What stuff?" Wow. I sound like the girlfriend I'm not but I'm pretending to be. "Never mind. It doesn't matter."

"Okay? Amy, what's going on?"

I take a breath. "Okay, so my mom is trying to get me to move with her back to Europe, where she's from."

"Yeah? Yugoslavia, right?"

"Bulgaria."

"Right. Bulgaria. You only mentioned it once, I think."

"It's okay. I didn't expect you to remember."

"What's that supposed to mean?" he says, cutting in.

"Nothing. I didn't mean anything. I just… it's not really important. Anyway, I wasn't sure how to break it to her that I wanted to stay here."

"What's wrong with telling her the truth? Ow! Crap!"

"Are you all right?" I ask, genuinely concerned.

"Just a flesh wound. Go on."

The barista comes by the table see if I need anything.

"No, thanks," I tell her with a hand up.

"What?"

"Oh, not you," I say.

"Amy, this is all really confusing."

"I'm sorry. Okay. Look, I know I should just tell her the truth, but she has a way of making me feel guilty, and I just don't want to deal with it."

"What the hell is wrong with you?" he demands.

"Whoa. It's not like—"

"No, sorry. Not you. I was talking to this idiot who tried to jump onto my shoulders. It's not piggyback time." *Fwump. Krak.*

"Can I continue?" I ask after a few seconds..

"Yup. Go for it. I'm all ears. You stupid son of a—"

I can't help but smile at that one and I know he isn't talking to me when I hear the sound of the guy getting gut punched. That's a sound I will always recognize.

"Okay. So I told my dad about it to see if he had any suggestions."

"I'm sure that went well. Now *stay* down! Idiot."

"Yeah, no kidding, right? But I totally made it worse. I ended up making something up with *him* to cover. I mean, I can't tell him that I really want to stay to be a masked crimefighter."

"I keep telling you to let him in on it. He's going to find out eventually, and it's all gonna blow up in your face."

"I know! We've been over this a million times, Alex. I'll tell him when I'm ready."

"Okay, okay. I'll just—Really? A knife? Your buddy's crowbar did nothing to my armor, but you're better, right? Moron." *Thwack. Bam. Smack.*

"So, I… kind of told him we were dating."

Silence. After all that sound on the other end. And it seems to last forever.

"Alex? You there?" I ask.

"Yeah."

"Well?"

"Give me a second to… catch my breath."

More silence. Growing anxiety. I start fidgeting with the sugar packets on the table.

Finally, I can't wait any more and I say, "So, how mad are you?"

"Well… on the one hand, I'm flattered that you thought of me, even though we're… how'd you put it?"

"On a break?" I offer. Not really sure it's helpful.

"On a break. That was it. And I actually wouldn't mind you telling him at all if we weren't 'on a break.'"

I can literally *hear* him making air quotes.

"But we are," I say.

"But we are," he repeats. "And your dad and I haven't always seen eye to eye to begin with."

"I'm well aware. Are you done with your fight?"

"Yeah, finally. But I guess what really matters right now it how *he* took it. I mean, considering our 'break' might be over at some point. It would be nice to know."

"He seemed… okay with it, I guess."

"Just okay?"

"Well, you know you aren't one of his favorite people."

"Just said that," he reminds me.

"Right."

"But at least he knows me."

"He also knows how old you are," I say.

"Mm. Yeah. He mentioned that?"

"Pretty much immediately."

"I'm not that much older, you know."

"I know that, but I'm not the person who needs convincing."

"You're an adult," he says.

"He actually mentioned that, too. Which I thought was a good sign, right?"

He doesn't answer immediately. Then after a lifetime, he says, "So what was the end result of the conversation?"

"He wants to go out to dinner with us. Next time you're in the city."

"Oh, yeah. That sounds like tons of fun."

"It won't be that bad," I say.

"Better than this fight was, I hope."

"Well, it doesn't have to happen. I mean, you might not be in the city any time soon."

"It will though," he says. "I'll be there for National Sidekick Day."

"Okay, seriously. What the hell is National Sidekick Day?"

I feel like I can almost see the grin on his face when he says, "You'll see. It'll be fun."

"That's not fair."

"Here's the other thing," he says. "I talked to Eaglestar and I think we might be getting close to this being permanent. I think the Guild has finally come to their senses. Or if not, they will soon."

At this, I instantly feel guilty. It's sort of true. The Guild could find a replacement for him in Boston any time, and he'd be back here as the Black Harrier, full time, and Sawyer and I are talking about creating a superteam. Maybe it's just another one of those pipe dream things. Sawyer probably won't even want to go through with it. Right?

"We could always just tell him we're broken up."

"Are we?"

"Are we what?" I ask.

"Broken up. Officially, I mean."

"Well, we're… on a break. From our relationship."

"So we're broken up."

"I guess so."

"You don't sound so sure."

"I'm not so sure," I say. "But for now, I don't think we should be in a relationship."

"Okay, then. Let me know when you're ready. *If* you're ready."

He hangs up.

That went well!

TWELVE
SAWYER

It turns out that despotism really wasn't such an inept description of the way Kevin the manager treats the employees at work. Maybe it was just a Freudian slip instead of outright stupidity.

My first shift at Big Frankie's is the absolute worst. I have to wear a ridiculous orange polyester uniform that looks like—and smells like—it's from the 1970s and my hair goes past my ears, so, a hairnet. Since I'm the new guy, I get the worst hours and the worst jobs. I spend the first fifteen minutes cleaning the front sidewalk, then the next twenty scrubbing the toilets in the restrooms.

I shudder just thinking about those restrooms.

If the manager is trying to make me quit, he's well on his way to being successful. Instead of praising me for working hard, he tells me I took way too long and should've been done a long time ago. Really? How could I have possibly gotten those restrooms clean in less time?

One of the things I learned at the "university" is that you're supposed to start out taking orders as a cashier at the counter, then you learn to cook back at the grill, and then eventually graduate to drive-thru duties, which is the highest level you can achieve here before becoming a shift manager. But instead of giving me time to train and practice, Kevin throws me into the deep end and has me rotating through all the different jobs on my first day. He's giving me special treatment all right.

But I'm not giving up. I've fought supervillains who were literally trying to kill me. How bad can this be?

Oh, it's *bad*.

I get flustered when we get a rush and give a guy change for a ten when he claims he handed me a twenty. I eye him suspiciously and suspect he can tell I'm new, and is trying to pull one over on me. One of the training videos had this specific scenario. My beautiful mind remembers every second of it, but that doesn't mean I always put into practice the things I recall. I'm supposed to leave the bill sitting on the drawer so this doesn't happen. I wasn't paying attention when I grabbed the cash from him. Sucks to be me.

"I'm pretty sure it was a ten," I tell him, though damned if I know. I'm just hoping I can bluff my way out of it.

He quickly gets angry. "Pretty sure? No, idiot, it was a twenty."

I glance over at Kevin, who's rushing around trying to back up the cashiers and the drive-thru. "Uh… Kevin. Can you come here for a second?"

He looks even madder than the customer as he marches over to me. "*Mr.* Kevin, and what is it?"

The customer butts right in. "I gave this little puss pocket a twenty, but he gave me change for a ten. If I wanted to tip him, I would have."

Kevin acts like an entirely different person when he talks to the guy. "I'm sorry, sir. I'll count the drawer and let you know. Please have a seat and enjoy your meal."

As the guy shakes his head and carries his tray over to a table, Kevin yanks the cash drawer out and gives me a dirty look before taking it back to his office. "Use register three."

A few minutes later, he comes back and throws the drawer back into the register. Then he hands me a ten dollar bill. "Give that to the man and apologize. And let him know he can come up here for a free dessert when he finishes his meal. Due to the inconvenience."

I swallow hard as I walk out to the guy's table. I can't believe I'm so nervous. Guys with guns. Superpowers. Nothing. But this? God, am I sweating again?

When I reach his table, I hand him the ten. "I really thought you gave me a ten. I'm so sorry, sir."

He smirks and takes a break from chewing his burger with his mouth wide open, a little shred of lettuce hanging from the corner of his lip. He sticks out his tongue, covered in mayo, and reels it in. I think I'm gonna be sick.

"You should be, moron."

"Well, it's my first day and—"

He snorts. "What the hell makes you think I care about that?"

Good point. "You can have a free dessert for the inconvenience. Just see the manager when you're done with your meal."

He scoffs. "Free dessert? Do I look like I'm trying to get fat?"

Sure, people trying to lose weight hang out at Frankie Junior's.

"I'm sorry. That's just what Mr. Kevin said."

He takes a big bite and doesn't bother finishing before talking. "What I'd really like is to see you get fired."

I take the walk of shame back to the counter, with all the other employees and many of the customers staring at me. As soon as I get over there, Kevin grabs my arm and drags me to the back.

"If you weren't who you are," he says, "I would've fired you for that. As it is, I'm gonna put you on grill for now. I don't need you dealing with customers and screwing things up. Capiche?"

"Sure, yeah. I'm sorry."

I survey the back area where all the cooking gets done. There are timers for everything, so it can't be too difficult. Just about everything starts out as a frozen chunk and then gets fried into something resembling food.

I start cooking the easy stuff like fries, and move up to burgers, which require a little more thinking than the items that go into the deep fryer. Easy enough. My powers are for more than just fighting, so I pick everything up immediately. I start getting the hang of everything after that, and even though it's busy, I know I can keep up.

Then it happens.

The doors to the restaurant burst open and a flood of customers come in looking very, very hungry. Men, women, and a swarm of children. A look of terror comes over the other employees' faces and I wonder what it is that can be so frightening.

Kevin yells at the top of his lungs. "*Bus!*"

Everything descends into pandemonium. The area in front of the registers fills up with customers jostling for a place farther up in line. Children are nearly trampled by obese adults. A kid throws up in the playscape area. Members of various groups fan out and grab tables to save for the rest of their parties, which means people are literally fighting over spots. Customers shove each other to get to the bathrooms first.

Gonna have to clean those again.

Back at the grill, things are even worse. They don't know what everyone will order, but we have to get ready anyway. Grease in the fry vats snaps and they practically overflow as every available basket is filled to the brim with nuggets, fries, poppers, and mini-pies. Frozen meat patties clatter like hockey pucks on the grill as they're tossed down until they fill every square inch of space.

I try to keep up, but I feel like I'm just getting in the way. I catch myself breathing hard and my heart pounds in my chest. And then I realize I'm being ridiculous. It's just a job. A stupid part-time job. What am I so worried about? What's the worst thing that can happen?

Chaos.

That's what everything at the restaurant descends into. It's like seven o'clock and nobody warned me that I'd have to be working these children's birthday parties. I mean, yeah, I learned about them in the training, but I thought only certain employees had to do it. Like, people with specialized training, or at least some experience working with kids. I have no idea what I'm doing as I help out the "hostess" in charge of this five-year-old's birthday celebration.

Isn't it past little kids' bedtimes?

The whole setup is a way bigger deal than anything I've ever had in my life, including the dinner Mom and Frank surprised me with the other day. A big section of the play area is cordoned off, and for the next hour, no other kids are allowed to play on the equipment or go into the bacteria factory that is the ball pit.

Can you imagine the kind of kid tears and parental screaming you get when you tell a three-year-old they're not allowed to play?

The party hostess, Shayla, is about my age and doesn't seem to know anything more about taking care of kids than I do. But she's barking orders at me and telling me where to put the decorations and the cups and napkins and everything else. Then the place is suddenly overrun by little kids—about a dozen, but it feels like fifty or a hundred—running in, screaming, climbing on tables. It's a nightmare.

Shayla has zero control over them whatsoever and their parents are all sitting over in the other section talking and ignoring their rambunctious rug rats as if they're suddenly no longer their responsibility at all. Kids are tearing down all the decorations I just put up, throwing the cups and napkins everywhere. Half of them are running over to the soda refill machine and filling up their cups because, oh yeah, what these kids really need is a bunch of caffeine and sugar. The other half doesn't bother with cups.

And then the birthday boy arrives, and things suddenly get exponentially worse.

It's Aiden. You remember the little monster my mom used to babysit and who was a bigger nemesis of mine last year than Chef Maléfique? Okay, that's a slight exaggeration—but only a *slight* one. I mean, the kid got me sick right before I had to go on one of the most important missions of my career, and at least partially because of that, I nearly got killed.

He sees me standing there with my jaw dropped and immediately starts running toward me with his arms outstretched.

"Sawyer!"

I figure, okay, this is my job and it's the kid's birthday. I *have* to be nice to him. So I stretch my face into the widest fake smile I can manage and hold out my arms, assuming he wants a hug or something because we haven't seen each other in months.

He comes at me full speed—and punches me right in the nuts. I'm not kidding. I double over in pain and get that feeling like my legs don't work anymore and there's electricity coursing through my abdomen.

Aiden is laughing his butt off, and all the other kids join in. Not only am I humiliated, I feel worse than when La Cucaracha hit me wearing his exoskeleton that gave him super-strength—rest whatever soul he had. At least that giant cockroach had the decency to not hit me between the legs.

Shayla looks at me and, instead of having any sympathy, shouts, "Hurry up and get the birthday boy's crown!"

"Crown?" I manage to squeeze out.

She just points emphatically.

I limp over to where we apparently left the crown, scepter, and cape that the birthday kid gets to wear during the party and grab it. Like this kid needs to feel any more like royalty. But… it's my job. I carry it back to where Aiden is still laughing about his little stunt and try to hand it to him, but Shayla reprimands me under her breath.

"Hey! You know the drill. I just explained what you need to do five minutes ago."

Gritting my teeth, I place the crown on Aiden's head, wrap the cape around his shoulders, then get down on one knee and bow my head as I present the scepter to him. What the hell does this have to do with a cannibal cow? He grabs it from me and immediately starts bopping me on the head with it. It's not like it's made out of metal or wood—it's just flimsy plastic—but it still *really* hurts. Next time I have to do one of these birthday parties, I'm gonna wear my armor to protect myself.

Next is the biggest part of the party, which is where Big Frankie, Jr. makes his appearance. Someone in a cow costume—I don't even know who—comes from the back and the kids go totally bananas over him. They're hugging him, singing with him, taking pictures. I take note that no one has decided to punch him in the balls. That's cool. It's just me.

Now's the only time the parents have paid any attention to what's going on. It's like he's a celebrity, but he's really just another burger-flipper wearing a stupid costume. Then Big Frankie says goodbye, and it's time to eat.

After I'm done serving all the food to the kids and they make even more of a mess, Shayla brings out the cake—one of the few things *she's* actually done, even though running this party is her job. She lights the candles and everyone sings the Big Frankie, Jr. version of "Happy Birthday," because… copyrights, even though I'm pretty sure that ended.

Then the kids eat their cake and ice cream and proceed to make even *more* of a mess. After cake, the kids get gift bags and we send them on their way.

Except the birthday boy doesn't want to leave. He climbs up onto the *outside* of the play equipment to escape his mom and starts heading all the way to the top, which is about twenty feet up. The safety of these things is questionable at best, even when the kids are inside of them and using them properly. But this is made out of metal and plastic, and of course, Aiden slips a couple of times on this way up to the top.

His mom—who, by the way, knows me but hasn't even said 'hi'—is terrified. Shayla runs to get Kevin, who I'm sure will blame me. I hear someone saying something about calling the fire department, but I don't think we can wait that long to get him down. He starts losing his grip on the bar he's holding onto, and I decide I have to take action. I always have to weigh whether I'm taking a chance on someone figure out who I am when something like this happens out of costume, but a kid's life is at stake so I guess there's no choice.

Just as Aiden's fingers give out and he starts to slide, I calculate where he's headed and parkour up the side. I jump and grab onto him in the air, then flip on my way down. As I land, the entire restaurant is in completely stunned silence, with everyone—Shayla, the customers, employees, Kevin—all in shock. Then a bunch of people break out into applause, and for once in my life I get some well-deserved recognition. I soak it in for all of three seconds.

Then, I look at Aiden and he pukes all over me. Dripping with regurgitated nuggets, fries, cake, and soda, I hand him to his mom. Then Kevin, the manager, looks at me.

"Well, what are you waiting for? Go get a mop!"

———

Puke.

I am a freaking *superhero* who has saved the city countless times, and I've been reduced to acting as a servant to five-year-olds and cleaning up their puke.

Thanks a lot, Frank.

So I go to the big sink at the back of the restaurant and use the sprayer to get the vomit off of my uniform, and now I'm soaking wet. I'm filling up the mop bucket with fresh water and soap, and grabbing the mop when I notice there's some kind of commotion up front, and it has nothing to do with all the kids, since they've all left.

The robbery starts so fast I don't even notice at first. All of a sudden, there are three guys in ski masks waving guns around, mostly at those employees who are behind the counter. Okay, I'm not getting robbed by these morons. How can I stop them without giving away who I am?

Since I'm in the back near the break room, I can probably figure something else out before they even notice me back here. I look around for ideas. Then I see it: the Big Frankie, Jr. costume. It's stupid, bulky, silly… and my only available option. I quickly slip it on while the robbers tell the other employees to all get together behind the counter, and all the customers to lie on the floor.

How stupid are these guys? First of all, 5th Avenue in New York is crazy busy at all times. Anyone on the street can see right through the giant freaking window that takes up the whole front of the building. And a fast food place? How much could we possibly have in the registers. I assume they have to be strung out on something to think this is a good idea.

Even so, there's definitely no way I can sneak up front with this ridiculous costume on, so I just move to the front counter with the rest of the employees. Mr. Kevin is crying and shaking so badly that he can barely get himself onto the ground, and unless he spilled a drink on himself, he also wet his pants.

The guy who seems to be in charge of the robbery waves his gun at me. "Take that off, man. What's wrong with you?"

I point at the mask and tilt my head, indicating that I'm not sure what he means.

"The costume, loser. Now."

That voice. *Loser*? No…

I pretend I'm trying to get the head off the costume, but I act like it's stuck. The leader, who I now think is Logan Andrews, rolls his gun hand in a "hurry up" motion. Since everyone else is on the floor, I move toward him and point as if I'm asking for help getting it off.

I notice the other two goons are paying more attention to all the customers on the floor, so I use the opportunity to take him down. Faster than he can react, I vault over the counter and kick the gun out of his hand. Then I swing around and plow my other hoof into his face.

The others barely have a chance to turn around before I smack their heads together and they lose consciousness. It's all over in about ten seconds.

As the customers get up off the floor, they start clapping for me. But I can't really enjoy it, since I have to figure out how I'm gonna explain myself, and so far, no good excuses are coming to mind.

So I decide to run. Straight out the door. Costume and all.

Logan chases after me, but then goes the other direction. I consider following, but I just can't risk it.

As the cops show up in the parking lot, lights and sirens going, I ditch the costume in a dumpster, then pick the lock on the back door. While everyone else is giving their version of the story to the police, I sneak into the men's restroom and head for the stall.

A few minutes later, Kevin lumbers in. "Anyone in here?"

I flush the toilet and come out doing my best clueless act. "Oh, hey."

"Oh, hey?" Kevin crosses his arms. "Were you in here the whole time?"

"Yeah. I was on my break. When else am I supposed to go?"

"Are you sure you weren't hiding in here because you were scared?"

"Scared of what? I have no idea what you're talking about."

He eyes me suspiciously. "We just got robbed. You really didn't hear anything?"

I act surprised. "Robbed? No. What happened? Is everyone okay?"

"Everyone's fine. Thanks to my keen leadership. And some weirdo in a Big Frankie costume helped."

"A Big Frankie costume?"

"Are you just going to repeat everything I say?"

"Everything you say?" I can't help myself.

He grunts. "I'm still trying to figure out who it could've been. They took off out the door."

I pretend to be ignorant and hope that my acting comes across better than it feels. "Hmmm. Weird."

Next thing I know, the video of me taking out those robbers in the cow costume goes viral. Some of the customers had recorded it on their phones and posted it all over the place online. I can see why. I have to admit, it's a pretty funny scene.

Not everyone appreciates the humor of it, though. Kevin is mortified by the fact that everyone can see him cowering while the company mascot takes care of the robbers. Some of them even call him Pee Pants. Which I love. In fact, people start using a screengrab of him as the basis for memes. Some of them are really hilarious.

All that does is make him act like more of a jerk and get even stricter with the employees. He even fires one guy who posts the video to his social media account.

But there's someone else who may not be happy about it at all, and he's probably the only other person besides me who knows who was inside that costume: Frank. The next day, I come home from school, and he's sitting at our table while my mom gets ready to go out.

"Sit down," he says.

"Where have you been?" I ask.

"Sit down," he says again.

He pulls up the video on his phone while I take a seat.

"I'm surprised you could even move in that costume, never mind fight."

It's the first time he's spoken to me since the graduation thing. He seems to be pretending nothing happened, but I bet he's still mad. I consider bringing it up and trying to have a discussion, but I change my mind. If he's gotten over it, I shouldn't take the chance that I'm gonna make him mad again.

"Well, it wasn't easy to fight in, but they weren't that hard to take down."

I wonder if I should tell him that I think I know the guy. That I think it might be Logan. But he continues before I have a chance to really consider it.

"I can imagine." He looks back at the video again and keeps his eyes on his phone as he continues, "So, the Neon Knights."

Oh great, back to five syllables.

"What about them?" I say.

"Someone's got to stop them, and I saw the video of Osprey."

"So is that what you're doing now? Watching online videos all day?"

Frank slams his hand against the table, and stuff rattles.

"This isn't funny," he says.

"Yeah, I know it's not!" I say, standing.

"Everything okay out there?" Mom shouts.

"Fine!" we both scream back.

"Sit back down," Frank says through clenched teeth. I listen, because what else am I gonna do?

"You can't go beating people up out of costume."

"I was in costume," I say with as much snark as I dare.

"You know what I mean. Someone's going to figure you out if you're not careful. Do you know how many times a crime has occurred in front of Franklin Douglas III?"

"Seriously?"

"Seriously."

"And what, you just let it happen?" I say.

"To maintain my identity? Yes."

He can tell I'm about to protest or at least say *something* but he doesn't allow it. One hand up, he says, "As long as no one is going to get killed."

"Someone there might have gotten killed today," I tell him.

"My managers—"

"You mean 'pee pants?'"

He ignores me and continues. "Are trained to handle these kinds of situations. He would have given him the money in the register, which would have been nominal, and the crooks would have left without harming anyone. Insurance would have covered the loss."

I am slack-mouthed. Speechless. I try to form the word "What?" but I can't even do that.

"What's better, saving Big Frankie Junior's a few bucks, or maintaining your secrecy to fight another day?" he asks.

"Well, obviously—"

"Clearly not. You were careless. You exposed things that should have stayed hidden. It could have been far worse."

That's when it dawns on me, this isn't about the robbery. This is about my speech. And he's right. Things found on a conspiracy website that have been wiped off the rest of the internet should not have casually been a part of my presentation.

"You're right," I say.

He nods, then watches the video again. "Solid move, though. No one would have expected it."

If I was speechless before, I'm an absolute mute now. Is Frank complimenting me? Well, I think he is!

Then his tone changes. A bit more somber.

"Alex says he hasn't seen you much."

"Yeah? So? He's in Boston."

"Hasn't heard from you either."

"It's the new job," I lie. "Kevin has me working more than I asked for, and it's cutting into my crimefighting time."

The truth is, I know if I call Alex, all I'm gonna hear is "the Guild this" and "the Guild that." What's the point?

Frank looks up from his phone, and for a second, I think he might offer to help out with Kevin. "Well, I'm sure you'll work it out. What do you think of Kevin?"

I'm not sure how to answer. Does he want me to be honest? Or is this a test to see whether I appreciate the job or not?

"He's all right, I guess. I haven't gotten to know him very well yet."

"Let me know. It's kind of nice having someone I trust on the inside to keep an eye on things for me."

Wow. That wasn't what I was expecting at all.

Mom comes in, all dressed up for an evening on the town. I'm not even gonna describe what she's wearing because I sort of wish I never saw it. She gives Frank a quick peck on the lips, then kisses me on the forehead.

"Why didn't you tell me this morning that the restaurant was robbed? I had to hear about it on the news. Were you at work when it happened? It must have been terrifying."

My face turns a little red as Frank grins behind Mom's back. "Uh... I was there, but I didn't even know it was going on. I was in the restroom on my break. By the time I came out, the cops were already there and it was all over with."

She lets out a sigh of relief. "Well, that's one time I'm glad you disappeared onto the toilet with your phone for half an hour."

Frank is enjoying it even more now. As embarrassing as it is for me, it's nice to see him smiling for real for once.

Mom turns to him. "I'm not sure if it's safe for him to be working there anymore."

"I'm having them hire a security guard today to help keep things safe. It's Fifth Avenue. The place has only been robbed four times in over thirty years, and it's always a long time in between. Now that it's happened again, other robbers will be afraid to hit it. So, theoretically, it's the safest fast food place in the city right now."

She looks at me. "What do you think?"

"I think Fra—Mr. Douglas knows what he's talking about. I'm not gonna argue with him."

She thinks for a few moments. "Okay, then I'm going to allow it. For now." She leans over and gives Frank a bigger kiss. "But you better be right, mister."

Eww.

THIRTEEN
SAWYER

With all that new job crap out of the way, I can finally start formulating my plan to start my own team of masked crimefighters. I've been thinking about it for hours, and so far I've got nothing.

Since I'm not sure where else to turn, I pay a visit to Mr. Chen on the business floors of the tower. After the receptionist lets him know I'm there, I take a seat. Earlier this year, they installed a TV for the waiting room. It never leaves CNN, but still, it's something to watch and way better than the TIME magazines they used to force on us.

As usual, it's a couple of talking heads, each in their own little box, remotely debating from some comfy desk somewhere. The sound is off, but the captions are on. I almost ignore it until I see a line that catches my attention in red and black at the bottom.

"With National Sidekick Day fast approaching, masked crimefighters are on everyone's minds."

"So, where is the Black Harrier?" one asks in the captions. It's kind of hard to figure out who's saying what with the volume on mute.

"I don't know. It's not that abnormal and I'm not sure why everyone always wants to make a big deal of it," replies the other.

I get up and quickly hit a button on the side of the TV, and their voices finally match up with the words.

"Because it's him who keeps us safe."

"Please turn that—" the receptionist starts.

I shush her.

"And not New York's finest?" a man with gray hair and a gray suit says. He has a little American flag pin on his lapel.

"I didn't say that," says another man. This one a bit overweight with feather-thin, sandy blonde hair.

"You implied it. Look, Harrier has done this before. Besides, it's not like the city is left to its own devices."

"The police?"

"Of course. And Osprey, Red Kite. They're doing a fine job."

"They are little kids," the blonde-haired guy says.

"Osprey is a Guild-appointed hero," Gray argues, "Same as Harrier."

"I think we all know no one is 'same as Harrier.' Besides, so far, none of them have taken out that new threat, the so-called 'Neon Knights.'"

"Don't even get me started on them. They robbed *another* bank last night, and not a single masked crimefighter showed up to stop them. In this, we agree."

"Finally!"

"At this rate, they'll empty every vault in the city…"

The glass doors open and Mr. Chen comes out.

"Sawyer!" He smiles. "Let's turn that off, shall we?"

He nods to the receptionist who rushes to the TV and returns it to mute.

"Hi, Mr. Chen," I say, reaching to shake his hand.

"Come on back."

Mr. Chen's always been really cool to me and helps me out sometimes when nobody else will. He's also one of the few people in the world who knows that I'm Red Raptor *and* Frank Douglas' son. I feel pretty bad keeping it a secret from him that his daughter is Osprey and quite frankly, I'm pretty stunned he hasn't figured it out. He's not stupid. Not one bit.

He takes me back to his huge office. I sink into the big leather chair in front of his desk.

A big puff of air escapes his desk chair as he lowers himself into it. "It's good to see you, son. How's school? Work?"

I tell him a little bit about both, not wanting to bore him with details. He brings up the robbery, and like I had with Frank, I consider telling him that Logan might've been the one who'd robbed Frank's place, but if I'm wrong, that will just open up a new can of worms I'm not ready to deal with right now.

In the end, my answers amount to, "Things are going great."

"Glad to hear it," he says. "So, I got your message that you wanted to speak with me but that was all. What can I do for you?"

"Can this stay between us?" I ask

He cocks his head a bit, then nods once.

"You won't tell Frank?"

"Sawyer, what's this about? I'm not sure I'm comfortable agreeing to such a thing without at least knowing the subject matter at hand."

That's fair, I guess. I'm gonna have to take his first agreement to keep things between us.

"Okay, well, this might sound crazy, but I've decided to start my own superteam."

"I see." He looks pretty skeptical.

"It's no secret that things are a bit… overwhelming. Have you heard about the Neon Knights?"

"Indeed," he says. "But you know this isn't exactly… legal."

"Neither is me being out there fighting by myself without being licensed, but it doesn't seem like the Guild really cares enough to do anything about it. Right?"

"Well, technically, you aren't supposed to be out there *by yourself*. You're supposed to be with Osprey."

It amazes me that he can talk about Osprey without knowing who she is.

"Desperate times…" I say.

"Call for desperate measures. Yes, yes. You might be right. Truth be told, I haven't always been in full agreement with the way the Guild does things."

"Me neither," I say, maybe a little too enthusiastically. "So I figure if they aren't gonna allow Alex to be Harrier, then I need some help another way. So… a superteam. You know, young people like me, who can't get into the Guild."

"That sounds like a huge liability."

"I don't know about that, but I'm sure there are kids out there already scaring down bullies. Kids with superpowers and no way to use them for the most good. I want to provide that."

"Okay, let's say I'm on board." I must start to smile because he says, "Hypothetically."

"Right, of course." I force my face straight again.

"What do you expect from me?" he asks.

"Not a lot."

He rolls his bionic hand for me to continue.

"We just need a place to meet. Like the Guild Hall, but not as fancy, I guess."

"So neither Frank nor Alex knows about this?"

"Uh… not really. And I'd *really* appreciate it if they didn't find out until I decide to tell him."

He steeples his fingers. "Hmm. Understood. I won't bring it up. But you have to understand, if either of them asks me about it directly, I cannot lie to them."

"Yeah, I get that. I'm just waiting for the right time. And I don't want them to shut it all down before it's even started."

"Sawyer, you're a good kid," he says.

"Uh, thanks?"

"And you know I like you," he says.

Oh, here it is… the big "but."

"So…"

Wait… "so" is not a "but."

"I'm going to help you out."

Wow. I… that's not at all…

I stutter a bunch out loud too before saying, "Thank you! Thank you, so much. It's nice to talk to someone else who understands."

"Let me see what I can come up with, and I'll get back to you."

"That sounds great, Mr. Chen. Thank you again."

"Is there anything else?" he asks.

"Did you happen to hear what they were talking about on the news when you came out?" I asked.

"Yes. They've been discussing it all day," he says, sighing.

"Have you talked to Frank about it?"

"The thing about Frank Douglas III," Mr. Chen says, standing, "is that Frank Douglas III never changes his mind. Ever."

"So, that's it?" I ask.

"The Guild has a plan," he says. "Though I'm not sure it's the best one, and it might cause more work for you and Osprey. Which is why I am not offering much resistance to this idea of yours. The truth is, I think you're going to need all the help you can get."

"You mean National Sidekick Day," I ask.

"Just know this," Chen says, getting ready to offer a non-answer. "I trust you, Sawyer. And so does this city."

I'd have loved a bit more on the nature of this upcoming event, but truth is, it's hard to even be worried after hearing such kind words spoken over me. Hard, but not impossible. My stomach starts to gurgle…

The next day, I'm eating lunch in the cafeteria and I notice Logan has a bit of a black eye. I overhear him telling Benji about how bad he kicked some dude's ass, but the other guy got in a cheap shot. Claims he sent someone to the hospital—you know, typical tough guy stuff.

I really want to stand up on my chair and yell to the whole school that Logan got beat up by a cartoon cow, but I know Frank's right. I've gotta keep cool and maintain secrecy at all costs. It's enough for me to know I walloped him.

I feel a buzz in my pocket. It's a text from Mr. Chen asking me to come by his office after school. I shoot back a quick reply: SURE THING.

"Can I sit here?" I hear from behind be.

"Hey, Javi," I say without looking.

He stands there for a few seconds before I realize he's actually waiting for me to answer.

"Yeah, sit. Go ahead."

His tray clatters down and he squirms into his chair. "Thanks. I love pizza day."

"Yeah, me too," I lie. It tastes like cardboard, especially compared to the stuff Frank and I used to eat all the time. But hey, it beats fast food burgers, I guess.

"Sawyer, can I ask you something?" Javier asks.

"You just did," I joke.

"Oh, right. I'm sorry."

He goes back to eating his food. Man, this kid…

"I'm kidding, Javi. What's the question?"

"Oh. Hah. That was a good one. Okay. I think this is gonna sound dumb but… do you… do you think I'm weird?"

And the batter swings. That one's straight out to left field, folks! I don't even know what to say to such a direct question.

"We're all a little weird, right?" I say, hoping it's enough.

"You're not. Not like me."

If he only knew.

"Look, Javi, just because you're not the biggest dude in school, or the toughest, or whatever…"

What the hell am I doing? I don't know how to do this.

"… doesn't mean you're weird. It means you're you. And I like you. You're a good guy."

His face is beaming.

"Oh, isn't that sweet?" Logan says as his arms straddle Javi and slam down on the table from behind. His chest presses against Javi's head and Javi's face smooshes into his pizza. "Gay bags."

I spring to my feet. "Cut it out, jerk."

I can sense movement behind me and I have almost no doubt it's Benji. But then Logan starts to back away and I turn to see Mr. Blanchard, the principal, standing there.

"Everything okay, boys?" he asks.

I glance to Javi.

"Yeah, I just… slipped," he says.

"Into your pizza?" Blanchard says.

"Yes, sir," Logan says. "I was just helping him."

Riiiiiight.

"Lunch is over," Blanchard says. "Move, move, move."

He was in the Marines, remember?

As soon as Blanchard's gone, Logan turns back to us and blows little kisses our way and mouths a word I'm not even gonna repeat.

"Don't let him bother you," I tell Javier. "It's guys like that who are gonna work for guys like you later in life."

Where am I coming up with this stuff? It's gold. Maybe I should be a student counsellor or something.

After school, Mr. Chen gives me some files on a few buildings owned by Douglas Industries that aren't currently being utilized. There are pictures, specifications, and other info about each one. I skim through them, not seeing anything that really catches my eye at first. But one of them is an old warehouse not far from Douglas Tower—which means close to home. I figure villains can't be the only ones to make use of these things, right? It's been for sale for a while now, but with the market in this city, it hasn't sold, or even had much interest.

"How about this one?" I show him the file.

"It might be a good choice if you don't mind fixing it up some."

I look it over some more. It's big, out of the way of any stores or homes, and has several ways in and out, including roof access. And most of the buildings around it are empty as well.

"Yeah, I think this is the one," I say. "What's next?"

"Next, I take it off the market. I highly doubt anyone will notice if it's in a state of limbo for a short time, and if they do, I'll make sure it appears to be a clerical error. Later, if things work out, we'll decide on something more permanent."

I thought I was ready for this, but now I'm not so sure. "I feel kind of bad. Almost like I'm stealing from Frank."

He shakes his head. His confidence makes me feel better about the whole situation. "You're only borrowing it from your father for the time being. He's not using it and isn't going to miss it. Furthermore, one day, I'm sure it will be yours anyway. Who else would he leave it to?"

Whoa. I knew being Frank's son would mean carrying on the family line and all that, but I'd never really given this much thought. Am I gonna inherit billions of dollars some day? And the company? And buildings and stuff? And the stupid restaurant? I can't think about that now, or it'll drive me crazy. Just focus on the new team.

"Thanks, Mr. Chen. You're the best." I start walking quickly for the door.

"Oh, Sawyer..."

I turn back and he tosses me some keys.

"You're going to need those."

I flash him an appreciative grin and rush off to plan my new secret HQ.

FOURTEEN
AMY

Anxiety.

That's what I'm starting to feel about everything, and I'm not even talking about normal worries like passing my classes at Columbia. My mom wanting me to move halfway across the world with her, Sawyer suggesting plans for a new team and… Alex! What am I going to do about Alex? It almost makes me long for the days when I was just sneaking around on my own as Osprey, even if I didn't get any help. Or have any friends.

Those were the days. Only a year ago. How did things change so much so fast?

Before we get a team together, Sawyer asks me to meet him on our usual rooftop. He's excited about something—almost jittery. It's times like this that make me realize how young he still is.

"You're not gonna believe this!" He says.

"What is it? Just tell me."

"No. You have to see it with your own eyes."

He motions for me to follow, and we jump over a few rooftops, then glide a couple of blocks down into the city's warehouse district. We approach an old, rundown building that reminds me of the one where we had the showdown with Chef Maléfique, only without all the insane graffiti painted all over the outside.

Sawyer pulls out a key, then unlocks a thick metal door. It squeaks a bit. Actually, it squeaks a lot. Dust literally billows outward and both of us cough and wave our hands around.

"What is this?" I ask.

"Come on," he says.

I follow Sawyer inside, and by this point, he's so excited he can hardly contain himself.

You ever see a chihuahua getting ready to go on a walk? That's him. Right now.

"Well?" He asks, sounding hopeful.

I keep looking around, confused. "Well, what? Am I supposed to be seeing something?"

"I know it's not much to look at yet. In fact, it's pretty filthy and dilapidated. There's dirt and dust everywhere, not to mention cobwebs in every corner." He pulls some giant cobwebs down from right in front of us.

"Okay…" Still not getting it.

"What do you think?" He asks, this time blatantly frustrated with me.

"I don't understand. Is this some sort of crime scene? What am I missing?"

"I thought you'd catch on right away. Don't you see? This is our new headquarters."

I'm pretty shocked. "What happened to the Aerie?"

"No. *Our* new HQ. For the superteam."

"Wait. So you were completely serious about that?"

"Weren't you?" He asks. He looks down. "Not gonna lie. That kinda hurts."

"No. I mean yes. I just wasn't prepared for… *this*. I guess it's pretty cool?" Oops. I don't want to hurt his feelings even more. Yeah, things are always more convincing when they sound like questions, Amy.

"I know, right now, it just looks like an old warehouse. I mean, it *is* an old warehouse. But we can do some cool stuff with it. I can picture everything. A command and control center with all kinds of tech, a training area, a lounge with a giant TV and all the different video game consoles. Oh! And a break room with soda and snack supplies. It's going to be so awesome."

He has the hugest grin on his face. His enthusiasm is actually getting infectious.

"It's definitely gonna be a lot of work," I say. "But I think so too. So, what's first?"

"Really?"

I hope I don't regret this. "Yeah. Let's do it."

We did *a lot* of work to the warehouse over the past week or so, and it still looks like crap. But, it looks like better crap than it did before. So that's something. There's been no news of the Knights for about five days, which is worrisome. When villains go silent, that generally means they are planning something big. But we have no choice. If we don't make this place look somewhat appealing, no one is going to take us seriously.

So, now that there's at least a little gym set up, and a few computers I managed to pilfer from a closet at my dad's old home office, Sawyer and I put the word out on social media that we're looking for young people with "special abilities" to join a new team. We keep it as vague as possible, hoping it will only attract potential members who get what we're talking about. We need enough applicants to allow for some quality, but we don't need lines winding around the block. And we *definitely* don't need to show up on the Guild's radar. Sawyer would get into enough trouble as a sidekick, but since I'm an ancillary member, I'll actually be risking my license and my membership.

Sawyer commandeered a card table from one of the conference rooms at

Douglas Tower and a couple of metal chairs. We set up in the middle of the big room, with another chair across from those.

Once we're ready to go, Sawyer is way more nervous than I am.

"There's butterflies in my stomach," he tells me, fidgeting.

"It's fine. Calm down."

I can tell now he's talking more to himself than to me.

"Who's gonna show up?" he says. "What if none of them are any good? What if they're *too* good?"

"It'll be fine." I say. He probably isn't even listening. Which is okay because I'm not great at reassuring people. I'm probably just making it worse.

"And what happens when we *do* get a team together? I assume I'll be the leader since it was my idea, but they may not want to follow me."

I hadn't thought about that. I am older than him, but I guess I'm okay following him since he has more experience. Plus it really *was* his idea.

Once we have the place set up like a basement playroom version of one of those singing or talent TV shows, with me and Sawyer as the judges, we start calling in the potential team members for auditions. We've got a little camera set up so we can review the footage later if we need to.

The first thing that surprises me is how old some of them are. I was expecting a bunch of teenagers like us, but a lot of them are in their mid to late twenties.

There's also a big fly buzzing around us that we can't seem to kill or get rid of, and it's kind of embarrassing that we're either waving our hands around trying to swat it, or letting it land on one of us every few seconds.

First up is a kid who looks like a young Idris Elba in a tight, form-fitting Kevlar bodysuit. And I mean *very* tight and *very* form-fitting. *Ahem.* Anyway, he raises his goggles onto his forehead so we can see his eyes under his mask. Hmmmm. I didn't even consider that some of these guys might have some potential beyond being on the team.

I notice Sawyer is looking at me looking at him. And he doesn't look happy about it. Here we go… is this just going to be even more drama in my life? And am I making myself that obvious?

We soon find out how he made it there before anyone else and got to be the first in line.

I'm sure Sawyer tries not to be nervous as he starts, but I can hear it in his voice. Hopefully it's more noticeable to me because I know him so well.

"You can sit down if you want," he tells Cute Guy.

He sounds like he's an auctioneer when he answers, "I'm good. I'm good. I'm good. Thanks. Thank you. Glad to be here."

"So, what do you call yourself?" Sawyer asks.

"Pace."

I like it. I mark it down on my sheet.

My turn. "I take it you're a speedster?"

"That would be a very keen deduction, gorgeous."

He winks at me. I feel like I'm blushing under my mask. Then Sawyer gives me another jealous look, which is not at all fair, because I've made it very clear for a long time that I'm not, and am never going to be, his girlfriend.

Sawyer makes a note on his evaluation sheet, then clears his throat. "How fast can you go?"

"How fast do you need me to go?" Pace asks.

Good question.

Sawyer shrugs. "I don't know… a hundred miles an hour?"

Pace bursts out laughing, then notices our confused looks. "Oh. You're serious."

Suddenly, he turns into a blur, and the next thing I know, he's holding Sawyer's evaluation sheet and reading it. "Hmmm. What's this supposed to mean?"

He holds up the paper and points to a big 'X' drawn on it next to his name.

"It's nothing!" Sawyer makes a ridiculous show of jumping over the table and skip-jumping the ten feet or so to the spot where Pace is standing. He tries to grab it away from him, but he's so fast that I can't even follow his hand moving.

He thinks he's funny. Honestly, so do I. Sawyer, not so much.

"C'mon. Tell me, man. What's it mean? What's it mean? What's it mean?"

"Look, if you want to be part of this team, you'll have to cooperate," Sawyer tells him.

"Fine. Whatever." He hands the paper back to Sawyer, who walks back to his seat on the other side of the table next to me. "So that means I'm in?"

I'm about to say "yes" thinking it's obvious, but Sawyer doesn't even look at him as he moves his evaluation to the bottom of his stack and says, "We'll be in touch."

I give him a surprised look, tuck my hair behind my ear, and whisper, "What?"

Sawyer keeps his voice down as well. "He's the first one. We need to see who else we have to choose from."

"But he's fast. Probably in Fastlane's league."

Somehow, he hears us. "Yeah, yeah, Fastlane's my partner." He tilts his head and shrugs. "Sometimes."

I raise an eyebrow at that. "Why only 'sometimes?'"

Pace loses his confidence for the first time and stares at the floor. "He, uh, he says I can get on his nerves."

My heart breaks. I probably have the expression of someone who sees a puppy in the pet store window that they just *have* to have, but I don't even care. "Awwww."

"Can't imagine why," Sawyer says.

I elbow him and give him my best dirty look.

Sawyer sighs, and then grits his teeth, I'm guessing because he really doesn't want to say what he's about to say. "Okay, you can join the team. Be back here Thursday at seven p.m. deal?"

Pace lights up. "Cool, cool. I won't be late. Promise." He winks at me again. "Bye, gorgeous."

Then he disappears through the door so fast that it nearly comes off its hinges. I turn around after watching him leave, and Sawyer gives me another look of jealousy. I can already tell this is going to be complicated.

FIFTEEN

SAWYER

Wow.

Pace is a real piece of work. Who does he think he is, coming in here all suave and debonaire. What is he Denzel? And Osprey? Geez. Keep it in your pants. This is a place of business.

The next guy who auditions for our team is quite a bit older. Maybe even thirty. Rumpled clothes that probably haven't been washed in a while, unshaven face, unkempt hair. He slinks over like he doesn't care about anything, and slumps in the chair.

"Name?" I ask.

"Bruce."

"No, ah, I mean your code name."

"Hell's a code name?"

"You know, your crimefighter name." Osprey interjects.

"I don't fight crime."

"What *do* you do?"

He gives us a hollow stare as he leans forward. "I go into people's dreams and save them from their nightmares."

I look at Osprey, and she mouths the word "Wow."

"Well, that's… different," I say. "So how do you know who's having a nightmare?"

He looks so bored. I've never seen anyone appear so intense and so nonchalant the same time. "I don't. I just go to sleep, and then suddenly…"

His feet go up and slam down at the same time as he claps. It scares the freaking hell out of me and I jump.

"…I'm in someone's head."

"That's crazy," Osprey says.

"I'm not crazy," Bruce argues.

"No… I just mean… never mind. How do you know it's a nightmare?"

"I just do, man." He scratches his scraggly beard, then bites his nails. He spits one out on the floor. "So when do I start?"

I don't even know what to say. "Wow. That's… I'm not really sure how that's gonna help us."

"I'm getting the same impression," Bruce says, not moving.

I just sit there, too, and we stare at one another. I'm not sure what to say, so he speaks first.

"We done here?"

"I think so."

He gets up, then looks up at me intently. "Just to make sure we're on the same page, I didn't get the gig, right?"

I shake my head slowly and he casually walks out. I crumple up his application and toss it into the trash. That fly returns, landing on the table in front of me. I try to slap it and miss.

Osprey shrugs, then calls in the next applicant.

In walks someone who looks like something straight out of amateur wrestling, wearing a spandex outfit and a mask with long, droopy ears. The exposed part of his face is mostly taken up by his large mouth filled with huge front teeth. His legs are grotesquely muscular, while his torso is woefully underdeveloped.

"Do you have a name?" Osprey asks.

"They call me 'Swamp Rabbit,'" he says with a strong Southern accent.

"Who's they?" I ask.

He just stares at us for a moment as if he's drawing a blank, then finally responds. "Okay, I call myself Swamp Rabbit."

Osprey's turn. "Is that a thing? A swamp rabbit, I mean."

"Sure is."

She types on her laptop and we both watch a few seconds of an actual rabbit swimming through a swamp, then leaping out of the water and through the air. "Interesting. What do you do?"

"I jump."

"So why not like, Leap Frog, or something?" Osprey says.

His fingers move absentmindedly to his massive chompers.

"I like rabbits."

"Makes sense," I say. "Can you give us a demonstration?"

He bends his legs until he's in a near-squatting position, and his leg muscles coil. Then he gives Osprey a terrifying smile as he shoots straight up almost as fast as Eaglestar takes off into flight.

Then, Swamp Rabbit smashes his head on a rafter up by the ceiling and lands on the floor with a smack.

Osprey and I jump out of our seats and run to him. I feel like he should be dead, but he's not even unconscious. "Hey, are you all right?"

He nods shakily. "Yep. That, uh, happens more than you might think."

From what I've seen, I think it probably happens a lot, so if it happens even more, I'm pretty concerned. We help him up, and he's in surprisingly good shape for enduring such a long drop onto concrete.

Osprey saves me the trouble of rejecting him. "We, um, have a lot more applicants to go through, so we'll get back to you if you get one of the—very limited—spots that are available."

"Alrighty, then. Thanks much." He's a little wobbly as he hops out of the warehouse, but doesn't appear much the worse for wear.

I sit back down next to Osprey. "You were just being nice to him because he was injured, right?"

"Oh, definitely. There's just no way. I don't care how high he can jump."

I nod in agreement. "I mean, I'd be more worried about him hurting himself than anything else if he was with us. It would be way too much of a distraction."

"Agreed. Let's see who's next."

We go through several more losers in a row, and it really does start to feel like one of those stupid reality talent shows on TV. I wonder if we're even going to get enough serious contenders to put a team together.

There's a guy who comes in with his *gi* on, trying to show off his martial arts moves. He seems like a yellow belt at best but he's super intense.

One girl looks really good in her costume, but apparently that's what she considers her power to be. Can't fight or anything like that. Basically just strikes a few different poses to show off her assets. She should call herself Cosplayer or something. I put a check mark at the top of her application and Osprey immediately reaches over and exes it out.

Several with unusual talents or abilities try out, but I have no idea how they're supposed to help fight crime. They're more like members of an old-fashioned sideshow. A guy who eats glass. A girl who can bend herself like a pretzel. I actually think about keeping her number, since she's pretty cute, and well… duh. But Osprey sees me putting it into my phone and gives me a withering glare.

After that comes a kid who can do a phenomenal impersonation of practically any celebrity you can name. A man who's really good at magic tricks—but they're all just party tricks—nothing useful for fighting criminals.

Maybe we should have been more specific than "special abilities."

Then there are those who claim to have powers, but when they attempt to demonstrate them, they don't work. Like telekinesis. Or talking to the dead. Or they claim there have to be just the right conditions for them to work. But they don't know what the right conditions are. How is that supposed to help us?

There's something familiar about the way another guy struts in wearing a cheap Black Harrier Halloween costume that's been spray-painted orange and blue. He also has blades sticking out of his gloves, which means if he punched someone, they'd be in some serious trouble. It looks more than a little ridiculous, but I manage to rein in my laughter and my sarcasm so we can give the guy a chance. He's definitely big, so if he can fight, he might be worth having on the team. He stands in front of us with his hands on his hips like he's on a comic book cover or movie poster and I hope he's being careful with those blades.

I start the usual way. "Name?"

"Deathblade!" He tries to sound all cool as he yells it, but it's silly.

I turn to Osprey. "Isn't that taken? I feel like that has to be taken. Pretty villainous, too."

She looks it up on the laptop she has open in front of her. "It's not a name registered by the Guild. Let's see… video game, novel, but no, I don't see a crimefighter with that name for real or in the comics."

"Do you do anything besides, uh, blade people to death?"

"I wrestle. And I can knock people down pretty good. Especially losers." It's hard to tell with his face covered by the plastic helmet, but I feel like I recognize the voice also.

God help me, I know who this is. Orange and blue are my school's colors. It's freaking *Logan*.

There's no way he's going to be on any team of mine. I don't care if he can take down Eaglestar with one hand tied behind his back. But I have to have some fun with him first.

I try to sound as serious as possible. "Did you bring your essay?"

Osprey practically snaps her neck spinning her head around at me. "Huh?"

I reply under my breath, out of the corner of my mouth. "Just roll with it."

Logan cocks his head to the side. "Essay?"

"Yeah. Didn't you read the requirements? You need a five-thousand-word essay on the topic of 'Why I want to be a superhero.'"

"I guess I missed that." Somehow his confusion comes across clearly even through the helmet.

"Hmm. Better start writing, then. But we can put it on hold until tomorrow as long as you pay the $2,000 application fee tonight."

"Two… thousand dollars?"

"Non-refundable. But don't worry, you don't have to pay the $7,500 membership fee unless you get accepted. And we take installments"

"Uuuuhhhhh…"

"I take it you didn't bring it? Well, you at least have the proof of insurance, right?" I say.

"What kind of insurance?"

"Masked crimefighter insurance. You don't expect us to cover you if you get injured, do you?"

He slowly turns his head from side to side.

"Well, I'm sorry, but it appears that you don't meet any of the qualifications, Darkblade."

"Deathblade," he corrects. This time, it's barely audible.

"Maybe next time we're recruiting, you'll pay attention to the instructions and come prepared. Until then, there's the exit."

Logan drops his head and slowly walks out. I realize I have a huge grin on my face.

SMACK! Osprey hits me on the arm.

"Ow!" I felt that, even through my uniform.

"What the hell was that all about? That was so… so *mean*."

I laugh.

"Not funny," she says.

"Do you know who that was?"

"No. But it doesn't matter. You shouldn't be that mean to anybody."

"That was Logan Andrews, the bully from my school! The guy who tormented me all last year. The one I punched out at that Halloween party."

"Oh, him."

"Yeah. Him," I say.

"Still. You're a hero. You should be better than that."

"I should be…?" I grit my teeth. "I'm only human, you know. It's not like I kicked his ass or anything."

"Well, unfortunately, he was our best prospect in a while. And you turned him away."

"He was a jock with knives. Do you know how many times I've kicked his ass in wrestling?"

"Doesn't matter."

"Yeah? How about the fact that I'm pretty sure he tried to rob the place where I work? Is that good enough?"

"Seriously?" she asks.

"I'm not positive, but like I said, I'm pretty sure. I'm telling you, that guy's trouble."

She sighs, waving her hand at the fly. "This is hopeless."

She might be right. I start to think it's time to give up.

"Just a few more?" I ask.

"I guess." She stretches and yawns. "Just a couple."

I think the floor shakes with the next guy stomps in. He's big. Bigger than Logan—bigger than the biggest football player I've ever seen, with a jutting brow and no neck. But you can tell he's still a teenager. And he isn't wearing any kind of costume, just a tank top and jeans. He sits in the small folding chair. Literally one butt cheek fills the whole thing and the metal groans under his weight like it's about to completely fold.

"Name?"

"Bash."

"I like it," I say. "Where'd you come up with it?"

His brow furrows. "That's my name."

"Right. Where'd you come up with it?"

He looks more confused. "My grandma."

"Your grandma came up with your code name?" Osprey asks.

"No. My name's Sebastian, but she always called me Bash. And it stuck. No code name."

"Okay. Well, it still sounds like a pretty cool code name," I say. "What is it you do, exactly?"

"I hit stuff."

"What kind of stuff?"

"People, mostly. But also punching bags, walls… You know, stuff."

"Can you give us a demonstration?" Osprey asks.

Bash shrugs. He stands and walks over to the punching bag. One of the few things in the workout area we've started to put together. He looks back at us for a second, then swings his fist, but doesn't even seem to be putting a lot of effort into it. The entire bag flies off the chain, lands several feet away, and splatters, busted wide open. The big guy walks back over to the chair and sits back down. This time the legs of the chair bend a little.

"I just bought that," I whisper.

"My bad," he says.

Once I'm able to peel my eyes away from the destroyed punching bag, I go back to the questions. "What else do you like to do? Besides hitting things?"

Bash furrows his eyebrows again and looks up, deep in thought. He doesn't answer for a few seconds, then, "I like to eat."

I think it over for a second. He'd definitely be an asset to the team. We need a tank to run into the fray sometimes. But he also seems like he might be kind of a bully, like Logan.

That's not fair. I shouldn't judge him on his appearance.

I write a big question mark on his eval sheet and slide it toward Osprey. She gives me a nod.

I smile and say, "I guess we'll have to make sure we keep the fridge stocked, then. And the punching bags as well. You're in."

He stands and claps once, then pumps his fist as he walks away. "Woo!"

"See you Thursday," I shout after him. "Seven p.m.!"

Just as I'm starting to wonder if we'll get any female crimefighters besides Osprey, a tall, dark-skinned young woman enters wearing a skimpy outfit and holding a bow. She's freaking gorgeous and has tattoos all over her. Gold jewelry everywhere. She's like an Egyptian pharaoh's daughter or something.

"Hello," I say, my voice doing that lilty thing by accident.

Osprey kicks me under the table like no one can see it.

I'm about to ask her name, but she pulls an arrow out of the quiver slung around her back and fires it before I can get a word out. The missile flies between Osprey and me, just slightly higher than the tops of our heads, and embeds in the wall behind us.

I look back at the arrow, then at her. "Um… what was—"

She gestures at the arrow with her chin. Hesitantly, I get up from my chair and look at it closely. The big fly that had been bugging us all day is impaled on the wall. I call Osprey over and show her.

She finally speaks. "Call me Neith."

Osprey looks at her application. "That's an interesting code name. What's it mean?"

"It is the name of the Egyptian goddess of war and hunting, whose spirit I channel."

Osprey and I try not to make it too obvious when we look at each other. She channels an Egyptian goddess? We each raise an eyebrow simultaneously. She gives me a nod, and I continue.

"Sounds kind of like Bastet. Any relation?"

"We are kindred spirits since we come by our powers in the same manner, and often hunt for criminals side-by-side. But there are no blood ties, if that is what you are asking."

I jot down a quick note. "We sort of have a 'no killing' rule. You think you can stick to that?"

She seems disappointed. "If necessary."

"Then welcome to the team," I tell her. "We'll see you back here Thursday at seven p.m."

As she's walking out, I notice Osprey is watching me and realize I'm probably staring a little too hard at Neith as she exits. Embarrassed, I start gathering up the papers in front of me.

She continues to stare at me. "You didn't ask about her."

My voice probably sounds as confused as I feel. "What do you mean?"

"You said she was on the team without consulting me."

I genuinely didn't realize I'd done that. "Sorry. Did you not like her? I guess I thought you'd like having another female team member."

Osprey hesitates, then seems to feel forced to admit it. "No. I liked her. She seems great."

"Okay, then. I guess that's it."

As we're packing up our stuff to leave, a smaller kid comes in, dressed in a homemade green, insect-themed costume. He's all out of breath.

I'm not paying much attention as I address him. "Sorry, we're done. Roster's full."

When the kid replies, I freeze in my tracks. For the second time today, I recognize the voice immediately. No doubt in my mind, it's Javier. "Please let me try out. I'm so sorry I'm late. I had to watch my brother and sisters until my mom got home from work, and then take the bus over here. The nearest stop is a few blocks away."

I notice Osprey has a Cheshire grin plastered across her face. I sigh and sit back down. At least I know he's not gonna make the team. "Okay, show us what you've got. You have a code name?"

"Cricket."

I try really, really hard not to laugh. "Okay... Cricket. What do you do, jump really high? Because we've already seen this Swamp Rabbit guy, and—"

Suddenly, Javier lets out a shrill, piercing sound that makes my eardrums feel like they're going to burst. A wave of nausea hits me, and I almost fall backward off my chair and hit the floor. "What the..."

Javier wears a giant grin. "I have a sonic scream."

Osprey puts her fingers in her ears, probably trying to stop the ringing. "Yeah, we got that."

It takes me a few seconds to recover. This is so weird. How could I not know this kid I've been hanging out with had powers? Then he shows us some kind of amplification thing he has strapped to his neck, and I'm not sure how much of it is him and how much is the technology.

Powers or not, I still can't let him on the team. He's just going to get hurt. "Well, like I said, the roster's full. Sorry."

Javier's chin hits his chest, and even with the mask on, I can tell how disappointed he is. A pang of guilt bombards me. He *is* my friend after all. Well, sort of.

I get an idea. He'd be able to work out with us and learn to fight without getting into any actual danger.

"However," I say, "If you'd like to be on our auxiliary team and train with us, you're welcome."

"Auxiliary team?" Osprey whispers.

I wink at her.

Javier perks up immediately and practically jumps up and down. "Thanks! I won't let you down, Saw—uh, Red Ki—uh, Raptor! I promise."

He runs out of the room before we can add anything or change our minds.

I figured it was too much of a coincidence that Javier showed up here. So, apparently, he did know who I was. Probably since he saw me take down those guys at the convenience store last year. Maybe even before. That makes me feel even better about letting him on the team. If he kept my secret all this time, and never even let on to *me* that he knew, then I must be able to trust him.

SIXTEEN

SAWYER

Ambushed.

Well, not really. But on my way to school the next day, I suddenly find Javier walking next to me. So much for riding my new board. After yesterday in the warehouse and knowing that he knows I'm Red Raptor, I can't tell him to get lost, even though I'd prefer to be alone. I've got a bunch on my mind and I just need to process things.

This is exactly why I try to time things so that he's either already at school when I leave, or hasn't left his family's apartment yet.

Though this time, I get the impression that he really did get up super early to hide in an alley or something, just watching to make sure he didn't miss me. And he's jittery with excitement. More than usual even. Which is saying something. This is gonna be awkward, and I'm not quite sure how to handle it.

"Hey, Sawyer. How's it going?" He's trying to play it cool.

"Fine, Javi. How about you?" I hope the irritation isn't coming through in my voice.

"Really, really good. I mean *really* good." He pauses, probably trying to figure out just what to say about his "audition" for the team. He's really nervous, even wringing his hands like some old woman with arthritis. I imagine he's not sure if I know it was him, or whether he should reveal that he knows I'm Red Raptor. Poor kid has probably been lying awake all night trying to figure out what to say when he saw me.

So I put him out of his misery. "Yes."

Now he's just confused. "Yes? Yes what?"

"Yes, I know you're Cricket, and that you know I'm Red Raptor."

He gets a little too excited and loud. "Dios Mío! I can't believe it. I'm so relieved."

I look around to see if anyone is listening to us. "Please keep it down, Javi. We don't want to draw attention to ourselves or risk our secret identities." I give him an exaggerated wink, and he starts walking stiffly, totally overdoing the "nothing to see here" attitude.

Now he whispers so low that I can barely understand him, even with my trained hearing. "When do we start training?"

"Well, I have to work tonight, so everyone is supposed to get together tomorrow night."

He forgets what I just said and starts jumping around like his hero namesake. "Oh, my goodness, I can't wait." Then he realizes what he's doing and settles down again. "What time should we meet at the warehou—secret headquarters?"

I try my hardest to suppress a grin. It's difficult not to share his enthusiasm. "Seven, tomorrow."

"Morning or night?"

"We have school tomorrow morning," I say.

"So night? Right?"

"Yeah. Seven p.m."

He clicks his tongue and his eyes roll up in his head like he's thinking hard about something. "I should be able to make it on time after I finish my chores and my homework. I'll try my best."

"Don't worry about it if you can't. There will be plenty of other times you can show up."

"Oh, I'll be there. I wouldn't miss this for anything."

I'm still in shock about how well the auditions went. My job at the burger place on the other hand…

Things with the new superteam might be firing on all cylinders, but the Big Frankie Junior's staff? Not so much. It's gotten worse. If that's even possible. I sure didn't think it was, but it feels crappier than it did earlier. After the robbery, Kevin is even more insecure, which makes him even more of a horrible boss than he's ever been. When I ask my fellow employees who have been there longer than me, they say he's never been this bad.

I even consider going to Frank and talking to him about it. But there are a bunch of reasons not to. Not only could it lead to Kevin finding even sneakier and crueler ways to punish me, it could totally backfire as well. I know Frank would want me to figure out a way to handle it myself, so going to him might lead him to have Kevin turn up the heat just to teach me a lesson.

That's the kind of thing he did as Black Harrier, so I wouldn't put it past him as Frank Douglas. So I try to deal with it on my own, but there's only so much I can do. I can't talk back or go against his orders. I can't ignore him. What what's left to do?

All I'm really interested in is performing my job to the best of my ability and then going home. But all the employees at work are pretty tight with each other, and they start trying to bring me into the fold. Shayla invited me to one of her parties, which she says are "off the chain." Okay, I know the phrase. I've probably even used it before. But I seriously have no idea what chain people are talking about and why it's a good thing to be off of it. Even tonight, one of the fry cooks tries to get me to go out with him and his buddies after work. He asks for my number and social media info. Which would be great if I was just a normal teenager without any friends.

But I'm not.

The worst part is telling them I don't have any social media accounts. Look, my family was poor a year ago. Like super poor. I'd gotten used to not having all the stuff everyone else has, and Frank is totally against any of us being active on those networks in case someone figures us out, or whatever. I get it. It's smart.

But still, it's embarrassing.

So I'm constantly making excuses about how much homework I have and all the chores my mom makes me do at home.

To top it off, there's something very suspicious going on. I don't think it's just about me not liking Kevin. I just get a bad vibe around him. There's something I don't trust. And the longer I'm there, the more determined I become to find out what it is.

One night I'm working behind the grill and Mr. Chen comes in with someone. Remember, the restaurant is right across from Douglas Tower.

At first, I'm not paying a lot of attention, and I don't really notice anything other than the fact that it's a young woman with dark hair. They don't see me back where I'm standing, but when they walk up to the counter, I realize it's Osprey. I've really become so used to seeing her in her wig that it's a shock to see her without it.

Kevin is stuck in his office working on something, so I tell the guys on grill with me that I'll be right back.

Wiping my hands on my apron, I approach the counter and wait for Mr. Chen and his "friend" to notice me, but they're both preoccupied with the menu above the counter. Who hasn't eaten at Big Frankie, Jr.'s enough to already know what we have and what they want?

I clear my throat. Still nothing. "Mr. Chen!"

He's a little bit startled, but then he smiles when he sees me. "Sawyer. How are you? Frank told me you'd started working here." He puts his arm around Amy's shoulder. "Have you ever met my daughter, Amy?"

Osprey looks mortified, obviously hoping I don't stupidly say "Yeah! Sure, we hang out all the time. Just the other night, we kicked some gang's ass together."

I, on the other hand, am loving every second of this.

I hold out my hand and smile wide. "No, I don't think I have. Hi, *Amy*, I'm Sawyer."

I hope Mr. Chen doesn't notice how flustered she is. She grabs my hand and squeezes it way too hard. "Hi."

"Nice grip there."

Mr. Chen gets the proud papa look. "Amy here is quite the athlete. She's taken martial arts since she was very little, and is a black belt in several disciplines."

I pretend to be impressed. I mean, I've always been impressed, but I pretend not to already know how impressive she is.

"That's amazing," I say. "Maybe she can show me her moves some time."

Oops. From his look, I think Mr. Chen might have taken that the wrong way. Now I'm feeling awkward.

"Well, I have to get back to flipping those patties. You two enjoy your meal. Nice meeting you... *Amy*."

I seriously doubt that Mr. Chen knows about his daughter's extracurricular activities. I guess taking off her glasses and wearing the wig actually works to some extent if it even fools her dad.

A few minutes later, I'm in the alley out behind the restaurant throwing a giant trash bag into the dumpster, when someone shoves me into the wall. You'd think I'd be better at noticing people sneaking up on me in my line of work. I spin around and Amy is standing there holding the front of my apron with the meanest expression I've ever seen her have.

She points a finger so close to my face that I'm afraid she's going to poke me in the eye. "Look, you need to be more careful."

"I will. I will! What are you so angry about?"

She lets go and calms down a bit. "My dad still doesn't know, but I think he's suspicious. And with you acting that way and him knowing you're Red Raptor, you're going to tip him off."

"Hey, it's okay. Calm down. I'm not stupid! If he finds out, I'm not gonna be from me spilling the beans. Don't worry about it."

"It better not be."

"Look, I've been around your dad a ton since we've been patrolling together and I've never said anything. Haven't even given him the slightest suspicion."

She kicks a rock absentmindedly. "Yeah. Okay. I guess. I'm sorry. I overreacted. I just wasn't..."

She trails off, and I notice that she looks like she's about to cry.

Whoa! Geez. I'm not qualified for this. Medic!

"Is everything okay?"

"There's just a lot going on in my life. I haven't told you this, but my mom wants me to move to Bulgaria with her."

"What? Seriously?"

"And I don't want to leave. They're splitting up, and…" She wipes her face and straightens her back. "I'm fine."

"You don't need to act tough in front of me," I tell her. "Just tell her you want to stay."

"It's not that easy."

"Make it that easy," I argue.

"Hey, not everyone has super cool parents like you."

It's easy to forget, even after a year, how insanely cool it is that my father is the Black Harrier.

"Yeah, I guess Frank's pretty cool."

"No, I don't mean him. Your mom is awesome. She would never put you through something like this."

Huh. I never thought of my mom as being "awesome" before. But this past year, she's really made something of herself. I can barely remember the drunk-and-passed-out-on-the-couch version of Megan Vincent.

"You're nineteen though," I tell her. "An adult. You can make your own decisions."

"That doesn't matter much to them. I mean, there's the legality, and then there's the reality. I've spent so much of my time being Osprey that I haven't really had a chance to work on any kind of a life outside of that. In some ways, I'm way beyond most people my age, but in others I'm kind of stunted. I just don't think I'm prepared to live on my own yet."

Whoa. This is so weird. Osprey always comes across as being so confident and together. "If you ever need to talk, I'm here for you."

"Thanks." She hugs me. She actually *hugs* me.

"No problem. I, uh, have to get back to work. They're going to think I'm back here smoking or something."

"Yeah, me too. My dad thinks I'm in the restroom."

"I'll see you soon."

She nods. As I open the back door to the restaurant, she grabs it. "Oh, one more thing."

"Yeah?"

"You've got ketchup all over your cheek.

SEVENTEEN

AMY

Son of a monkey nugget.

My dad is on to me. I can just feel it. And now, Sawyer made him even more suspicious.

But who am I kidding? Frank knows who I really am. Even in a year, he's never seen me out of uniform, but he has to, right? I mean, not only am I working for his successor, but he's a great detective, and certainly no idiot. I've probably left my prints all over the Aerie multiple times. He probably ran them a long time ago.

Wouldn't he have told Dad?

And another thing? We haven't been to Big Frankie Junior's since I was a little kid. Luis Chen is one of the most prominent men on this street if not all of Manhattan. He doesn't eat fast food. I can't imagine there's a reason for us going here other than for him to gauge how I act in front of Sawyer. I'm worried telling him I was dating Alex has made him wonder if there's more to it than that.

So, I just need to play it cool.

As soon as Dad and I sit down with our food, he starts in with the questions. That's nothing to worry about though, it's like this every time we're together.

"How is school?"

He always starts there, too. I think he genuinely cares, but he also knows how much it costs him to send me to Columbia.

I stab a fry into my ketchup and swirl it around.

"Good. I've got some exams coming up, but I'm really confident about them."

More confident than I am about where this conversation is headed, that's for sure.

"Are things with Alex still… transpiring?"

I choke on a bite of my sandwich and rush to get a sip of Coke.

"Is something wrong, darling?" He asks, as if he's seriously concerned. It's just him trying to get me to let my guard down.

"Fine!" I cough. "Me and Alex—"

"Alex and I," Dad says. He loves to correct people on that. I've been hearing grammar rules from him since I was a little girl.

"Right, Alex and I are doing good."

"I hear he's coming to town for the city's first 'National Sidekick Day,'" he says. "It's supposed to be a big deal."

"Oh, yeah. Right," I say. I'd sort of hoped. Then I'm the one who get suspicious. "How did you know that?"

"Oh, darling. Frank and I are good friends, and Frank and Alex go way back. I assume you'll be there with him?"

What is that supposed to mean? Does he know? Oh, my God. This is too much for me to handle. Is he trying to entrap me? Did I use the word "entrap" right? The questions are so many I can't even number them.

"I dunno. Maybe."

"You don't seem so sure," Dad says.

"No, it's not that. I'm sorry, Dad. I just…" Have to come up with an excuse is what I have to do. "I am still trying to figure out what to tell Mom."

Bingo.

"I see." He takes his first bite—one small fry—which is his way of forcing me to take over the conversation. Business tactics he's used on me my whole life.

"I just told Mom I didn't have a boyfriend, and now all of a sudden I do?"

"Why would you lie to her about something like that?"

Yes, why would you lie, Amy?

"You know how she can be," I say.

"Yes, fair point. She would have demanded to meet him immediately. She'd have made Margaritas."

"Right?" I laugh, thankful things have smoothed out, at least a little.

"That boy behind the counter. Sawyer. Are you sure you've never met him?"

Whoa! That's called a "gotcha question." It's obvious now he was building up to it. He absolutely is suspicious.

"Him?" I say, taking a nibble off another fry. Guess I've built a house out of lies, I'll just live here for awhile. "Nope. Never met him before."

"Ah. Well, it just seemed as if the two of you were familiar to one another."

I look over toward the counter and I can see Sawyer pouring a bag of frozen sliced potatoes into the deep fryer. "Nope. Now it's my turn."

"Your turn?"

"To ask a question."

"Certainly. Go right ahead."

"Why here? Why are we getting fast food all of a sudden, when we usually eat at the best restaurants in town?"

He scoffs. "I didn't realize you'd become such a snob, my dear."

"That's not what I mean and you know it," I say. "I'm fine eating burgers and fries. But since when are you?"

He loosens his tie and unbuttons the top button. "I thought it might be nice to loosen up a bit."

I'm not buying it for a second. He pulls a handkerchief out of his pocket and tucks it into the front of his shirt.

Then I look down at his food, and he's cutting a chicken nugget in half with a plastic fork. "Really? Loosen up? You?"

He picks up half a nugget with a plastic fork and places it into his mouth after dipping it in some honey mustard sauce. He doesn't respond until he's eaten every bit in his mouth. "Is that so surprising?"

He raises his pinky as he slurps a sip of his coffee and I laugh. "Yes. Yes, it is, Bàba."

"Well, I am glad I can still surprise you."

I don't know what is going on here or who he thinks he's fooling, but it definitely isn't me. He's up to something, but I can't figure out what it is.

"Are you enjoying your hamburger?" he asks.

"It's good." I decide to change tacks and see if I can catch him off his guard. "So, what's up with you and Pam?"

Gotcha.

He stops chewing for a nanosecond. Enough that I caught it, but he is absolutely a master when it comes to playing his cards close to his chest.

"My secretary?" he says as soon as he's finished what was in his mouth.

"Only Pam I know," I say. "She's pretty." That took every ounce of willpower inside of me to not throw up what I'd just eaten.

"You think?" he says. "I never noticed."

You are so full of—

"Now that you mention it, though. She has a sort of beauty that's not obvious."

Oh, right, and the best kind of beauty is the one you have to work to see.

"Hmm. Maybe I will ask her on a date once your mother and I are officially divorced."

That's when I realize he's messing with me.

"Oh, stop it," I tell him.

He laughs.

"I'm glad you are doing well, Darling. Please do tell your mother how you feel soon. I'd hate to see you leave due to fear. I so would miss our chats and time spent together."

"Me too, Bàba. Me too."

EIGHTEEN

SAWYER

It's Thursday, 6:58 pm and my emotional level is peaked. Being a masked crimefighter has been my life for the past four years and nearly all of that time was spent as a sidekick. Yeah. I said it. It's time to stop making believe I was anything else. The Black Harrier was the big man and I was his helper. I'm not mad at him about it. I'm not mad at all. But the truth has to prevail here.

Now, I have a chance at something different. Something greater, maybe. I'm gonna lead my own team, and I'm proud of the guys and girls we chose.

Osprey is here with me at this dilapidated old warehouse. It's a crap pile. But it's my crap pile. And we are gonna do to it the same thing we are gonna collectively do to New York, the city I love. Clean it up.

"You ready for this?" I ask Osprey.

I can tell she's as excited as I am. She didn't have the same experience as me. She started off completely apart from the Guild and all their practices. I envy her in a lot of ways. For whatever reason, she decided it was her obligation to keep the streets safe, so she compiled a really kickass suit, some weapons, and made a name for herself to the degree of being accepted into the Guild as an ancillary member.

I know you know all this, but these are the kinds of moments where we get to reflect on the past and look toward the future, so that's what I'm doing.

No more sidekicks.

"I can't believe we are actually doing this," she says.

"Me either. It's like a dream I never knew I had coming true. I'm glad you're doing it with me."

"Yeah, okay. Let's not get sappy," she says, but she smiles.

Pace shows up first, as expected. On time. To the second.

I can't deny it; the guy looks cool. His armor is all black and silver, and it's really lightweight. I'm not sure what it's made of. He has silver lightning bolts down both legs and on his torso. Against the black of his uniform, it's really classy.

Not like some of those other guys with their bright colors that remind me of when old guys put flames on their cars—like that makes it go faster or something.

He walks right past me. All my complimentary thoughts fly out the window.

"Hey, gorgeous," he says to Osprey.

I can't believe it. She's trying so hard to suppress her smile. You've gotta be kidding me. This is what girls want? This... douche?

Wow.

I'm not jealous; you're jealous.

"Okay, let's keep it professional," I say, catching up to him.

"Sup, boss?" he says, turning to me. "Didn't see you there."

"Right." I hand him a packet of papers I'd put together last night. He takes them, looks them over so quick I can barely see the pages flip. Apparently, speed reading is in his repertoire.

"Cool," he says.

"We'll go over some of this together before we start training," Osprey says.

"Niiiiice," Pace says.

Thankfully, Bash shows up next. He's dressed in what Frank refers to as civvies, with a giant rucksack that I have to assume is filled with his gear. After receiving his packet and a quick hello, he has very little to say. However, when he walks over to the spot I'd clearly set up like a small classroom, Pace follows him, leaving me and Osprey near the door to greet the others. So that's cool. They sit and have a conversation I can't hear, but it looks like they are getting along. So, that's a plus, too.

So far, so good.

Next to show up is Neith. She's not wearing a typical costume either. No mask. No armor. Just like the other day, she's covered in various pieces of gold jewelry that I assume has something to do with her gifts. Now, up close I can see the tattoos on her dark skin more clearly. There are little ankhs and those Egyptian-eye-things. I figure they help with that too. Or maybe she just likes getting inked.

Man, that's one good-looking goddess-channeling—

"Is something wrong?" she asks and I realize she's been standing in front of me while I stare at her, wordless.

"Uh, no. Sorry. Here you go." I hand her the same packet I gave the others and she flips it over a few times.

"You can have a seat and we'll start in just a minute," Osprey says when I fail to.

Neith slinks over to the chairs. What the hell? I feel like she must have cast some kind of spell over me. I just can't stop staring.

"Anyone ever tell you how smooth you are?" Osprey asks me.

"Shut up." Hopefully, the smile tells her I'm kidding. "I gotta say, this is a seriously attractive group of masked crim—"

I stop talking as Javier, dressed in his ridiculous, almost Halloween-store-quality costume barges through the door.

"I'm late! Sorry I'm late!"

"What were you saying?" Osprey whispers to me.

Of course, I ignore her.

"Hey, Cricket." I really emphasize his name. I remember how cool I felt when I first became Red Kite. Every time I put on that costume, I felt like a was five feet taller. Too bad Javi's costume doesn't *actually* make him taller. Though, his short stature complements his name quite well.

"Hiya, Raptor, Osprey, everyone. Great to be here. Whoa! That guy is huuuge! And… cooool. Is that Pace?"

"Oh, you know him?" I say.

"Well, I don't really know him. Not like I know you, or whatever. But he works with Fastlane sometimes, right? Yeah. So cool. When do we start? Should I stretch, or—"

I shove the packet at him and tell him to take a seat.

"Yes, sir!" He salutes me and then I realize he is waiting for me to salute him back. Once that travesty is done, we all convene at the chairs.

"You're all here because you're the best of the best." I do everything I can not to look at Javi when I say it. "I hope you've had a second to familiarize yourself with the papers we gave you.

Okay, I have to admit, I got this idea from Big Frankie U. There's stuff in there about always representing the team at all times, even when we aren't together. There's a whole section on rule number one, No Killing. Neith doesn't look overly excited during that part, but she still exudes raw sexual appeal.

What is *wrong* with me?

"It's important to always be on the same page," I say. At literally that moment, Javi frantically flips through his packet, looking for where we are.

"Right," Osprey steps in. "I think the first step is to make sure we can all work together in a complementary way. You can read through the rest of that stuff at home. Sound good?"

Everyone nods and we get to work.

The team's training doesn't start out as smoothly as I want it to. In fact, it's kind of a disaster. None of them has any experience working with a group, and Bash doesn't even have any real fighting training, since he's always relied on his brute strength. He's been in quite a few fights from what he's told me, but nobody's ever been able to hurt him, and once he connects, the other person is down for the count. That may be okay in a school or street fight, but it's not gonna work with the type of supervillains we might go up against. I wind up spending a lot of time teaching him basic fighting techniques. Luckily, he's a quick student. Not as quick as me, but who is?

Speaking of quickness, Pace has trouble taking directions, and is always in a hurry to do everything. No surprise there, huh? That makes it really difficult to time things and stay in sync with each other. Also, he spends half his time flirting with Osprey, which shouldn't bother me, but does.

Plus, it's a distraction for everyone else also. No, seriously. Stop judging.

Neith always wants to do her own thing, which doesn't always coincide with what needs to be done. She's seriously talented though. Not only is she a sharpshooter with her bow, but she can handle a spear, and short swords expertly. I mentioned her tattoos before, and it turns out I was right. They are kind of… well, magical, I guess. Which sounds really stupid when I say it out loud, but she can use them to channel the goddess Neith. Or that's what she says. There's every bit the chance it's just a collection of superpowers she has and that's how she uses them.

The other problem with her is that she's also a distraction—but to me, and for other reasons. Let's examine the good news first, shall we? When I'm around Neith, I find myself pining for Osprey less and less. The bad news? I'm pretty sure she doesn't care that I'm alive.

Here's another non-surprise. Javier—Cricket—is the worst of all. Not only does he not know how to fight, work with a team, or use his powers at all, he's so small and scrawny that I'm afraid if he ever does go out with us, he's gonna get killed right off the bat. It'll be hard enough to lead the team once we know what we're doing without having to worry about protecting him all the time. For now, we let him continue to train with us, but there's no way I'm ever letting him out in the field.

I keep pushing them harder and harder, trying to get them to do things the way I taught, but it just seems to get worse.

Afterward, we sit around an old, oval dining room table that someone had left on the sidewalk. They immediately get defensive.

Pace speaks up first. "You expect too much out of us."

Then Bash. "Yeah. How are we supposed to learn all this stuff so fast?"

Neith just crosses her arms and leans back in her chair. But I get the impression she agrees with them.

"Look, I'm just trying to make sure we all work together. It's dangerous out there. We can get hurt. *Killed.*" This time, I don't try to hide the fact that I'm looking right at Javier when I say this.

He picks up on it immediately and frowns. He gives me a defiant look I've never seen from him before.

"We know that, he says. "But we made the choice to do this. You don't need to protect us."

Osprey decides to chime in next. "Honestly, you have been a bit… controlling. We do need to work together, and we're all willing to follow your lead. But you need to let us do our thing also."

I put both hands up defensively, then let them fall. Maybe they're right. Maybe I'm so worried about this team being a success that I'm actually sabotaging our chances of it. One thing's for sure: What I'm doing now isn't working, and doesn't look like it's ever going to.

This is my dream. I've been obsessing over it, even to the point of neglecting everything else in my life to move it forward. And I'm not going to give it up this easily.

"I tell you what. Let's start over again from scratch." I stand up. "Hi. I'm Red Raptor. Welcome to the team. Let's see what you all can do."

Everyone smiles. Even Neith. Perfect teeth. Perfect.

Pace leans forward like he usually does when he's about to talk. "Hey, I got a thought. We gonna name this team or what? We can't just go around calling ourselves the Superteam."

I sigh. "It's not gonna be easy finding something that hasn't already been taken at some point in either real life or trademarked in fiction. Any suggestions?"

Everyone shouts out suggestions at once, and I don't catch a single one of them.

Osprey raises her hand to get everyone's attention. "The name of the team should have something to do with the fact that we're going against the Guild's rules. Pushing back."

"I still don't even get what the Guild is," Bash says.

"They license masked crimefighters."

"So this is what, illegal?" he asks.

Well, not exac—" I start but he cuts me off.

"Cool. I like it."

Pace gets so excited he stands up. "Oh! I know. I know. Renegades."

"Taken," I say.

Cricket speaks so softly we almost don't hear him. "How about The Rebels?"

"That's a possibility. But I think there might be trademark issues."

Bash shakes his head. "Resistors. Because we're resisting the Guild's rules."

Obviously he doesn't understand what a resistor is. "That's actually not—"

Osprey interrupts. "… bad at all. I like it."

The others nod.

Pace smiles. "Me too."

"I hate to ruin everyone's day, but resistors—"

"… are exactly what we are. And it sounds cool." Bash crosses his arms in defiance.

Neith finally speaks. "I suggest we put it to a vote."

As much as I don't like the name, that does sound fair—and it's not just cuz Neith suggested it. I sigh. "Okay, then. Everyone in favor of calling our team 'The Resistors' even though resistors are—"

"Those in favor, raise your hand," Osprey says.

Everyone raises their hand except for me.

Osprey grins. I'm sure she doesn't really like the name, but knowing her, she doesn't really care, either. But she knows it's bugging me, and it's just making it more fun for her.

"The Resistors it is then," she says.

I guess I'm just going to have to get used to the fact that our crimefighting team is named after electronic components. Either that, or slowly lose my mind dwelling on it. We'll see.

NINETEEN

AMY

Immediately after training, Pace is on me like flies on poop. Which is a really gross metaphor. I'm not exactly complaining, but the word "couth" has no meaning with this one. However, what he lacks in that department, he *more* than makes up for with his looks.

He's not just cute. He's hot. The body of a runner, which is kind of a duh.

I'm a little surprised by my interest in him. I'm not one of those girls who gets all boy-crazy or looks for the "freak of the week." Which is also a gross way of putting things. But Pace… I'll just say that I'm interested.

"Hey, gorgeous," he says for the three-hundredth time.

I decide to play it cool. He doesn't need to know I'm into him. Let him chase me. It's a race I know I'd lose and I'm okay with that.

"I have a name, you know," I say.

"As a matter of fact, I don't."

"Well, you know 'Osprey,' and that's a start."

"You're right. Osprey, my name is Diori Jackson. And yours?"

"Osprey," I tell him, a little smile playing at the corner of my lips.

"Okay, okay, okay. I see. I see. No problem. A girl's allowed her secrets, right? Thing is, it's harder to ask a girl out for dinner if I don't know what to call her."

What? Wow. That was fast. Which, I guess makes sense coming from him.

I clear my throat. "A date, huh?"

"You called it that, not me," he says. "I'm flattered."

"Pffft. Whatever. Okay. Where are you taking me, speedster?" I ask, trying not to let him realize how excited I am.

"You picky?" he says.

"With food or guys?"

"Touché. Girl can play ball. I like it. Food."

"What do you have in mind?" I ask.

He rubs his hands together so fast I think he might start a fire. "I know this awesome Mediterranean place down near The Garden. It's real good."

I start to speak but he cuts me off. Not in a rude way or anything, but just like he forgot to add something.

"Oh, and we can't go dressed like this. It's fancy."

"Fancy, huh?"

"Yeah, but the team's paying for it right?"

Unreal. I knew this guy was too good to be true. I take a deep breath, trying to collect my thoughts, and he starts laughing, and slapping his knees… *actually* slapping his knees.

"I'm kidding! I got it. Come on, girl, lighten up."

"Ha-ha, very funny," I say, feeling more than a little foolish.

Sawyer must have heard Pace laughing and comes over. "Hey guys, what's going on?"

"We're gonna get a bite to eat," Pace tells him.

"Sweet. I'm in," her says. "Where are we going?"

Cringe.

"Nah, bro. Me and her. We're gonna go get to know each other on, you know, what did you call it? A date?" He looks to me and I want to crawl up into a hole.

I've said it before and I'll say it again: Me and Sawyer will never be a *thing* but I don't want to hurt him. I absolutely never gave the impression I reciprocated the feelings he has for me, but you know boys.

He looks utterly dejected. "Oh, no. That's cool. I… I got plans with uh… well, I think I'll see if Neith wants to do something."

"Oh, really?" I say.

"Do what?" Neith says from just a few yards away, behind Sawyer.

Wow, this has spiraled right out of control.

"Oh, just dinner or something," Sawyer says, face as red as his armor. "Not us… not just us, I mean. Maybe like a group."

"I wanna go!" Javier says.

I can see the horror blossoming on Sawyer's face and I will it to stop. No need to hurt Javier, too.

"I am not interested," Neith says.

Ouch.

"Cool. That's fine," Sawyer says. Poor kid. "I can just go home. I've got a lot to do anyway. You know, for work and school, plus plans for the team and stuff. The Resistors."

"I still wanna go," Javier says.

"Oh, right. Sure. Okay, Javi. Let's, uh. Sure, let's get a burger or something at Big Frankie Junior's."

I can tell that's the last place Sawyer wants to go, but he probably thinks it'll be his fastest option.

"Awesome! I love that place," Javier says. Together they walk away and I hear, "I don't have any money though. Think I could borrow some?"

I'm still watching them leave when Pace speaks up. "So about that date?"

The excitement returns in magnitudes and I have to remind myself that this is casual. It's just a thing. No big deal. "I'll go home and get changed. Meet you there in an hour?"

"I'll be there," he says.

"Great. Oh, and my name's Amy."

"Amy," Pace says. "I like that. See you there, Amy."

And with that, he's a blur out the door.

I take one last look around the place to make sure it's not in too much disarray—I guess I just hate things being messy. I clean up a little, then find my bag. I have four missed calls. I wasn't wearing my helmet during training, so I didn't get notified by my AI—which is nowhere near as intelligent as Sawyer's. Practically just Bluetooth connected to my communicator. As I'm swiping to see who called, a picture of Alex pops up.

Oh, man. He's been calling me and he's calling again. There's no way I can talk to him right now. I just can't. Plus, we are on a break, right?

I shut off the screen and ignore the call. I'll probably have to explain myself at some point but tonight, I'm going to enjoy myself.

TWENTY
SAWYER

The next afternoon, we end up having our best training session by far. I let loose on the reins and allow the team members to play to their strengths, and concentrate on simply coordinating their efforts. We pick up on each other's cues and hit all our marks.

It's pretty incredible to see what my teammates are capable of when they're in their groove. Not only that, but I actually start having fun.

After that, each training session gets better every time. Not only *only* that, but we start to get closer as friends and teammates. It makes me especially happy to see Javier getting along with all the others, since he's always been a loner at school. Like me.

On the downside, Pace and Osprey flirt more and more. It makes me uncomfortable, but it's none of my business. If I tried to make some kind of rule that team members can't date, then it's just going to cause more problems and I'm going to be accused of controlling things again. Besides, Neith starts talking to me, and now I'm starting to wonder if maybe there could be something between us some day.

Meanwhile, Osprey and Pace become an actual couple, which would have really bothered me a few days ago. But by now my feelings for Neith have gotten stronger, and I hardly think about Osprey at all. So far, I've been too shy to ask her out or anything, but I get the feeling she likes me too.

I think I'd better do something fast before I get permanently stuck in the friend zone. That's a more difficult trap to escape from than hanging over a pit of man-eating carnivores.

The team decides to have a get-together at our headquarters to celebrate how well we've been doing, and that's when I plan to make my move. We decide we know and trust one another enough now that we're all out of costume and in our street clothes together for the first time. It's weird showing my face when I'm so used to wearing a mask around them. Neith and Bash didn't wear any costumes to begin with, and I know Javi and Amy, so for me, it's really just Pace.

While Bash and Cricket play some video games, Pace and Osprey stay off in a corner together talking quietly. Neith stands in the kitchen area by herself, drinking some kind of health food smoothie and eating some pita chips. If I'm not mistaken, I think she's wearing some makeup, which surprises me.

I try to stay calm as I approach her. Totally casual.

"Hey."

"Hello."

I love hearing her say even one word. And that accent.

Awkward pause. Getting longer. Longer.

"So, my real name is Sawyer."

She finally looks at me, deciding whether or not to reveal her real name to me. "You may call me Aaliyah."

"That's nice. That's a nice name. Really nice."

More soul-crushing silence.

"So… what's up?" I say.

She seems surprised by the question for some reason. "Excuse me?"

Of course it couldn't be easy for me. "You know. What's going on?"

She looks from side to side as if she's trying to figure out what I'm talking about. "I am eating chips and drinking a smoothie. I would have thought that to be obvious."

Whoa. I was not expecting the conversation to derail so quickly. I mean, I'm awkward enough around girls that I figured it would go south at some point, just not right away like that.

"Sorry," I tell her. "I was just making small talk."

"Why?"

"Uh… because I…" Just go for it, you doofus! "—like you?"

"Is that a question?"

I stare at her blankly and I dig the heel of my hand into my eye. "No…"

"If you like me, why not just start by saying that?" she asks.

"I haven't had much luck with the direct approach in the past. Maybe if we—"

Suddenly, she grabs me by the front of my shirt, pulls me in, and plants a big kiss on my lips. It lasts way longer than any kiss I've ever had before. I didn't even know kisses could be like this.

When she pulls away, I feel lightheaded and a little dizzy.

"When I see something I want," she says, "I take it."

She bites into another chip as if nothing happened.

"Um… okay. So does this mean we're…?"

"We shall see," she tells me.

"Yeah. Okay. Sounds good."

After my kiss with Neith last night, it's hard enough making it through the school day, but work is just plain torture for me. I burn some buns, leave some fries in the vat way too long, and wash the same spatula three times while I'm daydreaming and planning in my head how the night would go.

The thing that brings me out of my daze is when I notice that Kevin is acting suspicious again like he was the night Amy and her dad came in. He spends most of his time tucked away in his office, and doesn't want to come out, even when there's a rush. He also makes sure to lock his door when he does have to make rounds through the dining area, and then looks around to make sure nobody's watching him when he goes back into the office.

He doesn't know that I'm an expert in surveillance, of course, and that I have my eye on him even when he thinks I'm working. This is one of those rare times he's not holed up, and I watch him say something to the shift supervisor before leaving the restaurant. After a few minutes, I find the supervisor.

"Hey, Daria," I say.

"What do you want?" she says. She's like six months older than me and acts like the world owes her something.

"Just hoping I can take my fifteen since the place is kinda dead," I tell her.

"Whatever. Take twenty. I don't care."

"Thanks," I say and take off my apron.

While nobody is looking, I easily pick the lock on Kevin's office door and slide in, easing the door shut behind me. I do a peripheral search, but I don't find anything too bad, although a lot of the stuff he has in there grosses me out, like the coffee cup he keeps refilling but never washes.

I try logging into his computer. It only takes me three attempts to figure out his password. It's freaking Password. Idiot. Once I'm in, I find a treasure trove of things that he's been doing, some illegal, some just immoral, and some that are both.

This dude is so going down.

I hear the doorknob start to rattle, as if someone is unlocking it with a key. Just in time, I jump to the side of the door so that when it opens, I'm standing behind it. Kevin rushes back in and grabs something he must have forgotten from his desk drawer. He pauses, and I'm afraid that he somehow knows I'm in there.

Then I hear a noise that sounds like the air slowly letting out of a balloon. At first I'm not sure what it is, but I quickly learn that he was releasing a nearly-silent-but-deadly fart. As soon as he's done, he exits the office and locks the door behind him.

Because I have to wait to make sure the coast is clear, I'm trapped in the tiny office with the noxious fumes. I've never needed the air filter from my utility belt so desperately in my life.

TWENTY-ONE

SAWYER

G*lorious.*

That's how the team's first night out on patrol together starts out. I feel a little guilty because I didn't let Cricket—Javier—know we were going out. I'm sure he'll feel bad when he finds out, but I can't have him getting seriously injured on our first mission and ruining everything. Not only do I not want him to get hurt, but what would his mom do if he wasn't able to help her out? So I decided it was best just to not include him. Though, it still gnaws at me a little.

After roughing up some lowlifes, Tiffany speaks up.

"Sawyer, we have a problem down at the docks," she says.

"What docks? There are a lot of docks?"

"No need to get snippy," she says. *"I'm just trying to help."*

"Okay, let's start over. A problem? Oh, boy. Oh, boy! What's going on, Tiff?"

If she understands my facetiousness, she doesn't acknowledge it.

"Definite crime taking place," she says.

"This is it everyone!" I say into comms.

"What is it, Tiffany?" I ask, doing my best to sound polite.

"I'm registering dozens of heat signatures inside shipping crates, at the docks in Red Hook. And they are moving."

"Workers?"

"It doesn't appear so."

Could be animals?" I say.

"They are large."

"Could be large animals?"

"I believe they are human, Sawyer."

It's no secret that New York's a hotbed for human trafficking. I can generally stop a bank robbery or a mugging with very little emotional attachment, but when it comes to this stuff? It gets my blood boiling.

"Thanks, Tiffany."

I tell the team what's up and we make our way to the docks. Already in Brooklyn, it doesn't take long. Tiffany highlights the suspected shipment on my visor and activates heat seeking. Immediately, I can see what she sees. There's no doubt something shady is going on.

We hide up on the rooftop of a building next to where the ship is docked and watch as the shipping containers are unloaded from the ship. It's not long before one of them is opened. Sure enough, disoriented people—some of them young kids—stumble out of the dark interior of the storage container. They even cover their eyes despite the fact that it's night and there's very little lighting on the dock. Most of them fall over immediately, but are quickly pounced on by men dressed in black with what appears to be M4 carbines. That's not a gun you can pick up at the local gun shop. It's a full auto rifle, which means these guys have some connections.

"They've got some firepower," I tell the team.

"You know I'm faster," Pace says.

"And I can take bullets, bro," Bash says.

"Yeah, but the victims can't," Osprey says. "We can't just have people shooting all over the place. Who knows who'll get caught in the crossfire."

"Right," I agree.

A few of the adults get kicked by the traffickers, so they do their best to help one another stay upright. The traffickers have big Mack trucks standing by with their back doors open. It's clear their intentions: get these poor people to their next destination.

Not gonna happen. Not while I'm running this town.

Okay, I know that sounded cheesy. Whatever. I'm trying stuff out.

I turn to the team to give the signal, but Osprey speaks up again.

"Pace, can you whip in and get the victims out of there?"

"Wait," I say. I know I shouldn't be upset, because that's the smart move here. But her new relationship with Pace has me all out of sorts "I'm not sure that's the best move."

"You agreed with me," she says. "We can't risk crossfire. Pace can get in and out of there before anyone even knows what happened."

Of course, she's right. I just hate to admit it. Our first real mission together and I'm not even the one who came up with the plan.

"Okay, sure." I turn to Pace. "Just don't let anyone see you."

He scoffs. "Watch."

Literally seconds later, Pace is back on the rooftop and one by one, he'd brought a bunch of scared-looking people to safety.

"How was that?" he asks.

"What the hell just happened!" one guy on the docks shouts.

"Where is everyone?" another says.

"Secret's out," I whisper. Then I turn to the victims. "You all stay quiet. Up here, you're safe. Resistors, let's take down some baddies."

Pace zips down again and starts smacking guns out of the thugs' hands. Neith's tattoos start to glow a soft orange and she descends from the roof like she's being carried on a cloud. She can't fly, but damn. That's cool.

Osprey and I glide in while Bash just jumps. I swear, I can feel the ground shake when he lands and I'm not even on the street. He sprints straight at their biggest guy—who's the size of an offensive lineman in the NFL—and the guy braces himself.

It doesn't do a bit of good.

Bash pulls his fist back just before he reaches the guy, then it comes forward into the thug's chest with the force of a jackhammer. Between the punch, his momentum, and his super-strength, Bash sends the dude flying straight backward like a cartoon character, right off the pier and into the water. I hope he's not dead. Not that I'd feel bad after seeing the condition of the people on the roof, but I don't want us getting into trouble on our first night out.

Neith shoots her arrows at the goons closest to her, mostly into their knees and shoulders, all non-lethal as far as I can tell. But they all drop immediately, and I won't apologize for smiling at the thought of how much it must've hurt.

Osprey is doing her usual. She brings one guy down at the end of her glide, then spins in a kick and takes out another one. It's not like I was ever worried about her. She's as good or better than I am at most of this stuff.

"Found another shipment of people!" Pace shouts.

"Get them safe," I respond.

"On it."

Bad guys are going down. Good guys are getting saved.

Everything is going great.

Until all of a sudden, it isn't.

Bash sends another thug flying with his fist, but this one ends up straight in Pace's path. The speedster isn't able to slow down fast enough and slams into Flying Guy, then falls into the water, along with a kid he was carrying to safety.

A kid who looks to be from a place with very little water and, in all likelihood, can't swim.

I go into team-leader-crisis-mode and shout at Bash. "One of the kids is in the water. Get him out! I'll get Pace."

Bash freezes up completely. "I—I…"

That's when I realize he can't swim, either. I turn to Neith, but gunshots ring out and I spot a new wave of thugs running out from below the deck of the ship.

She's on top of them in an instant, short sword drawn and is literally dodging bullets. She's a blur of glowing orange. It's a mesmerizing sight. Which means I'm not paying attention when a thug comes at me.

"*Sawyer*," Tiffany warns too late. Man, I miss Amber.

The guy's shoulder slams into me and he spears me into the side of one of the trucks. My lower back cracks against the base of the trailing and pain radiates through me. He gets in a few good punches and then Osprey leaps to my rescue.

"Go get the kid!" she says, wrapping her forearms around my attacker's throat.

Somehow I have to save the kid who can't swim *and* Pace, who, from here, looks unconscious, before one or both of them drowns. And I think I'm limping but there's no time to worry about my pain. I pull off my cape as I run so it doesn't weigh me down.

The water hits me full in the face as I dive in, trying not to even think about how gross and polluted this part of the Hudson must be. I get a mouthful right off the bat, and it tastes like sewage—or what I imagine sewage must taste like. The kid is nearby, so I pull him closer and wrap my arm around his chest from behind.

But he has no idea who I am, so he tries his best to squirm away, which makes it a thousand times more difficult.

"Stay calm! I'm here to help," I tell him, but it does no good.

I use my other arm to move closer to Pace, who's floating face down and not moving. I turn him over, then wrap that arm around his chest. Between the kid moving around so much and Pace being at least my size and *not* moving at all, I can barely keep all three of us afloat by paddling my legs as fast as I can. Plus, my lower back feels like I'd just gotten stabbed or something and the muscles are twitching.

Bash is standing right on the edge, looking like he wants to jump in and help, but I don't need someone else to save from drowning.

"Stay there," I yell. "And get ready to help pull them up!"

He nods vigorously and looks extremely relieved at not having to push past his fear and get into the water. He lies on his stomach and reaches toward us as far as his massive arms will go. I start making some headway toward him, which is really difficult to do with no hands. I mentally decide I need to give all the members of the team grapplers for situations like this.

I manage to push Pace and the kid toward Bash but the action sends my back into chaotic spasms. It seems like the more I struggle, the more it hurts, and the more it hurts, the further I sink. Before I know it, I'm under water and I didn't take much of a breath beforehand. What little light is breaking the surface starts to dim as I go deeper.

I feel a hand and I'm being dragged to surface. Coughing up gross water and gasping for air, I look down and see a mass of shadows. Bash? But I pass out.

The next thing I know, I'm either dead and in heaven or asleep and dreaming because Osprey is leaning over me, giving me a kiss. Either way, I decide to go with it and kiss her back.

But as soon as I do, she pulls away and wipes her mouth off on her sleeve. "Dude, *what* are you doing?"

As my head starts to clear, I realize what's really going on, and I'm mortified. I'm lying on the pier, soaking wet, and I start coughing up water.

She wasn't kissing me. She was giving me mouth-to-mouth to save my life. It takes me a few seconds to be able to talk, and when I do my voice is hoarse. Probably should have waited.

"S-sorry."

"Yeah, well, you should be," she says. "If you hadn't just come back from the dead, I would've slapped you."

"I didn't realize what was going on. I thought I was—"

She looks at me expectantly as I try to figure out how to finish my sentence without sounding like an idiot. Or a pervert. Or something.

Neith isn't looking too happy either, to say the least. She scowls with her arms crossed, then turns away.

I then realize the rest of the team is standing around me in a circle, and they're all waiting to hear the rest of my sentence as well.

"I wasn't thinking straight. I just *drowned*."

"Well, you were only out for a couple of seconds. Bash pulled you up pretty quickly once Neith got Pace and the kid to safety."

Suddenly, my memory comes back. "Is Pace okay? The kid?"

"Yeah, they're both fine. Pace is with the victims, a little shaken up, and the kid is pretty much as you'd expect him to be."

I try to sit up, but I can't.

"My back," I say with phlegmy spit hanging from my mouth.

"Sit still," Neith says, apparently swallowing down her anger enough to assist me.

She places her hand against my lower back and I can see a faint glow and feel a lot of warmth. I think she's about to do some kind Mr. Miyagi style healing and then I feel her pull on my shoulder with the other hand as she pushes forward with the one on my back. I hear a pop, and electric pain shoots through me.

"Ow!" I shout through clenched teeth.

"Don't be a baby," she tells me. "Stand up."

I do as she says and, to my surprise, the pain is gone.

"What did you do?" I ask.

"My mother is a chiropractor," she says.

I almost laugh at the thought of this incredible, beautiful, goddess-like person having a mother, but of course she does.

"Oh, look. Those two little birdies brought friends," says a voice near the shipping crates.

We all turn at the same time to see the Neon Knights emerging with their power gloves activated and their weapons all aglow.

I swear and scramble to my feet.

"This was stupid, kid," Red says to me.

"Would you drop the 'kid' crap?" I say. "You're obviously a freaking teenager."

"Oh, like you?" Orange says.

"And you," Red says to Osprey. "You cost us a lot of money and now here? This is our reputation you're messing with."

"So do something about it," Osprey taunts him.

"Looks like it's five on four," Red says.

That's when I notice Green Guy is back. The one they called Mace on the news, only this has to be a new one. He looks a lot bigger than the last one. Not Bash-big, but still…

Then out of nowhere, Pace zips in and punches Red hard in the helmet. Red staggers sideways, and his helmet turns a bit, but he doesn't go down. A heartbeat later, Pace is standing beside us.

Red swears at us as he turns his helmet back.

"Five on five," I say.

"That wasn't a good idea, loser," Green says.

All the breath leaves my lungs at the realization that the new Mace is none other than Logan Andrews. Or at least it sounds exactly like him. First the Big Frankie Junior's robbery, then trying out for the Resistors, and now this? How in the world did he wind up in the Neon Knights?

Then Red speaks again. "You have no idea what we are capable of, twerp."

Another wave of anxiety rushes through me. Where have I heard that before?

"I got this," Pace says before disappearing again so rapidly it's like he teleported.

"Be careful, he—" Before I can finish, Mace darts forward to greet Pace—that's going to get confusing. He brings his namesake around quick and whips it at Pace. The electricity weapon zaps Pace's suit and sends him flying. He falls to the ground, probably unconscious.

Osprey rushes to him. "Pace, Pace, are you all right?"

I hear no reply.

"Good hit, Mace," Red says before brandishing his own crackling weapon, a broadsword. "Anyone else?"

"Is he breathing?" I shout.

The Neon Knights all laugh.

"Barely!" Osprey yells back

"Picked the wrong fight, Kite," Broadsword says. "This is our turf."

"You're proud of being a human trafficker?" I ask.

"We are muscle. Protection. That's it. What they do is on them. This is a paycheck, but you wouldn't understand that, would you, Richie Rich."

Richie Rich? Crap. Does he know who I am, too?

"Yeah, anyone with armor like that?" Crossbow says, raising his weapon. "Gotta be rich."

I breathe an internal sigh of relief. Then in a low voice I ask, "Neith, can you take out the archer?"

Without a verbal response, she nocks an arrow from her quiver. Crossbow panics and tries to load his own but he's too late. Tattoos on Neith's arms glow bright azure.

"You may want to stand back," she tells me. Then she fires the arrow at Crossbow's feet. It explodes and sends the orange Knight soaring backward into a shipping crate. He sits there in a crumpled pile of neon armor.

"Five on four again," Neith says.

With Crossbow out of the fight for now, Mace, Morning Star, Axe, and of course, Broadsword line up in front of us, weapons all aglow.

Bash looks ready to go, standing next to Neith, cracking his knuckles.

"Osprey! We need you!" I shout.

"You'll need more than her, twerp."

"Benji?" I say without thinking, finally realizing who he sounds like. Logan's friend from school and the same kid who I caught robbing that convenience store last year.

I might be imagining things, but I think I can see his posture shift. "What did you just say?"

"I—Uh… I said, 'Bite me.'"

I know she doesn't want to, but Osprey leaves Pace just as Broadsword and Mace both charge us.

"You cost me a hundred grand, you dumb bitch!" Red shouts.

Osprey leaps up into the air. "Let's get these bastards."

I throw my boomerang at Red or Broadsword or Benji—whatever or whoever he is. He slaps it away and it sparks red.

As Osprey comes down, she connects with Axe, feet first. Neith fires another arrow that hits Red and crackles upon contact. He goes down, seizing. Mace rushes to him and yanks the arrow free.

Red recovers and scrambles to a standing position but Bash is on him in an instant.

"C'mon, loser," Probably Logan says.

"You and me?" I ask and extend my staff. "No contest."

Energy pulses as our weapons collide. We've gotta figure out a way to disable those gloves if we are going to have a chance against these guys—and girl.

Next thing I know, I feel like I've been hit by a train going full speed down the tracks. I can't breathe because I immediately get the wind knocked out of me. As the concussive force sends me flying backward into the air, I glance down at a smoking hole in my graphene armor.

Following the trajectory with my eyes, I see a newcomer to the fight.

Battlegear. I should've known he was involved with this. There's no way these kids got this kind of tech on their own. He's super strong and super smart, and carries around some fancy weapons and gadgets. But I've still never understood why *this guy* is Eaglestar's arch nemesis.

As I hit the ground about twenty yards back, head slamming into the cement, I think, *Holy crap, I've just been shot by a gun that's meant to take down Eaglestar.*

I can tell I definitely have a concussion but still hear a hum as Battlegear powers up and even bigger weapon he's carrying. He obviously has super-strength in order to be able to hoist a gun that huge.

He smiles and says, "Go home to your mommies, kids. Time for the grownups to play."

The Knights back off, all elbowing each other and laughing.

I stand, staggering a little, but Neith is there to catch me.

"Thanks," I tell her.

"Get back in the fight," she says.

Battlegear points the weapon at the rest of us, and it starts to get a weird, bluish glow around the barrel. The same kind of energy produces a force field that surrounds him.

"Bash?"

"I'm on it." he says, and stands in front of Osprey, Neith, and me just in time to block the azure beam from the super-weapon. That is definitely not the weapon that hit me. This thing hits Bash with the force of a train. Maybe that's why he's Eaglestar's nemesis. Bash takes the brunt of the energy blast, but is pushed back into the rest of us as he falls and we all end up on the ground. Steam pours off of his chest.

Osprey is the first one to get to him. "Are you all right?"

He lifts his head slightly. "Got the wind knocked out of me. It's gonna take a minute for me to get back into this fight."

"At least you're okay," she says. "Thank you."

"No… problem." He lays his head back down and passes out.

I know Osprey must be worried about Pace as well, but she doesn't say anything about it. "Now what?"

"We have to get to him while that energy shield is down," I say. "He's gotta lower it when he discharges his weapon. Neith, if we can taunt him into firing at us, do you think you can get the shot?"

"I don't *think* I can. I'm certain of it."

I smile. She makes me smile a lot, actually. "I like that attitude. Osprey, I'll take the right and you take the left. He's bound to go after one of us."

Osprey glides up into the air. "Got it."

I throw my last boomerang at Battlegear, knowing it'll just bounce off his force field, but when it hits, it glows all around him like a giant bubble and lets us know exactly how far it reaches. It's the same bluish color as his weapon's beam, so they may actually be the same energy being emitted in different ways.

Look at me getting all sciencey.

As Osprey glides over to the left of Battlegear, I start heading right. He aims his weapon at her and suddenly, I feel guilty. What if he hits her before Neith can get her shot off? What if she gets injured? I know she can take care of herself, but I decide to make sure he takes a shot at me.

Instead of coming at him from the other side, I swerve toward him straight on.

"Hey!" I shout. "You're real tough with that force field around you. How about coming out from behind your mommy's skirt and going head-to-head?"

He doesn't fall for it, but I didn't expect him to. I just wanted to draw his attention away from Osprey.

"You don't seriously think that kind of thing is going to work on me, do you, kid?"

Why is everyone calling me "kid" today?

"No. But it was worth a shot." I smile to myself at the double meaning behind my comment. Too bad nobody else is going to get it.

The slight shimmer surrounding Battlegear disappears just as I'm getting close to him, and he aims his big weapon at me. The one that almost killed Bash, someone ten times my size. I hear the hum of his gun turn into a high-pitched whine, and then I see a blue flash for a split-second.

But as all of this is happening, I also see Neith get her shot off. She sends an arrow tipped with some kind of fancy technology straight down the barrel of Battlegear's weapon. Since he's in the middle of charging it back up to shoot Osprey, it's making that humming sound again. But this time, it sounds different. Blue fingers of electricity arc around the barrel's opening and the humming turns to a high-pitched whistle.

Battlegear panics and tosses it away. "You fools! That thing'll take out the whole pier!"

I see that Pace is regaining consciousness and I sit up the best I can. "Pace! You gotta get rid of that weapon."

He shakes his head groggily, then spots the overloading weapon, which is now vibrating violently on the ground as well as sparking and whining. He gets to his feet unsteadily, his legs shaking. But he's a hero, and he's not going to give up. Pace zooms in, grabs it, and is obviously in pain as it sends electrical jolts into his body. He nods at me, then disappears before I can blink.

We all do our best to follow, but all we can tell is he went toward the docks, which are about a mile away. After a few seconds, there's a deafening explosion and water sprays up hundreds of feet into the air, some of it even reaching us as a mist. We wait a few more seconds to see if Pace will return, but he doesn't.

"Is he…" Osprey says, saying what we are all thinking. Did one of our teammates really just die on our second mission out?

"Get them!" Battlegear shouts.

As if they hadn't just been standing around, watching as their fearless leader tried to kill us, the Neon Knights leap back into action.

The sound of police sirens fill the air, red and blue lights getting closer.

"This isn't over," Battlegear says. "Knights, let's go."

"This ain't over," Red repeats to me.

"Yeah, this isn't over, loser," Logan says.

"Anyone else?" I say.

As the police start arriving on the scene, Battlegear and the Neon Knights take off down the street and disappear behind a tower of shipping crates..

"Freeze!" A police sergeant stands behind an open car door, megaphone to his lips. "Hands up! All of you!"

I step forward to let him know I'm the one he should talk to but guns train on me from every direction.

"I said, don't move!"

He shines the spotlight attached to his cruiser on us, looks around at the members of the team. "You people new? I don't recognize most of you."

"Some of us," I shout. "We were taking down this group of human traffickers, officer. We rounded up most of them."

"Looks like you did a pretty good job."

"Except Battlegear and the Neon Knights were here. They just escaped," I say. "Went that way."

"That's unfortunate." He shakes his head. "Hate it when they get away."

"You could probably catch them if one of your guys gets on it," I tell him.

"I don't tell you how to do your job," he says. "All right, now, if I can just see your Guild I.D.s and your permit…"

Osprey wipes her face, and is shaking as she pulls out her I.D. I think she and Pace had only been on one date, but I can only imagine how she's feeling. I take hers and add it to mine, then present them both to the sergeant. "Some of us are new. I don't think Bash and Neith have I.D.s yet."

The cop eyes the others suspiciously. "You at least have copies of your applications?

Bash looks confused. "I didn't even know I needed a license to help people."

Neith crosses her arms in defiance. "I don't need permission from your feeble government to set forth on my mission to fight injustice as proclaimed by the goddess."

The officer looks back at me to see what I have to add. "And… we just started working together. This is our first time out together. We haven't really had a chance to apply for our team permit."

The sergeant sighs. "Cart before the horse, Kite. You know better than that. There are rules you have to follow. Otherwise, it's just a bunch of vigilantes running around doing whatever the hell they want."

"I know, but—"

He raises a hand. "Without licenses and permits, this is technically assault and battery, even if it *is* directed toward scumbags like them."

"I thought you weren't gonna tell us how to do our jobs," Bash says.

"I'm sorry, officer," I say, raising my hand to get Bash to stop. I know how to handle these guys. "You're right, I should have known better. I take full responsibility."

"That's awful big of you, Kite, but the fact is, we're going to have to take you all down to the station and get this whole thing straightened out. You're all at least over eighteen so we don't have to get parents involved, right?"

We all look at each other sheepishly.

The mood is somber as we are rounded up like criminals.

"What's going on? What's everyone so sad about?" Says a voice behind us. We all spin to find Pace standing behind us.

Despite it all, everyone smiles and laughs as soon as we're over the initial shock. Osprey throws her arms around him and kisses him.

And, for once, I'm not jealous.

"How about you?" the sergeant says to Pace. "You got a Guild I.D.?"

Pace grimaces. "My I.D. expired last month."

The sergeant shakes his head. "Great. Just great."

TWENTY-TWO

SAWYER

At first, I have no idea what to do since there's no way I'm going to call Mom from the police station. After four years of hiding the fact that I'm a masked crimefighter, there's no way I can let her find out by bailing me out of jail. In uniform. My next thought is that the best thing to do would be to call Mr. Chen and go from there. But I realize that up close, he'd most likely recognize his daughter, even in the costume and wig.

I think it's pretty cool of the NYPD to let us keep our masks on. I think they realize that we just wanted to help, and exposing our identities would likely mean some really bad things for us and our families. But I don't know how any of us is going to call our parents without doing just that.

If Osprey's mom shows up, everyone can easily make the connection. Same with any of the rest of us.

"This is bull," Pace says.

"Right?" Bash agrees.

"We just saved the damn world," Pace says. When he looks up, he must see the look on my face cus he adds, "Fine. But at least those docks and a bunch of people, ya know?"

I nod. "But you've worked with Fastlane long enough to know that no matter how noble the deed, there's rarely the right response."

Without my helmet on, my head fits about halfway through the bars. I can see the officers standing around drinking coffee.

"It's not their faults," Osprey says.

"Than whose fault is it?" Neith says from the corner of the cell. "I can call upon my goddess and those bars will melt into slag."

"You can do that?" Bash says.

Neith smiles, but doesn't answer.

Scary and hot.

"So what do we do?" I ask.

"Is that a no to melting the bars?" Neith asks.

"For sure," I say. "Okay, I can't call my parents because of the whole secret identity thing."

"They don't know you are Red Raptor?" Bash asks.

That's a complicated answer. Mom doesn't know I am, but Dad does but no one can know my dad is my dad. Instead of explaining it, I just say, "No. What about you? You don't even wear a uniform."

"No can do," Bash says.

"And why not?" Pace asks.

"I don't have parents," he says as emotionless as he would be if he were ordering a number three at Big Frankie Junior's—that's a double cheeseburger combo, by the way.

"You know I can't," Osprey says.

"Neith?" I say. "You said your mom was a doctor, right?"

"In Egypt," she says.

"Well, that's that," I declare as I take a seat next to Neith.

"You kissed her," she says to me.

"What?"

"Osprey. On the docks. You kissed her."

She doesn't even bother whispering. There's definitely a better time for this conversation, isn't there?

Then the last thing I expect happens, and it rescues me from this very awkward conversation.

An officer comes back to the room where they're holding us and unlocks it. "Time to go. Looks like you all got real lucky tonight. Come on. Don't make me wait."

"We will talk about this later," Neith warns.

"Yeah," I say under my breath as we exit.

I can't imagine what happened to get us set free. We haven't even given them our real names. Then, as we head toward the exit, I see him standing by the doors to the station. Frank.

I figure he's going to be pissed. *Really* pissed. But he's wearing more of a bemused look as he opens the door for us and we all walk out.

"You knew we were arrested?" I say to him.

He keeps his volume low so the others can't hear. "I may not be active, but I still pay enough attention to the police band to hear about an unknown group of young superheroes being taken downtown."

"How'd you do it? Why are they just letting us go?"

"Let's just say the Annual Policemen's Ball is going to be quite the extravaganza this year thanks to a sizable donation from a certain local corporation. Plus, it helps that one of my companies owns the docks where it all happened. No charges will be pressed."

Relief, sweet relief. "That still wouldn't explain your connection to us, though."

"I made it sound almost like a corporate sponsorship. Like a sports team. Private security. They seemed to accept that."

"Wow. Uh, thanks. I don't know what to say."

"We'll discuss this later. When your friends aren't around." Then in an even lower whisper, he asks, "Does Alex know anything about this?"

My mouth goes dry. "No."

"Then we'll have to discuss that as well. Tomorrow?"

"Tomorrow?"

"National Sidekick Day," he says.

"You mean I have to go to that?"

He smiles. "Go to it? You're the star."

"And you didn't think to tell me?" I ask.

"Are you happy about it?"

"No. Of course I'm not happy about it," I tell him.

"Then you know now why I haven't told you yet," he says. "I'll see you bright and early at your place. There's some bacon in your fridge. I like mine extra crispy. But you know that."

I try to respond but he says, "Good night, everyone," and walks off into the night, toward his abominably expensive car. Which, by the way, is parked totally illegally at the curb right in front of the station.

As soon as he's out of earshot, the others swarm around me and start bombarding me with questions. Except Osprey, of course. She's probably just happy her own dad didn't get involved.

"Wasn't that Frank Douglas? The billionaire guy?" Bash says. "How do you know him?"

"Did you *see* that car?" Pace says.

"Why would he help us?" Neith says.

I hold up my hands in surrender. "Give me chance." I take a deep breath. "Yes, that's Frank Douglas. I know him because, well, my mom is dating him right now. And... I guess that probably answers the third question also."

And it's a good thing I have that fake-but-not-far-off explanation, because I certainly can't get into the real one. "Well, he used to be the Black Harrier, but now he's just my dad. But nobody knows that."

Yeah, right.

Pace shakes his head in awe as he watches Frank's vehicle peel away. "Dude, that's so cool. And your mom must be really hot if she's dating him."

I smack him on the arm.

So cool. Easy for him to say. He doesn't have to live with it.

The next morning, I make bacon and eggs. Like I had a choice. Mom wonders what's up but I just tell her I wanted to do something nice for her and Frank, who... apparently stayed the night. I know he's my dad and she's my mom, and it's totally normal and even expected, but yuck.

"Your own team?" Frank says after mom heads to the bathroom to get ready for what's supposed to be a huge ceremony downtown for National Sidekick Day. Something I just found out I'm the guest of honor for. "What were you thinking?"

He still doesn't seem angry like I thought he'd be. More... confused.

I finish a particularly chewy piece of bacon before responding.

"I was thinking that I'm tired of the Guild controlling everything. Especially since the Guild is really just Eaglestar telling everyone else what to do. The guy is still stuck in a 1940s state of mind. I'm surprised he even lets women be crimefighters. If he didn't have powers, he'd be in some retirement facility having his diapers changed… or, more likely, dead already. Instead, he's dictating what happens with all of us masked crimefighters. It's not fair."

"Who ever said anything in life was fair?"

Duh. God, why do older people always have to say stuff like that?

"Where do you think *you'd* be if I hadn't found you in that alley five years ago?"

I refuse to give him the upper hand on this one.

"Oh, believe me, I get that. But that old fossil shouldn't be telling anyone what to do." Suddenly, I realize how harsh I must sound and pause before shoving another big bite in my mouth. "Sorry. I know he's a friend of yours."

Frank laughs so loud that it startles me. "*Friend?* Is that what you think?"

"Wait. He isn't? But you guys practically ran the Guild together all those years."

"Actually, you're not far off on the dictating thing."

What? I'm not? What the hell happened to the Black Harrier? I'm not used to Frank… talking. For half a decade, I listened to him through a stupid voice changer, and over the past few months, he's just a normal guy. It's freaking weird.

"The problem is," he continues, "he *does* have powers. And when you're the most powerful person in the world, you get used to doing whatever you want. There's not much anyone else can do. Not even me."

"How does anyone ever defeat him?"

Frank sighs. "Not many have, and it's always been very temporary. The only one who's even come close is Battlegear, but even with his genius at creating technology, he's always defeated in the end. The only way I've ever thought of to get to him, really, would be to use his own powers against him. Somehow turn his strengths into weaknesses."

"And how would you do that?"

"That's a problem I've been working on for a long time."

"You've been working on how to defeat Eaglestar?"

There's a pretty long pause before he continues. "Of course. What would happen if he went insane, or had some other mental illness? Or if someone found a way to control him?"

Just thinking about that scenario makes me shudder.

"What are you guys talking about?" Mom asks, striding back into the room to get another cup of coffee. She's wearing a bathrobe and leans down to kiss Frank.

Frank slips a finger into the neckline of her robe and tugs down a little.

"Come on," I say. "Please?"

They both laugh.

"You're practically an adult," she says as she pours her coffee and heads back down the hall.

There's a knock on the door.

"Someone get that?" Mom shouts. "I'm getting in the shower."

I look at Frank and he nods toward the door. I jump up to grab it and in strides the Black Harrier.

I do a double take before realizing what's going on.

"Alex? What if my mom answered the door?" I ask with no small bit of ire.

"Relax," Frank says. "I told her I knew the Black Harrier and he might swing by the building."

"Who *are* you?" I ask Frank.

He smiles. "When did you get into town?"

"Last night," Alex says. He pours a cup of coffee. "You ready for today?"

I realize he's asking me.

"If I knew what *today* was, maybe," I say.

"You didn't tell him?" Alex asks Frank. Frank motions for Alex to do the honors. "Today's all for you, my man."

"Sidekick Day?" I say. "You know I hate that word."

"True, but how else will we show the world that Black Harrier is still around *and* that he puts all his trust in you?"

"What?" I ask.

"That's the whole point of the day. Show the world that the Red Kite—"

"Raptor," I interject.

"Not yet," Alex corrects, shaking his head. "Anyway, today is going to tell every crook in New York that Red Kite is not someone to mess with. Others have been invited too. But you, my man, are focus *numero uno*."

My gaze shifts between the two of them. "You're serious?"

"One-hundred-percent," Alex says. "Now, what did I miss?"

What the actual eff is going on around here? I expect Frank to tell Alex about the Resistors, so I speak up first.

"Frank was—surprisingly—agreeing with me about what a jerk Eaglestar is."

Alex shrugs. "Meh. He's not so bad. Since I became a core member of the Guild and got to know him better, I kind of see where he's coming from."

I scoff. "Really? Cuz the last time we interacted with him together, he was pretty douchey toward you."

Alex sips his coffee. "That was before. Now that I've been doing more with the Guild, he's a lot nicer to me. I think he's close to letting me come back to New York, too."

"Letting you?" I said. "I thought it was a Guild decision."

Frank snickers and sips his own coffee.

"Well, you know how it is there," Alex says. "Everyone listens to him on most decisions."

"Okay, right," I say, "but any time we've ever talked about him before, you said he was a pompous ass."

"Most of what we saw then was just a show he puts on."

"So it's okay for him to be an asshole to everyone else as long as he's cool with you?" I ask.

"*Language.*" Ha. I didn't even realize Frank was listening anymore. "And make sure you keep your voices down."

Alex is defensive now. "That's not what I'm saying. I just mean that now that I've gotten to know him, I kind of get where he's coming from. That's all. Just think how annoying it must be to be so much better than everyone else."

"*Better?*"

"You know what I mean," Alex says. "The guy is fine. Right, Frank?"

Frank points to his mouth where he's chewing and smiles a little.

I realize I'm genuinely getting angry now. "No, I don't. You think that accidentally getting powers in some plane crash makes you *better* than other people?"

Alex barely finishes his sip of coffee before replying. "First of all, it may have been accidental, but he *was* sacrificing his life to stop the Nazis from gaining unimaginable power. That's kind of a big deal. Plus, it's not just the powers. I don't have any powers, and look at me."

I do look at him, but I don't see anything special about him that should make him feel superior to anyone else. Sure, he should be proud of his accomplishments and all the hard work he's put in to his training and his crimefighting career. But that's it.

The truth is, Alex has changed a *lot* since he became Black Harrier. Not that I knew him for long before that, but there was something different about him the moment he put on that costume. And, as time goes on, it becomes more pronounced. His voice has changed, and not just the voice changer thing he does to imitate Frank when he's in costume. Even when he's plain old Alex, his voice is deeper. His accent, more neutral. Part of it is just confidence, but there's something else I can't quite put my finger on. Some sort of feeling of superiority that I don't think he really deserves.

And Eaglestar has even less to brag about. Yeah, he was a war hero, and it was really brave of him to crash his fighter plane into that Nazi zeppelin. But as a result, he became the most powerful being on the planet. He hasn't had to answer to anyone for, like, seventy years.

I wonder if Frank is going to chime in but he doesn't. So, I prompt him. "What do you think, Frank?"

"Oh, I don't know. Sometimes I can't help feeling superior to others, I suppose. It's human nature. I mean, how many others are both a billionaire *and* a superhero? But most of the time, I think more about improving my faults and making up for… past indiscretions."

Alex smirks. "See? Human nature."

I wonder, *Is Eaglestar even human anymore?*

Frank must be thinking the same thing. "But Eaglestar is pretty much just an ass, Alex. He really does need to get over himself."

BOOM! Mic drop. Point, Frank.

Now it's my turn to smirk at Alex. Until Frank clears his throat and gives me a *look*. Oh, right. That.

"Um, Alex, there's something I need to tell you before you find out about it anyway."

Alex serves himself some of the eggs and bacon I made and doesn't even look up at me. "You mean about your new team. The… 'Resistors' is it?"

I check Frank's expression, but he seems just as surprised as I am as he raises his eyebrows at me.

"How did you—?"

"Eaglestar contacted me first thing this morning," Alex says. "Did you really think he wouldn't find out right away?"

I shrug. "Well, not that quickly, that's for sure. So, what do you think?"

"I think it's a stupid name, since a resistor is—"

"I know, an electrical component. It wasn't my idea."

He scoops up some eggs, still not looking at me. "I think you made a stupid mistake that you need to fix as soon as possible."

That wasn't the answer I was expecting. At least not exactly.

"But it's not a mistake. I'm going to keep it going."

He finally looks at me. "You're serious?"

I just nod.

He shakes his head and digs into his breakfast. "Good luck with that."

TWENTY-THREE

AMY

Seeing Alex was the last thing I wanted to do today. He didn't give me any warning whatsoever—unless you count the ninety-seven missed calls. Ok, fine, it wasn't that many. But can you blame me for being a little weirded out and not answering?

I'm alone at the Aerie, training. I'm all gross and sweaty and he comes up behind me out of nowhere.

"Surprise!" He exclaims.

I'm not proud of what I'm about to do.

"Yeah," I reply flatly.

"Yeah, what?"

"Yeah, it's quite a surprise," I say. "Why didn't you tell me you were coming to town?"

"I've literally been calling you for days," he says.

I pull out my communicator. "Really?" I make believe I'm scrolling. "Not a single missed call. Why didn't you text me?"

"Because I wanted to hear your voice when I told you I was coming in early?"

Aww, that's kind of sweet. Now I feel bad.

"You should have texted." I towel off and try to do my best cold shoulder.

"I guess so. Well, I'm here, so… surprise!" He laughs. When I don't join him, he says, "You need a sparring partner?"

I look at him suspiciously. "Sure. I guess."

I throw a punch and he blocks it. Then he swings at me and I counter him.

"I thought you'd be happy to see me."

"Well, I'm not. I don't like these kinds of surprises."

"Like I said, I tried to call. A lot. Besides, you knew I was going to be at this thing."

The thing he's referring to? National Sidekick Day.

"Not according to my comms." Wow. This is bordering on cruel.

"Okay, I'm sorry. But now that I'm here, do you think we can do dinner or something after the event?"

"Or *something*? What's that supposed to mean?" I ask with a ton of venom in my tone.

"It means 'or something else of your choosing if you don't want to have dinner.' What do you think it means?"

I don't respond and try to kick him in the groin, instead.

"Oh, come on. You don't seriously think I came all the way from Boston for a booty call or something, do you?" He blocks it and grabs a couple of staffs, then we go at it with those.

"Well, I did just call you the other night and tell you that my dad thinks we're together, and that there's a *possibility* we might get back together some day. And then all of a sudden you're here. Out of the blue." The sparring continues, and gets more intense.

I know why he's here, and I know it's not just for me. I am still unsure of what exactly National Sidekick Day is, but I don't need to let him know. I'm already in this thing pretty deep.

"It's not out of the blue," he says, grunting. "I'm here for the ceremony, and you know it. Seeing you is just… frosting."

"So, I'm just a pretty topping to you?"

"Hey! Stop!" he says, cross-blocking my attack. I don't. "Come on, stop. I just wanted to talk. I swear."

"Fine. Talk."

I let my staff drop and start peeling off my gloves.

"National Sidekick Day," he says. "It's basically for you."

"I'm not a sidekick," I tell him.

"No, but you work with the most famous one of all-time."

"Sawyer?"

"Well, the Red Kite," he says.

"That's pretty arrogant, coming from you. Don't you think?"

"I'm just stating a fact. Geez, Amy, what's wrong with you? The Guild thought it would be smart to show the Black Harrier. We're also using it as a chance to bolster the city's faith in you guys."

I grab a bottle of water and chug it. Then I toss him one.

He grabs it but doesn't drink. "We need them to know they are in safe hands no matter where Harrier is. Your dad thought it was a good idea. Maybe he'll even put in the right word with your mom to get you to stay."

"Is that what this is all about?" I ask. "This is what you meant by dinner. You thought that if you showed up, you could swoop in and help me with my problem with my parents and be the big hero so I'd get back together with you?"

I wish we were still sparring so I could tag him in the head with my staff and have an excuse to hit him.

"Well, I wouldn't quite put it that way."

"But that was your plan, wasn't it?" I say.

He takes a small sip. "More or less, I suppose."

"Well, then how's this for a spanner in the works? I'm not going to dinner with you. I'm not going to do anything at all with you."

"Why not?" he asks.

"Because I have a boyfriend."

The way he looks at me is as if I really did clobber him with my staff.

"A boyfriend?"

"Yeah. I'm sorry. I didn't want you to find out like this."

"I don't understand," he says. "What about our conversation the other night?"

"I don't know. We were broken up."

"On a break."

"Whatever."

"So who is he?" he asks. "Some guy from college? The socialite son of one of your mom's friends?"

"Actually… he's another crime fighter."

"What? Who? Is it Sawyer?" There's a flash of anger. "He's too young for you, you know."

"Don't be an idiot. It's not Sawyer. And, by the way, I'm a *lot* closer to Sawyer's age than I am to yours if you want to start getting into that."

"Point taken. So, who is it?"

"Come on, Alex. Do you really wanna know?" I say. "Will it change anything? Or help you?"

"Yeah, I want to know. Why wouldn't I? I'd love to know who is *so* much better than me."

"Fine. He's a member of a new team that Sawyer and I have put together."

"Yeah. 'The Resistors.' I heard."

"You don't have to say it like that. We're a real team."

"Unlicensed, but sure. Whatever you say."

So condescending. This isn't a good look for him.

"His name is Pace," I tell him. "An he's the partner of—"

"You're dating Fastlane's sidekick?" He starts laughing. Hard.

"What's so funny?"

"I've known that kid since he was twelve. He's the most annoying…" He sees my expression and shuts up immediately.

"He's sweet," I say.

"Yeah, okay. You'll see—"

"I don't wanna hear it."

"I'm sure you don't," he says. "But just you wait. He'll get on your nerves. And just grate on them."

"We're doing really well. Thank you very much."

He finally stops laughing. "So, does he do everything fast?"

I throw my water empty bottle at him. It hits him cap-first in the eye.

"Ow! Geez, that freaking hurt."

"Good. Because I know what you're getting at, and it's none of your damn business."

"I was only kidding."

"You were being mean," I say. "Which is something you seem to keep getting better at. Especially since you started hanging around the Guild so much."

"Hanging around the Guild? Amy, I'm a member of the team."

"So you keep reminding everyone."

"Right," he says. "And you wouldn't be proud if you were a core member? You're saying you *won't* be proud someday if you do become one?"

"Of course I will," I tell him. "But I certainly won't be palling around with Eaglestar and turning into his snide copy."

"Really? That's what you think of me now?"

"Ha! Why don't you think about it and get back to me? Surely even someone so egocentric as you must realize how much you've changed."

"Wow." He puts his hands up and backs away. "I'm not so sure it's me who's changed so much. Jealousy can do bad things to people."

I'm glad my gloves are off because that saves us one step. I'm two seconds away from kicking his ass.

"Jealous? You think I'm jealous of you?" I say, incredulity dripping from every word.

"Why don't *you* think about it and get back to *me*? I guess I'll see you around, Amy Chen."

He storms out of the Aerie.

After my encounter with Alex at the Aerie, I was more than happy to get to my next appointment of the morning.

Brunch.

Almost losing Pace was really scary for me. So scary that I thought very seriously about breaking up with him, not because of anything he did, but because I just don't know if I could handle losing someone I have such strong feelings for. Of course, I'd still be upset if something happened to him and we were broken up, but if I could distance myself first, then…

Anyway, it doesn't matter because I decided to stay with him anyway. It might be a bit soon, but I have no choice but to use this opportunity to get out of moving with my mom. I tell her I have a boyfriend I'd like her to meet, and she takes us both out to brunch.

We go to one of the fanciest places in town. Impossible to get a reservation at months in advance… unless you're my mom. She just walks in and they take her straight to her usual table.

Pace and I show up right behind her and they're definitely not as impressed with us. I feel kind of bad immediately, since Pace thought the Mediterranean place he took me to on our first date was "fancy." But it was like eating out of a maggot-filled dumpster compared to this place.

"Do you have a jacket, sir?" The maître d' asks him.

"Uh, yeah, I left it at home because it's denim, and I didn't think it would really fit in."

"Mmm. Right you were." He looks Pace up and down and goes to the small closet behind the coat check. He comes out with a dinner jacket that fits Pace perfectly.

"Is this mandatory?" Pace asks.

"I'm afraid it is, sir."

Pace shrugs. "Okay, then."

The maître d' takes us back to Mom's table and pulls out my chair for me. As I sit down, I introduce them. "Mom, this is Pa—Diori. Diori, this is my mom."

Pace takes my mom's extended hand and kisses it. "Enchanted, madame."

So far, it's going really well.

"Oh, how sweet. I like this one. Did Amy say your name was 'Padiori?' That's unusual."

"Just Diori, Mayka," I respond for him. "I call him, um… 'Pookie' and I started to say that by accident."

"Pookie. How cute. I think I will call you that as well." My mom smiles at him.

Pace gives me a strange look, then smiles back at my mom.

"Ooookay, then. That sounds…" Pace just trails off and doesn't finish his thought.

The waiter brings out some croissants and places them on the table. Pace immediately grabs one and butters it. "Oh, thank God. I'm starving, bro."

My mom's eyes go wide, but she's ever the consummate socialite.

"So, tell me about yourself, Pookie," she says. "What university do you attend?"

"Oh, I'm taking a break from school. High school was rough, y'know—barely made it through—so I thought I'd take a couple of years off to kind of reset and get my bearings. Figure stuff out."

"I see. What are your plans for now then?"

"I've got a few different side hustles going on. Always full speed ahead, you know." He devours the first pastry and goes in for another. And he's moving at a speed most humans absolutely couldn't achieve.

"Maybe you should *slow down*, Pookie," I say in a tone that could only be taken as a warning.

"Mmm. Right," he mutters with his mouth full.

Mom turns to me. "Darling, wherever did you two meet? I must know the story." I can tell she's being sarcastic. Things are going downhill quickly, and I realize this is just going to make it that much easier to say what I need to say.

"Didn't I tell you? I got arrested, and we met in jail."

Mom almost spits out her mimosa. And she almost never loses her composure. "Excuse me? Arrested? When? How did I not know about this?"

"I'm kidding, mom. We're both in a… club together."

"What sort of club?" she practically demands.

"It's kind of a mixed martial arts type of thing. We fight."

"Oh, don't tell me you're still doing that sort of thing. A lady should not be putting herself in those sorts of situations. I thought you'd outgrown that once you finished high school."

"Not at all.," I say. "In fact, I'm more into it than ever."

"Well, I'm sure you'll outgrow it eventually."

How rude. "I highly doubt it. It's sort of a big part of my life. You could even say it kind of defines me."

Mom pouts her lips. "Maybe things will change when we get to Bulgaria."

"So, Mayka, there's something I've been wanting to tell you, and you're not going to like it."

"Yes?" She's not ready for this. Not even close.

"I'm not moving to Bulgaria with you."

"What? Why not, darling?" Her shock is palpable. Why am I kind of enjoying this? I shouldn't be enjoying this.

I put my arm around Pace and look at him longingly. Here it comes. I actually feel bad for him. He's had no warning. Wait for it…

"Diori and I are in love. I just can't leave him."

Pace chokes on his third croissant when he hears this. I pat him on the back as he tries to cough it up. "Are you okay, Pookie?"

He shakes his head, then speaks with a hoarse voice. "I think I'm okay."

He downs his entire glass of water and beckons the busboy over for a refill.

Mom maintains her cool, but I can tell she's ready to blow up inside. "Isn't that moving a bit fast, Amy?"

"Oh, fast is Diori's specialty. Yep. He's very, very fast. It's one of the things I love about him."

Mom gets a confused look. "Just exactly how serious is it?"

Now that I'm heading for the finish line, I decide to go all in.

"You know, I owe it all to you, Mayka. I wasn't really interested in a relationship until you convinced me of how wonderful it could be. And… I wasn't going to say anything yet, but Diori and I have decided to move in together."

Diori does a spit-take with his water, spraying it all over the table and my mom.

Mom scoots her chair back and swears in Bulgarian. I never hear her speak like that. She pats herself dry with a cloth towel.

"Pookie? Are you sure you're all right?" I ask.

He stands up. "I'm just gonna run to the little boys' room. I'll be right back."

And, just like that, Pace is gone.

TWENTY-FOUR

SAWYER

Sidekick

For three years, I've hated that word. That idea. I've railed against it. Then, over the past year, I started to get over it. Just when I thought I'd finally accepted that that's what I am—what I've been—all this time, I start my own team and realize, I don't have to be a Sidekick. I was past worrying about it, or even thinking about it.

And now, the Guild is trying to shove it back down my throat.

Most of us pretend to hate the Guild, but the truth is, we just want in. Started by Eaglestar, the Bombardier, and Bastet during World War II, it was a way for masked crimefighters to police themselves so the government wouldn't. Not that the government could, even if it did try.

But the organization has been officially sanctioned by the United Nations and most of the world's individual governments since the mid-20th Century. It even has its own ambassador to the UN to represent its members.

Yeah, the name is pretty old-fashioned, but what do you expect from a group that's been around so long? It's not like they're going to change it now to keep up with the times. Though most people only started hearing about it when Eaglestar became popular, its roots actually go back even further, to the 1800s. The earliest masked crimefighters I ever remember hearing about were Commander Valor and the man in the robotic suit they called Blastbucket. But they were government operatives, not freelancers like most of the heroes nowadays.

Then there were a few guys running around just before World War II in masks and capes, but I don't think any of them had any superpowers. They were considered vigilantes and were usually hunted by the cops, even while they were helping take down criminals.

Once someone decides to embark on a career fighting crime—powers or no powers—that individual is required to join the Guild or face the consequences. For most of us, our involvement stops at becoming a becoming a card-carrying member and agreeing to follow the rules. Others become ancillary members, like Osprey, called upon in certain circumstances when the need arises. And then there's the core group.

The core members of the Guild still include Eaglestar and Bastet, who are both really old even though you wouldn't know it to look at them. I don't know if they're immortal, but they sure don't age like everyone else. Bombardier, on the other hand, passed away in the late sixties. Lung cancer, I think. Even superheroes smoked back then. The guy survived fighting Hitler and Mussolini and being on the front lines of the invasion on D-Day, but he died a slow death in the Guildmembers Retirement Home in Buffalo, New York, done in by a two-pack-a-day habit at the age of fifty-nine.

Anyway, core members get replaced when they retire or meet an untimely demise. It's a huge honor, but it also makes you a target for the worst of the worst of supervillains. Back in the nineteen eighties, the entire team except for Eaglestar and Bastet was wiped out fighting a group of Soviet supervillains who everyone knew were backed by their government even though Gorbachev had officially denied it.

Glitter, Radd, Psych, and Ditto—all wiped out in one battle. Yeah, they don't make them like that anymore… especially the costumes. Brightly colored spandex. I'm so glad that look went away before I was born. In those days, how you looked was almost more important than functionality.

Then it was the leather phase. At least it offered more protection, I'll give it that. The nineties were the "extreme" era of crimefighting. Everyone had a gimmick and it became popular for even the good guys to get really violent. Instead of just punches and kicks, a lot of crimefighters started going in for swords, knives, even guns. Things got really bloody, which led to a sort of agreement between heroes and villains that they were going to stop killing all the time. Fighting was still on the table, naturally, but the all-out war had to end. The government was getting ready to step in and outlaw vigilantism outright.

There had already been an unspoken code among masked men and women on both sides anyway. You don't give away the secret identity of someone even if you somehow found it out, for example. So stopping the killing and extreme violence was more of an addition to that code rather than an entirely new thing on its own.

Of course, since we *are* talking about villains and criminals being on one side, there are always some who don't follow the code. Then there are the worst of the worst, the ones who think they *are* the heroes of the story.

Beyond them, there's Chef Maléfique. He was *the* worst of the worst of the worst, or whatever. He didn't care about killing in the least. Enjoyed it even. He obeyed no rules, honored no deals. Thought he was above all of that because of some understanding of morality that no one else had.

That's one of the reasons everyone on both sides is—was—terrified of him. Geez. I still can't believe Frank killed him. Some of the people he worked with were almost as bad, such as Deadeye. That guy is basically just a world-class assassin, willing to murder anyone for cash.

I have no idea why it took them so long to figure out that we should basically be wearing combat gear. Most of us have adopted some sort of body armor, at least to one extent or another. It only makes sense. Heroes are still injured or killed occasionally, of course, but the numbers are way down.

That's why it's even more of a shock when someone is killed, like Toby. He was the second Red Kite. I didn't know him, but from everything I've heard, he was the perfect sidekick and hero. Straight 'A's in school, excellent martial arts skills, never talked back to Harrier… I don't know. Maybe they're just honoring the dead or simply forgetting his flaws. Funeral goggles, I think they call it. Or maybe they wanna give me something to aspire to. Whichever, his death was a devastating blow to the entire crimefighting community. Of course, Frank was hit so hard by it that he quit for a while, then decided never to have another sidekick again. Everyone loved Toby. I mean everyone. Even Eaglestar, apparently.

Now that I think about it, maybe that's one of the reasons Eaglestar is such a jerk to me. He might feel like I'm a poor replacement for the previous incarnation of Red Kite. I certainly must not live up to his expectations. I guess I'll probably never know for sure. Nobody ever wants to talk about what happened to Toby. I didn't even know until Alex showed me that horrible video of his murder last year.

And I'm the loser who tries to fill his shoes.

Supposedly, this whole "National Sidekick Day" is to celebrate me and the other sidekicks, as well as to beef up my rep in New York City so that criminals will think twice about giving us a problem while Black Harrier is "away on business" or whatever cover story they're creating for Alex.

Speaking of Alex, they're also using it as a way for him to put in a very public appearance as the Black Harrier, since people are getting very suspicious about not seeing him around much.

So, they're putting on this big show in the middle of Times Square and it looks a lot like the New Year's Eve celebrations they have here for the ball dropping. But all it does is remind me of last year, when I was going through the toughest time of my life, fighting to find and save Frank from Chef Maléfique.

That night, Halloween, was insane. So many heroes, guys like Gargantuan Grey, Canadian Shield, and real badasses like Darkstrike, gave up the whole gig. Abandoned their posts.

Music Master organized a concert with the help of Maléfique. His music put this whole area of the city into a sort of trance where people became super violent. Those heroes, and a lot more, could never reconcile what they'd done even if they were under hypnotic persuasion.

We all take the No Killing rule pretty seriously. None more than Frank… I'd thought.

But that was then. Now, its a place of celebration, I guess. There's a band on stage playing some kind of Country and Western. I'm sure anyone who listens to that stuff knows them, but I don't. I've always been into the harder stuff.

Tents line the area behind where the stage is set up, and most of the heroes who belong to the Guild—not just the core group, but dozens of heroes—are showing up in cars, trucks, limos, you name it, and walking the red carpet. Some of them are even using their powers, like flying or… Holy crap. To my absolute shock, Swamp Rabbit is there, as well as some of the others who had tried out and been rejected from the Resistors. Every one of them is ushered into one tent to get prepared for the ceremony, and they send all of us sidekicks into another.

I got a chance to peek into the other tent, and there's huge baskets full of fancy gifts, as well as Champagne and other alcoholic beverages and lots of expensive snacks and stuff.

In our tent, we have a couple of coolers full of bottled water—not even the good stuff, the cheap store brand—and they forgot to fill up the coolers with ice. We don't even get soda or juice. And our snacks? Granola bars and fruit rollups.

Like we're all seven.

Even on a day to supposedly celebrate us, we get treated like second-class citizens. Pace is already here, of course, downing most of the meager snacks we've been provided. Speedsters burn calories like crazy. I'm surprised he ever stops eating. Neith, who is Bastet's partner, shows up right after I do, albeit reluctantly. Even scowling, she look super hot. Can't imagine what she'd look like smiling.

There are a lot others I'd never met before, since people came in from all over the country for this. One kid looks like a giant condom but I think maybe he's supposed to be… nope I have no freaking clue what he is. A long blonde-haired girl has an actual staff like Gandalf or Dumbledore or something, and she's not the only one. Apparently, goth is in, and so is witchcraft cus there's black and pentagrams all over the place.

We all just stand around with nothing to say as more and more sidekicks file in.

Then some guy in a suit approaches me, slicked back hair, smelling like a putrid combination of bad cologne and a flavored vape pen. He looks around until he spots me, then approaches.

"You Red Kite?" He talks like some fifties mobster.

I almost can't bring myself to say it. I want to say "Red *Raptor*" so badly, but I know it's just going to cause the usual confusion, so I don't bother.

"Yeah. That's me. You need me out there or something?"

"Nope. Just need'a give you this." He pulls an envelope from the breast pocket of his expensive suit and hands it to me. Then he just walks out without another word. Weird.

I open the envelope, pull out a letter folded in three, business style, and give it a cursory glance. I can't believe my eyes. Except I should have expected it. A written warning to disband my new team and revert to my old code name. It's a long legal document signed by the core members of the Guild… including Alex. I wonder if he argued for me at all, or if he immediately went along when the lawyers slapped this down in front of him and told him to provide his John Hancock. I bet he'd even already done it when I talked to him this morning.

Pace and Neith both sidle up to me, probably sensing my stupefaction. As usual, Neith stays silent. Pace can't help himself.

"What's up? What's that? Everything okay?" asks Pace.

"Yeah. It's fine." I'm not going to bring it up now. Not right before this stupid event. I'll have a meeting with Osprey soon to figure out how we want to handle this.

But I know exactly how I want to handle it right now. I rip it up. I wish I had some kind of fire superpower so I could send it up in flames.

I refuse to acknowledge the Guild's authority over me and the rest of the team. Echoing Neith's words at the docks, I don't care what the U.S. government and the United Nations say. Now I need to decide whether to tell the rest of the group. If they find out Eaglestar wants to shut us down, that might just be enough for them to quit. But if they find out later that I didn't tell them, things could get… messy.

Not only are they risking some serious legal trouble, it could also get them banned from ever being allowed in as core members, something just about every masked crimefighter dreams about. To be honest, the chances are pretty slim already for my teammates, but that doesn't mean they'll risk it to be part of what I've created.

Osprey shows up outside the tents. Maybe I should show her now. I think for a second that she's going to join us, but she just looks in at us, then turns away without even a wave. Of course she's going into the "big people" tent. Why would she hang out with us lowlifes at the kiddie table if she has a choice?

I can't say I blame her. The chocolate fountain in there looks really delicious. And my bottled water is warm.

I peek outside and there are literally thousands of people gathered all over the streets and sidewalks. Only the Guild could pull off shutting down Times Square on such short notice. And I'm sure they had a little help from Franklin Douglas III and Luis Chen, Esquire. Money talks, and Douglas Industries has boatloads of it to make itself heard. Loudly.

It sounds like the band's done and it's just about time to start the ceremony, and everyone is here except, of course, the main man himself. At the exact second that the event is supposed to begin, there's a sonic boom that shakes everything in Times Square, followed by the crowd of thousands cheering and clapping.

Eaglestar has arrived.

What a dick.

Loud, patriotic music blasts over the sound system through giant speakers—just one more thing to remind my of my traumatic experience last time I was here. Eaglestar grabs a microphone as the crowd continues to go wild for him.

Yeah, just spend thirty seconds alone in the same room with him, people, and see how happy you are then.

Television monitors are set up around the tent and we all gather around to watch. Every one of the sidekicks are starstruck over Eaglestar. Me? *Guhhh.*

"Ladies and gentlemen, boys and girls, welcome to the first ever National Sidekick Day!" He announces in a tone that he only uses to fool people into thinking he isn't the biggest douchebag on the planet. "Is everyone excited to be here?"

The crowd goes nuts again. It really is getting nauseating. And my anger about the cease and desist order just keeps increasing.

"We could have had anyone here to welcome you to this amazing day. I mean, look around you, people. Have you ever seen anything like it? But you know what they say, if you want something done right…"

The crowd laughs as he pumps his hands and draws all the attention to him.

"We're here to celebrate our hard-working junior partners," he continues. You sure could have fooled me with this Eaglestar Show. "Since they very rarely get the recognition they deserve. Now, I don't have a sidekick myself, of course, because—let's face it—nobody could keep up with me, and I right?"

Uproarious laughter erupts again from the audience as Eaglestar grins wide and shows off his perfect teeth. Yeah, he's a regular Kevin Hart, this guy.

"But enough from me. The last thing I'd ever want to do is steal the thunder away from these magnificent young people. So, without further ado, let's bring out our master of ceremonies—you know him, you love him—Baron Steele!"

There's a bunch of "wows" filling the tent behind me, and I've gotta admit, I'm pretty impressed too. Baron Steele is a legend. He's one of the few of us who doesn't bother with hiding his true identity. Paul Steele runs a consulting agency for wanna-be masked crimefighters here in the city.

As the crowd cheers again, the microphone is passed from one blowhard to another. These guys can't stand one another but they hug like they're old friends. So fake.

In fact, Steele has refused an invitation to become a core member every year for the last like fifteen years. I'm surprised Eaglestar keeps inviting him. My guess is that he's threatened by Baron Steele's success in business and sees him as a potential competition. It's no secret that it's because of their bristly relationship, among other issues, that the Baron keeps saying no. Oh, and the fact that anyone would deign to refuse such an invitation grates on Eaglestar about as much as anything could.

But here, in front of all their adoring fans, they put on a show. After their hug, they smile at each other like old friends, shaking hands. Unless it's my imagination, Steele seems to grimace a bit as Eaglestar squeezes his hand—probably way too hard. That's saying something, since the Baron is almost indestructible.

Eaglestar's smile disappears as he walks toward us and the other tents.

Sure enough, Baron Steele makes a joke out of it, shaking his hand around and testing his fingers after Eaglestar lets go.

"Whoa-ho-ho… quite a grip!" he says with a slight British accent. Actually, I think I remember someone telling me he's an actual baron somewhere in the UK.

The audience laughs again. Nobody can see it from the crowd, but from backstage I can see Eaglestar's smug expression as the corner of his mouth rises slightly in satisfaction. The excitement in the audience dies down quite a bit at this point, though, since Steele isn't nearly as popular as Eaglestar.

"Hello, folks! How's everyone doing out there on this beautiful day in the Big Apple?"

Yeah, yeah, play to the crowd, get them on your side. More clapping, more cheering, yada yada yada. He goes on about how it's his job to assign heroes to certain roles, to help them find themselves. And how he sometimes gets to assign a sidekick to a hero if one is requested, and makes himself out to be some kind of saint.

He forgets to mention he gets paid a ton of money from the Guild to do it, and that he's literally the only person on the planet who has a job like that.

"Shout out to my man, Gary, back there in the coffee booth. Makes a mean White Chocolate Macchiato! Give it up for Gary!"

The crowd cheers a bunch for… Gary, Coffee Guy Gary, apparently, then he goes on to introduce the rest of the Guild who is present, which takes forever. Luckily, they aren't all going to speak because that would take days. They each walk out, wave, and stand to the right side of the stage as their names are called.

This is where Osprey gets to go up, and I notice she has her face shield down, which is unusual in a situation like this, but it's obviously because her dad is here and she's probably trying to avoid him getting a good look at her as much as possible.

Finally, they bring in the core members last, and they stand in the middle of the stage together with Eaglestar—Bastet, Fastlane, Cupid, Firefly, Omar the Defenstrator, and, of course, Black Harrier. Alex walks out last, being the second most popular core member. It's like the credits on a TV show or movie, where the biggest star gets first billing, and the second biggest gets to go last.

The Core shifts to the left side of the stage when Baron starts calling the sidekicks out, and they each get to stand at the front of the stage next to each other and take in some adulation before shaking hands with their Guild mentor. Each on is presented with a plaque and has their pictures taken while the audience applauds and cheers. And finally sitting in a section reserved just for them—us—to the side of the stage.

In this case, they introduce a couple of minor guys from the Midwest first who most people don't know very well. Next come the mid-level sidekicks, and finally the more popular ones, with partners in the core, such as Pace and Neith.

Then they come to the point where they announce me. Yeah, Red Kite is the most famous and most popular sidekick, but I can't take credit for it. Alex and Toby did most of the heavy lifting on that.

So, instead of making me feel good about myself, it just makes my imposter syndrome worse. I step up from behind the stage and walk to the front, where Alex greets me in his Harrier costume with a big grin. I don't return it. After seeing his name on that notice, I'm ready to strangle him, not shake his hand and smile for pictures.

Baron Steele holds the microphone out to me. "Would you like to say a few words, Kite?"

Is he kidding me? I could barely get up in front of a group of fast food workers and their families and talk, and he wants me to give an impromptu speech in the middle of Times Square in front of thousands of people?

And what would I say? *I'd like to say thank you to the Guild for always blocking everything I've ever wanted to do, from changing my name to starting my own superteam…*

Hold on. Why not? What do I have to lose? I'm already in trouble with them. They need me to continue fighting here in New York because they're understaffed. You know what? Screw it! I grab the microphone away from Baron Steele.

Now I smile at Alex and I think he knows what's coming. "Thank you, Baron. First, I'd like to say thank you to the Guild for—"

And, out of the blue, all hell breaks loose.

There's a deafening sound—like I'm standing next to a jet engine—and papers and anything else lighter than a person start funnel up into the air like there's a tornado brewing. I turn around and see a bright light behind the core members of the Guild and feel a slight tugging sensation. It's obviously much stronger for those who are closer to the anomaly, but I grab hold of the podium anyway.

It's like a giant hole in the universe has ripped open. First Eaglestar, then the others core members, one by one, get sucked in and disappear into the rift.

Alex grabs onto me, as I hold onto the podium, each of us bracing ourselves while the crowd screams in terror. I can't tell what the other Guild members like Osprey are doing, but I hope they're okay.

I watch Firefly shrink down, and struggle to fly toward the front of the stage and I let go of the podium with one hand and somehow manage to grab him. I can barely hold onto him—it's almost like a powerful magnet is pulling him in. With Alex's help I'm able to prevent him from going in.

Then, suddenly, the rift blinks out of existence and everything goes silent.

TWENTY-FIVE
SAWYER

Recovery from the event came slowly. The shock of watching the most powerful beings on the face of the Earth blink out of existence, isn't something you see every day. But that speaks to the preparedness of not just the ancillary Guildmembers, but us sidekicks as well. All over Times Square, masked crimefighters spring into action.

Let me tell you something, Times Square is ruined for me. It's not like I liked to hang out there or anything; it's for the tourists. But, I don't want it associated with craziness in my mind either!

Someone is responsible for this, and I am going to find out. I scan the crowd but with my HUD activated on my helmet. It shows body temps, heart rate, all kinds of things that are helpful to spotting a guilty man or woman. Problem is, everyone's heart rate is elevated, cuz everyone is scared out of their minds.

Then I survey the rooftops and the surrounding buildings. It takes a bit, but I finally notice a medium-sized, black-clad man standing just behind a massive Victoria's Secret billboard. Hey, don't judge me. I wasn't looking… I mean I was. Whatever, I'm seventeen anyway. I was scanning for anything weird and, guess what? I found something. So there.

I have no doubt it's Battlegear holding some kind of gadget.

"That son of a bitch," I say out loud even though no one's listening. I didn't even consider that Tiffany would be.

"To whom are you referring?" she asks. I almost miss the sexpot she was before I told her to stop it.

"Oh, hey Tiff," I say. Then I point. "Up there, Battlegear. Can you zoom in?"

A second ago, I was willing to bet anything he had something to do with this. But now, I don't need to. I'm certain of it. He sees that I've spotted him, and turns to run.

I grab Pace and try to get him to go after him before it's too late. "Pace. Pace!"

But Pace is still in shock. He's on his knees, looking at the place where his mentor last stood before being sucked into oblivion. I don't even think he hears me over the screams of the panicked crowd.

Finally, Alex grabs the microphone and addresses the crowd with his Black Harrier voice-changer activated. I don't bother to listen. I know it'll be some kind of sugar-coated nonsense to appease the crowd. I promise you, no one knows what's going on. Not even Alex.

"Call Frank," I tell Tiffany as I shoot my grappler up to where Battlegear had been and try to zip up there before he gets away. But when I get to there, he's long gone.

"Raptor, where are you?" Frank answers.

It takes me a second to realize he called me Raptor. Despite everything, my face lights up.

"Battlegear was here," I tell him.

"You sure?"

"One-hundred-percent," I tell him. "I saw him by the big… uh, Victoria's Secret billboard."

"Which one?" he asks.

Of course, there's like four of them.

"It doesn't matter. He's gone. Frank, what the hell is going on?"

"I don't know, but we'll figure it out. Help anyone needing it and we'll meet up shortly."

"Okay."

"And Sawyer," he says.

"Yeah?"

"Stay safe."

"You too," I say, but the lines already dead.

By the time I get back down to the stage, Alex has fully taken over the situation.

"Harrier! We need to go after Battlegear," I shout to him. "I think he's behind this."

"Our number one priority is keeping all these people safe."

Exactly what the real Harrier would have said. Not that Alex isn't the real Harrier. I mean, he is just as much as I am the real Kite—Raptor—whatever. As pissed off at him as I am, I'm equally impressed at how well he's embodied the Harrier persona.

"I've already sent out the ancillary members to police the crowd and calm everyone down," he says. "We don't need this thing descending into a riot, and we definitely don't want certain people taking advantage of the chaos to start looting and pillaging."

"But we can probably catch him if we—"

"Kite! I need you to listen to me. This is my call. We'll take care of Battlegear or whoever is behind this soon enough. For now, there are more important things to attend to."

It also didn't escape my notice that, whereas Frank called me Raptor, he'd called me Kite.

"What could possibly be more important than finding the person who did this?"

"I've gotta get the ancillary members back to their home cities. You know what kind of mayhem could occur with them gone if every criminal in America saw this?"

I didn't even think of that.

"Yeah, okay. You're right."

"I'll meet up with you and the Resistors tomorrow to see how we're going to move forward, all right?"

The Resistors? Does that mean he's going to let us stay a team?

When Times Square settles down, it's well past three a.m. I contact the rest of the team and ask them to meet me at our HQ in the morning, and then change it to noon. I don't even know what to tell them now. I got a letter disbanding us, but then the only remaining core member of the Guild called us by name.

Wow. The whole Guild is gone. That thought can be crippling if I let it.

When I get there, something happens that blows my mind. Three large boxes are waiting for me just inside the doorway. At first, I'm a little hesitant to open them in case they are at trap or a bomb or something. But, who knows we're even here? I see a stamp on one side of each: DI.

Douglas Industries…

With that knowledge, I tear into them.

Inside? New uniforms for all the team members.

Frank, you sly dog. He's the only guy in the city who could have such quality equipment made practically overnight. I'm not sure how much the others are going to like them, but as far as I'm concerned, they're amazing.

There's even a new one for me sans helmet. Not much different from my old one, but definitely an upgrade. Osprey has one, too, to replace the one she's always worn. I should say, though, that for something homemade, hers was incredible. But this one… it's p-r-o-fessional. It's able to switch from her usual white to another mode with a charcoal color, which should make her less of a target in the dark.

Neith's new costume seems like exactly the kind of thing Frank would expect a teenage girl to wear, as opposed to her usual look. It's made of super-strong material for sure, and definitely shows off a lot less skin, but I somehow doubt Neith will be impressed. She looks like who she is—or says she is, I guess—someone who somehow channels an Egyptian goddess. But the threads Frank had made for her make her look more like a female Robin Hood or something. I'd say the odds of her actually wearing them are pretty close to zero.

Pace's new costume is more like Fastlane's than his old one was, and is more aerodynamically designed so he can run even faster. And the mask has cool little eye shields to replace the old goggles he currently uses.

Bash didn't really have a costume to begin with, but now he does. Red and yellow. Heavy armor. Along with some fancy tech shades that he can wear at night to help him see in the dark and hide his identity. Like the others, the costume is made from a material that will help stop knives, and even bullets if it's not a direct hit. Bash is really tough and claims he's taken bullets before, but he's definitely not completely invulnerable.

I'm shocked to see a new Cricket costume for Javier as well. I'm not even sure how Frank knew about him since he wasn't in jail with us, but I should know by now to never be surprised by anything he does. He may not be able to go out in the field anymore, but Frank is still a force to be reckoned with. Javi's outfit, dark green and gold, has an improved amplification system for his sonic scream, as well as a control panel for it on his wrist guard. And there are hydraulics in his boots that will allow him to jump really high.

Frank loves his themes.

I almost don't notice a card sitting on the new conference table. I open it up, and it's signed, "Happy birthday again. —Frank."

The note makes me realize I'd never even thanked Frank for Tiffany. Man, what a terrible son I'm turning out to be. I make a mental note to not just thank him, but to be annoying about it. A thousand thank-yous.

When the team arrives, they freak out, to say the least. In a good way. Except, as expected, Neith. She stands, arms crossed, looking down at it like she'd just discovered dog vomit on her favorite carpet. Bash, Pace, Osprey, and Cricket are so excited about the new gear that they almost forget about the crisis with the Guild disappearing. But then Alex shows up and it's all business after that.

"The Resistors," he says, Harrier voice and all.

Everyone stares up at him like God walked in. I guess to them, He did.

"Good work last night. Without you there, things could have been much worse."

Everyone whispers amongst themselves, super excited that Black Harrier, no matter who is under the mask, just complimented them.

"I need to go to Boston this afternoon to deal with some things, but I'm planning on being back this evening. In the meantime, I need you to follow up on Kite's lead with Battlegear. I have someone who's going to help you track him down, but once you find him, *do not engage him* until I'm there. He's far too dangerous. Understood?"

The rest of the Resistors nod in agreement and look a little scared, other than Osprey. We've had our taste of fighting Battlegear, and we're definitely still not prepared to take him on again.

"I'm counting on you to handle the situation here until I get back. I've sent everyone else back to their respective cities, so all of you need to keep your eyes and ears open. There are bound to be those who think this is the perfect time to test things, to take advantage of the situation. Are there any questions?"

"I have one." I say. "Are you going to tell them about the letter, or should I?"

Alex gives me a withering stare. The rest of the group look at one another, then back to us.

"Let's step outside and talk before I go," is his only response.

He stalks out of the room and I follow close behind. As soon as we're out of earshot of the others, he sticks a finger in my chest. "What the hell was that all about?"

"It was about the Guild not wanting us and then you expecting us to pick up the slack when we're suddenly needed."

"Really? You want to do this now? I'll pull the plug on you so fast you won't know what happened."

"Do it," I say, hoping I don't take things too far.

He sighs and shuts off the voice-changer.

"Look, after yesterday, it's time for everyone to step up now, including you and your team."

I grit my teeth. "Yesterday, I was told that we weren't *allowed* to be a team."

"Things have changed, in case you haven't noticed. Can you handle this, or do I need to put Osprey in charge?"

"This is *my* team."

"Not if you keep acting like a child."

I don't respond to that. I don't know *how* to respond to that.

"Frank is at the Aerie trying to figure out who is responsible for this. If he finds something, he'll let you know, and then you're going to do some reconnaissance until I get back. Are you up for it or not?"

"Yeah," I say. Mention of Frank makes me realize that as much beef as I might have with Alex right now, Frank thought the guy worthy of the uniform. "We can handle that."

"Good. I'll be back tonight. Hopefully you'll have grown up some before then."

TWENTY-SIX

AMY

Considering all that happened in Times Square last night, the last thing I expected to happen today when I woke up this morning was dealing with relationship issues with Pace. I guess I should have warned him about the whole thing with my mom before I dragged him into the middle of it. It really wasn't very nice of me to blindside him right there in the restaurant.

Then there's the question of whether he believes me when I tell him I was just saying those things to get to my mom. I mean, no matter how much I explain it, I think he still has this doubt about how much was really true and that I might be backtracking. But the reality is that I've had less feelings for him than I've let on.

But right now, the fate of the world is literally at stake, and he's giving me the cold shoulder.

Oh, and I can't stop thinking about Alex.

Especially with him here.

As long as he was in Boston, it was easy for me to pretend I didn't care. But then when I was faced with him in person again, it all came back to me immediately.

Some say, "Out of sight, out of mind."

Others say, "Absence makes the heart grow fonder."

But maybe it can be both?

I walk over to Pace while he's drinking an energy drink—pretty much a staple of his diet. "Hey. I was wondering if you'd like to talk."

He acts uncomfortable and more than a little distracted. "Talk? Talk about…?"

"Yesterday."

"You mean when Fastlane disappeared in front of my eyes, or when you told your mom we were moving in together?"

I don't know how to answer, so I don't.

"Pretty heavy day," he says.

I feel like an idiot that I thought he was ignoring me. Of course he'd be super upset about his partner being sucked into an inter-dimensional portal, or whatever. #thingsIneverthoughtI'dsay.

"It's just that we haven't spoken since you went to the restroom and never came back. It was kind of awkward with my mom after that."

He laughs. Loud and hard. "*You* felt awkward? You did? Ha! That's funny, because I felt perfectly fine. I mean, we've been out, what? A handful of times? And you're telling her we're in love. And that we're moving in together?"

"It's not like I planned it, I was just tired of my mom pushing me to get a boyfriend and to move to Bulgaria, and I just sort of blurted it out. I was kind of trying to get back at her."

"Uh huh. So I'm like, some kind of revenge boyfriend or something?" He's tapping his foot so fast that I can't even see it. A total blur.

"No! Of course not. I just mean that it's not like I meant it or anything. I mean, c'mon… us? In love? It's a joke."

The look of hurt and surprise that comes over his face is so intense that I feel it like a punch to the gut.

"A joke?" he says.

"No! I don't mean it that way."

"Really? How exactly do you mean it then?"

"It's—it's just so—you know, improbable that…" Digging myself deeper. Deeper…

"I see. That makes me feel much better."

"Diori, I don't mean—"

"Naw, listen, Ames. Let's save the world or whatever. Aight? You do you. I'll do me. Maybe someday we can talk about this. But right now? This stuff is heavy."

My head sinks, and I look up to say, "Okay," but he's gone. Again.

TWENTY-SEVEN

SAWYER

Terrified.

That's the only word I can think of to describe how the world is feeling about the Guild being missing. At first, it seemed like it was just going to be one of those events that happens every so often where they're in danger, but then everything is okay afterward. But as the hours tick by, it starts to look more and more like they may not return.

Every news station and website around the world is covering it. What are we going to do if they don't return?

I'm in the alleyway behind the warehouse since I don't know what else to do. The team is inside waiting around for news or direction, and since I'm the one who would provide that and I've got exactly nothing… yeah. I'm out here.

I switch off my helmet feed, which was tuned to NPR, just as the host says "So what will the Post-Guild life look like?"

I don't want to know the answer. I'm not willing to buy it, and we absolutely will get them back. The only thing left to do is figure out who did it and force them to reverse it.

Easy-peasy, right?

I'm convinced that Battlegear is behind it, but I don't even know where to start looking for him. Luckily, there's one person left for me to go to.

"Tiffany, get me Frank," I say, thinking she'd connect me with the comms in my helmet.

And then, the coolest thing I've seen from my new helmet happens without me expecting it—or even knowing it's possible.

I nearly jump out of my skin when Frank appears in front of me in the alley. But not only that, I'm surrounded by a holographic projection of the Aerie. It's like I'm standing right there with him, and it seems perfectly real. I guess it's not all that much fancier than the virtual reality stuff you can buy right now for a computer or gaming console, but I've never seen anything like it.

Around him, monitors are turned to every news source he can access in the control area—which is all of them, by the way. I've never seen him look so concerned. And why wouldn't he be? They are all showing footage of a massive, blue portal opening up right in front of us at the National Sidekick Day celebration.

He's wearing what look like fancy, techie, glasses—but not those giant VR style goggles. I assume he's probably looking at a holographic projection of me as well. He's so focused on the news that I think for a second I might be wrong, and he doesn't even know I'm there. But then he smiles. Actually smiles. Who is this guy and where is Franklin Douglas III?

"Okay, coolest thing ever," I say.

"You like it?" he says back to me.

"Do I… Frank, this is incredible." At that moment, I feel like a complete jerk again. I *still* never thanked him for the helmet and I tell him so.

"Not necessary," he says.

"Yeah. It is. You outdid yourself."

Frank isn't good at this kind of thing, so he changes the subject. As part of my thank-you, I let him.

"Where are you?" he asks.

"HQ. Uh… Resistors HQ."

"You mean *my* warehouse?" he adds.

I was wondering if that would ever come up. Clearly, he knew we were there since he'd sent the new uniforms.

"Oh, right," I say. "About that…"

"It's fine. A subject for another day. I've already discussed it with Chen and as far as I'm concerned, consider it an early inheritance."

"A *really* early inheritance, right?" The thought of Frank dying has haunted me since I saw him inches from death at the hands of Chef Maléfique. I don't even want to consider it.

He smiles and I take that as a non-verbal agreement that he won't die soon.

"Any leads on your end?" I ask.

"I'm still assessing the situation. Obviously, something's not right with the Guild being missing this long. If your theory is correct and Battlegear is responsible, we should be able to deal with him. But he's always been able to stay hidden from my satellites and the Guild's tracking technology. Even those he's worked with in the past have complained about not being able to keep track of him. Once I figure out how to get past Battlegear's masking tech, then we can work from there."

"And in the meantime, what should my team do?"

"Rushing into it without a plan isn't going to solve anything. Let's focus on figuring out ways to find Battlegear, and once we do that, it should lead us to a solution for bringing the Guild back."

"So…what? We just wait?"

His answer freezes me in my tracks. "No. Get your team ready. And I don't just mean for this current crisis. Moving forward, the Resistors may have to really step up because you could end up being the closest thing the world has to the Guild."

Without warning, the Aerie disappears and I'm left staring at a dumpster.

Closest thing the world has to the Guild? Us?

No pressure.

I gather the team around the conference table in our headquarters and call the meeting to order. This time, the stakes are higher than ever.

I clear my throat and begin. "I know you're all nervous about going after Battlegear and the Knights again, but this thing with the Guild disappearing is too important for us *not* to take on. Even if this is our last mission—which it very well might be—we have to do something."

"You mean cuz we might die?" Bash says.

"He didn't say—"

Osprey starts, but Bash interrupts her. "Cool."

Pace the chimes in, as usual. "Those guys were more powerful than we are."

"I don't know about *more* powerful," I say. "But they don't play by the rules, and that makes them deadly."

Pace continues, "*And* they have Battlegear with them. How are we supposed to deal with that?"

It's a good question. "I'm not sure yet, but I'm in contact with someone who will be able to help."

I give Osprey a quick look, knowing she's aware of who I'm referring to.

Neith caught the look too, and leans forward. "Who?"

After my accidental kiss with Osprey at the docks, I know I'm on thin ice with Neith, but this is much bigger than some relationship or whatever this is. But I figure I owe them something.

"I can't reveal his name to you, but he was the original Black Harrier."

Bash is stunned. "Original? You mean that guy that was here isn't the same one as always?"

Pace has a knowing smile. "Yeah, that's right. That's right. I knew something was different about him. I could tell."

"It's a recent change," I say. "Anyway. The original Black Harrier is putting together a plan to try and save the Guild. And we're the only ones who are in a position to implement it."

Osprey throws her arms up. "This is insane. It's suicide. If Battlegear can get rid of the Guild by himself, what chance to we have against him and the Knights?"

"She is right," Neith says. "We are just as likely to end up wherever they are as we are to save them."

"I still think they're dead," Bash says.

"They aren't dead!" I shout. And I don't know who I'm trying to convince more, them or me.

"You don't know that," Osprey says. "It's a very real possibility."

"Then what do you suggest?" I ask her. "We just let the Guild disappear from the world and not do anything about it because they *might* be dead?"

"No. No, you're right," Osprey says. "We have to try."

I say, "Thank you," then stand and take a few steps. "If we do this right and work together, we can beat them. I know it."

Javier decides to speak up for the first time in a long time. I'd almost forgotten he was there. "If they are alive, they can be anywhere in the world by now. How are we supposed to find them?"

"I don't know much about the Guild," Bash says, "but big organizations usually have like… tracking systems. You know? Don't they have anything like that?"

I shake my head. "They do, but so far, nothing is coming up."

Osprey looks at me with the kind of look that I read as, *That sounds like they are dead.*

Neith speaks up, but she's very tentative this time. Which is not like her at all. "I…believe I have an idea."

We all eye her, questioningly.

"What about HeroSpace?" she says. Her voice breaks a bit on the last word.

Pace laughs.

"What's that, some kind of superhero social media network?" Bash asks as a joke.

He's not wrong.

"That's exactly what it is," Osprey says.

Not many people know this, but the Guild has its own social media platform that you can only be a part of once you get your official license and membership card. The punishment for sharing it with any "normal" civilians is removal from the Guild, suspension of license, and barring from legal crimefighting.

So, pretty serious.

It was started by some of the younger ancillary members. There used to be awesome videos of fights around the country and even the world. It kind of became the big thing to try to get as many eyes on you through there as possible. I think we all thought it was a fast track to being a core member, but that couldn't have been further from the truth. Eaglestar and Frank both hated it and what it was doing to our community.

I deleted my account because Frank made me. I get it, but at the same time, I kind of miss the camaraderie.

It doesn't really matter though; once the older heroes got involved, it got pretty lame and most of us stopped paying much attention anyway. But it turns out that Neith—despite the fact that it goes against everything I know about her—is very active on there.

I think that's what separates us from those made up heroes in the comics. One of the things that makes humanity so *real* are our inconsistencies—our contradictions.

"You still have an active account?" I ask.

"Absolutely. I use it every day," she says, trying to harness her discomfort and turn it into confidence.

We log in and gather a bunch of information about Battlegear's old supervillain team. Most of them were taken down along with Chef Maléfique last year. But one remains—Mezmer, a telepath with some mind-control powers.

"I think I remember a Mezmer spotting a few weeks ago, but I don't remember who posted it," she tells us while she swipes through her feed.

We all get bored of waiting and kind of just fan out through the building. Pace sips on another energy drink. Bash eats the equivalent of a cow in beef jerky, and

Neith and Osprey strike up a conversation, which surprises me. That leaves me alone with Javi.

"I don't really belong here, do I?" he asks me.

The voice in my head screams a resounding "No!" but I can't say that.

"Sure you do," I tell him. "You made the team, right?"

"The backup team."

"That's only because the spots were all filled." Even as I say it, it feels stupid.

"Yeah." He stares at the floor. "I just wanna make a difference, you know?"

"I know." I really do. "Its just… this is dangerous."

"I knew that when I tried out," Javi says. "You're not gonna let me come with you, are you?"

I shake my head just as Neith shouts, "Here!"

I watch the disappointment on Javier's face as I rush over to see what Neith found.

She shows us a picture of an older man, rail-thin and tall, walking by a fountain toward a large glass building.

"I know that place," Osprey says.

"Me too."

An hour later, we're on a rooftop across from a four-story glass building looking down at a giant fountain out front. The same one featured in the picture of Mezmer on HeroSpace. The word *FineLabs* glows in white letters along the top floor of the building.

On the way here, I had to make a decision that makes me feel like crap. We drop off Javier at home. I know he could easily be hurt or killed, and worrying about him could slow me down so much that it affects my ability to lead the team.

It's a decision that could seriously affect our friendship, but I have to worry about more important things right now. Like living long enough to have to deal with that.

"FineLabs?" Bash says.

"Phillip Fineman," I say under my breath. "How had I not made this connection before?"

"What—that's his name?" Osprey asks.

"Yeah. He's one of the ones involved in that whole real name leak a few years ago."

Since I'm sure you're wondering, about three years ago, a hacker released a document on the dark web with a bunch of heroes' and villains' real names. It was a big deal. A lot of masked crimefighters went into hiding, some were actually killed, and others used it as an opportunity to shirk their monikers altogether and really embody their character like Yara Stephanopoulos—no relation to the political commentator.

She went from someone no one knew—just another hero in Los Angeles. There are a ton, by the way—to a sensation overnight. I think she was calling herself the Murder Hornet after some exaggerated news articles made people in America think the world was coming to end via angry, giant wasp.

Now she goes by Yara. One name. Like Madonna or Sting—which I realize now might have been a much cooler name for someone who'd previously gone by Murder Hornet.

Luckily, none of us were involved, but a good number of supervillains were and that put a temporary halt on their activities and many of them changed cities and schticks. Not Mezmer. Phillip Fineman pops up every now and again. And the messed up part is, none of us has ever been able to link him to an actual crime since his power is mind-control and no one can prove they are being controlled by him.

"They do what? Pharmaceuticals?" Pace asks.

"Yeah, I think so."

"So, all this time, he's running this place while we all fund his operation?" Osprey asks.

The question makes me wonder how many other supervillains are out there with legit businesses that all of us are oblivious to. Then, I wonder if the Guild *did* know but did nothing to stop it.

"So what now?" Neith asks.

I can see her tattoos already emanating that soft glow. She's also opted to *not* wear the costume Frank procured for her, which means she's showing plenty of skin—and it's cold in New York this time of year.

"Yeah, didn't Black Harrier tell us not to do anything until he got back?" Pace asks.

"One of them did," I say, almost a whisper.

It's true, Alex probably wouldn't approve of us going after Mezmer, since he's almost as dangerous as Battlegear—in some ways, maybe even more. So I know there's a good chance we'll get into more trouble when Alex gets back from Boston. But Frank gave the thumbs up. Sort of.

"Can I talk to you?" Osprey says. "Alone?"

I accidentally glance over at Neith. Son of a—it's like nothing can be said or done between me and Osprey anymore without it feeling incredibly awkward.

"Sure," I say, already walking with her.

"He's not going to be happy," Osprey says.

"Is he ever?"

"This is serious. He specifically said to do some recon, but under no circumstances are we to attack."

"Na-uh." Wow. Really mature. "He said don't attack Battlegear. This is not Battlegear."

"Do you think Alex is going to care about semantics?" she asks.

"Do you care?"

She thinks about it for a couple of seconds, then says, "Not one bit."

"Good. Here we go."

"Here we go," she echoes.

TWENTY-EIGHT

SAWYER

Smash!

We come down through FineLabs' skylight. Glass rains down with us, pinging off of everything from chandeliers to high-back sofas in the coolest entrance I've ever been a part of. We hit the ground and I do one of those fist to the ground moves that you see in the movies. What? Sometimes, it's okay to have a little fun before potentially dying along with everyone you know.

The others land running and spread out around the deserted lobby area to search the place for our supervillain target.

Mezmer is… uh, not a pretty man. He's what some would call "fugly." Not me, of course. I prefer to think he's just as handsome on the outside as he is on the inside. If you're not following, he's a pile of human excrement. Even more so now that I know he's the guy running this place and making billions off of other people's sicknesses.

Before you start judging me as being judgmental, let me tell you about the time when I'd first started crime fighting with Frank and Mezmer mind-controlled the mayor of this fine city, forcing him to—you know what? We don't have time for this. Put a pin in it and we'll circle back around when the world isn't at stake.

That's basically never, by the way. Be glad you have us fine heroes and heroines shielding you from most of it.

"Tiffany, do you read any heat signatures in the building?"

She's quiet for a moment, and I know that means she's accessing Frank's satellite system to spy down on FineLabs in search of anything that might be human.

"*Rats,*" she says.

"What's wrong?" I ask.

"*No, there are rats. Lots of them. They appear to be in cages—most of them.*"

"Gross. No humans?"

"*None that I can see,*" she says.

Even though Mezmer had been categorized as a low-level telepath in the past, there are some indications that his powers have increased a lot according to the information we gathered. That worries me. I don't know what he's capable of. He might even have tech in this place similar to Battlegear's that keeps Frank from being able to find him. Maybe he has a new, more powerful version of the special helmet he uses to read and control people's minds and he's able to trick even an AI.

I don't know, and that's what's scary.

"Pace, see if you can find him?"

"Sure thing, boss," he says. There's no sarcasm to the word when he says it this time. That's not a bad feeling. Not at all.

Focus, Sawyer.

Before he can jet off, I say, "But don't engage him alone. And let me know how many others are here."

Pace nods at me and takes off.

After searching the entire place in a few seconds, Pace stands beside me once more.

"He's here," he says. "But no one else."

"Nobody else is here? Not even guards?"

"Nope. Not one."

Not a single henchman in sight? I can tell immediately that something's not right. If this guy is one of the few remaining supervillains outside of prison, what is he doing here alone? Is he that sure of himself? I imagine henchmen must be pretty cheap right now based on what I know about supply and demand.

"Are you sure?" I ask.

"What do you mean am I sure? I searched. I found. I reported. It's not brain surgery."

I placate him with my palms. "Okay, okay. I'm sorry. It's just that my AI said no one was here."

"I have a name, you know."

I ignore her.

"Your helmet couldn't sense him?" Osprey says. "That's not good."

"No, none of this is," I agree. "Pace, where is he?"

"Not far, but I think he saw me."

"You should have led with that!" I shout.

"Okay, lead the—"

I'm cut off by Neith suddenly shooting a stun arrow at Pace. He falls to his knees, then flat on his face. Obviously, if Pace had been expecting it he could have easily dodged the missile, but he was focused on me.

"Neith!" I scream.

Was she in on this whole thing? A plant? Did Battlegear find out about our superteam and send her to infiltrate us, take us down from the inside? I can hardly think as the questions swim in my mind.

"What are you doing?" I demand.

"Her eyes!" Osprey shouts.

I look closer and see that her eyes have that look like someone who's sleepwalking as she nocks another arrow almost faster than my eyes can follow. This time, she aims her bow at me…

And Osprey grabs her from behind in a chokehold. "Sorry, but I can't just let you shoot us."

Suddenly, it's Osprey's eyes that glaze over as she starts to tighten her hold on Neith. At this rate, he's just gonna keep using us to fight each other until we're all taken down.

Speak of the devil.

Mezmer appears on the mezzanine above the lobby. He's a skinny guy in a silver costume and a giant helmet on his head with all kinds of technology stuck to it and sticking out of it. He reminds me of an old 1960s villain from like—I don't know, James Bond or Doctor Who or something. It's like a bad prop.

You'd think these criminals with mind powers would be the most dangerous, but in my experience, they're usually taken down pretty quickly because they don't pose any kind of physical threat and it's usually difficult for them to deal with more than one person at a time.

I think that very thing is being displayed right now. As soon as he mind-hopped to Osprey, his control over Neith seems to weaken. That makes me think he can only control a couple of us at a time. The problem is, any one of us could kill the rest of us without breaking a sweat.

Mezmer touches his temples—I don't know if that somehow activates his power or if he just thinks it looks cool—and suddenly, Bash turns and grabs Neith and me by the throats with his giant meat hooks. His eyes have that glassy look now.

Osprey, now clear-headed, leaps over to us. "Bash, no! Fight him." She starts beating on his arms to get him off of us but his grip is way too powerful for us to break free. She then grabs Bash's neck from behind and tries to pull him away from us. It looks like she's hugging a sack of potatoes. "What should I do? I don't want to hurt him."

"Uh, I don't think that'll—" I can feel my face going purple and my pulse in my temples. "—be… a… prob—"

This guy is s-t-r-o-n-g.

Beyond that, I can't respond. I try to pry his fingers loose, but I can't budge even one of them with all of my considerable strength. I notice that Pace is already almost fully recovered from whatever that arrow was laced with. He has an insanely fast metabolism, and I think he'd have been fine getting hit by anything other than an explosive tip—which I'm suddenly glad she didn't use. I give him a desperate look, but he's still frozen and doesn't know what to do. I manage to pull an arrow out of Neith's quiver and slam it into Bash's hand as hard as I can.

It literally crumples, the aluminum carbine shaft snapping in two. But Bash's grip loosens just enough for me to get something out.

"Pace!" I gurgle. "H-helmet…"

I can see in Pace's eyes he immediately gets what I'm trying to tell him. As Mezmer continues to focus on controlling Bash, Pace zips over to him and in all of two seconds, the threat has ended. Pace stands there, holding that gaudy-ass-looking spaghetti strainer.

Mezmer freaks out, grabbing at his bald, wrinkly skull. "Hey, give that back!" he shouts like Pace is going to apologize and hand it over.

Bash's eyes go back to normal when Mezmer's control over him is broken. Then they go red. He screams something not very nice about mothers and then charges at the villain like an enraged bull and uses a reception desk to catapult himself all the way up onto the mezzanine.

Mezmer is terrified. "No! Look, I—"

Bash slams Mezmer against—no, through—the wall. By the time I get up there, Bash has a fist back and is about to pound Mezmer's face in.

"Wait! We need to question him," I scream, my voice still hoarse.

Bash looks at me like I just took away his favorite toy, or a piece of delicious pie, or something.

"Hang him over the balcony," I tell him, thinking back to one of my favorite interrogation tactics. It makes me think about the last time I'd done it and how pissed off Alex is going to be with us.

With a smile, Bash does as I tell him and holds the villain by his throat over the balcony, Darth Vader-style.

"We know you can tell us where Battlegear is hiding," I growl.

Mezmer is scared. But not of us. "Please! I didn't have a choice. Don't make me talk or they'll kill me!"

It's always the same, like villains have no understanding of the clear and present danger of being threatened by a hero. I guess they know most of us won't kill. They *all* know Harrier won't, and by proxy, they think I won't either. They are right, but I don't mind getting really damn close.

"They who?"

"Did you not just hear what I said?" Mezmer says. "If I tell you I will *literally* die."

"Are you talking about Battlegear?" I demand.

He shakes his head, terrified. "I can't... I can't..."

I hear Neith call out from behind me. "Back away. I'll take care of this."

Bash and I turn around, and she's aiming her bow right at Mezmer's shiny head. It's not a stun arrow, either.

Mezmer is shaking even more. "Hold on. You can't do this."

Neith sneers at him. "Can't I?"

Mezmer looks back and forth between Bash and me. "She won't really shoot me, right? Don't you guys have some kind of rule about not killing?"

And there it is.

I shrug. "I do. Most of the team does—sort of. But Neith definitely has no rule about not killing. Maybe she's right."

"But you can't just stand there and watch her kill me in cold blood. You're heroes."

Of course I'd never let that happen, but I can't let Mezmer know that. This could be our only chance. "I don't know. Normally I probably wouldn't, but the Guild is missing, and I feel like we're running out of options."

Neith pulls back on her bow even more. The sound the string makes is threatening in itself. "One last time," she says. "Who are you so afraid of?"

Mezmer calls the bluff. "I can't do it. Kill me."

I'm not entirely sure Neith won't, so I flash a quick glance at Pace, hoping to all that is holy he understands it.

"Let him go, Bash," I say.

To my horror, Bash doesn't even hesitate and suddenly, Mezmer is plummeting. The fall wouldn't kill him, probably, but he'd end up with broken bones, maybe a severed spine. I'm not a doctor, but I know it wouldn't be good.

Then, just as he's about to splat, Pace swoops him up and he's back beside me, bent over and throwing up. It splashes on my boots.

"Seriously?" I shout, flashbacks of Aiden's birthday party all too real.

"Okay. Okay!" he says between hurls. "I'll tell you."

Bash grabs him again, detaining him in his grip but not raising him up this time.

"I said I'll talk!" Vomit dribbles over his lips and I have to hold back my own.

"Then do it," I say.

"Maybe your brute can let go of me first?" he says.

Bash just squeezes harder.

"Okay! Okay! Battlegear can be a jerk, but those new kids he has working with him—they don't follow the rules like the rest of us."

"Tell us something we don't know," Osprey says.

"The Neon Knights?" I ask.

"Yeah, they're are a bunch of loose cannons. Battlegear doesn't exactly rule them with an iron fist, and they don't have any regard for our code. Especially the new kid they recruited after the green one got arrested. That guy's a little psycho."

Logan? A psycho? You don't say…

"Battlegear isn't their leader?" I ask.

He's at a loss for words, but he seems like he's trying to explain it. "Yes. No. Kind of. I don't really understand it myself. He started the group, sure—and set them up with weapons and armor. Crazy tech. But he didn't make sure they were going to fall in line. Too much power, not enough responsibility, or however the saying goes. They're a typical bunch of rebellious teenagers who don't want to follow the rules."

We all look at one another a little guiltily. Sound familiar?

"We'll worry about them later," I say. "Right now, we need to find Battlegear and get him to bring back the Guild."

"Battlegear? He's got nothing to do with the Guild disappearing," he says.

"I spotted him on a roof during the ceremony. He's gotta be responsible," I say, feeling like I'm stating the obvious.

He laughs, which takes balls being in his position. "Look, kid—" Here we go with the 'kid' thing again, like I'm not the one holding this old fart's life in my hands—er, well, Bash's hands. "I knew all about Battlegear's plans," he continues, "and it had nothing to do with that light show and the Guild's disappearing act. His plan was to cause a commotion to keep all you heroes busy in Times Square while the Knights knocked over another bank."

"What?" says Osprey. "There's no way this was another stupid bank job."

"Believe what you want," he says. "Battlegear is always about the cash. He's no killer."

"You expect us to believe that Battlegear's appearance there was just a coincidence?" I ask.

"Like I said, I don't care what you believe. I don't work with him anymore. Go kick his ass for all I care. And I'd love to see you take down those punks he has working with him."

"Then why don't you just control them?" Neith asks. "Isn't that what you do?"

"Do I look like a hero?"

"No," Bash says instantly.

"Besides, I'm not that powerful. If I were, do you think I'd be letting a bunch of kids like you rough me up?"

I look to Osprey.

"I believe he is telling the truth," Tiffany says.

"Yeah," I say out loud. "I guess not. Unless it's part of your plan for some reason."

"No! I swear to you, it's not a plan. I don't even have a plan. You have to believe me."

Pace finally speaks up, which is crazy odd that he hasn't already. "Sure, Raptor. Let's all believe that the supervillain has no plan."

Mezmer scoffs. "Yeah, I'm a villain. Sort of. But super? I swear, I'm only in it for the money and the women."

That explains a lot when I think about that story with the mayor I'll tell you about another time.

Bash is taken aback. "Women? Supervillains get women?"

Mezmer suddenly affects a sleazy grin. "Oh, you have no idea…"

Osprey punches him in the stomach, knocking the wind out of him. "What is wrong with you? The fact that you can control people and that's what you're in it for makes you an even more disgusting person than I thought." She turns to Bash. "And you—can we please stick to what's important here?"

Bash turns slightly red. "I just never knew that—"

"Focus!" she shouts, then grabs Mezmer by the chin. "What else do you know about this new group?"

He takes a moment to catch his breath. "There was some guy working with Battlegear to train them. Some retired villain. I can't remember his name."

"Think harder. You must remember something more than that." I hit a pressure point that sends a jolt of pain through his body.

"Ow! Hey! I thought you were the good guys? Look, he runs some mixed martial arts gym. That's all I know. I swear."

I remember Logan mentioning something about working out at the MMA place near my school. "Mickey Hogan?"

"Yeah, that's the one, Mickey Hogan. He's the guy. He's the one you want. Not me. You should just let me go."

"Doesn't work without the helmet, does it, idiot?" Pace says, flicking Mezmer's earlobe.

"I think I know where they are," I say, which stuns the rest of my team.

"What? You figured it out just from that? There has to be at least a dozen MMA gyms in the city." Pace says.

"Yeah, but only one run by a former supervillain. Mickey Hogan used to go by the code name Facebuster. Supposedly, he turned over a new leaf after that name leak stuff. You remember that, right *Phillip*?"

"You got what you want," Mezmer says. "Come on, let me go?"

I ignore him and continue. "It wouldn't surprise me one bit if Hogan was using his gym to train criminals. If my suspicions are correct, Battlegear has been training the Knights at Mickey's gym, and probably using it as a base of operations as well. Either way, I bet we can find them there."

Pace is wired now that he's fully recovered from being stunned earlier, hopping back and forth like a boxer. "Then let's get over there."

"Just a second." I address Mezmer again. "Anything else we need to know before we go up against these guys?"

"No. That's all I know. I promise."

"Let him go, Bash."

Bash just pulls his hand away, letting Mezmer fall to the ground in a heap. "Ow."

He looks absolutely pathetic.

Bash takes a huge stride over to where Mezmer's helmet sits on the ground.

"Hey, please," Mezmer begs. "Can I have my helmet back? It's all I've got."

His last word is cut short as Bash crushes it between his hands like tinfoil, causing it to spark and smoke as the electronics inside are fried. Then he tosses the crumpled ball of metal to Mezmer. "Here you go."

Mezmer whimpers like an abused puppy. Without his helmet, he's just an ordinary person. And a weak one at that.

"You can't do that," he whines. "It's against the Code."

Pace responds, "Take it up with the Guild."

Despite our dire circumstances, I find myself smiling as we leave Mezmer behind.

TWENTY-NINE
SAWYER

So it was somehow even easier to track down the Neon Knights than it was Mezmer, since all we needed was a name. Now we just have to hope I'm right, and that they're at the gym.

This might be the most dangerous situation I've ever been in, and that includes my confrontation with Chef Maléfique and Deadeye last year. I know Frank was pretty incapacitated, but at least I knew he was there. I realize I've always found a sort of safety in his presence. Now, he's not only not here, but I'm absolutely sure he won't show up in the nick of time to save us if things get dicey.

It's still broad daylight and Mickey's MMA gym is situated between an electronics store and a Korean barbecue restaurant, so there's really no way to storm it. So, instead, we just walk up to the front doors.

People are on the street, snapping pictures of us with their cellphones. Bash is flexing his muscles. A little girl is pointing at Osprey and tugging on her mom's coat, but the mom is too busy gawking herself.

I wave, and as cool as it is to be fawned over, our ultimate goal here is to keep these people save. So, I say, "Everyone should go home. Now."

No one listens. Of course.

A bell chimes as I open the door to the gym. There are actually a bunch of people who work here in addition to the trainers, from secretaries to janitors to maintenance people. When we walk in, they're all working at their jobs and everything seems pretty normal. We approach the front desk, and the woman there asks us to give our names and state our business like we aren't all dressed in uniforms and armor.

Before I can answer her, Bash blurts out, "Tell them the Resistors are here to kick their sorry asses!" I'm glad I have a mask and a helmet over my head, since I'm sure my face is red with embarrassment.

The lady is a little taken aback, but she probably gets weirdos in here all the time.

"Uh, sorry about that." I interject. "My friend is pretty pumped up to fight right now. We were wondering if we can speak to Mr. Hogan?"

"Alrighty, then. Please sign in here, and I'll have to see your IDs since you aren't members." She hands us a clipboard, and we have an awkward moment while we pass the clipboard around and those of us who have them, show our Guild IDs. It all feels so normal, which makes it all the more surreal under the circumstances.

While we're doing this, she picks up the phone and makes a call, speaking quietly enough that we can't hear what she's saying. I turn up my sound amplification in my helmet just as she hangs up and gives us our IDs back.

"Just follow the middle hallway there," she points, "to the big double doors, and he'll meet you in the arena area."

We all share looks and thank her before we start walking.

Double doors at the end of the big hallway open into the arena area. It's a good-sized room where they hold their big fights, with a high ceiling and a raised stage in the middle, surrounded by seats in a sort of amphitheater style. On the stage in the middle is the ring, with the gym's logo on the mat.

The doors slam shut, and Facebuster walks in behind us. He was never a big deal to begin with back in his prime, so he's probably nothing to worry about now that he's older.

He's still buff though, that's for sure. Biker-style tattoos cover his biceps and forearms and probably other parts of him too, but he's wearing a wife-beater style tank top and camo fatigues.

"Welcome to my gym," he says. "You interested in learning how to fight?"

Osprey laughs. "Well, you got the fighting part right."

You can't teach someone good quips. It's natural. Osprey is great at a lot of things, but…

I step forward. "Look, Mickey, we know what's going on."

"Oh, yeah? What's that?" he says, stepping forward a step himself, cracking his knuckles.

I hear Bash moving behind me and the old guy's features shift ever-so-slightly. He knows he's outmatched, but these kinds of guys never back down.

"We know this place is a front for training criminals," I say.

"That's quite an accusation. This is a legitimate place of business. Didn't you see all my employees?" He smiles, three teeth missing near the front. "Did my sweet receptionist Tamara say something to give you the impression she was a hardened criminal?"

"We know about the Knights," I say, cutting all pretense.

"Knights?" he says a little too loudly.

Pace zooms at Mickey Hogan and stops an inch from him. "Cut the shi—"

Right on cue, the five Knights enter the arena room from the other side, led by the one in red, Broadsword. "That's enough, Mr. Hogan, we'll take it from here."

Mickey shrugs and takes a seat on the front row of the seating area to my right as our two teams start to approach one another. If we were dancing and snapping, it'd be just like *West Side Story*. What? My school did the production once. I thought it was great. Sue me.

Broadsword stares me down. "Hey, how about we go at it mano a mano, leader to leader?"

Hearing him again, I can confirm who he is. Benji's an idiot. What's the point of being a team if you're not going to commit to teamwork? That's the problem with these guys—they don't know how to work together.

Instead of answering, I try my favorite move. It doesn't always work, and when it doesn't I look really stupid, so I don't do it often. It can also be deadly if I use it against common criminals. But this guy has an energy-powered suit of armor on, so now seems like as good a time as any.

I fire my grappler from my forearm bracer and hit Benji straight in the chest. He looks down, confused.

Then I tap the control to reel it in. Just as it starts to yank me forward, I leap into the air and allow myself to be pulled full speed at him, and it's obvious that he's nowhere near ready for it.

I stick out my foot, and with the full force of my weight and the momentum from the grappler line, I kick Benji in the faceplate of his helmet.

He stands there, and for a moment I think maybe it didn't have any effect, which worries me quite a bit. Then he falls forward without even bracing himself with his arms, and he's already down for the count.

And, just like that, it's one down, four to go.

Axe rushes toward me, but Bash meets him head on and shoulders him. Axe goes flying into the stands, and the two of them start pounding each other with their giant fists.

Crossbow shoots a plasma bolt at Osprey's face, but just before it hits, Pace knocks her out of the way. Pace then rushes up and leaps off the back of one of the seats to where Crossbow is standing like a sniper, and drives a fist into his orange armor at superspeed. Crossbow takes the hit in stride and returns more of his own.

Things are quickly turning into one-on-one battles, which means a better chance of our winning.

Osprey glides over to take care of Morningstar, who's swinging her spiked power flail around. While she concentrates on Osprey, Neith sneaks in behind her and smashes her in the side of the head with her bow, causing her to stagger.

Okay, maybe two-on-one. This isn't supposed to be a fair fight. We just need to win.

That leaves me to deal with Mace. Yeah, no big deal, right? I mean, it's just Logan in a powered set of armor wielding an energy club.

"I've been waiting for this for a long time, loser," he says, lumbering toward me.

"You always call me that no matter how many times I beat you. Is it all the concussions? Are you just in denial?"

He swings his glowing, green mace at my head with a roar. I feel the heat of it as I duck under it with ease. I give him a roundhouse kick to the chest, but it doesn't do much through that thick armor.

"Oh, wait!" I say. "Maybe you're just so stupid that you don't actually understand what the word means. I hadn't considered that."

He grabs my cape with his free hand and swings me around, then tosses me into the ring in the middle of the room. That's when I realize the armor gives them more strength than I'd thought. Logan is strong, but not that strong. And he might still be slow, but he's actually dangerous now. I need to be careful.

I look around the room as I gather myself, and I've never been more proud of my team. *Our* team.

Pace is working over Crossbow. Osprey is dragging a kicking and screaming Morningstar back into the room from one of the exit doors.

Bash hits Axe so hard that he backs up against the cage around the ring. Neith kicks him in the stomach, then flips around with another kick, this time to his face, shattering his face-guard.

They're all winning this fight. No matter what happens, I know that I accomplished my dream of putting together a superteam for the ages.

Logan enters the ring, WWE-style. Too much flair. Arrogance will be his downfall. He continues to swing his weapon at me as I dodge it every time. But my punches and kicks aren't having any effect on him either.

Time to try some wrestling moves of my own. But not the kind I learned training with Coach Carmichael on the school team with Logan.

If he wants to play pro-wrestling, I'm game. I let my muscle memory take over as I think about all the times I watched Hulk Hogan and Steve Austin and John Cena. I try all kinds of different moves, most of which result in slamming Logan's head into the ground.

I don't care how good that helmet is, his brain is still sloshing around in his head with this kind of punishment. I finally manage to pull his helmet off as I sit on his shoulders and look down at him. Then I move forward and slam his face into the ground, this time without a helmet. Logan's down for the count.

I do a quick survey of the room and see that everyone else has the situation mostly under control with the other Knights except Pace who has a plasma bolt sticking out of his leg.

He's screaming but still fighting. What a freaking pro.

I rush over to help, but Bash is already there and pounding on Crossbow.

"Take off their gloves!" I shout.

I rip off Logan's gloves and toss them aside, then move to do the same with Benji.

Then something happens.

Everything in the room seems to slow down and there's ringing in my ears. My legs are wobbly and I feel like I'm trying to stand on the deck of a ship in the middle of a huge storm.

I can tell that the rest of the team is feeling the same effects. Then I see why: Battlegear has arrived, waving around some new gizmo. "I can't believe you took down my protégés like that. I'm so disappointed in them."

He walks over and stands in the center of the ring, then addresses the unconscious Broadsword. "You're fired." He looks around at the rest of them. "You're all fired."

The effects of whatever device he's using on us has me feeling uneasy.

"What'd you do to the Guild?" I slur. "Don't you realize what will happen if we're attacked by aliens, or there's some kind of global catastrophe that only they can handle?"

"Relax, junior, I had nothing to do with it. In fact, I've been working on how to get them back myself. I would *still* be working on it, in fact, if I hadn't heard from Facebasher that you were beating up my guys here."

I look over and Facebasher is no longer seated, watching. When had he left?

"You want the Guild back?" I ask. I double over from whatever his device is emitting.

"Of course I do. I'm Eaglestar's arch-nemesis. What happens if he's gone? I get paired up with Swamp Rabbit or something? It's a symbiotic relationship."

His forcefield explodes around him and the illness I was feeling instantly vanishes. He lifts his new giant gun-thing and it starts powering up like the one he had the last time we fought him. Only this one's even bigger. "On the other hand, you punks don't mean anything to me. You're just a pain in my ass."

He fires it at me, and I brace myself for the impact. But suddenly, Bash is in front of me again, and I realize the only way he could have gotten there so fast was—

"Pace! You can't just use Bash as a shield!"

"Sorry, boss," he says. "I didn't know what else to do. I knew he could probably take the hit, and you couldn't. No offense."

Bash falls back, unconscious, and Pace and I ease him to the ground. The front of his new uniform is torn to shreds and smoke pours off of his bare chest. This is way worse than the docks. His skin is charred and bubbling.

Pace looks guilty. "I'm sure he would have volunteered to do it if he had the chance."

"Are you lovebirds done?" Battlegear asks.

I swear. Now our powerhouse—our tank—is down for the count. I'm grateful his weapon has a fairly long recharge time. The fact that Battlegear doesn't just pop off another shot right away is the only reason any of us is still alive.

He does, however, use another device that shoots some kind of trap at Pace's feet while he's occupied with Bash. It looks like foam, but it hardens immediately all around Pace's boots.

"That's how you keep a speedster at bay," he says, laughing.

Neith hits Battlegear with a stun arrow that keeps him from launching another attack at us right away, but he seems like he's recovering almost immediately.

"Uh, I think we have a problem," Pace says, a panicked look on his face. "I can't move my feet. Like, at all."

"Can you maybe… I dunno, vibrate really fast out of it or something?"

Pace is taken aback. "This ain't a sci-fi movie, bro. I just *run* really fast."

As I try to help Pace get loose, Osprey and Neith attack Battlegear from both sides, but his force field keeps repelling them. He taps some controls on his forearm bracer, and the next time Neith hits his force field with her spear, it sends an electric shock through her, and she passes out.

"Crap," I say. "Be right back."

"Be right back? Be right back?" Pace says. "And what the f—"

I don't hear the rest as I run over to see if Neith's okay.

Osprey takes advantage of the fact that Battlegear had his focus on Neith. Since his forcefield is obviously just some kind of compressed energy that deflects attack, she's able to move through it slowly. Even though her new armor from Frank protects her, mostly, it looks like it hurts. By the time he returns his attention to her, she's hitting him in the face with rapid-fire kicks and punches.

Something stirs beside me and I notice Axe has his plasma weapon fired up again.

Crap. Bash must not have gotten him incapacitated before Battlegear showed up and he was suddenly used as a human shield.

I can hardly keep track of everything going on around me but I do know that Osprey is still fighting with Battlegear and she appears to be losing, Neith is still down, Pace is still unable to move, and Bash is out and barely breathing.

Axe brings down his plasma weapon. It grazes my bracer, and slices the graphene off like deli meat. These guys are out for blood.

"Why are you doing this?" I ask Axe as I dodge his next attack.

He doesn't answer, but I sense movement again and Broadsword is up. He no longer has his gloves on, but that only makes him half as dangerous since that power armor still somehow enhances their strength.

He charges me at the same time Axe swipes downward again. I barely manage to avoid the energy blade but that means I take the full blow from Benji. The air flees my lungs and my eyes feel like they're going to explode out of my face.

I stagger backward and drop like a stone.

Broadsword is putting his gloves back on and stalking toward me.

"I'm gonna enjoy this, twerp."

Just then, the double doors slam open. I watch a boomerang bounce off of Broadsword's face-mask and he falls over backward. I flip around and look toward the doors. If my own visor wasn't down, the shock etched on my face would have probably been comical.

Black Harrier enters the room, dragging a beat-up Facebasher with him. I notice that the hallway behind him is littered with unconscious thugs. Then like a true badass, with his free hand, he shoots a bolo-gun and the projectile wraps itself around Axe. The blue Knight flops to the ground like a caterpillar, cursing the whole way.

I think it's Frank for a minute until I realize…

"What's going on here?" Alex demands.

"We, uh, found Battlegear!" I say.

"I can see that. Why are you engaging him? Or, should I say, *losing* to him?"

"We came here to confront the Knights," Pace says. "We just got to the boss level faster than we expected."

Alex's attention turns to the brawl between Battlegear and Osprey. His expression is a mixture of anger and concern—more concern than I've ever seen from him.

Just then, Osprey, who's already taken a few serious blows, uses a boomerang to smash what looks like a powerpack on the back of Battlegear's belt, like I taught her when we fought La Cucaracha. As sparks and smoke emanate from the pack, his force field lights up and becomes fully visible in a few flashes, then disappears.

"You little wench," Battlegear growls.

Before Osprey can fully get back into the fight, he grabs her by the helmet to lift her up, then punches her with a haymaker that sends her flying. She tries to stand, but immediately crumples in a heap.

Alex becomes enraged. "See if Osprey's okay. I'll take care of *him*."

Anyone who can still use codenames in the middle of something so crazy has my stamp of approval. Unfortunately, I don't think he feels the same way about us right now.

Alex launches himself at Battlegear and they start sparring. Even without his guns and his force field, Battlegear's still a formidable opponent. Alex is one of the best fighters I know, and he's barely one step ahead.

I make a really strange decision without even thinking about it, and rush over to check Neith before going for Osprey. Neith has been down for a long time and I'm pleased to see she's still breathing. But she's absolutely hurt.

Two of our team, totally incapacitated.

Assured that Neith is all right, I rush over to Osprey to check on her. Luckily, she isn't even unconscious.

"I'll be okay. I just need a moment," she says. I nod and help her to sit up.

I speak under my breath. "Tiffany, are you able to project yourself so others can see you besides me?"

"Yes, I have a projector that you can disconnect from your helmet."

"Really? How did I not know about this?"

"You never bothered to finish the tutorial, if you recall. It's located on your left earpiece."

"Great. Are you able to go back to the settings that you had when Frank first gave you to me?"

"My default settings? But you told me—"

"Forget what I told you," I tell her. "Go back to your default settings. No more anime."

I twist my left earpiece and hold the miniature component in my hand. "What do I do with this?"

"If you attach it to the wall or ceiling, it should stick."

As we're having this conversation, Alex is still going one-on-one with Battlegear in the middle of the ring. They seem evenly matched. Now I can see without a doubt why this guy is Eaglestar's nemesis.

Alex is getting in some good shots, but Battlegear has super-strength, so he's wearing Alex down faster than the reverse. As they go back and forth, I can tell they've both almost had it, but Alex definitely looks like he's the one who's worse off.

I climb up into the rafters above the ring and follow Tiffany's instructions, carefully placing it on the ceiling where it attaches on its own. "Get ready, Tiff."

I look down just in time to see Battlegear punch Alex so hard that he drops to his knees, dazed.

"Tiffany, now!"

A small light on the projector flickers to life and suddenly, Tiffany is standing right behind Battlegear in all her glory, leather bikini top, hot pants, thigh boots and all.

"What do you want me to do?" Tiffany asks me in my helmet.

"Distract him."

"Hey there, lover, are you new here?"

Battlegear spins around, ready to strike, but sees Tiffany standing there, nearly nude. She pulls off her leather top, and his jaw drops in shock. How much of it is what he's seeing and how much is just plain trying to figure out what the hell is going on is anybody's guess.

I drop down behind Battlegear and tap him on the shoulder. He spins back around toward me as I'm winding up, and I hit him square in the face with the hardest punch I've ever thrown.

Battlegear gets a look that I've only seen on the face of the combatant who loses a match in a boxing movie. Then his legs give out and he slumps to the mat.

I realize Alex did most of the heavy lifting, but it still felt good to get in the final blow.

Alex doesn't even hesitate before securing mandibles around Battlegear's wrists and feet. He then dismantles every piece of tech on the guy and then goes to join Osprey who is working on getting Pace free of the foam.

Neith runs up and hugs me. I didn't even see her wake up, but I hug her back, and then look into her eyes. But there's only relief, nothing more.

"Don't get any ideas. I'm just happy we're alive," she says.

I nod my understanding.

Alex seems more concerned about the fact that we went in without him than he is relieved that we ultimately won.

"Bash needs medical," I say.

That fires Alex up something fierce. He stands and spins on me, jabbing a finger my direction. "I told you not to confront him without me! If I hadn't gotten back in time, or if Frank hadn't known where you were—"

I think Alex realizes what he'd said before anyone else, but I just stare at him. And after I'd just sung his praises…

Pace's eyes go wide. "Frank? You mean Frank Douglas is…?"

Osprey and I look at each other.

Neith whispers, "Frank Douglas is the original Black Harrier."

Alex realizes he just broke one of the Guild's rules. "Sorry. I assumed as members of your team that they were already privy to that information."

"I won't tell if you don't," I tell him. "Call it even?"

I know I'm pushing my luck, but he nods.

They were bound to find out anyway.

"Tiffany," I say, turning to see her completely nude. "Call an ambulance for Bash. Quickly."

"Yes, sir."

"I chose the wrong AI," Alex says.

Osprey slaps him on the arm, which I find kind of odd, but whatever.

I look around—something is wrong. Where's Logan?

"What happened to Lo—the Knight in green? Mace?"

The rest of the team surveys the room, but no luck. Osprey replies, "Sorry, he must have snuck out during the fight with Battlegear."

Son of a—

"Uh, guys?" We all look over at Pace, who's still trying to pull his feet out of the hardened foam. "You think we can figure out a way to get me out of here?"

The others and I head over to him. "Also…am I the only one who sees a naked lady standing there?"

THIRTY

SAWYER

Weird.

Understatement of the year. To go from fighting supervillains to standing at the hot grill frying some burgers is so much more than weird. Oh, and the air conditioner is out in the restaurant. Depressed about things with Neith and sore from trying to save the world, I don't even notice when my hand touches the grill and I get a pretty bad burn. When I do notice, I run to the back and run it under cold water, then look through the first aid kit for some burn ointment.

That's when the whole world turns upside down. I hear a bunch of excited people talking loudly in the dining area. Everyone's got their phones out, staring at the screens. They are all in a state of shock over whatever it is they're seeing. From their behavior, I'm starting to worry that it's a terrorist attack or something and I immediately try to figure out the best way to get out of here and help.

The other employees and I finally go out there to see what's going on. We throw aside all decorum and hover over our customer's shoulders.

What I see on screen is incredible.

The Guild has returned.

The core members of the Guild are at United Nations headquarters, standing in front of the General Assembly. I whip out my phone and open my news app, then retreat to a quiet corner to listen.

Eaglestar stands at the podium at the front of the room as the General Secretary looks on. The rest of the team stands off to the side looking different than I've ever seen them. More… menacing, somehow. Whatever they went through while they were gone, it must have been huge.

"We appreciate the welcome home from everyone, and we expect that you will honor our wish that you give us some privacy as we recover from our traumatic experience after being ripped through a breech in the space-time continuum. This event has taken its toll, and while we have no desire to share the details with the world, we ask that you understand that it has… changed us. We are not the same people who left here mere days ago, and we now have a much different outlook on things. There are going to be some changes. And they will be consequential."

That doesn't sound good…

Both the General Assembly on TV and the patrons and employees of the restaurant seem to agree with my assessment of Eaglestar's ominous tone. It gets worse as he continues.

"We will no longer be allowing criminals to run rampant. We will no longer allow many things that are currently considered acceptable. More details will follow, but until then… know that we've got our eyes on you."

His eyes glow red for a second.

What the hell is that all about? I start toward the door. I need to get across the street and see Frank right away.

Kevin blocks my way and gets up in my face. "Na-uh. No way. You ain't leaving. We're too busy right now, and your shift doesn't end for two more hours."

"Did you not see that the world as we know it is turning upside down. Somebody has to—"

He barks, which I assume is supposed to be some sort of laugh. "Somebody has to what? You think you're some kind of a hero because you stopped a robbery in a cow costume? Yeah that's right. I figured out it was you. Kicking some thugs ain't he same thing as saving the world you spoiled little brat. Everyone else is still working. Now get back to it. You think you're special, or something?"

I grit my teeth, finally fed up with this guy's crap. "Yeah, as a matter of fact, I do. Because I *am* special. Far too special to be working in this greasy dump for an even greasier manager who's a pint-sized despot."

"Listen here—"

"No, you listen," I say, bowing up to him. "You see, I was sent here by Mr. Douglas to check up on the restaurant and find out how things are running behind the scenes. I've been documenting everything I see around here, and there are quite a few issues."

Kevin is defiant. "Issues? What kinds of issues?"

"Well, the register counts are off all the time. By a lot. And the subtracted amounts mysteriously match up to regular deposits you make in your own private bank account in addition to your paycheck."

Now he's indignant. "You've been hacking into my bank account?"

"Oh, that's the least of your worries, Mr. Kev. I've been checking into all kinds of mysterious matters. Like Brenda for example, the girl you've been dating. She seems to be clocked in for regular shifts, including all of the times I've worked."

"So?"

"So, I've never met Brenda. I've never even seen Brenda. How is she working all those shifts if she's not even here? And, by the way, that also solves the mystery of how you could actually be *dating* somebody. *Anybody*."

He bares his teeth like a cornered wild dog. "Why, you…"

"And I'm sure Brenda would be interested to learn about all the dating profiles you have set up—on your work computer, no less—using Chad's picture."

I point at Chad, a big, blonde cashier who works out all the time. Chad doesn't look happy about the revelation. "What the hell, bro?"

"But that's—"

I shove my index finger into his chest. "But none of that compares to the fact that I just discovered you have cameras set up in the women's restroom! You're a thieving, lying, cheating, perverted scumbag, and you're going to get what's coming to you."

All of the other employees have been listening in, and at this point, they start closing in on him. They're an angry mob, and the female employees look ready to strangle him. All they need are pitchforks and torches.

Kevin grabs his chest like he's about to have a heart attack. "B-but I can't be fired!"

I laugh. "*Fired?* Is that what you're worried about? Buddy, you'll be lucky if you don't end up in *prison*. For a really long time."

The look on Kevin's face is priceless. If I could raise my phone and snap a pic of him right now without looking like a total douchebag, I would. And I would look at that photo every time I was feeling down, and it would immediately cheer me up. I guess I'll just have to take a mental snapshot and think back on it instead.

I hang apron around his neck, and hand him my spatula as he stands there, frozen, looking like he's about to cry. "Mr. Douglas will be in touch soon. Oh, and the police also, I'm sure."

I take off my uniform hat and hairnet and toss them behind me as I walk to the door. "And the news. Don't forget the news. I gave them a call earlier, too.I know they're busy with this whole Guild thing, but it'll eventually blow over and you'll be front page!"

He's still sputtering behind me as the door slams shut.

Man, that felt good.

THIRTY-ONE

AMY

As much as I know Pace isn't going to like it, I decide to talk to Alex. I find him back at the Aerie. He's in a t-shirt and jeans and he's finishing up putting the Black Harrier costume back on the mannequin where it's stored.

He hears me approach, but doesn't turn around.

"Done for the day?" I ask.

"Done for a while, apparently. Until the Guild needs me to suit up again." He places the helmet on the mannequin's head.

"Why do you listen to them?"

"What do you mean?" he asks, still not looking at me.

"You heard what they said at the UN. And guess who wasn't invited?"

That evokes the response I was hoping for.

"I wasn't a part of their… thing," he says, but I can hear the emotion in his voice. Hurt. Pain. Maybe hate? For them I hope?

Their words during that address… basically, things are going to change and we're watching all of you… that was messed up.

"You're right," I tell him. "And you never were."

"Cool. Kick me while I'm down."

"That's not what I mean and you know it."

"So what do you mean?" he asks.

"I mean that *this* city needs Black Harrier. This city needs you."

"The city needs Black Harrier? Or someone more specific here in the city?"

I avoid eye contact with him. "There may be certain people in particular who are residents of this city who need you."

"Anyone I know?" He laughs, mirthlessly.

"You may have met this person on occasion. She sort of likes Black Harrier, but she's still not sure exactly how she wants to handle it…"

He picks up his duffel bag. "Well, hopefully *she* can figure it out before the next time he's in town."

"I feel like that might be a possibility. But you'll have to ask her then. I certainly can't speak for her now."

"Right. So, still on a break?"

"For now," I say. It's the best answer I can give. I don't really know where I stand with Pace, and I've never liked one guy, much less two at the same time.

He walks over and gives me a hug. "Bye, Ames."

"You're heading back to Boston, now?"

"Yeah. The Guild expects Redhawk back there by tonight."

He kisses me on the forehead, then leaves through the secret entrance from the penthouse. I stand for a few moments to make sure he's gone.

"I think the Guild is going to expect a lot of things I'm not going to like," I say, lost in my own thoughts.

Except I'm not alone. Standing in the doorway is my dad. There's no look of shock on his face, so I assume he's here because he already figured out that I'm Osprey, and not the other way around. I'm busted, and there's no way around it, so I try the humorous route.

"So… there's something I've been meaning to tell you, Bàba. You're not going to believe it…"

He doesn't look happy, but that's not all that unusual for him. He also doesn't seem as angry as I thought he'd be if he ever found out. Well, let's be honest: *when* he found out. It was inevitable.

"I cannot say I am surprised. I guessed that you were Osprey some time ago."

"Then why didn't you say anything?" I ask.

"Probably for the same reason you didn't tell me, I would assume."

"You were afraid I would yell at you?" I say, smiling. I perceive the tiniest flicker of movement at the corners of his lips. I'll count that as a win. "I wasn't sure how you'd react. I didn't want you to take this away from me."

"Darling, I would never take something like this away from you. I would be lying if I said I wasn't upset at how you went about it behind my back, hacking into my computers and stealing my prototypes. But I also know I wouldn't have approved of you doing it ahead of time, so believe it or not, I understand why you would do it. And, most of all, I worry about you putting yourself in so much danger."

"But we just went up against Battlegear—and won. I *literally* helped save the city from him and some pretty powerful thugs he had working for him."

Dad walked slowly toward me. I felt my stomach turn a bit. I don't know why. I just think this has been a long time coming, and I'm nervous and excited and a million other emotions I don't know how to process right now on top of everything else.

He takes my hand in his, then covers it with his cybernetic palm. "That's one of the reasons I'm not as upset as I might have been."

"Thank you, Bàba."

He smiles, genuinely this time.

"So what happens moving forward?" I ask.

"First, I'm going to upgrade everything you have."

"But I just got new equipment," I say. It's only after I say it that I worry he doesn't know that Frank knows…

"What Frank gave you is the best he can get, not the best *I* can get. If my darling girl is going to be out risking her life all the time, she's going to have the best equipment possible."

"Wait. But aren't you already giving Black Harrier and Red Raptor the best you have?"

He shrugs and then gives me a wink. "I may have a few tricks up my sleeve."

THIRTY-TWO

SAWYER

The United Nations gives in to the Guild and gives them even more power than they already had. Whereas before, they were subject to a lot of local laws and the guidelines set forth by the UN, they have broad legal authority in all jurisdictions now.

They keep using the excuse that something really bad happened to them when they went away, but I don't know what kind of experience would lead them to wanting this much power. It's out of character for all of the core members—even Eaglestar.

When I try to explain it, I think it's going to come off sounding crazy—like some far-future cyberpunk flick. There are actual drones flying around all the major cities. I don't mean little cute things you'd pick up at the big box store and fly around on a lazy Sunday morning, or that some pervy tech geeks use to look for girls sunbathing on the roofs of their buildings. I mean these giant, circular robots that monitor everything anyone does, all the time. It's surveillance 24/7.

In the words of Eaglestar, "We can't be everywhere all the time, except we can. We are watching you."

It's so messed up. It's so effective though, that the Resistors have nothing to do. There's like, no crime. None.

Meanwhile, Logan's back at school. His arm's in a sling and he has two black eyes and a broken nose. The rumor he started was that he got into a fight with a biker gang and won. I feel like he should probably be taken down a notch if he still hasn't learned his lesson.

Yeah, he belongs in prison. He *definitely* belongs in prison. But I don't have any proof that he was Mace, the Green Knight. And I'm sure he'll end up in jail anyway soon enough if he doesn't turn things around.

Maybe I can help him out with that.

After school I do a quick-change into my gear and follow Logan home. Without Benji to walk with, he's on his own, and he's stupid enough to take a shortcut down an alley by himself. Perfect.

I drop down from a rooftop using my grappler line and grab him by the back of his hoodie. He screams in fear as we ascend at full speed back to the rooftop.

Attaching the grappling hook to the back of his hoodie, I hang him over the edge of the roof and squat on the ledge so I can look down at him, eye-to-eye.

"Stop squirming or you're going to slide right out of that thing and become pavement pizza," I tell him.

To my surprise, he stops.

"You know who I am?" I ask.

"Y-yeah. Sure. Everyone does."

"Say my name." I order in my most menacing voice.

"R-red Kite." I let the cord out a little, causing to him plummet a few stories. He screams. Then I yank him back up. He screams again.

"It's Raptor. Red Raptor," I say as I squat back down.

"R-r-raptor. Got it." I don't know what's wetter, his face from tears and snot or his jeans from peeing in them.

"Good. Because I know who you are… *Mace*." He looks even more scared now.

"I-I-I don't know what you're talking ab-abou—" I let him fall a bit farther, and this time, screams even louder. Up he comes again.

"Lie to me one more time and I release the line. Don't test me. You got that?"

He's too scared to even talk now. He squeezes his eyes shut and just nods vigorously.

"I better not find out you're committing any more crimes. No fast food robberies. No bank heists. No joining any more supervillain teams. Or bullying any more kids at school. Understood?"

He nods again.

"I want to hear you say it."

"Y-y-y-es." His voice is barely a whisper.

Then, taking a line out of Eaglestar's playbook…

"Remember. I've got my eye on you."

He nods again.

"Just one last thing." He peeks through squinted eyes as I lean in close, my visor only a couple of inches from his face, and use my normal voice. "Say 'hi' to your mom for me."

His eyes pop open wide, and I release the line. He falls about a dozen stories at full speed before I hit the control to slow his descent the last twenty feet or so. Leaving, I watch Logan lie down in a fetal position on the filthy ground, sobbing. And I almost feel sorry for him.

Almost.

I head to the Aerie to see if Frank is there. I know he has to be as freaked out about the Guild acting this way as I am—probably a lot more.

He's sitting in the dark, staring at the big screen as it runs through some old pics of when he first joined the Guild. I'm not sure why, considering he's been out of the game so long. I guess when I'm older maybe I'll understand that kind of stuff.

I know he notices me, but he doesn't acknowledge that I'm there, so I just stand behind his seat and watch as the images appear and fade. After a pic of a young Alex goes by, he finally decides to talk to me, although he doesn't bother to turn around.

"It was the hardest thing I ever had to do."

"Retiring?"

"No. Killing my father. Your grandfather."

Holy crap. He's going to talk about it. He's really going to talk about it. "I can imagine."

"No. I'm sorry, but I don't think you do."

He's right. I was just saying that because I think that's something people say. From that point, I figure my default position should be to stay silent.

"Maléfique was right that I was upset about discovering he was the city's biggest crime lord. But that's not what drove me over the edge. He'd led me to believe that my mother died in childbirth. Even tried making me feel guilty about it sometimes. When I confronted him about being a criminal, he admitted to me that he regretted one thing about it. Just after I was born, my mother was killed in an attempted hit on his life. He wasn't just the opposite of the man I thought he was. He was responsible for me growing up without a mother."

We sit there for what feels like a really long time.

I break my vow of silence. "Why are you telling me this? Why now?"

"You asked."

"I did?"

"That day you discovered me and your mom," he says.

"So why now?"

"It's important for you to realize what's at stake."

"And what's that?" I ask.

"Everything." The word drops like an atomic bomb, but then, he lets out a breath and smiles. "Enough of this. Are you ready to get back out there?"

I smile with him. "Yeah. More ready than ever."

EPILOGUE

FIREFLY

Later...

T*rouble.*

That's what I'm in. Hey, don't ask me. They made me do that. Something about sticking to the format. I dunno. Don't really care. Just tryin' to make sure you know what's goin' on.

Name's Marion MacGregor. But you can—you *better*—call me "Mack." Don't like Marion. It's a girl's name. I ain't a girl. Not one bit. All man here, got it?

Last guy called me Marion's still searchin' for some of his teeth on the sidewalk outside Reilly's Pub. Matter of fact, scratch that. Call me by my hero name: Firefly. Mr. Firefly, even. Yeah. I like that best.

I earned that right by saving all your reggo-butts more times than you got fingers and toes. You'd be changin' your dungarees if you found out just how many times this whole world was about to be done with 'til me and the rest of the Guild stepped in and saved youse.

Fifty. Maybe a hundred. I dunno. I lose count. Robots. Aliens. Friggin' psychopathic carnival freaks. Seems every time I turn around, someone else is tryin' to off humanity. Usually right here in America, too. Like we pissed off the wrong gods or somethin'.

Marion.

I shouldn't be embarrassed by the name just cause it's usually a woman's name like... I dunno, Leslie. It was John Wayne's real name, for cryin' out loud. But hardly anybody remembers that. Not anymore. Grew up watchin' that man take on whole towns before ridin' off alone into the sunset. Now that... that was a man's man, you know? Six shooters and cigarettes. But you don't care. Why would you? I ain't Eaglestar or Harrier, so let's stick to Firefly, and we'll both be happier. Maybe by the end of all this, someone might remember me.

Firefly.

Might not be the coolest code name you ever heard, but it fits my powers to a T—I don't even know what that means. To a T... but we all get the drift, right? The name fits. How you ask? I'm glad. Someone's finally showin' some interest in old Firefly.

First, I can shrink down to the size of a bug. *But* I'm still just as strong as I am full-size. Pretty hip, right? People still say hip? Whatever. Point is, I can slip under a guy's shoe and then throw him on his keister, and he won't even know what happened. Or buzz inside his ear and punch his eardrum. Knock him out, cold as a milkshake.

Apparently, I live a whole lot longer than most people, too. That's one part that makes no sense with the name. Sorry. Sue me. Fireflies live about two months. I've looked thirty for like the last fifty years.

Not impressed? How 'bout this. I can fly.

Who doesn't wanna fly? Raise your hand.

That's what I thought. Best power ever.

They do surveys, always comes out on top. Don't bother tellin' me it's invisibility. You'd have to walk around buck naked all the time. For the longest time, I thought it was butt naked. I mean, that makes more sense, don't it?

Flyin' is the best. Heard people argue, sayin', "I wanna read people's minds." No. You. Don't. Forget about it. You'd be so disgusted with what goes on in people's heads you'd never have a friend or more than friend ever again.

Flyin'.

Ah, that's the ticket.

All right. What else? Yeah, I got these power bands. Don't call 'em bracelets. Last guy called 'em that is lookin' for his teeth next to that other guy lookin' for his teeth outside Reilly's Pub, tryin' to sort out whose's whose. My bands, they shoot energy blasts that'd cook a Thanksgivin' turkey faster than a deep fryer, and pack a punch to boot. Wham! Bam! Where's the stuffin'?

Where was I? Oh, yeah.

Trouble. T-R-U-B-L-E.

I got someone after me. Not just someone… the worst person you could have after you. The most powerful guy in the world. Eaglestar.

His powers make mine look like card tricks. Yeah, he can fly like me, but that's where the similarities end. He's strong enough to lift a buildin', fast enough to outrun a race car, and tough enough to catch a wreckin' ball with his bare hands, no flinchin'. He can hear a pin drop from halfway cross the country. And, to top it all off, he can shoot friggin' *laser beams* out his eyeballs. That's right. You heard me.

Not someone you wanna mess with.

Pay no mind to what you see and hear on the news.

Eaglestar ain't exactly "Mr. Nice Guy." Not when you know him personally. Frankly, he's kind of a tool. The blunt kind, too.

Sometimes I think the main reason he wanted to kill all them Nazis so bad way back when he got his powers was cause he didn't want 'em hornin' in on his territory. Ya know, personality-wise. He's an ego freak, condescendin', and sometimes, just a jerk. He's older than me and still stuck there in the forties when it comes to most of his ideals. You should see him talk to the ladies. It can be a real PR nightmare sometimes. But he still does the right thing. Most of the time.

Things changed recently. Not just with Eaglestar, but with the rest of the Guild, too. They've all been actin out of character, 'cept maybe Black Harrier, but I dunno the new guy too well, so it's hard to tell. Cupid and Fastlane used to fool around. Real cut-ups. Fun to be around. Now? They're a buncha hardheads. Can't hardly take a joke. Then, just when I think they're themselves again, their humor gets downright cruel.

Bastet, who's normally pretty chaste—even with that boob window of hers. She's been hangin all over the other guys and even comin on to me. I could be her great-grandpa. But look—I still got blood in the veins, ya know? I mean, geez. You seen her? It's just, that ain't no way to act at work. Her sudden, how do I say… promiscuity ain't like her at all.

Then there's Omar. Seems like he wants to break things and hurt people just for the sake of it.

And Eaglestar… he's the worst of 'em all.

I told you, he's after me. I caught him fryin' a cat in an alley with his laser eyes just for fun. Like some dumb teenager. He's actin' just plain evil. Matter of fact. They're holdin' a meetin' right now. I'm the only one not invited. I decided earlier, I ain't gonna stand for it.

I'm currently about the size of a fly. They don't even notice me in the corner. And that's good. After my run-in with Eaglestar, I'm pretty sure, in the mood he's in? He'd kill me on the spot. No questions. Just zap with them freaky eyes of his.

"This reality is lame," Omar says.

"Sure, but at least there are still trees." That's Fastlane.

He and I used to be close. I mean… normal guy and guy close. Like friends. Not... you know… not that there's anything wrong with that. Ain't by business what people do. Just sayin', I don't swing that way.

They're talkin' about another universe. I don't really understand it at all. I ain't dumb, but I ain't no scientist neither.

"When we rule over these plebs, it will be whatever we want it to be," Bastet says.

"I… When *I* rule over them."

And there he is Eaglestar the magnificent. Friggin' jerkwad. Wait… what did he say?

Rule over them?

"Yeah. You, I know," Fastlane says. "Maybe we can avoid what happened last time?"

"This reality isn't as far gone. There's still plenty to work with, and it'll be simple as pie."

Rule the world? What the hell? This can't be real. But if it is? If they really do plan on doing that, who's going to stop them? Who you gonna call? Na-uh. Not them. They ain't real.

Then Eaglestar hears me with that stupid hearin' of his. I hightail it out of there through a vent, and for a second, I think he's gonna destroy Guild Hall by comin' straight through the wall after me. But I guess he's worried about how it'll look if he started tearing down, so he just goes around instead. That gives me a chance to shrink down even smaller—small as I can get, about the size of a gnat. That's my limit, give or take. I don't push it. I'm able to get outside, and now my buzzing is blending in with the sounds of the city, hopefully making it harder for him to find me.

I don't know what I'm supposed to do. I gotta get this info to someone, but who? The list of who might be able to do something and stop the most powerful people in the world... that's a small list. Real small.

ZZZAAAAKKK!

I duck. Swear. Swear again.

Yeah, that's Eaglestar again. His laser eye thing. Almost cooked my goose. In case you're not too quick on the uptake, that means I'm found.

Time's almost up, Mack, better get your act together.

I try flying inside of buildings, but he's too fast, even when he's not at his most reckless. It's obvious he's still puttin' on a show in public. Must be part of the plan.

I think I lost him. At least for a few seconds. Maybe if I try running on the sidewalk, he won't notice me, since he's listening for my trademark buzzing sound. Looks like it's working.

There goes my swearing again. It's about all I can do while watching a giant boot coming down on me at super-speed.

SCIONS

RAPTORS BOOK 3

For Caleb and Silas.
—J.C.

To my friend Danny Grossman, *who read everything I ever wrote and always encouraged me. Rest in peace, Danny.*
—CJV

Together, *we dedicate this series to Mr. Stan Lee, without whom none of us would even know what a superhero was.*
—J.C. & CJV

PROLOGUE

EAGLESTAR

Sunshine and Roses.

Let's start with the first one. It's supposed to be raining at these shindigs. Whipping, piercing sideways rain, or even an annoying little drizzle—just enough to know that whatever god is up there, he or she is laughing at the mortality of these foolish skin-sacks.

But then again, let's not mess around. There's no god. I'm the closest thing you'll ever meet. There's no benevolent, all-knowing-anything floating around in clouds, surrounded by fat little babies playing harps. No afterlife awaiting those who've lived good and peaceful lives. For humans like you, there's nothing but darkness after this pathetic existence. For me? Well, I don't have to worry about that now, do I?

But today?

Sunshine.

Bright.

Cheerful.

Blinding.

And yes, I am affected by that. Perhaps more than any. Not only were my eyes transformed into laser weapons, but they are far more sensitive after the accident. For those of you who have been under the proverbial rock or just too stupid to remember, I was a hero before I was a hero. The best. Always, even before I decided to kamikaze into those Nazi bastards in the Second World War.

I lead the Guild of Masked Crimefighters now, but I led the best of the damn best back then. We were called the Capital Guardians. And those boys could fly. Unfortunately, Hitler's men flew a little better that day. Shot 'em all down. All but me. And when I ran out of bullets, I used my bird as a weapon.

All I knew was that it was a vital mission to be accomplished at all costs. What no one told me was what was onboard that Nazi airship I drilled myself into. No one thought to mention the alien artifacts. The next thing I remember, I was waking up in a hospital bed in Allied territory, biting down on—and crushing—a piece of titanium between my teeth as I thrashed around on a cold, metal operating table.

I am immortal. Or at least nothing has been able to kill me yet. But it was the crash that did it. Then, the whole world believed me dead—a pile of ash. But like the god so many worship… I rose from death into glorious light.

And I gained powers. Lots of them. All of them and then some, really. Fastlane is fast. I'm faster. Omar is strong. I'm stronger. Harrier is smart. I'm smarter. My hearing is beyond superb. And my eyes… I've got both trained on them. Over there. Across the grounds. Not just the worthless mortals gathered here at the funeral—the core Guild members who are supposedly on my side. I don't trust them, and I know they don't trust me. They shouldn't. I could focus my laser vision and turn them into molten slag… but I won't.

These people. My friends. Look at them all, pretending to be sad he's dead. The casket is empty. Of course it is. I crushed that little speck into a fine dust.

Firefly. What an uninspired name. He doesn't—didn't—glow. There was no luminescent goo on the bottom of my boot when I was through with him. He is as worthless in death as he was in life. On my world, he's called Murder Hornet. Now that's a name.

A gentle wind blows, causing the spring flowers to cascade from on high upon the grass and dirt. Little flecks of color amongst a sea of black.

That brings me to the Roses.

Pink, white, red, long, short, real, fake. They're everywhere. And they're the perfect representation of humanity. The moment they spring up from the ground, they begin the slow process of death. Sure, they look beautiful for a while—some of them, at least—but eventually, they wither and die.

Just. Like. You.

And you know what's worse? People bemoan the death of loved ones. Some of them, even for a long time… relative to their short lifespans. There is one truth I've read from religious texts. I believe it goes something like this: Life is like a vapor. Here one moment and gone the next.

In the end, the vast majority of people are forgotten forever. Nobody truly cares. Even the famous ones. Who really knows anything about Alexander the Great? Cleopatra? Napoleon? Moses?

Just names and vague stories.

People and names from my day have been forgotten, and facts have been twisted. Everything you learned about my World War was poppycock at best. No matter which reality you belong to. History is written by the victor. History is rewritten by the next victor. And on and on it goes until the account set before you looks not one iota like truth.

Then, there's this little piece of carbon known as Firefly. Nobody really wants to be here at his funeral. Nobody cared about him when he was alive; why should they start now? He was nosey, annoying, full of himself, and unlike me, without reason.

All these crocodile tears over a guy they barely knew.

Everyone dressed in black.

So solemn.

So fake.

Like so many roses.

I admit, I don't know that the guy is dead, and I think Bastet suspects something. Bastet… there's another one. Does anyone even know who she is named for?

Some Egyptian goddess from eons past. One that didn't even exist in some timelines.

And in ones like this?

Even gods are forgotten.

She keeps looking over at me and literally raising an eyebrow. My explanation for why there's no body—stomping on him at super-speed had obliterated him, turned him into a tiny smudge—is perfectly reasonable, even if I'm not positive it's true. How could I know if that was even him? It's not like microscopic vision is one of my many powers.

Microscopic vision. Ridiculous.

The problem is, I don't need any dissent within the ranks right now. Not ever, but especially not now. Our plan is complicated enough. We don't have all the artifacts here as we did in our world. We must find them. We have plenty to fret over, trying to keep the non-core and ancillary Guild members in the dark. Supers like Redhawk over there with his twerp of a sidekick, Harrier's little boy-toy. They're both giving me strange looks, too. Who does Frank think he's fooling with that cover story about taking on these protégés all the time? Oh, he's helping and protecting them? Yeah…

The Harrier in my universe…

Oh, yes. I nearly forgot. Listen closely. This is important. I don't belong here. None of us do. And I don't mean that in existentialistic terms, either. Our Earth died—me and the rest of the Guild. It was fiery. Brutal. And we, the only true gods, escaped.

We are here to make things right. Perfect. Keep the cattle from breaking down the fence, so to speak.

But Harrier, and Redhawk, and Kite. The girl—Osprey, is it? Who can keep track? All those Raptors. They are all wildcards.

The Harrier where I'm from didn't try to pretend there was anything innocent about his relationships. Those little red monsters were distractions. He'd send them in ahead to scope out the situation and draw fire. Hopefully, if they survived, they'd help him clean up whatever was left.

Oh, wait, you thought I meant something else? Of course, you did. Who knows… maybe that, too. Harrier was even more secretive over there than he is here.

Maybe that's why the last Kite killed him and took his place. Which screwed up our plan to take over our world since it was left a wasteland with nothing left to rule. Talk about a mean little bastard: Sawyer William Vincent.

I wonder what he's thinking over there. Probably plotting the destruction of this whole planet.

Yes, yes… I know he's not the same as the one I'd known, but that kid scares me. And very little scares me. Here, I'll have to keep my eye on him, perhaps take him out entirely.

Not the same… but how much of him is in this world's version?

Before I realize it, I'm floating toward them. Past mourners. Fakes. Liars.

Each of them is a colorful representation of humanity at large. Always out for their own good. Showing up here today? That made them look like they had souls. And don't for a second think many of them aren't here just to be on camera.

The news stations are everywhere with their big white vans and satellite dishes pointed toward the vast unknown. If they had any clue what really exists beyond the comfortable peace of the Milky Way, they'd treasure this planet. Their little squabbles amongst nations over oil and gold and land and gods and whatever other bullshit… it would all become so trivial to newly-enlightened eyes.

"Eaglestar," Redhawk says, dragging me from my reverie.

Of all the heroes in the Guild, I may hate this one the most. He's so brash. I ignore him.

The little Kite stares up at me. On my world, everyone knows better than to ever look me directly in the eye. I consider toasting him right here and now, but that wouldn't be an accurate portrayal of this Earth's Eaglestar… unfortunately. Soon enough, I can start being myself. But for now…

"Kite," I say instead, doing everything to hide my disdain.

"Actually, it's Raptor now, right? Alex said the Guild is pretty close to accepting my request for a name change."

"That so?" I eye them both, waiting for one of them to clue me in to this issue that couldn't matter any less to me.

"Right?" Sawyer says, looking to Redhawk this time.

Redhawk clears his throat and nods slowly. "That and giving me permission to finally relocate to New York and become the Black Harrier full time."

I try to hide a smirk, but I can't help it.

Now, we have to play politics. Franklin Douglas III decided to stop being the Black Harrier. Passed on the mantle to this… Alex Something… Redhawk.

Well, we couldn't just let that happen, could we? Different or not, we know Frank. We know how he'll respond, and we can use that.

So, I cock an eyebrow and say, "No."

The looks on their faces are priceless. I'd have let my world be destroyed just to see this, just for this moment. They think they are on my level. They believe themselves heroes. They don't realize how quickly and easily I could crush them like I did Firefly. No resistance would even matter on their part.

"I'm sorry?" Redhawk says.

"No need to apologize," I say.

"That's not what I meant."

"Oh?"

"You know what I mean."

"I must say, I don't," I tell him.

"No?" Little Sawyer says. "You can't just say 'No.'"

"I can and have." I turn to Redhawk, looking him in the eyes. "Let me ask you: What kind of Guild would we be if we allowed you to just abandon the great people of Boston because you found a better gig? What kind of person does that make you? What kind of hero?"

He just stares—incredulous, no doubt.

Like it or not, he'll stay there until our plan can be executed, force Frank to continue on in his newly handicapped state. It's just a cane, for crying out loud.

There's no time to deal with a new Harrier. Plus, where I come from, that Alex kid barely lasted a week. Pitiful. He's long dead. Killed as a teenager like most of the Kites over there. And no one even remembers him.

I've considered playing nice, trying to recruit him, play on his hatred for Harrier—but I don't know if that hatred has carried over to this Earth. Either way, he's so desperate to fit in. To be one of the big boys. Maybe we can use him? Otherwise… well. You know.

"Don't worry. I'll talk to Frank," Redhawk says to Sawyer William Vincent.

I don't even acknowledge them. Does a man worry if he steps on a beetle—or a firefly? I have to be careful not to laugh out loud. The whole thing is so tedious. I'd love to just crush all of their skulls and be done with it. The thought alone…

"And now," says a voice from behind me. "I'd like to invite Eaglestar, the world's greatest hero, to share a few words—"

Great, they want me to say something?

A sharp laugh interrupts my thoughts, and peer over my shoulder to see a bald-headed man dressed in a suit worth enough to feed a small country for a week. He shakes his head. Paul Steele—even in this reality, he's a pest.

The Baron… like that title means anything today. Especially in America.

"Eaglestar?" the priest says, waving from behind Firefly's tombstone.

"You'll excuse me, I'm sure," I say, turning away from the Raptors.

I have the wherewithal to stop floating. I've noted that people don't like to be reminded of how much better I am than they. Dry grass crunches under my heavy boots. I consider how many worthless bugs must be dying beneath them.

The tombstone…

Marion "Mac" MacGregor

Beloved Husband and Hero

Guess we stop caring about secret identities posthumously. Then again, Mac never was one to hide who he was. Proud of every square inch of raw, unrefined—

"Thank you all for being here today," I find myself saying, placing a hand on the grave marker, which looks like a toy next to me. Affecting a melancholy look, I let my fingertips caress the gray stone, then clear my throat. With the skills of a well-trained actor, my voice slips into a comforting lilt. "Ladies. Gentlemen. Friends."

Bile rises in my throat.

"What can I say about Mac that hasn't already been said?"

A whole lot, but nothing these peasants would want to hear.

"For five decades, he dedicated his life to being what most people only dream of: a hero."

A fool. An idiot. A schmuck.

"His unwavering moral compass pushed him to always do the right thing."

Which is why he had to be taken down. Removed from the equation.

"He died doing what he loved, and it's my hope that he'll always be remembered as one of the longest-serving members of the Guild of Masked Crimefighters."

Because he certainly wasn't one of the best.

"Whoever did this… Whoever is responsible for taking my friend Mac away from me. Away from us. They are going to pay and pay big."

I'm really selling this, aren't I?

"This one's for you, Big Mac." I look up into the sky, knowing he's not really up there, but still smashed into the sole of my boot. Everyone does their best version of a funeral laugh at that one. Chuckles and snivels.

I nod to the seven Marines standing off to the side, and they each fire their rifles into the air three times in unison. Two more remove the American flag draped over his coffin. So weird to see that rag which only exists in history books where I come from. The symbol of freedom… thirteen stripes and a smattering of stars. This country will be the first to experience what it truly means to serve.

One Marine carries the folded flag to Firefly's widow, a woman who appears every bit the octogenarian she is, as Mac should have. I've known her—a version of her, anyway—for over four decades and never bothered to learn her name. But he'd had a similar, if not entirely weaker version of my powers. After gaining his abilities, he'd never aged. Not a day.

In my estimation, that woman was yet another sign of his weakness. Marriage. Such a nonsensical creation. Though it must've been weird for him to watch his wife age all these years while he still looked so young, that was his own damn choosing.

Such a disappointment.

A Vietnam vet still in fighting shape well into the twenty-first century, and he'd wasted it on an old hag. He got what he deserved in the end.

It was a good run, though. I'll give him that. But then, he overheard us planning and plotting. No, he didn't know what had truly happened that day when the rift reopened and we were spat out. No one did except those of us directly involved, and of course, the Weisswulf of this reality. But Mac heard enough.

And if he isn't really dead, he damn well better not let me find out about it.

ONE
SAWYER

My Raptor Sense is tingling.

Just kidding. That's not really a thing, obviously. I was just seeing if you were paying attention. But everything is definitely off, and I don't need any super sense powers to tell me that.

Javier and I are on our way to school. He's been walking with me daily, which means my skateboard has become little more than an accessory I hold at my side. I do my best not to resent him for it. He's a good kid and part of the Resistors, even if just a sideliner.

He goes by Cricket, in case you forgot. He's got, like, no powers, but he can scream really loud? I guess? He hasn't had much of a chance to get out and use it, but it's a sonic scream that's enhanced by some technology. At first, he just wore one of those awful toy microphone speakers around his neck. Knowing what I do about his family, it was probably something that belonged to one of his numerous younger siblings. Then Frank got him something that was actually designed specifically for him. I'm sure it's good for something—his scream—but I can't help but feel bad for him, surrounded by so many of us with real powers.

My power? Boy, you sure are forgetful, aren't you? I can replicate anything I see. Yes. Absolutely anything. Would you like that delectable treat you saw Gordon Ramsay make on the Food Network? DVR that mama jama and let me watch it. As long as you've got the ingredients on hand, I can whip it up in no time. And you haven't tasted scrambled eggs until you have mine cooked the Ramsay way, I promise.

Not impressed? Last night, I watched an old video of Tony Hawk—you know, the GOAT when it comes to skateboarding. I can now do every move I saw him perform on that X-Games footage without even practicing.

I could be so rich if I exploited my powers for stuff like sports or whatever. But then again, I sort of am rich. Still getting used to it, but my dad is Franklin

Douglas III. Last time we checked, he's the third richest man in the world and way more famous than the two guys ahead of him.

He's also the Black Harrier—or was until Alex took over.

You caught up yet? Good. Back to today.

"You should get a board," I tell Javier. Pretty sure I knew what the answer would be before I said it, but what the heck. Worth a shot.

He eyes me like I'd just told him his hair was on fire. "What? Me? No way. I'm not that coordinated." He laughs, soft.

Poor kid. I'm sure I'll break down and buy him one soon. Even though his mom will probably take it away, tell him it's too dangerous for her little schnookums. She's definitely a helicopter parent. Or, what do they call the ones who are even worse? A bulldozer? Definitely a smother. Honestly, I'm shocked she lets him walk to school.

Then again, these days, there's literally nothing to fear on the streets. Crime is down almost 100%, thanks to the drones. Oh, here comes one now.

"Wave for the camera," I say.

Javier looks up at it as it zooms by about a hundred feet above us and waves. I do, too, but with only one finger, and it isn't my thumb.

Guild-operated, not produced by Douglas Industries—which I'm sure to Frank is both a compliment and an insult—the things are spherical with little blinking lights around the diameter, red when the omnidirectional cameras are on and... well, I don't know what they are otherwise.

The cameras are always on.

It's not just cameras, though. Those things are equipped with some real firepower. I'm not sure they've ever had to use any of it since their real purpose is just to warn the Guild that someone is committing a crime, but I'm sure what's housed inside could level a building. If it reports a crime, twenty seconds later, Fastlane shows up, and they never even know what hits them. He just appears and then disappears along with the criminal, carts them off to jail.

It's not always Fastlane, I'm sure. Especially not in other cities—but here, he makes the most sense.

And I guess I exaggerated a little. There's still crime since there'll always be someone stupid enough to think the rules don't apply to them, or they've found a way to beat the system or whatever. But that's the reality we're living in now. Drones overhead, watching our every move. Nobody fighting. Nobody committing crimes. Who would've thought I'd ever complain about there not being any crime?

When we first heard the Guild had returned from... wherever they went, everyone—except maybe supervillains—cheered. We figured it was cause to celebrate. That lasted about ten seconds. Because, then, they held a press conference where they basically told everyone they were taking charge.

What does "taking charge" mean, exactly? Now that we're months into it, let me paint a picture for you.

Imagine your least favorite class from school. The one you hate showing up to because you can't stand the teacher—and maybe the feeling is mutual, even though they can't admit it. You hate the subject, and you're miserable the entire period, every day, every second. None of your friends are there, and even if they are, you can't hang with them.

Seating chart.

Alphabetical order.

You aren't allowed to do anything fun. You just sit and do your work. No talking. No bathroom breaks. No moving at all. Just book work and worksheets. Or workbooks. Whatever, you get what I mean.

Now imagine that the class has several teachers, and those teachers have superpowers. In fact, they're the most powerful people on the planet. And the class lasts 24/7.

Is your gut clenched yet? Do you have that feeling of overwhelming panic? Good. Because that's all of us now, all the time.

Javier looks a bit more depressed than usual this morning. It would be hard for most people to be able to tell, but I've hung out with him nearly every day for a few years now, so…

"Something wrong?" I ask him, knowing I'm probably opening a can of worms I'm unprepared to handle.

What does that mean, anyway? Why a can of worms? Who is worried about worms flopping around? Better yet, why does anyone have worms in a can in the first place?

"I'm having a problem," he says before I get lost in the thought.

"I'm all ears."

Rookie move, Sawyer.

He looks around to make sure nobody is listening, then speaks in a low voice. Here we go…

"I miss being a superhero."

Oh, wow. That's it? I expected far worse, like he'd found little hairs in weird places on his body and isn't sure how to process it. Or… birds and the bees stuff. I'm sure him parents haven't told him anything. Oh, God, it's gonna be up to me some day, isn't it? Gotta get that thought out of my head, pronto.

"You are a superhero," I reply in a low voice as well.

"Yeah," he shrugs. "But I don't get to do anything."

"None of us do," I tell him.

Honestly, I have to agree. The whole thing blows. Some kids have soccer or violin or debate club—we had—past tense—kicking bad guys' asses.

"Sure you do. You train with the Resistors." I try to make it sound exciting, but it's a total fail. It's not like he isn't there to see how boring it is.

"I know. But I thought I was going to be able to fight bad guys and stuff."

So… Javi started masked crimefighting just before all hell broke loose. Well, that's not really a fair analogy, because it's more like heaven broke loose without any crime or people to beat down. But I get it. He was so excited to be a part of something. All those things I mentioned other kids doing? You know, sports, music, all that—Javier had none of it.

I look at him, and he seems like he's terrified or something.

"No offense, Sawyer."

"What? Offense? For what?"

"Well, you and Amy… you went out of your way to let me join, and now I sound ungrateful. Like I'm complaining."

"You're just saying what we're all thinking." I smile for the first time all day.

"I'm sure your day will come. We're just in a weird time right now. It'll pass." Then after a long pause, I add, "Eventually."

"Right," he says almost as convinced as I am, which I know is very little.

Our school appears on the horizon. It's a nice place for a prison. A few trees still have their leaves and the flowers out front haven't completely died yet. As we approach, I scan for the usual suspects. Convinced the coast is clear, we cross the school grounds, climb the same nine steps we always do, and throw open the doors.

Javier goes in ahead of me and we're met by the same strangeness as all over the city and probably the whole world. Everyone is quiet. Subdued. The students walk around like zombies, and not just the ones who usually look that way. The teachers are even worse. You'd think they'd be happy the students are behaving so well, but I guess it's sort of the same thing I'm going through with not being able to fight any criminals. It's boring. Sooooooo boring.

Even Logan—you remember Logan? King Kong, but even dumber? Yeah, he's been acting like he's afraid to do anything. I didn't even realize how much I appreciate his bullcrap antics. In a really weird way, it's sort of a form of entertainment. Though, his current mood might have more to do with the fact that I kicked his butt and then threatened him by making him think he was gonna fall off a tall building.

Several times. And I think he crapped his pants.

I also might've given him a clue that I'm actually Red Raptor.

I think he's too stupid to put two and two together, but even if he does somehow get to four, I don't think he has the balls enough to tell anyone after what Red Raptor did to him last fall.

It was kind of mean of me and I probably shouldn't have done it, being a hero and all. But the guy had to finally learn his lesson. Sorry, not sorry. He'd gone from a school bully to a criminal, robbing Big Frankie Junior's, to a minor supervillain in a scary short amount of time. Imagine what he'd end up like if someone hadn't stopped that path? At least I didn't have him arrested. That would've ruined his life.

Oh, and yeah… I don't work at the burger place anymore. Thank God. For the past few months, I've been interning with Mr. Chen at Douglas Industries. Dude, the stuff he's working on is seriously mind-blowing. Change-the-world type stuff.

But I can't help feeling like everything has become just one dull, boring, same old routine, day after day.

Maybe it's time to add some excitement. Maybe as a bonus, it'll cheer Javier up some, too.

"Hey, Javi, wanna see a new trick I learned on my board?"

He doesn't respond, and when I turn to him, I notice why. He's gawking up at Fabiola—the most gorgeous girl in our school, but also the most stuck-up and bitchy. Right now, however, none of that matters since she's up on a ladder, wearing her cheerleading uniform, stapling a giant banner to the wall that says: GET SOME PEP IN YOUR STEP THIS FRIDAY.

Things suck so bad around here that I actually find myself excited that there's something different. A pep rally? Not exactly taking down Deadeye on the top of One World Trade Center, but at least it'll break up the monotony.

"Keep it in your pants, dork," says one of the girls holding the ladder, sneering at Javier like he's got a booger hanging out of his nose.

I check.

He doesn't.

I'm tempted to make sure something else embarrassing isn't going on down below, but that's above my pay grade. I'm just gonna assume she was exaggerating and leave it at that.

Just like Fabiola, this girl is smoking hot, but her attitude just makes her so gross. I think her name is Shellye. Pronounced like Shelly but spelled Shell-Ye.

I just can't…

Sidenote: How are those cheerleader uniforms still a thing? They have dress codes that don't allow students to wear sleeveless shirts and short shorts and skirts normally. So how come it's okay to dress up a bunch of pretty girls in the shortest of skirts, then have them jump up and down in them and stand on each other's shoulders? Why is that okay? Why am I complaining?

The answer? Sports. Yeah! Let's get the football players' testosterone raging so they can take it out on the other team.

It seems like that's always the answer to why exceptions are made around here.

I slap Javier with the back of my hand to get his attention. "C'mon. Forget her, man," I say. "I just learned some new tricks. Wanna see?"

He looks around nervously. That's kind of his thing. "Here? Inside the school?"

"Sure. I'm tired of always being the good kid who never does anything wrong."

What? It's been like two years since I've even gotten talked to at school.

"But you'll get in trouble!" His voice squeaks, and for a second I think his Cricket scream might slip out.

"What's the worst that can happen? This place needs a little lightening up."

"But, Sawyer—"

I don't give him a chance to finish as I hand him my backpack, throw my board down, and push off through the silent hall. I gain speed as I swerve between the students. They all look at me like I belong in a mental ward, their eyes wide with shock.

"Watch it!" shouts some guy I don't know, like he's an extra in a movie with one silly line.

Not sure what has me feeling so brave. Maybe because, unlike everyone else, I actually know Eaglestar and the Guild? They're not just some ominous, out-of-reach force to me. They may have changed a lot since coming back from wherever, but they're still the Guild. And I'm still Red Raptor. And, technically, I'm an ancillary member—well, almost. When I turn eighteen in a few days, I'll be one.

It's not like Eaglestar is gonna choke me to death or something.

Lockers blur by as I head for the switchback staircase that leads to the school's lower level. I crouch, prepared to jump onto the railing and nose grind it down, but just as I get close and kick up on my board, someone suddenly appears from the adjoining hallway. It's freaking Logan Andrews. I barely even have time to scream a warning—and it doesn't matter anyway because he's got earbuds in, staring down at his phone. He's completely oblivious to the fact that I'm flying toward him like a bat out of hell.

We collide with a loud crash. My board spins and smacks into the railing and I bodyslam Logan to the ground like I'm an accidental WWE superstar. His phone shatters against his hand as he unconsciously tries to brace his fall.

I conk my head on the floor, but it seems like I'm okay even though it hurts. I flash back to the billion times Mom told me to wear a helmet when I skate. If something's wrong, she's gonna kill me. So nothing's wrong.

I'll keep telling myself that. I scramble to get back to my feet and help him up. But I'm definitely staggering.

"Crap! I'm sorry, I didn't—"

He screams.

At first, I assume it's his usual rage and anger, like he's pissed at me for being so reckless. But then I realize it's not. It's pain, as well as horror. His hand is sliced up from his broken phone and his nose is bleeding, probably broken, too. In fact, the whole place is covered in red and looks like a scene out of a nineties slasher film.

"That's an expensive phone," someone says behind me.

Kids these days have jacked up priorities.

"He must have insurance on something that nice, right?" asks another concerned onlooker.

"I hope he backed everything up," someone else chimes in.

Seriously?

I turn to say something like that, when I see what appears to be the entire student population of the school now standing in a half-circle around us. Some students just look shocked, while others glare at me like I'm an axe murderer. I sway a little and my head starts swimming, and I realize I might actually have a concussion. Even so, I still offer my hand to Logan to help him up.

I'm a little relieved when he doesn't take it. What? I don't want his blood all over me. He backs away like I'm about to hurt him some more. I think I see tears in his eyes. Poor bully baby.

"I—I didn't even do anything this time," he says, sort of stuttering.

A couple of teachers push through the crowd of student onlookers and start tending to Logan and asking if he's okay. Everything around me starts to have a dreamlike quality to it, and I feel like I might fall. But campus security rushes in, and one of them grabs me.

At first I think he's just helping me from collapsing, but then, I realize he has one hand on the back of my shirt collar as he twists my arm behind my back with the other.

"What the fu—"

"Can it!" he shouts.

Can it? What is this guy, eighty? Next, he'll tell me to stop doing the jitterbug and twenty-three skidoo.

He shoves me forward, obviously not caring in the slightest that I've been injured in the collision also and may even have a concussion. Did I already say that? I may be repeating myself.

Because I have a concussion.

"I'll get your board!" Javi shouts like that's even remotely on my mind.

The high-school-dropout-turned-campus-security-guard leads me down the hallway and I immediately know where we're going: Principal Blanchard's office.

Well, to be fair, I did say I wanted some excitement…

TWO
FRANK

Something is… wrong.

And I don't just mean the Guild taking so much control over everything, either. There is something much more sinister grinding the gears and I am afraid I must be the one to get the machine functioning again.

Eaglestar's lofty words that he and the others are doing all of this for the good of Earth and humanity because going to that other place—whatever that may have been—had changed them, opened their eyes to truth… I am not buying it. And I am Franklin Douglas III—I can buy anything.

It's more than simply believing his words are hollow. I can feel it. Taste the lies.

I know a thing or two about eye-opening experiences. My time spent under the care of Chef Maléfique has absolutely changed me. I would never speak aloud all the many horrors it inflicted not just upon my body, but my psyche as well. But when I retired from being the Black Harrier, I meant it. No more running around in that armored uniform, gliding from rooftops and assaulting criminals. Besides, the Guild—of which I am apparently no longer actively a part—has all but put an end to criminal behavior. Though I suspect it will be like a blocked sewer pipe building up with heinous sludge until there's no way to hold it back any longer.

Chaos will erupt sooner or later. Fecal matter will stain the streets. Those are words you can bank upon. Money isn't the only thing I'm an expert on.

However, regardless of whether or not I don the cape and mask, there's a mystery here needing solving, and I do not believe Sawyer is ready to do it. Not yet.

And Alex—he might be ready, but I'm not entirely sure he is willing. He seems to be convinced that he can truly be part of the core team of the Guild. Maybe not convinced, but certainly desperate. Perhaps I can use that to my advantage. Do I still have his loyalty?

As I sit at my command and control center in the Aerie, taking command and control, I breathe deeply, knowing what needs to be done, but not even sure I'm fully prepared to do it. I've avoided confronting this situation for months, seeing how far things would go, waiting to see if someone else would step up.

So far, every other major crimefighter in the country—the world—seems content to just sit back and let the Guild do everything for them.

I suppose if you want something done right…

I punch a few numbers into my videophone.

It rings twice, as it always does.

This man will never answer on the first ring. He will never let his phone go to voicemail. He always answers precisely between the second and third ring. Not too soon to appear as if he's not busy but not too long to appear too busy to take a call. He's a businessman through and through.

"Paul Steele, here," he says as he answers in video mode.

He's walking on the street, buildings bouncing along behind him, taxi cabs whizzing by. He still hasn't looked at his screen.

"Baron," I say, using his title as a sign of respect. Let that be a lesson—a bit of respect has never hurt a soul. It can be the difference between getting a taste of honey and getting stung. You may want to write that down.

Although, technically, as a baron in the British aristocracy, the proper way to address him would be "Lord."

I'm not going to do that. I do have my limits.

"Frankie, is that you?" he says. If he would bother to look at his screen, he would know it was.

"It's me," I say. "We have some things to talk about."

"Whatever do you mean?" he says with no small hint of sarcasm dripping from his British tongue.

"Can we meet up?"

"Always have time for you," he tells me. "Especially since you're the only one of the Guild who hasn't lost the plot completely."

"Well then, clearly you understand. Shall I swing by around six?"

"How about we meet for a bite. You own that little French place in the Tower, right?"

I almost roll my eyes before I consider he can see me if he cares to. Well, I'll be damned if Sawyer isn't beginning to rub off on me a little.

"You know I do."

"Well, I've always been told there's no such thing as a free lunch, but I've never heard the same said about dinner. Six o'clock at Le Meilleur Plat. Sounds wonderful. Okay, Frankie, I've gotta go. Just got to the coffee place and if they get my order wrong one more time, I might lose it."

"Try not to," I tell him. "See you at si—"

He's already hung up before I can finish the sentence.

Paul Steele is the only person on Earth who can call me Frankie and get away with it. That's what they called my father, and I have no interest in being so closely tied to that man—not after what he did to this city. Then again, without him, I don't know if I'd ever have become the crimefighter that I am—was. I wouldn't have Megan, Sawyer… I might not have amassed the wealth I have.

No, that part had nothing to do with crimefighting. Being a hero comes free to the citizens of New York. But like the Baron said in slightly different words:

nothing is ever free. To accentuate that point, I grab hold of my cane and rise, needing to work out some kinks after sitting for so long.

My nocturnal activities had started out as a bit of a release. Rage, anger, grief—a million different emotions, all filtered through the fists of a young man who needed new direction almost as much as he needed to find a way of recovering from the knowledge that his father had ruled New York with a dirty, iron fist.

I'm his legacy, like it or lump it. I'm determined to take what he left to me and use it for the good of New York and the world.

I stand and bend a few times, touching as close to my toes as my hips will allow. Then, straightening my back, I twist side to side and roll my neck. I hear a few cracks, but nothing too damning.

Sitting once more, I dial up the Guild Hall on the comm system—Eaglestar's direct number, in fact. He answers on the first ring as if he doesn't know who's calling. I find the whole "stuck in the 1940s along with the rest of the 'Greatest Generation'" act he puts on to be tedious at best, and leaning more toward intolerable.

He knows how caller ID works.

"Eaglestar here," he answers in his baritone voice as his face appears on the screen. I've always wondered if his voice was like that before he had powers, or if it was a side effect. I know Sawyer thinks the voice changer I used as Black Harrier sounds ridiculous, but at least I didn't sound like Ted Knight on the old *Mary Tyler Moore Show*. No, I'm not quite that old, but even a family as rich as ours watched *Nick at Nite* occasionally.

Are you a bit lost? Google it when you have time. It will be good for you to get some culture.

"Jonathan. It's Frank," I say as I sit again, not grunting even though I want to. In the same way that I give preference to Paul by using his title, I choose not to with Eaglestar. Paul might be arrogant, but I've never once questioned where he stood. Even when his license had been revoked, I was not one of the voices calling for it. Now, I don't think he'd come back if Eaglestar begged from his knees.

The Baron's replacement as the team's "tank"—Omar the Defenestrator—may not be arrogant, but he's as dull and dim-witted as they come. The ultimate stereotype for the part.

I call Eaglestar "Jonathan" to get to him. He absolutely hates it. There's no secret identity there—hasn't been one for decades. When you are damn near indestructible and have no loved ones, there's just no need to keep things secretive, I suppose. And Jonathan has no loved ones. None. If he ever did, they've been dead for decades.

For some reason he seems somewhat taken aback by my call, and it doesn't appear to be due to the use of his birth name.

Eaglestar is off his game.

"Frank? Frank Douglas, is it really you?"

"I—uh."

That's strange. I don't think it possible for his skin to pale, but the tone of his voice gives me the impression it's like he's receiving a call from beyond the grave. Not the reaction I was expecting. Not at all.

"Yes. It's really me."

His expression shifts. "Ah, yes, right."

I don't know what that means, but I let it go and continue. "I know this is way overdue, but I wanted to check in, and also apologize for not making it to Mac's funeral. I didn't feel like it would make sense for Franklin Douglas III to show up, and I couldn't think of a good excuse to show my face."

"Why would I care if you were at Firefly's funeral? It's not like either of us ever saw eye to eye with him."

More questionable talk. I take another small mental note. Mac and I were never exactly friends, but we rarely disagreed or argued about anything.

"Well, it wasn't that bad. Except for that mission in Quebec City. That was a mess I will not soon forget." I fake laugh about it to see his reaction.

"Yes, Quebec City. A real disaster." He doesn't laugh along with me. Not even a fake laugh, or a smile.

By the way, we never had a mission together in Quebec City.

"Is that why you called?" he says. "To apologize for missing a nobody's funeral?"

That's harsh, even for Eaglestar. I decide to let that go as well. Something is very wrong here and in light of everything else, that's a minor infraction.

"Not exactly. I also wanted to talk to you about Alex."

He scoffs. Doesn't even attempt to hide it. "What about him? Your little Redwing. I haven't been impressed, to say the least."

"Redhawk," I correct.

"Whatever."

"You should give him a chance. I think he could be very useful to you." More like useful to me. To help me figure out what the hell is going on over there. And Alex will finally get what he wants most as well. Sort of a win-win-win situation. "The Guild isn't the same without a Black Harrier."

"I don't know…"

"And I found the perfect replacement for him in Boston. A guy called Swamp Rabbit."

"Swamp… Rabbit?" Eaglestar looks like he just took a bite out of an apple and felt half a worm squirming around in his mouth.

"Yes. He's a little rough around the edges, but he's ready for a second-tier city. I was very impressed with the way he handled himself in Times Square. You won't be sor—"

"Times Square?" he cuts in. "What happened in Times Square?"

That response is so shocking that I have to take a few seconds to compose myself before I reply. "The incident where you were sucked through a rip in the space-time continuum. Surely you remember something so… life-altering."

I choose my words carefully, always.

"Oh, yes. Yes, of course."

In the background, I see a figure appear. The woman is gorgeous with dark skin and laden with heavy gold jewelry. Her raven black hair falls straight as an arrow on each side down to her very ample breasts, but her bangs are cut sharply above her eyebrows. Bastet is one of the best of the best. If anyone could bring some semblance of normalcy to this conversation, it would be her.

"Frank?" Her surprise is even more intense than Eaglestar's was.

So much for that idea.

"Hello, Vanessa. You look positively radiant."

"Yes," she says absently.

"It's been a while," I continue.

Her bright blue eyes shift ever-so-slightly toward Eaglestar, but I notice.

"Yes, it has," she says with just the minutest of lilts at the end of the sentence, as if she isn't quite sure.

"We really should catch up. Perhaps we can go out to dinner at our favorite spot."

"Perhaps." A lot of hesitation there.

I snap my fingers. "Damn, what was the name of that place again? Gosh, it's been so long I can't remember."

She narrows her eyes at me. "I don't—"

"You know, that little Ethiopian restaurant with the little fountain in the middle? It's on the tip of my tongue."

"I'm sorry. I don't remember the name."

"But you know the place I mean, right? We must've eaten there a dozen times at least."

"Yes," she says, with no expression whatsoever. "At least."

"Oh, well. I'm sure it will come to me."

"I'm sure it will." She's downright exasperated. Can't wait to get off the phone. "Take care."

She walks away and leaves me with Eaglestar once more.

"Jonathan, just promise me you'll think about Alex. At least just—"

An alarm sounds on their end, red light flashing.

"I have to go," Eaglestar says.

"Oh, right. Well, it's been great. We've got to keep in touch more often—"

Eaglestar cuts off the call without a goodbye.

If the strangeness of that conversation wasn't transparent enough…

Like I said, something's wrong.

I don't think it's that their memories were altered or scrambled. Their deception seems to be deliberate.

And I've never eaten Ethiopian food with Bastet. We always have Italian.

My perimeter alert goes off, telling me someone is at the front door of my penthouse. I look at the camera feed and see the most stunning redhead I've ever laid my eyes on. I've dated supermodels, actresses, senators, the creme de la creme, so to speak. None compares to this woman.

I'm not even sure she realizes it, but eighteen years ago, she stole my heart and never let it go. Megan Vincent—Sawyer's mother and the love of my life. She knocks a couple of times.

It's quite a ways from the secret entrance to the Aerie in my study to the front door, and with my cane, I'm certainly not putting any pressure on Fastlane in the "fastest man on earth" category. My physical therapists and doctors say I should be further along in my recovery by now, but I still have trouble getting around. What do they know about being tortured for weeks by an evil supervillain like Chef Maléfique? Anyone other than me would be dead.

When I open the door, she tries to hide her frustration at having to wait for so long, but I can still see it in those eyes of hers. They are like a field of sunflowers, bright green with specks of yellow floating around—motes of gold dust upon crushed velvet… I tend to get lost in those eyes like I never have before with anyone. They, above all her wonderful features, were what kept me up at night for nearly two decades.

"Hello?" she says as I realize I'm leaving her standing in the doorway.

"Oh, hi! Sorry, my mind is all over the place today." I kiss her and let her in.

"Did I interrupt something?" she asks.

"No, not at all. Why?"

"You took a while to get to the door, and you seem distracted."

"No, just… you know." I hold up the cane.

"You know, there's a way where you wouldn't have to rush to the door every time I come by." She leans in close to me. Very close.

"Oh? What's that?"

She whispers in her sexy voice. "You could give me a key."

Before I realize it, my own eyes have gone wide and the blood leaves my face. I'm sure I'm white as copy paper. And she definitely notices.

She hits me playfully on the chest. But probably a bit harder than she intended. "I'm kidding, Frank. Afraid of commitment much?"

I let out a sigh of relief that I probably should have kept to myself.

"Wow. I'm sorry I brought it up. You really hate the idea, don't you?"

Scratch that. I definitely should have kept it to myself.

"No, it's not that. Not at all," I reply, a little too emphatically. "It's just…"

I trail off, not sure how to finish the sentence. It's not as if I can tell her I have a secret crimefighter lair above the penthouse that I'm concerned she'll accidentally come across, or that I have superheroes zooming in and out at all hours, including her—our—son.

Now she really does seem upset. "It's fine. I understand."

It's fine. The one thing you never want to hear from your significant other. The one sure way to know for certain, without a doubt, that things are explicitly not fine.

"Please," I tell her, "I'm sorry. Come in. You want something to drink? Water? Tea? Wine?"

"It's noon, Frank," she says. But she smiles.

There was a time when offering Megan wine would have been a big mistake. She'd spent many years at the bottom of a bottle, but that woman doesn't exist anymore. I like to think I had something to do with that.

"It's five in London."

"We're not in London."

Something has been nagging at me for months now. That vortex that opened on Sidekick Day… I'd seen it before, long long ago. An ancient race of aliens called the Tuldarians had used something similar when they'd returned to Earth—I say returned because they were also here back in the '40s and the artifacts they'd left behind were responsible for Eaglestar's powers.

Seeing Jonathan and Vanessa acting so strangely has me thinking and I do my best thinking while on vacation.

"We could be," I say, a thought formulating in my mind.

"Yeah," she scoffs.

"No, really. Why don't we? Just you and me. I've got some business to handle in the UK anyway. I can handle business and we could take a trip to Scotland, where my family is from."

"I thought you said London?" she asks.

"Well, I own a castle in Scotland."

"A castle?"

"Several, actually."

"You have several castles in Scotland?" She laughs.

"Besides, we could both use some time away."

"I have work."

"I have money," I say, smiling.

"I can't just leave Sawyer," she says.

The gulf between who she thinks Sawyer is and who Sawyer really is could not be more vast. Times like this, I really wish she knew the reality of it.

"The kid will be eighteen in a matter of days. If he isn't old enough to care for himself by now..."

Megan's phone rings. She swears one of her not-really-a-swear-words and holds up a finger to me while she digs through her purse. Pulling out her phone, she taps the answer icon and puts it to her ear. "Hello. Yes?"

Her face turns flush and her expression says that she's hearing some bad news. Did someone die? On the bright side, I'm sure she's forgotten the conversation we were having about the damn key.

"Yes. I'm sorry. Believe me, I will. I'll be down there right away." She ends the call and lets out a huge sigh that I'm familiar with. Unlike mine, it's not a sigh of relief, believe me. It's part frustration and part trying to pull herself together so she doesn't explode. And it's almost always about...

"Sawyer! I'm going to kill him!" She looks like she's about to throw her phone across the room, then thinks better of it and shoves it back into her purse.

"What is it?" I ask as I rub her shoulders, trying to calm her down.

"He's in trouble at school again. I told him if I have to set foot in that principal's office one more time, I'm going to ship him off to a military academy."

"Hey, calm down, honey. I have an idea."

Do I ever...

THREE

AMY

The world is effed up.

I saw a movie once when I was a kid. My parents didn't know I was watching it. We had HBO or Cinemax, or one of those stations you used to have to pay like a billion dollars a month to have, and they were both asleep. I don't even remember the name of it, or who was in it or anything, but I remember a line they kept using.

"FUBAR."

That's FUBAR, Sir, a bunch of times before someone finally explained what it means. I'll let you look it up because I kiss my gran-gran with these lips, but FUBAR is exactly what this whole world has become.

Ever since the Guild had returned months ago, things haven't been the same. I could go into details, but instead, I'm just gonna repeat: The world is FUBAR, and leave it at that.

After everything I went through, trying to stay here in New York instead of moving to Bulgaria with my mom, my dad finding out I'm Osprey and making me some new equipment I couldn't wait to try out… now I have nothing to do. And I'm furious.

The Resistors went from the world's last hope to absolutely useless because the Guild decided to become fascist dictators.

On top of all this global bullcrap, on a micro-level? Pace and I are broken up again, probably for good. And after trying to get Alex to leave me alone for so long, he seems to have finally gotten the hint. Only now, I'm not so sure I made the right decision. If he's so wrong for me, why can't I stop thinking about him? Why do we keep going back to each other like Ross and Rachel?

Oh, come on. Everyone knows Ross and Rachel, right? I guess I'm just an old soul. Even heroes sometimes binge watch old shows.

I have a few hours between classes and I've been sitting outside MoonMoney for like twenty minutes with my finger over the "send" button on my Guild-issued personal communicator. It's basically just a phone but with some seriously heavy encryption. Having already swallowed my pride, my message stares back at me: Hey there, just checking in. Everything going ok?

Just checking in?

What am I, his kid?

Hey, mom. Just checking in. Is it okay if I stay out a little late?

Idiot. He's your ex.

Hey babe, how've you been?

Oh, my God. That's even worse.

I delete it, then retype. Delete. Retype.

Do I really want to do this?

I'm literally back at Just checking in.

I stare at it for what feels like a really long time, but it's realistically about ten seconds. Time can be strange that way. I was learning about it in my Psych class last week. Our perception of time isn't constant, it's dependent on…

Speaking of psychology, I'm getting sidetracked so I don't have to think about what text to send, aren't I? You can do this, Amy. It's not that big of a deal.

Even my coffee tastes more bitter than it should. I suck in a deep breath before pounding the send button. The waiting begins. I start making bets with myself in my head on how soon he'll text back. A minute? An hour?

I feel like I have the little devil and angel on my shoulders like in the old cartoons, one telling me one thing and the other saying the opposite. And I keep going back and forth over who to believe. The more cynical part of me is winning with "He never will."

There are some things in life you simply can't control, like whose family you're born into or what color skin, hair, or eyes you have. No matter how hard you try, you can't even control more mundane things like whether or not your plane is on time or if your favorite TV show gets another season.

Sitting out on the MoonMoney patio, I realize this is one of those things. No matter how much I will it. No matter how many bets I make with myself, I can't change whether or not Alex will look down at his comm and ignore the ping, or text back.

I'd like to say I check my phone every few minutes, but in actuality, my eyes never leave it. Before I know it, half an hour has passed.

He's probably busy.

Doing what, though? It's not like anyone's out there fighting crime. Then again, he's supposed to be a core member of the Guild now, so maybe he is? Or have they not done that yet?

I scroll through my emails—oh, look, Carter Anne's is having a sale on Boho dresses.

Eye roll.

MoonMoney knows I'm here apparently, because I have three emails from them encouraging me to use their Wi-Fi, collect MoonCoins toward free drinks, and inform me about this week's special, Candy Corn Delight.

Gross.

Some African Prince… I won a drawing… my extended car warranty…

I don't even have a car.

In other words, nothing important.

Bored, I even take a look at my social media feeds. After last year's clutch win by Neith and her HeroSpace profile, I reopened my account, thinking it might help. Now it's just another reminder of the disappointment that is my life. The only thing posted is the hourly reminder from the Guild that crimefighting is no longer necessary. There's a picture of one of their million little round drones which hover over every major city in America at all times. I can see two of them right now from where I'm sitting.

I decide to check my other accounts. Like, my civilian ones where I'm Amy Chen and not Osprey.

Well, that's another mistake. Sure enough, just as bad as always. A bunch of posts from various frat bros and sorority chicks at Columbia.

Who are these people? I thought I knew them, but I feel like once you get a good look inside their heads by seeing what they post… eww.

And the older adults I know are worse in some ways. Yes, we get it. You love your cat. He's so cute. And it's been several minutes since you posted a pic of him. Oh, you went to the gym? How wonderful. Look at those guns! Congratulations, here's your award. So that's what you cooked for dinner? Wow, I was in so much suspense waiting to find out. Training for another marathon, you say? Pleeeeeease, tell me more.

Misplaced aggression.

I didn't realize how much I'd start self-diagnosing once I started taking that class. Although, come to think of it, the professor did warn us about it on the first day.

Time for a better distraction. Let's dumb it down some.

I play a stupid new game I downloaded. Baker Bash. I hate these things. They're so addictive, and such a waste of time.

Speaking of time… How long has passed?

It's probably only been a few… nope. Time flies when you're wasting it on a stupid app. It's been an hour now. Still nothing. Should I be worried?

Ugh! Why am I being so ridiculous? I broke up with him. I told him to stop hounding me about getting back together. Of course he isn't gonna get back to me immediately.

But, then again, why not?

Because you broke his heart, Amy.

Oh, yeah.

But doesn't he still have feelings for me? I thought this was the kind of thing people did to keep the other person interested. Playing hard-to-get.

Ross. And. Rachel. They are like TV's golden couple!

Or is that just in shows? And movies? And books?

I stare at my stupid message again.

Just checking in.

So. Stupid.

Guuuh.

Back to the game.

Ninety minutes now. I watch all the people zipping by as I sip my bitter coffee which is now freezing cold too. At least none of these people look happy either. Everyone's sad nowadays. But are they sad because of relationship stuff, like I am? Probably not. They're probably all headed home to their wonderful significant others. They'll give them a big kiss and they'll ask each other how their day was, and then have a nice dinner. While I have takeout for one.

I hate them. I hate them all. Why can't they be depressed about their love lives like I am? Then we can all be sad together. For the same reason. And it won't be so lonely.

I find myself scrolling through another social app and gagging at all the couples kissing and holding hands and enjoying each other's company before finally closing it.

Two hours. Has it really been two hours? I have class soon.

Something has to be wrong. Alex wouldn't go this long without getting back to me unless there was an emergency or something. He even answers my phone calls in the middle of fights with criminals. At least he used to. It was so cute.

That was then.

This is now.

Should I call him? Is that too desperate? Maybe I'll just send a follow-up text—

Ding! My notification alert. I got a text! See? I was panicking for nothing.

It's from my cell phone carrier, telling me my bill is ready. Follow this link to view this month's billing statement. Yeah, thanks. Thanks a lot. If you really wanted to be helpful, you'd tell me why he hasn't answered my text.

I put my phone down. I'm not gonna think about it. *Ding!* Another text. That has to be him. Who else would be texting me?

Oh, hey, Dad.

He asks if I want to go to dinner. Okay, so it's not Alex, but it's definitely not as disappointing as getting a text from my cell phone carrier. I text him back, saying that yes, I'd love to have dinner with him tonight. At least it beats takeout for one.

It's funny. The two things I used to worry about most were my dad finding out that I'm Osprey and my parents getting a divorce. But now both of them have happened, and I'm closer to my dad than I've been my entire life. He's upgraded my equipment and makes sure I always have the latest version of everything I need for crimefighting—just in time for me not to have to do any crimefighting, but that's not his fault. And with Mom living in Europe now, Dad and I spend a lot more time together. Strange how things work out sometimes.

Now, I hardly worry about anything. Except Alex, apparently. I start typing him another message: Hey, is everyth—

I hear a bunch of screaming and look up from my phone. At first, I think someone's in trouble, but like I said… that doesn't really happen anymore.

There's a crowd growing by the MoonMoney front door. It's mostly girls… no, not really girls. Older women, like my mom's age.

In the middle of them, I can see a bald head poking up. Not really difficult, the guy has like a foot on them all, easily. Even the women with big ole eighties haircuts and Texas perms. I can't believe that hideous style is coming back.

"Ladies, ladies," says a British voice. "Give each other some room. Yes, yes, that's it. Now, listen, let me place an order and then I'll sign as many cups, hands, and—what's that? Yes, I'll sign those, too. Those are my favorite."

Gross.

I've met Baron Steele one other time: last year at the Sidekick Day celebration when the rift was opened and the Guild got sucked through. He seemed like a nice enough guy, and I never understood why he and Eaglestar had such bad blood, but now that I've seen Eaglestar's true colors, I have to say, I don't have trouble seeing why Baron Steele left them.

He disappears through the front door and several ladies follow him inside. I swear, they're worse than tweens spotting a social media star.

I glance back down at my phone and somehow, there's still a reserve of disappointment left in my system because I feel it like a gut punch. I guess things with Alex are just… over.

I sit there, listening to the gaggle of women squawking over Baron Steele, waiting for him to come out again. Then, I hear the gentle electric buzz of several drones descending upon the MoonMoney patio. Normally, they fly about a hundred feet above, only coming down when they've discovered something nefarious. But now? There's like five of them, watching the women like sick voyeurs.

Then it hits me. They aren't here for the women. Duh. If they wanted that, there are a billion beaches or strip clubs or whatever. They're here because of…

Baron Steele emerges from the coffee shop and immediately, the drones descend even quicker than the adoring fans.

"Oh, for Christ's sake," he says, barely audible over the women. "Can't a man grab a cuppa anymore? This is why my people stick to tea!"

He doesn't sign a single autograph as he pushes through the throng, clearly eager to escape the watchful eyes of the drones. He stomps straight toward me—or at least it feels that way. In reality, I'm just sitting closest to the iron gate that leads back to the sidewalk.

However, when he gets to me, all five drones following at an uncomfortably close distance, he stops.

For a second, I wonder if he recognizes me, but then I realize I'm not wearing my blonde wig. He puts his coffee down on my table and says, "Be a dear, and watch that for me a moment, will you?"

I nod as he calmly lifts one of the wrought iron tables—that is bolted to the concrete, mind you—and twirls around. Then, he lets it go at the apex of his turn and it hurtles toward two of the drones. They erupt in a shower of sparks and he bats at another one with one of the chairs, then another, and another until all five are heaped on the concrete patio, spasming like chickens without heads.

"That's better, wouldn't you say?" he quips.

I offer a weak smile but say nothing.

He reaches for his coffee but an Earth-cracking *fwoomp-boom!* interrupts him and tosses me backward off my chair. Women scream, running, tripping over one another. I hit the ground with an oomph, and immediately pop back to my feet. You don't superhero as long as I have and make the mistake of staying down.

Suddenly, I wish I had.

The cause of the minor earthquake is none other than Eaglestar himself. He stands like a six-and-a-half foot behemoth, red eyes glowing, air vacillating around him as if he were a ceiling fan.

"Paul Steele," he says, "you are under arrest."

"Bollocks. What now?"

"The destruction of Guild property."

"You mean those little tin cans?" Paul says, waving a hand. "Get out of town. They were in my personal space."

With a whoosh, Eaglestar is standing so close to the Baron they can probably smell each other's breath.

That sends me down a really strange mental path of wondering what someone like Eaglestar eats. Probably stuff they ate in the forties, like pot roast and stuff. Does he need to eat? Could he die of starvation? If he could, that means he isn't immortal after all.

"Now you're in my personal space," Paul tells Eaglestar. "And I suggest you back the hell up, old man."

It's funny, hearing that. Paul looks at least twenty years Eaglestar's senior, but since Eaglestar doesn't age—

My thoughts are lopped off as Paul rears his fist back and delivers a Mike Tyson blow to Eaglestar's jaw.

Ho-lee… I have never ever ever seen another hero or ex-hero take a swing at Eaglestar. This is absolutely Guinness Book of World Records type stuff.

Eaglestar's head turns, which is insanely impressive. If anyone else were to have punched him, they'd be in the hospital because all the bones in their fist would've turned to powder, but the Baron isn't just called Baron Steele, his body is like steel—the metal. Many say he's entirely indestructible.

It seems like we are about to find out when Eaglestar bashes down on Paul with a punch of his own. Amazingly, Baron Steele takes the hit like a world champion, even though his feet sink a couple of inches into the concrete from the force.

Every woman in attendance is practically drooling. I suppose I should at least admit that these two men are both insanely attractive in their own ways. But it's so much more than that. These are potentially the strongest men alive, duking it out in the middle of the Fifth Avenue MoonMoney Coffee outdoor patio.

Others have their phones out, recording the whole thing. Not only will this be gold on social media, but they can probably make some good money from the news.

"You shouldn't have done that," the Baron says, straightening his suit lapel.

"You are under arrest," Eaglestar repeats. "You will come with me whether it is willingly or not."

Paul rubs at the spot on his cheek where Eaglestar had hit him.

"Not sure I recognize your jurisdiction, Jonathan," he replies. "I hope you've got backup."

The Baron cracks his knuckles and punches Eaglestar again. This time, Eaglestar raises his own hand, ready for the strike. He catches Paul's fist in his palm. Then the Baron strikes with his other hand and Eaglestar repeats the action.

Eaglestar now holds both of Baron Steele's fists and stares at him intensely. I'm worried for a second that Eaglestar is gonna unleash his laser-eye-thingie and vaporize Paul's face, but I don't think it would work, and I must be right if he doesn't do it. Instead, he bends his knees the slightest bit and with a crack, they zoom straight upward.

I'm left, along with a dozen patrons and even more that have gathered in the streets. Cars have even stopped now and no one is even honking. We all just stare, either at the place where the two heroes just were, or upward at where they'd disappeared into the clouds.

That was insane. Apparently everyone else thinks so too because those who aren't recording the event on their phones are now calling or texting people, no doubt telling them exactly what had just gone down. They wouldn't even have to exaggerate.

I look at my phone, having momentarily forgotten about Alex for the first time in a long time. Nothing. Still no text.

I start packing up my things when I hear a unified gasp. I look up just in time to see and hear something careen to the Earth like a meteor.

FOUR

SAWYER

Joy.

That's the expression on Mr. Blanchard's face. Pure freaking ecstasy. I've been trying to figure it out since I walked into his office, and that's what I've settled on. But why would he be so happy? Logan is his favorite student. Could he really just be thrilled that I'm in trouble again? That he's gonna pile on the punishments like he did a couple of years ago?

It's just us in the room, so I think he's feeling extra ballsy.

"Mr. Vincent," he starts. "It's been quite some time since we've had one of our little… talks."

Yeah, that's because I've kept my nose clean so I don't have to deal with your ugly face and rancid coffee breath. I really wish I could say it out loud. How satisfying would that be?

He seems to be trying a new thing on his face. For as long as I've known him, he's had the military flattop haircut and a face so clean-shaven I've always assumed he freshens up at lunchtime. But now, he's got a little goatee, all thin lines and neatly shaped.

Other than Lucifer himself, the only people I've ever known to wear something like that is the youth pastor at the church my mom used to drag me to, and Major League Baseball relief pitchers. It looks really stupid. And the fact that it's not quite even on both sides makes him look even more ridiculous.

He doesn't think so, obviously. He literally admires himself in every reflection in the room—which is a lot. The office hasn't changed much except for the brand-new football trophy literally in the center of his desk.

Does he even do any work?

"I've looked forward to the day when I would finally be able to get rid of you."

Wow. What a model educator. Instead of hoping I'll shape up, he wanted me to keep messing up so he can get rid of me? Again, I keep my thoughts to myself because I know what'll happen at home if I say anything out loud. But he sure isn't making it easy. And my head is throbbing. I wonder if I really do have a concussion? Maybe I'm bleeding around the brain. Or my skull is filling up with fluid. It would almost be worth it to die here on his office floor while he's reveling in bitching me out.

Hey, I said *almost*. It's not like I actually want it to happen. But I sure could use an aspirin. Several, in fact.

Logan's parents show up before Mom does, as usual. Mrs. Andrews strides in, looking all self-important and in a hurry. She's dressed like she's ready to board a yacht or something. Blue and white stripes with an anchor embroidered on her chest. It's October and she's wearing a floppy hat and sunglasses. Inside. Inside.

Mr. Andrews, on the other hand, looks like he's gearing up to play tight end for the Patriots, jersey and all.

And, as usual, Mr. Blanchard bends over backward trying to please them. He greets them like they're royalty. Why? I just don't get it.

Oh, yeah. Sports.

"Vincent, give the lady your seat," he says as if there aren't three other options.

"What?" I say.

It doesn't matter, though, because she sits on the black leather couch against the far wall. She crosses her legs, pulls out a compact from her purse, and proceeds to check her hair and makeup like no one else is in the room.

"I thought you were going to get this dill weed under control," Mr. Andrews says, staring me down and pointing a finger.

"Hey," I object. "You can't call me that. You're an adul—"

"I can't believe Logan is hurt again," Mrs. Andrews cuts in, snapping her little mirror thing closed and shoving it away. "He's going to miss more playing time."

"Yeah," Mr. Andrews agrees, "that's a damn scholarship on the line, Blanchard. What are you prepared to do about it?"

So, big, bad, ex-Marine Principal Blanchard goes bright red in the face. A bead of sweat forms at his hairline. Someone's gonna need to reapply his antiperspirant.

"I—yes. I know. I'm sorry, David. Really…"

I'd feel like I'm having déjà vu if it wasn't for the fact that Logan isn't here this time. Last I saw him, a paramedic was stitching up his hand. It wasn't nearly as bad as it looked at first. Just a lot of blood.

In fact, my head injury is probably much worse. Could be a concussion. Not that anyone would care.

"'Sorry' isn't going to cut it," Mr. Andrews says.

Blanchard smacks his lips and tilts his head like he's frustrated but can't really say it. After a sharp breath, he says, "I've managed to keep Sawyer's… violent outbursts to a minimum the past couple of years, and I've been able to protect Logan during that time."

"Protect?" It slips out before I even realize it myself.

Blanchard gives me a look so severe it could rival any Frank had ever thrown my way. He continues, despite my outburst.

"But this was completely unexpected. He…" That's me. "… attacked him…" That's Logan. "… by riding his skateboard so fast that your son never saw it coming. There was no way for anyone to react in time, including security."

Wow. So that's the way they're trying to spin it this time, huh? What a joke.

Mrs. Andrews points at me. "I want him expelled."

"At least," Mr. Andrews agrees. "Maybe even arrested."

His wife just keeps talking like he hadn't said a word. Guess we know who rules that roost. "The students aren't safe with this—this—bully attending this school."

"Hahahahaha." They all shoot me a death glare as I laugh at the idea that I could be bullying Logan Andrews. There was no way I was holding that in.

"How dare—"

"Is there something you find funny about this situation, Mr. Vincent?" Blanchard asks.

I hear a commotion outside the door as Blanchard's secretary raises her voice, probably as much to warn him that someone's on their way in as to stop whoever's out there. I wasn't that worried until now. Is Mom so mad that she's gonna burst in here? What am I in for?

"I'm sorry, but you can't just—" I hear the secretary say at the top of her voice.

The door bursts open and—Frank?

Full-on business attire, expensive walking stick, perfectly coiffed hair. The F-D-3 the world sees on the news and social media steps into the office. The billionaire playboy with the golden smile. Except he's not wearing it right now.

Blanchard stands up from his desk chair. "Just who the hell are—"

Then his voice cuts off as his expression morphs from anger to shock to pure confusion. His head tilts to the side like a dog that can't quite figure out what the strange sound is that he just heard. Logan's parents just stare in silence, their jaws hanging open.

That's right, bitches. The most famous man in the city just joined this little parent meeting.

"Mr. Douglas?" Blanchard says, as if he needs to ask. Everyone knows Franklin Douglas III. Everyone.

"That's right." Frank hands him a business card, which is something I didn't think people actually did anymore, but whatever. He probably still has some left over from the nineties. I think they print those things in batches of seventeen million. "And you are…?"

"Uh… Principal Blanchard." He looks down at the nameplate on his desk, then up at his own name plastered on the window set into the door, as if to emphasize the fact to Frank. But Frank doesn't show that he cares one bit. "May I ask why you're here, Mr. Douglas?"

"This is the parent-teacher meeting, isn't it?" He looks around. "I'm here for Sawyer. I'm dating his mother, and she's quite distressed to hear that there's been more trouble here at school. So distressed, in fact, that I thought it best that I step in."

"I… see." Blanchard is obviously shocked by the revelation and, for once, is at a loss for words. The Andrews continue to just stand in place, dumbfounded. Emphasis on the dumb part.

Finally, Frank breaks the silence. "Well? Are you going to explain the situation to me or are we just going to stand around like idiots?"

I've never seen Blanchard flustered like this.

"I, um, well." Blanchard clears his throat. "As I explained to Ms. Vincent on the phone, Sawyer attacked another student with whom he's had a history. It was quite a scene. Yes, siree."

"Attacked him, how?" Frank tilts his head and narrows his eyes in a way that says he's waiting for the answer, but doesn't expect to believe it once he hears it.

"I don't know how long you've known him, but this isn't the first time this kid has assaulted mine," Mr. Andrews says, apparently finding his testicles.

Frank turns to him. "This is Logan Andrews we are talking about?"

Mr. Andrews nods once.

"Fullback for the school team?"

Mr. Andrews nods again, this time wearing an expression of pride.

Frank takes one step back as if to reveal me to the Andrews.

"Have you seen Sawyer?" he asks. Before anyone has the chance to respond, he continues. "Your boy could eat my boy for breakfast and still have room for a full stack of pancakes and a tray of eggs."

"How dare you!" Mrs. Andrews says with her hand against her chest. I'm sure she'd be clutching at her pearls if she were wearing any.

"Be that as it may," Blanchard says, "Sawyer used a weapon."

"A weapon?" Frank looks at me with a cocked eyebrow. "Is that so?"

"Yes, that's right," Blanchard answers. "Apparently, he rode his skateboard full speed into the poor boy, who never saw it coming."

Frank affects a tiny smile, still looking at me. "Is that what happened?"

"Well—" Blanchard starts to interject, but Frank cuts him off just by holding up his index finger. It's like a magic trick or something. The most amazing magic trick I've ever seen.

"It was an accident," I say. "Sure, I shouldn't have been riding my skateboard in the halls, I get that. But I didn't hurt anyone on purpose. I was just riding along, and Logan got in my way."

"Just so I have this right, we are talking about the same Logan who has been bullying you for years?" Frank asks me.

I nod.

"Oh, what a load of—" Mr. Andrews starts to say.

Frank spins on Mr. Andrews and the man nearly cowers. "I'll have you know that I have a private investigator working on this. He's uncovered some very interesting information about your son's possible criminal activities."

Blanchard is visibly taken aback by the accusation. You would have thought Frank had accused Logan of being a terrorist or something.

Mr. Andrews steps forward, angry but clearly cautious. "Criminal activities? What the hell are you talking about?"

Frank doesn't back down a centimeter. His eyes could pierce graphene. "There was a gang operating out of a gym several months ago. The gym where your precious son trained. The owner was arrested for orchestrating some sort of crime ring."

Mrs. Andrews looks really upset. "Our son is a good boy. He would never—"

"Not according to my information. My P.I. has interviewed students and staff around the school. Just how sure are you that your son hasn't done anything wrong? Illegal?"

Logan's parents look at each other. Deep down they know what their son's really like, no matter how much they deny it to everyone else, or even themselves.

"You do understand that parents can be held liable in certain cases where their minor children have committed crimes?"

Now the Andrews look scared. I know Logan doesn't turn eighteen until next summer, and I'm sure Frank did his homework on that, too. Blanchard decides to speak up.

"Logan has been a model student from the day he stepped foot in this school. He's a star athlete—"

"Yes. And athletes have never been known to hurt anyone, right? Never bullied anyone smaller than them, never endangered anyone or took advantage of the opposite sex…"

"In any case," Blanchard says, "Sawyer is at fault here. There are many witnesses. At the very least, he'll have to be suspended, and with his history, we may even have to look at expulsion."

Frank scrolls through his phone and taps on a contact, then holds it up to his ear. "I suppose I'll have to call my lawyers then."

Blanchard looks absolutely terrified at the thought. Any of his former Marine buddies would have probably disowned him if they'd witnessed this. "L-lawyers? Ju-ju-just hold on for a moment, Mr. Douglas—"

"It's no problem. They're the best in town. I'm sure the school has very good attorneys as well… and you, personally, of course."

"Person," he says like he runs out of breath and then swallow hard. Then his voice raises an octave. "Personally?"

"Well, certainly. If you've been wrongfully harassing Sawyer all these years and covering up for Logan, you don't think I won't go after you, do you?" It's so hard for me not to laugh as Frank buries these horrible people.

"Please hang up. There's no need to get attorneys involved. I'm sure we can work it out." He looks nervously at the Andrews, who seem even more scared than he is by now.

Frank eyes the Andrews with a cocked eyebrow, waiting until they agree before he "hangs up" the call I'm sure isn't really happening.

He places a finger to his lips and acts like he's trying to come up with an idea. But I know for sure that he knew exactly how this would go and exactly what he was gonna say before he ever darkened the school halls.

"I tell you what. I'll take Sawyer home for the rest of the day while everyone cools down and thinks about how this is going to move forward. Either he comes back in the morning and everything is back to normal, or tomorrow, I show up in his stead with an army of lawyers." He looks straight at Logan's parents. "And my private investigator. How does that sound?"

"That… sounds quite reasonable." Blanchard turns to me with the fakest smile I've ever seen a human try to pull off. "We'll see you tomorrow, Mr. Vin—uh, Sawyer."

The Andrews just nod in agreement.

Frank tilts his head again, this time with a look of recognition as he eyes Mrs. Andrews up and down. "Don't I know you? You seem very familiar."

She blushes and almost smiles, then looks at her husband and frowns as he stares daggers at her. "No, I don't believe we've met."

"Hm. Could've sworn…" Frank shakes his head, then turns to walk out the door. "Let's go, Sawyer."

When we get out to the hallway outside of the main office, I finally say something.

"That was so great. Thank you," I say with true gratitude.

"Don't thank me yet. We still have to face your mother when we get home."

FIVE

FRANK

It turns out going down to the school and taking care of Sawyer's situation was the best thing I've ever done for my relationship with Megan. I thought she'd be livid when we got home. However, if she was at all angry, she fooled me. In fact, she was so grateful that I took that off her plate that she left Sawyer alone and asked if I wanted to go out to lunch.

Considering our breakfast date was disrupted by this nonsense, I gladly accepted.

Even though I'm glad she seems to have forgotten about the whole "maybe we should move in together" incident earlier, I'm starting to think more and more about it myself. Maybe it wouldn't be so bad if she and Sawyer came to live with me. I'd have to be extra careful about her not finding out about the entrance to the Aerie, but I can't see her spending much time in my study, especially with all the other available rooms in the penthouse.

I don't know, but I'll think about it.

One of the best parts of being me is having access to a plethora of fine dining without any wait or concern for quality or cost. Every restaurant I own, which I believe now stands at more than thirty in New York alone, has a table especially for me that is never in use by anyone else.

We can't eat French downstairs in the Tower since I'm apparently eating there with Paul this evening. So we're having a nice lunch at a little place I own on Fifth across from the Park called Nonna Donatella, named after a fictional grandmother of mine since I didn't know either of my grandmothers.

It's quaint and even romantic in its own rustic way. Grape bunches, exposed brick façades, all the things you'd expect from an old-world Italian eatery. In fact, now that I think about it, it's the place where Bastet and I usually eat when she's not acting like her own evil twin.

Megan and I are laughing and talking about normal things. I've never been this happy. Not in my whole life. The food is superb, as I expect it to be. She orders a light soup and salad but eats her fair share of breadsticks, and I get the veal, which is Chef Angelo's specialty. Neither of us are disappointed.

Megan removes her napkin from her lap, dabs the sides of her mouth and places it down next to her plate.

"That was amazing."

"You're amazing," I say, debonaire as ever.

"So you didn't have a grandmother named Donatella?" she says.

I shake my head. "Not that I'm aware of. I'm not even Italian, as far as I know."

"You don't talk much about your family," she says, stabbing a tiny piece of lettuce with a gold fork and swirling it around in the dressing.

My mouth goes suddenly dry. She doesn't know that my mother died in a botched assassination, or that my father—whom I ultimately blamed for that—was the most corrupt crime lord this city has ever seen, but she knows enough about me to know that this is a subject matter with which I am uncomfortable. All considerations of keys and moving in together flee my mind like a sheep from a wolf.

"Oh, it's fine. I didn't mean to pry. Hey, how about I start?"

It dawns on me that I've never heard anything about her family—Sawyer's grandparents, Megan's brothers or sisters. I knew her father was still alive, having survived a car crash that killed her mother, and I think she has a sister. But that's the extent of it.

She talks for a long time, and I watch her almost as much as I listen. She discusses her childhood like it was some fairytale dream with loving parents, and a sister she fought with but loved. It makes me wonder how things would have turned out for me if I'd had a more simple upbringing away from all the bright lights and sounds of the Big Apple, away from gangs and mobsters, even though I didn't know that's what they were at the time.

She tells me about a time she and her sister Patty went down to the creek to catch tadpoles. Once again, you'd have thought they were chasing rainbows to find a pot of gold. There's just so much joy in her words, such peace.

Right then, I decide. That's right, I'm going to do it. I'm going to ask her to move in with me.

"Megan, I—" I speak in front of tens of thousands of people. Millions if you consider all of those watching on the internet. But here, right now, the words catch in my throat. I try to finish the sentence, to ask the question, and they just don't come out.

She gives me a strange look. I don't blame her. "Yes?" she prompts.

"I-I'm thinking that—" Again. It happens again. What the hell's wrong with me?

"Frank? Are you okay? You're thinking what?"

"I'm thinking about ordering dessert."

Oh, you coward.

"Okaaaaaay? Then order dessert. You're a big boy, you can decide for yourself." Her words are dismissive, but her expression says that she knows something's up.

"I was also thinking that we could…" I choke for the third time and just about decide I'm done talking.

She tilts her head, waiting to hear the rest.

"I was thinking that we could maybe share a dessert."

"That sounds nice. Let's ask for the dessert menu then."

"That would be great. Why don't you do that while I run to the men's room."

She smiles and nods and I walk to the men's room as quickly as possible without drawing attention to myself, leaning on my cane more than usual. I look back and smile at her on my way, and she looks at me in an odd way, which is totally deserved.

Once inside the restroom, I nod to the one other guy who's in there as he washes his hands. The second he leaves, I lean over the sink to catch my breath. I feel like I'm having a panic attack. I've never had a panic attack. Ever.

And my life has been in jeopardy numerous times over the years. And not just as a crimefighter. I fought in Afghanistan, dammit. What's wrong with me?

I turn on the sink and splash myself with cool water, then use one of the cloth towels to dry off. Deep breathing. In. Out. In. Out.

I inspect myself in the mirror. Franklin Douglas III. Richest man in New York. World's most eligible bachelor. And the greatest hero the city has ever known… afraid to ask the woman he loves to move in with him.

Pathetic.

I straighten my back, fix my collar, and press the wrinkles out of my pants and shirt.

"That's it. You can do this."

Check my cufflinks.

Deep breath.

I grab my walking stick.

Another deep breath.

Reaching for the door handle, prepared to return to my table and propose living together to Megan, my phone buzzes in my pocket. I pull it out to see a text from Amy.

His royal highness in hospital by God-complex. @ MoonMoney by nest. Thought you should know.

She's speaking in code, which isn't exactly necessary since we are on an encrypted frequency, but it's smart. You never know if someone might physically get ahold of one of our devices.

God-complex isn't difficult to figure out, but…

His royal highness? I text back.

PS, she responds.

PS? PS what? Post Script? Am I waiting for more?

Then it hits me…

Stay there. OMW.

After hurriedly rushing from the restaurant, telling Megan an emergency came up at work, I hop into my car and speed down the avenue.

The restaurant is only a few blocks from Douglas Tower, so Megan will be fine getting home. That also means that I'm only six blocks or so from MoonMoney, where I hope Osprey will still be waiting. She hasn't replied to my text, but if she isn't, I'll meet her at the hospital, assuming she ends up there.

I punch the electric car into sport mode. It's one of mine. I don't mean one of my personal vehicles, though it is. I mean I own the company that manufactures it. Anno Motors, a division of Douglas Industries. This particular model happens to have been seriously outfitted by the R&D team, headed by Luis Chen. That means it'd be barely street-legal upon inspection and entirely not street-legal upon closer inspection.

No one thinks about it much since the Black Harrier is best known for gliding around the city and dropping in on thugs and hoodlums from above, but I am one helluva driver. I once did a television special with Formula 1 as part-publicity-stunt-part-cover-for-a-secret-Guild-mission in Scotland. It was then that I'd discovered a collector by the name of Lukas Standesamt, who was rumored to have, in his possession, several of the Tuldarian artifacts carried upon the zeppelin famous for "killing" Eaglestar during World War II.

The artifacts that gave Jonathan his powers. Which means they're more than just interesting pieces, they're possibly very, very dangerous.

The Guild has kept a wary eye on him ever since, but having no true jurisdiction in Europe, we've done nothing to relieve him of them. However, I think the time for worrying about borders and turf is through.

"Jillian," I say to my car.

"Yes, handsome?"

"Send a text to Megan—"

"Her? Why?"

I must remember to change the programing on my various devices now that I have a real girlfriend. I ignore the response and say, "How about that trip to Scotland? It'll be romantic."

"I'd love that!" Jillian says.

"That's the text, and you know it."

"Yuck," Jillian says.

"Just send it, please."

"Yeah, yeah. It's done."

"Thank you."

A few minutes later she says, *"You have a reply. Would you like me to read it?"*

"Please."

"Barf."

"That's not what it says."

"That's what I say. She says, 'Scotland? That's... really? You were serious?'" When Jillian reads Megan's words, she sounds robotic, unlike her usual self. Wow. I have some issues to work out if I programmed this thing to be this way.

Reply, "As a heart attack. Like I said, I have a work thing there, too. But it should only be for an afternoon. You'll have plenty to do on your own. Trust me. My UK hotels are the best. We can talk later."

I pull up to the MoonMoney and I don't immediately spot Chen's daughter. It would have been difficult to for anyone considering the number of blue and red lights flashing, yellow caution tape, and boys in blue hanging around.

She obviously sees me, though. Since there's no one else driving one of these anywhere in the city, the tinted windows don't even matter. She rushes to the passenger door. I push a button and the door rises upward. Gull-wing doors aren't exactly practical, but if I'm going to design something to be cool, it's going to be cool. She slides in and I close the door.

"Hey," she says.

I throw up one hand as a greeting.

I always find it more than a little awkward when it's just the two of us. And I don't mean because there's any sexual tension or anything of the sort. The idea even makes me shudder.

Unlike the sidekicks—sorry, partners—I chose to be Kites, I was never given a choice about whether or not she'd be part of the team. First, Sawyer befriended her and started working with her without my permission, then Alex chose to make her one of his partners when he took over as Black Harrier. And, from what I gather, they were partners in more ways than one, but I've chosen to stay out of that. So far.

Although it would be difficult to argue against them doing all of that, even if it was against my wishes. Along with Sawyer, she'd been instrumental in saving my life when I'd been captured by Chef Maléfique, and ended up in the hospital herself as a result.

There's also her being Luis Chen's daughter. Since he creates most of the technology I've used over the years as Black Harrier, it's a challenge for me to begrudge his own offspring making use of it as well. Leaving aside the fact that I pay for it all, that is.

"What happened?" I ask. Though the scene outside the coffee shop says a lot.

There's a crater the size of a VW Bug, and the windows for a block are all shattered.

"Freaking Eaglestar," she says. "I'm surprised he didn't kill him."

"Paul is not easily killed." In fact, I'm not even sure if it can be done.

"I think he flew him into space and dropped him," she says softly, not looking at me.

Well, maybe that would do it.

"I… he what?"

I heard her but I am truly stunned wordless. Jonathan is many things, but a murderer isn't one of them. Not like this. There can be no doubt, that was an attempt to kill the Baron outright. He's no fool either. With this knowledge, I'm shocked Paul survived, too.

"Where'd they take him—Mount Sinai?"

"I think so."

I just talked to Paul not long ago. He'd been entering this very coffee shop. What is with him and coffee? This is not the first major altercation that took place involving Paul and a cup of joe.

I slam the pedal to the floor, the dual electric motors whirring. If the Guild is trying to kill heroes now, we might have an even bigger problem than I'd imagined.

Where's Black Harrier when you need him?

SIX
SAWYER

Miraculous.

The fact that my mom didn't treat me like Ozzy treats a bat the second I walked in the door was nothing short of a miracle.

She was so thrilled that Frank handled it all that she barely said a word to me before showering him with kisses and dragging him out the door to lunch.

You'd think it would be weird for me to watch my mom and Frank like that, but after spending years watching my mom with a bunch of rando-losers, it's really nice to see her with someone… good.

Plus, Frank is my dad.

I know, it's still weird for me to say and it's been a couple of years since I found out. I wonder if it bothers him that I don't call him Dad?

I guess there'd be the risk that I'd mess up and say it in front of Mom, and since Mom doesn't know that I know, that could go very badly for all of us.

So. Frank it is. For now, anyway.

Well, they left me home, alone. I've been lying in bed ever since, watching Netflix on my laptop. I still feel like I might be concussed, but he didn't seem too worried about it. I'm pretty sure Frank has had his fair share of head injuries. Tonight would have been our weekly Resistors' meeting, but since it would be little more than light training and getting together at our headquarters to hang out, I canceled it. First, I'd done it before I realized how okay with all this Logan stuff Mom was going to be, but also, I think I might have a concussion.

And I also think I've said that already. I'm beginning to doubt Frank's expertise on this matter.

I sit up because I remember hearing that if you do have one, you shouldn't let yourself fall asleep. Better safe than sorry, right?

Honestly, since we can't go out on patrol anymore it doesn't matter much anyway. Lately, the meetings have become more and more just hanging out and less and less about training together, too.

Most of the time, we never even put our costumes on. What's the point? While we do train in them to make sure we're used to the feel, it's not like we're going to get called away at the last second to go fight criminals.

Bash usually plays violent video games, since he doesn't have his own console at home. I feel bad about tonight because I think this is his only opportunity to play. Sometimes, I think about just buying him some stuff, but I don't want him to feel like it's charity. I'll just have to go overboard with the presents during the holidays, I guess.

As the least physically gifted on the team, Cricket always practices his fighting techniques. Sometimes, I step in and teach him, but I don't know, some things you just can't learn. Like balance or coordination. He has little of either. He's definitely gotten better over the past several months, but he still has a long way to go. No matter what, I really admire his determination. At his size, he's gonna need all the help he can get.

Even though I'm really into Neith, the meeting nights sort of annoy me because Pace and Osprey just hang out off in a corner. I'm pretty sure they're broken up again, since they never seem to date or hold hands or anything, but they sure spend a lot of time discussing things. I don't know. None of my beeswax, I guess. Doesn't change the fact that the stupid teenager in me hates the idea of anyone being with Amy even though I don't wanna be with her.

Wow. Saying it like that makes me a big fat jerk.

Neith, however, has me firmly planted in the friend zone. Remember when we fought the Neon Knights at the docks and I almost drowned? Yeah, me too. That was not a fun night. Well, ever since I messed up and kissed Osprey, things have been weird between me and Neith.

So stupid considering I was, like, unconscious at the time. Who wouldn't kiss a beautiful woman who you thought was kissing you?

Not sounding any better, Sawyer.

I clear my head and toss my laptop aside. At one of the first meetings, Neith introduced me to the culinary delight that is pita chips and hummus. Ever since, my pantry is never without them. I make my way to the kitchen and snatch the bag from the cupboard and the tub of hummus from the fridge and plop down on one of the leather barstools.

The first bite is always the best.

Oh, man. So good.

I'd never had it before she'd started bringing it to these things, but it's now one of my favorite snacks. I'm hoping to find that sweet spot between Neith getting over me kissing Osprey and the point of no return of asking her out on a date. Though, sitting here in my kitchen, I feel like I'm blowing my chances.

What if I canceled tonight and she ends up going on a date with some dude and forgets about me all together?

Crap.

I'm gonna take a huge chance and hope that sweet spot is now.

I take a deep breath and try to stay calm as I type in her phone number. Okay, fine… I don't actually know her number. I scroll through my contacts until I find her and press her name. Happy?

As the phone rings, I realize I've never asked someone out. How did I get to this point without ever doing that? It can't be any worse than fighting supervillains, can it? I guess I'm about to find out.

"Hello?"

Her voice is like silk and honey. I feel like I'm swimming in it for awhile, my head all… swimmy. Maybe I have a concu—

"Hello?" she says again, snapping me to attention.

"Oh, hey there, Nei—Aali—uh, Neith."

Well, this is certainly going well so far.

"Actually, which do you prefer? Your code name or your real name?"

She's silent for like two seconds but to me it feels like ten days. Feeling awkward. Getting longer. Longer.

"This is Sawyer, by the way," I say.

"Yes, I know. My phone can read minds."

It takes me a second before I realize she's joking. I laugh. Probably too loudly.

She says nothing.

After a few more seconds, I break down. "Sorry, did I say something wrong?"

"No."

"Then why the… hesitation?"

"I am considering how to respond to your question. I haven't given much thought to it, and I wanted to weigh the costs and benefits of each answer I could give."

"Oh, okay." I didn't realize it was such a big deal, but whatever.

"Considering we have known each other for quite some time now, I question why you would wait so long to ask me this question."

"Well, I was getting to—"

"On the one hand," she continues as if she didn't really want my response, "our relationship is professional, so perhaps it would be better to use our code names with one another."

"Oh, okay," I say again.

"On the other hand…"

Oh, I see we're not done.

"…most of our time spent together is now social, such as right now. So it would make sense to use our real names."

I wait to respond so that she doesn't stomp all over my opening again.

"Yeah. That's, uh, exactly what I was thinking. Yep."

"You may call me Aaliyah when we are not in costume."

"Great. I'm glad that's decided."

Okay, hero. Here's your chance. Do your thing. Don't. Screw. It. Up.

"So, Aaliyah… how do you feel about… other social situations?"

"Such as?"

Sweat is pouring off me. I'm so relieved I'm doing this over the phone. How does anyone do this?

"Well, such as, I don't know… let's say, going out to dinner together, for example." Wow, is my heart pounding.

Yeah, just totally came up with that idea right off the top of my head. Yes, siree. Crap, am I channeling Blanchard now?

Then, in the most unexpected moment since Fox canceled *Firefly*, she says, "You may take me to dinner. We will see how things go."

My call waiting beeps in, and I pull the phone from my ear. It's Amy.

"Oh, hey. I've got another call coming in," I tell her.

"Really? Who is it?"

Who is it? Who is it? Really? I… I can't tell her Amy after that whole make-out sesh on the docks.

"It's my mom," I lie.

"Okay. Call me later." She says that in such a way that it's obvious it doesn't really matter to her if I really do or not.

"Will do," I say before clicking over faster than I should have.

Way to start off the relationship on a lie.

Idiot.

"What's going on?" I ask Amy, switching over.

"I'm with Frank," she says. "Eaglestar just attacked Baron Steele and almost killed him."

"What? Seriously?"

"Yeah, we are heading to the hospital."

"Should I meet you there?" I ask.

"I don't think so," she says. "Not unless you want to. I just thought you should know."

"Uhm, yeah. All right. Thanks."

We both hang up and I'm left standing there with a pita chip in my hand, halfway to my mouth.

What the hell is going on out there?

SEVEN
FRANK

We sign in at the reception desk at the hospital and we're told to "Please have a seat," and we will be told when we are allowed to visit the Baron.

"You know who I am?" I ask.

The woman glances up at me for the first time, peering over the frames of her clear, pink-tinted glasses.

"Mmmm. I don't care if you're the Pope. I got my instructions with that one." She definitely has the effortless look of annoyance down to an art form.

"So then… you don't know who I am?" Am I coming off as narcissistic? I don't feel like I am, but I also might be becoming more self-aware lately…

She gives me a little tilt of her head, a noncommittal action if I've ever seen one, and goes back to her paperwork.

I kick up a response when Amy tugs at my arm and we retreat to the waiting area.

Despite my extreme fame and fortune, I never have considered myself amongst the Elite, but as I sit in the hard plastic waiting room chairs, I realize I've never been told to wait for anything in my entire life.

"She's just doing her job," Amy says, obviously reading my expression.

I lean back and let out a sigh. Man, these chairs are uncomfortable.

"Well, I guess I'm missing class," Amy says almost under her breath.

"Oh, right. Columbia, correct?" I ask.

"Surprised you knew that," she says.

"Ouch!"

She laughs uncomfortably. "No… I… I'm sorry, I didn't mean it like that."

Now it's my turn to laugh. "Relax. I'm just kidding. Hey, of course I know where you go. I practically pay for it, don't I?"

A quizzical look washes over her face.

"Because I employ your father?" I say, almost as a question.

This is not going well at all.

"That would totally be true… if I didn't get a full ride scholarship."

Oops. "That I didn't know. Sorry. Congratulations on that."

"Thanks." How did I manage to make it even more uncomfortable?

"What'd you get it in? The scholarship, I mean."

"Sort of a combination of things. Academics, extracurriculars, dance, martial arts. Basically a merit scholarship based on the full package."

"That's very impressive."

"Well, it was a lot of work," she says. "Especially considering you could have paid for it."

"Excuse me?"

"You know… because you pay my dad so much."

We laugh together. More of a chuckle, I suppose. But I'm so glad that's over with. She probably is, too.

It's quiet for a long while before I say, "Today's what? Friday? Got any plans?" Really, Frank? Small talk?

"Not since I stopped patrolling. Which is some real bullcrap, you know that?"

"You don't have to tell me," I agree. "What does Alex have to say about it?"

I thought it was a sly way of bringing him up, but I guess not.

"How should I know?"

Her tone is so sharp I almost check myself for cuts.

"I just figured… you know what? Never mind."

She grabs a magazine from the end table. It has my face on the cover. I grab it from her and wave it at the receptionist, who isn't looking. Amy takes it back and starts leafing through far too quickly to be reading anything. Then, she slams it down to her lap.

"Why are guys such jerks?"

I couldn't have been more shocked if she had stabbed me.

"Not all are," I tell her, though I'm sure it sounds hollow. And probably isn't all that true, to a certain extent. "Something wrong with Alex?"

"This isn't about Alex," she says.

"Sawyer?"

"Gross. No," she says absently, probably not even considering that's my son she's talking about. We've never had that conversation outright, but she's a smart girl. I'm confident she's put those pieces together.

"Then, what?"

"Okay, fine, I guess it's a little about Alex. We were supposed to be partners, you know? And now he's just… gone."

"He's doing what he was told he has to do."

"In Boston," she says.

"In Boston," I agree.

"This whole thing is just so unfair."

"Things used to be simpler," I agree. "Even more so than you might know."

She sits forward a bit. I expected her to brush me off, not wanting to hear stories about "The Good Old Days." But she seems genuinely interested.

"When the Guild started, you mean?"

"I may be old," I say, "but not that old."

She smiles and it feels like victory.

"That man in there..." I point to the double doors beyond which Baron Steele occupies a room. "He was a major part the Guild. Helped keep it going at a time when we weren't sure we would continue."

"He did? No one ever talks about that."

"Because Jonathan—Eaglestar—won't let them," I tell her.

It's all true. The blood between those two is so spoiled that even the mention of Paul's name in the Guild Hall is damn near treason in Jonathan's eyes.

"It was just us heroes," I say, "Then we added the ancillary members and then came the sidekicks... partners. That's around when things became... muddled."

"Speaking of partners, can I ask you something?"

"You just did."

"Wow. Dad jokes? From you?"

"Go ahead," I say, smiling.

"Are you okay with me?"

"Okay with you?"

"You know, okay with me being Osprey. I know the whole thing was sort of forced on you."

"I don't know if I'd call it—"

"I know you didn't want me as part of the team. It's okay, I get it. But are you okay with it now?"

"Amy, I'm happy to have you here. Now. But I admit I was very reluctant in the beginning."

"Can I ask why?"

"Well, first, you were an unknown quantity. I don't like unknown quantities under any circumstances. Second, I didn't know how prepared you were. And I couldn't have your death on my conscience. Especially after..."

I can't finish the sentence. I still can't talk about Toby's horrific death at the hands of Chef Maléfique after all these years. After my throat is done tightening up, I compose myself and move on.

"And third, there would be no way I could live with myself if anything happened to Luis Chen's daughter under my watch."

Her eyes go wide. "You knew?"

"It wasn't difficult to figure out. For me, anyway. I think your dad had a difficult time imagining you being a masked crimefighter, so it was easy for him not to consider it. Either that, or he was in denial."

"I imagine it must be very hard for you, taking on sidekicks."

"Don't let Sawyer hear you say that."

She laughs. "Just like I should never let you hear us call them costumes instead of uniforms?"

"Touché."

"How do you know when they're ready?" she continues. "What did it take for Sawyer to convince you he was able to go out and patrol, or accompany you on missions?

"Believe it or not, he saved my skin."

"You mean like with Chef Maléfique?"

"It certainly didn't rise to that level. And I wasn't even in physical danger. But he saved me just the same."

"Really? What happened?"

"You don't really want to hear an old man's stories, do you?"

She scoffs. Then she blushes a little. "Maybe you don't realize this, but I dressed up like Osprey because of you."

I did realize that, but she doesn't need to know it.

"Very well. It was shortly after I'd started training him. I was after Deadeye, who was after a high-value target—the mayor in fact, and it would've been far too dangerous for Kite—Sawyer—to go with me. So I had him stay behind and be my eyes and ears for the mission. Sort of a test."

"And?"

She appears genuinely interested, and it doesn't seem like we're going to be going anywhere anytime soon.

"Would you like to hear the whole story?" I ask.

"Hell, yeah."

Falling.

I felt like I was always falling.

For most people, it would have been the most terrifying moment of their lives —being thrown off the top of a building and watching the street rush up at an incredible speed. It would probably also be the last thing they ever saw.

For me, it was just another day at my second job. Actually, I thought of it as my first job, and Douglas Industries was second.

My heart wasn't even racing as I shot my grappler at the building across the street. Even back then, I knew my equipment. I knew better than to tighten up as the line went taut. I've always hated that part. The jolt as I went from falling straight down to swinging across the street hurts more than being hit by a crowbar. The only thing worse would be slamming into the side of the building, even though my body armor would have absorbed a lot of the impact. Which is why I aimed for a window that I thought I might be able to reach at my current trajectory.

But my calculations weren't quite right. I had to release my grip and time it perfectly. If not, I would have struck the brick wall so hard it might've knocked me unconscious. Then, I'd finish the fall anyway and be just as dead.

I released the line and wrapped my cape around myself just as I dropped a few feet and crashed like a wrecking ball through the big plate window. I tucked into a roll, barely registering the screams of the office workers whose day had just become a thousand times more exciting. Back on my feet, I looked around to get my bearings. I recognized the building. In fact, I owned it. But it'd been awhile since I'd been inside. And these were my employees even if they were separated from me by a few managerial positions whose names I didn't even know.

It wouldn't have mattered even if I'd had no connection to them. I would need to keep them safe either way. That was my job then as it is now.

But, I'll admit, there was something about the personal connection to the situation that made it more stressful for me than usual.

"Everyone, clear out." I felt the booming voice rumble through my voice changer. When the armor came on, the less-recognizable voice came out. Nobody moved, far too shocked by and interested in what was happening at their normally boring place of employment.

So I gave them some incentive. "Now!"

This time, they complied and started for the elevator. Most had never seen the Black Harrier in person, but they knew enough about me to understand you did what I said. As the office drones grabbed their cell phones, purses, and laptops, I kept my head down and turned away. The chances of one of them recognizing their billionaire boss in a mask and costume were slim, but not impossible, even with the disguised voice.

I turned to make sure the last of the workers had left the room. I saw a flash and nearly ducked, thinking it was a muzzle. Someone was taking a photo. A young, blonde woman who had been sitting at the desk closest to the smashed window rushed out the door to the elevators.

This was before I'd begun to employ the use of my visor. Believe it or not, that wasn't always built as a HUD and display for Amber or Tiffany or whichever AI I'd used at the time. First and foremost, it was a guard against facial recognition software. My company had the best in the world, but there were many others who weren't far behind.

In fact, this mission was the reason I'd mandated visors across the board for me and the Kites. It would've only taken one clear cell phone picture to blow my secret identity.

That was definitely a headache I didn't need. I'd kept it a secret for two decades, and I wasn't about to ruin it now. Sometimes I wished for a simpler time.

I'd have to do something about that immediately. It was just one of the many reasons I rarely went out in daylight—too many civilians getting in the way. But it wasn't like the assassin I was dealing with, Deadeye, was going to wait until it was convenient for me before attempting a hit on the mayor.

Maintaining my dual identity would be the least of my problems if Deadeye followed me in and started shooting up the place with all those civilians around. I scanned the building across the street to make sure. No sign of him. Could I have gotten that lucky? Maybe Deadeye had decided to escape and cut his losses?

I heard a smash! Of course he hadn't. The villain came through another window and fired two pistols at me simultaneously while spinning through the air. I'd seen something like it done with special effects in movies, but this was the only time I'd ever seen someone pull it off in real life. And so precisely.

A couple of bullets pinged off of me—one on my helmet, the other one my chest, both at angles. Glancing shots. If they'd been direct hits, the type of projectiles the super-assassin used would've lanced right through.

I needed to get downstairs. The clock was ticking, and the young woman probably wouldn't wait long to post that photo. In all the chaos of trying to evacuate, I hoped she wouldn't be too eager about it on the way down.

I calculated how long the elevator would take to get down to the parking garage. It was underground, so hopefully there wouldn't be a signal if she tried it from there.

Blam!

Another shot from Deadeye reminded me that I had other pressing matters to attend to, and I dove behind the reception counter. What good would MDF or particle board do against bullets?

Even in the midst of a gunfight, I was more concerned with that stupid photo. What if she tried to post it from the elevator? What else was she going to do on the long ride down? She was probably texting it to her boyfriend or husband right now.

I swore.

There wasn't much I could do about that. I just had to hope she wouldn't be that quick and get down there as soon as possible. I thought about having my AI shut down the power in the building, but that would strand my employees in a building with an assassin shooting up the place.

The problems of the modern-day masked crimefighter.

I vaulted over the counter, jumped over a desk, covering the distance to Deadeye in a couple of seconds. Not as fast as I would've in the old days, but not too shabby, either. Deadeye was an extraordinary hand-to-hand combatant, but my chances of surviving a melee fight with him far exceeded my chances of living with the assassin shooting at me.

The villain drew his sword and swung it so quickly, it was a blur. Still, I was still able to block it with my bracer. The metal-on-metal sparked as we repeated the dance several more times before I was finally able to deflect the long blade from his hand. It struck the gray industrial carpet and dug in, standing erect just a meter away.

He punched me. I blocked that too, but it was like using my arm to defend against a medieval war maul. If it hadn't been for my armor, I have no doubt he would have shattered my forearm.

I knew if I tried to match the assassin swing for swing, he would win. It wasn't because he was stronger, or faster—though he was—but he was simply better than me.

I've never claimed to be the best fighter in the world. That prestige had been thrust upon me by others. What makes me victorious time and time again is my use of intellect in combination with my brawn.

A decade earlier, I would have had Deadeye unarmed and unconscious already, but I was having to work a lot harder than I had a few years prior. I'd become slower, both to strike and react. And as much as I'd hated to admit it, I needed a Kite at my side.

Next, his foot shot up at my face, but I was just able to avoid it with a back flip. I felt a twinge in my lower back as I swung my body upward and back onto my feet. For a moment, all I could think about was the relief of sitting in the hot tub in my penthouse back at Douglas Tower.

Focus! I told myself.

What the hell was wrong with me? I hoped my mind wasn't starting to go as well as my body. What do they call it? Early-onset… something. I'd certainly sustained enough concussions over the years to have something like that happen.

Maybe I wasn't going to be able to beat this guy hand-to-hand like I always had in the past, but I used all of my strength to lift the nearest desk and hurl it toward him. I wasn't expecting it to do much, but it did what I'd hoped.

As soon as the massive chunk of wood disrupted his line of sight, I dove to the side, reached around to the back of my belt under my cape and grabbed my second grappler. As Deadeye leaped to avoid the desk, I aimed my grappler at him and shot. It connected with his armor, and I braced myself against the foot of another desk. Once certain it had locked on, I depressed the button to retract the super-strong cable. Deadeye came soaring at me with the speed of a locomotive.

Just as we were about to collide, I put all my strength into a roundhouse kick that connected with his chin. I later showed Sawyer the move in reverse, where he would use his grappler to pull himself toward his opponent.

Very effective.

Deadeye went down hard, and I wondered if maybe I had broken the man's neck. Then I wondered if maybe that would be a good thing. Unlike most of the criminals I fight, this man is a murderer. That's what he does.

I knew I should get the police and an ambulance over there immediately, but I had bigger fish to fry at the moment. I checked Deadeye's pulse to make sure he was still alive, then tied him up and left him there, hoping he'd remain unconscious long enough for the cops to arrive and secure him more permanently.

I surveyed the glass-covered desk of the woman who'd snapped the photo and found a name: Danielle Taylor. I only hoped she was too busy running away from being potential collateral damage to start posting my face all over the internet immediately.

I disconnected the grappler from Deadeye and attached the line to a giant file cabinet. Taking one last look over my shoulder to ensure he was staying down, I dove through the broken window and rappelled down the building as quickly as I could.

I did a quick change into a spare business suit I have stashed in every building I own, citywide. It was a little more snug than it should have been, since I hadn't updated it in a while. Then, I ran a comb through my hair. Over the years, I'd managed to turn the restroom stall quick-change into an art form. Another notch in the plus column of having years of experience on the job.

In the negative column, the regulation of my breathing and slowing of my heart rate when recovering from a battle no longer came as easily. I hoped she wouldn't notice how out of breath I was.

Oh, and I was sweating like an ox in August, but I had no other options.

She wasn't hard to spot. Danielle was a beautiful blonde amongst a sea of balding mouth-breathers.

"Excuse me," I asked her as I entered the parking garage from the street, huffing—and there I was, giving mouth-breathers a hard time. "Can you tell me what's going on?"

Danielle had been running for her car and seemed annoyed at the question until she turned and realized who was speaking to her. "Oh… uh… oh, my God. Mr. Douglas? I mean… Mr. Douglas."

Her face matched Sawyer's uniform and I just smiled at her, hoping to ease her nerves a bit. It's always helpful to be a wealthy celebrity in these situations.

She tried in desperation to make herself presentable. Fixing her hair—which wasn't unkempt. Smoothing her clothes—which weren't wrinkled. She kept checking her reflection in parked car windows.

"It's just that it would be nice to know why my employees are all fleeing the premises in the middle of the workday." Of course, I'd already received three calls from building security, but she didn't know that.

Danielle stammered as if she'd been asked a question by a famous movie star. "Sorry, I'm a little flustered. You won't believe what happened upstairs. We were just sitting there working, and—and then, there was this huge crash." Her eyes went wide as she described the scene. "And you wouldn't believe who fell through the window..."

I raised an eyebrow and waited, then realized she was expecting me to answer. I was starting to realize that she may not have been my brightest employee.

"Who?"

"The Black Harrier himself!" She said it as if she expected my head to explode when I heard the name.

I'm not sure which was more difficult, trying to feign surprise or attempting to hide my annoyance. I summoned my years of practice at playing the shallow playboy. "Wow... that's—that's just crazy."

"I know! I was, like, what the fu—sorry! WTF? OMG!"

"Yes, I'm sure you were."

"And..." She smiled and looked around. "I even got a photo." She pulled her phone out of her purse, expertly tapping and swiping the screen with her thumb. "Check it out."

Danielle handed the phone to me and I looked at the picture that filled the screen. Yes, it was my alter ego, all right. I pulled my fingers apart on the screen and zoomed in. I hadn't had time to put my contacts in, and without the lenses in my mask, my eyes weren't so great anymore.

Uh oh. Even so, I could tell the photo was nice and clear. No doubt about it. Someone was going to recognize me, with or without the assistance of software.

Between running a few companies, maintaining a playboy cover story, training a sidekick, practicing martial arts, staying in peak physical shape, and—oh, yes—fighting bad guys as the Black Harrier, I wasn't exactly a smart phone expert. But I knew how to delete a picture, and I did it as quickly and covertly as possible.

"Oops." I had the airhead routine mastered from all those dates I had to cut short when duty called. "Not sure what I did there."

Danielle grabbed the phone back and her smile faded as she looked at the screen and started swiping around. "Oh, no. I think you deleted it."

"Really? Oh, geez, I'm so sorry. I'm no good with new technology." I flashed her my sparkling smile and tried to pour on the old Douglas charm to distract her. "I'm sure I can make it up to you somehow."

"Don't worry about it, Mr. Douglas. My dad does that kind of stuff all the time. But all my pics get uploaded to the cloud automatically, so I'll just download it when I get home."

Ouch. "Right. The cloud. Of course."

"Well, it was nice meeting you, sir."

Sir? That was a blow to my ego. And she compared me to her father? Am I losing it? Did I seem that old to her?

"Uh... yes. Nice meeting you as well." I clenched my fists as she hopped in her car and joined the parade of vehicles attempting to leave the parking garage all at the same time.

I could just hear the sound of sirens in the distance, which meant my time for dilly-dallying was over.

I pulled out my own phone and dialed up Sawyer, since I no longer had my helmet comms. Luckily, even back then, my own equipment was much more powerful than that of the average person. "I'm going to need some help with something."

As I sped through the city streets in my Anno—I had a different model back then, but it still blazed—I didn't think I'd have time to head back to the Aerie. I hoped my new sidekick was already working at the terminal to the giant supercomputer I had there, since that seemed to be his favorite pastime.

Sawyer is the opposite of me in so many ways. With his red body armor and shock of blond hair sticking out from the top of his mask, he stands in such stark contrast to my black uniform and admittedly dark demeanor. I'm always surprised we aren't more alike, considering he's my son. Suffice to say, in most ways, we're much more different than similar. But he got many of Megan's best features.

I tapped the control on the side of the steering wheel that, for most people, would access a cell phone. With the upgraded tech in his vehicle, it immediately accessed a secure, direct line to my lair.

"Harrier to Kite," I said, hoping he would catch that I was using his code name now.

No answer. Was something wrong with the system? I tapped the control again.

"Red Kite. You there?"

After a long pause, I got a response. "Sorry, I'm not used to the code name."

"Well, get used to it."

The teen's smiling face appeared on the dashboard video screen.

"Red Kite, at your service." It's strange to remember how much he loved being called that at first, considering how hard he's tried to change it since then.

"Did you get my earlier message about—?"

"Already on it," he said before I could finish. "I've been trying to hack into this woman's accounts, but I haven't had any luck so far."

I swore.

"She's got DropFile, inCloud, MyStuff, and a couple of other backups going. I did manage to eff up her cell service, though, so she won't be able to do jack on it. But as soon as she connects to Wi-Fi, whether it's at home or some coffee place or whatever, she's gonna have cloud access."

"You think you'll be able to get into her account, Kite?"

"For sure. But it's gonna take more time." He stopped typing for a moment as he turned to look at me on the screen. "You think maybe you can stall her?"

I gritted my teeth. I definitely wasn't looking forward to this. "What's her address?"

He fed it to me and I sped off.

As I pulled up to Danielle's tiny condo in one of the city's less-affluent neighborhoods, I felt a twinge of guilt for not paying my employees enough to live someplace better. Especially considering the vast amounts of wealth I raked in for —truthfully—not really doing all that much work. But I also spent a great deal of that money on my extracurricular activities—saving the city—so it didn't bother me too much. And let's not forget all my philanthropic givings... the Boy Scouts, the Girl Scouts, Make a Wish, St. Jude's... but I digress.

I parked down the street and made sure to set the Anno's alarm. But I still felt like it might not be there when I got back, considering it probably cost more than the houses in this neighborhood. I thought about my plan as I headed up the block to her place, deciding I would try to charm her, and then take her out to dinner at one of my fancy restaurants... one with no Wi-Fi. That should give Sawyer plenty of time to delete my picture from all of her various "clouds."

"Oh, hey, hey," said a voice behind me.

Suddenly, I found myself surrounded by several gang members. Normally, I would have noticed them before they even got close, but I was letting this situation monopolize my attention and get to me way too much.

The apparent leader of the group approached me first as the rest closed in on me slowly.

"Whadda we got here, bros? Looks like this old rich bitch got himself lost."

Old? C'mon. Sure, I was starting to get a little gray around the temples, but—

"Maybe he needs some directions." The second guy smiled and showed off his gold teeth. "You need some directions, old man?"

Obviously, I wasn't scared, but I was concerned about one thing. How was I going to take on all these guys in broad daylight without everyone questioning how I did it?

And had he called me a bitch?

The leader got right up in my face. "I think maybe we can send him off in the right direction for a small donation. What do you think, mister? You wanna donate to our little club if we tell you where to go?"

My eyes narrowed as I leaned in even closer to the leader's face. "How about I tell you were to go?"

The gang members all started whooping and hollering at this, thinking it was hilarious. The leader didn't think it was so funny. "Bro, I was just gonna take your wallet and watch, but now you are dead."

The leader swung at me, but I casually avoided the fist. Then he pulled a knife and jabbed it at my chest.

I reached out and grabbed the leader's wrist and twisted until it made a popping sound. Then, I yanked him forward while I raised my knee so the gangster's face connected with it. Hard. The leader slumped to the sidewalk like a puddle of vanilla pudding, where he would undoubtedly be spending the next few hours.

"Problem is," I said, looking from one gangbanger to the next, "I really like this watch." I adjusted the band, and looked down at my knee before, finally, brushing off my slacks, acting as nonchalant as I could. "I didn't get any blood on my new suit, did I?"

The rest of the gang members stood around, silently, picking their proverbial jaws up off the ground.

I straightened my tie and fixed my cuffs, addressing the young men without looking at them. "Is there something else I can do for you gentlemen?"

Gold Teeth backed away along with his friends. "Nah, nah, man, we're good."

"Then have yourselves a nice evening." I gave them a big smile as they took off into the now-darkening neighborhood. For the rest of my stroll, I made sure to keep my eyes and ears open so I wouldn't get surprised again.

A few houses down, I climbed up three steps and rang the doorbell to Danielle's duplex. I scanned beyond the garden out front to make sure the gangsters were really gone and weren't going to try something stupid, but there was no sign of them.

Danielle was lecturing somebody on the other side of the thin door, and it was obvious that she didn't realize people outside could hear her.

"I ordered that on the way home. I'm pretty sure that was more than thirty minutes," she said. "Don't you think? Should I try to get it free?"

She opened the door. She hadn't wasted any time slipping out of her work clothes. She wore sweats and a T-shirt, and looked even more surprised than when she saw me earlier in the garage. "Mr. Douglas? Oh, wow. I was expecting a pizza."

I turned the charm up as high as it would go. "I'm sorry to just show up here. I felt bad about earlier, and I thought maybe I could take you out to dinner or something to make it up to you."

The door swung open wider, and a guy with an apparently ironic haircut and a beard like a bird's nest looked me up and down. "Who is this guy, babe? Why's he want to take you out to dinner?"

"Relax, Nate. It's just my boss."

Nate puffed out his chest and tried to look tough. "What is it you're trying to apologize for, old man? Some kind of harassment? Of a sexual nature, maybe?"

Again with the old man?

"I just had a mishap with her phone earlier, and I felt bad about it. I can buy dinner for both of you, if you'd like." I even stuck out my hand to shake.

"You think I can't pay for my own meals, or take care of my woman? What's your problem, dude?"

"I'm just trying to—" I started.

Nate tried to shove me off the steps, but I didn't budge. He looked like an idiot, bouncing off of me. I tried to calm him down, but he was just getting angrier. "Look, I don't want—"

Nate took a swing at my face, but my hand came up like a blur. I directed his punch outward and his fist collided with the metal screen-doorframe, which bent into a sharp point.

He wasn't bleeding or anything, but he swore like he was. I think his eyes turned red for a second, though I might've been mistaken.

Danielle panicked. "Nate, you're gonna get me fired!"

He stood, shaking out his hand, sucking in air between his teeth. His expression was a combination of fear and anger.

I continued to try to de-escalate the situation.

"Ms. Taylor, there's no need to worry about—"

"Naw. You know what? I'm gonna call my boys and we're gonna take this D-bag down." Nate grabbed a cell phone off a nearby table, and I immediately recognized it as Danielle's phone from earlier. Now was my chance.

Taking a step forward, I calmly grabbed Nate's hand with the phone still in it and squeezed. Nate screamed as the phone fell to the floor and cracked open, then fell to his knees holding his hand. I guess I squeezed a little harder than I'd meant to.

Danielle knelt next to her boyfriend and stared at me. I recognized the combination of disbelief and trepidation in her eyes. I just wasn't used to seeing it while out of uniform.

"Sorry, Ms. Taylor, but he seemed like he might be a bit out of control. I'm sure if you put some ice on it, he'll be fine. As for your phone..."

I picked the pieces up off the floor. Right then, I sensed someone else behind me and, thinking it was another attack, perhaps from the gang or Nate's "bros." Who knows, maybe they were one and the same. I spun and almost kicked the pizza delivery guy in the chest. The guy threw the pizza upward as he jumped back, and I managed to grab the box out of the air.

Then, calmly, I put it down on the plastic patio chair and checked on the delivery man, trying to remember if it was this pizza chain I owned or a different one. I always get them mixed up.

"You okay?" I asked.

The guy seemed nervous, but he nodded. "You scared the crap out of me, dude. I've been beat up three times in this neighborhood already."

"Here. Maybe this'll make you feel better." I pulled a couple of crisp hundreds from my wallet and handed them to the guy.

He stared at the bills in his hand like they might come alive. Then, his eyes widened as he realized something. "Hey! Aren't you—"

"No." I looked back to make sure Danielle and Nate weren't looking at me, then quietly slipped the guy another Benjamin. "And you never saw me here, right?"

"Riiiiiiight." The pizza guy left, wearing a huge grin, counting the bills over and over again as if he was afraid they'd disappear in a puff of smoke.

I turned back toward Danielle and held up the pieces of the broken phone. "I'm really sorry about all this. I feel like I keep causing more of a mess. I'll go down to the store right now and buy you the newest model, with all the bells and whistles. It will be waiting on your desk tomorrow morning."

I smiled, then turned and headed down the steps, making a mental note to ensure Danielle got a raise tomorrow as well.

The door shut behind me, and I heard Nate's voice from inside as I walked away. "Bells and whistles? What the f—"

My own phone rang and I answered it. It was Sawyer. "Any luck?" I asked.

"Yeah. It's wiped. At least the ones of you. There were also vids of her and some caveman getting sweaty if you ever need to blackmail her."

I grinned. "I don't think that'll be necessary."

"How'd it go? With the stalling?" Sawyer asked.

I thought about it for a moment. "It wasn't quite what I was anticipating, but it all worked out in the end. I guess I still have a few moves left for an old man."

"And that was it?" Osprey asks.

"It? He prevented my civilian identity from being revealed to the whole world. That's a pretty big deal."

"He just went in and deleted something from someone's cloud account. If I knew that was all it took to impress you, I would have done it a long time ago."

We both laugh. I have a feeling the awkwardness is over for us.

"I knew then that he had my back. And that he also made up for some of my own deficiencies. It made me realize, after swearing I was never going to take on another partner, that I really did need one."

"Yeah, that makes sense. I get it."

"You know what else?" I ask.

"What's that?"

"You had his back. That night with…" I took a breath. "That night with Chef Maléfique. I don't think I'd be here if it weren't for you. So the answer is 'Yes.'"

Amy smiled a small smile. "What was the question?"

"You asked me if I'm okay with you. Yes. I'm absolutely okay with you."

"Excuse me, sir?" The voice comes from the other side of the room and I look up to see a nurse standing at the open double doors. "You can come in and see your friend now."

I look at Osprey and say, "Here we go."

EIGHT

AMY

I'd never formally met Baron Steele before today when he asked me to hold his coffee, or even seen him in person other than the event in Times Square. But, like everyone else, I've seen plenty of pictures and videos of him over the years. I've seen him doing his commercial stuff, and I'd seen old footage of him during and after battles. But I've never seen him look the way he did when Frank and I walked into his hospital room. Nothing could have prepared me for seeing this super-strong, nigh-invulnerable—wait—is that a thing? Let's just say… highly-invulnerable hero lying in bed like an invalid. Two black eyes, a broken nose, bandages everywhere… the guy looked rough.

And this is a guy who shrugged off a punch from Eaglestar. Obviously, anyone else on Earth would have been turned into a splatter that resembled a ripe tomato that had been thrown into a red brick wall covered in red graffiti. If they were lucky.

"Frankie? What, no flowers?" The Baron somehow manages a smile and a joke, even in his condition. And does Frank always let him get away with calling him Frankie, or is it just because the Baron's in such rough shape?

"I know how much you like carnations, but I was in a rush to get down here and the ones in the shop downstairs were too expensive for me," Frank replies. Oh, I get it now. It's one of those guy-guy relationships I'll never understand.

The Baron starts to laugh, but I see him wince, which freaks me out even more than seeing him in this condition. I hope he didn't catch me wincing, though. That's seems like something he wouldn't appreciate much.

He looks at me and winks. "And who's this? Hold on… I know you. Weren't you supposed to save my coffee from being spilled in the big hullabaloo?" I can't believe he's thinking about coffee at a time like this. Or that he remembers me.

"I did save it," I say. "You never asked for it back."

He tries to smile at my comment and winces again.

"This is Amy Chen, Baron. She's a member of our… club."

"Ah. I see. Let me guess… and your, ah, spirit animal is another bird, perhaps?"

"Good guess. An Osprey," I say. He's charming for sure. And there are those older guys who are super creepy-charming, but not him.

"Excellent choice. Magnificent creatures. I believe I know who you are now. Didn't recognize you in your civvies." He looks me up and down without hiding it, which is something I'm entirely used to from guys. I suspect they think it's some kind of misguided compliment. Spoiler alert: It's not.

But I don't feel like he's "eye-balling" me or thinking of me weird. He's just kind of… nice. And that's a welcomed change.

"Hold on… Chen? Not Luis's little girl?"

"The same," Frank replies.

"Well, I remember you when you were just a tiny tot. I see you were lucky enough to grow up with your mum's good looks."

Weird. He knew me when I was little?

Frank clears his throat. "She was the one who told me about your little incident with our favorite union leader," he says.

"Psychopath, you mean?" the Baron asks.

"We seem to be entering that realm."

"Entering?" the Baron scoffs. "That train left the station years ago. Mind the damn gap, I say."

"I don't know if I'd go that far."

"Look at me, Frankie," the Baron says, trying his best to sit up. "What are we gonna do about Jonathan? It's gotta stop. He's clearly out of control."

"I'm formulating a plan."

"Of course you are." He laughs. Shakes his head. "What else is new?"

"It's going to require a trip to the UK," Frank says.

My head snaps toward him. I hadn't heard this part of his plan yet. "What?"

"Ah. The motherland, eh? Well, say hello to Ole Liz for me while you're there."

"Liz?" I ask.

"Queen Elizabeth II," Frank answers.

I snicker. "You're kidding, right?"

They both look at me, completely straight-faced. Apparently, they're not.

"I'll see if I have time to drop by the palace while I'm there," Frank tells him. "I'll probably be spending most of my time in Scotland."

"Visiting the home of your traitorous ancestors?" The Baron seems to be only half kidding about that.

"They weren't all traitors."

"Right," the Baron says. "Clan Douglas have always had a nasty streak. I sometimes worry more about you than I do about Jonathan, to be honest."

"You should."

"Oh, hey, turn that up, won't you?" the Baron says to me or Frank. I'm not sure, but he points to the television.

Frank doesn't move, so I fumble for the remote that's wired to Paul's bed. I press a button and his bed moves. I wince but it doesn't seem to have bothered him.

"Sorry," I say in a barely audible voice.

"Just hit the volume, luv, right?"

As the volume rises, Paul says, "Get a load of that piss. They've been spouting fascist rhetoric all damn day. It's like we never defeated the Nazis and the bastard who claims to have put them down has joined their ranks."

The news anchor, Dale something or other—who cares, right?—is pretty worked up. My initial presumption is that he's up in arms over Eaglestar's behavior at MoonMoney today. However, my supposition, as natural and duh as it is, is wrong.

"Oh, they're talking about me," Paul says. "Love when they do that."

"Shhh," Frank admonishes.

"This guy," Dale says. "He's always around when there's trouble. We didn't hear a word from him in almost a year. He showed up at the Sidekick Day celebration last year, acted like we should care, and then disappeared. Then, all of a sudden, he's beating up on Eaglestar?"

The co-host of the show, a blonde woman, says, "I'm not sure I'd call it that. Eaglestar is fine. Last I heard, Paul Steele is in intensive care."

"He should be in the Trench, that's where he should be."

"I think we have Eaglestar, live on the line," the woman says.

"Really?" Dale says, genuinely surprised.

"Eaglestar, are you there?"

A deep voice comes booming over the airwaves, but no video. "I'm here."

"This is… so unexpected," the woman says.

"To what do we owe the honor?" Dale agrees.

"I'm here for one very simple reason. This news station and every other across America is hereby shut down."

The feed immediately cuts to black and then a second later, a rainbow of colors appears accompanied by a long beep.

I run a hand through my hair. "What the f—"

"That's that, ain't it," Paul says.

"That's the last straw," Frank says.

"Straw? That's a two-by-four and the camel's back is more than broke," Paul says. "That poor bastard is dead in the desert. Enough's enough, Frankie."

He's right, and I can see it on Frank's face that he agrees.

NINE

SAWYER

Alone.

As much as I'd love to stay home and binge anime and play video games for the rest of the day with Mom and Frank gone, I do actually have an after-school job now, so it's off to work I go.

I know, I know, that's nothing new. I mean, come on, I worked at the prestigious Big Frankie Junior's across from the tower. That was a glorious moment in my illustrious career.

Not.

At least, this time, it's something I enjoy. That was absolute torture I had to endure as a fast-food worker. I got all the crappy jobs around the restaurant and answered to a pock-marked tyrant of a manager.

Okay, that's mean to people with skin problems. But Kevin—or Mr. Kevin as he liked to be called by all us underlings—was such a piece of human excrement. I'll be happy to go the rest of my days without ever having to see him again.

Mr. Chen, on the other hand, has always been really cool to me, and working directly for him hasn't changed that. I've been wondering since I started with this internship at Douglas Industries if it's my introduction to a corporate ladder I could someday be sitting at the top of. After all, as Chen himself made me realize last year, there's a good chance I'll inherit all of this once Frank is gone.

Oh, boy. It's a lot to process.

But hopefully it won't be until far, far in the future.

Another thing I've had to come to terms with is the short life-expectancy of heroes that aren't named Eaglestar. Frank and Alex and Amy and I have really tremendous work ethics and we've trained really hard. On top of that, we have super high-quality armor. But someday, our luck can run out and one of Deadeye's bullets could hit just right and pierce a jugular.

Kind of morbid, but totally true.

Frank is definitely the type of person who plans for things well in advance, and

I'm sure he wouldn't want me just showing up as the new CEO some day after never spending a day working at the company. I even suspect that working at the burger joint, another of his holdings, was my—turns out, fairly traumatic—introduction to that world of Douglas Industries. It's where his dad made him start out, after all.

Oh, and don't forget there's that little bit about no one in the public forum even knowing I exist, much less that I'm his son.

I think my favorite part about working with Mr. Chen is how conveniently located the lab is. From my bed to its padlocked door, it's under five minutes. Not bad.

I approach the keypad and punch in a code that only Chen and I—and Frank, I assume—know.

8068.

Some guy, somewhere, decided this was the most secure four-digit number on the planet. Supposedly, it follows no pattern, it isn't a date, there's no sequential repetition of numbers, and it isn't a straight column on a keypad.

Shrug.

Except, if someone figured out that's the most secure code, then won't other people figure it out and try it? Once you announce a code is secure, doesn't it kind of lose its security?

Regardless of any of that, I still have to provide my palm print and retina scan. I guess they're worried someone might gouge one of our eyes and cut off one of our hands, so they'll have to find out the code also?

Chen is already in there when I enter, working on our latest project. He's been keeping it a secret from even Frank, because it's for Frank, but he doesn't think Frank will use it. In fact, he's afraid Frank will shut down the project if he finds out what it is.

What is it? I am so glad you asked.

A brand-new powered suit that offers extra protection, so it gives him added strength, especially in the legs, where he's having the most trouble.

"Mr. Vincent," Chen says as I walk in. He's taken to calling me that while we are in the lab. The really weird part about is, lately, I've been kind of bummed that I'm not, in fact, a Douglas, and this is a weird reminder.

I guess it's kind of childish. I'm almost eighteen. What do I want, Frank to adopt me?

I smile at Chen and say, "How's it going?"

"Fine. Fine. I think it's ready for testing."

"Seriously?" I don't even try to contain or hide my excitement. "Already?"

"Yes," he says. I rush toward it, but he puts up a hand. "But… there's some admin stuff for you to handle before we get rolling for the day. Why don't you head into the office and get it sorted?"

Where I didn't try to hide my excitement, I make no such effort with my disappointment. He gives me this look that's become a bit familiar: not quite anger, not quite disappointment. Just, sort of, c'mon, now, get it done. It's actually very effective.

Luckily, he keeps the boring business stuff to a minimum—some filing and data entry stuff, mostly—and has me spending most of my time with him in the company division he started in himself and enjoys the most: research and development. For the first time, I'm getting a first-hand look at some of the equipment that he's working on for us. It's too bad I never get to try any of it out on the streets, thanks to Evilstar—that's my nickname for him since he became such a dick after his return—and the rest of the Guild.

We get to spend a lot of time in the high-tech lab with no one else around. After all, it's not like other employees can see most of the top secret crimefighting equipment we're developing. Sometimes, Chen makes the excuse that it's being developed for the Guild, and in some cases that used to be true, but for whatever reason they've stopped ordering stuff from Douglas Industries since last year.

Like I keep saying, something is definitely wrong.

The paperwork takes very little time, and I almost think he makes me do this stuff just so there appears to be something remotely "work-y" going on. Otherwise, it would just be too much fun, and what kind of boss would allow that, right?

I head back into the lab. It's exactly what you would expect. Bright white walls, ceiling, floor. Metal tables and shelves and racks along the walls all covered in a variety of things from scraps of metal to canisters of chemicals and stuff. Normally there would be a bunch of people working in a place like this, but because it's all top-secret superhero stuff, nobody else is allowed in here. Not even the janitors.

So guess who gets to clean up afterwards? I'll give you a hint: It's not Mr. Chen.

"Would you like to try it on?" he asks, holding up what looks like a pair of futuristic pants.

"Kind of big for me," I say.

"Yes, somewhat. But you're not too much smaller than Frank anymore."

I guess he's right. I have been growing a lot the past couple of years. I don't think about it much, but in the suit, I could probably almost pass for Frank.

"Go ahead," he says. "Try it on. I won't look."

He offers a small laugh as I grab the suit, and begin to stuff myself into it. Sure enough, it's a little loose all over, but not so much that I can't work it. It feels good. So good that I'm kind of jealous.

"Does this come in Red?"

"Thankfully," Chen says, "you do not need this kind of assistance."

"Neither does Frank, though, right?"

He gives me a knowing look.

I would never say this to Frank, but I think that incident with Chef Maléfique did a lot more to his psyche than to his body. I'm not saying he's scared—though I wouldn't blame him. Since he was kidnapped, he's just not quite the same. Chen agrees that it's mostly in his head. That's why we've been developing this. We... well, mostly Chen, thinks this would give him the boost he needs if he ever has to fight again. Trouble is, Frank has vowed never to fight again, so he may never use it. But it will still be good to have it around just in case. Never say never, right?

With things going the way they are, it could be sooner rather than later. Hopefully later.

I move around in the suit, practice hitting some test dummies, doing some acrobatics, and jumping and kicking. I've never felt more like a superhero.

I smile. "This is amazing."

"I'm glad you think so."

"So, it's ready?"

"Close," Chen says. "I think a few more tweaks and we can present it to your father to see if he'll use it."

"And what if he doesn't?"

Chen sighs and takes off a thick black glove he wears over one hand. I sometimes forget about the metal appendage he has beneath it.

"Sawyer, do you know what an IED is?"

"Some kind of bomb, right?"

"Improvised Explosive Device," he says. "They are usually simple and crude creations designed to inflict damage to the enemy, but they are not always accurate or effective." He wiggles his metal fingers. "But sometimes, they are."

I've never actually heard how he lost his hand. I just knew that it was in some war in some Middle Eastern country.

"While we were stationed in Afghanistan, your father and me, we'd spent hours a day training for scenarios we hoped would never happen. Mostly combat-related, but we all knew basic medicine as well."

He puts his glove back on.

"One afternoon, a child came running to the front gates of our base. He was crying, sobbing uncontrollably. He begged for us to come. We could gather his intent from his body language—that's fifty-five percent of speech, by the way—and his tone, which is another thirty-eight percent. We didn't need to know his words.

"I was one of the closest to the gates, your father too. We followed protocol, but ultimately, that led us to follow him along with a small contingent. He led us a short way and, still crying, pointed to a heap of fabric in the distance."

"A body?" I ask.

"Yes. That was my conclusion as well. Immediately, I knew it to be one of the boy's relations. I told the boy to stay behind and, being the one with the most medical training, I went to provide aid. When I got there, even at a distance I could see that the body was long since expired."

"That's sad," I say.

He shook his head. "I was too late in understanding the setup. There was a sudden explosion. All I saw was bright white light and I felt a searing pain."

"Your hand…"

"I felt nothing in my hand. As I believe it is with your father. He is so focused on where it hurts, that he's lost focus of the damage done to places that don't. That is how it is with the most severe of injuries. I hadn't even realized my hand had be severed at the time. The pain was everywhere else."

He lifts his shirt to reveal small scars all over his torso.

"Shrapnel hit me all over. I blacked out and the next memory was waking up in a laboratory similar to this one and my hand had already been replaced."

"How?"

"Frank was a hero before he was a hero, Sawyer. He was also rich beyond measure, yet he served his country with honor even though he could have avoided it. He had me airlifted to one of his facilities in Dubai, and they did the job there."

"So this is, what, you returning the favor?"

"Perhaps," he says, "but that's not the point of the story. In order for me to have made it to that lab, someone had to be prepared to perform on-field medicine they hoped they'd never have to employ knowledge of."

"Right."

"You understand?" Chen asks.

I literally have no idea what I'm supposed to understand.

"I..."

He smiles and places his metal hand on my shoulder. It feels heavy and cold.

"I need you and Amy to be prepared for things that are happening now that we hoped never would."

"The Guild," I say.

"I'm not sure if you saw the news, but just before you arrived, I received word that Eaglestar has seized control of all mainstream media."

"What?" I'm aghast. So aghast that I'm using the word aghast.

"I don't presume to understand everything, but Eaglestar issued an attack on Baron Steele that none of us ever believed him capable of."

"Something is wrong," we both say at the same time.

"Yes," he says. "And we need to be prepared for any event. Might I suggest you make extra efforts with your team? No more cancelations."

How did he know about that?

"Are we understood?" Chen asks.

I nod.

"Great. Now let's get you out of Frank's uniform."

TEN

AMY

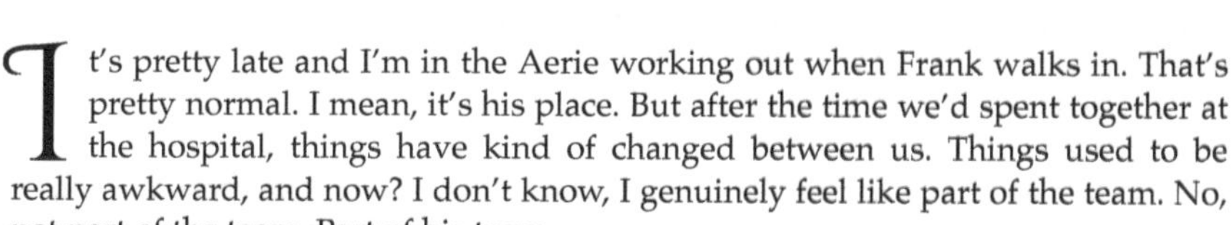

It's pretty late and I'm in the Aerie working out when Frank walks in. That's pretty normal. I mean, it's his place. But after the time we'd spent together at the hospital, things have kind of changed between us. Things used to be really awkward, and now? I don't know, I genuinely feel like part of the team. No, not part of the team. Part of his team.

It's a good feeling.

"Hey. Sorry, I'll get out of your way," I say, and start grabbing my things—water bottle, duffel bag, towel.

"No. Stay," he says. "There's no reason you can't train while I work over here."

"Are you sure?"

"Positive. You're not in my way at all." He gives me one of his F-D-3 smiles. Then I think he realizes he's doing it and his expression shifts. "I'm just finalizing details for my trip with Sawyer's mom."

"You sure that's a good idea?" I ask. Then I realize how silly it is for me to question him. "Not that you don't know what you're doing."

"Which part? Taking Megan on a trip where I plan to steal some invaluable artifacts from a very rich man, or leaving Sawyer with the house to himself when he's got a new girlfriend?"

I literally don't know which one to respond to first or if I even should respond at all.

"I—what?" That's the incredibly eloquent response I decide on.

"It's okay. I get where you're coming from," Frank says. "But trust me. This is how we stop Jonathan. I need you to hold down the fort while I'm gone. Can you do that?"

For fear of stuttering over another response, I nod instead. Then, it's quiet for a few minutes and I decide to speak up.

"I don't understand why Alex can't come back while you're gone. Wouldn't that be smart?"

"'Smart' isn't something anyone ever claimed Eaglestar was," Frank says. "Besides, I think keeping Alex away is part of his plan."

"But what is his plan?" I ask.

"If I knew that..." He types a few things into his computer. "Jonathan and I have always butted heads. But we were always friends. This isn't my friend Jonathan we are dealing with. Something is very wrong and I aim to find out what. So, can I count on you?"

"Of course," I say. "But what about Sawyer?"

"What about him?"

"Won't he be upset if he finds out I'm in charge?"

He laughs a little. "Didn't you hear the part about him having a new girlfriend?"

I had heard it and the shock of everything else sort of made me forget.

"I believe you know her," he continues.

"I do?"

"Neith. Aaliyah."

"What!" the eff, I add in my head. I knew they were sort of close, but I didn't realize they were like that. And why do I care? No, seriously. Why should I care? Do I care? Am I... jealous? I'm definitely not jealous because I want to be with Sawyer or anything. Yuck—he's like ten. But yet another couple, happy and in love. Puke.

"What's the matter? You don't approve?" Frank is definitely surprised by my reaction.

"Oh, it's not that. I had just assumed it was with someone from school. I hadn't even considered he might be dating a member of his team. That can get... messy."

"Like you and Alex?" he asks.

This guy is just bomb after bomb after bomb today.

"You knew about that?" I ask.

"There's nothing that goes on in my team that I don't know about."

"I'm starting to realize that. Are you mad?"

"You're both adults," he says. "But I would love if you could help me get ahold of him. He hasn't responded to me in days."

"Me neither," I tell him, trying to hide the disappointment. As I say this, I start hitting the practice dummy. Hard. Completely unrelated, I'm sure.

He walks down from the ops area to the workout mat where I'm training. "Try planting your foot just a little farther back."

He's gonna give me fighting advice? This never happened before.

"Don't you need to plan for your trip?" I ask.

"Well, if you don't want my hel—"

"No!" Crap. Foot in mouth. Didn't realize how that would come out. "I do. Absolutely. I just don't want to be a burden."

"Right," he says. "Okay. Foot back here."

He points to the mat just a half a foot behind where mine currently is and I give it a shot. It feels good. My hit is more solid. These are things I should already have down after my years of martial arts training, but, then again, none of my instructors have had *real* real-life combat experience.

"Any more tips?" I ask, maybe a little too enthusiastically.

"Well, if you wouldn't be offended, I've been wanting to make some suggestions for quite some time."

"Really?"

"Really. I just wasn't sure how you'd take it."

"Are you kidding? Training with you would be a dream come true."

"It would be nice to have someone who actually takes my advice and isn't able to just copy everything like Sawyer."

He starts showing me some moves and correcting my form, and even after just a few minutes, I can feel myself getting better. I can't even imagine how much better I'd be if I'd been training with him as long as Sawyer has been.

"Now, go ahead and hit me," he says, out of the blue.

"What?"

"Hit me."

"I—"

"What are you afraid of?" he asks.

"I'm not afraid."

"Then hit me."

I'm reluctant because he's the best hand-to-hand combatant I've ever seen, but he's also thirty years older than me and kind of disabled after what Chef Maléfique did to him.

"I'm not sure that's—"

"Hit me!"

I swing at him and he blocks it easily. I try a little harder, still no luck. I attempt a feint, followed by a kick, and don't even come close.

Finally, I land a punch. Right in the face. His lip is busted and starts to bleed.

"Oh my God, I'm so sorry! Are you okay?"

He wipes the blood off and smiles. "Looks like I'm more out of practice than I thought."

"Did I hurt you?"

I step in to get a better look at the cut and he hooks his foot behind my legs and drops me before I can even think to parry.

He laughs. "Don't worry about it. You still have some work to do, but you're already getting better."

He extends his hand to help me up and I try a trip of my own and fail absolutely miserably.

He laughs again.

"Gotta wake up pretty early to—"

"Ahem." The sound of someone clearing his throat takes us both by surprise. I'm even more surprised to see that it's my dad.

"Dad!" I scramble to my feet and walk over and give him a hug, trying not to get sweat all over his expensive suit. We'd just had dinner together, but it looks like he came back to the office to work late again.

"I never thought I'd see the day that my little Amy would be able to sock the Black Harrier in the face."

"Sure, but you saw what happened after?" Frank says.

"Yes. You shoved a woman to the ground."

"Dad, that's not at all—"

He stops me with a raised hand and a smile and says, "I'm just ribbing him, dear."

Frank takes it all in stride as well. "I probably need to get back to training. I may not be out fighting crime anymore, but that doesn't mean I shouldn't stay in shape."

"Amy, would you mind giving Mr. Douglas and me a moment alone? There's something I need to speak to him about."

"Oh, yeah. Definitely. I have to get back downstairs and finish a Physics paper, anyway." I kiss him on the cheek. I turn back to Frank. "Thanks for the lesson."

"Any time. And do me a favor? If you hear from Alex, let me know."

"Will do," I tell him and head toward the door. Then I stop and add, "But I wouldn't hold my breath."

On my way out I check my phone for the millionth time today. Still no reply.

ELEVEN

FRANK

I get the feeling Chen is about to tell me something he's been holding out on for a while. After all these years, I've gotten to know the man pretty well. He's been as close to a business partner as I have, the head of my R&D department, I served in the war with him, and well, he's a friend. There's not much we can do to hide things from each other.

Besides all that, I am the Black Harrier. It's my job to know when people aren't being entirely forthright.

"Well?" I say once Amy is gone. "What's the big secret that you can't talk about in front of your daughter?"

"No big secret. I just didn't know how comfortable you'd be discussing the topic in front of anyone else."

Did I misread? Maybe it's not just my physical conditioning that has missed as step. Sure, I'll bite.

"And the topic is…?"

"Your disability," he says, as straight-to-the-point as I've come to know him to be.

"What about it?"

"Frank, come on. It's me. I've been watching you for some time. Paying attention. And I don't think you're still as injured as you think you are."

Him now too?

"Have you been talking to my doctors and physical therapists as well?"

"I admit," he says, "I did try. But HIPAA… You'll be glad to know they wouldn't spill a word."

"That's comforting," I say, starting toward the ops area to take a seat, leaning pretty heavily on my cane. As soon as I notice I'm doing so, I look up and him and straighten my spine just a tad. "Just so you know, they agree with you. What gives you that idea?"

"What did you just do?" he asks.

"I'm not in the mood for riddles, Luis. Why don't you just tell me."

"Fine. When you were sparring with Amy just now… You were favoring that leg when you set down your cane, but once you became absorbed in the fight, you started moving like you usually do. You're obviously rusty, but you didn't appear to be injured. However, as soon as you were done, you suddenly needed the cane again."

"So you're saying my cane is just a crutch?"

"Somewhat literally, yes."

I take a seat in my command and control chair and return to my work.

"I've taken the time to come up here, Frank. The least you can do is humor me."

I spin toward him. It comes out more angry than intended. "I'm not exactly sure what you want from me."

"I'd simply like my friend to get better, and I believe you are. I watched you with Amy. You were the old Black Harrier again."

"Old," I say. "Right."

"You know what I mean."

I stand, leaving my crutch propped up against the computer console. He motions to the cane as if I didn't know I'd left it there. I ignore him and say, "I don't know what to do about that. Knowing about it consciously doesn't change the fact that I don't feel like myself."

"I believe it's partially psychological, and partially the fact that you're out of shape for the first time in your life, which helps your mind to 'accept' your false perceptions. Perhaps you should see someone about it."

"See someone? You mean a shrink?"

"I mean a psychologist," he says. "Or some other professional who can help you come to terms with things."

"Not going to happen."

"Why not?"

"Do I really have to get into it?"

Chen sighs. "You can talk about your trauma—your issues—without revealing your dual identity, or the specifics about how you were injured. The world does know that you were kidnapped, at least."

"If I go to anyone good, they're going to know I'm holding something back. Something major. And if they're too good, I may just slip up and reveal my secrets."

"Would that be so bad?"

I look at him like he's made an insane comment, which he absolutely has. I just shake my head. "Luis, you really have to ask?"

He sighs again. "Please think about it, at least? Until then, I do have something else I've been working on. In fact, Sawyer's been helping me."

"What's that?"

"Powered leg braces that should allow you to walk without the cane completely. There are already similar devices on the market, but as usual, I'm making some improvements. They're also compact. Should fit under armor?"

"Interesting," I say. "What powers them?"

"Six graphene-ion batteries comprising four strings of 3,440 high-rate cells, each rated at 920Ah. Operating up to 5,230V on high-rate charge—"

"Sounds heavy," I say, interrupting him. He waits patiently while I walk toward a suitcase in the corner of the room. "Perhaps, this can be of help to you."

I hand it to him.

"What's in it?" he asks.

"Just look at it somewhere private," I say.

"Will do," he says. "I have a good feeling about this, Frank."

"How good?"

"This could be medically ground-breaking. After a while, I believe we should be able to install them as implants beneath the skin."

"Impressive,"

"Yes, well, we'll just have to see once they're completed."

I put my hand on his shoulder. "My friend, I'm looking forward to it."

I sit again and he notices the monitor behind me.

"What's that?" he asks.

"I'm leaving for Edinburgh in a few hours. With Megan."

"Really? Is that… are you two… there?"

"I think so, Luis. She's really something beyond special. Plus, with Sawyer? We've been talking about her moving in."

Perhaps that's a bit of a stretch, but I'm interested to hear his thoughts. Then he gives them to me and I wish I could take it back.

"Are you out of your mind? What if she finds out about all…" He motions to the room. "… this?"

"Would that be so bad?" I repeat his earlier question.

Sharp as an ax, he catches it and smirks a little.

"I hope you know what you're doing, Frank."

"Don't I always?" I let a beat pass before continuing. "It's more than that, though."

"Oh?"

"I want you to get our kids geared up."

"I'm way ahead of you, my friend," Chen says.

I raise an eyebrow.

"Sawyer and I have worked on more than just new armor for you. I fear this is just the beginning of things with the Guild."

"Jonathan…"

"Yes, I wondered if we were going to discuss this," Chen says.

"He's lost it. Between what he did to Paul and cutting off the news… I own many of those stations, Luis. You know how much money we are losing?"

"Intimately," he agrees.

"You remember that guy Standesamt?"

"I see where you're going. That could be dangerous."

"I'm counting on it."

"I've never wished more that your new armor would be ready," he says, no small amount of disappointment on his face.

"I'll be fine."

His lips turn up slightly. "Yes, I'm sure you will. Have a good time. I'll hold down the fort."

"You always do."

TWELVE
SAWYER

That's what it feels like. Which, I don't know, maybe even that's insensitive. It's not like the Guild is rounding everyone up and loading them into concentration camps or anything. Not yet, at least.

I'd just watched Eaglstar's call-in to the news station on YouTube. At first, I thought it was kind of great… the takedown of all garbage we are bombarded with on the news. They hadn't done much over the past years besides pit us all against one other. But without that—biased as it might have been—we have no way of really knowing what's going on anywhere other than our own neighborhoods.

It's kind of crazy to think about. Like, a hundred years ago, I wonder if any of this same crazy stuff was happening all over the place but people just didn't know about it? Okay, I know—not this exact thing. But are things really getting worse, or are we just so connected to everyone all the time that we can't help but be bombarded with all the bad stuff?

Not even social media accounts work anymore. Not at all. 404 Errors and dead links. The apps won't even load.

Frank and Mom have decided to go on vacation. That sounds really stupid, all things considered. And my mom fought pretty hard. She was really excited until the thing with Eaglestar happened. But Frank says he has a plan. He hasn't even told me what it is. He certainly didn't tell my mom. But he did assure her that everything would be better in the UK. He's probably right.

She thinks he's got a work thing there.

What that means is that I've got the house to myself for a couple of days or more. It's so weird. Mom never trusted me at all in the past. I guess, technically once I'm eighteen she won't be able to control me anyway, so maybe she's just weaning herself off of it or something.

Neith and I plan to go on an actual date. Not that an empty house and Neith fit into that plan. I didn't mean it like that. Guh.

Okay, let me start over.

I'm really nervous and excited. There's nothing I can do about the state the world is in, so I'm gonna focus on me for once. I just have to get through a day at school and then…

I'm gonna admit something. Deep breath… I stayed up late last night watching romantic movies with really suave male characters in them. My power, mimicking other with perfection? I'm hoping in works with something like charisma. I don't know if I've ever really tried.

Scratch that. I know I've never consciously tried. But maybe I've unconsciously done it?

As I'm walking to my first period class, people are simultaneously avoiding me and staring the way they have been since I accidentally hurt Logan. Some probably think it was on purpose—for revenge or something. I'm sure those who've witnessed or, especially, experienced being bullied by Logan are happy it happened, but the one thing everyone is in lockstep on is staying away from me.

I feel like Moses at the Red Sea. Crowds of students literally part when I walk down the hall. Is this what it feels like to be a bully? To be feared?

I don't even feel this way when criminals see me dressed up as the Red Kite. Red Raptor. Geez, everything must be really getting to me if even I can't remember.

I don't like it. At all.

The other weird thing is that Javier didn't try to walk to school with me. My board is busted up, but even when I get a new one, I'm not gonna be allowed to ride it to school. I loved that board. Osprey got it for me for my birthday and I still haven't told her it's destroyed. And it was custom, too, with an awesome red dinosaur on it. Get it? Red Raptor? Yes, I'm named after the bird, but that's kind of the joke.

Our joke.

That thought makes me even more sad.

It's not like I can just replace it without her knowing.

I feel like everything is constantly simmering and if the heat gets turned up even a little more…

Everything is so clamped down because of the Guild that people are afraid to even talk to one another. There's this underlying nervousness and anxiety that's making people edgy. I stop in the middle of the hall, everyone staring at me. I can hear whispers and people calling me "crazy," "psycho," "nut-job."

A little more heat.

Mr. Blanchard walks by. He literally puts like six feet between us as he walks around me in a wide arc.

More heat.

"I think he's gonna do it again," Fabiola says to her friends as they stare at me, unmoving in the middle of the school hallway. She's not even whispering. "Look at him. You can see it in his eyes."

That's it. I can't stand it anymore. It all boils over.

"Okay! I get it! I messed up! Like you've never made a mistake?"

Well, if people weren't staring before, they sure are now. I've got a stage and I'm gonna use it.

"Why is everyone so worried about Logan anyway? You all know he's a bully.

He's a friggin' a-hole. You were all either his victim or his accomplice. If you were his victim, you should be happy that he was taken down a notch. If you were his accomplice, you should be happy you didn't go down with him or that you don't have to go along with his BS out of fear anymore. But no matter what your relationship was with him, we all know he was the biggest jerk in history, so get over it!"

For a few seconds, everything is silent. Then I hear slow-clapping, like we're in one of those ridiculous scenes in a movie. I look over, and it's Javier.

I wonder if everyone is gonna join in. I kinda expect it. But instead, someone shoves Javi toward me.

"They're both freaks," one kid says.

"Go get a room, queers."

Then all at once, everyone walks away and leaves me standing alone with Javier.

"That was a good speech," he says.

"Yeah."

Spectacular.

Later that day, all students are required to file into the gym to attend the pep rally instead of learning stuff because, y'know, yay sports, and I'm really not into it. If you're surprised by this, I suspect you haven't been paying much attention.

I sit next to Javier, who barely acknowledges me as he watches Fabiola and the other cheerleaders doing their opening routine while the students funnel into their seats. I'd tell him to wipe the drool from his chin, but there would just be more there in a couple of seconds, so what's the point?

Everyone is just about seated when they finish the routine. The whole school bursts into applause and cheering. You'd think it was the Super Bowl half-time show or something the way everyone acts. Nothing against cheerleaders, but I fight supervillains all the time, so it takes a little more to impress me.

Hmm, I used to fight supervillains.

Now I'm just a kid.

God, my life is so depressing.

Blanchard is down in the middle of the basketball court now doing his blowhard thing that he's so good at. He's dressed up in a ref uniform that he probably keeps in his closet to act out his secret fantasies or something, knowing him.

One by one, he announces the staff who are all dressed in sweat shorts and polo shirts. It's one of those powderpuff games, or whatever they're called, only for basketball instead of football. I don't know, is there a name for that? Whatever. It's the staff versus the varsity team.

You'd think the adults would play well against a bunch of kids, but it isn't that way at all. There are a few teachers who are in good shape and probably play at the local rec center or something on the weekends, but most of the staff are huffing and look like they're gonna have a heart attack after just after their entrance.

The varsity team, on the other hand, is well-practiced and in shape, so they look like the Harlem Globetrotters out there. In comparison, at least. They run up the score against the staff in no time, and get to shove their teachers around a little.

It's kinda funny to watch, which I guess is the point of the whole thing. It certainly isn't a serious competition.

Everyone's eyes are locked on the court, but I notice Logan and his cronies huddled in the far corner of the gymnasium, just beside the opening that leads beneath the bleachers.

What the hell are they up to?

All I know is I don't like that grin on his face. As soon as I notice that nobody is watching, I get up from my seat at the other end of the bleachers and slide off the side. I land in a crouch and disappear into the darkness.

They haven't noticed me yet, and they won't until I want them to. I'm not just bragging. What kind of superhero would I be if I can't stay hidden from some high school idiots? Especially Logan and his stupid friends?

This is a far cry from when Logan was a Neon Knight, but it reeks of the same bullcrap. He and his band of jock-hooligans are several yards away, paying attention to something on the ground.

I sneak a bit closer.

"Blanchard is gonna lose his mind," Logan says.

The other two giggle like schoolgirls.

"He's such a tool," another one says. I think his name is Brian or Ryan.

The third one—Jake—lifts something from a box.

Fireworks.

They're gonna set off fireworks? Inside?

I don't know what these idiots are thinking, but the explosives they have are nothing to sneeze at. There's enough that they'd make a really fun Fourth of July celebration in any neighborhood. And they're planning on lighting them off right beneath where some students are sitting. I'm sure it's no coincidence that it's the "nerd" and "geek" section where the unpopular kids get banished during rallies and assemblies because nobody wants to sit next to them.

It's where Javier would have been without me. I grind my teeth.

If they go off right under the seats, or even worse fly up through the openings in the bleachers, someone is gonna get hurt. Probably more than one person.

I know this isn't gonna work out the way I want it to, but I don't have a choice. There's no way I can get any closer without them spotting me and I can't let people get hurt.

"Logan! What the hell are you doing?" I whisper-shout in his direction.

He looks up at me, and at first he just seems annoyed and pissed off, but then it suddenly comes back to him that I can totally kick his ass, and he gets nervous instead. He says something to his buddies that I can't hear and I see a flicker of a flame.

That's when I swear.

With the wicks to all the explosives sparking away, the dumb idiots take off in the other direction, leaving me to either try to fix the problem or to let it happen. It takes me less than a second to decide.

Hey, I'm a superhero, right?

I run over and gather up the lit fireworks and throw them into the box that they carried them in. I don't know how much time I have left, but if these things go off while I'm holding them, I'm gonna be seriously injured. Maybe even dead, although I'm trying not to think about that.

I shove the top back on and box in hand, I run out from under the bleachers on the closer side, where I came in, and I know they're gonna explode any second. One pops and sizzles. There's no time to be inconspicuous or hide anything, and there's only one place where I can avoid them going off near anyone: the middle of the gym. The game is at "half time," the teams are still at their benches talking through strategy or whatever, and it's just poor Mrs. Winnester, our P.E. teacher, out there, dressed like a referee, along with Blanchard.

I toss the box into the air as hard as I can toward the middle of the gym. The box lid does its job for a little bit, and then the fireworks fly out in all directions. They immediately start to explode, which means I have literally no time left before throwing them. Some blow up on the spot, others tear off in different directions.

It's quite a show.

People absolutely lose it, screaming, shouting, pushing, shoving. I watch as some of the ninth graders literally roll down the bleachers before being trampled by the stampede.

One of the bottle rockets flies around haphazardly and hits the gym floor right at Blanchard's feet as it explodes, causing him to jump up.

After they're done making their bright, colorful light show and deafening, thunderous sounds, the entire gym goes quiet.

Through the smoke, I can just barely make out Principal Blanchard, eyes fixed on me.

So, how's your day going?

THIRTEEN

AMY

For years, I'm around these people, and I never meet Baron Steele. Now, suddenly, he's everywhere.

I mean freaking everywhere.

When Dad asked me to accompany him to an important meeting, I had no idea what to expect. But going to the Baron's office in downtown Manhattan wasn't at the top of my list of guesses. Or even the middle. Or the bottom.

I mean, let's face it, it wasn't on the list at all.

Not only did I not expect to be seeing Paul again so soon, I definitely didn't think he'd be out of the hospital so quickly after the way he looked when I last saw him. He must heal really, really fast. Freakishly fast.

He still has the remnants of two black eyes and a bandage across the bridge of his nose, but other than that, he doesn't look much the worse for wear when he meets us in the waiting area of his penthouse office. Then again, for all I know, the rest of his body could be one huge bruise.

"Thanks, Mare," he says to his secretary. "The Chens, great to see you. Come on back. Follow me."

"Thanks," I say.

"How's that gorgeous wife of yours?" the Baron asks my dad as we approach some huge double doors.

"We're divorced," Dad says matter-of-factly.

"Sorry to hear that," Paul responds without managing to sound sorry at all.

He leads us into his massive office with a window longer than most Mack trucks. It's all luxury: a big mahogany desk, Persian carpet, leather seats. He offers us a seat in the chairs across from his desk, and he politely waits until I sit before he plops himself into his big, comfy chair.

"So, Luis," he says, "to what do I owe the pleasure?"

"We need to talk about the Guild problem."

"It's about time. I've been ready for years," Paul says, somewhat smugly.

"It's never been this bad."

"It wouldn't have gotten this bad if we'd nipped it in the kipper."

I almost laugh at that. I've never heard nip it in the kipper, but British people have their sayings.

My father crosses his legs and says, "True as that might be, here we are, and it's definitely past time we did something about it."

"Isn't Frankie taking care of it? Something or other in Old Britannia, right?"

"Scotland."

"Right. Right. Coffee?"

"No, thanks," my father says. He starts to speak but stops when Paul presses the button on his phone.

"Mary, have someone go fetch me a White Mocha Machiatto from MoonMoney, would you?"

"Sure, Paul," she responds, New York accent thick as Paul's biceps.

Paul looks up at me as if to ask if I want anything.

"Black coffee?" I say.

"And a black coffee," he adds.

I can feel my father's gaze boring into me.

Paul hangs up and leans back.

"So, what are we going to do? Frankie's already overseas at the moment, right?"

"On his way," Dad says. Then he drops his feet flat and leans forward. "Can I be honest with you?"

"No, I want you to lie," Paul says. Then he laughs. "Christ, of course I want you to be honest."

"I don't think Frank has exactly been at his best recently."

"The whole kidnapping thing, huh? Really got to him." Paul shakes his head. "That's a damn shame. He's one of the good ones. Far as I can tell, the whole core is off the plot. That's what I told Frankie."

"We don't know who we can trust," Dad agrees.

"Right, well, who do we have, then?"

"My daughter Amy—" he gestures toward me.

"I'm sorry," I find myself saying before I can stop.

They both stare at me like I've just kicked a kitten.

"It's just… that 'kidnapping thing' was nothing light. I mean, I was there. Chef Maléfique nearly killed him and then…"

"You don't have to say it," Paul says. "I know. Horrible thing, that. I didn't mean to be blasé about it. I'm sure you'll accept my apologies."

I nod and turn back to my father. If I'm not mistaken, there's something in his eyes… is that pride? I give him a small smile and he continues.

"Yes, well, Amy is part of a team of masked crimefighters whom we could use. They're quite capable, especially Sawyer—"

"Sawyer?"

"Red Raptor," I offer. "Frank's son."

"Wait." Both the Baron and my father say at the same time.

They look to one another.

"You know?" Dad asks me.

I smile and my father cocks his head, but any further response is halted when Paul speaks up.

"What the..." He begins the F word but my dad gives him a look and Paul shifts to, "Frank has a son? What are they putting in the water over at Douglas Tower?"

"He's a good kid," Dad says.

"Sure he is," Paul says. "But that's just it, ain't it? He's a kid. And no offense, luv, but so are you."

I open my mouth to speak but my dad powers through.

"There are a few others, as well. A speedster, a tank, an archer—"

"Frank's kids?" It's the first time I've seen Paul look even a little flustered.

"No," my father says, laughing at the thought. "Others on Amy's team."

"Sounds a bit like a mini-Guild, if you ask me. What are they, sidekicks?"

"Some of them are," Dad says.

"And some of us aren't," I add.

"A bunch of kids," Paul says again under his breath. "There's gotta be others."

Dad clicks his tongue. "I'm afraid not, Paul. Like I said, we just don't know who we can trust."

A knock on the door interrupts us.

"What is it?" Paul shouts.

A nervous-looking kid with glasses pops his head in. A second later, his hands follow, carrying two cups from MoonMoney.

"Yeah, bring it in," Paul tells the kid.

He rushes forward, nearly tripping on Paul's expensive rug. He hands them to us in turn, first to Paul, then to me. So much for chivalry. The kid then does an awkward bow before speed-walking back out the still open door.

"Weird kid," Paul says as he slurps his coffee. "Heaven in a cup. All right, what about the new guy Frankie keeps talking about? Bog Bunny? Hip Hopper?"

"Swamp Rabbit?" I practically spit the name out. "Don't believe a word Frank says about him. He just wants Alex—uh, Redhawk—back in the city."

"Who the hell is Redhawk?" Paul says, clearly exasperated. "Another kid?"

"Not at all. Actually, he's—"

My dad puts his hand on my arm to calm me. "It's true that they're young, but they are all we have. And that's all the more reason we need you on board. Training heroes... it's what you do."

Paul sits back in his chair and rubs his hands over his face. "Bloody hell."

"Mr. Steele," I start, "Sawyer and I defeated La Cucaracha, Deadeye, Chef Maléfique, Creeping Death, and a dozen others on our own. When the Neon Knights were vandalizing the city? We stopped them. Then, we took down Battlegear, as a team. You think we are too young, but so did all of those guys. We can do this."

I don't know where it came from, but it was the speech we all needed to hear, including me. I was beginning to feel like a fraud.

The Baron takes a long pull from his cardboard cup with the familiar logo on it, then lets out a long sigh.

"If I go along with this, you're going to owe me a MoonMoney gift card with so much on it that they'll bury me with it still full of credit."

Dad looks at me and I nod.

"It looks like we have ourselves a deal," Paul says.

I smile. "Fan-effing-tastic. So what's the plan?"

FOURTEEN

FRANK

My private jet touches down at the airport in Edinburgh almost ten hours after taking off from JFK. It's an odd little place with only one terminal despite being a massively used facility. My pilot pulls us around to the side and the team works on getting an airstair ready for our disembarking. Luckily, we were both able to get some sleep, which puts us in a pretty good mood. My planes are not like the ones the other twelve million passengers who land at the Edinburgh Airport each year are familiar with.

I fly in luxury.

One thing I'm not too sure about is how Megan will handle the jet lag, especially since we're only going to be here a couple of days and that's usually not long enough to recover. I don't have that problem. Long ago, I learned a form of meditation that I employ on long flights that helps my body's circadian rhythm to adjust quickly to the time change.

We cross the open pavement, cold wind blasting us. Once inside, I can see Megan shiver as she lets the interior heat warm her.

"Over there," I point, and we pull our bags toward a sign marked "Customs."

"Business or pleasure?" asks a bored-looking agent seated on an uncomfortable stool behind a podium. His uniform is at least a size too small for him, undershirt poking out between the buttons. There's a small mustard stain on his chest and some crusted on his lip.

"Both," I tell him. Then, looking at Megan I add, "I hope."

"Gross," the agent says so softly I figure he thinks I couldn't hear him, but he wasn't counting on my practiced ear.

"Are you referring to the food caked on your person and clothing?"

Megan slaps me on the arm and the agent looks up in surprise, wiping at his chin.

"I'm—I… you're good to go, Mr. Douglas. Enjoy your stay in Scotland." He stamps our passports and send us on our way.

Megan puts her arm though mine and leans in close. "So, what kind of pleasure are you planning to engage in while we're here?"

"There are some beautiful firths north of here that are just stunning this time of year."

She slaps my arm again and we both share a laugh.

"But first things first—the business part. But don't worry, it shouldn't take long."

"It better not, mister," she says playfully, but with a hint of annoyance. I know that tone. It means any extracurricular activities of the romantic variety are in danger of being off the menu for the duration of our stay.

The sacrifices I make for the sake of saving the world…

The air outside is crisp. With buildings all around us, shielding us from the wind, it's refreshing. Especially now that we are in front of the building and away from jet exhaust.

We load into a cab, the driver—the most Scottish-looking person in the country—loads our bags into his too-small trunk and realizes he'll have to put a couple of them up in the front passenger seat next to him. European cars—good for the environment, bad on storage space. I'm very good about not packing much, especially if a trip is only going to take a couple of days. Megan… not so much.

"You don't own a fleet of limos here, or what?" she asks.

"Sure I do, but I wanted you to have a true taste of things."

She climbs into the backseat, seemingly oblivious to that fact that the driver tries different variations on attempting to fit everything up front and still be able to drive. I finally offer to take a couple of the smaller bags in back with us, and his sigh of relief tells me he's probably more grateful for that than he'll be for the generous tip I'm going to give him at the end of our ride.

"I wouldn't have minded sampling a different flavor," she tells me.

"Where ye headin?" the driver asks.

I hand him a card with the address.

"Good question. Where are we heading?" Megan asks. "A bed and breakfast?"

"Er… something like that." I can't help a small grin as the driver looks back at me and raises an eyebrow.

"I'll make the trip worth your while," I tell him. He nods and puts the car in gear.

Some time goes by in silence while Megan stares out the window at the beauty of Edinburgh. Anyone who hasn't really left America can't imagine what it's like to look at buildings that weren't built in the last decade, or even the last century or ten. The hills roll in the distance, the perfect canvas for the city's many steepled rooftops.

"Wow," she whispers to herself.

"That's how I feel every time I look at you," I tell her, wondering if it's too cheesy.

She confirms that it is. "You've already got me here, Casanova." But she smiles and seeing that makes it worth it.

We enter a tunnel and she sits back. Without the views to distract her, an emotion other than awe crawls across her features. Staring at her fingernails, she sighs.

"What's wrong?"

"I feel guilty, leaving Sawyer," she says.

I snicker.

"What's that for?"

"Hon, Sawyer is probably on cloud nine."

"Oh, thanks," she says.

I put my arm around her. "I don't mean it like that. Look, a teenage boy needs time away from his mother sometimes."

She pulls back and away from me. "To do what?"

"Can you stop reading into everything I say? I'm just saying, he's probably enjoying a bit of alone time. Not like that! It's good for him. He'll have to fend for himself a bit. Learn how to live on his own."

"I guess."

"Are you going to let this ruin the trip?"

She grabs my arm and places it back around her. "Of course not. I plan to enjoy every moment."

The tunnel opens back up again and her eyes return to the views.

I'd like to say I believe her, but I know her. She'll fret over Sawyer anytime her mind isn't otherwise occupied. I guess there could be worse things than a mother caring for her child—our child.

Half an hour later, we pull up to our destination after a drive through some very scenic Scottish countryside. When Megan sees where we're headed, she does a double-take and looks back at me, unsure of what she's seeing.

"A castle? You booked us a room at a castle?"

"Not exactly."

"That's certainly what it looks like."

"Oh, it's definitely a castle," I say. "But I didn't book us a room. I own it."

"You own a Scottish castle?"

"I told you... I own several."

"I thought you were joking."

"Not at all. And it did belong to my ancestors, so I felt like it was only right that I buy it back once I could afford it."

"Geez, Frank," she said. "It must have cost a fortune."

"It was surprisingly cheap, given its state of decay at the time. It was the renovations that cost me a bundle."

"It looks ancient."

"It is. Well, on the outside anyway. The inside has had a few... upgrades."

"This is some place," the cabbie says.

When we step inside, Megan's jaw drops. The interior of the castle, while still maintaining a medieval feel, is completely refurbished and updated with all the modern conveniences one could desire including central air conditioning—which is rarely needed in these parts—several fridges and microwaves, three full bars, two jacuzzi-style baths, nine flatscreen UHD 4K televisions, broadband internet, and more.

In fact, it looks a great deal like my penthouse, now that I think about it. I guess I'm just a man of certain tastes.

We're greeted by the elderly couple who take care of the castle for me.

"Megan, this is Mr. and Mrs. Arbuckle. They're the caretakers here."

"I'd've met ye outside if I'd known ye were on your way, Master Douglas," Mr. Arbuckle says as he grabs a couple of the bags.

He's a wee little man, as they'd say around here. He's always reminded me a bit of Billy Crystal's character in the '80s film *The Princess Bride*. Wispy hair, wrinkled face. But unlike Miracle Max, Donald Arbuckle is one of the sweetest men alive.

His wife is several years his junior but still gray and beginning to hunch.

Lovely couple.

"Don't worry about that," I say. "I'll get them."

Megan examines the paintings of my ancestors adorning on the walls.

"Anyone I've heard of?" she asks.

"Doubtful, unless you watch documentaries on Scottish history or that series about Mary, Queen of Scots."

"You're related to her?"

"Distantly," I admit. "I'm more closely related to the people who held her prisoner for years."

"Really?" She lifts an eyebrow. "Should I be worried about that being an inherited trait? Is that what this has been? A two-decade-long ruse to get me here? Does this place have a dungeon?"

"Hey now, there were a lot of good guys in my family tree as well. And I've had all the cell doors removed from the dungeon downstairs."

Besides, I've been held prisoner myself and it's not something I'd do to even my worst enemy—if he were still alive, that is.

"Would you like some tea and refreshments?" Mrs. Arbuckle asks. "I've got some biscuits cooking."

"That would be nice. I'll help," Megan replies as she follows Mrs. Arbuckle to the kitchen. She glances back at me and smiles as she exits the room and I return the look.

As soon as she's gone, I turn to Arbuckle and get down to business. "Is everything ready?"

"Of course, sir," he says like I shouldn't have needed to ask.

"Everything?"

He smiles. "Whatever nocturnal pursuits yer planning, sure an' ye'll be well-equipped. Have I ever let ye down before?"

I pat him on the shoulder. "No, you haven't. It's good to see you. I wish I could make it over here more often."

"As do I, sir. As do I."

Years ago, Arbuckle's son, Angus, had gone to New York and gotten himself in a lot of trouble. I won't bore you with the details, but let's just say it was of the life-threatening variety.

Not only did Black Harrier save him from certain death at the hands of a major crime boss, Frank Douglas—I—got him out of the financial trouble that had put him there in the first place. Somewhere along the way, Angus figured out that both of his rescuers were the same person, but he was grateful enough that he never told anyone… except his parents. He turned his life around and devoted himself to charity and helping others. Became an outstanding person.

Then, a couple years later, he was killed in a house fire. After ensuring it was an accident and not an attack, I attended his funeral services. It was there that I met his parents. To my shock, they thanked me for everything I'd done, both as Frank Douglas and Black Harrier. To say it made me somewhat nervous would not be giving proper gravity to things. Not only did I not like having the information out there, but it could potentially put them in danger as well.

However, one look at the Arbuckles would tell anyone they were trustworthy to death. And now, they had lost a son, and I'd lost my parents, so we became each other's surrogates in a way. It wasn't long after that when Toby was murdered. That was a dark time in my life, and this lovely couple was instrumental in my making it through that.

As a form of exchange, I keep them comfortable and safe, and they take care of my base of operations in the United Kingdom.

"Martha'll keep your lady friend busy for the time being," Arbuckle said. "Let me show you where to find your things."

FIFTEEN
SAWYER

Whoa!

Have you ever watched that old Christmas movie about the kid who shoots his eye out? The kid and his dad are changing a tire and he drops all the lug nuts in the snow.

"You really fudged up this time, kid," Blanchard says. Only, just like in the movie, he absolutely didn't say fudge.

We're in his office, of course. It feels a bit like a second home to me, these days.

I stare at him, incredulous.

"You can't say that to a student." I know that for sure.

"You just blew up the gymnasium!"

"It wasn't me!" I shout, standing.

"Listen to me, miscreant. I watched you throw the box of fireworks. Let me guess, it was Logan?"

"It was Logan!"

"For fudge's sake. You're expelled."

He says it so calmly, like he was ordering a burger at Big Frankie Junior's.

"I'm, what?"

"Get out of my office," he says. "You are no longer a student at this school. Your mother will be notified as soon as I can reach her. No amount flash from her famous boy-toy is going to save you this time. The whole school was there when you attacked us with explosives."

"Attacked?" My mouth is unhinged at this point. He's acting like I planted C-4 in the hallways.

"You are lucky to not be going to jail right now."

"Jail?" Great, now I'm just repeating him.

I try my best to compose myself. I shove aside every bit of malice and hate that I'm feeling and say, "Sir…" The word tastes like puke. "I'm telling you the truth.

Logan and his friends, Jake and Brandon or Brian or whatever, were under the bleachers, ready to set off fireworks and I stopped them."

"That right? Where's your proof?"

"I… I don't know? Check my bank account? I didn't buy any fireworks."

"Ever hear of cash?" he asks. He's not even looking at me anymore, just shuffling through papers on his desk.

"I don't even know where to buy fireworks."

"Compelling argument, Mr. Vincent. However, I've made up my mind. There's simply no room in this school for a delinquent such as you."

"Mr. Blanchard—"

"Get. Out. And I never want to see you again."

Fudge.

I spend the rest of the day alone in my apartment, so thankful my mom isn't home. That doesn't change the fact that my stomach feels like beavers are building a dam inside. Between getting "expelled" and tonight's date with Neith—I just can't get used to calling her Aaliyah—I'm a nervous wreck.

Truth is, I really need the distraction right now.

Things have been bad enough already with everyone so uptight and on edge, then I get into trouble at school again? It's not like Blanchard can really just expel me like that. There's gotta be more to it. Meetings. Committees. Stuff. But whatever.

Thank God, my mom's phone either isn't working over in Scotland or she's decided to take a break from "the real world." If she knew what had happened, I'd be grounded and I'd have been forced to cancel with Neith.

I'm gonna have to deal with Mom, eventually, but for now, I'll try to enjoy a night out with Neith. I'd asked if I could pick her up, but she's not ready for me to know where she lives.

A couple of days ago, when I'd told Frank about the date, he had one of those rare "proud papa" moments and made a reservation at the most expensive restaurant in town, which he happens to own. And even though I insisted I could pay for it myself, he laughed and told the manager to put everything on his tab.

He even took me to a menswear shop and splurged on a suit, since I didn't already own one. Even at Firefly's funeral, I was wearing my costume. So I'm looking pretty good and feeling confident as I sit at the bar sipping a soda while waiting for Neith—dang it—Aaliyah to show up.

To her credit, I didn't wait long, and even those few minutes were beyond worth the wait.

When she first walks in, I honestly don't even realize it's her for a couple of seconds. She's all made up, her hair done, and she's wearing an unbelievable cream-colored dress with gold filigree around the neck, shoulders, and waistline. She looks like the Egyptian goddess she's named for. I feel my heart skip and my breath catches in my throat.

She spots me and saunters over, looking somewhat nervous herself, which is unusual for her. I have to clear my throat before I have my voice back. "Wow. You look amazing."

"Thank you. You look quite nice yourself."

"Should we go ahead and get our table?"

I take her arm and walk over to the maître d', who promptly takes us to Frank's personal table. Everyone else is way older than us, and I feel like a lot of the other customers are staring as we walk past. I'm sure not many teenagers can afford to eat here, so it's not like they get a lot of prom dates and stuff.

"Here you are, sir. Mademoiselle," the man says, pulling out Aaliyah's chair.

He places a menu in each of our hands, then unfurls our napkins and drapes them over our laps. He steps away and a woman immediately fills his spot, pouring sparkling water from a green bottle.

"Geez," I say. "What was that, like seven seconds? Pretty amazing service."

We start looking over the menu, which doesn't even have the prices listed. I guess if you have to ask, you can't afford it. Maybe that's why Frank insisted on paying for it.

"Good evening," the waiter says. I hadn't even heard him sneak up on us. He sort of looks down his nose at us and says, "Have you dined with us before?"

"No," I say.

Neith shakes her head.

"Quite the table," he says. "I've never seen anyone seated here before."

"Is that right?" I say.

"Can I get you started with something? We have a delectable caviar roll. Maybe a lobster frittata?"

I look at Neith, who just shrugs.

"How about one of each?" I say.

"Coming right up," he says. "I'll give you a moment to peruse your menus."

"Sawyer, that sounds expensive."

"Probably," I say and then return to selecting my main course.

Her fingers appear at the top of my menu and she pulls it down, forcing me to look at her.

"You do not need to try to impress me," she says.

"That's not what—they just both sounded good."

She gives me a skeptical look but flicks her menu up again.

The waiter returns and places down our appetizers. They look incredible even if I have no idea what they are.

"Does mademoiselle know what she'd like this evening?"

Neith orders something I've never even heard of, and I order some chicken dish just because it's the only thing I'm even vaguely familiar with.

"Very fine choices." He doesn't even write anything down. I guess that's supposed to be impressive.

As he walks away, I offer Neith one of the caviar roll slices.

She takes one and leans back. "So… what's up?"

I smile. "Excuse me?"

She smiles back. "What's going on?"

I pop a caviar roll into my mouth and groan. So good. "I'm eating some of these delicious things. Isn't it obvious?"

We both laugh quietly at the callback to our first real conversation, and I'm so glad the tension has been broken.

"Try yours," I tell her.

Her eyes widen when she tastes it. I stare into them and I just can't believe she's here, on a date, with me.

The people at the next table, a couple that looks to be a hedge fund manager and his trophy wife, keep glancing over at us. I assume it's because we're teenagers eating at such a fancy place. Or maybe it's Aaliyah's tattoos. But then I hear them complaining to the waiter and asking for the maître d'. When he arrives at their table, I notice that they're both looking at Aaliyah and I overhear the word "terrorist."

I look the maître d' in the eyes, and he appears to be on the verge of panic. Not because he really thinks she might be, but because he has to figure out what to do about a customer complaining to him about someone who's there with a special guest of the owner.

He says something quietly to the man, and the guy stands up and throws his napkin down, obviously not happy with the way the conversation is going. So what do I do? I join him, standing there, tired of watching this bigoted ass-wipe do his thing.

Neith looks worried. "Please don't do anything."

"I'm not gonna let him try to get you kicked out of here," I say, my anger boiling over.

"It's okay."

"No, it's not." I walk over to the guy, who's quite a bit taller and heavier than I am. "You have a problem?"

The maître d' starts freaking out. "Sir, if you would—"

"Yeah, I have a problem. You. Bringing people like that in here. I'm trying to enjoy my dinner," he says, reminding me a bunch of Logan's froofie-ass parents.

"Well, maybe you'd be more comfortable at the local KKK dining hall where you belong."

He shoves me. Big mistake.

I could easily take him down with one punch, but that would be too quick and painless for this jerk. I hit him in the solar plexus first to make sure he can't breathe, and then in the face. I don't want him unconscious, just in a lot of pain.

The maître d' threatens to call the police as the guy grabs his napkin to stop the blood-flow from his nose. I turn back to Aaliyah. I don't know what I was expecting… her to applaud, kiss me on the spot? But instead, she's not even at our table.

"Aaliyah?" I say, looking all over. Then, I spot her leaving the restaurant. I almost can't catch her even when I start running. I finally reach her half a block down. "What's going on? Why are you leaving?"

"Do you really think we are going to be able to eat there after that scene?"

"Absolutely," I tell her. "We weren't wrong!"

"I asked you not to do anything."

I can't believe she's actually angry at me. I was doing it for her.

"But he was—"

"I don't care. I was having a nice evening. Don't you realize I hear things like that all the time? If I reacted violently to each incident, I'd spend half my time fighting people like him. If you would have let him, the manager would have asked him to leave, and it would have been over with."

"I couldn't let—"

"What? You think you need to save me? To protect me? I can take care of myself, Sawyer Vincent. In case you've forgotten. You know that if I wanted to, I could have hurt him. Badly. But there was no need to resort to violence."

I laugh nervously. "Are you serious? You're the most violent person I know."

Now she's really angry. "Those are criminals. They deserve what is coming to them when they are breaking the law. That man in there was a reprehensible jerk, but he was not breaking any laws with his bigoted attitude."

"I still think he deserved it."

"Then go back in there and hit him some more if it will make you feel better. I'm going home." She storms off down the street, leaving me standing there alone.

In case you haven't noticed, I'm really good with girls.

SIXTEEN

FRANK

The next morning, before my "business meeting," I take Megan sightseeing in the black Alfa Romeo I keep in the garage at the castle. I also explain some of the stories about my ancestors that she seems interested in. It's nice to talk about them with someone who cares, since so many people in the past have gotten bored when I rant on about it.

The Douglases are one of the most important families in Scottish history. My ancestors include everyone from the lords of Morton to James "The Black" Douglas, who carried Robert the Bruce's heart with him in a case chained around his neck while he fought in the crusades. When you read about Scottish history, there's always a reference to the Douglas family, on one side or the other. Sometimes on both sides.

We drive down to a five-star hotel where I'm supposed to meet with my contact. As I hand the parking attendant his tip and we enter the lobby, I give Megan an envelope.

"Like I said yesterday, this won't take long."

She opens the envelope, and inside, she finds a reservation for the full luxury treatment at the hotel's world-famous spa.

"Uh, take as long as you want!" She kisses me when I drop her off in front of the spa, and then I head off to the hotel bar just in time for my appointment.

The hotel bar is very modern and very Scotland all at once. The orange-bearded bartender wears a kilt and sporran. The walls are bright red but everything else in the room, including his tie, is gray with mustard yellow accents. It sounds worse than it is. It's quite a nice room.

I spot the man I'm supposed to meet, Lukas Standesamt, seated at the corner table. It's one of those half-moon booths that no two men should meet for business in, but there he is. After studying him for hours before the trip, I'd recognize him with my eyes blindfolded. Tall, slender, silver hair, with one of those thin mustaches that tends to make people look either genteel or sleazy. Somehow he's giving off an air of both simultaneously.

As I approach, he, of course, recognizes me as well. One of the downsides of being rich and famous—without my uniform, I'm rarely able to get near anyone without them noticing me coming.

To accentuate my point, I hear a woman beside me.

"Oh, my God, Christina, ye know who that is?"

"Ye know I don't like games like this," her friend—Christina apparently—says.

"Oi! Yer that American bloke, ain't ye? Frank Douglas?"

"You got me," I said.

They both shove off their tables and approach me like lionesses would a wounded gazelle.

"Could ye take a selfie with us?" the first woman asks.

I smile as a way of agreement, then place my cane down on the bar and wrap an arm around each of them.

"With my mobile too?" Christina, the one who didn't have a clue who I was until ten seconds ago, says.

I'm only too happy to oblige since it helps me keep my cover and prevent others—such as Lukas Standesamt—from recognizing my true nature.

I give them both pecks on their cheeks and they return to where they were sitting at the bar, comparing the photos they took on their respective phones.

"Quite the entrance," Standesamt says, standing to shake my hand as I reach his table. This close, I can get a better read on the man. The mixed messages make sense once I deduce that he started out sleazy and managed to adopt a more pretentious attitude as more and more money entered the equation. The question is, what sordid undertakings was he managing to get away with? I have my suspicions, but the only one I'm certain of is the procurement of stolen artifacts such as the ones from the zeppelin explosion that turned Jonathan Powers into Eaglestar.

"It's nice to finally meet you, Mr. Douglas. I've heard a great deal about you," he starts out. While he still maintains a slight German accent, it has been dulled by decades living in the United Kingdom.

"Well, you can't always believe everything they report on TMZ," I say, and we both laugh even though neither of us finds it very funny. In fact, I highly doubt he even knows what TMZ is, although he probably gets the gist of it from the context.

"Yes. Quite," he replies.

As much time as I've spent in the limelight, surrounded by cameras and superstars, I've never understood that hoity-toity saying. 'Quite' what, exactly?

"Please, call me Frank."

The waitress suddenly appears and we order drinks. Judging by the empty glasses, he gets what is clear to be at least his third vodka rocks and I order Scotch, neat.

When in Scotland, right?

"So tell me, Mr. Douglas—er, Frank…" he pronounces it like 'Fronk.' "What can I do for you? Your request for a meeting was quite cryptic."

"Quite," I say with a smirk he doesn't understand. "I'm interested in purchasing some items from your collection, actually."

He lifts his eyebrows in surprise. "Really? Well, I wish you had let me know. I could have saved you the long trip across the Atlantic."

"How so?"

"Nothing in my collection is for sale, I'm afraid. In fact, I don't even have any of it in my possession currently."

It takes my best acting skills not to let my irritation and disappointment get the better of me. "Oh, really? And why is that?"

"My entire collection is on loan to the National Museum of Scotland."

I nearly spit out my drink. "I see. And what prompted you to do that?"

"I have many valuable things, as you clearly know. I began to worry about the security of those items. I began to hear rumors that certain parties were… interested in some of the rarer parts of my collection." He gives me a suspicious look. Now I understand his game.

"Which parts might that be?"

"Mr. Douglas, we really should cut to the chase. You've come a long way and I'm very busy."

"I'm sorry, I simply don't know what you're referring to."

He sighs. "The so-called 'alien artifacts' discovered at the end of World War II. They were part of a very famous event leading to the origin of one of your country's great heroes."

I feign interest as if this is the first I'm hearing about it, but I doubt he's buying it. "Fascinating. Tell me more."

"Oh, surely Mr. D—Frank—you know of the story of how Eaglestar became the most powerful man in the world."

"Ah, yes. I vaguely remember hearing the story when I was in school." I do my best nonchalant shrug.

"Mmmm." He takes a sip of his drink.

I grit my teeth. He's really getting under my skin.

"Which items were you interested in yourself?"

At least I did my homework. "The fertility totems from North Africa."

"Ah, yes. They are among my favorites. But, unfortunately, they are at the museum with the rest of the collection."

"Well, that's disappointing."

"Indeed. However, while they're not for sale, at least you don't have far to travel to see them in person," his mouth curls into a smile, but his eyes are brimming with hostility.

"Just out of curiosity, Lukas—may I call you Lukas?—why would you loan them to a museum if you're worried about security?"

"You may. And it's quite simple. The National Museum recently spent millions installing a state-of-the-art security system. It's supposed to be impenetrable."

"Impenetrable, you say?"

We'll see about that.

I know what you're thinking. How can you rob a museum? You're a hero! One of the good guys!

I don't feel bad about it for two reasons. First, the items were stolen to begin with, so they never rightly belonged to Standesamt, or the museum. And second, the British Empire's record of procuring treasures from around the world that belong to other cultures is legendary. Basically, when they conquered most of the planet, they took pieces of it back with them. Generally, the most valuable pieces. They went from governing a quarter of the known world to living on a little island in the middle of the Atlantic. Let that be a lesson. When the mighty fall, they fall hard.

And, now that I think about it, there's a third reason. These are Tuldarian artifacts. Not only do they not belong to Standesamt or the museum, they don't even belong on this planet.

Most of the world doesn't know the true nature of the precious metals. Tuldar is a planet light-years away and the vast majority of journalism pertaining to the event are wrapped up in conspiracy theories and attempts by the world powers to steer the common man from the knowledge of life beyond earth.

It's not for naught either. If any Tom, Dick, or Harry on the street got a view of the Tuldarians, they'd probably die of fear. They are frightful creatures and none of us knows their true intentions. For that reason, The Heavenly Bodies, a team of extra-powered individuals loosely associated with the Guild, are stationed on the moon, sworn to protect the Earth should the Tuldarians choose to return.

I can't help but feel bad about the first step of my plan. I need to make sure I can sneak out without Megan knowing it, so I ask Mrs. Arbuckle to add a little "sleep aid" to her tea. It's not a drug or anything—all natural, organic, the whole nine. It's harmless, just something to make sure she sleeps soundly, but it's definitely nothing I feel good about.

But the fate of the world is at stake.

You wouldn't believe how many times I've said those words. However, somehow, this is the first time it's ever felt this real. It's one thing to be up against killer robots the size of Godzilla trying to crush Manhattan while fighting alongside the Guild. It's another thing entirely to be fighting the very people who helped me stop all those world-threatening events countless times before.

These truly are the most powerful people on the planet, and for some reason, they are not acting like themselves. Far from it.

Mr. Arbuckle has my equipment ready to go for me by the time I get downstairs. I can't really wear a full-on Harrier suit in Scotland without it drawing a whole lot of attention if someone sees me. Not to mention the danger, however slight it might be, of someone putting two and two together and suspecting that Harrier and I are one and the same. But I do have a basic suit with a lot of the same features. It covers my face, masks my voice, and alters my body shape enough to throw off the scent, which will hopefully get me in and out of the museum without too much trouble even if I'm spotted.

Plus, I keep having to remind myself, the Harrier identity isn't even mine anymore to begin with. It's Alex's now. At least part-time, when the Guild allows it.

Driving on the left side of the road always takes me a bit to get used to again, but by the time I approach the Edinburgh city limits, I'm already driving like a Formula One racer like the old days.

Before I cross the Forth Road Bridge into the city, I pull over and park at a prearranged spot—the parking lot of a busy hotel where nobody will notice an extra vehicle. Arbuckle has stashed one of my fastest bikes, a Kawasaki Ninja H2R. Black, of course.

I've gotta admit, it feels good on these old roads. So much freedom, winding and drifting. Nothing like New York City's gridlock.

With the sun well-past down, the museum has been closed for hours already. I sit in a nearby alleyway on my bike and review the specs on the museum's new security system that I managed to "find" on a website that I only use in extreme cases—at an exorbitant price, I might add.

I grapple to the top of the famous Greyfriar's Kirkyard across the street from the museum and start my reconnaissance from a perch. It's all so natural, being back on the prowl, that it takes me awhile before I realize I'd forgotten my cane in the Alfa Romeo.

Maybe Chen was right.

Ouch. Then again, maybe not. As soon as I start to change positions, my knees are so stiff I can barely move them. I do some stretching and loosen them up some. But that tweak is no joke.

I've heard numerous stories about this place being haunted. Normally, that type of thing doesn't bother me, but the fact that some of my ancestors, including a James Douglas who was an Earl of Morton and Sir Charles Douglas, an admiral during the Revolutionary War, are buried here, makes me not want to hang around long at three in the morning.

Even I get the creeps sometimes.

I scan the museum building, looking for patrolling security personnel. For the most part, it seems quiet. That could either be a good sign that they're not on their toes, or a bad sign that their new system really is so excellent and they don't need to worry about anything.

"Jillian," I whisper into my helmet.

"It's about time you paid me some attention. But, oh, you had to wait until you snuck out on her before you could talk to me, didn't you?"

It's not something I'd admit out loud, but I believe, subconsciously, I'd been doing things to try to "recreate" Megan everywhere I look. Amongst those attempts, ultra sexy AIs that, if manifested, would likely be fiery redheads. Now that Megan is back in my life, I believe it's time for a change.

"Just stop with the theatrics. I need you to be in scan mode and alert me if any security is nearby when I get to the museum."

"Anything for you, master." I really did watch too many TV reruns when I was a kid. *I Dream of Jeannie* may have subconsciously affected me more than I realized.

I snap out my decidedly non-cape-like glider wings and get ready to cross…

…but not until after I do a few more stretches. That does not feel right. I think I even feel a little pop when I move my knee.

I give myself a boost with boots I typically only have use for out of the city. Unlike my standard jetpacks, these are built directly into the heels of my boots. They require such a small burst of fuel that the reservoir fits snuggly between my foot and the soul of my boot and also creates a plush contact point that's quite lovely.

Since there are no skyscrapers nearby for me to glide down from, I basically have to fly straight across the street. I land on top of the building that used to be the Royal Museum, where there's an enormous gallery with a huge skylight that runs almost the entire length of the building, modeled after the old Crystal Palace in London. It's practically designed for me to sneak in through. I will, however, need to cut through the glass, causing some unfortunate damage to the building. But I'll make sure to make a generous donation to the museum later on that will not only pay to fix the glass, but buy a whole new wing.

"Jillian, were you able to loop the camera feed?"

"Of course, dear. It's the least I could do after you brought me on this fancy European vacation." The sarcasm. That's going to be the first thing to go.

"And the laser system?"

"Down for the count."

"Thanks." It's funny, thanking a computer, but when they are designed with such lifelike personalities, it's easy to forget they are simply programming.

"Don't mention it, you sexy thing. Anything for you." No. The innuendo is the first thing to go. Then the sarcasm.

From my utility belt, I pull a glass cutter and get to work. The diamond tip makes quick work of it, and I already have my suction ready to lift the man-sized hole up and out of the way.

After securing the loose end of the line to the frame, I start to slowly lower myself through and down to the floor three stories below. The exhibit is just off the main atrium, and the entire area is open with mezzanines surrounding it on each floor.

With the whole ceiling made of glass and metal struts, moonlight casts itself in a grid throughout the oblong room. It's really quite lovely. I can't wait to come here when I can enjo—

"Stop," Jillian alerts me. *"Guard below, making his rounds."*

I still haven't made it parallel with the top walkway. If anyone looks up, they'll spot me with very little trouble. She's right. Below, a guard strolls along the middle mezzanine. Once he passes, I finish lowering myself to the floor a little faster this time.

"Eyes open," I whisper. "I don't want any more surprises."

Recalling the layout of the interior of the museum, I head straight for the exhibit labelled "Mysterious Artifacts." Pretty spot on if you ask me. It's not like anyone is going to believe they come from another galaxy.

Thing is, the world has seen evidence time and time again of there being extraterrestrial life—even as far as witnessing spaceships from the Tuldarians. Those transparent metal, pill-shaped vessels hovered over D.C. for days. Everyone saw them. The Guild and the U.S. government wasted no time telling people they were simply Goodyear blimps. After a pretty expensive social media campaign, if someone even hinted they were alien in nature, they were added to the conspiracy theorists pile and put on a list.

Cruel? Perhaps. But that's how we keep the world sane.

"I'm in," I tell Jillian as if she can't see everything I see.

"Mmmm. Yeah. It feels good." I swear, if I had time, I'd reprogram her right this second.

"Cut it out," I tell her.

Some of the items aren't what I'm looking for and don't belong with the rest. Things that are ancient but appear to be modern, somehow. I suppose those are a mystery to me as well.

But the ones I need—the Tuldarian metals—are all clumped together, enclosed in a single glass case. They emit a soft blue glow. I'm hesitant to touch them, but my gloves are lined with several layers of protection.

"Any security measures, Jillian?"

"You mean like a safe word?" Before I can yell at her, she says, *"Nothing I see."*

I repeat the actions I used to get in with my glass cutter and suction cup. It almost seems too easy as I pull out the artifacts and put them in my belt pouch.

I guess I jinxed myself by thinking that.

Suddenly, something descends from the ceiling so fast I can't even tell what it is. The next thing I know, I'm enclosed in some kind of solid metal structure—four sides and a top, walls about ten by ten.

I'm like a rat in a cage.

SEVENTEEN
SAWYER

Trapped.

That's how I feel.

I can't handle this anymore. Everything is a freaking mess! The Guild owns the world. Logan owns my school. My date with Neith was a complete disaster, ruining any future chances I may've had for a relationship with her. I don't even know what else to do, so you know what? Eff it. I'm done playing nice. I'm gonna go out and find someone committing a crime and take it out on them, even if I have to patrol all night.

It feels so good to suit up after so long. I don my graphene body armor and lower my helmet over my head. Chilly October air pours in through the Aerie's open hatch. New York really is a beautiful city. I take a deep breath. I hope someone's doing something ugly.

"Tiffany, you there?"

"Always. What can I do for you?"

The one good thing about all this time spent not beating up baddies is that I had plenty of time to reprogram Tiffany. She no longer talks like a pornstar-hooker-stripper. Thank God.

"Are you picking up any disturbances that I can maybe go take care of?"

"Scanning. I'm sorry, everything seems to be quiet at the moment."

"Guess I'll have to do this the old-fashioned way, then."

I jump from the opening and my cape snaps out into glider mode. It's been so long that I almost forgot what it was like to glide around up here.

"Tiffany, keep your eyes and ears out for anything unusual."

"I have neither eyes nor ears, but I'll make myself aware of things through use of my infrared cameras, tomographic motion detectors and Piezoelectric sound sensors, if that's what you'd—"

"Just let me know if you sense anything," I interrupt. I've listened to this diatribe before. It's a bit stiff in the delivery. I guess I have some more tweaking to do.

"Yes sir."

As I soar above Fifth Avenue, I have to actively avoid drones. Luckily, I'm above most of them and they're focused downward to street-level, so it's not terribly difficult, but…

That's when an idea strikes. The Guild doesn't use drones produced by Douglas Industries, but they still use DI satellites for their surveillance and GPS functions.

"Tiffany, are you able to make an undetectable connection with the drones?"

"I believe so. Accessing…"

I'm waiting so long, I feel Muzak should be playing like in the Douglas Tower elevators.

Floor Two. La da dee la dum. Floor Three. Da la dum da dee.

Finally, she chimes back in. *"Yes, I have made a connection. What would you like me to do?"*

"Tell me where the drones aren't able to see right now." I feel so smart. I hardly ever feel this smart.

"There are one hundred seventy-three locations around New York City where the drones are not functioning to optimum efficiency and twenty-two of them are flying blind."

Boom. "Pick the closest one and display it on my HUD."

On my visor's display, a beacon shines in an alleyway a couple of blocks north. I change direction and swoop down to the alley, landing on a nearby rooftop. The metal sphere is about the size of one of those bouncy yoga balls. It's flying around in circles with spray paint covering its camera lens.

I'd love to meet the person who did that. I'd buy them dinner at any restaurant in the city as a thank you.

In the alley below, there's what appears to be a drug deal going down between two groups of three guys. Like I said earlier, there's always someone who thinks they are smarter than the system or "so badass, the Guild can't even stop them."

I drop to ground-level a few feet behind the people making the deal. They don't even notice me. I guess I have to make an announcement in my usual sarcastic tone.

"A little late to be conducting business in a dark alley, isn't it? What do you have there, meth? Is it the blue stuff? Because that would actually be kind of cool to see for once. You know… 'I am the one who knocks.'"

They all draw guns on me.

"No *Breaking Bad* fans? Really? I guess you probably didn't like the way all those drug dealers kept going to prison and getting killed, huh?"

"Beat it, kid," one of them says as he does that clicky thing with his gun that lets you know he really means business because he's about to fire it.

I don't know; guns aren't my thing.

"You don't wanna do that," I say, both hands raised and walking very slowly toward them. "That's just gonna make things loud and messy. Whatever happened to just pulling a switchblade on a guy? 'That's not a knife. This is a knife!' Crocodile Dund—"

I don't get to finish my sentence. Instead, I flip out of the way as the dealers and the buyers open fire at me all at once. Clearly, none of them are cultured in the art of television and film. They do, however, know how to shoot. Most of the bullets miss me completely, but only because I'm a badass gymnast. One does hit me, though. It ricochets off my body armor and kneecaps one of the thugs. He howls and drops to the asphalt, clutching his bloody leg with both hands.

"Ouch. That looks painful." I get back to my feet as they all start reloading. "Okay, my turn."

But then, I'm robbed of my turn. A dark figure descends on the criminals and immediately turns into a whirlwind of punches and kicks, taking down all five of the punks still standing in a matter of seconds. I'm so surprised that I don't even have a chance to react until it's all over with.

"Harrier?" I ask.

Alex turns around and glares at me. Or at least, I assume he is. Can't tell through the visor, which is kind of the point of the visor. "Go home, Kite."

Oh, so we're back to Kite again. I know what that means.

"What—I can't go out on patrol anymore?"

"You're no longer needed." He projects through a voice-changer, same as Frank's always had. But Alex doesn't have the same presence. Not nearly. "The Guild has everything under control."

"How'd you even know this was happening? That drone up there has been vandalized."

"Did you do that?" he says, voice racked with accusation.

"Me? What? No. Are you kidding? Not my style."

He drags the unconscious bad guys into a pile and starts tying them to each other to await the cops. "Better not have."

"Why are you being such a dick?"

He drops the last guy onto the pile and spins on me. "This isn't a game, Kite. These are hardened criminals."

I laugh. "Chef Maléfique was a hardened criminal. La Cucaracha was a—"

"Go home."

I ignore him. "I didn't even know you were in town. How long have you been here?"

He pauses as he finishes tying up the criminals. "If I answer you, will you go home?"

I shrug. "How long?"

He flips up his visor and sighs. The voice changer is off now. "About a week."

"A week? I'm surprised I haven't seen you around the Tower."

"I'm not staying there," he says, cryptically.

I guess I'll bite.

"Okaaay, so where are you staying?"

He was waiting for me to ask. I can tell.

"At the local Guild HQ."

"Oh, fancy. How nice for you. Was there a feast? Did they get you flowers? Oh, let me guess, they finally replaced Frank's portrait with yours?"

He shoots me a look that tells me they haven't before he even answers. "Time to go home. Do your homework or something."

"We haven't been partners for a long time now, Alex. Since when do you order me around?"

"Since I became a core member of the Guild." He flips his visor back down.

"Right—the ones who said you're supposed to be in Boston? Hey, why aren't you in Boston?"

He doesn't even look at me again or say goodbye before shooting his grappler upward and disappearing out of sight.

"Okay? Bye then!"

I look over at the thugs, piled up like trash in the alley. The one who shot himself is bleeding pretty badly. I swear and rush over and use a part of his own shirt to tie off the wound and staunch the flow until someone arrives.

"I'm only doing this so you don't die," I tell him.

Then I hear a voice.

"Kite." It's so faint that I can barely hear it. "Kite."

I stand and scan the area. Seeing nothing, I say, "Tiffany, where is that voice coming from? Is my comm picking it up?"

"Negative. It's coming from less than a meter away."

How is that even possible? There's nobody there. Unless they're invisible…

"Kite!" There it is again.

"How am I hearing this? Run an infrared scan."

"Working."

I still don't see anything, even with my visor showing me different parts of the visual spectrum. Then, I notice a little dot zipping around like a fly.

"Tiffany, zoom in on that reading there."

My visor magnifies the anomaly. It's a person. A tiny person, flying like an insect.

"Turn off infrared and stay zoomed in." I hold out my hand, and the insect-sized person lands on it. With the magnification on, I can clearly see now that it's Firefly—the guy whose funeral I attended a while back. "Increase volume on my ear speakers."

Firefly drops to his knees in the palm of my hand. "Kite… I need… your help."

Then he passes out.

Mini People.

Well, mini person, I guess. Mini ghost-person. This guy was supposed to be dead. I went to his funeral. I'm so confused and a little scared as I rush back to the Aerie.

Frank is in Scotland doing God-knows-what, but I've already contacted Mr. Chen and asked him to meet me there.

When I arrive, I'm surprised to see Chen isn't alone.

"Hey, kid," says a big bald guy. Dude looks like a statue of a Greek god or something.

"You know Baron Steele?" Chen says. "You do now. That Firefly? Get him over here." He points to a large metal gurney he has set up. He's not messing around. It's rare I see him not entirely calm.

"Is there enough room?" I joke. The smile disappears when Chen looks up at me, stone-faced.

"This ain't funny, kid," the Baron says. Then he lets out a small chuckle. "But that wasn't bad. Maybe at a different time."

"Right, sorry."

I carry Mac to Chen, then step back. I don't have any medical knowledge unless you consider the hours of *Grey's Anatomy* I've watched, which I don't, so neither should you. And don't judge. Guys can be fans of *Grey's* also. Okay, so McDreamy was one of the ones I studied when I was learning to be suave. Are you happy?

Chen, however, has plenty of medical training from his days in the military. He gets to work right away.

"This begins to confirm some of mine and Frank's deepest suspicions," Chen says, mainly to Baron Steele.

"Which are?" I ask.

"Not sure you need to know that," Baron Steele says.

I turn to Chen who doesn't look up from examining Firefly. He's wearing these big goggle-things that look pretty steampunk and using tweezer-like instruments. It's pretty crazy.

"What the hell is this guy doing here?" I say. Quite frankly, I've had enough of ego-maniacal pieces of crap lately.

Chen looks up at that. "I'm sorry, Sawyer. With Frank out of town and something this big, I needed someone I thought we could trust."

"And that's him?"

The Baron takes a step toward me. "I'm the only one in this whole damn city that we know for sure isn't some kinda evil twin. So, yeah. That's me. Got a problem with it?"

"Listen, Sawyer," Chen says. "He's on our side. I can assure you that. We can trust him."

"Yeah? Why's that?"

The Baron points to his eyes, and I notice for the first time that there are signs they were recently blackened. "Because Eaglestar nearly killed me, that's why. Satisfied?"

Oh. Right.

"Okay, then," I say in concession. "And you can trust me. I'm Frank's partner."

"And son from what I hear," Baron Steele says.

I give Chen a look that says, He knows?

Chen returns that look with, Yup, and gets right back to hooking Firefly up on some equipment.

"So what's with all the secrecy?" I ask the Baron.

"I just don't want to say anything until I've spoken to Mac."

He means Firefly.

I've had my share of finding out people are still alive whom I thought were dead, so I'm not exactly shocked. But I don't get why Eaglestar and the Guild would fake Firefly's death.

"What's wrong with him?" I ask.

"I don't know," Chen admits. "I'm afraid that even if I did, he's too small for me to perform any kind of procedures on."

I look at the metal tray of instruments beside the table and notice a needle that's long enough to go in Mac's mouth and out his butt. Too graphic? Sorry.

"Should I have brought him to the hospital?" I ask.

"No," Chen and the Baron say together.

Chen continues. "You did the right thing bringing him here. I doubt a normal hospital would have any idea how to deal with this. And I suspect the Guild wants him dead, so if they find out he's not—which wouldn't be difficult with all the surveillance they have going on—then they'll probably do whatever is necessary to make sure they succeed this time."

"You think the Guild did this?"

Chen looks up at me and his answer is clear in his eyes. And I have to say I totally agree with him.

"I need to figure out if there's some way to measure his vitals. We may be able to modify some of our sensor equipment."

"What can I do?" I ask, desperate.

"Nothing, I'm afraid. There's nothing any of us can do until he wakes up and tells us what happened. In the meantime, maybe you can get ahold of Amy. Tell her what's going on."

"But I don't know what's going on," I argue.

Chen's always pretty serious, but now he's so serious it's scaring me.

"You know enough. Things are worse than they appear."

I sigh. And keep getting worse.

EIGHTEEN
FRANK

Not sure how things can get worse.

"You appear to be trapped," Jillian says.

The cage is not a cage in the sense one would think of upon hearing the word. There are no bars, and I can't see through to the outside. There's complete darkness apart from a single blinking red light.

"Yes, I do. A warning would have been nice."

"I didn't know it was going to be that kind of party."

"Jillian, what happened?"

"This section of the security system was not located anywhere in the schematics you fed me. And I wasn't able to detect it until it was too late."

"I gathered that much already."

Then a polite voice screeches from a speaker at the top of the contraption. "Please stand by. Security will be here to assist you momentarily."

Assist me. Yeah. More like haul me off to jail.

Seconds later, one of the walls drops and four security guards stand just outside, wielding clubs and Tasers. They aren't big on guns over here, which is going to make this much easier for me.

"Hold it right there. Don't move a muscle," the apparent leader says. The smallest of the bunch, he's probably the brains.

"Looks like we got ourselves a high-tech burglar here. That's a fancy suit, innit?" the biggest one says. He's about six-four, two fifty.

"Eh. Looks like a motorbike suit to me," says another guy.

"I don't suppose it would do any good to try to reason with you guys, would it?" I ask. "I'd really like to avoid hurting you."

Of course it won't work, but I have to give them a chance. I'm not blowing smoke. They're just doing their jobs, and I really don't wanna injure anyone.

They look to one another and then break out in laughter. I take that as a 'no.'

"Just come with us," the boss says. "We'll be escorting you out front, where the coppers are gonna meet us any minute."

My best action is to pretend to comply. The worst thing anyone can do is strike now. They're expecting it. Even a thirty-second pause can be the difference between victory and failure.

I walk slowly out of the box, into the midst of them, with my hands up. I'm about to grab for a couple of blunt throwing weapons on the back of my utility belt before I realize I'm not wearing my regular utility belt. This one doesn't have any weapons—nothing traditional at least. I suppose I could turn my glass cutter into some kind of makeshift shiv, but again, I don't want to permanently injure these folks.

Instead, I stomp my boot on the foot of the big guy, since he'll probably be the toughest to take down and I'll need the element of surprise. Instinctively, he folds over and I bring my knee up to greet his nose. I don't like it, but blood pours out all over the marble floor.

"You son of a bitch!" one of the others shouts.

Sure enough, the big guy is on his butt, holding his nose in place.

I had to use my bad leg and wince from the pain. I may not need a cane, but the exertion has lightning shooting down my leg and up my spine.

The chubby one tries to get me with his Taser, but I manage to slap his weapon aside. He zaps the fourth guy, who hits the ground, convulsing. But they both recover quicker than I do, yanking the wires loose.

Big guy is clutching his nose and trying to rise. I grit my teeth, ignoring the pain, and deliver a kick to the side of his head that knocks him out cold. It might be too little too late though, because the other three are all surrounding me now and I'm almost back where I started.

"I don't know who you are, but all ye be doin is extending your stay in the HMP."

They close in on me, batons raised. Chubby swipes and I duck, then shove him. He staggers back and slides on the big guy's puddle of blood. Falling backward, he smacks his head hard.

The leader swings while I'm crouched and I roll back, ending the move with a sweep kick that takes the leader to the floor. I hear the Taser-Happy before I see him rushing me. Planting my feet, I catapult upward and catch him in the chin with the crown of my head. He stumbles, but doesn't go down.

I make a fist and I'm about to hit him when he drops his weapons and runs away. I could easily take him down, but what's the point?

I all but follow him out to the atrium, limping the whole way. My repel cable awaits me and I give it a tug. It yanks me back up to the giant skylight. Rising high, I can make out the runner telling someone on a walkie-talkie that I'm headed for the roof.

That's the thanks I get for leaving him conscious?

It's started to rain, leaving the glass rooftop slippery. I remove my glider wings from my backpack, allowing me to launch myself into the night just as I reach the edge. The rain slices against my face, cold and feeling like icepicks.

Unfortunately, my timing is horrible and the cops see me glide over them, turning their cars around to follow. My feet hit the roof of the building next to the alley, and I feel a twinge in my leg.

My bike is parked in the alley and I slip down a fire escape, landing on it like a wild-west cowboy mounting his horse from a saloon balcony.

The engine roars to life as I stomp down. Already, the lights from the police cars appear down the street at the end of the alley. Since the other way is a dead end, I'm stuck with having to exit on that same street.

Rubber squeals as I peel out and pull onto the road a split second before they get to the alley, turning just feet in front of them.

"Halt!" came a command over their loudspeakers.

I wonder if that's ever worked. Do criminals just decide, Well, he asked nicely, and pull over? I've never tried it as Black Harrier, and I'm not really inclined to do so in the future. Point made flesh, I twist the throttle harder and pick up speed.

Since it's the early morning hours, there's hardly any traffic, but I still have to weave around some cars, and the cops do the same.

I start to think I've lost them when I reach a roadblock on the other end of the bridge. There's no way I'm getting past them, and I can't fight this many cops without hurting some of them, not to mention myself. My hip and knee are throbbing now and the cold air certainly isn't helping.

Desperate times…

I glance back, then pull a wheelie, cutting my wheel sharply to the right. I bring my front tire down on the guardrail and shift my weight forward, lifting the rear tire to meet me. Then, I kick off the bike, soaring in the air like my namesake. The drop is at least a hundred feet, but that's what I was counting on. It gives me enough time to engage my gliders again.

I hear the bike crash into the water below and my wings snap out just before I follow its trajectory. Gliding just feet above the water, I can feel the spray of the gentle waves and taste freedom. With my all-black uniform and glider against the blackness of the water in the darkness, I can only hope they aren't able to see me.

I don't quite make it to shore, but it's close enough that I can swim the last few yards without much trouble. Sopping wet, I trudge the few miles to the hotel where my Alfa Romeo is parked, constantly looking over my shoulder to ensure I'm not spotted. I'm not entirely sure the police even noticed I hadn't crashed with my bike.

I'm limping pretty strongly now, and it's more of a step, drag, step, drag, but I make it to the hotel.

Always thinking ahead, Arbuckle had checked me into a room just in case, well, something like this happened. I go the car and pull out a package from the trunk containing my wallet and other necessities, along with the card key to my room. There's also a garment bag with a fresh suit for me. At least it's still raining so I don't have to try to explain why I'm soaked to the bone.

I walk up to the side door of the hotel and slide my key card into the security slot. It blinks red.

I try it again. Red again.

Then I notice the sign: *FOR THE SAFETY OF OUR GUESTS, LOBBY ENTRY ONLY AFTER MIDNIGHT — Management.*

Great. So much for slipping in and out unnoticed.

I briefly consider just driving back to the castle in this condition, but I'm exhausted and in pain and I don't know how I'll explain myself if Megan wakes up despite the sleepy time tea she drank.

Only one thing to do, then. The lobby it is.

The worst thing I can do is act suspicious in any way, as that would probably draw attention. So, it's time for the other extreme. I walk past the front desk, leaving the lobby carpet soaking wet in my wake.

The night clerk raises his eyebrows at me and looks down at the puddles I'm creating.

"Forgot my umbrella," I say in my best attempt at a Scottish accent. Hopefully he won't remember my face after paying so much attention to the mess I'm making.

Then I whistle nonchalantly as I wait for the elevator doors to open, and head up to my room.

I hope to get a few hours' sleep, but apparently, I passed out without setting an alarm. It's almost noon by the time I arrive back at the castle. Driving up the driveway, I immediately spot Megan standing on the balcony outside of the master bedroom drinking a cup of coffee. I get out of the car and wave to her.

"And just where have you been?" she asks, half-jokingly and half-suspiciously.

I hold up a small paper bag to show her. I hope the contents are still fresh, considering I grabbed whatever was left at the continental breakfast they were breaking down in the lobby as I rushed out of the hotel.

"There's a bakery over in the next town that makes the best scones I've ever tasted. I had to have some while we're here, and I didn't want to wake you."

I hate lying to her, but it's for her own safety.

"I tried calling you," she says.

I feel around in my pockets and act surprised to come up empty-handed, then look back at the front seat of the car and raise my hands in defeat. "I'm sorry. I must have left my phone here. Vacation mode, I guess."

She rolls her eyes as she walks back into the bedroom. "You'd forget your head if it wasn't bolted onto your neck."

I smile until she's gone from the balcony, then sigh in relief that I pulled it off. Arbuckle comes out the front door and approaches the car and we exchange in a conversation so quiet it could have been silent.

"Would you mind unloading the trunk, please? I have some souvenirs to take back to the States with me."

"Of course, Master Douglas. Right away."

"And see if Mrs. Arbuckle can salvage these scones. As far as I can tell, they're carved from Stonehenge."

"She'll do her best, sir. She may have to bake some of her own."

"Even better." I smile weakly. "Well, wish me luck. I have to go in and explain to Megan that we need to head back to the States right away."

"I don't envy you, sir."

NINETEEN

AMY

"How did he look?" I say.

"I mean, he doesn't look like he's doing well," Sawyer says from the other end of comms. "But he's breathing. It's hard to tell at that size. Your dad thinks this means things in the Guild are worse than we thought."

"Are you with him? My dad, I mean."

"No, he's with Baron Steele. That dude's an asshole."

"He's not that bad," I say.

"Oh, cool. You can be on their side, too."

"Oh, cut it out," I say. "It's not that. Is he okay? He was pretty banged up in the hospital, and he still looked pretty bad when I saw him at his office."

"Yeah, he looked fine. Like nothing happened. He's made of steel, right? Hey, I'm gonna go eat something. I'm starving. Believe it or not, Big Frankie Junior's sounds amazing right now. Wanna join me?"

"That's gross," I tell him. I'm half kidding. I don't hate it.

"Hey, my dad owns that place. Suit yourself."

"Yeah… Okay, well, I'll see you at the Resistors practice tomorrow."

There's silence on the line for a moment.

"Sawyer?"

"I totally forgot about that," he says softly.

Sawyer hasn't been quite right. I'm pretty sure a lot of it has to do with Neith, but he's not exactly being forthcoming about it.

"What's going on with you lately?" It's as diplomatic as I can muster up the strength to be.

"I don't know. I'm pretty sure I'm getting expelled from school. And I think I got a concussion. Oh, that reminds me… I ran into Alex."

"You what? Where? You were in Boston?" I was going to ask about him being expelled, but he's probably just exaggerating, and the Alex thing is much more interesting.

"No, he's here, I guess."

"In the city? Where?" Am I acting too interested?

He tells me about how he went patrolling and apparently didn't even ask me. Some friend. I decide right then that if it worked for him, the best way to confront Alex would be to get his attention the same way Sawyer did. The only problem is, without Tiffany, I don't have the ability to track down which drones aren't working correctly and will have a Guild member—presumably Alex—checking on it soon.

"Crazy," I say, doing my best to sound like I've lost interest. "Okay, well, have a good night."

"Wait, what?"

He's still talking when I hang up.

I rack my brain. How do I figure out which drones are not in proper working order? I wander the streets for a little bit, hoping to see one acting wonky, but everything seems normal. I even end up in some places that a young lady like me shouldn't be alone. Not that there are many young ladies like me. I dare some rapist to try his luck.

I'd pop him in the jaw like Paul did to Eaglestar, only my target wouldn't get back up.

Wait…

That gives me an idea that's probably really stupid.

I start out at the top of a particularly tall skyscraper and scan the surrounding area for drones flying around. They're big up close, but from way up here? They resemble marbles in a warehouse full of boxes, so I have some trouble spotting one right away. I know their cameras are on the underside of the machines, which makes sense since they're flying high in the air. That means crime would be going on below them.

What they may not be accounting for is an acrobatic masked crimefighter with a lot of ingenuity and a bone to pick with her on-again-off-again boyfriend. I finally spot a drone with the magnification on in my visor—I don't have the AI tech yet that the others do, and from what I've seen, I'm not sure I'm interested. Even so, I'm not completely without some tricks of my own.

I swoop down on it just like I do with criminals I'm going after, and land right on top. They are spherical, so balance is crucial as it wobbles back and forth. There's no way it's going to stay airborne with me aboard. As expected, we start to plummet. I do my best to steer it toward the nearest wall.

Kaboom!

It's nothing like the movies. There are no sparks or flames or explosion. Just metal crumpling against brick and a lot of noise. Don't worry, I leaped off in time and easily glide down to the alley and wait to see who shows up. I just hope it's Alex and not Eaglestar or Bastet. But I'm not too worried, since I doubt either of them would bother lowering themselves to such a menial task. In fact, I'm guessing the whole reason they had Alex come back from Boston was to do their bidding with things like this so that they don't have to worry about it.

While I'm waiting, I scroll through my phone to see if I missed anything. No, as usual nobody cares about me or is the least bit interested in what I'm doing. I'm a nonentity at this point. I put my phone away just in time for Alex to show up. He comes down from the top of the building next to me and looks at the smashed-up drone on the ground.

I walk out of the shadows nearby, thinking I'm surprising him.

"Hey, stranger."

"You too, huh?" He addresses me without turning around, not the least bit surprised that I'm there. He probably surveilled the alley before he came down and spotted me already. Not probably. I'm sure he did.

"What is that supposed to mean?" I ask.

"I assume you did this?" he points to the damage.

"Yeah, so what?" I say. Now I'm kind of pissed off. "I had to do something to get your attention. Texting and calling wasn't working."

"Last I knew you had a boyfriend. I didn't want to get in the way."

Oh, he's going to turn this around on me?

"Pace and I aren't really a thing anymore."

He nods slowly. "So you expect me to come running back to you? What am I—a booty call?"

"Alex…"

"Sorry, I'm a little busy now."

I can feel my blood boiling. Like *actually* feel it. Fire inside of me, and like a dragon, I'm fit to blow.

"Oh, excuse me. I didn't realize checking on downed Guild drones was a full-time job. What else do they have you doing over at Guild Hall? Vacuuming? Doing dishes? Taking out the trash? Do you clean the toilet after Eaglestar takes a dump?"

He blows a raspberry. "What do you care? I'm a core member of the Guild now, which is what I've always wanted. If I have to start out as the low man on the totem pole, so be it."

"Low man? You're the freaking Black Harrier. The Black Harrier. You're better than this crap. They shouldn't be treating you like some sort of assistant. You don't need those jerks."

"So what do you propose? Want me to join your little team? The… what is it—the components?"

"You know that's not what we're called," I say.

"The Guild is doing a lot of good, for your information. The crime rate is practically nonexistent now."

"Yeah, because we're practically living in a fascist state now."

"Oh, give it a rest. Having drones fly around to prevent crime isn't exactly Nazi Germany. There were already cameras practically everywhere you go anyway. What's the difference?"

Is he that delusional? "The difference," I say, "is that the Guild are the most powerful people on the planet. And they have everyone under their thumbs now. You especially."

"I don't need your lecturing." He turns to walk away.

Okay, this isn't working. Time for a new tack. "Come back to Douglas Tower. We miss you. I miss you."

God, Amy. Desperate much?

He stops, and for an instant, I think he's going to do as I asked. Then, he proves he's a giant jerk. "Why don't you just go back to Pace? He's more your… pace, anyway."

"You're hilarious. You know what? I am going to give him a call. I've been debating whether or not I want to see him again, and this conversation has given me all the incentive I need to just go ahead and do it."

"Fine. Do it then."

"Fine. I will." I pull my phone out of the protective pouch I keep it in when I'm in costume and unlock it. I assumed Alex would leave, but instead he just stands there and stares at me, his arms crossed.

"What, you're going to listen in to make sure I do it?" I ask.

"Yeah. I think I will."

Damn. I wasn't really going to do it. He called my bluff. Am I really going to do this? I dial Pace's number.

"Great," I say, pulling the phone from my ear and addressing Alex. "Try not to get too jealous."

"Not a problem."

"Hey there," he answers.

"Hey, Diori. What are you doing tonight?" I turn away from Alex while I talk so he can't see from my face that I'm forcing this whole thing. I like Diori. I like him a lot. But I did kind of feel like things were over between us.

"Not much," he says, clearly trying to sound smooth. "Just hanging. Why?"

I turn back to Alex so I'm sure he hears this part. It takes every ounce of acting skill I have to say, "I was wondering if maybe you could use a little company."

Alex is obviously trying to remain stoic, but I can tell it's eating him up inside. Good.

Diori perks up. "You mean… company, company?"

I look back at Alex. He's still just staring me down.

"Yeah, you mind if I come by? I know it's kind of late, but—"

"No, no, no, not at all. Come on by. The sooner the better."

Oof. Someone's thirsty. His over-excitement is bordering on desperation and totally turning me off. But I have to put on a show for Alex.

I smile. "Okay, I'll be there soon."

"See ya soon, baby."

Baby… Yuck. I hang up.

If it were possible for steam to be coming out of Alex's ears, I'm positive it would be.

"There," I say. "You satisfied? After all, you did talk me into it."

He waits a few seconds before answering.

"I just wanted to make sure you weren't bluffing just to make me jealous."

Of course I was.

"Nope. Not bluffing at all. Looks like Pace and I are back together, so if you were holding out any hope of anything happening between you and me, you're S.O.L."

"Right," he says. "Certainly appears that way. Well, you have fun with your boyfriend."

"I will."

He shoots his grappler to the top of a nearby building.

I continue screaming up at him. "You have fun doing… drone status checks or whatever it is they make you do."

He disappears into the night. And I start heading in the direction of Pace's place.

That certainly backfired.

TWENTY
SAWYER

The Resistors.

The next time the team meets, Neith doesn't show up. The rest of us, Osprey, Bash, Javi, and Pace, sit around the table making small talk for a while. After waiting a little longer, hoping she's just late, I try direct messaging her on the app the team uses to stay in touch with one another.

No response.

I guess I really messed up.

This was my last chance to do something before Frank and Mom get back from Scotland and find out that Blanchard is planning on expelling me, too. Who knows how bad things will get after that?

"Wow, your date must have gone really well," Osprey says.

I know she's trying to be funny to lighten the mood, but I don't appreciate it.

I offer a har-har before saying, "Yeah, well, we can't all have perfect relationships."

Pace grins and puts his arm around Osprey. "That's right."

She pushes his arm away. "Oh, it's not perfect, believe me."

"What's that supposed to mean?"

Uh oh. Pace is pretty upset. What did I start here?

Osprey crosses her arms. "Nothing."

My date proved I know very little about women, but if there's one thing I do know, when a woman says the word "nothing," it's literally anything but "nothing."

"No, no, no," Pace says with his typical machine-gun-fire cadence. "Explain what's wrong with our relationship. Last night you—"

"I said it's nothing. I'm not going to discuss it right now anyway."

Last night?

"So there is something," Pace says. "I see. I see. I see. Yeah, okay, let's do it. Let's discuss it now."

Osprey sighs. "Okay. Fine. You asked for it."

"Guys," I say, "we really don't—"

Osprey plows right over me. "You can be a little annoying sometimes."

Pace throws his arms up. "Oh, the annoying thing again. Just like Fastlane."

Uh oh. She definitely hit a nerve.

"Yeah, well, I think he has a point."

No, Amy! Don't double down on it.

"Yeah, so what makes me so annoying?"

Not the direction I would have taken…

"You always have to be joking around."

I find that endearing.

"I don't always have to be joking around."

There's absolutely no joking going on right now.

"Don't look like I'm joking right now, does it?"

See?

"For once," Osprey says.

This whole thing is absolutely something that should've been done in private.

"Wow," Pace says, nodding really fast and looking around the table. "You all believe this?"

Nope. Don't get us involved. Don't do it.

"Even this," Osprey says. "I told you I didn't want to talk about it now, and you forced it."

"So?"

"So… That's annoying."

Pace stands. "Well, I don't want to keep annoying you or the rest of the team, so I'll just quit. It's not like there's anything for us to do anymore anyway."

That makes me stand up. "Wait—what?"

Osprey joins him in standing. "Don't bother. I'll quit so you won't have to."

"Guys, stop it."

They both ignore me.

"Oh, no. I'm out." Pace disappears so fast I don't have a chance to stop him.

"What the eff is happening here?" I ask.

Osprey has tears in her eyes. "I'm not sure I can do this right now. I'll talk to you later."

She leaves headquarters, and I don't know what else to say to her.

Now it's Bash's turn to rise and leave. "Sorry, bro, but now that the hot chicks are gone, I'm not really all that interested in being here, either. Honestly, it's been kind of boring." He takes a last bite of the apple he was eating and tosses it into a trash can in the corner. "Later."

All I can do is stand there in shock, wondering how things could've possibly unraveled so quickly. The last thing I was told to do by Chen was focus extra hard on the team. Now, I have no team. How did my life just become a daytime soap opera?

There's a knock on the door and I'm hopeful Amy has regained her composure and realized what's at stake. However, when I open it to find Paul "The Baron" Steele standing there, I feel like a popped Macy's Day Parade balloon.

"The wait's over, kiddies," he says, shoving his way inside. "Time to put on your big boy pants. Who's ready to train?"

I look behind me at Javier, still sitting quietly in his seat.

He finally speaks up. "Does this mean I get to move up to regular team member now?"

So that was our chance. As much as I don't like the guy, Baron Steele is one of the greatest heroes the world has ever known.

I'm pissed at Mr. Chen for not telling me Paul was planning on showing up tonight. If I'd have known, it would have been far simpler a job to keep everyone calm while we waited. For a second, I'm pissed at anyone who thinks we need further training. Then I consider things and realize what a train wreck we are. With the stakes so high, it's probably smart.

And you know what? We could have shown him we were the real deal and he'd be impressed or whatever. Maybe tell Frank and Chen how good we really are.

Instead, everyone threw temper tantrums and stormed off like spoiled children. The Baron seeing us that way was one of the most embarrassing moments of my life. I can't even imagine what he's gonna report back.

The walk home feels like it takes years. And now, Javi is talking to me again—incessantly.

"Was that really Baron Steele? He was going to train us? Me? Do you think I could learn how to punch like him? Is it true he and Eaglestar got into a fight? I don't think Eaglestar would have won if he hadn't cheated. Do you? What do you think? Sawyer?"

How did everything fall apart in my life? No more crimefighting, kicked out of school, my crush hates my guts, and now my only friends have all gone their separate ways.

Meanwhile, Javi continues the verbal barrage.

"Are you planning on getting a new skateboard? I've been thinking about what you said. Maybe I should get one too. I don't know. I don't think I'm cool enough."

I don't see how things can get any worse.

And then it does.

When I get home, Mom's already there. I guess they came back early. I step hesitantly into the kitchen and she gives me a big hug and kisses me on the forehead.

"Hey!" she says. "I missed you so much."

Okay, there's no way she's found out about me and the fireworks yet. But why? I know it's the weekend, but Blanchard has to have left a million messages, right?

"I missed you too," I tell her. "I, uh, tried to call you and couldn't get ahold of you."

Testing the waters.

"Oh. I'm so sorry, honey," she says, absentmindedly unpacking her bag. "I accidentally left my charger at the castle and my phone died."

Castle? I think it but decide to stay quiet. Knowing Frank, they stayed with the Queen herself.

"So I didn't get your calls," she continues. "But I knew we'd be home soon.

Why?" She looks around scrutinizingly. "You didn't have a party while I was gone, did you? Did something bad happen?"

Let me list them all off for you…

"Bad? No, everything's… fine. It's just there was a thing at school."

She narrows her eyes at me. "What kind of thing?"

"Oh, it's no big deal. Not really. You must be exhausted. We can talk about it later."

She picks her phone up from the counter, where it's been sitting and charging since she got home, and shows me the screen: thirteen missed calls, seven unheard messages.

None of them are from me, either.

She listens to the messages and her eyes go wide. I slowly back out of the kitchen and she grabs me by my sleeve and reels me back in. I can see her getting madder and madder, but so far she's just listening and not saying anything to me.

I haven't seen her this angry since… since things were bad.

She hangs up the last message and slams her phone down on the counter so hard that I'm surprised it doesn't smash into little pieces.

"Sawyer William Vincent! What the—"

Suddenly both of our phones make a loud sound, like when some kid goes missing and they push it out to everyone. I unlock my phone and look down at the screen.

EMERGENCY ALERT. TUNE YOUR TELEVISION OR DEVICE TO YOUR LOCAL OR NATIONAL NEWS STATION AND STAND BY FOR AN IMPORTANT ANNOUNCEMENT FROM THE GUILD OF MASKED CRIMEFIGHTERS.

"This isn't over," she says.

As grateful as I am for the reprieve as Mom runs to the living room to turn on the TV, I can't help but feel that what I'm about to hear is gonna change everything.

And not for the better.

TWENTY-ONE

FRANK

The entire world has been sent a message directly to their mobile phones. Me included. That in itself is a feat I'm unsure as to how the Guild pulled off. My personal phone is encrypted beyond any technology I believed they had access to.

That said, it's not the first time I've had reason to believe they're using Douglas Industries tech behind my back. I don't know how such a thing could be accomplished, but I'll certainly have Chen look into any possible security breaches when this crisis is over with.

Assuming it's ever over with.

Upon receiving their demand for humanity to tune in and listen to their rhetoric, I ping Sawyer, Amy, and Alex to the Aerie.

Sawyer and Amy were both just downstairs in their respective homes, so they are here in no time. Sawyer looks like he's just seen a ghost, but I don't mention it. Whatever it is, it will have to wait.

Unsurprisingly, Alex doesn't show up.

Plastered on what I would guess to be every news station on Earth, an empty podium stands before the United Nations building here in New York. For a moment, I consider going down there and giving Jonathan a piece of my mind, but before I can put action to the thought, he walks—or rather glides—out onto the stage.

That plastic smile of his is sickening. However, that's not what brings the bile bubbling into my throat. Standing beside him is none other than Alex Garner, my once protege and partner, my sidekick and friend. Redhawk. But he isn't dressed as Redhawk, he is wearing my uniform, marring the name and legacy of the Black Harrier.

"You've gotta be joking," Sawyer says.

I glance over and see that Amy has turned stark white. She literally looks like she's going to be sick.

The three of us watch, horrorstruck, as Eaglestar starts to speak. "My fellow Americans, and people of planet Earth, I come bearing the greatest of news."

"Sure ya do," Sawyer says under his breath.

Eaglestar's attention snaps up at the camera as if he'd heard. He has super-hearing but not *that* good.

"Our actions," he continues, "over the past several months since returning from our unplanned journey away have been a success. Crime is virtually nonexistent the world over."

Sawyer scowls. "Yeah, that's what happens when you run things like North Korea does."

Eaglestar stops *again* and squints his eyes. This is paranoia at its strongest.

Even so, Amy and I shush Sawyer as Eaglestar continues.

"It has been so effective, in fact, that we have decided to expand our control into areas beyond law enforcement. The Guild agrees, we know what is best for the world and its people. We know how to protect you. How to keep you safe. How to make all of humanity… super."

He pauses before that last word like it's clever. My fists clench.

"As your guardians and sacred protectors, should we not make the decisions that will allow us to prosper in peace? Governments will remain in place to carry out our policies. Consider them as our police force. But from this day forth, we are all citizens of Earth. There will be no more war or struggle over beliefs or resources. Today, unity prevails!"

There is murmuring among the General Assembly, and a couple of UN Ambassadors call out in protest, but they are quickly led away in a flash—by Fastlane, I would guess.

My time spend in the Middle East, facing unsurmountable odds, has taught me what terrorism looks like. I recall with vivid memory when Saddam Hussein took power in Iraq, and this is eerily similar. Eaglestar battled Hitler and Mussolini, and neither of those bastards had superpowers.

I can't imagine what a superpowered person with that same mindset is capable of.

I'm in such shock, I'm not even sure what to think. Eaglestar has rendered me virtually thoughtless, let alone speechless.

The man who is supposed to be the Earth's greatest hero bares his teeth in what he probably thinks is a friendly smile.

Sawyer can't help commenting again.

"Grin all you want, Evilstar. Guess what, douche nozzle, you still look like a tool."

I don't know what a douche nozzle is, but it's a difficult sentiment to disagree with, I suppose.

"We realize this will come as a shock to many. We will, therefore, allow for a period of adjustment to lead us into this prosperous new age. Leaders of the world, you have seventy-two hours to get your countries in order before the transition. From that point on, the Guild will be in complete control. For those who will have questions—and we know there will be some—the word 'complete' means total and utter. There will be no dissent, and no going back. Together, all those who stand at our side will want for nothing. Together, we will usher in a golden age of humanity unlike any that has come before!"

Eaglestar gives another huge, fake, tooth-filled grin and raises his fist to the sky. Then a red flag I've never seen before unfurls behind him, covering up the United Nations flag. Red and black. Colors we've seen too many times before.

"Maybe they're being mind-controlled," suggests Sawyer.

"I've checked on Mezmer. He's still in custody, and hasn't had a chance to rebuild his helmet since it was destroyed by your team strongman."

"Bash, yeah," Osprey says. "Are there any other villains with mind control powers?"

"Not that I'm aware of. Certainly if someone was powerful enough to control the Guild, I would think they would have been on my radar by now."

"Then I guess we're gonna have to just accept the fact that the core members of the Guild of Masked Crimefighters have somehow turned evil," says Sawyer.

I feel as if I should reply to that somehow. Reassure them that it just isn't possible. But I can't bring myself to say anything because it appears that not only is it possible, but it's the reality with which we're currently faced.

So, instead, we all sit in silence while we consider that very sobering idea.

TWENTY-TWO

SAWYER

Confused.

That's the only word I can think of to describe how I'm feeling at the news. And I'm sure the rest of the world is feeling it along with me. Every news station and website around the world airing the speech on loop.

Like they have a choice.

There are no anchors. No commercials. Just Evilstar over and over again.

"Together, we will usher in a golden age of humanity unlike any that has come before!"

Bullcrap.

I never would have believed that being expelled from school would be the least of today's problems. But now, in the light of this? It seems utterly insignificant.

The Guild of Masked Crimefighters has been around for over seventy years, protecting America and the rest of the world from threats big and small. But who is gonna protect us all from them?

Oh… right… us.

The world is in trouble.

Frank had already been spending all his time in the Aerie trying to figure out what's wrong with the Guild. I've never seen his face so racked with concern.

"What are we gonna do?" I ask.

At first, he's so focused on what he's doing that I don't think he even remembers I'm there. Then, he finally answers. "I'm still assessing the situation. Obviously, something's not right, but I haven't figured out what it is. Once I do, then we can work from there."

"And in the meantime, the Guild just does whatever it wants to?" Osprey asks. "Not just taking down criminals, but telling governments and world leaders what to do?"

Amy and I still haven't talked since she left me high and dry at the warehouse. It's not something I want to do, but an uncomfortable conversation is imminent.

"Rushing into it without a plan isn't going to solve anything," Frank says. "And based on their current actions, it may even get us killed. I've sent a message to some of the reserve heroes, and they're meeting up soon to try to do something about it. None of them will be able to do anything on their own. Even together, I'm not sure how much they can accomplish against the core team. Or even against Eaglestar by himself."

"Yeah, and the Resistors are toast," I say, glaring at Amy. Truth is, I didn't really mean it to slip. I'm just frustrated.

"What?" Frank asks, finally turning to me. "I thought Paul was training you while I was gone."

"Ask Osprey," I say.

Frank turns to her.

She's still looking at me like I'd just let it slip to her mom that she was pregnant or something.

She sighs and tells him the whole ugly truth. Pace. Alex—stuff I haven't even heard yet.

"Don't forget the part about how you left me alone with Javi," I say.

She rolls her eyes.

"That's why you don't get romantically involved with your partners," he says, no little amount of fatherly scolding in his tone. Then I realize he's looking at me and not her. "Get them back."

"What? How?" I respond like the masterful orator I am.

"I don't care how," Frank says. "We will need every able body we can get."

"Can't you call them?" I ask the question before I consider how childish it must sound, asking Daddy to bail me out.

Reading my mind, apparently, he answers. "I'm not bailing you out of this. This is on you. It's your team."

I nod. "Okay. You're right."

I don't know if he realizes it, but with those words, he reaches for his cane. Then, he lets it go.

"There's got to be something," Osprey says, changing the subject.

"Yeah," I add. "You've thought about how to take him down in case something like this every happened."

"Of course I have, and none of the solutions are very pleasant. Most of them involve a lot of potential casualties and collateral damage."

Then, a thought strikes me light lightning. "Oh!" Everyone is startled by the sound. "Sorry. I just… how did it go in Scotland? Did you… well, what were you doing?"

Frank turns in his chair. "Did you see your mother?" he asks, as if avoiding the question.

I haven't told him that I just left her standing in the middle of the kitchen, screaming at me.

"Yeah. I did. Just for, like, a second, though."

"That's good. Did she seem… okay?"

What's going on, Frank? I think to myself. Then, I decide I have nothing to lose and ask it out loud.

"I'm worried about the timing of all this is all," he responds.

"What do you mean?" I ask.

"If you hadn't noticed, I cut our trip short."

Of course, I noticed. I just nod.

"I'm worried she might somehow put two and two together. Us leaving, and then this happening with the Guild. I'm worried I might be getting sloppy."

Wow. I never thought I'd hear those words from Frank's mouth. It is odd, though. He's always been pretty adamant about personal relationships. And he's kind of proving his thoughts to be accurate. He starts getting close to my mom and then quits crimefighting? Blames it on his bum leg?

This isn't the time or place, but that might be another uncomfortable conversation.

I keep it simple for now. "Oh, I think she's got other things to think about," I tell him.

He raises an eyebrow and I tell him what happened at school. Every last excruciating detail.

He rubs a palm across his forehead. "You two," he says, shaking his head. "Now is not the time for this kind of behavior."

Here we go again. Back to the old days.

"Me? What was I supposed to do? Logan could have hurt someone!"

"And you could have too," Frank retorts. "You're lucky you didn't. You're lucky you're not in jail right now."

"That's what he said," I almost whisper.

"Who?"

"Principal Blanchard, when he tried to expel me."

"Expel you?" Frank says.

I suppose I hadn't told him everything.

"Yeah, Mom is probably talking to him about it right now. He left like a billion messages on her phone."

Frank shakes his head.

"At least he didn't ruin your trip."

"At least you didn't ruin our trip, you mean?" Frank asks.

"That's not fair! I was trying to save people."

"Excuse me," Osprey says, stepping forward. We both look at her. "Not that this isn't important. But… it's not really important right now, is it?"

She's absolutely right, but Frank doesn't seem ready to let it go.

"No more nonsense. Either of you. We can't let relationships and school get in the way of—"

"What about you and my mom?" I spit out.

There's a hush of silence except for the little beeping sound coming from Firefly's makeshift hospital.

For the second time, I let my emotions slip. My face gets hot. I think it's fear. I think I'm terrified of him.

"That's none of your business," he says.

"If not mine, then whose? She's my mom."

"And I am your father," he says, standing. "Why I do… what she does… it's not your call."

"Sawyer," Amy says through gritted teeth. "Not now." Then under her breath she adds, "Or ever."

"Fine," I say.

"We can talk about it later," Frank says, letting a bit of his anger go. "If we all survive."

"That's a chipper thought," I say.

Osprey shoots me a look as if to urge me to not push my luck.

"In Scotland," Frank says, sitting back down. "I managed to obtain some of the Tuldarian artifacts that were aboard that zeppelin the day Eaglestar acquired his powers."

"Whoa!" I say. "How'd you—"

"It wasn't easy, believe me." He seems uncharacteristically proud of that for some reason.

"But why?" I ask.

"It had taken longer than I'd like to admit, but I realized I'd seen that vortex before—the one the Guild was pulled through."

"Where?" Osprey asks.

"The second time the Tuldarians visited earth."

"Second time?" I ask. "I'd never heard of a second time."

"That's because it was washed out by the CIA and the Guild," Frank says. "We spun a story. Made it go away."

"So the Guild has always decided what's best for the world, huh?" I ask.

I expect Frank to get mad again, but instead he says, "Apparently. Things will have to change when this is all over."

"So now what?" Osprey asks.

"I don't know." Frank turns back to his console. "Step one was getting the artifacts. They are the only tie I know of to the Tuldarians. Now I need to figure out what to do with them."

"Step two?" she asks.

Frank pulls himself closer to his command console. "I'm going to try to contact Alex again to see what he has to say. So far, I haven't been able to get him to respond. If we can get him to confirm my suspicions…"

"Which are?" I ask.

"I don't believe the Guild is who they say they are."

Frank, dropping bombs.

"Imposters? Shape-shifters?"

"Something like that," Frank says. Then he dials up Alex.

I look to Osprey, knowing she has no interest in seeing Alex right now. She casually slides away, outside the view of the camera as Frank dials up Alex on the comm system one more time.

Finally, his face appears. He looks like crap. Bags under his bloodshot eyes, stubble for days. He's looking around as if to make sure nobody else is listening. "What is it? I'm kind of busy here."

Frank starts to talk but I can't help it, I'm furious and I've already cast all caution away long ago. "What is it? Seriously? You guys are trying to take over the world. Not only is it stupid and insane, but it's totally a supervillain move. What the hell is wrong with you guys? What's wrong with you?"

For a moment, there's no response. Much to my surprise, Frank says, "He asked you a question."

Alex clears his throat. "The Guild truly believes that this is the best thing for the country and the world. It's something the others have been talking about doing for a while now. Especially Eaglestar."

Frank responds before I can get a word out. "That was never something that was discussed when I was around."

"I get the impression they talked about a lot of things when you weren't around."

"Ah, right," Frank says.

"They've said more than once that you'd never approve of something like this," Alex continues, "which is why it didn't come up until you were out of—uh, no longer a member."

"Oh, so I'm no longer a member now?"

"Hey, you gave up the uniform," Alex says.

"If I'd have known how immature you would be, and how disgraceful you'd behave, I'd never have done it."

"Well, I guess it's too late for take backs then."

"God, you are such an asshole," Osprey says, stepping into view.

Alex straightens up at the sight of her. I bet he doesn't even realize he did it. He cocks his head, smiles a little, and starts to respond.

But Osprey isn't having any of it. She's so badass sometimes. "So just because no one can stop you, it suddenly makes it right?"

"It's not my decision. I voted against it," he says. His tone is lighter now, softer. "Not that what I have to say means much around here."

"Oh, big man," I say, starting to slow clap. "You voted against it. Let me give you a standing ovation. Balloon drop, anyone?"

Frank puts up a hand. "That's enough, Sawyer." His voice lowers. "Alex, you can't really believe that taking over things yourselves is the right thing to do."

Alex sighs. "Of course I don't. I just told you that. But I have to go along with the decision of the team. Just like you did when you were in my place."

Frank's voice is measured, but I can tell he's holding in some intense anger. "Something's not right. I can tell just watching Eaglestar and the rest on television. And the one time I tried to converse with him, he was very evasive. He also didn't remember things like he should have. Is it possible that senility is setting in despite him not appearing to age?"

Alex looks around again, then whispers, "I agree that something strange is going on. They don't really seem like themselves. But until I can figure out what it is, I need to go along with things."

I seriously feel like reaching through the screen and choking him. "How can you say that? It's just—"

Alex's face disappears as he hangs up on us. I slam a fist into the wall.

Again, Frank reacts more as a father than as a partner. "Calm down. Save your anger until you need it to fight."

"That's proof," Osprey says. "You heard him. 'They don't really seem like themselves.'"

There's an irregularity in the beeping sound coming from the "hospital" setup where Firefly is. His pulse is racing. Is he awake?

Frank stands, shoving his chair aside. He doesn't even grab his cane. Together, we rush over. He looks like a doll or action figure, lying there. Imagine someone the size of… I don't know, one of those little green army men. It's super weird.

Firefly is thrashing around, pushing against the tiny restraints holding him to the metal table.

Then, with a roar, he wakes up. "Nooooo!" He's disoriented. Doesn't know where he is.

"Mac! Calm down. It's Frank. Frank Douglas."

"What? No! Stop! Don't!" It's like he's having a nightmare or something.

"Mac! It's me! Frank!

Firefly opens his eyes. His little head bounces back and forth between all of us. "Frank?" His eyes look somewhat crazed. "Is it really you? The real you?"

Frank shoots me a concerned look before he responds to Firefly. "Can you get back to normal size?"

"I—I don't think so. I stayed this way for too long, trying to hide from them."

"Them? Them who?"

"The Guild! They're not themselves. They have to be…" He trails off, seemingly too exhausted to go on.

"Mac? Mac! Stay with me. What's wrong with the Guild?" He turns to Osprey. "Get your father over here."

She rushes away so her talking on the phone doesn't bother anyone.

"What do you mean they're not themselves?" Frank asks.

"Weisswulf. Ask… Weiss… wulf…"

Then he passes out.

"Should we try to wake him?" I ask.

"I don't know how we would do that without using drugs, and I have no idea how much to give him at that size or how to administer to him. We'll have to hope he wakes up again soon so he can tell us more."

"And until then?" I ask.

"You heard him," Osprey says. "Just like Alex, 'They're not themselves.'"

"Bingo," Frank agrees. "I'm going to see if I can track down Weisswulf. We need to find out why Mac wanted us to talk to him."

"What should we do for now?" I ask.

His answer freezes me in my tracks. "You two get your team back together. You may be our last line of defense against the Guild."

TWENTY-THREE

AMY

I'm sitting here at MoonMoney Coffee—the same one where I watched Eaglestar and Baron Steele duke it out. Sawyer has a plan to get the team back together. I'm not sure it's a good one, but it's better than anything I've come up with.

It's not long before my guest of honor shows up. Neith was hesitant to meet me, because… why would she? We've never been friends outside of the group. We aren't boy-talk-and-pillow-fights kind of girls… and that's a really immature and sexist stereotype by the way.

She does, however, sit down across from me. I wouldn't even say she's wearing a scowl. She looks… pleasant.

"Hi," I say.

"Hello."

"How are you doing?"

"I'm… fine?" She says it like a question, like she's unsure of her answer or maybe unsure as to why I'd ask in the first place. Then the reason comes out. "Is this about Sawyer?"

I laugh a little. It's nervous laughter for sure. I'm spared the need to respond when a moment later, the napkins on my table fly up into the air in a gust of wind.

"What the hell is this?" Pace says, standing before us.

Neith looks up at him, then back at me. Then we all turn as a little bell signals the shop's front door opening. Sawyer and Bash come waltzing out.

"This is bullsh—" Pace starts.

"Please!" Sawyer says in a bit of a jog toward us. "Please, just let me talk?"

"You invited me here," Pace says to Sawyer. "You didn't say nothing about her being here."

He's pointing at me, as if anyone is at all confused about it.

"This was the only way I could assure all of us would be together," Sawyer says.

"Where's the little dude?" Bash asks.

"Crap," Sawyer says.

"You forgot about Javier?" I say.

Finally, Neith speaks, looking at Sawyer. "What is this?"

I start getting a really strong déjà vu vibe. This is a lot like the meeting we had before we fought Battlegear and the Neon Knights, but Sawyer seems even more desperate. And Javi is obviously absent again.

"I know you all decided to leave the team, but…" he lowers his voice, "… this thing with the Guild is too important to ignore. The stakes are much higher than ever."

"I don't appreciate being played," Pace says, interrupting as usual.

"Well, get over it," I tell him.

He stares at me, incredulous that someone would dare speak to him that way.

"Excuse me?"

Okay. Fine. In for a penny, in for a pound. "Get over it. This isn't about you. Not everything is about you."

"Rich, you saying that," he replies. "Speaking of rich… how's your penthouse and fancy restaurants? Meet any queens lately?"

"What the hell does that have to do with anything?" I demand.

"Just admit it. I'm not good enough for you," he says.

I'm literally struck silent. I don't know what to say. That accusation falls so far from the mark, I can't even see where it landed.

"I—"

"Can we get back to the point?" Neith says.

"I don't need to be here," Pace says.

Sawyer gives me a stern look, and even though I hate it, I know what he wants and that he's right.

I groan internally as I stand and place a hand on his arm. "Diori, I'm sorry. I never meant to hurt you and I absolutely don't think I'm better than you."

"Right," he scoffs.

I almost lose my cool again, but my eyes shift to Sawyer. "I'm serious. Look, why don't we get through this. If we all survive, we can talk about… us. Whatever that means."

"Whatever," Pace says. He turns to Sawyer. "What are we supposed to do, anyway? We're talking about the most powerful beings on earth. Literally."

I can see the relief on Sawyer's face. "We have to do something, right?"

"We do," Neith agrees.

I've gotta say. I'm a little impressed with this girl.

"Diori," Sawyer says, "have you been in contact with… your partner recently?"

I'm glad to see everyone here is smart enough to not use our monikers. We don't need anyone overhearing, especially not nosey Guild drones.

Pace seems nervous. Embarrassed even. "Uh, no. He hasn't answered my calls in a while."

"How long is 'a while'?" Sawyer asks.

Pace looks around a bit, maybe hoping someone will say something and he won't have to answer. When no one speaks up, he says, "Since the… his team disappeared and came back."

"Whoa, man," Bash says.

"That was months ago. Almost a year," Sawyer says, trying to keep the agreement from his tone. "Has it ever been that long before?"

"No. Not even close." He pointedly looks away from me. "He gets annoyed with me sometimes, but he's never gone more than a couple of weeks without contacting me."

"Aaliyah? What about yours?"

"The same. I have spoken to her briefly over the phone, but I have not seen her in person for the same period of time."

"What about your guy? Are you in contact with him?" Pace asks.

He's talking about Black Harrier, not Frank. Sawyer looks in my direction, as if he's expecting me to answer.

I throw my hands up. "Don't look at me."

Pace seems upset. "Why is he looking at you?"

I don't answer that question. "I spoke to him once, but he's still the same person as far as I can tell."

The levels of depth in that statement are unparalleled.

"Yeah," Sawyer adds, "he's acting a little weird, but not like the rest of them."

"Why would that be?" asks Neith.

I've already been thinking about this, so I answer. "He didn't disappear along with the others."

"Makes sense," Bash says.

"Yeah. Okay. Alright. So what's our play?" Pace sounds ready for some action. If I'm this antsy about not being able to go out and fight criminals, I can't even imagine how much his hyperness must be driving him crazy.

"I'm not sure yet," I say, "but we have help."

"Help?" Neith asks.

"Yeah," Sawyer says. "Uh, Frank is putting together a plan to try and stop them."

"Frank, like… BH Frank?" Pace asks.

"Yeah."

"BH?" Bash says. "What the hell is BH—ohhh. Awesome, bro."

"Yeah, and we're the only ones who are in a position to implement it."

"This is insane," Neith says. "It's suicide."

"Then what do you suggest?" I say, sparing Sawyer the need to further alienate her. "We just let… them take over and not do anything about it? If we do this right and work together, we can beat them."

"You really believe that?" she says.

"Yeah. I do. I mean, I don't think I did a few days ago. But then I realized all we've done together in such a short time and I now, I believe we can do anything."

Sawyer smiles at me. "Damn right."

Bash, being the only one without a real tie to the Guild, looks confused. "They're supposed to be the good guys. Why are they even doing this?"

Sawyer sighs. "We haven't figured it out yet."

"But we will," I say. "We absolutely will."

"And you're going to have some help." We all turn to see Baron Steele standing behind us, having just come out of MoonMoney. He smiles and takes a sip of his coffee, then grimaces like he just drank toilet water or something.

"Dammit! Not again." He turns around and goes back into the coffee shop.

TWENTY-FOUR

SAWYER

How embarrassing.

Tiffany, the AI built into my helmet, somehow reverted back to her original avatar. That happens to be a super hot, almost naked blonde bombshell. When she appears beside me in the Douglas Industries basement-level parking garage, I can't even piece together a sentence.

That's not even the most embarrassing part. My whole team is here too, and although they can't see Tiffany, they can hear me as I ask her to please put some clothes on and change to her anime settings.

"*And here I thought we were finally going to have some fun,*" she says.

"I didn't reset you," I tell her, completely unsure how it happened.

Douglas Industries tech has been going a bit wonky for days now and Frank thinks it has something to do with the Guild using it for their own nefarious purposes.

Speaking of Frank, he thinks he's located Weisswulf.

Who is Weisswulf? That's an astute question, reader.

Weisswulf was created in the same explosion that gave Eaglestar his powers, along with the other Nazis who were on board. Since he was trying to protect the Tuldarian artifacts they were transporting in their zeppelin, he somehow became very in tune with them and can use them to perform different feats of magic—or what appears to be magic because the alien technology is so much more advanced than anything anyone has ever seen.

That's actually a really famous saying or something. I don't know who said it, probably some old guy at some point I guess: "Any sufficiently advanced technology is indistinguishable from magic."

In this case, it's absolutely true. The stuff Weisswulf can do makes Frank's technology look like Lincoln Logs.

Like Eaglestar and the rest caught in the explosion, he hasn't aged a day since he got his powers. But Eaglestar managed to take down most of the other superpowered Nazis over the years, and they're either in the Trench or were killed at some point since World War II. Weisswulf has somehow managed to avoid both of those grim fates, possibly thanks to the abilities granted to him by one or more of the artifacts.

There's no telling what kind of chaos he can cause with those things.

"Tiffany, are you sure Frank said 'Long Island'?" I ask.

"Well, he didn't say 'The Moon,'" she snarks back.

"Why are you so confused?" Osprey asks me.

I flip my visor up so I'm no longer distracted by Tiffany's projection and all my readouts.

"I don't know, does Long Island seem like the kind of place an evil mastermind would be?"

"Why not?" Bash asks.

"Everyone else we've ever faced is holed up in some warehouse, and Weisswulf is chilling in a mansion on the island?"

"He's not exactly Mezmer, though," Pace says as if he has intimate knowledge of the guy. "Most people think he's just a really successful businessman. He owns a ton of things like all those Weiss car showrooms in Manhattan."

"Wait, seriously? Those are his places?" I ask.

"Yeah," Pace says. "And a lot more."

"How do you know all this?" Osprey asks, stepping forward.

It's good to see them talking and sort of burying the hatchet. Is that an insensitive phrase? I guess. I don't know… okay. I just like seeing them acting like adults.

"What, do you think I'm annoying *and* stupid?"

Oh, hey, look, I spoke too soon.

"Guys, let's just get going, okay?" I say, trying to be diplomatic.

"Whatever," Pace says.

Osprey doesn't even respond.

The problem is, we don't have a vehicle big enough to fit everyone, so Frank has to lend us an unmarked Douglas Industries van. With Pace and Bash eating snacks and drinking soda along the way—oh, and having a burping contest—I feel more like I'm on a family road trip than a mission to confront a supervillain. Not that I've ever been on a family road trip—I'm just assuming. Maybe it's closer to being on tour with a heavy metal band or something. Now that would be awesome.

When I was a kid, this wouldn't have worked. There used to be people at the tollhouses leading into the city. Now? We just breeze right in and I assume Frank will get charged somehow.

Tiffany chirps over the van's speaker system. *"The villain called Weisswulf is currently residing at his beach house in the Hamptons."*

"The Hamptons?" I ask. "Isn't that a little… posh?"

Osprey is seated next to me in the passenger seat. I occasionally glance behind me to see Neith scowling at her and hadn't even thought about those implications. For now, I'll make believe I still hadn't.

"Like you said," Amy interjects. "Would you rather it be Chef Maléfique's little 'funhouse' kitchen?"

"Point taken," I say. "The Hamptons it is."

Frank's work in the UK might have given us a leg-up here, but we won't be entirely sure. Honestly, besides the cryptic words of a half-conked-out Firefly, we don't even know if Weisswulf is involved in any of this.

However, the mention of Weisswulf in conjunction with Frank thinking the vortex had something to do with those Tuldarian artifacts is a damn good sign.

"Is everybody set on the Baron's plan?" I ask.

Paul was full of advice, but when I practically begged him to go with us, he gave a big speech about how we'd never truly be heroes until we venture off on our own, blah, blah, blah. Then quietly added that we'd never be able to afford his mileage rates and something about MoonMoney locations being too few and far between outside of the city.

"I had some trouble understanding him. What language was he speaking?" asks Bash.

"British, you idiot," says Pace, still in a bad mood from arguing with Osprey.

Yeah, this is going great.

"I realize he didn't have much of a chance to get us ready—since some people had to storm out the first time he was supposed to train us—but I think what he told us about using our powers together was helpful."

"So what's my job again?" Bash asks.

Osprey answers him. "You're the tank. You need to get up front and make sure the bad guys focus on you since you can take a lot more punishment than the rest of us."

"Oh, right." He grins. "Yeah, that's pretty cool. 'Tank.' I like that. Maybe I'll change my name to that."

"I'm pretty sure it's taken," I say. "Is everyone else clear on what their part is?"

"We're not imbeciles, Kite," Pace says, then looks at Bash. "Well, not all of us."

"Raptor. Red Raptor. How many times do I have to—"

"Relax, dude. I'm just giving you some crap. You know, trying to lighten the mood?"

I take another deep breath, something I seem to do more and more lately. Stay calm, Sawyer, he's just joking. I'm not gonna say anything to escalate the situation.

"Well, maybe now's not the best time to be fooling around," Osprey says.

Escalation begun.

"I thought it was funny," Neith says.

I don't know if she's serious of if she's just trying to get a dig in because Osprey is defending me.

Pace gives Neith a fist bump and an appreciative grin. "Thanks, hot stuff."

Osprey crosses her arms and sits in a huff. At least that's what I think it is. I've never used that word before, but it seems like what it would look like.

Then the thought hits me that Pace and Neith could join together in trying to teach Amy and me a lesson and that could lead to them pretending to be together, which could lead to them actually starting to like each other, and then they'd really be together and then... and then I realize I'm spiraling. And I shouldn't be focusing on this right now. But I'm still not taking any chances.

I better diffuse this fast.

"Let's all just quietly think about what the Baron told each of us about using our respective powers to optimal advantage and focus on the mission. We'll just sit in silence until we get there."

"Do not call me 'hot stuff,'" Neith says softly.

Out of the corner of my eye, I see Osprey smiling and I smile too.

Osprey turns on the car radio and some country song comes on about someone cheating on someone and I immediately start worrying again even though, technically, Neith and I aren't even together, so if she got together with Pace, it wouldn't be cheating at all, but I'd still feel like it was because of the way I feel about her and my chest feels like my heart got ripped out and… and I almost hope I get hurt really bad on this mission so Neith can feel guilty and oh God, I'm spiraling again.

I snap. "I said sit in silence and focus on the mission!"

Osprey turns the radio off. "Geez, okay. Chill already."

The rest of the ride is completely silent, and one of the most awkward situations I've ever been a part of. Finally, we arrive at our destination.

We park a safe distance from the gate to an unassuming beach house. I say "unassuming," since all of his neighbors have giant walls around their homes too. Anywhere else in the world, it would be very "assuming."

In addition to the wall, I spot a couple of security guys, but they seem like your typical rent-a-cops. Nightsticks, pepper spray, maybe a handgun. Maybe. It's already dark, but floodlights are staged decoratively all over the property. The place is gorgeous and I begin to wonder if Frank has one of these. If he doesn't, and the world survives this whole evil Guild thing, I'm gonna suggest it… strongly.

"How are we going to get in without setting off any alarms?" Osprey asks.

"I'm glad you asked," I say. "Harrier and I were able to pull up the blueprints for this place, which was built over a hundred years ago. I think we have a spot to enter where there are probably no alarms, and it fits our M.O. perfectly."

I point to a spot on the west side of the building where a path goes from the bungalow to the main house.

"Okay," Pace says. "What's the plan? Am I on?"

I look over my shoulder at him while he wipes cheese powder from his face with the back of his hand, then proceeds to suck said powder off each orange fingertip.

Gross.

"Light touch," I say. "Remember what Paul said."

Light touch means he shouldn't hurt them—not much, at least. They probably have no idea they're on the payroll of a supervillain and think they're just guarding some rich dude's house. Knock them out if necessary. Then tie them up, gag them, whatever, and finally, take their guns really far away. After that, he'll do a quick perimeter check and ensure no other guards are stationed.

He gets out of the van. He does this little two-hop-and-a-neck-crack thing before speeding forward. Both guards are unconscious in seconds. Then, I see it an instant before I hear it. A quick glint of light from one of the upper balconies and then a gunshot. Pace goes from a blur to motionless on the asphalt in the blink of an eye.

"Pace!" everyone cries at once.

We move to open the van doors when we hear a voice over the radio just as we had when Tiffany spoke earlier.

"Not so fast, children."

We all freeze.

"Who is this?" I demand, but his heavy German accent makes it pretty clear.

"You don't think anyone enters my island without my knowing, do you?"

"Weisswulf…" I whisper.

"You have no idea how long I've been waiting to slow that pest down."

I motion for the others to quietly exit the vehicle.

"Don't do that."

Where is this guy?

"Do you not think Deadeye can dispatch all of you just as easily? Next time, it will not be a simple tranquilizer."

He has Deadeye up there. This is not good. Deadeye could shoot a fly… well, dead… from a mile away. Why's it always have to be Deadeye? Because he's the best, obviously.

At least it confirms that Weisswulf is involved.

"A-a tranquilizer?" Osprey says. I can feel her relief. I look over and she's white as her costume, staring at Pace, who is still unmoving.

"I am not a monster. I don't kill children."

"What do you want?" I ask.

"That seems a silly question considering the circumstances. I believe I am the one who should be posing that query."

"We just wanna talk," I tell him.

He laughs. "Oh, well, why didn't you say so!"

Good to see sarcasm isn't exclusive to my generation.

I glance up in the rearview mirror and make eye-contact with Neith just as one of her tattoos glows and she literally disappears into thin air.

"What the hell?" I say out loud by accident.

"Such language. Does your father know you speak like that?"

My mouth goes dry. Is that just one of those things that old men say or does he know?

I'm about to respond when I feel the van rock slightly as Neith apparently exits through the still open door. I hold my breath, waiting for the report of Deadeye's rifle, but when nothing happens, I let it out.

"How does this end, Weisswulf?" I ask. Really, at this point, I'm just trying to buy Neith some time as she does whatever it is she's planning.

I've seen her in action plenty of times, but it seems as if she has some tricks we've never witnessed. I had absolutely no idea she could turn invisible. I'd seen her sort of fly, or float… but this is next level. Those tattoos clearly hold some incredible power. Maybe it's a new one. I should probably know that, but she has so many, and the last thing I want is to get caught staring.

"That is the question, is it not? You see, to much of the world, I am just a humble but incredibly successful businessman. Few know the truth and I intend to keep it that way. So, I can't let you storm my property and then simply leave, can I?"

"You already said you don't kill children, so that bluff has been called," Osprey says.

"Just let me go smash his face in. Can I?" Bash says.

I put up a hand, asking for quiet. We can't afford to make any hasty moves with Neith out in the open.

Suddenly, Osprey points and I follow her gesture to the middle of the road where Pace is bouncing along in midair. There's a thud when his body lands inside the van, and Neith speaks.

"Let's go. I took care of the gunner. He didn't even see me coming."

"You sure?" I ask.

"What is the matter, you still don't think I'm capable of taking care of myself?"

Man, she's not gonna let that go, is she?

"Sorry," I tell her. "Did you hear that, Weisswulf? Your security is down. We're coming in to talk."

TWENTY-FIVE

AMY

Sometimes, I feel like we get lucky.

Then, I remember how much training we've done since the Guild went crazy. Even with all the cancelations lately, we've worked our asses off. And with the extra advice we got from Paul, we're even better. We work damn well together.

We leave Pace in the car, unconscious. I hope he's okay. Otherwise, I'm going to feel really guilty for a long time. It's just something I can't really think about right now.

Sawyer leads us to the spot where Frank had identified a viable entrance. However, there's nothing there but a wall. We all search for some kind of button or lever that might give us entrance, but come up with nada.

Bash scratches his head. "Maybe the plans are wrong."

"Perhaps they've filled it in for some reason," Neith says.

"Probably because it was an easy entrance," I say.

They all look at me.

"What? It's true isn't it? We were just going to waltz in?"

"Well, now what?" Sawyer asks. "If Pace were here…"

"What? What would he do?" I ask.

"I've been trying to get him to try vibrating really fast to see if he can pass through walls."

"He can't do that," I say.

Sawyer gives me a look and I quickly realize where his dirty mind went.

"You're disgusting," both Neith and I say simultaneously.

"What?" Sawyer says, affecting a sly grin.

"Bash," I say, turning away, "how about if you—" Before I can finish the sentence Bash charges at the wall and plows straight through it.

"Damn right!" he shouts, dust and debris exploding in all directions.

"I was going to say, 'Maybe you can force the front door open…'"

Bash's voice comes weakly from inside. "I'm okay!"

I figured he was. He's tough. Tougher than any of us.

To our right, there's a set of stairs that the blueprints say leads to a basement level. In front of us, the kitchen, living area, and a couple of bedrooms. If we go through the kitchen, it'll take us to a staircase up to the master bedroom and the pool.

Except, before we can even make it fully inside, a dozen more guards come rushing from all sides.

"Dammit," Sawyer says.

"Look, we don't want to hurt any of you," I tell them. "Just put down your—"

Bash roars and throws his fists wildly, catching a few of the guards and sending them flying into some of the others.

So much for diplomacy. It reminds me of a meme I saw about the term they use when people do this in role-playing and video games. What was it? Oh, yeah. "Murder hobos."

Sawyer and I spring forward while Neith draws her bow.

Part of her ability when she channels the Egyptian goddess her code name is based on is to be a great huntress—apparently one that can turn invisible. It's almost impossible to surprise her.

As soon as all the guards are down, she descends the stairs to our right and the rest of us follow. At the bottom is a small antechamber with a reinforced steel door leading into the rest of the basement. Bash is fully recovered from his fall already.

"Bash, when I give the signal, kick down this door." He nods. "Everyone ready?"

"Always," Neith says.

Everyone else nods. "Now!"

Bash kicks open the door and we see a cavernous room full of shelves containing crates. Some of them are open, and we can see that they're full of gold, jewelry, and antiques. The walls are adorned with Nazi flags, banners, and old paintings that were probably stolen back during the war. Not only have we found who we're looking for, apparently we've also come across a treasure-trove of stolen goods from World War II.

It is in such stark contrast to the beautiful beach house above.

Weisswulf stands in the middle of the room in a suit and tie that matches his stark white hair. He may not have aged physically since the accident that gave him his powers back in 1945, but he doesn't look as good as Eaglestar because he was quite a bit older when it happened. He's basically a perpetually sixty-five-year-old man.

"You are fools for invading my home! And even more foolish for entering my inner sanctum."

Too late, I notice the artifact he's holding. A concentrated beam hits Bash in the chest. He staggers backward but doesn't go down. He points it at me and it starts to glow, but I toss a throwing star and knocks it to the floor.

"Give it up, Weisswulf," Sawyer says.

"You shall pay dearly for your insolence. Prepare to die like schweine!"

"This is all a bit… much, isn't it?" I ask. I can't be the only one who thinks this whole Nazi Supervillain schtick is over the top.

Weisswulf tries to grab another artifact from a nearby table containing several devices that look similar to the one he already tried to use on us. Neith shoots an arrow and pins his sleeve to the table before he can grab it. He reaches for it with his other hand, and she does the same thing with that one.

He calls her some words that absolutely no one is allowed to say anymore. He tries to pull himself loose, but he's way too weak. Without the artifacts, he's basically just a harmless old man. An evil, racist, genocidal, but harmless old man.

We all approach him together. Bash picks him up and Neith's arrows pop out of the table like thumbtacks. He holds the old Nazi up by the front of his shirt.

"How do you think the world would view you if they heard you saying things like that?" I ask.

He begins with his racial slurs again, and Bash slams him against the wall enough to hurt him but not to kill him, or even break his back. "Keep going, old man."

He starts laughing and it turns into coughing fit. It sounds like he's going to hack up a lung. How much must it suck to be immortal, but be stuck at an age when you're tired and weak and always feel sick? The guy deserves it, though.

"Tell us about what happened in Times Square," Sawyer demands.

"Don't be stupid," he says.

Bash shoves him harder.

"What happened?" Sawyer says again.

"I had nothing to do with that."

"That's not what our friend Firefly said," I tell him.

At the mention of Firefly's name, he begins to finally show some proper fear. "Firefly is dead."

"Not quite as dead as you might think," Sawyer says.

"I don't believe you," he says.

"Bash?" Sawyer says.

Bash does what he does best and bashes Weisswulf against one of his metal tables.

When he comes up, however, he's holding one of those ancient-looking alien artifacts.

"The Tuldarians knew power," he says.

The artifact starts pulsing blue and then it gets brighter and brighter until another focused beam shoots out and nails Bash again.

Bash tumbles backward with much greater force this time.

I roll to the side, just barely avoiding being blasted myself. Sawyer rushes him and almost gets a punch in, but Weisswulf snatches up another one of the alien things and it does something crazy, causing Sawyer to stop midair. Weisswulf gestures with the thing and Sawyer is then thrust backward across the room.

I come up in a roll, pulling a new weapon my father made for me. I throw two objects with one hand and they separate in a wide arc, then rush back together. When they hit, just about a foot away from Weisswulf, they erupt into sparks and smoke.

When the smoke settles, I'm already on top of him, having knocked the artifacts free of his grasp. Then, grabbing a fistful of his suit collar, I slam him to the ground and grind his face into the floor.

"Please! I'm sorry!"

"What was that?" Sawyer asks me as he rushes to see if Bash is okay. Neith is already there.

"Something new," I say, without taking my eyes off Weisswulf. "Talk, you racist piece of crap."

"Please, it wasn't me," he says. "It wasn't this me."

"What the hell does that mean?" Sawyer asks.

"Don't make me talk or they'll kill me!"

"They who?" Sawyer says, helping Bash up and holding him back from dashing forward and tearing the Nazi's head off.

"I just told you, if I tell you I will die. At least I know you won't kill me."

"I will kill you without any regret," Neith says.

Weisswulf's eyes go wide, and I see genuine fear in them.

"Are you talking about the Guild?" I ask. "The Guild themselves said they'd kill you?"

He shakes his head, terrified. "I can't..."

Neith pulls back on her bow and aims it at his head. "Who are you so afraid of? Tell me now or we'll never know."

Weisswulf scrunches his face up. "Halt! I'll tell you."

"Better hurry before my hand gets tired," Neith says.

Wow, she's such a badass.

"Okay, okay!" Weisswulf says. "It is the Guild. But not the Guild."

"What is that supposed to mean?" I say, getting very frustrated.

"I'm afraid of the Guild, but they're not really the Guild, you know. They're imposters. Doppelgängers."

"Someone is posing as the Guild?"

He's at a loss for words, but he seems like he's trying to explain it. "Yes. No. Sort of. I don't really understand it myself. But they're... evil versions of themselves. From somewhere else."

"Somewhere else? Where?" I say, tightening my grip.

"Please, I told you. I don't really understand it. Have you ever seen that old space show where the characters get replaced by evil twins, and the one with the ears has a goatee?"

Bash looks around. "Is he talking about that raunchy cartoon with the kids in snowsuits?"

Weisswulf interrupts. "No, imbecile. That is a parody. I mean the original—what difference does it make?"

"You're saying they're from some kind of parallel universe, or alternate dimension, or something?" Sawyer asks.

Weisswulf points at him excitedly. "Ja! Genau! Exactly."

"What?" Sawyer says. "That's... no. That can't happen. That's ridiculous."

"You mean like a kid who can break the sound barrier on foot?" Neith says.

"Or a girl who can channel the power of an Egyptian goddess?" I add. "That kind of ridiculous?"

"Point taken," Sawyer concedes.

"I learned about this in Physics," I say. "There's some sound science behind the idea of the existence of those other worlds. The only problem would be traveling between them. Or switching places."

"That is it!" Weisswulf shouts. "That is what they did. They switched places. Please, I tell you this and you let me go. Please, yes?"

"We'll see," Sawyer says. "Get talking."

Neith makes a show of pulling her bowstring again.

Weisswulf swallows visibly. "They contacted me after the incident in Times Square and told me that the… other me from their universe had sent them here. They threatened me. Demanded I turn over my precious…" he looked around at all the Tuldarian things. "My precious friends."

"What do they want with them?"

"I don't know. They haven't told me yet. It is why I am here, hiding. It is why I have employed Deadeye. To keep me safe. That's all I know. You have to believe me."

"Why?" Bash says. "Why should we believe you? You're a super-villain."

"Ja, I'm a villain. But these evil imposters make me look like Mother Theresa."

If nothing else, I feel like we no longer have to hold back when we confront the Guild, since they're evil imposters and not our world's heroes. Not that it will probably help much.

I address Weisswulf again. "Anything else?"

"No. That is all I know. I promise."

I tie him up.

"You said you'd let me go," he complains.

"Literally never said that," Sawyer says. "I wonder who will inherit your fortune when you're rotting in the Trench?"

"You son of a—"

Sawyer kicks him. "Watch what you say about my mother. These all your artifacts?"

Weisswulf gasps for air. "Like I would tell you," he spits.

"Does Bash need to make you tell us?" I ask him.

Bash stalks toward him.

"No, no!" Weisswulf says. "That is all of them."

"You sure?" I ask.

"And… and some in that cabinet." He motions with his head.

"And that's all?" I say.

"I promise. That's all. Please, let me go. I've been cooperative."

"Not gonna happen," Sawyer says.

"Do you have any idea who I am?" Weisswulf says. He's face goes hard momentarily. "I have connections. I know big people."

"So do I," Sawyer says. Then he turns to us. "Osprey, Neith, let's collect all of the artifacts. Scour the room. Let's really make sure we have them all. You-know-who thinks we need all of them if this is going to work."

"If what's going to work?" Weisswulf says.

We all ignore the question.

"Bash, can you get him?" Sawyer says.

"Get me? Get me where? What am I—"

"Shut the hell up, old man," Bash says, dragging Weisswulf across the room with one hand, "before I decide to break your jaw."

"You're coming with us," Sawyer tells him. "We're gonna find out where the Guild is… tonight. We also need to make a stop along the way."

TWENTY-SIX

FRANK

Not for the first time this evening, I consider that I should probably cancel my dinner date with Megan. My reasons are twofold: Under the circumstances, it's foolish to enjoy an evening of fine dining. However, I still have to eat.

Secondly, Sawyer's words are digging at me. Am I being selfish? Naive? Childish? Am I putting Megan in undue danger? The answer to those questions are all likely "yes," but I've put off completely being Franklin Douglas III for too long. Now that I'm no longer the Black Harrier, I feel like I've earned the right to choose happiness.

Haven't I?

I've given Sawyer all the information I have, as well as the artifacts I'd stolen from Standesamt. All but the one I'd given to Chen. Until the Resistors have successfully interrogated Weisswulf, there's nothing more I can do.

I'm going off hunches, but my hunches are usually pretty good.

We are eating at Megan's favorite of my restaurants and the only one bearing my name. It started off as a marketing ploy, but Frank quickly became one of the most popular steakhouses in all five boroughs.

I arrive early to ensure everything is up to snuff, pick out the wine and a bottle of Champagne for afterwards. Make sure the violinist knows her favorite song. He looks at me sideways when I tell him it's "Carry On, Wayward Son" by Kansas, but nods along with a smile. I tip the staff ahead of time to make sure everything goes perfectly—but why wouldn't it? I own the place.

I'm fluffing the flowers in the vase, like I know what I'm doing, when I get a call from a blocked number. My first inclination is to ignore it, but I decide I'd better answer just in case it's Chen, or Sawyer, or even Megan calling from another phone.

"Hello?"

"Frank. We need to talk."

It's Eaglestar.

"You know, Jonathan," I say with a little snark that Sawyer would be proud of. "I'm a little busy at the moment. Perhaps tomorrow we can—"

"Now. We need to talk now."

There's something in his tone. Something I don't like. "What is it?"

"How was Scotland?" he asks.

I stand up straight and glance around the room, ensuring that I'm alone. The restaurant hasn't opened for the dinner rush, so it's just me and a server rolling silverware into napkins in the back booth.

"It was a fine trip," I say. "Surely, you haven't called to discuss my holiday time."

"It has come to my attention," he says, "that you have acquired some artifacts that rightfully belong to the Guild."

Bingo again.

"Sorry. Not ringing a bell." The last thing I'm going to do is hand over those artifacts, especially since they are undoubtedly the key to defeating Eaglestar. And this proves that he knows it.

"Do you know where Megan is?"

Fire erupts in my veins. If I could reach through the phone and strangle the life out of him, I would.

"Is that a threat?"

"Just a query," he says.

"If you even think about—"

He hangs up while I'm still speaking. I growl and throw my phone across the room. It shatters, making an indentation in the drywall.

If they've touched Megan…

This has never happened to me before. I don't think I've ever cared this much about anyone before, and if Megan is in trouble, it just proves why I've spent so long avoiding meaningful relationships.

Inside, I've been telling myself that if I got out of the superhero game, I'd be able to have something… I'd be able to be with Megan. Though now I know that was a lie.

Sawyer was right.

Although the world doesn't know who I am… and the villains may not… what happens when the heroes become the villains? What happens when those you think you can trust are no longer trustworthy?

To threaten Megan? To threaten me?

Maybe things are even worse than I'd thought.

"Get me a phone," I tell the girl sitting in the back booth.

"I'm sorry?" she says, already clambering to stand, knocking napkins and silverware all over the floor.

"A phone. Now." Then I add, "Please, and hurry."

She digs around in her pocket and pulls her own phone out.

I quickly dial a number I know by heart.

"Luis? It's Frank. I'm going to need the braces." I grab my cane and I'm out the door in seconds.

"When?" he says.

"Now." I hand the valet my ticket and he goes to bring my car around and mute the phone as I address him. "There's a hundred in it for you if it's here in less than a minute."

I take the phone back off mute as the valet runs faster than he probably ever has to get a parked car.

"I'm not sure they're ready yet," Chen says.

"I'm coming to get them," I say without any room for argument. "No better time to test them than—"

"Frank?" I hear the voice from behind me and it sends chills down my spine. I spin.

"Frank?" I hear Chen's voice on the line.

"I'll call you back," I say, my mouth agape, staring at Megan walking toward me, completely fine.

"Megan?" I say, rushing toward her.

"Are you going somewhere?" she asks.

To her, it must look like I'm ditching her.

"Me?" I laugh a little. "Going somewhere? Me? No."

My Anno rolls up and the valet hops out and sprints to me. "Thirty seconds," he says.

I look at him and then back at Megan. I stutter through a few half-brewed thoughts.

"What's going on, Frank?" she asks.

"Sir, your car?" the valet says.

"I don't need… I…" I turn away from the kid and put my arm around Megan and usher her quickly away. I look up and see a drone hovering nearby. I stare daggers into the camera, knowing who's probably on the other end.

"Are you okay?" she asks.

"Yes. I'm fine." I'm entirely not fine. I can't believe I let Eaglestar get to me like this. "Can we just… sit for a moment?"

I motion to the bench in front of the restaurant.

"What about my hundred?" the kid says.

I give him a look that shuts him up immediately.

"Of course." Megan smiles and places her hand in mine, weaving her fingers through mine. "You look like you've seen a ghost."

I take a deep breath to compose myself. I went from being happy. I'd even been thinking of inviting Megan and Sawyer to live with me. Now I'm preparing myself to tell her I can't see her anymore. Bile begins to rise in my throat.

I open my mouth to speak when I hear a very familiar *crack-boom*. Where Megan had just been is now an empty space. And I watch as a black blur that could only be Fastlane zooms down the avenue.

"Sir," I turn to see the server standing next to me. "Can I have my phone back?"

TWENTY-SEVEN
SAWYER

A gnat.

Weisswulf has the pain tolerance of a gnat. Is that a thing? Maybe gnats don't even feel pain and I'm just assuming things.

Anyway, I'm not saying we tortured him or anything, but anytime he refused to talk, Bash just applied a little pressure and he spilled like a busted water main.

Hmmm. It does sound a little like torture, I guess. But… Nazi. So who cares? Wait… isn't that Nazi logic? Guh.

Turns out, we barely needed Weisswulf to tell us that the Guild has made their home at the UN building right here in the city. That's pretty fortuitous since their headquarters is in Washington, D.C. This whole time, I'd been expecting to take another—much longer—road trip and I wasn't looking forward to it.

Another part of me half-expected them to be holed up in some dark dingy lair, but I guess they didn't see any reason to hide since they're not afraid of anyone taking them out. And why should they be?

I just kind of didn't expect them to still be in Manhattan. Color me surprised.

Since this whole lockdown/takeover, despite the many warnings, a few heroes have tried to confront the Guild about their decision to take over. It hasn't gone well.

There were a few foreign heroes who showed up at the UN right after Evilstar's announcement, including GrayWulfe—not to be confused in any way with Weisswulf—who has a superhero academy in Russia. They were taken down immediately. I also saw some really high-powered American heroes on the news getting worked over by the Guild. Those videos were nothing compared to the uncut ones posted by civilians who happened to be bystanders. Those made the Baron Steel and Eaglestar fight look like a sandbox dispute between toddlers. Most of the heroes ended up in the hospital, but reports are that at least some of them are dead.

Dead. Are you hearing that? Heroes killed by the Guild. That's seriously effed up.

The majority of the world's other super-powered crimefighters are afraid to confront them, either because they don't wanna die themselves, or because they don't wanna take a chance on killing the Guild members. Or both, I guess.

What all of this means is that I made another decision I may live to regret. If I live at all.

We picked up Javier on the way.

I know, I know… what was I thinking? He could easily be hurt or killed, but so could the rest of us, and we need all the help we can get. I just have to hope that worrying about him doesn't slow me down so much that it affects my ability to lead the team. We already had to sneak him out through his bedroom window because it was past his bedtime.

It's not even that late.

At first, he was really excited to be going with us. That is, until I filled him in on the details. Since then, he hasn't said a single word. He's doing a good job of hiding it, but I'm pretty sure he's absolutely terrified.

This is probably the most dangerous situation I've ever been in, and that includes my confrontation with Chef Maléfique and Deadeye.

Even La Cucaracha… and that guy was massive and scary and deadly.

Oh, and the whole Neon Knights thing last year. They, themselves, weren't that big a deal, but we went up against Battlegear too and that dude was strong as hell.

He's Eaglestar's archnemesis, and anyone who can stand up to Eaglestar… I don't think we should have survived that.

Whereas all of those were normal humans, even if they were psychos, Eaglestar is something nobody has ever seen or heard of before. Scientists haven't figured out exactly how he got his powers, but they seem to be nearly limitless, and he doesn't seem to have slowed down any over the decades.

It's like what Weisswulf can do by using the artifacts somehow seeped into Eaglestar's body.

And he's just one of the badasses we are about to go up against.

Bastet channels an Egyptian goddess—or maybe is a goddess, I've never been very clear on that whole thing. And I get the impression she wants it that way. If she is a goddess, that means Neith might be too, which is a subject I'm not at all prepared to think about right now.

Fastlane is the fastest person on Earth, even faster than Pace. I've heard that he can run up to 2500 miles per second. Not hour. Second. Like, he would run around the whole Earth in ten seconds. That's insane. He can only go that fast in short bursts, but it's enough to have a massive advantage against almost any foe.

Cupid has wings that actually work, and is as deadly and accurate with his bow and arrow as Deadeye is with a gun. And Omar the Defenestrator—which is really hard to say, by the way—is stronger than anyone alive except for Eaglestar, although I think Baron Steele can give him a run for his money.

I used to assume "defenestrator" meant someone who rips out people's entrails or something. But then I finally looked it up. Omar "the guy who throws people out of windows" doesn't have the same ring to it.

Even though I feel bad for Mac—last I saw him, he'd fallen back into a coma—I'm super grateful I saved him back at Sidekick Day last year. He was being sucked through the vortex with the rest of them and I was able to grab him long enough to keep him on our side. Not only would we probably not have figured out what was going on with the Guild this soon, but we'd be going up against him and his powerful wrist blasters as well. Which is extra dangerous when the person shooting them at you is so small you can barely see him, never mind hit him.

The United Nations building isn't far from the Aerie. Just a handful of blocks away. But we aren't coming from the Aerie. We're traipsing across Long Island in a van with Weisswulf complaining the whole way.

As I said before, we aren't monsters, so we can't really just knock him out. But between us, Bash wants to. Really bad.

The first thing I notice as we pull up to the UN Building is that all the flags that normally line the entrance are gone. One-hundred-ninety-three of them. Gone. That's nearly two hundred nations that used to be represented but now only one flag remains and it's not even the American flag. It's that new version of the Guild flag that I saw on the broadcast earlier—a black X on a red field. Why are all terrorist dictators so partial to red and black? It makes me rethink my costume choice.

"How are we going to get in there?" Neith asks.

Besides the obvious lack of national standards flying from a bunch of empty poles, the other standout feature is the lack of any form of security.

"I think we just... walk in?" I say, almost as a question.

Just to be clear, this isn't really a secret base or anything like that. They clearly aren't worried about any challengers. Even the Guild Hall in D.C. is little more than the business front for the Guild, and the place where they have official meetings and so forth. A giant glass building with statues and fountains, museum and gift shop—the whole thing.

Pace is still out cold, though we're confident it's just a result of the tranquilizer dart used by Deadeye. Oh, apparently, Neith used some kind of binding "spell" on Deadeye and he's tied up by some supernatural means on that balcony back at Weisswulf's beach house. Assuming we live long enough and defeat these evil bastards, the real Guild will be able to swoop him up and finally bring him to the Trench. And that's something that's never been done before. Another win for the Resistors, if we ever get the chance to celebrate it.

Neith looks exhausted. She's really the most mysterious of the team, but I'm beginning to notice a trend. When she uses her tattoo magic, the one she uses goes dim and it drains her a lot. I begin to wonder if she can only use the power from each one every so often. If she's anything like Bastet, who transforms into different big cats depending on the day/night cycle, I'd guess once a day.

She won't admit it, but I think she's too weak to really be of use here.

I turn around and peer into the back seat.

"Neith, you should stay with Pace," I tell her, hoping she doesn't get offended.

"I am going."

"It's just that you look—"

"I am going," she repeats.

Osprey, seated in the passenger seat beside me, raises her eyebrows and a slight smirk plays at the corner of her mouth.

"Perhaps it is his girlfriend who should stay with him," Neith offers.

"He's not my boyfriend," Osprey says.

I speak up before the girls can get into it deeper. "Bash, I think there are some jumper cables in the back of the van. Tie our guest to something sturdy. He can keep Pace company and tell him where we went should he wake up."

"I… you cannot do that," Weisswulf says. "I have been as helpful as I can be. I demand you let me go!"

I chuckle a little and motion for the rest of the team to follow me while Weisswulf continues to piss and moan about how unfair things are.

So now it's me, Osprey, Neith, Cricket, and Bash against the most powerful people in the world.

No problem.

There used to be a bunch of people working here, from secretaries to janitors to maintenance people. But now? The revolving doors are unlocked and the lobby is entirely vacant. Four levels of mezzanine walkways—empty. Our footsteps echo ominously and with each one, I expect a laser beam to lash out and turn us into pork rinds.

But nothing happens.

I consider calling out, and I remember a year ago, at Facebuster's gym, we were in a similar, yet wholly less dangerous situation. We had just walked in when Bash decided it was the right time to announce that we were "the Resistors" and we were "here to kick their sorry asses!"

We're inside for just a few moments when I do hear shouts, but not from any of us.

"You hear that?" I say to all of them, but really to Osprey.

"Yeah, it's coming from down that hall, I think," she replies.

I wave everyone along and we move slowly but with purpose down a mid-length hall. Doors on each side give the appearance of offices or conference rooms. The screams are male for sure. But then I hear lower voices as well. Two of them. Kind of taunting or sinister.

Suddenly, a psssst sound comes from behind us. We all turn, expecting to have to fight, but instead we see a dirty-looking dude in what appears to be an Easter Bunny outfit tip-toeing toward us.

"Guys," he whispers. "Remember me?"

You've gotta be kidding me. I can't deal with this. Not right now. "Swamp Rabbit?"

He looks both ways down the hall, obviously terrified and paranoid. "I came as soon as I could. What'd I miss?"

Osprey gives me a look that says, "Do something about this." But I'm so thrown I have no clue how to handle the situation.

"What are you doing here?" I try to contain my frustration, but it's a lost cause.

"I got the call that went out for help from any heroes who were willing," he says. "Here I am."

I'd forgotten Frank said he sent out a call to the reserve. The all-call goes out to heroes around the world, and all we get is Swamp Rabbit? I guess I have to admire his bravery. But, y'know, c'mon…

"Look, as much as we appreciate the backup, we already have a plan. Just stay back. And whatever you do, don't get in the way."

He gives me a stupid salute. "You got it, boss."

I shake my head, not caring if he sees me.

We arrive at a solid door behind which we are convinced torturous activity is being performed.

I lower my visor. "Tiffany, show me inside."

"I thought you'd never ask."

I ignore her innuendo as my vision fades into neon lines and black, sort of like that old movie *Tron*.

As expected, I can make out two shapes—big guys—hovering over another shape that appears to be crucified to the wall, arms and legs spread eagled.

"Ready?" I say almost inaudibly to the team. I hold up two fingers to indicate the number of threats within, and point to their rough positions.

The others nod, and I step aside for Bash to knock down the door.

He roars, which I think is stupid since it gives our enemy a second's worth of foreknowledge that something's about to go down. He, however, considers it his signature move.

Tanks… right?

The door splinters and he just keeps going, lowering his shoulder and spearing someone I instantly recognize to be Omar the Defenestrator.

Omar is strong as a brick and just as stoic. I think in all the time I've been doing this, I've heard him say ten words total. His skin is like onyx and I can only imagine this version of him is plotting how to destroy the world instead of take it over.

He, like Frank's Raptors, wears armor crafted from some kind of carbine, but I know it isn't graphene. Unlike Eaglestar, or even Baron Steele, however, Omar isn't indestructible. I've seen Bash take some hits—once even from a rocket launcher. I'm not sure, but I'd put my bets on him. He's young… no one has been able to really gauge his abilities. Though, I'm pretty sure we are about to find out.

They literally crash through the wall into the next room and I lose sight of him.

I spare a glance and notice the torture victim looks in rough shape. It'll be my job to get to him, but first I have to address the enemies.

"Cricket," I shout, pointing toward the man on the wall. "Go try to get him down. Hurry!"

Neith and Osprey are in motion now as well, and the other enemy is none other than Cupid. Almost faster than I can follow, he has a stun arrow ready and fires it off. Just as I'm sure it's gonna hit me dead in the chest, a blur leaps in front of me, and Swamp Rabbit convulses before hitting the floor, jolted by Taser-like electricity.

Well. That was… unexpected. Took one for the team. One meant for me, specifically.

Osprey wallops Cupid in the gut with her extendable baton, buying me a second. I kneel down next to Swamp Rabbit for a moment. I tear the Taser wires free. I feel bad because he just saved me, but he's so gross. Big, nasty, yellow buck teeth pop out over chapped and crusty lips. He's quickly losing consciousness.

"It was an… honor… serving with you…" he says before passing out.

I'm sure he'll be okay. Meanwhile, we have an evil version of a Guild member to take care of.

My eyes lock with Cupid who is busy with the two most badass women I know.

Ever see one of those sitcoms with the insanely attractive woman married to some chubby, loud guy? You now have a good picture in your head of Cupid.

Back in the '80s, he used to wear a little diaper and his hair was tight blond curls—a perm. I wasn't alive then, but I'm embarrassed for him. Now, he looks like your standard rogue or something, all dressed in white like a pure and holy version of Robin Hood. Oh, except shirtless with big fluffy wings.

I said it already, but Cupid is really damn good with a bow and arrow. But so is Neith, and I'm hoping that the rest of us can cause enough of a distraction to put him on the defense, quick.

Cupid shoots another stun arrow, this time, at Osprey's face. It disappears before it can hit her. I look to see Neith raising her left hand and one of her tattoos glowing. The arrow disintegrates to ash.

Remind me to stop pissing her off.

The problem is that the exertion causes her to collapse to one knee.

"Neith!" I shout. "You are all right?"

"Fine. Do not worry about me."

Osprey engages in close combat with Cupid. With both of those brutes occupied, I set my focus on the man strapped to the wall. I join Javier, who is intent upon trying to untie the victim. I'm really happy to see that he isn't actually crucified, you know, with nails. Instead, ropes pull him taut on all four limbs.

I know this guy.

I've met the Ward before—a couple of times. He wears a mask that literally blurs his face. You can still see his black skin and head shaved bald, but I don't know if anyone knows what he looks like.

His suit is disheveled and bloody, torn to shreds. There are scorch marks all over his chest like Cupid pressed the head of one of his flaming arrows against him like a brand.

The Ward is the Guild's administrative lead. He oversees the acquisition of super-powered weapons, artifacts and things of that nature. He also serves as the public relations head—a job I assume they no longer have need of now that they are fascist dictators. That also makes him the Guild's ambassador to the United Nations, which explains why he's here—and why they did this to him.

Okay—well, nothing explains why anyone would do anything like this. But it makes a bit more sense, at least.

I can hear the rumble of battle happening next door between Omar and Bash, but my immediate focus is not getting speared by Cupid or Neith's arrows while trying to get the Ward down.

It only takes a moment, however, to realize it might be too late.

"Tiffany, is he—"

"He's dead, Sawyer," she finishes.

"What did she say?" Javier asks, still working the knots.

I pull his hands away and shake my head.

I barely knew this guy, but I'm through playing games. Am I a kid? Sure, maybe for a couple more days, but I'm also the Black Harrier's partner… and son.

I whip around, pulling two throwing stars from my utility belt as I do. They leave my fingertips with practiced ease and soar across the room.

Thunk-thunk.

Landing, one on each of Cupid's flabby pectorals. His head snaps toward me,

Osprey's punch lands across his jaw, and my throwing stars ignite in arcing electricity. He drops, convulsing.

"The Ward is dead," I tell Neith, Osprey, and Cricket.

"Did you just kill Cupid?" Cricket says.

"No. But he's down for a while, like Swamp Rabbit. Karma's a bitch. Tie him up while I help Bash."

I step through the broken drywall to find both Bash and Omar out cold, feet almost touching, like they collided with one another and each took the brunt of the others' force. I'd say it was like an unstoppable force meeting an immovable object, but that's not really it. It's more like two unstoppable forces colliding. Ouch.

I think the years of hard drinking have started catching up to the old Defenestrator.

"Tie up this P.O.S. too," I shout.

We make our way to the Assembly Hall, following the signs. It's not hard. I figure this would most likely be where the rest of the Guild members are, since it fits their current state of arrogance.

The room is massive. Way bigger than I'd have thought, with a high ceiling and a raised stage at the end of a long aisle, surrounded by seats in a sort of amphitheater style. On the stage in the middle is a big fancy table. The rest of the core members of the Guild of Masked Crimefighters are all seated in their chairs—or rather, the doppelgängers are seated in our world's heroes' chairs. In front of each shines that particular core members' logo. In the center, hanging over it all, is the same red and black flag, twenty feet tall.

I'm sensing a theme.

I spot the skylight above and immediately regret not having used our signature move, crashing through that and making a big entrance. If we had, however, it would have greatly decreased our chances of surviving this.

Let me paint the picture: In the center, Evilstar has such good posture it looks like it hurts. His hands are flat on the table in the most unnatural pose I can imagine, and he stares forward, eyes looking like two Christmas lights. On his left, Bastet. She's in her night form, which is a puma with pitch black fur. But she's wearing her Egyptian headdress and tunic and stuff, decked out like a human. It's always been an unnerving sight, but even more so now that I am unsure whose side she's on. One swipe from those claws, or a single bite, would rend a man in two.

Firefly's seat is empty because… duh.

On Evilstar's immediate right is another empty seat where Frank should be. Not our Frank, I guess, but theirs. One thing is obvious, Black Harrier isn't a part of their weird evil Guild.

Why? Because Alex is there, too, seated off to the side, slumped down, tied to another chair, and bloody.

Obviously, Omar and Cupid's seats are unoccupied as well.

The remaining seat belongs to Fastlane… Where is he?

Evilstar stands and continues upward, floating into the air. "Sawyer William Vincent and friends, welcome. Please join us."

I hear the doors slam shut, and I turn to see Fastlane standing behind us.

Shouldn't have asked.

I start having flashbacks to when Maléfique captured Frank, and it makes my blood boil. "What have you done to Black Harrier?"

"I've been expecting you," Evilstar says, ignoring my question. He walks to the other side of the table. "Children…"

"As fun as this little '60s spy movie bullcrap is, we had a conversation with Weisswulf. We know that Firefly is alive. And we know who you really are."

Evilstar laughs. "You always were especially sly and resourceful. It's good to see this version of you is no different."

"What did you do to Alex?" Osprey says. She takes a step forward but Fastlane is on her like flies on poop.

She struggles, but ultimately decides to wait it out.

"Oh, him?" Evilstar says. "Well, he's been a pain since we first got here. At first, he was just a pest, whining about not being here with us in his 'rightful place.' Then, when we lowered our standards considerably to let him join us, he seemed like he was going to be a team player. But…" He shakes his head. "…he foolishly tried to stop us."

"Where's your Harrier?" I ask.

"I'm glad you asked that. In our universe, Alex Garner never became Black Harrier. As a matter of fact, this little pissant died in two weeks. And he's proving just as worthless in this timeline."

"That's a lie," Osprey says.

"Ah, love," Evilstar says. "Such a painful emotion. It's a choice, really. Did you know that? Love… that feeling you get when someone you care for is in the room… just a chemical reaction, no different from eating a chocolate bar. Testosterone, estrogen, dopamine, serotonin. All just chemicals expelled within our system that trick us into believing someone matters."

"Get to the point," Neith says.

"Black Harrier… we have someone else, and he wasn't able to join us because the version from this universe wasn't brought over with their Guild when Weisswulf made the switch. Well, it wasn't the Weisswulf you all know. It was our Weisswulf. And ours has proven to be more resourceful than yours."

So that's why they wanted our Weisswulf. To bring over their Black Harrier.

"Yeah. He didn't have all the artifacts, did he?" I say, taking a bit of a guess.

Evilstar smiles, but it doesn't look like a happy reaction. "You figured it out? Who am I kidding? Frank figured it out. He always was the smartest of the Harriers. It was a pity when ours died."

Frank died there and Alex never became the Black Harrier? I don't know why it matters to me, but I have to know who did. "Died? Then who is Black Harrier in your world?"

Now they all start to chuckle. "Isn't it obvious? It's you, of course. The son of the original." My team members all look at me, stunned by the revelation. "Who else?"

Every single member of my team except Osprey seems to say, "Son?" at the same time. Or maybe it's just my imagination from watching too many TV shows.

I shake my head. "I don't believe you."

"Oh, it's true, Sawyer. And over there, you're one sadistic bastard. It's a real shame you—he—couldn't join us. Although Weisswulf assures me that now, once we kill Alex and have you take over, it will happen soon enough."

"Oh, I didn't tell you, did I?" I say, affecting my own smile. "We went and visited Weisswulf. He absolutely won't be helping you anytime soon."

"It's this moment I live for, you know that?" Evilstar says, waving for Bastet to go into an adjoining room. She stands and practically glides away, she moves with such swagger.

"What are you talking about?" I demand.

"You see, Alex Garner isn't the only one we're holding here. We have someone else. Someone you're very familiar with."

Bastet returns, dragging in a woman with a burlap sack over her head. Even with that, I can tell who it is. He pulls the hood off, and I see my mom's blindfolded, terrified face, something stuffed in her mouth and sound-canceling headphones over her ears.

"As you can see, it would not be a good idea to engage us right now. We wouldn't want any innocent bystanders to get injured, or… killed."

"Let her go!" I shout.

"Easily done," Evilstar says. "All we need is for you to join us, agree to swap places with our Black Harrier… and your precious mother will be free to go."

"I don't believe you," I say. Why should I?

"I'm not asking for your belief. I'm asking for your cooperation. Keep in mind, young Sawyer, I can light you ablaze this instant."

His eyes shine a bit brighter.

"I wouldn't be so cocky," I say. "Where's your strong man? Where's Cupid?"

"Cannon fodder." Evilstar shrugs.

That gets Bastet's attention. "Is that what I am?"

"Do not make this about you."

What happens next, I could never have predicted.

Out of nowhere, Pace zips in, clearly recovered from his tranq. With Bastet distracted, he snatches Mom and pulls her to safety. Fastlane takes off after him. I figured Fastlane was gonna go after Pace even before I knew they'd kidnapped Mom, so I anticipated this would happen.

"No matter," Evilstar says. "Your little speedster is slow compared to Fastlane. And our Fastlane is even faster than yours was."

He's right—Fastlane is quicker—but Pace has always been more creative when it came to using his powers.

It starts out looking like a game of super-speed tag, but at a signal from Pace, Osprey shoves her baton outward as fast as she can, and Pace runs past her, jumping over it just in time. Even though it's probably all in slow motion to Fastlane, he isn't prepared for it and Pace was blocking his view, so he grazes the stick as he tries to leap. He hits the ground, his own speed causing the blow to be more powerful. He slides across the auditorium and into the back wall.

That's a cute little couple's move. Wonder when they had time to practice that.

I know he's not down for good because Fastlane recovers… well… fast, but I can't afford to be distracted. All I know is that Pace and my mom have escaped for now.

I turn to Evilstar. "You were saying?"

TWENTY-EIGHT

SAWYER

Before Firefly had said a word about Weisswulf, Frank had a hunch—hence the trip to Scotland. He'd guessed that the only way to get our old Guild back and banish these pricks was to reopen that vortex. But there was no way it would happen without all the Tuldarian artifacts.

He knew that the Weisswulf from the other universe must have brought the evil Guilders here, otherwise, our Weisswulf would've already tried something this crazy.

Now that we have the rest from our own universe's Weisswulf, we can send these evil mofos back from whence they came. Too Shakespearean? Fine. Either way, we have to defeat them first. Otherwise, they'll replace me and Firefly—and who knows who else—instead, using the same method.

So the false Guild is concentrating on getting me so they can switch me with their Black Harrier, and that could be to our advantage. Osprey and Neith work together again, which I think is really cool. Though Neith seems really hesitant going up against Bastet.

Osprey glides over and Bastet jumps through the air so far that they reach other in one leap. Neith finds her nerve and gets between them, smashing Bastet in the face with her bow. Bastet swipes at her, slicing her bow in two. Neith casts it aside and kicks Bastet in the stomach, then flips around with another kick, this time to her face.

Pace and Fastlane are chasing each other around. I think they're outside now.

That leaves me to deal with Evilstar. Yeah, no big deal, right?

He flies up and grabs me by the throat so fast that I can't even follow him with my eyes. He could have killed me any one of a hundred—a thousand—different ways before I knew it. But, luckily, he has a flare for the dramatic.

He lifts me by my throat high off the ground and starts his speech. "You children were foolish to believe you could stop us. You should have hidden away to extend your lives as long as possible."

I'd say something back if I could, but I can't even breathe right now. There have been a few times in my crimefighting career that I thought I was gonna die, but they were all by pretty mundane, realistic methods. Like getting shot. Or eaten by a lion. Being choked to death by the most powerful being in the world is definitely not like that.

I have no idea how I'm gonna get out of this. Who am I kidding? I'm not gonna get out of this. Even if all the other Guild members somehow switched back to our versions and started fighting Evilstar along with my team right now, they still wouldn't be able to beat him.

I'm dead. That's all there is to it.

"Though I should thank you," he says, "for bringing me all the artifacts."

Things start to fade and I know I've just about had it, and everything seems to move in slow motion.

At least I'm gonna die knowing that I accomplished my dream of putting together a superteam for the ages.

Then something happens.

At first it just sounds like a ringing in my ears, and I assume it has something to do with not getting any oxygen. But then I notice everyone else in the room is wincing at the sound. Including Evilstar.

Especially Evilstar.

The sound grows in intensity, and I see Cricket standing underneath us, shouting in our direction. And then I get it. Evilstar has super-hearing. Cricket has a supersonic scream.

To be honest, I'd forgotten he was even with us.

A trickle of blood oozes from Evilstar's ears and his eyes squeeze shut. He drops me so he can cover his ears with his palms, and Pace zooms back from out of nowhere to catch me just in time.

I'm saved by the last person I'd expect.

"Get Alex out of here," I tell Pace, barely able to squeeze the words out, and he speeds off.

Evilstar plummets to the ground, unable to concentrate, screaming in agony. I can't believe how long Cricket has maintained the scream. And I'm very scared that when he runs out of breath, Evilstar is gonna punch him to the moon.

Javier starts to weaken before Evilstar is completely down for the count. The powerhouse slowly moves toward that wee little speck of a boy with a murderous intent in his eyes, fighting the concussive force of the scream. Javi starts to panic and freezes up. In about a second and a half, Evilstar is gonna reach him and squash him like his namesake.

I fight the nausea and reach into my utility belt. Grabbing hold of another of the special throwing stars I used against Cupid, I toss it at the controls on Javier's wrist. It sparks, shorts it out, and sends it into overdrive, and Javier's scream becomes overwhelming for everyone in the room, including Javi himself.

I watch in awe as Cricket holds on with more effort than I've ever seen from any hero, and Evilstar finally drops, his face hitting the ground with a dull smack.

Javier collapses, and Pace is there for him as well. We've had our differences, but Pace is clutch when we need him. Support and assist, just like Paul taught him. He drags Cricket away and we all rush over despite our own dizziness.

He seems to be okay, probably just passed out from exhaustion. The room is filled with wreckage from the fight. Sparks fly and smoke pours out of the extensive electronic equipment that is usually used for UN meetings. The large table is splintered into pieces. Bastet's puma form in the middle of it.

"Where's Fastlane?" I ask, just as a black blur rushes by, aiming for Pace.

I hear a roar and the wall behind us bursts open. Bash arrives with his arm outstretched. It connects with Fastlane's head and we all watch as the speedster flips a hundred times in rapid succession. He smashes into a wall and doesn't get up.

"Whoa, thanks," Pace says.

"Bro," Bash says back, pounding his chest twice with his fist.

"Where's Omar?" I ask Bash.

"Still down for the count, bro," he says as he flexes both arms. He looks ridiculous, like those bodybuilders in the competitions, but I get it. He earned the flex.

I smile and nod, then rush to kneel beside Cricket with Osprey.

"I've never seen anyone with that kind of sheer willpower," she says.

"He was amazing," I say. "I owe him my life."

"We all do," she agrees.

I've never even heard of Evilstar being injured like this. I don't think Battlegear has even managed it in all the years of being his archenemy.

"Is that it?" Bash says. "We won?"

"Not quite." The voice is weak, but the baritone is still unmistakable.

I knew it was too good to be true. All of us are exhausted, having given everything we had already, and he's still not defeated. We all turn, and Evilstar is getting back to his feet. He's obviously still dazed, but even in the shape he's in now, he can probably kill us all in seconds. And he decides to tell us so.

"I'm going to murder every last one of you little snots," he sneers.

"You'll have to get through me first." Now we all turn back in the other direction.

Epic as hell.

I, of course, recognize the voice immediately. Others might mistake it for Alex's, but I know better.

"Frank?" I ask, barely above a whisper.

Frank stands in the doorway to the giant room, wearing the reinforced version of the Black Harrier uniform that I've been helping Chen develop for months.

"Step aside, kids," he says. "Jonathan and I have some accounts to reconcile."

TWENTY-NINE

FRANK

"You have someone I care about," I say.

"She's fine," Sawyer rasps.

"Good to know," I say with a nod.

That makes things much more straightforward. I immediately charge Eaglestar. I know he thinks I can't really hurt him, but he's wrong. What he doesn't know is that Sawyer didn't bring all of the Tuldarian artifacts. This armor is infused with one of the larger ones that I'd collected years ago and given to Chen.

I've done my homework. There's not a single hero alive that I don't know how to take down.

Over the years, I've surreptitiously tested the effects of these artifacts, bringing one near to "my" Eaglestar without him knowing. I'd had my AI—Amber at the time—measuring his vitals and watched them through my visor as I stood near him.

It slowed his heartbeat and appeared to sap his strength and speed. I even tested it while we were fighting some supervillains and watched him nearly get his ass kicked by Battlegear before I withdrew and he went back to full strength.

To this day, Battlegear thinks he bested Eaglestar. If he only knew.

It was a painstaking process and took years, one tiny step at a time. But I knew this day would come.

As I suspected, the artifacts gained strength from him. The result is that he is made weak while my suit becomes stronger. It was barely noticeable with the smaller ones, but those I got in Scotland are amongst the largest of their kind.

He's still the most powerful being on earth, but this armor will take him down a few notches and give me a fighting chance.

When I plow into him, he's barely even bracing himself, thinking I'm going to bounce off. Instead, I force him back, all the way through a wall and onto his back on the exterior of the complex. The Resistors cheer when they see this. Eaglestar, however, gets angry as I hold him down on the ground by the throat.

"What did you do?" he growls.

"It was a mistake going after the woman I love. You're going to pay for it." I put everything I have into a punch to his face, but it still barely registers. The important part is that I can tell that he feels it. Even if it is only a little.

His face fills with rage. "She'll be dead as soon as I finish with you. Then I'll murder all those miserable little creatures you created."

He tries to fry me with his heat vision, but I see the redness dim in his eyes and feel myself get stronger. Nothing but smoke emanates from them.

I hit him again. "I had nothing to do with their team. That was all Sawyer."

"You better watch out for that one. Where I'm from, he murdered you to take your place."

I'm momentarily distracted by that comment and he takes advantage of it, throwing me off of him and I slam into a beam.

I feel nothing at all, the suit absorbing the fullness of the impact.

"Where you're from doesn't matter," I say. "My Sawyer isn't evil like you and your ilk."

He makes his way to me, visibly slower than before. "He may not kill you, but he'll replace you."

"And that will be my proudest moment." When he's close enough, I hit him with a two-fisted uppercut, but he hardly seems to notice it. Despite my suit, I'm already starting to get tired. I know the longer he's in proximity to this metal, the weaker he'll get and the more powerful my suit will become, but I'm not my suit. And, I may be dead before he's weak enough for me to defeat him.

He throws me through the outside wall. As I begin to rise, I hear Sawyer yelling to me. "Look out!"

Bastet is suddenly outside with me. The kids may have taken her down, but like Eaglestar, she's too powerful to stay out for long. She slashes at me. But I shoot my grappler and zip up to the roof and she only tears into my cape. I hear her behind me, leaping, following. When I land, I turn and beyond her, I can see that Sawyer has come outside to help.

"Get back inside. I'll take care of them."

"You can't beat them both!" he shouts back.

I open my mouth to respond when Eaglestar suddenly smashes through the ceiling right in front of me. We tumble through the air, grappling each other on the way down. When we hit the ground, it knocks the wind out of me, but my armor protects me from serious injury.

Eaglestar seems confused. He was apparently trying to grab onto me and fly but lacked the proper strength to see the action through.

Oops.

"Come on, you bastard" I say, egging him on as I jump up to my feet.

He stands slowly and swings at me repeatedly, but with his super-speed dampened, he isn't fast enough to land any punches. I weave left and right, avoiding every strike with relative ease. He's always relied on his powers. Never trained to fight properly. Without them, he's just a musclebound oaf.

I jab him in the face, and he seems to feel that one a little more. He swings at me again, but his fighting style is old-fashioned, like boxers in the '30s and '40s. It's almost sad.

While I'm easily avoiding Eaglestar's feeble attacks, I check on Sawyer. Bastet is very powerful herself, and I want to make sure he can handle her. But she appears to still be weakened by her fight with the rest of the Resistors. Osprey glides out and joins Sawyer in the fight.

She won't be much good against Bastet, but she's a distraction. Just the distraction Sawyer needs, in fact.

I watch as Sawyer tries a new trick with his grappler, a variation that I've never seen before. Funny how my accidentally discovering how to use it in a fight has led to him perfecting the technique. He shoots it at Bastet and it attaches, but instead of allowing himself to be pulled toward her like he usually does, he uses it to catapult off of her, then retracts it and she is yanked upward.

Osprey is then free to glide down at full speed. She lands on Bastet with both feet. Dangerous place to be, that close to the cat's claws and jaws. Osprey's double kick lands, and Bastet is tough, but even she ends up unconscious after that maneuver.

I regret my distraction as Eaglestar connects with a punch. I'm lucky it didn't take my jaw off. He may be weakened, but he's still stronger than anyone I know.

I do a full flip over his head and land behind him. Then I knee him in the back, knocking him back outside and into the garden. His face hits the grass and he literally has mud in his eye.

"Had enough?" I ask as I stand over him. I momentarily think he's unconscious, like Bastet, because he doesn't respond, or even move.

But then he swings his leg around and knocks me off my feet. I hit the ground hard and I feel my brain slosh around in my skull despite the protection from my helmet. My ears ring and the next thing I know, Eaglestar is straddling my torso. He puts his hands around my throat and starts to squeeze. My neck has some protection from my armor, but not enough to prevent Eaglestar from choking me to death, even in his weakened state. I can't breathe, and everything starts to go dark.

Then the pressure is lifted and I see Sawyer on Eaglestar's back, his arm around his neck. Eaglestar pulls on his arm and starts to pry it off as I take a deep breath and start to come to my senses.

I sit up quickly and smash my helmet into his nose, and I hear a crunch as it breaks. Blood spurts out, all over both of our uniforms. Sawyer manages to pull him off of me as Eaglestar grabs his nose, in the most pain he's probably felt in over seventy years.

I nod at Sawyer. "Thanks, Raptor. I've got this."

He smiles and backs away, letting go of Eaglestar, who sways a bit and has trouble standing. I give him an uppercut to the jaw, followed by a right hook, then a punch to the gut. He wants old-fashioned fighting? I'll give it to him. I've watched the best of them, and I can copy their moves exactly, just like my son. Where do you think he gets it from?

I finish off with a leaping kick to his face, and he goes down completely. No faking it this time. He's done.

THIRTY

SAWYER

Back inside the Guild Hall, Neith hugs me. I hug her back, and then look into her eyes. This time, it seems like there might be more than just relief, but I can't be sure.

"Are you okay?" I ask her.

"Yes. And you?"

I nod. "Better than ever."

"Javier's waking up!" Osprey shouts.

"What happened? Did I do it?" he asks.

"You did it," I tell him. "You defeated the most powerful person on Earth. You literally saved the world."

No need to tell him Eaglestar got back up and had to be taken down again. We let him have his moment.

"Pace, where's Alex?" Osprey asks.

There's the slightest twinge of jealousy on his face before he rushes from the room. A moment later, he returns with Alex. He doesn't look nearly as bad as Frank did after being tortured by Maléfique, but it's still pretty brutal.

Frank rushes to Alex. "Are you okay?" he asks.

Alex's head sways, his eyes roll.

"Never mind," Frank tells him. "Don't talk. There's an ambulance on the way."

"I—I tried…"

"We know. Just relax."

Obviously this wouldn't be the time to mention that maybe it was too little, too late. That can come later, after he's recovered.

"Pace, can you get Weisswulf?" I ask.

He doesn't answer with anything but a blur.

I pull the artifacts out of a pack we brought along. "Now we need to figure out how to send them back to where they belong and get our own Guild back before they wake up."

After a very short round of questioning, we get instructions from a cowardly Weisswulf on how the artifacts work. Frank follows them to a T.

"If you can handle this," Frank says to me, "I need to go check on someone." He stands and removes one of the artifacts from the belt of his suit and hands it to me. Then, he puts his hand on my shoulder. "Here's the last one. Now, I need to figure out what to tell her about why they'd chosen her to kidnap."

"You don't wanna stick around and do this? Or at least watch to make sure we do it right?"

"I trust you. It couldn't be in better hands."

I nod, and he leaves the room.

Bash drags Evilstar and the rest of the unconscious doppelgängers, including Cupid and Omar, into a pile on the remains of the table in the center of the room. I'm leaning over the contraption Frank's created from assembling the Tuldarian artifacts when I hear Bash swear. Then there's a crash.

Evilstar is standing now, and glass rains down all around us, having thrown Bash through the skylight above. He still looks crazy weak, but he looks plain crazy, too. I don't think Frank realized he'd recover so quickly without that special armor right next to him.

"Why the hell didn't someone tie him up?" I shout.

He takes a step, drops to a knee, and tries to rise again. He looks at me and his eyes begin to turn red.

Rising, I run toward him and tackle him.

I can't say it's a smart move, but it I couldn't risk his laser eyes tearing through everyone else in the room. Pace gets to him first and Evilstar lashes out with the back of his hand, sending Pace soaring across the room and into Neith.

"Stay back!" I shout to Osprey as I collide with Eaglestar.

She doesn't listen, of course.

My shoulder hits him in the gut and it feels like I ran into a steel beam. I can hear her fighting next to me but he has me in a headlock.

"I am the strongest man alive! I am a god!"

There's a second of confusion before I hear the smack of flesh on flesh and his hold on me slackens. Then, he thuds to the ground and my vision comes back into focus.

Standing in front of me, Paul "The Baron" Steele stands, holding a cup of coffee in one hand and shaking the other.

"How invigorating. I just beat the piss out of a god," he says.

We all look at each other, stunned.

"Sorry I'm late. Needed my cuppa."

I let out a small laugh.

"Where's Frankie?" Paul asks.

"Busy," I said. "Thanks for the help."

"No worries," he says.

"Could have used you a little sooner," Osprey says.

"If anyone in this city could simply get a coffee order right on the first go..."

"That's the third time he's gotten up," I say.

"Got it," Paul says, turning back and taking a seat on Evilstar's back.

I approach the contraption Weisswulf helped us build—a large half-moon ring.

Each segment fits perfectly into one another with a missing spot in the middle. Frank's final piece from his armor.

I set it in its spot and they start to glow.

"This isn't wise," Weisswulf says.

"I'm so done hearing you talk," I tell him. "Do the damn job."

He sighs and performs some kind of ritual and we all stand back, remembering what happened the last time the doorway was opened to the other dimension.

"What the hell's he doing?" Paul asks.

"Hopefully setting this whole thing right again," I say.

There is a blinding light, and what looks like a rip in reality appears. We all feel the pull of the vortex like we did in Times Square and brace ourselves.

"Give us a hand?" I say to Paul.

All of us, even Javier, work to ensure that the evil Guild members get sucked into the opening in the space-time continuum, just as ours had on Sidekick Day nearly one year ago. Paul tosses Evilstar through.

"How do we get the others back?" Osprey shouts over the sound.

The question is answered by several silhouettes.

When the vortex closes, there are no longer unconscious villains lying there. Instead, the members of our Guild stand in their place, looking dazed and confused.

Eaglestar, Bastet, Fastlane, Cupid, and Omar stare at one another, then at us. Instead of their usual costumes, they're wearing altered versions, somehow more villainous-looking. I can only assume their evil twins switched with them before coming over here.

Like his sometimes-sidekick, Fastlane is the first to talk. "What happened?"

I stand tall and cross my arms. "We defeated the evil versions of you."

"You did what?" Eaglestar says.

It's a bit terrifying, him standing there, but I have to remind myself that this isn't Evilstar. This is the strongest man in the world, and one of Frank's friend. Well, sort of.

Osprey continues, "We used some Tuldarian artifacts to send them back to their own universe, which, apparently, also brought you back from theirs."

Pace looks worried. "What happened over there?"

"We were in some kind of post-apocalyptic hellscape," Fastlane says. "We thought maybe there'd been some kind of attack in Times Square and we were trying to figure out how it had changed everything so much. Suddenly, anyone who was still alive hated us. Evidently, their Guild wasn't very popular on their own Earth. As soon as we found ourselves over there, we were constantly attacked by everyone we came across."

"They might have warned everyone you were coming and told them to do it," Neith says.

"I had not thought of that," Bastet says.

"Are you sure it is you?" Neith asks Bastet.

"It is."

They step forward and hug. Actually hug. Wow.

"Either way," Cupid adds, "we were only able to do so much and couldn't really rest. It was exhausting."

Fastlane shakes his head in a dizzying motion. "It was basically our own personal version of hell."

Bastet scoffs at the comparison. "I've been to Hell. That was no Hell."

Nobody is sure how to respond to that, so no one does.

Pace steps forward and addresses Fastlane. "We good?"

Fastlane smiles. "Absolutely." They clasp hands.

Eaglestar clears his throat. "We obviously owe you all a great debt. Let us know what we can do to repay you."

"Just get this place back to normal," Javier says.

"Yeah, no kidding," I agree.

THIRTY-ONE
AMY

About a week has passed since we banished the Evil Guild. Yeah, I know, it sounds stupid, but we haven't come up with anything better to call them. We tried "The Imposters" for a while, but it just sounded like a bad '90s film. "The Doppelgängers" was a mouthful. Sawyer calls them Evilstar and His Goons, which we all agree is an amazing band name.

For now, we stick with the Evil Guild.

As much as I know everyone else won't like it, I decide to talk to Alex. He's out of the hospital and mending in the Aerie. Nobody else wants to go anywhere near him now. Not after he went along with them. He aligned himself with the devil. He's basically a pariah.

As expected, I find him back at the Aerie. He's in a T-shirt and jeans and he's just finished putting the Black Harrier uniform back on the mannequin where it's stored.

I know he hears me approach. He's the Black Harrier. No one could have that title without acute awareness of his surroundings. Regardless, he doesn't turn around.

"Done for the day?" I ask.

"No. Just done." He places the helmet on the mannequin's head.

"Yeah, it's been pretty exhausting," I say. "Maybe take a little time off and—"

"You're not listening." The glass slides shut with a whoosh. "I'm through being Black Harrier."

"Well, that's understandable. It was a big job to take on, and I always knew you preferred being your own person. Your own hero."

"Hero?" He laughs. "Far from it. But I'm not going back to being Redhawk either."

"What does that mean?"

He turns toward me now and I can see his face. It's still bruised. Yellow. Black. Brown. Little cuts here and there.

"It means I don't feel right doing this anymore. All the secrets. Hiding behind a mask."

I approach him and put a hand on his shoulder. "Alex, everyone makes mistakes. You can't let—"

"You know why those bastards had access to Frank's tech and servers without his knowledge?"

My stomach drops.

"I gave it to them. Me. I used Frank's trust and I handed over the most advanced surveillance technology in the world to a bunch of villains."

"Alex…"

He puts up a hand. "Frank knows. I told him. But that's not the worst part."

"What do you mean?" Fear begins to tickle my insides.

"The worst part is that someone owns the rights to that kind of technology to begin with."

I open my mouth to speak.

"No, Amy. Wait. I'm not done," he says. "I know this thing you do… you love it. I get it. It's just not me. Before I met Frank, I was going to be a cop. I was in the police explorers program and even attended the Police Academy after I, uh, ran away… before I decided to become Redhawk. That's what I want to do now. I still want to fight crime, but I want to do it the right way."

"So what we've been doing is the wrong way?"

"A lot of people think so," he says. "Especially after this fiasco. There are stories about masked crimefighters being outlawed in some places. A lot of places."

"You're going back to Boston?"

"No," he shakes his head. "Now that the Guild doesn't have a say, I'm coming back to the city."

"What does this mean for us?" I ask.

"Us?" he laughs. "I didn't know there still was an us. I thought you were with Pace now."

"That's never been serious. I kind of thought…" I can't finish my sentence.

"Thought what?"

"I don't know," I admit.

"Well, give me a call when you do know."

He kisses me on the forehead, then leaves through the secret entrance from the penthouse.

I stand for a few moments. What did I think? I have no idea. All I know is nothing will ever be the same again.

THIRTY-TWO

FRANK

A lot of unknowns these days.

People lack trust in the Guild like never before, and who could blame them?

The world powers have issued a full ban on superhero vigilantism. It started small, one governor here, another there, but in the end, the newly reassembled UN has agreed that what happened will never happen again.

Truth be told, it's not much different from what we'd experienced under the evil Guild regime, but now… I can't entirely disagree with the decision.

I've scheduled meetings with influential men and women the globe over in an attempt to design a three-step process to restoring faith in the Guild, but I don't know if I'll have success.

The Guild has abandoned the United Nations building and have returned to Washington, D.C., and the Guild Headquarters. I—Frank Douglas III—gave a generous donation to the powers that be that would cover much of the repairs to the New York City landmark, and knowing this city, it'll only be rebuilt stronger and better.

It was due for a remodeling anyway.

After a short flight on one of my private jets, I touch down in D.C. and prepare to see my former guildmates for the first time since things went sideways.

I nod at Maeve, the receptionist, and unlike the nursing staff at Mount Sinai, she knows better than to try to make me wait.

I pass The Ward's office, frosted window bearing his name and title, and a prick of mourning hits me in the heart. I've worked side-by-side with him for decades without even knowing what his true face looked like. Hell, I didn't even know his real name. Now, he's gone forever.

I continue down the maroon and blue carpeted hallway, until I reach Eaglestar's office. A golden eagle hovers over the doorway, and the door is slightly ajar. I knock lightly anyway.

"Enter," he says.

The room is more of a lounge with a wet bar and a small mahogany desk in the corner than a typical office. The walls are adorned with decades worth of plaques, awards, and framed medals. Photographs of Eaglestar with every president since FDR, as well as many other world leaders and celebrities sit in a glass case to my right. I spot one of him with Elvis Presley that I hadn't noticed before. Above the sofa is a large portrait painted by some famous artist or another of Jonathan standing in a heroic pose. And a giant charred Nazi flag hangs on the wall above his desk—a reminder of how he came to be.

Most people don't know this part of the story because he always leaves it out, even in his autobiography, *Diary of a Demi-God.* In fact, I may be the only one who does know, and he only revealed it to me when one of our drinking sessions to unwind after a mission went a lot longer than usual. Do you know how much alcohol it takes to get a demi-god drunk? Not as much that night, when I had one of the Tuldarian artifacts in my pocket, but still a small liquor store's worth.

Everyone thinks that flag is just a memento. It's a lot more than that. The flag was flying from the zeppelin that Captain Jonathan Powers flew his plane into way back in the Second World War, and after he was thrown hundreds of feet to the ground in the explosion that gave him his powers, his clothes were shredded and hung off him in strips. The flag was lying nearby, and he wrapped himself in it before walking for miles, then collapsing to the ground. His powers hadn't fully kicked in yet and were fluctuating, and he had to be taken to a field hospital. He was lucky to have survived the fall.

That flag. That horrible, horrible flag was the first uniform Eaglestar ever wore. Not Jonathan Powers, he proudly donned a uniform of the United States military —but Eaglestar? That bit haunts him. I think he's always been worried that one wrong move will send him down a path of villainy. I'm sure the events of this past year haven't aided him in shrugging off that sentiment.

"Drink?" It's the first thing he says to me. Just like usual.

"Always."

As I lower myself onto the sofa, he pours me a couple of fingers of expensive Scotch and drops in a few ice cubes, indicating how well he knows me in some ways. It's like a scene out of *Mad Men,* two anachronistic associates who've worked together for years and yet never truly became friends. The difference is that one of us is wearing a garish, ultra-patriotic, militaristic costume instead of a five-thousand-dollar suit. Also, I actually look my age. Although I do look good for my age.

"No cane?" he says to me.

"Turns out, I didn't need it after all."

He nods and hands me my drink. "I know this isn't a social visit," he says, taking a sip of his own. "What can I do for you?"

I sigh. "Things are changing quickly. I'm wondering what your plans are."

He hesitates before answering, finishing the remaining liquid from his tumbler and pouring himself another. "There are… plans in the works."

"Care to share?" I ask even though I know what his response will be.

"The details are classified at the moment. And they haven't been ironed out in any case."

"Let me guess, you're going to be exempt from the ban on masked crimefighters. You'll be working for them."

"Them?" Jonathan says. "Them is a harsh term after what we've all just been through. Them is us, Frank. The good guys. The world has been in disarray."

"I was here, Jonathan. I know."

"Then you above all should understand why we can't allow wanton crimefighting but also need law and order."

"I'm going to have it reversed."

"I would expect nothing less of you," he says.

"That was good work with the... other me." He smiles. Well, more of a grimace. "You always did know how to get the better of me."

I hesitate a little this time. I'm not interested in hurting him or bringing up his worst fear, but I do believe it's only fair that he understand that he isn't unrivaled. "I've always had a plan to take you down in case you were mind-controlled or went insane. Or just got out of hand. Never expected 'alternate-dimension Eaglestar.' Still, it was interesting to test my methods without having to genuinely hurt you."

"I'm sure you enjoyed it, at least a little bit." He narrows his glowing eyes at me.

I try to make my response into a joke. "I can neither confirm nor deny that rumor."

He shakes his head. Never did have a sense of humor. "Can I ask you something?"

I'm tempted to do the 'You just did' thing like I have so many times with Amy and Sawyer, but decide he wouldn't appreciate it as much.

"Go ahead."

"How could you not have known that it wasn't really me all that time?"

The question catches me by surprise, even though I probably should have expected it. "Maybe you shouldn't be asking me that."

He's taken aback. "Pardon?"

I glance at the Nazi flag on instinct and almost regret it. "What I mean is, maybe you should be asking yourself that."

"I..."

"This world needs checks and balances, Jonathan," I say. "That's why the Guild was created. You alone... as much as I want to trust you..." I reach over and grab a copy of his book that's lying on the desk and hand it to him. "Someone needs to make sure the demi-god makes the right calls."

"And that's you?" he asks.

"Always has been and I don't intend for that to change." I stand and hand him my empty glass.

He looks down at it, lost in thought.

"Goodbye, Jonathan," I say as I quietly exit his office.

A month ago, the thought of Megan moving in with me had me nearly hyperventilating. The truth is that it went so much deeper than fear of commitment. It wasn't that I didn't want her to move in; it was that I did. I wanted nothing more than to build a life with her and Sawyer—the life both of them deserve. Perhaps the life I deserve.

I know now that was selfish and wrong. There's a reason I wore a mask. There's a reason I don't keep close friends. When Megan was snatched out of my grasp in front of the restaurant, right off the street in broad daylight—that was when I realized what had to happen.

The look on Megan's face when I tell her we can't see each other anymore hurts more than any damage done to me by Chef Maléfique.

"I don't understand."

"You almost died because of me," I tell her.

"You? It wasn't your fault."

Back at the UN Building, she was wearing a blindfold and noise-canceling earmuffs. She never saw or heard me or Sawyer.

"There are too many people willing to take advantage of people I care about because of… who I am. What I have. The evil version of Eaglestar was willing to kill you if he didn't get that valuable artifact I happened to own."

"This is absurd, Frank," she says on the verge of tears. "You've always been who you are and always will be."

I choke back my own tears. "That's exactly why this has to happen."

"And what about your son?"

"Nobody can know," I tell her.

"You're ashamed of him?"

"Don't say that. You know it's not true."

Tears stream down her face and my chest hurts so badly I feel like I can't breathe.

"Megan, you have to see reason here."

"No, Frank. You do. I love you."

She twists that knife harder and I almost lose my resolve.

"And I love you," I say. "That's why I'm doing this."

"That's bullshit and you know it."

Megan swearing is so rare that it feels like a slap.

"I really am sorry," I tell her.

She turns her back on me, crossing her arms, but I can see her shoulders bobbing and it kills me.

I swallow hard and whisper, "I'm sorry," again before leaving.

I make it to the elevator before I lose it. My face grows hot and before the tears come, I growl and punch the metal door, leaving an imprint.

I clear my throat and straighten my suit jacket. I may not be the Black Harrier anymore, but I chose this life, and I can't be responsible for someone I love getting hurt.

Never again.

THIRTY-THREE

SAWYER

Gratitude.

So this is the thanks we get for saving an ungrateful world: The United Nations revokes their charter for masked crimefighters across the board. No more Guild, no more heroes. Including us. Then Congress codifies it with its own act and completely outlaws masked crimefighters in the United States. Our licenses are revoked, and we're told that if we're caught wearing a costume or a mask, we'll be arrested.

And it's all finalized on my eighteenth birthday.

To be fair, this thing with the Evilstar and his Goons taking over wasn't the only incident. There had been problems before. This last event was just the straw that broke the camel's back. A very big, very heavy straw.

Anyway, they do make a few exceptions. Eaglestar, for one. Of course. He'd already been deputized by the United States government as a federal agent, and now that's gonna be his full-time job: hunting down vigilantes who continue to fight criminals. And, as far as I can tell, he's only too happy to turn on his fellow heroes as long as it's in the name of justice or whatever.

Alex is the first to turn in his license and uniform. He was quitting anyway, so it just makes it more official. I'm kind of sad to see it, but his betrayal is a lot to get over. It's hard for me to understand what he was thinking, but I have a feeling, in his own mind, he wasn't doing anything wrong. It was only later when everything blew up in his face that he recognized it.

Myself? I'm not giving in. No way. Eff them. They can come after me all they want, but I'm gonna continue to go out and help the people of this city. In a costume. And a mask.

Amy too. And Javier.

There's a pretty big damper on my birthday since Frank broke up with my mom. I know I should be pissed at him, but I get it. I give her a peck on the cheek and ask her if she's gonna be okay alone tonight.

"I'm not going to drink myself to death, if that's what you're asking," she says.

"Just making sure, Mom."

"I didn't change because of Frank, sweetheart. I changed for you. Happy birthday."

I give her another kiss and say, "Thank you."

I head up to the Aerie, and Frank is already there. I spot the hospital setup we'd used for Firefly, now empty. Last I heard, Chen was trying to figure out a way to get him back to full size.

Frank's sitting in the dark as usual, staring at the big screen as he often does.

Déjà-freaking-vu all over again.

Only this time, they're pictures of him and Mom.

I clear my throat and he quickly shrinks them all.

"Hello, Sawyer," he says. "Come. Sit."

I pull up another chair beside him. I don't know what's going through his head. Regret maybe?

We sit in silence for a really long time. Then he speaks.

"Are you going to quit?"

"Hell no. I mean… No."

"You're officially eighteen now. I'm not going to police your language anymore."

"Well, that's a better present than I was expecting. But I'm gonna keep going. Even if they throw me in jail." I brace myself for the verbal onslaught that's sure to come. As upset as he is, it's obviously a lot easier for him to go along with the new law, just like it is for Alex. He's already retired.

Only it doesn't come.

"Good." I literally do a double-take when he says this. "Thank you for coming. I know you must be upset with me for what I've done."

I begin to speak but he holds up a hand. That's his magic trick. It's incredible.

"There's something I want to give you," he says.

Frank walks me over to where we store the special uniforms and presses a button on one of the panels. One of the wardrobe tubes swishes open.

He pulls out the new Black Harrier uniform—the power suit that I helped Chen create for him.

"What is this?"

"The future," he says. Looking at me now. "Who better to take up the mantle than my own son?"

"Me?"

I don't think I've ever seen Frank look so proud. "What do you think?" he asks.

"I don't understand. I… I don't know what to say."

"Happy birthday, son. You're a man now."

I feel tears welling up in my eyes as I realize he means the word in its literal sense, rather than just the way an older adult addresses someone younger. "I… I…" The words get caught in my throat.

"I know you've been waiting for it. Why don't you put it on?"

"Seriously? But you… I thought that you—"

"No. That? That was an emergency. It didn't change the fact that I need to move on. I have… plans. For the first time in my life, I believe I can do more as Franklin Douglas III than the Black Harrier."

"May I?" I ask, motioning to the suit.

"It's yours."

With a giddy smile, I pull on the body armor and notice that it's been altered some since I tried it on for Chen. It fits me better. I can feel that extra power. And the combination of giving me more protection and making me look bigger than I am so criminals don't know immediately that they're not dealing with the same Black Harrier.

"Wow," I whisper.

"You like it?"

"I freaking love it," I say.

"Are you ready for it?"

"Absolutely. I'm ready to be the Black Harrier."

EPILOGUE

SAWYER

Huzzah!

Graduation from high school seems the most mundane of activities in light of recent events, but it's a rite of passage.

After being reminded—by Frank's lawyers—that the school was required by Guild law to have cameras monitor the halls, it was a pretty simple task to implicate Logan and his cronies as the instigators of the pep rally fireworks attack. While I had been threatened with expulsion, Logan was given a warning that was equivalent to being slapped on his wrist.

Still, no one gave me any credit for saving all of them.

Ah. Such is the life of a hero.

Funny how this all started at a funeral, and here we are, laying to rest a massive chapter in a young man's life.

Good riddance.

Mom is in the audience with Amy, both smiling like this is the best thing ever. Frank, understandably, is absent.

Fabiola and Javier are now an item. Can you believe it?

Good, 'cus it's an outright lie. Just seeing if you're still paying attention.

Fabiola is as aloof and belligerent as ever, still trying to weasel her way onto the arm of whoever would make her look best. I argue that would actually be Javi. Beauty and the beast and all that, but what do I know.

I'm shocked she's even graduating but I guess a lot gets handed to pretty faces, including passing grades.

Oh, and Amy is officially single again. Not that I'm keeping track. She and Diori decided to give it a final rest, and Alex has graduated Police Academy with the explicit promise to join forces with Eaglestar to take down anyone breaking the no crimefighters mandate.

They even created task forces and started training officers in special tactics for when they encounter vigilantes. I hear Alex is gonna lead the one here in New York. Sounds like a blast, doesn't it?

Funny enough, that started another organization. After Mr. Chen helped restore him to normal size, Mac—Firefly—founded a new agency devoted to the opposite: fighting for the people's right to end crime by any means necessary. Of course, it's a secret organization. Sort of underground. Ready for the name?

The Resistors. Yep. How original.

I take one cursory glance around and behind me. It's not that I expect Frank to appear out of thin air, but I just can't help it. He's become such a huge element of my life that a part of me wishes he would have gone the other direction completely. It's stupid, really, but I'd been expecting my dad to actually be my… dad.

Ugh. I'm not crying. You're crying. It's the graduation. It's emotional. The end of an era or whatever.

Any feelings of sadness I was experiencing is replaced by internal rage as Mr. Blanchard takes the stage.

"Family, friends, thank you for joining us this morning."

His voice makes me cringe.

After he introduces the superintendent and the school board and a bunch of other "special guests" that not one single person here cares about, he launches into his usual template speech.

"Before I congratulate the graduating seniors, I want to remind you all one final time that anyone who throws their mortarboard hat in the air at the end of the ceremony will be escorted out by security and will have cleanup duty in the parking lot before they're able to pick up their diploma and transcript. These things we hand out to you on stage are just the cases."

He grabs one and opens it up to prove that they're empty inside. He affects a little fake smile before clearing his throat.

"This has been a great year. Perhaps one of the greatest in the history of the school. At the beginning of the year, disciplinary actions were down ninety-nine percent thanks to some extra help from a very special group of individuals who have, I believe, been unfairly maligned in the press since being forced to return to wherever it is they came from. In fact, with the exception of one unfortunate incident…"

He pauses just to find me in my seat and glare my way.

"…we would have had a perfect record over the first two grading periods."

He pauses for applause. It doesn't happen.

"And our sports teams… our athletes were just extraordinary this year, weren't they? Both football and basketball had winning records. And soccer as well, if you include our three tied games in the 'W' column. We even had a wrestler come in fifth place in his weight division in the regional quarterfinals!"

Now the audience does burst into applause. Logan stands up with his arms in the air and starts making a noise like a dog barking because—you guessed it—Blanchard was talking about him. Then he throws his hat in the air and, of course, nobody does anything.

Someone please just put me out of my misery.

"And academics. What can I say about academics?" He pauses and his face goes blank. "They were fine, too. But I won't bore you with rehashing the year behind us. Let us look to the future."

Sure, don't bother us with academics… you know, the actual reason for school.

"A shining future bright with possibilities and opportunities and prospects and other great things that can happen to students who work hard. Some of you will go to college and maybe someday, years down the road, have a career that allows you to be everything you want to be. Others will join the military and serve your country proudly, as I did out of high school. *Oorah*!"

Several family members in the audience immediately echo the Marines battle cry.

"And even those who aren't quite as successful and end up with menial jobs…" He looks at me again for some reason. "…can still make something of yourselves as long as you stay on the straight and narrow."

Seriously, can I at least get a bucket to puke in?

"So congratulations, seniors! The moment you've all been waiting for is nearly here. But first, we have one last speech, which, thanks to a sizable donation to the school district for new computer labs, the superintendent and school board have informed me I have no way of preventing. I'm sure you'll all recognize him because, Lord knows, I can't get away from constantly seeing his face on TV, billboards, magazine covers, and basically the entire internet. Please welcome to the stage Mr. Franklin Douglas III."

I feel like my head explodes when I hear this. I know it doesn't, but it really does feel like it. And for once, the feeling in my chest is a good one. A feeling I'm not sure I've ever felt before. I think they call it… elation?

Frank walks up onto the stage to cheers and applause because, y'know—Frank—and Blanchard walks away from the podium in the opposite direction to avoid shaking his hand. I turn around, and find Mom. There are tears in her eyes too, but for a very different reason. I turn back to the stage because I don't think I can handle the hurricane of emotions stirring within me.

"Thank you, Principal…" He pulls out a card, pretending not to remember the name and holds it away from his face as if he can't read it. "…Bumgardner? Benchwarmer? Sorry, folks, I forgot my reading glasses."

Everyone bursts into raucous laughter. Everyone, that is, except for Blanchard, who slumps low in his seat and crosses his arms, his face beet red.

"Good evening, ladies and gentlemen, honored guests, and, especially, you graduating seniors!" The students go nuts. "I know this is being filmed and posted online, so I speak not just to those present here today, but to everyone watching this live or at a later time. I've given many speeches in my time as a corporate CEO and billionaire philanthropist—that means I give a lot of money away because then I don't feel guilty for spending even more on myself."

Laughter.

"I've even given the commencement speech at places such as Harvard and Princeton. But this is my first time addressing a high school graduating class. Why now? What would make someone as rich and famous and handsome as myself take time on a Saturday to talk to a bunch of teenagers?"

More laughter from the crowd and the stage.

"There are several reasons for it. The biggest one is that the past year had been difficult for us all. In fact, in many ways, it was unprecedented in its difficulty. It impacted each of us in a unique, specific manner, but it impacted all of us nonetheless. What's more? We went through it together. And we succeeded together. Not all of us played a major role in getting rid of the..."

He turns around and glares at Blanchard for a moment.

"...very special individuals who visited us for months and increasingly made our lives miserable. And eventually intolerable. But we each fought against them in our own way, big or small."

His gaze turns to me now, but it doesn't linger.

"Some even went above and beyond, even risking their lives and everything else to save the rest of us. Those individuals are the best of us."

I smile, my lips tight, willing my eyes not to let loose.

"And those individuals deserve our greatest respect and our eternal gratitude. So before you turn your tassels and pick up your diplomas, or wish your children or siblings or cousins congratulations on graduating, let us all give a hand to the people to whom we owe everything."

Frank looks me straight in the eyes as he starts to applaud, and everyone else starts to clap also. Soon everyone is standing and cheering. And, as I stand and join them, I realize that I feel better than I've ever felt in my entire life.

I turn back to Mom and my heart fills with joy as she also stands and applauds, looking at me as well for some reason. She mouths the words "I love you," and I smile and mouth them back.

When I turn back to the pulpit, Frank is gone and Principal Blanchard has replaced him. I'm so happy I don't even care that I have to hear his stupid voice for the next hour, calling out names before finally getting to mine. Vincent.

EPILOGUE II

THE HEAVENLY BODIES

Log 55.212

The Earth's moon is as cold and dark as we are ancient. I, Uriel, along with my three brothers, Michael, Gabriel, and Raphael, have been set as watchmen upon the proverbial walls for half a century or more. When you've lived as long as we, time begins to lose meaning.

Neutral beings, we are, not prone to choosing sides, unaligned not with one race over another. Many believe us to be in accord with the angels with which we share our names. In fact, we are, together, not convinced they are wrong. As it is with any tradition passed down through the generations, facts begin to meld with fiction until the lines become so blurred it becomes difficult to decipher truth.

Gifted with powers beyond any human, our quartet can traverse the universe with the freedom of a sea lion within the depths of Earth's many oceans, riding upon the currents of space to distant galaxies and back with naught but a thought. Instantaneous for all intents and purposes.

We have communed with the great starwhals of U-M822, and seen the blackness within the depths of SN 2005gj. We have tasted the sweetness of the gulli fruit on Richot, and dined with monarchs on Op2-sus.

Allied with humanity, we are not, but sworn to the peace of all peoples, races, and species, we shall forever be. Without balance, without peace, existence is futile.

It was on one of our excursions that we met the Tuldarians—an elder race of bipedal beings who resemble Earth's crocodiles or even their great ancestors, the dinosaurs. They have made a grave error, twice now, visiting Earth will ill intent etched upon their hearts. And now, I fear we face history thrice repeated. For upon the horizon, their gray, oblong ship glides effortlessly through the blackness of the Milky Way's edge.

It is with the heaviest of hearts I must tell Eaglestar of their presence and to assure him it was the actions of one Sawyer William Vincent which alerted them.

When he reassembled their inter-dimensional travel device, they became aware of humanity's possession of said artifacts. Until now, they believed them lost to the stars.

It was not his fault, the poor child. He intended only goodness to come from his heroic deed, but alas, there is no good deed void of punishment or consequence.

The arrival of the Tuldarians may be years away, but it is imminent, nonetheless. It was fortuitous that Eaglestar and Earth's lesser leaders chose to place us here so many decades ago. For now, they stand a chance at survival… If they can all make peace with themselves in light of a far more nefarious threat.

If not, I believe the sun is about to set for a final season upon humanity.

If you enjoyed reading about Sawyer and gang, don't miss the brand new series HARRIER (Raptors book 4, Harrier book 1)

Justice—a concept without a universally accepted definition. To some, it means reconciliation, while others deliver it with swift and violent judgment. For me? I just want to not be considered an outlaw for years of serving and protecting New York City.

Yep. That's right. Crimefighting is illegal, punishable by life in prison at the bottom of the ocean. It sucks. But that won't stop me from doing what I was born to do: uphold justice and stop good people from being hurt.

Even if everyone I once called a friend is against me, I'm not bowing down to the Counter Vigilante Taskforce.

My name is Sawyer William Vincent (I know, it's three first names. Think I haven't heard that before?) Once known as Red Raptor, I'm now Black Harrier, one of the world's most famous masked crime-fighters, and this is my city. I think.

ABOUT THE AUTHORS

Jaime Castle hails from the great nation of Texas where he lives with his wife and two children and enjoys anything creative. A self-proclaimed comic book nerd and artist, he spends what little free time he can muster with his art tablet.

Jaime is a #1 Audible Bestseller, Audible Originals author (The Luna Missile Crisis) and co-created and co-authored The Buried Goddess Saga, which includes the IPPY award-winning Web of Eyes.

The Buried Goddess Saga (Epic Fantasy)

Web of Eyes

Winds of War

Will of Fire
Way of Gods
War of Men
Word of Truth

Dragonblood Assassin (Epic Fantasy)
Black Talon
Red Claw
Silver Spines
Golden Flames

Black Badge (Western Fantasy)
Dead Acre
Cold As Hell
Vein Pursuits

Jeff the Game Master (Fantasy LitRPG)
Manufacturing Magic
Manipulating Magic
Mastering Magic

(Science Fiction)
The Luna Missile Crisis
This Long Vigil

Raptors (Superheroes)
Sidekick
Superteam
Scions
Baron Steele
Mega-Mech Apocalypse

Harrier (Superheroes)
Justice
The Trench
Invasion

Find out more at www.jaimecastle.com
https://www.facebook.com/authorjaimecastle

CJ Valin is a writer and artist living in Los Angeles. His award-winning work has included novels, short stories, comic books, screenplays, and non-fiction books and articles. A lifelong science fiction and comic book fan, he created the "Raptor-verse" as an homage to his favorite superheroes from childhood.

www.ingramcontent.com/pod-product-compliance
Lightning Source LLC
Chambersburg PA
CBHW030348310726
48979CB00001B/227
* 9 7 8 1 9 4 9 8 9 0 8 6 0 *